VOYAGE TO ALPHA CENTAURI

Michael D. O'Brien

Voyage to Alpha Centauri

A novel

IGNATIUS PRESS   SAN FRANCISCO

Cover art by Michael O'Brien

Cover design by John Herreid

© 2013 Ignatius Press, San Francisco
ISBN 978-1-58617-832-1
Library of Congress Control Number 2013909309
Printed in the United States of America ⊗

The Voyage

By Neil Ruiz de Hoyos

Edited by Phillip R. Cowan and Hui F. Zheng

Abbey Press

Title: The Voyage.
Author: Ruiz de Hoyos, Neil, 2029–2122 E-y.
Editors: Cowan, Phillip R., and Zheng, Hui F.
One volume, 788 pages; Standard Tongue.
Translations of original English language manuscripts NRdH-1,
-93, -94, -211. Supplementary documents: original Russian
language mss. AY-1, -2; excerpts from Chinese language ms.
XAL-1, and English language ms. TSE-1; Manuscript collection,
Central Library of Queensland.
Translators: Yusupov, Anselm P.; Zheng, Hui F.; and Oldfield,
Maria T.
Publisher: Abbey Press; Abbey Press Publication Number AP
259-14.
Date of Publication: 8 September 259 RP-y.
Archives of the Commonwealth Catalog Number 21,803.

THE VOYAGE

Being the true, candid, and unadulterated account of yet another great leap for mankind, mixed with the personal memories, irritations, and ramblings of Neil Ruiz de Hoyos

by Himself
(for his future edification and entertainment)

Home is where one starts from. As we grow older
The world becomes stranger, the pattern more complicated
Of dead and living. Not the intense moment
Isolated, with no before and after,
But a lifetime burning in every moment
And not the lifetime of one man only
But of old stones that cannot be deciphered.

—T. S. Eliot, *East Coker*, in *Four Quartets*

A week from now I leave this sanctuary—my home, my solitude, my consolation. I have almost completed packing, though I remain haunted by a sense of the unreality of what is about to happen. Even so, without warning, my heart begins thumping with the thrill of it. At other times, I am full of fears, regrets, fragmentary thoughts. I am a little at a loss for what to do with myself.

This morning I puttered about the cabin and greenhouse, touching beloved objects, standing still for long moments, pondering the turquoise cube on my desk, the budding cacti, and the riot of cosmos flowers blooming in the yard I have never mowed.

In the entrance hall, I stroked the horse's skull, like an ancient saint absorbed in meditations on mortality. I recalled the day, years ago, when I had found the skeleton in a ravine higher up on the mountain. The bones were bleached white, the metacarpal broken, the remnant unshod hoofs proving that it had been a wild mustang—a loner. I had brought the skull home to keep me company.

"So long, ol' pard", I said to him, and went out onto the front porch.

Sitting on the steps, I gazed out over the crowns of *piñon* trees to the blue haze of the valley below. I grew drowsy, despite the mug of strong illegal coffee I sipped. I closed my eyes, and from across the void of more than sixty years came the memory of a time when I was eight years old:

In the predawn light of what promised to be an exceedingly hot day in July, I awoke in a trailer park on the outskirts of Las Cruces, New Mexico. For no reason that I might have offered to myself, or to my parents sleeping in the other room, or to the dog yawning on the end of my bed, nor to the cats meowing outside the kitchen door, begging for scraps, I knew that this was the day for which I had prepared throughout the previous year—ever since I had reached the age of reason, as my mother called it, on the feast of my First Holy Communion.

I patted the dog, slipped into my shorts, and pulled a woolen vest over my T-shirt, for the night chill was still on the land. After strapping sandals onto my feet, I dropped to my knees beside the bed, and from beneath it, I pulled a cardboard box on which I had printed in red crayon: *Property of Neil Benigno Ruiz de Hoyos.*

The box contained necessary materials, some of which I had purchased at the flea market; some of which I had made with cast-off tin, bolts, and wire; and a single most beautiful item which I had found in the dump, discarded by wealthy people. It was a glass bell. Like all of the other handbells in the box, it made its own distinctive sound, which at the moment, for the sake of my parents' need for rest, and for the sake of my mission, I did not employ.

Carrying the box with the greatest care, I passed through the doorway of my small room into the kitchen, and quietly opened the door to the yard. The dog tried to step out behind me, but I pushed him back.

"Stay, Rusty, stay!" I whispered. "I'm goin' alone." I closed the door on his whines and set off into the silent maze of trailers, heading in the direction of the great mountains. It was not my task to reach the mountains, for, though they towered above the city, they were far. My destination was the desert. I would recognize the place where I must go when I found it, I was sure, and I felt also that it would not be a great distance from my home, though it would be better if it was far enough that sounds could not be heard by the people in the encampment where my family lived among a hundred other families no different from my own.

As I trod through the sagebrush and octopus plants, a frightened chaparral bird cried out in alarm and bolted, and a few steps beyond that, a small rattlesnake slithered away from my path, causing me some alarm of my own. Then came a whiptail lizard that darted from under a rock overturned by the toe of my sandal, its long tail rasping my ankle as it disappeared against the dust. Followed by a kit fox running through the bushes to my left.

Not long after, I stopped on the brink of a dry arroyo and put down my box. There, I huffed and puffed until my breath eased, all the while watching the sky turn colors and the tips of the mountain melt from rose into gold.

For a moment, I hesitated, because I sensed the importance of what I was about to do, though why it should be so I did not question. Now, I opened the box lid and removed the bells one by one and set them in a row on the gravel. Then, after dusting off my hands, I picked up each one and shook it. The morning air was warming, yet cool enough that the sounds were sharp and made small echoes on the rocks. One old brass school bell—clang-clang. One small painted bell from India—tinkle-tinkle. Two I had made myself, the first a cone of aluminum with a nut on a string—klonk-klonk—and the other a tin cup with a bolt on a wire—binga-bang. I was very fond of them but did admit that their sounds were not as nice as the others.

Finally, the glass bell. It was shaped like a regular handbell, cut with crystal designs, chipped and cracked, but still very fine. I grasped the handle and shook it. The glass bead inside swung and made a high ding-ding-ding. I shook it again. And then I kept shaking it, making a beat, a rhythm that made my feet tap in time and a song rise in my throat. First a hum, then a warble, no words, no meaning, just a trickle, like water flowing through an arroyo in spring.

Now I was dancing up and down and all around, shaking the bell harder, lifting my legs, throwing back my head, warbling and hooting and laughing. I danced in circles, I danced in lines, I crossed the pattern back and forth and made a circle again, and as I looked up and up, I closed my eyes. Singing, singing, I heard the arroyo roaring in my ears with sweet, fast waters, smelled cactus flowering and perfuming the air, and felt the wingtips of birds brushing my face, my bare arms, and my legs.

I did not know why I was doing this, did not pause to think about it. It was a good feeling, so happy, so happy, and that was reason enough. And with arms lifted high in the air, on and on I danced until the sun burst over the eastern mountains and the land filled with gold.

*

Then another memory surfaced, a time when I was fourteen years old: One Saturday afternoon in October, I stepped quietly through the scrub brush with a .22 rifle in hand, stalking jackrabbits. During the past hour, I had stopped from time to time and turned about-face, catching my dog in the act of following me.

"Go home, Rusty", I said in my most commanding voice. And Rusty would turn around and amble homeward with his arthritic gait, only to reappear again a hundred yards farther along.

Frustrated, but feeling some affection for the dog's loyalty, I walked back to him. Rusty promptly sat down on his haunches and let his tongue loll out. I patted him on the head and tried to explain. "You're too old for this. Look at you, you're a wreck. You make all kinds of noises, and the jacks can hear you a mile away."

Rusty responded with panting and drooling, and a wide dog smile.

7

"Look, you gotta go home. If you want some stew for supper, you gotta beat it. Now scram."

Rusty put on his doleful look, heaved a great sigh, got up, and ambled away homeward. Ten minutes later, he was back. I decided to ignore him and trust to my luck. There was a breeze blowing now, and I was downwind, so it wasn't an entirely hopeless situation. Not long after, I came to a place that seemed familiar to me, and then I recalled that it was the dry arroyo I had sometimes visited when I was a child. I smiled and shook my head. There on the brink of it, right there on that spot, I had danced and sung and shaken my bells—thank heavens, there had been no witnesses.

I sidled down the bank onto the riverbed and turned north on it. There were snakes in the shadows of the banks, I knew, but it was autumn, and I wasn't too concerned. I had shot dozens over the years, as had my father, and caught hundreds more on the glue plank I set for them in the crawlspace beneath the trailer.

Now and then a rustling in the bushes at the top of the bank drew me out of the bottom, gun at the ready, safety off, eyes squinting in the bright sunlight. But there was nothing. I went back down into the arroyo and continued to walk. It was like a wide road through the rough desert, a highway really. It was interesting to look at all the rounded stones, to think that once a year they were under water after the rains. Like looking through a telescope or a microscope, seeing what was usually hidden. Like people, in a way. You could always see their faces but never really know what was going on inside of them.

I was thinking especially of a girl in my high school, pretty, shy, and sweet. I would like to talk with her. I would like to ask her to the dance next month, my first, maybe her first too. But I wondered if it would come to anything, because I intended to drop out of school next year when it became legal for me to do so. I needed to get a job. There was a factory in town that made special cardboard boxes for fruit growers, minimum wage but better than nothing. Or maybe I could do seasonal work in the fields, though usually the Mexican migrants snapped up those jobs, willing to work for next to nothing, below minimum wage.

I needed to build an extension on the trailer, just a plywood box, a new room. I loved my home, but my bedroom was child-size, the bed so short that my head and toes touched the walls, and the ceiling so low that when I stood up my hair brushed it. Also, the well in the yard needed a new pump. My father was having no luck finding a job in Santa Fe. My mother never earned enough at the café. She was always worried, big things and small things.

"Benigno," she had called after me as I walked out of the yard in the direction of the desert, "watch out for snakes."

"I'll be fine, *Mamacita*", I called back. "I've done this ten million times. You gotta stop worrying about everything."

"You're right, I know. Still . . ."

Still. I had heard her say it more times than I cared to remember: *Still, Benigno, the world is a dangerous place.*

Even though there was some Scottish in her blood—her grandfather, a prospector named Neil—she had always called me by my second name, because it meant "friendly" and "kind". My Hispanic buddies at school told me it suited me, though they said *Beanpole* and *Stilts* would be good too. Punch you on the arm, tease you without mercy, then bring you home to their trailers where their mothers served you a Mexican meal, the best in the world. They were good guys. A few of them looked something like Spaniards, and most looked half and half, with Indian blood. The Aztecs, I called them. They were friendly and kind too, but don't ever get them mad. Like my very own self, brown skin, black eyes, with the exception of my totally insane, thick, blond hair that stood on end and needed a hay scythe to crop it down.

Mamá had a point about snakes. My sneakers were falling apart, and lately I'd grown so fast there were two inches of ankle showing beneath the cuffs of my jeans. Another reason to find a job.

A few minutes later, I rounded a bend in the arroyo and, without noticing it, stepped on a diamondback rattler that lay coiled on a flat rock. It leaped and bit me just above the ankle. I stumbled sideways and fell onto the stones, the gun clattering away. I reached for it, and fired wildly in the direction of the snake, but it was already disappearing into a crevasse in the rocks.

Inspecting my leg, I saw that the swelling around the fang marks was spreading quickly. I unbuttoned my trail knife from the kit at my waist, clenched my teeth, and cut two slices into the flesh. There was no way I could suck out the poison, so I used both hands to compress the area around the wound and squeeze out as much as possible. The blood dripped, but the fangs must have hit deep, because the swelling was worse now, and it felt as if someone was putting a blowtorch to my leg. Using my belt, I made a tourniquet below my knee, and stifling a cry, I cut deeper. As the blood began to flow, I tried to stand up, intending to hobble home as fast as I could, praying for time.

But it was no good. I felt dizzy, and now there was a corona of light around everything. I took a few steps, then collapsed. My head ached, and I could not keep my eyes open because the sunlight was another kind of fire.

Without warning, something wet and hot laved my face. I pushed it away, but it returned, along with whimpering.

"Rusty", I croaked, frightened by the sound of my rasping voice. "Rusty boy, go get *Mamá*."

*

During the year following this event, a high school teacher visited me in the hospital, and later at my home in the trailer park. He brought books. These were mostly about science. Natural history, astronomy, a bit of physics, and a bit of math, things that he thought might help me with my lagging studies. I had never been a good student, and now it seemed that I would become one of Education's countless casualties. But with little to do other than staring at ceilings and lavishing a good deal of affection on my dog, my attention was hooked, and then engrossed. I began to read in the subjects that had been arbitrarily brought to my attention, and begged for more. At first, my mind felt strained to its outer limits, and then the thing caught hold and I simply devoured. Five years later, I entered a college in Santa Fe, New Mexico, majoring in physics.

The Ship

I went into the little boat
I had crafted with wood and tears.
I rowed it to the true horizon
Beyond the gate of my fears.

—Xue Ao-li, *Beijing Poems*

I awoke from a dream of remembering. I do not mean that I awoke remembering a dream, though I did that too. The dream itself was about remembrance: the act and the mystery of it.

I had fallen asleep somewhere near mid-Atlantic and did not open my eyes again until the captain of our thirty-passenger Tesla announced that we were about to cross the west coast of Africa. Details of the dream were clear for a few seconds: I am lying on a bed in a little boat. I am very frail, older than I am now. An elderly woman is seated on a chair beside me. She is East-Indian, dressed in a turquoise sari. There is such love in her face—a beautiful face, the eyes wise but childlike. I feel great love for her, though I don't know who she is. Or maybe in the dream I had loved her a long time. In the dream, I seemed to know.

After I awoke, the feeling of love burned quietly inside me. This was natural enough, a pleasant illusion generated by my chronic aloneness, I suppose. Was she that girl I met in Santa Fe half a century ago, grown old? Was the dream a longing for what might have been? Probably it was. Yet, in the strange ways of dreams, it had seemed so real— for a few moments more real than the objective reality of the aircraft that was bearing me on the first stage of my journey. I also felt an urgency in it, as if it was exhorting me: Remember. And remember remembering. Even as the details begin to fade, I record it here in order not to forget it.

Love. How to write this word without prying the lid off a Pandora's box of illusory images and misinterpretations. If I had paid any attention to it throughout my life, my greatest achievement would not have become reality. I would not be going where I am now going.

For more than a year, I had been marveling over the photographs of the *Kosmos* and reading a constant stream of reports, the standard medium-security documents sent to all scientific personnel, just to keep us informed. During the past six months, there had been, as well, the regional meetings mandatory for anyone who hoped to take part in the expedition as essential staff or as a token presence. I was a token. It had not been forgotten that my theoretical work was at the foundations of the project, but neither was it overestimated. An army of space technologists, engineers, propulsion experts, astronomers, designers, and so forth had taken the mathematical formulas and turned them into the living dream. I had fulfilled my purpose, and it was only the government's sociopolitical agenda—that is, public relations and the self-image of the member states cooperating in the venture—that ensured my involvement at this late stage.

Thus, obeying instructions from the administration, I flew at the appointed time from America to the great northern desert in Africa, and after the rather lengthy three-hour flight, we began our descent to the airstrip of what I presumed was the ship's base station. We came in from the west, and because the station was nestled in the hollow of hills I was not afforded a view of the *Kosmos* itself, which I thought must be in the desert beyond. Viewed from the air, the administrative complex looked to be a small city of white, single-story structures spreading horizontally throughout the valley. It was not on any map that I knew of, despite its considerable population, more than ten thousand people, none of whom were visible at the moment, since they would be hiding in the shade to escape the blaze of the sun. The pilot cut the jets as he switched to hover power over the tarmac, and then descended vertically. When we touched down, he taxied the Tesla off the end of the strip and into an underground hangar. This proved to be a cavernous expanse of concrete, the largest man-made structure I had ever seen. It was filled with hundreds of parked jets, much like an autopark in more cosmopolitan settings.

A disembarkation tube clamped itself onto the door, which opened in an instant, permitting me and my fellow passengers a graceful exit. At the end of the tube, each of us was welcomed by an official escort, one per person. Mine was an efficient young woman with digital identibadge embedded on the breast of her uniform, a smile on her face, and a script that she recited by rote, albeit employing my name, position, and honorifics with admirable ease, as if we were long acquainted. Then she led me along a hallway, the ceiling illuminated by an unknown source, the piped air refreshingly cool. My cowboy boots clomped arrhythmically on the floor of shining white marble, while her stiletto heels clicked rhythmically beside me as she made polite chat.

Arriving at the main reception area, I was delivered to the initial security screening and passed through without too many problems. Eyebrows were raised over the compact survival kit clipped to my belt, containing my old fold-knife and other small items. I explained that it was a medical device for the pedicare of crippled feet. They hesitated, then waved me through the scanner. I was lucky. And my status helped, as well as the pathetically exaggerated limp I had produced for the occasion.

My flight was not the only one that would arrive today, and I knew there would be hundreds of specialists on the *Kosmos*, not counting service personnel. The ship could accommodate a thousand, I guessed, judging by the dimensions outlined in the information package. However, to sustain such a large number of people for nineteen years without the aid of supplementary resources would make for certain restrictions.

We Americans, along with a contingent of Koreans and Brits who had just arrived, were guided to a platform and into a rapid transit tube. We sat down on the plush seats, gazing out the windows at blank white walls, and when the doors hissed closed, we were propelled through the heart of the hills. Five minutes later, the machine stopped, and we stepped out onto a platform that appeared to be the lobby of a grand hotel. It was indeed a hotel, though one with a very selective guest list. Like all other buildings I had seen so far, it had only a single story above ground. I was to learn that there were eight more, below ground. A distinctive quality of this edifice was that one whole side was open to natural light, built on the slope of a hill facing north, away from the sun.

My room was scented with a vaguely oriental perfume, the soft carpet was subtly colored, and the furniture lean in design but luxuriously upholstered. The bed looked like something you shouldn't lie down on because you would never want to get up again. Framed artwork had cosmic themes: Hubble-8 galaxy photos, the new station on Mars, and an imaginative depiction of the planets of Alpha Centauri. The latter image appeared to be hand-painted, though I expect it was machine made. When I drew back the curtains to see what lay beyond, I had my first sight of the ship. There in the desert, about a mile away, she rested on her cradle. She was immense and very beautiful.

At first I just looked, amazed, shaking my head. Stunned, actually. The photos and diagrams I had seen had not imparted her three-dimensionality—not even my home holoscreen had conveyed the impact of her substantiality. Neither had the media images captured the sweetness of her ovoid form, like one of those beautiful white stones one finds on beaches in diverse places of the world, the kind you hold in the hand, not wanting to let it go. You always take it home with you. Always. Beauty is radiant wholeness, balance, harmony. The ship was a perfect manifestation of these. It was also the apotheosis of latent power. A week from now, the power would be unleashed.

*

Days of briefing followed, lectures from department heads, giving us a sense of the complexity of the expedition as well as delineations of responsibility. There will be flight staff and scientific staff for the voyage itself, and another set of scientific staff for investigation of the planet. Also some tagalongs, such as myself and a few famous names. I haven't yet met everyone.

The hand-out sheets we received at one briefing tell us that the warm bodies are divided into the following categories:

Ship's flight crew (total 60): captain and subsidiary ranks, navigation people, communications, liaison staff for the following categories.

Service staff (total 200): food, cleaning, laundry, mundane troubleshooting, all of which is grouped under the title "Maintenance" (our basic needs).

Scientific staff for voyage (total 171): subcategories as follows: botanists (8); physicians (12); nurses and paramedics (18); pharmacists (8); astronomers of various kinds (10); atmosphere controllers and recyclers (16); atomic fusion engineers (12); technicians assisting the aforementioned (6); anti-matter gurus/overseers (8); computer fail-safe watchmen (8); odd and sundry experts in extremely obscure fields (17). Add to the above categories the following social sciences: psychologists/counselors (16); psychiatrists (4); sociologists (8); community facilitators, a.k.a. social engineers (20).

Scientific staff for destination planet (total 238): There is some overlap with voyage scientists, because certain people will be working during the voyage and also working on the planet. I've subtracted these duplicates to arrive at the following figures for those who will work exclusively at on-ground exploration: botanists (20); zoologists (20); biologists (22); chemists (13); geologists (26); land transport staff (18); pilots for the four ship-to-ground shuttles (8); physicians (4); data analysts (12); astronomers (4); anthropologists (7); archaeologists (16); linguistic geniuses (10); assistants to the aforementioned (10); military support technologists, a.k.a. security and protection from aliens (48).

16

Tagalong (total 8): Nobel prize scientists (5); aging trillionaires who contributed money to the project (2); nephew of the current Federation president (1). Stowaways (uncertain).

And there we have it. The *Kosmos* will bear a known 677 people from our home planet to planet Alpha Centauri A-7, our closest neighbor in the galaxy, just next door, a mere 4.37 light-years away. (See attached list, names, and positions of all personnel.)

*

Well, here we are at last. Theory metamorphosed into solid fact. I recall the day I stood before a microphone in the concert hall in Stockholm, to deliver my acceptance speech of a Nobel Prize for Physics. It was, in fact, my second Nobel Prize, a distinction that has rarely occurred in the history of the Foundation. My previous award had been shared with another physicist, but this one was for me alone, specifically for my work in the dynamics of anti-matter enhancement and catalyzed fusion power. It was all on paper, but interstellar flight was now no longer unthinkable. The "mechanics" were within the range of human capacity, and I had mapped it out. I was forty-seven years old at the time.

I remember clearing my throat, adjusting my eye glasses, and shuffling my papers as the audience waited. I paused, feeling the ache in my ankle, recalling for a moment my vulnerable humanity. Throughout most of my life, I had lived with it and not given it much thought, regretting only that I had cut too deep with the knife and severed things that should never be severed—tendons, nerve connections. Perhaps the wound had also saved my life. Then, for no reason whatsoever, none at least that I might have articulated for the attending king, the scientists, and other dignitaries, I saw myself as a small boy dancing in the desert, yearning upward, and ringing a bell.

*

The "hotel" contained a facsimile floor of the ship, with sample rooms, our new homes. We were encouraged to familiarize ourselves with all the amenities in them, but I refrained from doing so, since I wanted to be surprised. However, I learned at a briefing session that there would be one cabin per person. Claustrophobia in a sealed container, no matter how large the container, could wreak havoc on the mission. People need both public and private space, indoors and outdoors. I picked up through conversations in the hotel restaurant that the rooms are small but comfortable, like ocean-liner cabins for second-class passengers. I wondered if *everyone* would go second class.

*

This evening, all the voyageurs were instructed to attend a "special" briefing session held in the conference hall. Gathered together as one body, we were first informed of something we already knew and had been reminded of during the previous year: Unmanned probes had been sent out to the mystery planet, which is usual with space exploration. They had been launched eight years ago, at the time when the *Kosmos* was well along in its construction. However, we were now told, almost as an afterthought, that they and subsequent unmanned probes would not arrive at the planet ahead of us. They had not been powered by the advanced propulsion system that would drive the *Kosmos*. They were, in a word, *slow*.

There was a good deal of rumbling in the audience when we heard this, because we had presumed (with blind trust) that the authorities had done things properly. We had assumed they already knew a great deal about the planet. As it turns out, they know nothing much at all, only that it is situated in the HZ—the habitable zone "likely to be hospitable to life". Earth's best instruments confirmed that it was certainly *there*, orbiting around AC-A, and gave a general idea of its size and behavior as a satellite to its sun, but little more than that. Readings of the light coming from the planet give early indications of a significant spectrum "edge", which theorists believe may be a biosignature in its atmosphere (if there is an atmosphere). Of course, theorists abound and are not infrequently proven wrong, scientists though they be.

We now understood that the images we had thought were high-resolution telescope photos, which we had pored over so thirstily, were computer-enhanced pixel clots and artists' renditions. The facts, in fact, were conjectures. The announcement was hastily followed by a torrent of highly technical data, stirring speeches, psychological manipulation, and no real explanation. There was much emphasis on the delights of being surprised. As I listened, I fumed quietly to myself and thought that nineteen years of one's life was a lot to invest in a surprise that might turn out to be a dead rock or, alternatively, a fulfillment of the worst fantasies produced by the entertainment industry. I realized, as well, that my own excitement over the cosmic quest had dulled my scientific instincts, my healthy skepticism, my habitual need to know more before making a big leap. I too had relished the element of surprise.

With only a few days remaining until the launch, people can still back out, but I doubt that anyone will do so. Our anger smolders into vague disgruntlement, fading out under the lure of adventure, the feeling that regardless of our blindness we are still pioneers of a kind unprecedented in the history of mankind. I must admit that this is also the case with me. What do I have to lose?

Nevertheless, my suspicious nature has analyzed the situation downward and backward through the layers of propaganda. I may never know the truth of the matter, but I think what happened is this: The political situation on Earth is getting darker and messier than it has been for the past century of relative calm. Controlled, imposed serenity will take you only so far, considering the volatile nature of human beings. Global authorities *need* this expedition, since it is just the kind of marvel that will pull the eyes of mankind away from our troubles. The length of the round-trip journey is ideally suited, politically and socially, to give our rulers enough time—nineteen years onboard relativity time, longer by Earth measure—in which to tighten the lid on the steaming pressure cooker.

I would add to this another factor. Apparently, the two trillionaires are in their eighties. And that means they will probably not live long enough, or remain in sufficient control of their mental faculties, to derive any pleasure from the project. My guess is that they threatened to withdraw their funding if the voyage was delayed beyond their lifetimes.

After giving the situation some thought, I feel sure that if the authorities had been forthright from the beginning I still would have agreed to be part of the expedition. It's the manipulation that really irritates me.

I should also mention that little bags of psyche candy were tossed into the audience. Skeptical at first, then masterfully flattered, then hooked, most of us extended our sweaty palms toward our global caregivers. Among the treats they offered was the announcement that there will be no internal surveillance during the expedition. It took some moments for this to register in the hundreds of brains present in the audience. Then for the faces to change from blank to puzzled. Lack of surveillance was unthinkable.

Here is a sample of the flattering explanation: "You are the most intelligent and responsible scientists in the world, and thus from the moment of departure until your return to planet Earth, there will be no need for social infrastructure security measures."

*

Tempting as it is, I will refrain from sarcasm. To be perpetually observed is as basic to the natural order as breathing without thinking about it, or in more alert moments, to feeling the wind on one's cheek. It is simply background. One strains to imagine that there was a time in mankind's history when the worst sort of surveillance you might suffer from was a bad-tempered neighbor peeking through the curtains of his house in order to keep tabs on your comings and goings, as fuel for gossip. But we of a later age have been born into the culture of omnipresent inspection by invisible authority. All lives are examined lives.

I think it unlikely that during the voyage we will be entirely without the presence of the pests I like to call "botflies" and "tapeworms". Mankind is not supposed to know about these instruments of the State. The former, like the botfly larva, burrows deep into walls and lives on the flesh of one's privacy, so to speak. I regularly repaint the interior walls of my home with a latex magnetic mixture that confuses signals. The tapeworms are another matter. They look like semitransparent insects, about one inch long. They fly around your home. They fly around everywhere as a matter of fact. Several years ago, when I first noticed them and learned that they are impossible to catch by hand or by manual fly-swatter, I quietly—very quietly—invented a little solar-generated gismo that I keep on my back porch, exposed to the elements. It looks exactly like a twirly weather vane. It is not a weather vane. It's a killer of bio-electronic parasites. Some mornings I find the porch littered with their corpses.

They have dwindled in number recently, sometimes disappearing for a week at a time, but always followed by an infestation. I once examined a sample under a microscope. The thing is simplicity at its most brilliant: nanotechnology, of course, with strands of larger carbon fiber. It's a flexible semi-opaque tube, looking disturbingly like a tapeworm, but with bulbous head, eyes, and gossamer wings. Its organs are microcircuits powered by photosynthesis; its head is a vid-cam nodule; the thorax is the transmitter. There's no inkling about where the transmissions go or who monitors them. How on earth anyone could keep track of the millions (perhaps billions) of images sent in to their home base, I can't begin to guess. Maybe they have

20

a computer-filtering system to catch troublesome behavior profiles and flag audio words.

I suppose there must be countless tapeworm casualties on any given day throughout the world, as they are swallowed by birds or smashed during thunderstorms, etc. On the other hand, maybe there aren't many of them after all, and only a few are sent out to keep an eye on problematic individuals. So far, no human beings have paid me a surprise visit in order to find out why there are so many casualties around my place. I designed my little swat machine with—how shall I put it?—with astute integration of engineering and visual aesthetics. I am very, very clever. I should say, rather, that I try to learn from my mistakes.

*

The night before we were to board the ship, there was a farewell banquet in the hotel's grand ballroom. I was placed at the head table with thirty other dignitaries, including a number of heads of state, nabobs, and potentates. My reputation was but one of numerous entities exhaustively displayed, filmed, and photographed. I declined to give an interview. Thankfully, I had not been asked to deliver a speech for this historic moment. Others did this quite ably. There were many speeches. Wine flowed, tears flowed. Later, a band swelled with its overtures, and a dance began. At that point, I went back to my hotel room for a well-earned rest.

The next morning a rapid transit train—a soundless floater—took us all out into the desert. On the way there, I discovered that the ship was *five* miles away, which confirmed that the *Kosmos* was larger than the biggest ocean liner ever built. According to specs, she is 1.0 kilometer long, 0.25 kilometer wide at midriff, and 60 meters high. As we approached her, I saw that there were no windows, no angles, no external protuberances; she was as smooth as an ivory egg. The hull's metal was not, strictly speaking, a metal. It was a new alloy of some kind. The ship sat snugly in its nest, the latter a monumental gridwork of spars composed of another kind of super-hard alloy, extending a few meters beyond both ends of the *Kosmos*. It was hard to tell which was the bow and which was the stern because the craft was perfectly symmetrical, without defining features.

We exited the train onto a platform that stretched the full length of the ship. Despite the size of this promenade, it was crowded with media people and state dignitaries come to wave good-bye. Fortunately, badly dressed elderly gentlemen do not attract the eyes of roving reporters, and thus I was able to board without anyone recognizing me. There were ten wide gangways leading into the underbelly of this elegant whale. Our ramp was midway along the length of the body. Crossing over, we entered a spacious lobby and were met by crew members in dark blue uniforms. On the breast of each was a logo badge, three illuminated stars above the ship's name. I noted in passing that the name was stitched on uniforms in a variety of alphabets; presumably, this had been predetermined according to the native language of each passenger and his assigned greeter. There were a lot of languages being used in the lobby. My official greeter's badge was in the Roman alphabet, and he engaged me in Spanish.

"Dr. de Hoyos, the captain and crew welcomes you aboard the *Kosmos*. It is an honor to meet you, sir."

"This thing sure is big", I said, gazing about the lobby and shaking my head in amazement. He looked confused for a second or two, then conducted me via an elevator upward to Concourse B, the floor on which I would be living. We exited into a long, long hallway, eighteen feet wide, with countless numbered doors along both sides. My room was situated nearer to what I presumed was the stern, about a third of the way back, numbered B-124. My guide typed the access code onto a digital keypad embedded in the wall, informing me that it was my date of birth. I could change the code to anything I liked, he said; just check the procedure in the Manual, which I would find in my desk drawer. The door whispered open, disappearing sideways into the wall. With that, I entered my own little room, my home for the next nineteen years.

Tomorrow is departure day.

*

Next morning:

After the final passenger was locked inside, the ramp doors were closed and hermetically sealed, their joints practically invisible.

As I said, the *Kosmos* rests on a cradle that is as long and as high as the ship itself. Both bird and nest must escape the force of gravity. The cradle will be powered by forty-eight anti-matter engines, with an assist from the anti-gravity devices that were developed in the decade after I won my second Nobel. Anti-gravity alone is not sufficient to over-come Earth's pull on a ship this massive, but when it is combined with the thrust of anti-matter, we will be lifted without undue violence through the Earth's atmosphere until we are free. The ascent will be felt as 1.5 times Earth's gravity, and thus we will be subject to some temporary discomfort during the process. Once we are in orbit, the cradle's engines and anti-gravity will be turned off, and the ship's internal gravity simul-taneously activated, restoring our sense of onboard normality at 1 EG, earth gravity. The cradle will then uncouple from the ship, and remain in permanent orbit as the axial skeleton for one of the new space sta-tions scheduled to be built during the next two decades.

After separation, the *Kosmos* will be maneuvered into position by stellar navigators, with bursts from its four anti-matter engines. Then we will begin to move forward into infinity, accelerating steadily throughout a five-month process that will take us to 56.7% of light-speed, our maximum velocity. Apparently, we will begin the journey by passing through the plane of our solar system. Doubtless this is for the visual drama, to be broadcast back to Earth. Since Alpha Centauri and the Centaurus constellation are 60.8 degrees below our orbital plane, we must change course before we reach the orbit of Neptune, thus avoiding the rather congested Kuiper Belt—which, with eighty to a hundred thousand objects, each exceeding 100 km in diameter, is no small traffic hazard.

The ship is vibrating. I hear the faint rumble of the engines.

Day 3 of Voyage, outward bound:

I will dispense with the standard day/month/year references, those signposts that we pounded into infinity as if into solid ground. Such references would be precise only "back there". Of course, Einstein-Minkowski's theory of the space-time continuum has been amply ver-ified by numerous experiments during the past century. And thus the onboard clocks present two reliable readings side by side: (a) Earth time, Greenwich, calibrated to the hour of our departure, and (b) ship time. Lift-off was arbitrarily established as Day 1, 00:01 hours.

Even so, I am dissatisfied with both measurements. Which of the two is real time? What, in other words, *is* time? What is objectively *real* in an arena where space has three dimensions and time has only one, and they are unified into a single phenomenon? This old mathematics-physics chestnut was cracked long ago, but now we will live it outside of paper and at over half the speed of light when we reach maximum velocity months from now. By that point, though our experience of time (in sensation and measurement) will be felt as normal, we will be about 20% slower than the passage of Earth time. Thus, for every year on Earth (365 days), only 301 days will pass on the *Kosmos*.

*

During the first two days, I could only goggle, gape, listen to my rapidly beating heart. Clichés came rushing to my mouth whenever other human eyes caught mine. We are all, I think, quite astonished. To live inside a dream. To languish in the warm arms of a myth. To tap-dance on an algorithm. Yet here we are.

*

We are accelerating in multiples of Earth gravity, which we do not feel, since the complex negotiation of onboard gravity with actual thrust gravity is flawless, the design extrapolated from Dr. Rodney Nihman's magnificent work at the Royal Astrophysical Institute and his own research foundation *Gravitas*. Rod died twelve years ago, but not before seeing the small, prototype one-man ship accomplish exactly what his equations predicted. Without this component, the voyage would have been technically possible but humanly unendurable: if the ship's internal gravity devices had never been invented—those magical mechanisms that sustain our own independent sense of normalcy—we would be reduced to unconsciousness in short order.

*

This is going to become a whopping great journal if I put everything on paper. They try to discourage hard copies here. The Manual encourages passengers to use digital memory files, since each cabin has its own minimalist personal computer (oddly named, "the *max*"). But I love the sound of my fountain pen scratching on paper. I brought along spare nibs and enough ink cartridges to last a lifetime. The two reams of paper, five hundred sheets each, ate a good way into my baggage allowance, though the allowance is ridiculously arbitrary. Weight is not really a problem; storage space in our "personal apartments" is the problem.

They like to make us feel at home. This is evidence of foresight on the administration's part, because they know we're going to be spending a lot of time together, all six hundred-plus of us, like passengers on a cruise ship that does not reach its port of destination until nineteen years after raising the anchor. More like illegal emigrants locked into a metal shipping container. A comfortable container, mind you.

My own apartment is presumably designed for upper-class passengers. Officially, we are all equal, all "crew". It may be that some of us, including myself, are "more equal", even though we are here for symbolic reasons only. I wonder where the trillionaires live and how they live. And do the grease monkeys in the engine room get a residence as nice as mine? There is no mechanical engine, no grease, but I suppose there are grades of service personnel. Do their swinging hammocks crowd together down in the hold?

I like my little home. Well, I had better like it, because it's all I've got to live in for a very long stretch to come. I am homesick for my cabin—my real cabin. Log walls, cedar shake roof, wood-burning stove (legal if owned as a historical artifact, illegal to actually use), my rock garden, the stream, an occasional wild trout. I ache when I think of the greenhouse, my cacti experiments, my chainsaw (also illegal). Alas, it was confiscated last year by the inspector who spotted evidence of crime in my back yard.

"Looking for tapeworms?" I queried, hoping to throw him off track.

"I don't know what you mean by tapeworms, Dr. de Hoyos", he said, with a severe look. "But I recognize woodchips when I see them."

"Uh-huh. And you just happened to be passing by my remote abode with your band of merry eco-police."

"You have destroyed a tree without authorization, sir, and under Article 4978b3, you have committed an indictable—"

"All right, all right, all right. The truth is, the chips are from a diseased pine, and I was trying to stop the progress of the pine-bark beetle before it infected the surrounding forest."

"Why didn't you contact my department for authorized removal of the afflicted tree?"

"I was concerned about the danger of disease spreading before the department responded."

He smirk-sneered at me—understandably, because it was a lame excuse. They always respond, instantaneously, rappelling down from their hovercraft in the most unlikely places. He warned me that unless the firewood was turned over to his response team, he would be forced to take me to court. I refused, arguing that the tree had grown in my own back yard; I had planted it when it was a sapling. Not convinced, he ordered a thorough search and confiscated the entire five cords of sweet dry pine I had split and stored in my garage. He also showed me the satellite photo of my off-the-chart heat emissions. I pleaded guilty. My two Nobels prevented imprisonment, but I had to pay a hefty fine.

It's interesting that they allowed an eco-criminal like me onto a ship like this. But I suppose they decided that banishing me from the voyage would have been a PR loss with too high a cost.

As you can see, my good self, my very old self of the future, my ship's cabin is fourteen feet long and about ten feet wide. (Digital photo attached.) Both outer and inner walls curve a few degrees, parallel double parentheses, but the end walls are flat. The walls, ceiling, and floor are made of some new material, neither metal nor plaster nor fiberglass, in an off-white hue that hints at early morning sunlight, which I presume is for soothing the ever-unstable human propensity to moods. When I draw my finger down a light strip beside the door, the ceiling and walls glow with whatever intensity I desire. There are three lamps for focused reading, round mini-spotlights that can be slid along the wall to any position one prefers. They think of everything!

The bed is nowhere to be seen until you press a tiny, glowing button by the door, and a slab projects into the room. Touch another button, and a compartment rises from beneath the slab, containing pillows. The bed is dressed with linen sheets and a light wool blanket. Real linen and wool: no expense has been spared. Press another button, and a synthetic wood desktop pops out of the facing wall, a padded spinal-friendly seat automatically unfolds from beneath it. The desk is equipped with the inlaid *max*, symmetrically positioned beneath its wall screen (invisible when not in use), plus a single drawer for stationery materials, containing at present only a mini-printer and the resident's guide, a wafer-thin e-book of 2,200 pages, titled *The Manual*, a kind of sacred scripture for the voyage.

On another wall, inbuilt drawers contain clothing. More buttons—closet doors disappear into the walls, no sharp edges to hurt an old fellow during storms at sea. Note of interest: I brought along my jeans, smoke-cured checkered shirt, and bush jacket. My fang-proof cowboy boots were frowned upon at the security screening, but I got them through with a bit of haggling. Doubtless, everyone has brought enough clothing to last for decades, and apparently the holds are full of replacements if they should be needed. The closets are stocked with standard issue apparel such as socks and underwear made of syntho-fabric. I popped these offending items into the recycle bin on Concourse D. Hopefully, no one can trace them back to me; I hate being nagged.

In addition to my 140 square feet of space, there is a bathroom. This cubicle contains a stainless-steel toilet, sink, and shower stall, efficiently designed for a smaller bio-mass than mine, and thus it is a little cramped. The bathroom cabinet contains some unusual we-care-about-you stuff, with a digital audio prompt encouraging me to make use of all the "optional" life enhancement technology:

A HUMVS (holistic universal medical vital signs) stick-on patch, preferably affixed to the skin at the center of the chest, calibrated to send continuous messages to an automatic receiver in the medical clinic on my deck. Despite regular urgings from my G.P. in Santa Fe, I have always declined using the dang things, which I call humvees. Some people have them implanted in their bodies. I can't for the life of me understand why healthy people would want to have an electronic parasite invade their interiors or cling to their exteriors. Parasites of any kind fill me with loathing. Also, I don't want to obsess on my health, such as it is. If I'm going to die, it will probably be by choking on a squirrel bone or falling and hitting my head on a nice natural rock. Not that any of the above is logical. It's just that I hate the … Oh shut up, Neil! Quit the crabbing!

Another item in the cabinet was a mood sensor tab, which the voice advised me to wear affixed to the bone behind one of my ears. If you're feeling low, or panicky, or really, really angry, the tab flashes appropriate colors (friends will notice and rush to your aid), and a tiny voice speaks up, urging you to proceed at once to the medical clinic on your floor.

In addition to the aforementioned, I found a transparent envelope containing three "serenity" pills: "A sample for your pleasure and relaxation. Additional prescriptions available from your physician."

Okay, then! Three tabs and three pills into the toilet bowl. Voice command—flush! Done. Now I can proceed with my life, fully exposed to the dangers, the uncertainties, the pains, and the beauties of human existence.

Back in my main room, I found a few more things offered for my consideration:

Transparent eye inserts, not unlike large contact lenses. These items, upon voice command, will trace luminous data across your field of vision, disappearing after a few seconds so you don't stumble over furniture or bump into people. Need the date and time, need to know the room temperature, need your position on the ship, need directions to simply anything on board? Just ask, and it will send you an instantaneous reply. Three levels of communication choice: visual only, audio-visual, and subliminal. For the squeamish, there are traditional eyeglasses that perform the same functions, though the subliminal is not guaranteed to be 100 percent accurate, due to inconsistencies in human neuron receptivity. Uh, thanks, but I can live without either of them.

Then there was the holography entertainment mask, so soft, so conforming to one's face, with voice command for thousands of films and other entertainments. Lie down on your bed and relax. Don't worry. Be happy.

Ear inserts for practically infinite audio choices—educational, scientific, cultural, musical. I tried it out for a few minutes. Nice. However, though haunted by the feeling that I might be making a mistake, I pulled them out of my ears. Nah, I told myself, why not go all the way! If I want thoughts, I'll think. If I want music, I'll hum. And I can always get much of the aforementioned services with a little extra effort, via the traditional method, by accessing the *max*.

There were other amenities, all of them so fascinating, so user friendly—and so very tiresome. I crushed the smaller items under my boot heel, and disposed of them down the toilet. The larger items went the way of the syntho-sox, into the communal, hopefully anonymous, recycle bin.

We are supposed to wear grip slippers whenever we venture outside our rooms. I will comply with this because the floors do tend to be a bit slippy. Lack of foresight is evident in this detail. Why didn't they install non-skid flooring? I would prefer to go barefoot in the hallways, but I have found from experience that exposing my feet in public spaces makes other people nervous. A Quasimodo lurching through the town square. Within my little cosmic homestead, however, I go barefoot. The floors and walls are set to body temperature—just like summer weather in my real home—though it can be lowered if I wish.

Along with the copious voice memos that I hope to record in my *max*, I will keep a more slender paper record of my observations, thoughts, ruminations of dubious quality, and useless asides, anything that strikes me along the way. I am interested in textures, nuances, surprises, more than the wonders of technology. If I should ever return from this trip, these will provide some amusement in my old age—my actual old age. I am now how old? Sixty-eight, I think. Just checked my personal profile in the archive, and yes, I am sixty-eight.

If space/time theory is inaccurate, proving to be limited in ways we did not foresee, or alternatively, more complex with event-dimensions that we could not have guessed, these personal age measurements may become meaningless by Earth time. In any case, I am still free to play with imaginary scenarios. If I survive the voyage, I see myself returning to my little garden in the Santa Fe mountains only eighty-seven years old, by ship time, a relatively young old man. Thank heavens for modern medicine! That will give me a few good years to collate these notes into a book, and maybe a few bonus years, after that to slip into alzheim2, maybe a3. By then, it won't matter to me at all.

Day 4:

Yesterday I made my first onboard notations, but must not omit mentioning a happy meeting that occurred on Day 1:

On every deck, there is a large panorama room, at the fore and aft of the ship, eight "theaters" that offer a view of outer space. Irrationally, I presumed that the view from the topmost public deck would give me a higher perspective. After doggedly climbing the stairs to A, avoiding the elevators for the sake of my general state of fitness, I entered the chamber to find that a crowd of people were already present, gazing raptly at the receding planet Earth. The panorama wall was a hundred feet wide and twelve feet high, displaying a scene that was not so much what one would see through a window overlooking space but rather the absence of a window, the absence of anything that would prevent the entire contents of the ship being sucked out into the void. I knew that there was indeed a wall there, in fact several layers of walls, but the effect was disconcerting, a 3D digital luminization of data the onboard scanners were transmitting to the screen in a resolution of 1.7 megapixels per cubic centimeter.

At the moment, the picture was in real proportion, the planet the size of a softball, the moon a shrinking golf ball. Within a few hours, the Earth would be no larger than a bright star, and Mars would appear on the left side of the screen. Then, the optics people would probably magnify the image for a quick fly-by view of the colony.

The crowd thinned a little, and I edged forward into a gap at the front. I watched for a while, enthralled but still disbelieving. When an elbow nudged me pointedly, I looked down to see the face of Xue Ao-li smiling up at me, shaking his head as he used to do at Princeton when we were young and had stumbled together upon some mathematical key that would, we felt sure, unlock further mysteries.

"I read the passenger list, Neil", he said. "I can't tell you how happy I was to see you on it."

"Me too, Ao-li. When I spotted your name, I thought, this is great news; nine years will be sufficient to get reacquainted."

"I agree. However, I must quibble with you about the time frame, since you seem to posit a one-way ticket. We have, I believe, nineteen years, voyage relativity time, to catch up on our news."

"You're right. But we should subtract the year spent on the mystery planet, since we will be somewhat focused on whatever we find there."

"True. Now, tell me why I know so little about your later life when we spent so much of our youth together."

"Forgive me, Ao-li, I've become the world's worst correspondent. I did read your article in last month's *Ion*, but never dreamed you'd be on the ship."

"Nor I, you. The world's most famous recluse. Why don't you answer your mail?"

"I ran out of stamps."

"Neil, Neil, postage stamps disappeared from Western civilization more than three decades ago."

"I know. I was preoccupied at the time."

"Working on something now?"

"Nothing very big. Just tinkering with the Bohr radius, pulling in some new research into adiabatic ionization energy, and other fun topics."

"That's fairly common stuff. Taking it to the nth?"

"Trying to see if it's possible. Infinity is alluring, of course. But in my golden years, I'm just having a little playtime. It's my conjecture that fairly common stuff still has some surprises for us."

"My sentiments exactly. Otherwise, how are you?"

"Very well, Owly."

Xue laughed in his discreet manner. The nickname had material-ized years ago when side by side we had hammered out the paper that won us the Nobel. His given name, Ao-li, combined with his horned rim glasses, had been too much of a temptation. In combative moments, Xue had called me Nil—for *Nil Carborundum Illegitimi*.

We watched the Earth receding for a time. People around us came and went. No one was saying much.

When the moon was no larger than a white bead, Xue asked, "What would you have done with your life, if you had had the choice? I mean other than what you actually accomplished—which, if I may say so, is not inconsiderable, since we are standing, as we speak, upon one such work."

I bent my knees in reply and simulated an up-and-down bounce. "This is Nihman's doing", I said. "My work was supplementary."

"Dr. Nihman has given us the ship's gravity, Neil, but you have given us the voyage itself. And you haven't answered my question. What, I venture to ask again, would you have done with your life?"

"I don't know. Haven't given it much thought."

"Surely you had dreams. Everyone has them."

I dropped my eyes. Such questions probe too deeply, though they may appear to be no more than casual pass-by scans.

"A man has only one life", I said. "But I suppose, if I'd had the time, I would have done a number of things."

"Such as?"

"I would have liked to play the cello."

"Mmmm, interesting", said Xue, with a nod of encouragement. "What else?"

"Basketball. I always loved basketball. But with my leg . . ."

"Truly amazing. And?"

"I would have traveled."

"You're traveling now."

"I mean on Earth. Climb a high mountain, swim in the ocean, see exotic places."

"Exotic places?" He spread his arms with a smile, indicating our present surroundings.

"When I was younger, I dreamed of living in a houseboat on Lake Dal in the valley of Kashmir, at the foot of the Himalayas."

"Intriguing."

"And you, Owly, what would you have done?"

"I think, dear *Nil*, I would have transformed myself from a physicist into a Shui-mo Master."

"That's some kind of martial arts, isn't it?"

Xue bowed, in mock oriental style, and said in his most artificially polite tone of voice: "No, honored sir; it is freestyle, water-ink painting on silk paper. But to be honest, I would have ignored all the arts on our beloved home planet in exchange for my own personal particle accelerator."

"Still trying to catch those little things that buzz around faster than lightspeed?"

"I would like to. Alas, no one has ten billion *Uni* to lend me for the proper butterfly net."

"Or to grant you", said I, with a shake of the head. "Perhaps they don't really understand the benefits to be derived from producing a black hole right here on Earth."

"I think you mean to say right *there* on Earth."

"Yes, right there."

We returned to gazing out the window.

"Alas, indeed, Ao-li, you soar, but you remain established, standing firm."

(Note to future archivists, if there be any, ages and ages hence: The Mandarin root for his given name is *Ao*, to soar or to roam, and *li*, to stand or establish. As you can see, such a name readily lends itself to various interpretations. Between me and my old colleague, there was much wild and friendly jousting.)

"Make no oxymorons, Neil, nor any of your Fermi jokes, or I will strike you with a martial art."

"All right. A truce, then."

"A felicitous truce."

We grinned and returned to our last view of a blue pearl floating in the infinite sea.

"She dwindles and dwindles", Xue said, in a reflective tone.

"Good-bye, O fairest world, good-bye", I soliloquized. "O blue gem in the heavens, where mankind dwells in love, and no man's hand is lifted against another, and the gifted realize their every dream, and all things sing, and the light grows gold when the bells ring."

"Good poetry needn't rhyme", said Xue. "Besides, you shouldn't tell lies."

"Lies? No, I was just dreaming."

Day 7:

I have spent two days exploring the ship from bow to stern, crow's nest to bilge tanks, so to speak. Actually, I don't have security clearance for the top and bottom levels.

There are six decks. Four of these, Concourses A through D, are accessible to everyone on board. Above the topmost public deck, A, there is the flight deck KC (*Kosmos* Command), which houses the control centers and crew quarters. Below D is the propulsion department and other services, recycling, atmosphere, electronics control, storage holds, gravity generators, etc. Titled PHM. Ordinary folk can't get down that far without knowing a code for the elevators or emergency exits. Emergencies? And where, precisely, would we exit to in an emergency?

There is a vast cafeteria on every concourse, A through D. Each has its industry-size kitchen and a battalion of cooks. Here, all meals are self-serve from a buffet, and free of charge. If one prefers to dine out and be served by a waiter, each concourse offers a large "restaurant", artfully designed for a feeling of intimacy, with décor and food expressing European, Asian, African, and Indian themes, respectively.

Bistros and theme-pubs abound. On deck D, there's a pub devoted to British "fish and chips", which are served in facsimile newspaper cones from the early twenty-first century, just for added effect. There's an eternal line to get in. On deck C, there's a single smallish café where you can order American-style hamburgers and fries. There's always a line here too, despite the sad fact that the "meat" has never trotted about on four legs. It's protein of some kind but manages nevertheless to sizzle and make the last remaining carnivores in the known universe (myself included) water at the mouth.

Let it be noted that at every feeding place throughout the ship, all such traditional animal-source foods are ersatz, usually vegetable protein genetically altered for maximum nourishment, chemically enhanced for flavor. Most other items in our diet are also simulations. Only in the specialty restaurants is it possible to order authentic natural food, mainly grain-base, as well as a few beverages such as tea and coffee and select wines (astronomical prices). Such real items are a minority

33

on the menu, and there is no guarantee that they will remain available throughout the voyage. Hydroponics, however, promises an unceasing supply of salads.

Note to self: You ain't rich, buddy, so do try to stick to the mega cafeterias and carry your own tray. Bistros, cafés, and the aforementioned fancy restaurants offer food and drink that must be paid for by the individual. We all have a "bank account", containing whatever credits we imported personally to the ship from our home accounts, combined with the *Uni*-credits allotted to everyone on board. Of course, all earthly monetary systems are contractual agreements about what a currency is worth, what it will buy. The truth is, nothing is produced on board. Nothing is really bought and sold, just the rearranging of materials to create illusions of semi-independence. Maybe somewhere among the passengers an enterprising soul is whittling a penny whistle with a pocketknife, and he might barter it for something he desires. The marketplaces echo with emptiness, haunted by ghosts. In fact, there are no marketplaces whatsoever. The only real estate is one's personal room, and according to ship's rules, these cannot be swapped. I wonder why not. What's to stop us? Later in the voyage, I might try to break the rules, just for fun.

There are a lot of civilizing elements, such as the numerous artworks along the hallways, affixed to interior walls in recessed alcoves. Apparently, there are two libraries and a single film theater on every concourse. Also, every floor has a DEC (digital environmental chamber). I've never submitted myself to one of these, not even the big omni-sensory in Santa Fe, where for a thousand *Uni*s you can spend three hours floating in the total illusion of a sandy beach in Florida, or an autumn walk through the Vermont woods, or scuba-diving in the Pacific, or relaxing in a Tokyo sushi-bordello, etc., etc.

I might try out the DEC experience later in the voyage, but for now I prefer reality—or as close as one can get to it in our flying city. At ship's midpoint, there is an atrium that creates a canyon soaring from its base on level D to its transparent polyplast ceiling above A. Visible through this layer is a blue "sky", across which puffs of "cloud" occasionally wander. The arboretum is rooted on the atrium's floor. I estimate the entire space to be about 150 feet wide by 400 feet long, a kind of central park with walkways and trickling brooks. Only certain kinds of South American trees reach as high as B, since all trees are young, though by the end of the voyage, they will have grown much higher. The air is sweet with increased oxygen and the natural scents of real leaves, bark, seeds. Perpetual birdsong fills the air (artificial sounds, which I suspect will become quite irritating with the passage of time). The purpose of this atrium is not scientific; it is aesthetics and consolation for the potentially claustrophobic—which is all of us.

As I said, the ship is 60 meters from bottom to top—approximately 180 feet, a small apartment building. (Excuse me, while I interject at this point: I have always appreciated universal *unimetric* in my work. However, I loathe the way it has become an offense to use the older measurements such as Imperial Yankee. I think I'll just revert to the latter whenever I feel like it. A human foot [my good one, anyway] is a handy measuring stick. Pardon my mixed metaphors.)

Doing a little computation combined with guesswork, and factoring in a floor thickness of two feet, I came up with these estimates:

- Topmost deck, KC, is probably 20 to 24 feet high. There may be subsidiary decks within its confines.
- A, B, C, D are each 12 feet high from floor to ceiling, for a total of 48 feet. Add to this the floor thicknesses of 2 feet each, and we get a total of 56 feet. Let's call it 60.
- Bottom level—P (Propulsion), H (Holds), and M (Maintenance)—is not accessible by A-to-D passengers. In the Manual's diagrams of the ship (illustrations, not engineer's blueprints), these departments are represented as positioned on the same floor, which would be about 80 feet high. Housed on this level are anti-matter/fusion engines, gravity apparatus, recycling plants, atmosphere control (oxygen regeneration and purification), and other basic services, including our stores of food, and the four ship-to-planet shuttlecraft, as well as wheeled and hover vehicles for planetary exploration.

Day 18:

I stopped a young fellow outside my door today, as he went past, guiding a soundless suction cleaner along the hallway.

"Who takes out the garbage?" I asked him.

"No one, sir. Everything gets reprocessed."

"Everything? Even the toilets and kitchen slops?"

"Uh-huh. We've got a pretty good separation plant in the basement."

"Really?" I said. "Are you saying that the water in my taps may have been passed through, er, other systems?"

"Yup."

"What about dust? Do you have uses for it?"

"Yup."

"Composting in the gardens?"

"Some of it. After separation, the organic goes to biology for a look-see, and then to the garden people. Non-organic goes downstairs. But I'm not sure what they do with that stuff."

Downstairs, I suspect, is the anti-matter department. It's interesting to know that even microscopic non-organics do something useful. As for the organics, well, there must be a lot of it lying about the place. For example, there is a vacuum bath available at the physical exercise centers. You stand naked for five minutes in a warm, windy suction chamber, and everything not rightly clinging to you is whisked away to become something else. Dandruff becomes part of a ripe tomato. Having your entire body vacuum cleaned is exhilarating—it always makes me laugh—and it's faster than a shower, with less waste of water. Of course, we're encouraged to shower too, for social reasons. Nothing is really wasted. Ingenious, but a little disturbing.

Day 24:

Throughout my life, I have tried to limit e-mail and voice mail. I have disciplined myself to check it only once a week. Interestingly, it is more than three weeks since I last felt the urge to check. The *max* gives me total service that accesses Earth as well as the all-ship's communication system. This morning, I opened up my inbox and found several hundred messages waiting for me. It took a day to wade through them all. There was nothing really personal, nothing that needed a reply, just official "bon voyages" from all manner of institutes and space agencies and publishers with contract offers. The only message that edged in the direction of intimacy was one from the president of the Association of Cactus Growers of America, who said that the gang in Santa Fe would really miss me, and could I please bring them back an "alien prickly pear", if I should find any on that planet. I sent back a one-line message promising I'd keep my eyes open.

36

Day 25:

There are scads of public lectures scheduled for anyone interested in hearing them. These can be attended in the privacy of one's room by keying in the event via the *max*. Alternatively, one may be physically present in the theater where lectures are delivered. We have so many experts on board it's unlikely that topics will be exhausted.

A social animator invited the five Nobel guys to give the inaugural lectures. We are a dry, dusty lot, but our fields and our prizes will probably draw a few people. The first, mine, is tomorrow night.

Day 26:

Close to two hundred people showed up, filling the theater. Since I am an old hand at guest lecturing in universities, I delivered an erudite and perhaps baffling address derived from my NP materials, spiced up a bit with conjectures about warped-space/warped-time and gravity effects, drawing the audience toward the climax with my final words:

"Does relativity relativize *existence*? We may *feel* that it does, since our psychological/perceptual/conceptual bearings are determined by planetary-based measurements, and tend to blur and even disorient us in the face of principles of cosmic physics. Yet relativity has no pretensions to being an ontological system. Indeed, philosophy may in the end prove to be a more coherent model of existence than physics."

As I had prearranged, at this point, the screen filled with photos of Alpha Centauri. Hubble-8 is now parked outside the orbit of Pluto-Charon, giving us the best shots of our destination we've ever had.

The star Alpha Centauri is of course a close grouping of three stars: the white binary stars Alpha Centauri-A and Alpha Centauri-B, and the red dwarf Proxima Centauri (or AC-C), which revolves around the two binaries. Proxima is technically our closest neighbor, but so dense, so packed magnetically, that we will give her a wide berth. AC-A is a tad larger than our sun, AC-B a tad smaller.

37

Then came the zoom photo of AC-A. Her planets appeared, all eighteen of them, in wondrous diversity, colors, sizes. Three of them are considerably larger than our Earth, but do not qualify as gas giants. Binary stars are unfavorable to the formation of giants.

Then the zoom to AC-A-7, the planet of our desire. The seventh out from the system's sun, slightly larger than Earth, slightly farther from its sun than Earth is from our sun. The advance probes that were sent out into the deep several years ago compose a telescope array about twenty kilometers wide, which gives us data integrated into an image the size of a pea. Increase the magnification beyond this, and we get a blur composed of square pixels. But it *is* blue, which may be gas clouds or may be water. Our onboard telescopes will give us steadily improving pictures, the closer we get to the destination.

I wanted music to accompany the visuals. After considering the soaring violin in Vaughan Williams' *The Lark Ascending*, and the saccharine arias of Ciccoletti's latest opera, *The Seas of Mars*, I had discarded both in favor of the magnificent drama of Holst's *The Planets*.

As the symphony progressed, a tremendous stillness settled on the crowd. Strangely, many people in the audience began weeping, mostly women, but also a few men wiping their eyes. The audience sat in silence for a few minutes, then left the auditorium one by one.

Day 27:

After an early breakfast, I went down to the arboretum and found that the lighting had been dimmed, with only pinprick lights along the pathways to guide nocturnal strollers. I was alone, like an old man in a park walking his dog just before dawn. The birds had been turned off, and the sound system was playing one of Mozart's concertos for wind instruments. I sat down on a bench and closed my eyes.

Later, a gardener passed by and spotted me in the shrubbery.

"Morning, sir."

"And a good morning to you", I replied.

"It's only 0600 hours, but I could turn on the sunrise, if you'd like."

"No thanks."

"People usually start coming around 0700. That's when I turn on the birds. Would you like the birds now?"

"No, the Mozart is excellent. Is classical played every morning? If so, I'd make a habit of sitting in."

"You're welcome any time, night or day. The music isn't always classical though. I like variety, so we do a lot of ethnic and folk. African. Celtic. Some soft Blues."

"Jazz?" I asked.

"I'm a Jazz-fiend myself, Neo-Orleans and Post-J, but I listen to it in my own room."

"How about Ancient Rock?"

He frowned. "We don't do that to the trees." He shook his head. "It warps proper molecular growth. Inhibits budding, flowering, fruiting. But with Mozart, Bach, the softer kind of Chopin, even some of the quieter Beethoven, you get an unusual response."

"Such as?"

"Increased growth rate. The stems and leaves gradually turn toward the speakers, as if they're yearning for the source."

"You're sure you're not imagining it? They can't possibly *enjoy* classical."

"Well, they don't have personalities, but there *is* significant positive response. It's entirely bio-based, of course."

"Of course."

He paused, musing, and said, "We're bio-based too."

I refrained from launching a strained discussion of the nature of intelligence.

"It's their spirit", he went on. "Spirits communing with each other."

Yikes, a philosophical gardener! I beat a hasty retreat.

Day 28:

Half-asleep, I sat bolt upright in bed and clicked on the spotlight. Grabbed a sheet of paper and my fountain pen:

Proposition A: The phenomenology of Music presents a coherent, universal "language" based in physics.
Proposition B: Music is a sensory manifestation of wave theory.
Proposition C: Music is wave as manifestation of "spirit".
Question: If all of the above is true, what is "spirit"?

39

Day 30:

Me and the cleaner guy have struck up a kind of trans-class chumminess. He told me his name is Dwayne. I told him mine is Neil. His masklike face hides a sardonic sense of humor, which can be evoked after you stay with him a while in discussions dominated by his stock responses: Yup. Nope. Maybe. He ejected me from my room this morning in order to give my personal space its mandatory monthly hygiene scrub. He used an odd assortment of tools, including old-fashioned rubber gloves, a sponge, and a bucket of antiseptic water. A traditionalist craftsman. I stood out in the hall, watching him work, and asked him where service personnel have their quarters.

"Downstairs," he said.

More digging brought forth the interesting information that even people with the lowest status have their own private rooms, like everyone else. His is on level D, mine on B, the trillionaires on A. These privileged folks, he tells me, have a luxury suite. (It seems that hierarchy is unavoidable in human affairs.) His own room is pretty much like mine, he says, maybe a couple of feet shorter, no desk, but bigger on the entertainment side of things for after-hours diversion.

"Films?" I asked.

"Yup."

"What kind of films?"

"Good, bad, and ugly."

"You mean the old cowboy film?"

"Huh? I don't know any by that name. But there's quite a range." He paused, flicked me a look, and added: "Not that I'm home on it." He cracked a droll smile, then got back to work.

Great guns! Thus, we have dialogues too, and I find they are as fun as any I've had so far, and better than my technical discussions with Xue. Dwayne and I are linked by nostalgia for the culture of the wild west, sagebrush and cactus, coyotes yipping under full moons, garish sunsets, etc. He is originally from rural Nevada but got scooped up when state borders were changed, and Los Angeles was declared one of America's ten metro-states. He was employed by a space technology firm for some years, has a degree in process engineering, another in computer science, but is glad to be on board the *Kosmos* as a glorified janitor.

Dwayne showed me how to access the films through a special key on my *max*. It quadruples the wall screen and pops up a menu, which has more than three hundred and eighty thousand titles to choose from. After he left, I shut it down and tried to forget the access procedure. Where are my cacti when I need them?

Day 60:

A few sociological observations:

Flight crew wears dark blue uniforms. We don't see many of them during our daily life. Occasionally, I spot them in the restaurants or bistros, rarely in the cafeteria feed-lots. Other staff members have uniforms too, when they are on duty. For example, the kitchen staff wear white, two-piece outfits with hair nets. Medical staff wears robin's egg blue, same design. Maintenance staff (cleaning, laundry, etc.) wear pale green. Social facilitator staff wear ordinary business suits with neck ties (identical for male and female facilitators). When off duty, all working people dress themselves in a rather narrow selection of ordinary clothes—whatever was trendy at the time we left Earth.

Women seem to be more inventive than men in this regard. They either have queen-size wardrobes stashed away somewhere, or they are constantly busy making alterations. Many of them must have brought needle and thread on the voyage. Intentional anachronism: none of them know what a needle or a thread is. They probably have electronic gadgets that unravel seams and stitch the cloth into new shapes. Jewelry is also a big item.

They are very vulnerable to stylistic herd mentality, for reasons which throughout my entire life I have never—never—been able to understand. This year they all wear their collars up, touching their chins; last year they had no collars on their blouses and wore pantsuits, with cleavage. The year before, it was demure lace at the throat and a skirt from the waist to the knees, below which the pant legs remained black elasto-cling, unhealthily constrictive. The skirt has risen to mid-thigh in recent months. How do they communicate to each other what they must do next?

My own sartorial standards are simple and unchanging: cowboy boots, jeans, checkered shirt, red bandana around my neck, and my thousand-*Uni* tweed blazer over the upper torso. Strapped to my waist is a frayed leather belt. Clipped to it is the trusty survival kit I bought during my teens with my first wages, containing the old fold-knife, flint, and compass. You never know when you might need to hijack a jet or find your way back to your home planet.

Day 110:

I try to put in two or three hours each day, working on pet theories, doodling with unified field conjectures, inventing mathematical neologisms (Neil-ogisms), having my fun. It keeps the mind alert and stimulates motivation with the promise that I just might extend the frontiers a little. However, after three months of it, my attention is wandering. I am experiencing what I have so rarely felt in my life, a sense of "boredom". When I first realized what was happening, I felt a stab of fear. Would this infect me more and more, I wondered? Would I become a tiger, pacing a cage, and end up frothing at the mouth and clawing the walls of my room? Or (more apt) would I become a flea bouncing frantically inside a matchbox? Such hallucinatory prospects paralyzed me for a few moments, and during this brief but horrible event, I glanced at *max* (don't capitalize him, Neil, for heaven's sake, don't capitalize that name!), afflicted with a sudden craving for a film to watch. Socially approved escape mechanism number one. An escape encapsulated within an interstellar escape mechanism of epic proportions, a multitude of escapes stacked one inside the other, like Chinese boxes or Russian Marushka dolls.

I tore my eyes away from *max*—from *the* max—pulled on my snake bite boots and went for an angry, limping hike all around the four concourses, avoiding every elevator and driving myself up and down the stairways. It helped. But it left me a little rattled.

I gotta get out more!

Interesting how my written notes have become fewer and farther between. I make entries in my voice diary each day, small memos, noting the names of those whom I meet: for example, my weekly chats with Xue, and also the nonscheduled exchanges I've had with the astronomer Strachan McKie of the Royal Observatory in Edinburgh, designer of the new tower at the ROE, author of many brilliant, somewhat idiosyncratic books—yes, the very man after whom the McKie Ultra Deep Field was named—that apparently empty corner of space where he discovered about three thousand new galaxies and more than eighty new quasars.

Encounters with McKie are neither lengthy nor memorable, seasoned as they are with his crabby comments and complaints, his antisocial nature demanding that human interaction be kept to the minimum, unless a subject arises in conversation that interests him (i.e., quasars). By coincidence, I brought along on the voyage my well-thumbed paperback copy of his book on quasars, not knowing he would be aboard. White-haired, cranky, tall but bent like a bad penny nail. I like him. He's a misfit like me.

Also, there is Dr. Maria Kempton of Sydney University, whom I first met in a lounge one evening when I was feeling shiftless. She initiated the conversation, asked if I was Dr. Hoyos the physicist. Inwardly I sighed, since I am not dedicated to my reputation. A lively irrational discussion with a real child would have been so much more rewarding, but, alas, children are entirely absent from our little venture, and are a somewhat endangered species back on our home planet.

Kempton is in her early sixties, but it took no stretch of the imagination to see that she had once been a lovely young woman. She opened the exchange by mentioning that we have something in common because we are both lapsed members of Mensa.

"You have lapsed?" I exclaimed with feigned shock.

"Yes, long ago. High IQs don't guarantee that you remember to keep your membership renewal up to date."

I knew why I had once been a member—I had been badgered into it by Xue for reasons of prestige—but I was curious to know her reason and asked why she had joined the elite brain club.

"Well, I was very young", she said with a thoughtful look. "It was pride in the beginning. And loneliness. The desire to find people with whom I could discuss things without them wondering if I was a dysfunctional, masculinized gnome."

"Which you very obviously are not", I replied with a little bow, dropping my cowboy accent, since I quickly realized she is one of those totally honest people you meet from time to time.

"Thank you, Dr. Hoyos."

"Please call me Neil."

"Neil. I'm Maria."

I asked about her area of expertise. Microbiology, she informed me, then launched into an intriguing conjecture about what kind of life we may find on our destination planet, that is, if we find any life. It is possible, she says, though by no means certain. However, AC-A-7 is in the Habitable Zone, is about the same size as Earth, about the same distance from AC-A as Earth is from our sun; moreover, AC-A is only a little larger than our sun. These "abouts" and "littles" represent immense distances and quantities, and thus we can only hope to find life there.

"Even if we do", she added, "the planet could be millions of years younger or older than ours, and whatever life it may have could be either extremely primitive or dying out in its end phase."

"Then there's the various sorts of ionizing radiation", I added, "which we have no way of measuring at this point."

"Mmmm, yes, the gamma rays and x-rays, you mean. Without sufficient shield, I suppose that would put an end to things pretty quick."

"They'd never get started, actually."

An enjoyable conversation. It concluded with her showing me photographs of her grandchildren. Yes, she has more than one. Apparently, she and her husband had three children, since Australia was the last state to sign the one-child global policy accords. Each of their children married and produced a single legal child, for a total of three! She's a very lucky woman. A strange joy took hold of me as I examined those bright shining faces. This was followed by a cordial goodbye on both our parts, and an agreement to talk again if we should happen to bump into each other.

As I said, there is a great deal to interest me on board, everything from the hydroponics garden (they have a good selection of vegetables, succulent vine fruits, and vividly colored flowers), to the arboretum (a wide selection of trees from every continent), to chess games in the commons, aerobics tracks around the ship on all four concourses, flights of stairs, sports and exercise rooms, and libraries.

(Note to myself: I really, really must read the Manual more carefully. I recently discovered that indexed under ship's services are the libraries, more than I had stumbled upon during my first exploration of the concourses. Taking a peek into one of them, I had assumed they were all the same: digital, "oak"-lined, full of arm chairs and fake fireplaces burning fake logs, visually appealing but lacking any tactile books. Today, however, while roving through deck A, I stumbled upon the single actual library, containing close to twenty thousand volumes, intelligently selected.)

Despite the myriad choices that lend themselves to keeping one active and interested, this does not consume so much of my day that I am deprived of an opportunity to make voice records in my e-diary. But I notice that I've lately been skipping days at a time. This written journal suffers even more from such lapses. Does consciousness change with the alteration of space-time? I would expect so, but it is not really measurable. Maybe the anorexia of the journal entries is no more than a case of my wrist muscles squeaking their little protests. "Stop writing all the time, Neil", they say. "Just enjoy life." My ankle hurts more than usual; I'm not sure why. I'll make an appointment with a doctor. There are plenty on board. Hmmm, now whom should I choose? Or do they choose for us? Guess I'll find out.

Day 121:

It turns out that they do indeed assign specific lists of potential patients to specific doctors. It would be interesting to check out the lists, to see who got who, and try to figure out why. I think they keep this information confidential since it would encourage musical chairs and create logistical havoc, human beings being what we are. My physician is a young East-Indian lady, Dr. Pia Sidotra. She's a specialist in tropical medicine, infectious diseases, and toxicity (industrial/chemical accidents). Graduate in General Medicine from Mumbai University, surgery from Université Pierre et Marie Curie in Paris, tropical medicine at Djakarta U.

During our first consultation, I tried to keep my defensive forcefield up. I don't automatically trust doctors. I especially don't trust young, brilliant, women doctors. First of all, they are professionals in highly prestigious positions, which implies that they have successfully navigated the world we live in, and are almost certainly very pleasant creations of the government, full of clone thoughts regarding basic human questions. In my experience, they have issues to work out. It may be said, to their credit, that they have to strain to be detached, even though practitioners in their field generally treat humans like bio-mechanisms. But ladies can slip into caring too much,

45

and thus they tend to overcompensate by becoming harder than men. They are also so thorough and good at what they do that in the end it's just easier to die than to endure all the trouble and testing they like to put a person through. Give me liberty or give me death, I say.

In any event, that was my attitude when we shook hands and began the consultation. She surprised me, however, by initiating a battery of oral health questions, using a pencil on paper on clipboard on knee.

"That's antiquarian of you", I opined. "One might go so far as to say anachronistic. I hope you approve of anesthetic for surgeries."

"In extreme cases", she said, with a small smile.

"Well, I'm a really extreme case."

"I can see you are." She paused and glanced down at her clipboard. "Dr. Hoyos, we've received no transmissions from your HUMVS here at the medical center. Of course, it's your choice to wear one or not, but according to medical law, I have to inquire about it, to make sure you haven't lost the transmitter without realizing it."

"I just decided not to use it."

She made a check mark on her paper.

"Test done?" I asked. "Did I pass?"

"I need to take your vital signs first."

After she had wrapped a pressure band around my arm and tapped a button to take the readings, I asked her if she had chosen to have a humvee implant or patch for herself.

"Neither", she replied quietly, without taking her eyes off my beeping graphs.

"May I ask why not?"

"I've always been concerned about the long-range effects of wave transmissions on living cells—only as an amateur interest, you understand. Perhaps an overly suspicious one."

"I've been concerned too, for other reasons."

"Physics?"

"No, philosophical—only an amateur interest, you understand—combined with general ornerariness."

Again she smiled.

"Would you like to know your vital signs results?"

"Just a summation, please."

"You're a very healthy man for your age. How do you keep fit?"

"I attribute it to fresh air, fresh water, natural and illegal foods, minimal electronic wave exposure, certain criminal activities that harm no one but myself, and so forth."

"Excellent", she said.

She hadn't tripped over the words *illegal* and *criminal*. This was one unusual doctor.

"And how about exercise?" she asked.

"Only mental. Theoretical physics keeps a guy on his toes."

And so it went. Our conversation, which had begun so stiffly, became free-form banter. She told me that, much as she admired my achievements in science, reading theoretical physics had always shut down her higher brain functions. I reassured her that this was probably true for most of mankind. She mentioned that she likes the novels of Charles Dickens and Indian love songs. I told her that I once saw a Bollywood film, but the love song put me to sleep after thirty minutes of uninterrupted passionate chanting.

By now, I realized she was something of an anomaly: an authentically charming person, humorous, sensitive, definitely not a clone-thinker. Her eyes sparkled, and she waggled her head a little whenever she made a joke. Later, on the way back to my room, I suddenly burst out laughing when I got one of her subtler ones.

I should mention that she told me my right wrist may need no more than a little rest and penetrating muscle cream, but she has also scheduled more extensive tests. My ankle interested her a lot: the scar, the limp, the neurological damage, the story that goes with it. In the telling, I tried not to embellish.

"You were lucky", she said.

"I had a good dog."

"Was his name Lucky?"

"No, his name was Rusty."

"A good pal."

"The best."

"Without Rusty, the history of the human race would have turned out quite differently."

"Aw, shucks, Ma'am, you exaggerate my importance", I drawled.

"Shucks, Dr. Hoyos, I don't think I do."

If I'd had a Stetson hat, I would have popped it onto my head and squinted into the sunset. When you're sixty-eight years old, you can get away with being coy, shuffling in the direction of a mild

47

playfulness without alarming beautiful young women. They just see Dad, and chuckle.

Day 137:

With pen in my left-hand fingers, I'm scratching this explanatory note. Right wrist diagnosed with median neuropathy—carpal tunnel syndrome. I needed surgery. It's done. Hand and wrist in cast. (Attached digital photo, self-made with left hand. Sorry for blur.)

Dr. Sidotra asked me if I want her to open up my ankle and do some tinkering with a team of neurologists. I said no. Told her I like my limp, it gives me character.

Day 153:

The ship is now cruising at maximum velocity. We are slightly above half-lightspeed. This will put us in the neighborhood of the sister stars around nine years from now. Some time will be lost in deceleration, which begins five months out from our destination.

Day 204:

Feels good to be writing again. Not much to write home about. I've read a lot of books since my last entry (see attached list). Some loss of the finer mind/brain/motor control in the fingers. Pia says it will return with practice. I don't want to waste paper, so make do by scribbling with the stylus on the *max*'s imprint tablet. Seems to work well, since there is some improvement as long as I keep sending messages along the neuron paths, waking up the little fellows in my wrist and hand, one by one.

Day 206:

I woke from a strong dream last night. In it, I was as old as I am now. An elderly woman—an East Indian woman—was seated beside me.

48

We were on the afterdeck of a wooden houseboat, holding hands and watching birds flying over a lake. There was lapping water, floating water lilies perfuming the air, a slight breeze. A soaring mountain range rose above the far shore. The woman turned to me, and I saw that there was great love in her face, a beautiful face, her eyes wise and innocent. I was in love with her. In the dream, it seemed that I had loved her a long time.

She said, "You know me, Neil."

I answered, "Yes, but what is your name?"

When I awoke, the feeling of love burned quietly inside me, lingering a little. It has been such a long time since I felt anything like that. Tears started running down my cheeks. I put a stop to it quickly.

Day 291:

Rereading this journal some months after the above entry, I discovered that I had a similar dream on the flight from America to Africa. (See entry, 13 October, 2097, Earth base–Africa.) So, two dreams about an Indian lady, one of them occurring before I met Pia. The women in the dreams didn't look like Pia grown old, nor was there the sense of Pia-ness. Though I am fond of the few Indians I have met during my life, I have no exceptional attraction to them. Well, there was one, that girl I met at college, though it came to nothing. What was her name? Raina or Ryka, if I recall correctly. No, it was Raissa.

Obviously my subconscious is sending me oddly consistent cryptic messages. I am feeling my old age, am approaching the crest beyond which is precipitous decline. Yet I remain lonely for what might have been, for a family of my own, for a legacy of human lives to bequeath to the future. A torch hurled across the abyss of time. Too late for all that. Emotionally, dreams can suffice for reality. About the objective future, well, we must leave that to the future archivist, if there be a future for our sad little island-universe race.

I don't feel much like writing. The visual screen shows no change outside the "window". It's beautiful, but static; the channel never changes. Only AC-A-7 has changed. It is closer but still a blur.

The human mind is stimulated by change, motivated by meeting the challenge of novelty or threat or pleasure, rewarded with the sensations of being instrumental in altering environments, and will

49

persevere in this as long as there is some degree of perceivable progress. People turn to knitting baby booties, doing crossword puzzles, collecting rare coins; they may even make an effort to understand $E=mc^2$ or to study the genetic adaptations of cacti, but in all cases, they need to see some fruit of their labors.

We weren't permitted to bring personal flora or fauna on the voyage. Only the ship's official botanists and zoologists have authority in those departments. Our first step on the planet will be absolutely sterile, just to make sure we don't ruin someone else's ecosystem. Wise move. Still, I do wish I could have smuggled on board my little potted *Echinopsis chacoana*, with its splendid white flower, and also *Opuntia polyacantha*, with its brilliant crimson blooms. What a consolation it would be to have one's own personal organic friends to care for in this lonely universe. Like humans, they are a combination of prickles and glory. Alas!

Day 299:

Speaking of prickles, and not much glory, Dr. Strachan McKie waxed personal today when we ate together in the cafeteria. It began when he banged down his tray on the table, sat himself across from me, and commenced: "They're bona fide idiots up there on the secret deck."

"Why do you say that, Stron?" I asked, intrigued.

"They're protocol zombies, that's why. I just had a talk with the chief flight astronomer, and asked him why the hell the on-planet astronomers aren't invited upstairs. He said something to the effect that personally, *personally*, he'd be ever so pleased to have me take part in the cabal, but it's against the rules. Against the rules, he said, the sniveller."

Then followed a stream of colorful Scottish invective. The mood tab behind his ear began flashing an ugly red. I heard a faint tinny voice coming from somewhere near it.

"Shut up!" he bellowed, and tore the thing from his skin. Fuming, he tossed it onto the floor. Then he opened his shirt front and ripped a humvee from his chest, throwing it onto the floor as well.

"Ouch", he snarled, since his unpremeditated violence had made him lose a few white chest hairs.

"Why would such a sensible idea be against the rules?" I pressed.

"What?" he barked.

"Why is it against the rules to have both sets of astronomers getting together?"

"They don't want any cross-pollination."

"Intellectual cross-pollination, you mean?"

"Right. He says they want two sets of eyes observing from different perspectives. Triangulation. Depth perception."

"Sounds like nonsense to me, Stron. It's good policy in some fields, but I can't for the life of me see why it would be useful to astronomers in our situation. You're all in the same spot, aren't you? And you still will be when we land on the planet."

"Exactly", he growled. "So what's going on here?"

"Maybe nothing more than knee-jerk territorialism."

"Maybe. At best, it's knee-jerk compartmentalization, minus the knee."

I laughed. "Well, I wouldn't let it get under your skin. Surely, they don't see any more than we see on the public screens."

"Aye, but they do get to look at a whole lot more instruments than we do. I want to see the spectrographs. I want magnetic readings, gravity aberrations, full-spectrum wave records—the lot."

I now recalled that among his many achievements, Stron is the discoverer of the spectrum factor that is widely known in the astronomy community as the "McKie edge". This is a light anomaly that he posits as a bio-signature of chlorophyll-bearing photosynthetic plants in atmospheres where ozone, oxygen, and methane are present.

"You want to see the edge", I said.

"Damn right, I want to see the edge! But the boys upstairs want to keep it all to themselves so they can write the definitive papers on the big discovery. One small step for a man, one giant leap for the onboard astronomers."

His face was now flaming, his hands clenched.

"You may be right", I said. "Still, it's not worth a heart attack."

That brought him up short. He glared at me with one eye closed.

"What's your favorite sport?" I asked.

"My favorite sport?"

"Yeah. Mine's basketball. What's yours."

"Don't be ridiculous, Hoyos. And don't distract me. This is serious."

"I know it's serious. Answer my question."

He snorted. "Curling."

"Stones on ice?"

"No, not just stones on ice. Not tin box rinks and artificial ice with synthetic stones smacking while the vidcams blink-blink-blink."

"Then what . . . really . . . is curling?"

"You're a tricky man, Hoyos."

"I know. So, what's real curling?"

Stron sat back and closed his eyes.

"Curling is every sense you can imagine uniting in concentrated ecstasy. It's art. It's war. It's history. It's sheer poetry." He opened his eyes. "*Hard* poetry, you understand."

"That's an interesting insight. In what way is it hard poetry?"

"Imagine a frozen loch, braced by mountains, thick, clear ice, blue-green, all the snow blown off by an angry wind. Imagine the pure air, your cheeks flushed with the cold, the oxygen pumping through your blood, thoughts clear, feelings high. You hear the sound of a real rock rumbling along the echoing ice and smacking another rock, sending it in a trajectory, with angle, speed, and distance all estimated, subject to the vagaries of nature."

"Like billiards."

"Only superficially. With curling, you have total joy, total investment of the body, mind, and soul, not escape from the self. But these paltry descriptions are a disgrace. There are no words to express its beauty."

"I'd love to learn the game some day. If we ever return to Earth . . ."

"If we ever return to Earth, you come to Scotland. Not the tourist's Scotland, mind you. You come and see me."

"I will."

"I think you mean it, lad."

"I do mean it." And I did.

The flame was waning from his face, burred humor lurking on the frontiers of his personality, the hands curled around his knife and fork but no longer clenched. You wouldn't want to be within eight feet of him if he had a claymore sword in his hands, but he was, almost certainly, the greatest living astronomer in the world.

He threw a huge chunk of scrambled "egg" down his throat and peered at me with some interest. "Heard your lecture. Very good."

"Thank you."

"Would have been better without the gawdawful music."

"Tastes vary. I hear people liked that part."

"No accounting for taste. Your gravity conjectures match my own."

I leaned forward. "Do they? Tell me more."

He did, and I listened, growing increasingly amazed by what this great mind had conceptualized. At the end of it, he pushed back his chair and stood. "Do you take a drink?"

"I'm not much of a drinker these days. Though I do like a dram now and then."

He grinned. "Good. I've got just the right stuff for you. *Coom wi's.*"

In a little art alcove on Concourse C (under a Picasso-lady cut into pieces and badly reassembled), we sipped clandestine thirty-year-old whiskey from a flask that he produced from inside his ratty tweed blazer. First, he checked up and down the hallway to make sure no one would happen along and see us.

"We needn't hide in corners, Stron", I said with a laugh. "There's no surveillance on board."

He said nothing in reply, just fixed me with an intimidating look.

"Oh, I get it. You don't want anyone and everyone lining up for a free drink, right?"

"Wet your gullet while you can", he growled, pushing the flask toward me again.

When we were comfortably fuelled and mellowed, he told me he had to get back to work and further informed me that he had decided we should talk again. And so, I hope, we shall.

Day 300:

Many people have voyage-related jobs. More than two hundred others are here only in view of planet-work, and thus have a lot of free time on their hands. Recalling my own nasty bout with claustrophobia and aimlessness, I wondered how they fill their idle hours, when, in fact, all their hours are idle hours. Or so I thought. I asked Stron what he does to cope with this. He told me that he needs three lifetimes to complete the papers he's writing. He says he is also performing experiments in a private laboratory.

"You need a laboratory for astronomy?" I asked.

"Different research entirely, Hoyos. I've developed a fascination for physics."

"Wonderful, Stron, wonderful!"

"'Tis indeed. However, though I hate to disappoint you, it's not astrophysics to which I'm referring. Nor theoretical physics. More a practical application: the relationship between hydrogen and oxygen and various organic compounds and how they behave under pressure and heat, the condensation process—that sort of thing."

"Ah", I said, bored.

I asked Dwayne the cleaner guy what he does to make his off-hours pass quickly.

"Books", he replied.

"What kind of books?"

"All kinds."

"And what about the other maintenance people?"

"Plugged in."

"Pardon me?"

"Plebeian mind-nummers."

"They like Math?"

"Numb. Numbing. Nummers, not num-bers."

"So, what are plebeian mind-nummers?"

"The old maximum e-drug. Surfing, vids, films, holo-porn."

"Digital environmental chambers?"

"DECs? Yup, there's a lotta people hooked on them too."

He paused and looked me squarely in the eyes for a moment. "Um, I think you should avoid using the *max* as much as you can, Doctor."

"Really? Why?"

"Uh, it's addictive. Sorry, I gotta go now. Bye."

I had supper with Xue and raised the topic of boredom, something from which he has never suffered. I was certain he would have projects on the go, and I was right. We also chatted about the problem in general: the nine years of time to kill for more than two hundred people on board.

"Didn't you know, Neil? Didn't you read the contract you signed?"

"That ridiculous contract, Owly! No, I most certainly did not read all 180 pages of it, including the numerous appendixes and small print. I'm still trying to make headway in the Manual, and that's 2,200 pages."

"Right. But in principle, it's better to read the documents you sign, don't you think?"

"Yeah, in principle."

"Well, my point is, in the contract, it states that the scientists who are designated only for planet work are mandated to do research and write papers during the outward bound flight—'as a contribution to humanity' the contract says. It may produce some useful developments, but I believe it's mainly a make-work project to keep people busy."

"I see. And why don't I know about this? Nobody's making *me* do research."

"You really didn't read the fine print. The contract exempts the Nobel winners from that stipulation. I expect they thought we'd suffer from the opposite problem, too much intellectual eagerness."

"Well, they're wrong, at least in my case."

Later, in the lounge, I happened upon Maria Kempton and asked her if she was doing "mandated" research.

She frowned. "Yes, well, we have to, don't we? Otherwise, they would dock our pay and *mandate* counseling sessions with DSI."

I shook my head. "Sounds kind of pushy to me."

"We signed the contract", she shrugged. "It was the only way to be part of this expedition. Fortunately, we're permitted to choose our own topics."

"Have you chosen yours?"

She smiled. "I've got a project on the go. It's a sociological study."

"That's a big leap from biology."

"Yes, but the overseers don't see it that way. They think everything about humanity is biology. Care to read my manuscript?"

"Uh ... in all frankness, Maria, ... much as I ..."

She laughed. "Good. A healthy reaction, Neil. You don't have to read it. But let me say this: While I *never* tell lies, I do sometimes enjoy having a little joke. May I give you a thumbnail sketch of my thesis?"

"Of course, please, sketch away and don't hold back."

"Did you know that for the past three generations the declining kangaroo population has been a problem in Australia?"

"I thought their overpopulation was your perennial problem."

"Right, ever since colonial days. But about seventy-five years ago, the ratio of human to roo began to reverse itself. Protein-deprived Aussies began to kill the creatures in large numbers, as well as the rabbits imported in the 1800s, which are the real pests, since they strip the country bare and multiply at astounding rates. Then the Green governments made it illegal—endangered species and all that. Aussies, as you may know, are a race of former criminals, and most of the time, we just function on basic common sense. Despite the laws, the roos and rabbits continued to decline, and the country continued to get greener. But that didn't please the Greenies any. Their real, if unstated, problem was with people. So the mask came off, and they demanded an increase in the human depopulation controls. A lot of people wound up as residents of state zoos."

"Pardon me?"

"Uh, prison. The one-child accords were signed later, in my generation. You know the rest."

"And you're writing a history of this?"

"Let's just say I'm writing a case study—the true case study."

"That's risky."

"The first hundred pages will be so nuanced and so loaded with socially responsible jargon that the readers won't know what's coming. If I do it carefully, they'll be nudged ever so gradually into seeing reality, despite their lifetimes of sucking in state and media propaganda."

"I didn't know you were a terrorist, Maria."

"And proud of it. Privately, I call my book *Out Malthusianizing the Malthusians*. Its official title, registered with the DSI oversight committee, is *Relevant Biofactors in Macropod Marsupial Population Statistics in the Australian Continent, 1886 to 2096, Volume I*. Like it?"

"Love it."

"If I ever complete the darn thing, it will be filed away in the computer and probably never read, not even by anyone capable of getting past the first few pages."

"Somebody might read it. Maybe when it's archived back on Earth one day."

"Maybe. If they ever do, it could keep a few DSI overseers off the streets. Shock the future-shockers, you see. By the time they get wise to me, I'll be a very, very old lady sitting in a rocking chair on the porch of a cabin in the Simpson Desert, eating roo pie and rabbit stew."

Day 302:

Xue cornered me in the lounge, where I was observing the inter-gender, interracial courting rituals of young scientists enclosed as specimens in their own experiment. It was amusing, it was interesting, it was entirely predictable. They're all so brainy, but they do appear to have emotional lives, though in various degrees of openness. They are not stupid about the potential follies, yet they devise new forms of conversational gambits and body language that initiate relationships without commitment. Silly young folk, they will fall in love with each other regardless of all that armor—*amour* conquers armor every time. Inevitably, some heart-blood will flow in communion or spill out through open wounds. That is standard practice in our world, of course, but here we have a clinical chamber in which it is possible to observe at close hand any mutations that might arise.

Civil marriages are legal back on Earth, though uncommon. Most people just bypass the paper work and settle the issue with a post-coital shake of the hands. However, official civil unions have been banned from the voyage because the sociologists and psychologists pre-determined that they would make the social infrastructure too com-plicated (housing, cheating, legal hassles, divorces, etc.). Of course, sexual encounters are perfectly legal for all who desire them, but these remain a matter of private negotiations between the parties involved. All of this is in the contract everyone signed.

In addition, most of the younger set were sterilized during the pre-flight stage, to which they had agreed because it doubled their wages. I declined DSI's generous offer for several personal reasons, though not from any illusions that I might become the progenitor of a clan of little Hoyos. Doubtless, a few staff members have retained their potency or fertility, taking the long, long view that one day they might like to create a human child. This small minority, whom I heartily applaud in the secrecy of my thoughts, adds a certain mys-tery to the voyage. I presume that sexual encounters are indeed hap-pening on board, and perhaps the fertile ones give to the situation the flavor of Russian roulette. Contraceptives sometimes fail, human relationships are a mess, and I hate to even think about it. Moving on quickly . . .

What was I talking about? Oh, yes, Xue cornered me in the lounge.

"Something for you, Neil", he said with a bow and presented me with a slip of rice paper.

"Shui-mo?" I asked, taking the paper delicately into my hands, feel-ing something akin to reverence. On closer inspection, I saw that it was a calligraphed poem.

"I wanted to add a ship on a sea, implied rather than articulated, since elegance of line is everything in Shui-mo. After consideration, however, I decided this would make a hybrid of two languages. No, let the poem alone speak to Neil, I told myself."

"Thank you. I will treasure it."

The poem:

> My little boat is made of ebony;
> My flute stops are pure gold.
> Water loosens stains from silk;
> Wine loosens sadness from the heart.
> With good wine, a graceful boat,
> And a sweet girl's love,
> Why be jealous of mere gods?
>
> —Li Po, 8th century

Four magnet beads now hold it to the wall beside my pillow. Laying my weary head down to take my rest, I read it fairly often. One apprehends the invigorating winds of Asia, perspective, horizons.

Day 307:

There was another highlight this week:

In order to stave off ennui, I decided to learn a new language, that is, Kashmiri. Of course, Hindi or Tamil, even Urdu, would probably be more useful in the long run, but one must have dreams, and I have not given up the fancy I once had as a young man—to live on a boat in my extreme old age, drifting through the floating lotus gardens of Lake Dal in Kashmir, lulled to sleep every night in sub-Himalayan breezes scented with water lilies and by the frantic mesmerizing music of northern India. Mesmerization begins as stimulation but ends as stupor, and in its best form, as sleep.

(Aha! Here is the source of my recurring dreams. I now see that my subconscious popped the old Indian lady into the waterscape, just to humanize it.)

In any event, while browsing in the book library, I happened to seat myself in an armchair beside a man of Indo-European appearance, who was reading *Moby Dick* with close attention. When he inserted a finger between pages, closed the book temporarily, and gazed upward into his own thoughts, I cleared my throat and broke his concentration. I need not write down every word of the convoluted discussion that ensued. In short, he is Dr. Dariush Ibrahimi Mirza, a philologist (one of six on board), originally from New Tehran, specialist in the Iranian languages, Persian, Pashto, Kurdish, as well as ancient Indo-European and Semitic languages. He taught at Cambridge University before he was invited on the voyage. Regrettably, he has never studied Kashmiri.

In manner, he is exquisitely polite, in temperament diffident, but a technical question easily catapults him into soliloquies or lectures. Exactly, *exactly* what I want. Later, through a search on the main computer, I learned that Mirza is a surname suffix that indicates nobility. Like everyone else on Earth, he is a democratic person, yet there lingers in his style the ethos of an older age: rich and monarchial. He is a very concentrated scholar, non-humorous, overgenerous with detailed facts that can mean nothing to anyone outside his field. He tells me he hopes to find evidence of civilizations on the planet, living or extinct, so that he can apply his skills to deciphering their writings. We have agreed to pursue a joint study of Kashmiri, since this language has similarities to other Indo-Aryan languages more familiar to him.

Day 341:

Our study progresses most amiably. We have developed a ritual of having a drink together after each session. The bistro on Concourse B serves alcohol diluted in various fruit juices, which I suspect are not quite organic but do taste like the real thing. Syntho-inebriation loosens sadness from the heart, Li Po might have said. Of course, alcohol consumption is strictly limited. The bartender knows who we are (each passenger has an identicard, which is scanned into his debit/credit account). There is not much to purchase on a pleasure cruise like this, and besides, all of our needs are more than adequately met. Still, it's beneficial for morale to go out for a meal or a drink. It's playacting, but most people indulge in it—more and more as the journey progresses.

I can now remember—and say—fifty-eight Kashmiri words. I trotted them out for Dariush this evening as he sipped his mango drink and I sipped my pomegranate. When I had finished my recitation, he applauded with childlike enthusiasm. Then, tilting his head back and closing his eyes, he recited three hundred words or so. I listened to it all, impressed and silenced—mesmerized, one might say. I went to bed early and dreamed about a place I loved when I was a boy, the desert near Las Cruces.

Day 365:

A year! It went by so swiftly. What did I do with myself? I can't remember a lot of it. In a circumscribed community, one's life is relieved from tedium by the highlights of significant events: a surgical operation, a spark of affection in another human being, a shared interest, a mini-crisis. There is also relief in gleaning bits of knowledge, be it pithy or frivolous. The ship's main computer holds pretty much everything recorded in human history. Apparently, each individual *max* contains about 25 percent of what's in the master computer, this reduction due to a sensible avoidance of repetitiousness and amateurish material. If we want to, we can always access the master at terminals in the libraries. For example, my *max* gives me a choice of 5.7 million references (from twenty-nine thousand articles) on the subject of high-energy photons; the main computer offers one hundred and forty-two thousand articles on the subject. It would take me about three trillion years of constant reading to have a look at every page on my *max* alone, abridged though the little gismo may be.

I know very well that e-surfing is a drug, addictive for shiftless people like me. Regardless, just for fun the other day, I said "search" into my *max*, and then the words, "conflict resolution between iguanas". Seven thousand entries popped onto the screen. I said "mumbo jumbo pudding" and got three hundred entries. Then I spoke random gobbledygook, and got no entries. A good sign, because it means the computer is really thinking. Still trying to confound the cyberbrain, I said, "tuna wars". To my surprise there were 2.3 million entries. I had no idea there had actually been wars over tunafish generations ago.

I tried to beat the system one more time, and said "pine-bark beetle revolts—word specific override". Bingo, success at last! I had whittled it down to three entries. Imagine my surprise when I discovered that two of the three were articles in little New Mexican online journals, reporting my arrest by the eco-police some years back. The third was also about the arrest, a damage-control, propaganda article in the *Santa Fe Times* written by the regional director of the department that arrested me. Ah well, it's nice to know I've been recorded by history. Nobel guys are a dime a dozen, but genuine eco-criminals are rare.

Eight more years to go.

Day 492:

Not a good sign. Not good at all. Months have passed since my last entry in this written journal. Numerous human encounters and private musings have occurred in my life since then, but I lack the motivation to recount them on paper. I have plenty of paper and my wrist is fine now, but my mind seems to have lost interest. At best, I dictate a weekly entry of significant happenings (or not so significant) into my voice diary. I can't understand the gap. I have decided to get a grip on myself and squeeze out some written things—anything—a discipline that may invigorate me. My regimen of physical exercise continues without interruption, but that is only because I hate feeling decrepit. The mind is a subtler dimension, hidden, and its private struggles can do much damage, even turning you into one of those irrational street-persons of times past, who babbled their cryptic genius to strangers cornered on sidewalks. I do not want to become a ghost that haunts this ship.

In my experience, scientists in old age tend to become obsessive, focusing entirely on minutiae in their own fields, growing ever more myopic, indifferent to their surrounding world. One has to work at broadening the range of interests. But when I make the effort, I sometimes sigh and ask, "What's the point?"

My sense is that love is the ultimate motivator. It takes a multitude of forms, this love. First and foremost is the reasonable love of self—in other words, self-respect. Then there is the love for expanding the horizons of knowledge for the benefit of others, many who are not yet born. If there is no aggravated pride in it, nor any feeding of a false persona, then it is an altruistic kind of love that seeks no personal reward other than the satisfaction of knowing that one has enhanced the life of others. It is a kind of fruitfulness. Is not this yearning toward fruitfulness written in the code of all human beings? I think so. Nevertheless, we can be totally blind to what we're about when we pursue certain lines of activity. And I wonder why this yearning mostly dries up in the desert of human relationships. In a real desert, even a cactus will flower.

Scratch the verbiage I have penned above, and ... what I'm really saying is, I'm lonely. Ah, poor me, ol' hound dog baying at the moon.

Day 495:

It's been more than a year since Dwayne and I struck up our relationship—lone cowpokes sittin' round the campfire tradin' stories. Yup, nope, maybe, and every now and then a flash from his surprisingly well-stocked vocabulary. Not too long ago, over a game of traditional checkers, I asked him to stop calling me Dr. Hoyos.

"Dunno if I can do that", he replied, after giving it some thought.

"Call me Neil", I said with a tone of command. "After all, I called you Dwayne practically from the start."

"Uh-huh, but that sort of fit right."

"The whole world calls everybody by their first names, so why don't you?"

"Whole world calls what ain't family, family, and what ain't free, free, and what's up, sideways or down altogether."

"Could you repeat that, please, Dwayne?"

"I mean the hierarchical relationships in human affairs are really quite skewed, Dr. Hoyos."

"Hierarchical? Where did you ever learn that word?"

He shrugged and failed to offer further response on the matter. Instead, he made a move, and said, "King me."

Every now and then, I bump into Stron McKie lurching down a corridor. He squints, beckons me into an alcove, and there we sip his clandestine whiskey. Today we went into covert mode beneath a marble statue—Greek, I think.

"What on earth is this?" I gestured to the statue with disgust, in a state of mild alarm, actually.

"This", said Stron, with a glint in his single open eye, "is the *Laocoön*. Observe, Neil, observe what we are as a race. Look at him wrestling with the snakes. Here's the poor fella trying to warn his countrymen that the gift horse is hollow, full of enemy soldiers, but the Trojans won't listen. And those wretched gods won't help either. They're the worst of the lot. It's them that sends the snakes out of the sea to devour poor old Laocoön and his sons."

"Er, Stron, do you think we could move to another spot?"

"Sure, why not."

We headed down the concourse to the next alcove and slipped inside. This one contained an abstract painting by someone named Rothko. The label informed us that its title was *Untitled*. Swaths of mulberry blur. Very nice, but I've seen better carpets.

"Forty million *Uni* for that one", said Stron, with a distinctly sarcastic tone.

"Let's go", I grumbled.

The next alcove contained *Whistler's Mother*, or possibly a fine, hand-painted copy.

"That lady is a clone of my old Gran", said Stron. "She too was overfond of the wee dram."

So there we stayed, and there we enjoyed our drams.

Some scientists turn to Art in old age, some to golf, some to philosophical reflection, seeking a unified field theory of simply everything, with a door wide open to the meta-everything. It can take the form of religious philosophy, or it can take the form of cosmological aesthetics, but in all cases, it is a yearning forward to something. Something bigger than our petty selves.

Perhaps that is why mankind has agreed to invest its resources in this voyage. We seek to spark our own global imagination, to experience vicariously the thrill of discovering the unknown *other*, be it an empty planet or an inhabited one. Why do we hope for aliens, our hypothetical long-lost brothers somewhere out there in expanding infinity? What does this yearning tell us about ourselves? That we are a very lonely race? That we are communal beings, expanding outward as our very universe expands? Alternatively, why would some (a small minority) hope that we are alone? Would this latter model assure us that we are a unique phenomenon? I don't know. My attitude is one of wait-and-see.

But I digress. Today, in the interests of expanding my own horizons, I dug deep into my luggage (a nostalgia item, a nineteenth-century, Wells Fargo saddlebag) and brought forth from this trove a gemstone, four inches square, a turquoise cube carved by the hand of an Apache, Zuni, Spaniard, or late Americano. I had unearthed it in the desert while hunting rabbits during my second year at university. Among its intriguing characteristics are lines inscribed on six sides, indicating its mathematical octahedron; in addition, there are pinpoint bores for the zonohedron vertexes. I tried to explain to Pia what an anomaly this was, but I lost her after a reference to three-dimensional Euclidian space.

"It's beautiful", she said.

"It's yours", I replied.

Her face lit up as she held it (reverently) in the palm of her hand. She said nothing, her eyes growing moist. Then I noticed a silent thought arise behind the tears: Why is he giving me this?

I put on my cowboy act, made little jokes, and exuded paternity, just so she wouldn't be troubled by any false notions about my motives. But how to explain to an extremely lovely, feminine, highly accomplished young woman that you simply are glad of her being. You wish to enrich her life, tell her stories that will, perhaps, extend her own horizons a little farther. You admire her. You wish to thank her for making the sacrifices that have helped her become what she is. To speak such words would ruin them. Let the little stone speak.

She thanked me in a quiet voice, and said that she would *cherish* it. An old-fashioned expression, quaint, endearing. I grinned, slapped my knees, and stood up, told her I had to go see about a horse. She laughed and we said no more.

Day 511:

Why do people give gifts to those they care about? Often it's something the recipient doesn't really need. Lately, I've received a couple myself. One thing for certain, in my case, it ain't physical attraction or romantic delusions. My guess is that it's a variation on what I feel for Pia. They're saying they're glad I exist, glad I'm here on the ship with them, that somehow I make their lives more interesting. A physicist who limps along the corridors with his game leg, dressed in jeans and smoky checkered shirt, shod in cowboy boots, and gets reprimanded by a "social animator" for wearing them in the cafeteria, brightens up their day. They appreciate that I'm a bad old boy who just might shoot a bandito but would never, never insult a lady or be so thoughtless as to perform experiments that would suck them all into a black hole of absolute gravity. People are either irritated by "characters" or admire them disproportionately.

Today I received another gift. This one from Dwayne. How he got my e-mail address, I cannot guess. In any event, there suddenly appeared on my *max* screen an image of a middle-age cowboy in a wide sombrero, squinting at me, blowing smoke off the barrel of his six-shooter. The voice-over said in a rough, growly tone, "The only good alien is a dead one."

Last year he gave me (as a hand-written, hand-delivered note) his personal communications code, explaining that I could use it if I ever needed help accessing films on my *max*. This would bypass the normal bureaucratic procedure for calling service personnel and consequent delays. Ferreting about in my desk drawer, I found the slip of paper and typed in the numbers, summoning the suspected culprit. When he came online in audio-visual mode, I said, "Thanks for the message."

"Yup", he said, not even cracking a smile.

"Do you realize how politically incorrect that caption was?"

"Yup."

"Do you really want to kill aliens?"

"Nope."

"Who's the guy in the photo?"

"An actor. Twentieth-century guy."

"He's new to me. Was he a real cowboy?"

"Maybe."

"It would be a thrill to be one, wouldn't it."

After a short pause, Dwayne asked, "You mean, be an actor or a cowboy?"

"Cowboy."

"Then, yup."

"Lots of danger."

"It's a tough job, but somebody's gotta do it."

We signed off. I wracked my brains for something to give him in return. Nothing came to mind. Chinese poetry would hardly do. And I doubt he's interested in Heisenberg's uncertainty principle. Maybe the dialogue is the mutual gift.

Day 604:

Maria Kempton's husband was killed by a kangaroo.

Really, I'm serious. Life is very strange. Stranger still, she tells me that she first met him decades earlier when he saved her from another aggressive kangaroo. At first, I wondered if she was putting me on. But as she told the story, the tears in her eyes laid this suspicion to rest.

"We were on a tour", she said. "Most of us were new faculty at SU. I'd never met him before, hadn't even noticed him. The bus stopped for lunch in the outback, at a station where in those days people tried to make a living by raising sheep. I loved the desert, very dry but not as barren as it seems. Of course, I'd seen kangaroos and wallabies in the zoo, but not in their natural habitat. I wanted to see one up close, and spotted a young joey nibbling grass behind the roadside café where we were eating. I tiptoed closer and closer to him, with my camera in hand. Its mother bounded over and kicked me. I tried to get away, and tripped and fell onto the ground. The mother began to kick me harder, and I got some cuts, plus a lot of bruises. Out of nowhere, Edwin—my husband's name was Edwin—Edwin came running with a stick and threw himself between me and the kangaroo. He beat it back, and it leaped away into the desert with its joey. Edwin was cut too, bleeding more than I was, actually. By then, everyone from the bus came running."

"A brave knight", I said.

She nodded. "He was."

The freak incident that ended his life occurred some forty years later, on a family holiday. A male kangaroo attacked him while he was down on his knees looking for botanical specimens at the edge of the desert. No one was able to determine why it happened. The animal just came in a fury, without provocation, kicking and slashing like a maniac. Before he could rally, one of the claws severed the jugular vein in his neck. Maria, their children, and grandchildren threw rocks at the kangaroo, and it retreated. Edwin was dead within a few minutes.

"So you see," she said, "when I received the invitation to be part of the staff on the *Kosmos*, I felt ..."

I know what she felt. A chance to escape the pain of unbearable loss, to explore something bigger than tragedy, and perhaps to make a new beginning toward the end of one's life.

I said none of this. Just squeezed her hand and excused myself.

I've been doing some research and have learned that kangaroos are usually not aggressive; it's very rare for them to attack a human without provocation. I found the news of Edwin's death in an archive file of the *Sydney Morning Herald*. One muses on whether the kangaroo that was the occasion of his meeting his wife was the ancestor of the kangaroo that killed him. On the next page was an article by an eco-politician, writing about the need to obey the endangered species laws, under a banner headline: *Save the Kangaroo!*

Day 717:

I asked Dwayne what he is paid for his janitorial services.

"I mean," I said apologetically, "I hope they're paying you good wages."

"Very good", he said.

"Not that you can spend it, really. I'm curious to know why the large number of service personnel continues to work so diligently, while the rest of us sit back and enjoy a sabbatical."

"This way we get to come on the voyage. That's payment enough for most of us. But we also get double the pay we'd be earning back home. With no place to spend it, other than a meal out now and then, this means that in twenty years all us deck-swabbers and bottle-washers will be able to retire young. I'll be forty-eight years old when I see Earth again."

"Not a bad employment opportunity."

"And an adventure thrown into the bargain."

Recalling that sterilized people get double pay, I said, "Uh ... forgive me for asking, but do you hope to be married some day?"

"Yup."

"Hope to have children?"

I had used the plural, as in illegal. He fixed me with a cool, level stare. "Yup."

"What will you do when you retire?"

"Buy a small ranch, raise horses, and ... raise children."

"A worthy dream. May it become reality. By the way, have you ever seen the Santa Fe Mountains?"

We talked on about his dreams for some time. He had thought everything through in great detail. He wanted a family, independence—big horizons. I told him about my real cabin in the mountains. His eyes got all visionary as he tried to imagine it.

"So you dreamed too, Dr. Hoyos", he said at last.

"I did. It took patience and ingenuity getting there. It cost a lot. I don't mean money."

"I know you don't mean money. You mean the way things are."

"Yes, the way things are."

Day 730:

Second year completed. No changes in the panorama outside the window, at least none that my eyes can detect. Only the three sisters are slightly brighter, their magnitudes increasing at snail's pace. Telescopic zoom now gives us AC-A-7 as a well-defined sphere, very small, no surface details visible.

Day 819:

Here I am again, the lapsed journalist. Nothing much to report. I have at least five hundred Kashmiri words tucked away in my head, enough to make me functional in a certain state of northern India. Dariush the Great is master of a vocabulary numbering upward of three thousand words. He is not competitive about it; he is an enthusiast. We enjoy simple conversations in Kashmiri. Who could have predicted this for my life!

Stron's drinking is getting worse. Where does he find the stuff? I'll bet he stashes it in that little highland castle he calls his room. Nevertheless, he is always coherent.

Maria is doing well. She does a lot of knitting in public places, and younger folk gather around her. She has made many friends. Every home needs a mother, and she's great at it. Maria the truly Great.

Pia and I joke whenever we meet, just to keep things on an even keel. I believe she has found somebody to love among the flight staff. I see her nose to nose with him in various bistros now and then. The symptoms are unmistakable. I am pleased to observe that I am happy about it, since this reaction reveals to me that my affections are unselfish. How unseemly it would be, indeed pathetic, if the case were otherwise. Poor old Quasimodo.

Day 846:

Memory. My father.

I was seventeen years old, not yet graduated from high school. Hadn't kissed a girl, not for lack of optimism. Still succumbing to mad crushes that remained entirely hidden from other human beings. My main distraction from this sweet desperation was reading science and pursuing an obsessive-compulsive habit of killing snakes. Hundreds of them fell before my wrath each year. I harvested them from the glue board daily with unhealthy glee. I stalked them in the desert with unflagging determination. I had purchased my first set of cowboy boots by then, with money earned at the box factory during summer break. The boots were snakeskin laminate with a diamond pattern. I got a lot of teasing about it at school, but this ruffled not a feather of my homicidal soul—more accurately, my serpecidal soul. I wore the boots along with leather chaps whenever I went out into the desert with my .22, and later my .303, which blasted my victims conclusively. Later, a shotgun—even more satisfying.

I was a bit deranged at the time, but my parents understood, even approved.

That year, my father and I had built onto the trailer a plywood box extension that became my new bedroom. It seemed a mansion to me, with a ceiling taller than the trailer's. It had inbuilt bookshelves, stuffed full in short order. I kept a collection of rattler tails in a jar on a shelf. My mother insisted on a crucifix on the wall near the foot of the bed, so that I could look at it every night before falling asleep and see it again upon waking. But I was lapsing. My new religion was all about justice in *this* world. It had a single dogma. Nailed to the outside wall on the backside of the trailer were three whopping great rattler pelts, two diamondbacks that I'd shot in the bushes at the edge of the trailer park, and a sulphur yellow black-tail, which I'd shot out of a *piñon* tree. They were protected species, but I didn't give a rip about that. I could have gone to jail for what I'd done, but I was never caught. The neighbors never told on me. They all hated snakes too.

Yup, I was seventeen years old and angry about fate, about life (though rather glad to have it), plus the other standard teenage stuff. I had pimples, my ears stuck out too far, and all of this was snarled up with the unfairness of the limp. I knew that I could never be part of the basketball team. Never.

My father was now working as a heavy-equipment operator, outside of Santa Fe, pulling in good money. He and my mother had agreed that any extra should be invested in saving to put a down payment on his own dump truck, which would enable him to operate independently of the big guys. But this meant delaying the purchase of a home of our own. He drove down to Las Cruces on weekends, hoping that our beat-up 2031 Hydra would make it there and back again. He'd bought the thing, used, for a thousand *Unis* and disconnected its solar power and hydrogen apparatus, re-rigging it for compost-biomethane fuel. I think he bought it mostly because the logo looked like a guy in a cowboy hat. I always wondered if the Malaysians designed the logo with full knowledge that they were making a great big Yankee joke. I rather doubt it.

(Note: Back home in my real cabin, I have five rusting Hydra logos nailed to the wall of my garage. Also some snakeskins. They will have disintegrated by the time I return—the skins, I mean, not the cowboys.)

So, this one Saturday afternoon, we were prowling along the arroyo bed, both of us with .22s in hand, earnestly looking for the snake that had messed up my life three years earlier. I think in retrospect that his earnestness was less than mine, but his intention was strong, a commitment to justice. Or maybe just showing me I wasn't alone.

We had no luck, then or later, in finding any big rattler in the arroyo. Perhaps it died of old age, but I hope its life ended badly.

The day was hot, and we were sweating hard. We agreed to take a break and climbed up out of the arroyo, searching for something to sit on. Not far away, we found a fallen mesquite tree. It's not common to find one of them down because it has a long taproot. But this particular tree had tried to grow out of a pile of stones, and at some time in the recent past, a high wind had done the job. The ground was littered all about with its dead leaves and screw-beans. We kicked the thorns off the trunk to make safe sitting places, and deposited ourselves accordingly. It was a nice moment.

"We need a fire", said my father.

The weather was hot as blazes, but we both knew what he meant. I gathered mesquite twigs and made a heap of them, with dry bean pod as kindling, then fired it. I added larger branches as the flames caught hold. The smell of burning mesquite is the best perfume in the world. Smiling, we sat back down on the trunk, taking sips from our canteens.

I can't recall how long we remained without speaking. I remember only that the silence was comfortable, though it seemed to stretch longer than usual.

At last, he said in a raspy whisper, "Benigno, I'd cut off both my legs if I thought it would help you walk straight."

I froze, choked, sad, happy, unable to say anything because my father was not a man to express emotions.

I nodded and nodded, but he was looking somewhere else.

"I know, Papa", I said, when I could find my voice.

Standing up, he whacked the dust off his jeans with his hat, squinted into the lowering sun, clicked his tongue, and said:

"Yup. We got maybe an hour before we should head for home. Let's go get that rattler."

We never did get the rattler, but it didn't matter so much after that.

Day 867:

I often overhear people in the cafeterias comparing notes on their DEC experiences, clearly a very popular recreational activity. Everyone on board has a right to a monthly free suspension of reality in these digital environmental chambers. I thought I should give it a try, reminding myself that I could always walk out if I didn't like it. I signed onto a waiting list for the chamber on my floor, and after three weeks of waiting, it was my turn.

The DEC on deck B is situated on the central avenue, halfway between the ship's bow and stern. In the "hospitality foyer", I was greeted by a comely maiden, who offered me a mobile screen listing hundreds upon hundreds of "environments". Friendly and helpful, she walked me through the index, suggesting things like "Be an Actor in a Hollywood Crime Drama" (extremely popular), "An Afternoon in the Louvre" (also a hot item), "Swimming with the Blue Whale", "Lost in the California Redwoods", and so on.

"Got any deserts?" I interjected at one point.

She frowned and continued to search the index. "We don't get many requests for that", she murmured, absorbed in her work. "Maybe you're the first. Oh, yes, here we are—four entries. The Sahara, the Gobi, the Great Australian, and the American Southwest."

"I'll take the American."

She smiled with pleased approval. Her accent was American, I think, or omni-continental, and I could tell she was professionally happy for me. In any case, she led me into a labyrinth of halls and adjoining rooms from which came the faint sounds of people at bliss in their environments of choice. As we entered my chamber, I saw that it was the interior of a white sphere with a flat base platform.

"I'll need your identicard, Dr. Hoyos", she said with a slightly more formal air. I fished it out of my back pocket and handed it to her.

"Now, for specifics", she continued. "Do you prefer the total sensory or just the visual/audio package?"

I explained that I didn't really know what either of the options entailed.

"Well, if I may suggest, I think you'll want to try the total sensory. As you know, the DEC is free, but for an additional fee you can enjoy smells, touch, taste, and the psychological experience of total reality. It's more than watching a movie. Far, far more, and you get it with just a teensy sip of a delicious enhancer beverage."

"What's the cost?"

"Five hundred *Unis* for two hours, one hundred extra for each additional hour."

"Thanks, I'll just take my free hours."

She nodded with a whiff of disappointment, told me to lay myself down on the centrally positioned anti-gravity foam pad floating above the horizontal base of the sphere.

"I'd prefer to sit on the floor", I said. "Can we get rid of the flying carpet?"

She firmed her lips, nodded again, and tapped her remote, making the pad descend into a rectangular orifice that opened in the floor. A panel slid across it. Another tap, and the anti-gravity unit descended and was likewise capped. I sat down and crossed my legs, Indian style. She went out, closing the door quietly behind her. A minute later, a subtle musical theme swelled from invisible sources. The lights dimmed, and on the sphere all around me there materialized three-dimensional blue sky, desert vistas with horizon and mountains, a circle of sagebrush around me, a hawk soaring above, the sounds of wind and bird cries, a coyote yipping.

It was a fascinating display of technology, and half an hour of it was pleasant enough, though before long, it began to stir up too much longing. Beside me, a campfire crackled with a pot of coffee burbling on it. I was suddenly irritated by the lack of smells. I wished I'd taken the drug. Instinctively, I wanted more and more and more. I wanted it to be real. I wanted to go home! Of course, I knew I was being seduced, regardless of the illusion of choice, but more worrisome was the realization that I was on the verge of not caring about the cost, nor about the abandonment of my self to someone else's manipulation of my subconscious.

I got up, pushed open the door, and left, never to return.

Day 985:

Pia has been encouraging me (read, nagging me) to conquer the pull of lethargy by taking up swimming.

"Oh yeah", I said with a laugh. "I heard there was a swimming pool onboard."

"It's on level D. I do laps there every morning", she replied.

I begged off, pleading that I had once nearly drowned in the Rio Grande, my single attempt at swimming during my post-snakebite youth.

"It's usually crowded", she said, ignoring my excuse. "I suggest you go at odd hours. Are you a night owl?"

"Definitely. Is there a shallow end?"

"Definitely."

She went on to tell me that regular swimming would exercise my whole body without jarring any joints. It could even improve my limp.

"Give it a try, Neil, maybe in the middle of the night, when it's quieter."

Thus, for the sake of undeclared Platonic love, I agreed to give it a try. I passed a few days of ambivalence, however, before making the final decision to locate the pool. I checked the index in the Manual, impressed yet again by how much the *Kosmos* contained. It struck me as sensible that the ship's designers had placed the pool near the bottom. If there were leaks, neither Picasso nor Rothko nor Whistler would be soaked (the gravity generators are situated on PHM, in a ship-length component, which in an ocean-going vessel would have been called the "keel").

I thought I might go between three and four in the morning when few if any passengers would be there to laugh at me nervously paddling about in the kid's end of the pool with my rubber ducky.

Day 987:

At three o'clock this morning, I got up, dressed myself in my khaki shorts and T-shirt, slung a white towel around my shoulders, and padded barefoot (illegally) down Concourse B to the staircase. The lights in the concourses are dimmed from midnight until six in the morning, but there's plenty enough to see by.

Arriving at level D, I turned left and walked toward what I think is the rear end of the ship (its symmetry still disorients me) until I came upon a wall sign displaying a little manikin doing a crawl in waves, with illuminated arrows pointing to a cross-avenue. I followed directions and arrived, in due course, at a physical recreation complex somewhere midway between port and starboard. The pool area faced the corridor, with a wall of transparent floor-to-ceiling panels. Within, a glimmering blue sea, perfectly still, without a ripple or a shark fin, awaited me. I made a burbling noise like a man speaking under water— the word "Open". An effeminate electronic voice oozed in reply, "Repeat, please."

"Open", I said in plain Spanish. The doors slid apart and I entered.

The ceramic tile borders were warm underfoot. There was no smell of chlorine, no sound of lapping, no lifeguard. The atmosphere was uterine, an audible hush. At the other end stood a high diving board. At the near end, steps led down into the pool. I descended and gingerly dipped a toe into the water, which to my pleasant surprise was body temperature, then waded out farther until I was submerged to the sternum of my chest. I laughed, and, using my good leg as a spring, I jumped upward and slapped my hands on the surface, sending tremors concentrically in all directions. The waves chattered at the edges of the pool.

I jumped up and down for a few minutes, gleefully making tsunamis until an old nonsense song awakened somewhere inside me, just notes of music without any lyrics. I threw my head back, warbling and hooting and laughing, submerging and spluttering, then rising and singing again. I felt so good, so free, so young.

For the sake of historical accuracy, I should mention that I do know how to swim. I just lost my taste for it when I nearly drowned all those years ago in the Rio Grande. Pausing in the *Kosmos* pool, I let the waves subside, seeing again that decisive event as if it had occurred this very morning:

I was fifteen years old. I limped badly in body and mind, morosely certain that I had recovered as much as I ever would from the damage done by my knife. I was angry as hell about it, brooding and keeping to myself. I shunned my old friends because their vitality was a constant reminder of my loss, and because we no longer could do anything interesting together.

Late one afternoon, I headed out toward the desert in the direction of the arroyo where the snake had got me. I had a .22 in hand, and I was bent on vengeance. At the edge of the trailer park, I happened upon an old buddy of mine, an Aztec named Alvaro. He and his pals (whose names I cannot now recall) were sitting on stones in a circle, playing cards and passing around a brown paper bag from which they sipped. I saw that they had only just opened the bottle since they were still pretty sober and their humor was congenial.

"Hoyos," called Alvaro, "come and play with us."

"Nah", I growled. "I got something to do."

"How come you give us the cold shoulder all the time?"

I grunted, shrugged, and limped onward into the chaparral.

Alvaro sprang to his feet and came running after me. He jumped in front to block my path and grabbed the strap of my gun, bringing me to a full stop. He was several inches shorter than me but tough as rawhide, brown-skinned, black-haired, not much Spanish in him. He had a reputation for being loyal to anyone he befriended, for drinking underage, for petty crime, and for ferocious courage.

"That's no answer!" he barked.

"Only answer you're going to get", I snarled back.

I knew him well enough to see that he was about to fly into one of his enormous tempers and pop me on the face with his fist. Instead, with flaming eyes and flaring nostrils, he caught himself, and after looking my bad leg up and down, he met my eyes.

"Come on, Benigno, don't be like that", he said in a cajoling tone. "Me and the *muchachos*, we're going swimming."

"I don't swim", I replied in my most surly manner, trying to shake off his hand.

"You lie! You used to swim with us all the time."

"What about the cops? They catch you swimming and drunk, you're in big trouble."

"Didn't you hear? Big crash on the interstate, ten-car pile-up. Every cop in the region's over there, so no one's looking our way for once."

Scowling, I considered his invitation.

"Come on, *chico*, don't act like a *gringo*."

"It only takes one cop or a DSI to catch you", I said. "Then you're dead."

Alvaro was an illegal, as were some of the other *muchachos*.

"You want me to hide in the sand hole all my life?" he said. "I been fooling them ever since red flower days."

"It only takes one mistake."

"I don't make mistakes. Besides, you're legal, so nothing's going to happen to *you*. Scared to get your feet wet?"

"I ain't scared."

"Then come with us."

In those days, I was aware of little more than my chronic rage; I had not noticed, until that moment, my loneliness. Thus, despite my filthy mood, I went with him. We walked back to the card game, which the players packed up in short order, and then we all crept through the mesquite trees in the direction of the river. I dragged myself along at the rearguard, taking my own un-sweet time about it.

We sat in the bushes by the Rio Grande for a couple of hours, playing cards, sipping from various bottles, smoking cigarettes, watching the sky in case any DSI hovercraft showed up unexpectedly. I drank more than I had planned. The rage was gone, leaving a rotten though not unpleasant melancholy in its wake. I didn't say much, but I couldn't help smiling at the crazy jokes being tossed around. The Aztecs were in high spirits, and I began to feel somewhat improved myself. When the sun set and twilight threw a nice cover over us, they crawled out of the bushes, stripped down to their undershorts, and plunged into the water, hooting and screaming. I did not join them. I drank some more and watched.

At one point, Alvaro came up out of the river and stood on the shore, beckoning me in.

"Come on, Hoyos; don't be scared; the water's great."

"I ain't scared", I snapped, slipping back into my mood.

"Yeah, you're scared. You think life's gonna hand you a tortilla full of *mierda* every day of the week."

"Yeah, well it does. It already did."

"So?"

"So, I'll just sit here and wait for the next pile of *mierda* to hit."

"Coward!" he mumbled, with a haughty look.

If he had shouted it, I wouldn't have been provoked. But the way he said it, as if he meant it, triggered something in me. I stood up and hobbled down to the shore and pushed him hard on the chest. He staggered and fell into the mud. He leaped up and pushed me back. My balance was not great, due to the leg, and I fell into the mud. I tripped him. Then we flew into a punching match, yelling and thrashing about in the horizontal position. Some of the *muchachos* swam toward us to break it up.

We both scrambled to our feet and resumed punching. I hit him hard on the nose, and it began to bleed. He landed a good one to my stomach, and I doubled over, down on one knee. Then I threw myself at him, tumbling us both into the water, where the bashing and adolescent roaring went on for some time, until, I suppose, we had both exhausted ourselves. At that point, the Aztecs arrived, separated us, and hauled us back onto shore. The bottles were passed around, cigarettes were lit, and a good deal of joshing was launched by the others in order to defuse the situation.

I looked at Alvaro warily.

He looked at me warily.

Then we both started laughing—uncontrollable, cathartic laughter. He fell down on the mud and rolled around, guffawing and bleeding, holding his belly. I dropped to my knees, gasping and bleeding, and pretty hysterical too.

"H-h-hoyos", Alvaro crowed when he could speak again. "Today I will not kill you. Do you know why I will not kill you?"

"No. Tell me why you think you will not kill me, though you would not be able to do it anyway."

"I will not kill you because your Mama and Papa saved my life when I was a red blossom kid. And your Mama she taught me how to read; she gave me education because I cannot go to the school."

"Fair trade", I said.

On an impulse, I tore off my clothing and lurched toward the river, screaming as I dove into the water, and the last sound I heard was the cheering of the Aztecs.

The river was colder than I thought it would be. My unused muscles went into violent spasm as the current swept me into deeper water. I struggled against it, trying to swim, but I was full of alcohol and drained by the fistfight. I went down in a panic and only survived because Alvaro dove in after me and pulled me up from the bottom.

He and his pals dragged me onto the shore and knocked the water out of my lungs at the very last minute before I was to expire and go onward prematurely, anonymously, Nobel-less, into eternity.

Eight months later, Alvaro was shot to death by an undercover mall marshal while trying to get into a sandwich machine at a shopping complex in Tucson, Arizona. At the time, he had been hitchhiking through the Southwest, looking for under-the-radar farm work. He was having no luck, and the day he died he was desperately hungry. When the news reached our village, I decided then and there never to swim again.

Standing in the *Kosmos* pool all these years later, I sighed, remembering Alvaro, wondering what he might have become if given even a fraction of a chance. In his honor, I did a dog paddle from one side of the pool to the other, forcing my legs to resist the pull of gravity, also resisting my psychological need to touch bottom. I did just fine. Then I performed something like a breaststroke back and forth. This was followed by a crawl. I did a few more lateral laps and really liked the feel of it. The pain in my lower leg and bad ankle was down to minimal.

Finally, winded, I stood up in shallow water and surveyed the inland sea. The waves I had made were still kissing the distant shores. Eyeing the diving board, I shook my head emphatically. "No way", I murmured, and meant it.

But then it crossed my mind how pleasant it would be to tell Pia that I had done real lengths. Taking a deep breath, I eased my body forward and launched into a long, slow crawl. Little by little, the old muscle memory returned, some of it sluggish but mostly not. At one point, I stopped to tread water and let my legs glide downward. My toes no longer touched the bottom. This gave me a moment of near panic, but I pressed onward, resuming a carefully paced and deliberately meditative crawl above the suction of the abyss.

I touched the distant rim and turned around for the homeward journey, arriving where I'd started with neither mishap nor undue alarm nor water in the lungs. It was a great feeling to have mastered an old enemy after a lapse of more than half a century.

I did a few more lengths. On the final one, I was struck with a moment of awe when I realized that I was lazily performing laps in a miniature body of water within a vessel that was, itself, doing one great lap on an infinite sea. The micro-abyss within the macro-void. I could not tell which of these I was afloat upon. The *Kosmos* was speeding toward AC-A-7 at around one hundred and seventy thousand kilometers per second, a velocity impossible for the human mind to conceptualize, except abstractly. The ship was doing the unthinkable, conceptualizing and actualizing simultaneously. And I, swimming in the opposite direction at the moment, was maintaining a speed of about one kilometer per hour.

The immensity of it, the apparent contradictions of it, seemed visual for a second or two. It stunned me and immobilized me. Fortunately, this occurred in shallow water. I got out of the pool and dried myself, feeling my mind stretching to breaking point. And because I did not want it broken, I shook off the images of proportion and relativity and returned to my room for a sleep, which proved to be a luxuriously deep one.

Day 1002:

Today, my first invitation to visit the home of a neighbor. It was triggered when I stopped Xue in the hallway and asked if I could make a copy of the poem he gave me and pass it on to someone else. He agreed without hesitation, then asked me to come along to his room because he wanted to show me something.

I won't embarrass the poor fellow by leaving a detailed paper record of what his room looks like. Let me at least say that while it is structurally identical to mine, the difference can be seen at every turn. It is pin-neat. It is obsessively neat. It is pathologically neat. The few books on his shelves are arranged according to finely sliced categories. There are no photos beaded to the walls. It looks like no one really lives here. Back home in my real cabin in the mountains, I have high-class litter everywhere and keep adding to it: stacks of books on side tables, my writing desk a heap of papers, fascinating phenomena from nature sitting on window sills, a giant wasp nest hanging from the rafters, a magnificent horse's skull in the entrance hall, waiting to greet my hypothetical visitors, etc., etc. By contrast, Xue's cell is a shrine devoted to pristine oriental order.

"Are you a Buddhist, Ao-li?" I asked him upon entering his little home away from home.

"No, though I am sympathetic to its aesthetics."

"A Confucian, then?"

"I admire the concepts of harmony in the Dao, but no, I am not a disciple of Confucius in the religious sense."

"You keep a real clean house."

"It is restful, and conducive to clear thought."

"You should get out more, have a little fun."

"I'll make an effort."

"Don't tell me you spend all your time doing physics. You gave me that poem, after all. And there's your Shui-mo too, though I haven't seen any evidence of it."

"I will show you when my skills are more developed."

"Well, it's good to see you've got some diversion."

"Mastery of different languages, rational and supra-rational, is an essential part of comprehending harmony. Macrocosm, for example, cannot be truly understood without the celestial language that derives from beyond it."

He was getting all obscure on me, which is a trait of his. I was still absorbing the aforementioned when he said, "I have something to show you that may illuminate the answers to your many questions."

He went to a closet cupboard, said what I think is the word *open* in Chinese, and the door vanished sideways. Within, sitting alone on a shelf, was a sculpture of some kind. He picked it up carefully and brought it to me.

It was dark metal, very old, spotted with rust. A stag with a great rack of antlers, about eight inches tall by eight inches long. Sitting on its back, side-saddle, was a little man reading a scroll with intense concentration. The deer's head was turned sideways, looking at me.

First it made me laugh, so whimsical did it seem, as if this were the artist's intention. Then I felt a subtle kind of . . . of what? Some kind of happiness maybe?

"Obviously not a literal scene", I said.

"Correct, not literal."

"But what does it mean? What is it saying? How old is it? Where did you get it?"

"So many questions, Neil. Let the image speak."

I did, and he observed me in his peculiar Xue way, quietly smiling to himself.

"It's really beautiful", I sighed. "But I don't pretend to understand it."

"It is a depiction of the spirit of poetry."

"Ah", I said, handing it back to him.

Day *1003*:

The sculpture was given to Xue years ago by his father. His was a family of artisans who for generations have made such things and sold them in a little shop on a side street in a poorer section of Beijing.

Today, while surfing, I found a surprising quote from the nineteenth-century British novelist Charles Dickens. Recalling that Pia likes his books, I decided to e-mail it to her, along with Xue's Li Po poem, addressing my message to her name, care of her clinic, since I don't have her private address. Before tapping the send button, however, I reconsidered.

> Electric communication will never be a substitute for the face of someone who with their soul encourages another person to be brave and true.
>
> — Charles Dickens

Whew, what a close call! I deleted the message and wrote it out by hand on a sheet of my white bond paper, which I folded into an airplane with her name on the wings. I took it down to the clinic to deliver it personally, but Pia wasn't on duty, so I asked one of her colleagues to give it to her. Li Po was also delivered as an airplane. Dreams take wings.

Later in the day, there was a knock at my door. I said, "Open", and the door disappeared into the walls. No one was there. Suddenly a brown arm and hand appeared and fired a green paper airplane into the room. The door slid shut. Astonished (no one has ever come a-calling before), I picked up the airplane. Inked on it in purple script were the words: *Thanks, pardner.*

Day *1005*:

Earlier today I gave a copy of the Li Po poem to Dariush. He read it and seemed thrilled. This evening after our usual study session, as we were sipping our drinks in the bistro, he said in Kashmiri: "I must tell you, Neil, that the poem stirred something in me. These intuitions emerge from the hearts of every race and at every period of history."

"This is so", I replied sagely (in English). "Human emotions produce universal images."

Replying in that language, he said, "By the word *heart*, I do not mean the emotions. I mean the deepest intuitions in the soul."

"The soul. A much-debated topic."

"Indeed."

"Are you saying you believe it exists, that it's more than just the flashing of synapses at a subtle neurological level, which stimulates a particular zone of the brain?"

"I believe it is more than that. Would you not agree that one can map precisely the ancient road that passes through the lands between Rome and Naples in Italy, and at the same time, one may remain largely ignorant of the men who built that road in ages past, and equally ignorant of the vanished civilization that passed to and fro on it?"

"Forgive me, Dariush, but the analogy is flawed."

"As are all analogies. But, oh, look at me; I am distracted from my subject, which is poetry. After you gave me the Li Po this morning, I did some research. By the way, where did you find it?"

"The physicist Xue Ao-li gave it to me."

Surprisingly, Dariush convulsed into chortling laughter (I have never before seen him crack a smile) and threw his arms in the air.

"Oh splendid", he said. "How interesting these coincidences. You see, I, too, have brought you a poem."

"Really?" I sat back, chuckling nervously. *This is a little weird*, I thought to myself.

"Yes, yes", he went on, "Yet, before I give it to you, I must explain that my composition is only loosely based on the original. Though the sense is close, the wording and some images are slightly altered."

With a deferential nod of his head, he handed me a sheet of paper, upon which were lines penciled in a crabbed script. "It is based on a fourteenth-century Kashmiri poem by a mystic named Laleshvari", he added as I began to read.

[The paper inserted here]:

82

The Lamp of Knowledge

O my elusive lamp of knowledge,
Your flame fanned by a throat's soft flute
Reveals my soul's plight;
Darkness is around me now,
And I within it sealed.
Yet may I bring forth my light
As seed locked within the soil
Will break the surface of the field
And bear its golden fruit.

I looked up, intrigued by this apparently new enthusiasm. His eyes shone, black and eager; he looked just like a badger emerging from its winter hole at the first breath of spring.

"Interesting", I said. "But I can't say I really understand it."

"That is fine, Neil, that is fine. A poem is a good seed, no?"

"No. I mean, yes. Er ... maybe."

Our discussion concluded with more crypticism on his part. As we were parting to go our separate ways, Dariush gazed at me with a fond, paternal look, which was quite odd, since he is at least five years younger than I am.

"Your background is Spanish, is it not?" he asked.

"Spanish-American, with a drop of Scottish thrown into the mix. Do you know Spanish?"

"Regrettably, I do not. None of the Romance languages are within my sphere of scholarship. As you can see, I have made an effort to master English, with its subtextual Romance influence, but this is because it is a necessity in the present world, after Chinese, though I am only superficially conversant in the latter's major tongues."

"I must introduce you to my friend Xue Ao-li."

"Please, this would benefit me—such a man, such a language, and a shared poetic interest. Regarding your own background, however, I am more interested in the symbolic and historical influences."

"I know a bit of my own history, but about symbolic influence I'm afraid I'm a nitwit."

"Ha-ha", he laughed—the second time in our acquaintance—and wagged his index finger pedantically at me. "The seed, Neil, the seed!" Then he went off down the concourse without a backward glance.

Day 1006:

Memory: My mother.

Our suburb of Las Cruces was called Sunnyview Acres. It was sunny all right. The hundred or so trailers in the community were ovens that for a good part of the year baked the brains of all those who lived inside them. Most of us were Hispanics, with a scattering of Vietnamese and less-affluent Québecois (who called themselves "snow-birds").

From spring to late autumn, residents kept discarded rubber tires on their roofs, covered by sheets of splintered plywood scavenged from the local dump and held down by more rubber tires. This kept the trailers cooler than they might otherwise have been, but even so, certain months were brutal, the community dominated by lethargy, bad moods, drinking, and domestic squabbles. The good, the bad, and the ugly lived side by side.

Mostly people were good. A majority of families were intact, each with a mother and a father. There were plenty of children.

My mother had been born in southernmost California. Her culture was Mexican and very Catholic. My parents worshiped at Mass once a week when a traveling Franciscan friar parked his old pickup truck in the dusty "plaza" at the core of Sunnyview Acres and rang a hand-bell to call the faithful to prayer. A surprising number of people attended. He heard confessions beforehand—there was usually a long line for this—and afterward he offered the Mass using the truck's tailgate as an altar. I liked him because he was sincere, simple, kind, and handed out candy to the children just before packing up to drive on to his next mission territory. People supported him by giving auto-fuel and food. It was technologically impossible (as well as illegal) to transfer *Uni* credits to him. He didn't have an account anywhere in *this* world. He was a dedicated man, since in those days the churches were closed, due to the indifference of a once-Christian nation and, sporadically, government crackdowns on organized religion.

We were not organized, but we were religious. Fray Ramon called us his "parish". How it came to be that so many Catholics had congregated in one spot, I don't know. The elderly ladies with rosary beads and lace headscarves were forever reminding us that *Nuestra Señora*, the Mother of Christ, had inspired our families to come together, each via a diverse chain of circumstances, without any planning on our parts. The truth is, few if any of us had chosen to live here for spiritual reasons, and I think all of us would have made our escape in a flash if circumstances had allowed it. Nevertheless, it was not an unhappy community.

There are so many things I remember about my mother. I mentioned that she had a tendency to anxiety, which in retrospect I realize was not unfounded. But that was not a big part of her personality, certainly not a big part of my experience of her. Most of all, she was a person who loved. She loved me, my father, the children of the neighborhood, the infirm and the ill, pretty much anyone who crossed her path. It was she who first called Sunnyview Acres "our village". And, I believe, she made it so. This was partly due to her personality and partly because our people were not exactly ecstatic about living in a parking lot for the socially undesirable. Calling it "our village" made it a home.

She was always heading out of the trailer on this or that errand: a pot of soup for an invalid, helping at the birth of a child, teaching little ones to read, patching up a quarrel between neighbors, making birthday cards for the motherless or the fatherless. She was never an interfering sort, but she had a knack for showing up in people's crisis moments and disarming them. Everyone loved her. The old ladies called her *Madrecita*, little mother. And so she was to many.

One of her major traditions was the making of *piñatas*. Three times a year she made them—for Easter, the feast of *Nuestra Señora de Guadalupe*, and Christmas Day. December was my favorite month of the year, the temperature mercifully cooler, but mainly I loved it because it was a time crammed with anticipations, since the latter two feasts were only weeks apart. As *Mamacita* put it, the newborn Jesus was "the little King of the poor". The Virgin of Guadalupe was "she who overcomes the devourer" or (more emphatically) "she who crushes the serpent's head". And that was just fine by me.

I recall the numerous *piñatas* my mother made over the years, from the time I first began to walk until I left home for college. As big as a pumpkin, each one was unique, each an elaborate creation. First she inflated with her own breath a big latex balloon—she had long ago purchased a boxful from a man who used to sell lighter-than-air helium balloons at a novelty shop in Albuquerque. Over the balloon, she laid strips of scrap paper soaked in a paste made from flour and water. Layer after layer went onto it, until, days later, it was hard and dry enough for painting. She used brilliant colors applied in flamboyant designs. Sometimes she tied red wool tassels onto the seven spokes that radiated out from it, sticks that she poked into the body. It was the common Mexican custom to use spherical clay pots covered with colored paper, but my mother felt this would be a waste of a good pot. Moreover, she derived such pleasure from her creativity that even if a host of such pots were at hand I don't think she would have used them.

The seven horns, she explained to me when I was very young, represented the seven deadly sins. If we could smash all the horns without breaking the *piñata*'s body, there would be an extra prize. Then we could break the *piñata* itself, which according to her symbology represented the breaking of our wills so that the good inside of us would spill out for others.

In later years, I read that other interpretations are widespread among Hispanic people, but all things considered, and not without some bias, I prefer hers.

For the children of the village, the prime objective was never the overcoming of deadly sins or the human will. We liked our wills very much and exercised them whenever we could get away with it. At that point in our lives, we had no knowledge of any but a few of the unmentionable sins. No, we were after the treasure inside the *piñata:* the dried fruit, salted almonds in tiny cloth bags, confetti, a child's dime-store ring that sported a huge "diamond", and, above all, the candy in a variety of flavors and wrappers.

She always completed the *piñata* the day before a feast, and together we filled it through a hole in the top, gleefully adding anything we could find that would excite a child's heart or tongue. When we were ready, my father tied it up with strong cord, and then we all went off to bed, smiling in the darkness of our rooms.

The *piñata* was our gift to the village. My mother was in the habit of standing in the middle of the makeshift dusty plaza at sunset on a feast day and wildly clanging a brass handbell to summon anyone who might be interested. When a crowd had gathered, and a bonfire of mesquite brush was flaring nicely, my father slung the *piñata* cord over a rope stretched between two trailers on opposite sides of the plaza. He hoisted it up where it swayed deliciously above our heads. Usually a few old men would appear, strumming their guitars, and a few younger ones with beer bottles in their hands showed up to watch the event—remembering what they had felt when they were children.

The mothers of the community would organize the children, anywhere from thirty to a hundred, depending on the ebb and flow of the population. They would hand out sticks and shout strident orders that the littlest ones must be given first crack.

The smallest made valiant efforts to whack the giant *piñata*, but my father would pull on his rope and make it gently dance up and down and swing this way and that. Hardly ever did *los pequeños niños* cry over their failures, because they knew they would get a reward later and also because they were shy of all the attention. Soon everyone was laughing and shouting encouragements. This part took a long time, but it warmed us up. Now and then a deadly sin would suffer a glancing blow and tilt sideways.

Then the next rank of children, a year older, would have a try. One by one, each child took his turn. Now my father's evasive actions demanded more ingenuity. A few more horns got smacked, one might fall off entirely and cracks appear in the poor *piñata*'s body. This was greeted by maniacal cheers and shouts to bring on the next age group.

Usually by the time the ten-year-olds were up to bat, everyone was chanting:

> *Dale, dale, dale; no pierdas el tino,*
> *Porque si lo pierdes, pierdes el camino.*
> (Hit it, hit it, hit it; don't let your aim go astray,
> Because if you lose it, you lose your way.)

Even the dignified Vietnamese, who usually clustered in an ethnic group, broke ranks and danced and chanted in their language, scooting their children into the lines of the hopeful. At last, the twelve-year-olds would line up for their turn. My father was sweating by then, the old men were strumming madly, the crowd had worked itself into a fever.

The older children had the biggest challenge of all. Each would be blindfolded. Seasoned veterans of the event, they leaped about and swung the stick with amazing dexterity and intuition, listening for the tell-tale swish of air and the hum of the ropes. Crack-smack-crack. Now the will was sagging, with numerous fractures and hints of its treasure showing, though as yet unspilled.

Finally, some lucky soul would give a terrific, well-placed blow, and the *piñata* would collapse, disgorging is contents in a shower. The children rushed in, as did a few clucking mothers, who prevented the

87

scene from becoming a free-for-all. Many times, when I was one of the youngest, an older boy or girl would help me gather a few candies and trinkets, lest I be swept aside in the melee.

Day 1008:

Within the past week, I've had three cultural encounters. This is unprecedented. I am not a culture guy (except for a few favorite music composers). Yet out of nowhere, a poem, a sculpture, and a literary quote have unexpectedly been dropped into my mind and now reside there. I don't think there's a probability theorist on board whom I could consult about it, and thus I'm left to my own interpretation.

It's alluring to develop theories out of coincidences, but if you let it go too far, you can slide into delusional states of consciousness. Then you see messages and confirmations in everything. It's projection, of course. Like believing the Appian Way or the Egyptian pyramids were made by aliens. Loss of objective context is the problem. If the faulty mode of ingesting and interpreting reality is not corrected, it degenerates still further into hearing "voices".

During my university years, I enjoyed some friendly dialogues with one of my profs, a super-intelligent guy. As we got to know each other better, he sometimes took me out to lunch and expounded his private theories about absolutely *Everything*. His reasoning, his context, was totally articulate. He explained (and demonstrated with impressive facts drawn from all the sciences) that Martians had planted human life on Earth, and that there were "guides" from that race still among us, benevolent and disguised, helping us to "mature" into a higher consciousness, moving us toward the era when we would take our proper place in "the galactic community".

I raised the objection that the guides didn't seem to be doing a great job of it, considering the messes we earthlings kept getting ourselves into.

Solemnly, he replied: "Neil, that is because we so rarely listen to them. Their voices are speaking clearly, but we are deaf."

"Do you hear the voices?" I asked.

"Yes", he nodded, reverently.

When the first expeditions to Mars had completed their exhaustive studies and reported that there never had been any form of civilization, nor any sapient life, on that planet, my prof simply adjusted his inter-pretive lens.

"There was a catastrophic change in the environment, and they were forced to move."

"Why didn't they move here to our planet?" I asked. "It's a pretty nice planet."

"Their motives are the highest, very pure, and it is against their principles to interfere dramatically with the evolution of more prim-itive sapient species. Guidance, yes, but never a mass immigration."

"So, where did they go?"

"They wouldn't have gone very far away from us. They remain Martian in identity, maintaining their distinct cosmological role, but it is my belief that they now dwell on a planet of one of the stars of the Alpha Centauri system."

And so forth . . . .

Day 1095:

Third anniversary of lift-off. Everyone is out celebrating in the res-taurants and social centers. The hallways echo with the revelry of mer-rymakers, long past bedtime. As for me, I spent the day reading articles by twentieth and twenty-first-century radio-astronomers on the topic of planetary magnetism.

It prompted a memory of something I'd learned in college but had forgotten: Einstein's negative reaction when the evidence started pour-ing in that the universe is expanding. He refused to believe it, got real irritated, and wrote unpleasant notes to the offending scientists and journals. He didn't *want* to believe it, even though his own work had provided some of the theoretical basis for the discovery. He was, in a word, *emotional*. To the man's credit, he later publicly admitted that he had been wrong. So interesting—even with geniuses, compartmental-ization disguises our subjectivity.

I took a shower, had a good afternoon nap. Read some more. Checked my message box—nothing but my annual tax bill for the cabin in the mountains. It made me feel emotional, unscientific. Quick as a jack-rabbit, I sent back the payment code, which will reach the scribes in Santa Fe 1.5 years from now. I had thoughtlessly neglected to make arrangements before leaving home to have taxes automatically deducted from my bank account. This worries me. Will they confiscate my cabin and 0.75 acres of nearly vertical woods for unpaid back taxes? Are they that heartless? Surely, someone will explain to them that I am away on a rather important trip and will return.

The latest messages from Earth are now dated 1.5 years ago, and the time lapses between them are growing, since they must cross an increasingly greater distance in order to catch up to us. In the meantime, AC-A-7 expands. The telescopes show a planet not unlike ours, with variations of dark and light blue, moving weather fronts, as well as stable surface formations that look like continents. A majority of these masses are dark green. Pale green, ocher, and tan areas ring the equator. Both poles have a white cap. The image is still very small, and even with computer enhancement (a guess, not a fact), details are too indistinct to be sure. But things are looking up. We may be able to land.

Day 1096:

Today, as we shared the weekly drink in our favorite bistro on Concourse B, Dariush expressed interest in the customs of my family.

"Did you, the Spanish-speaking people of the Americas, have unique celebrations or distinctive symbolic traditions?" he asked.

"We did."

"And do the people continue their practices in our times?"

"I don't think so. Though it's possible some of it remains in remote places, villages perhaps, or individual families."

I recounted in detail the *piñata* festivals I had enjoyed as a child. He listened with shining eyes, as if he could see it all.

"Wonderful, wonderful", he said when I was finished. Then, curiously, a melancholic expression washed across his features. He dropped his eyes and remained in silence for a time.

Looking up, he said, "I too was raised in a small place. It is a village on the shore of the Caspian Sea, at the foot of the mountains. We had beautiful traditions. Poetry and song. Storytelling was a great art in my family. Also the most delicious foods. My mother was very gifted in the making of sweets. She made sugar-date bread, poppy-seed pastries, halva with nuts and cardamom. Oh, I miss them very much. My father was a scholar, and from this, you may properly conclude that he was not a wealthy person. That is why we children enjoyed simpler lives than people now live. I swam often in the great sea, which was my joy, and I fished. When I was a boy, it was difficult for my parents to keep me out of a boat. It was a good life we lived there. We were far from the cities. Of course, it was not then possible to go to Tehran."

"Had it been built when you were a boy? I thought ..."

"I refer to the old capital. We could not go there because of the radiation, you understand. Did I mention that my father was blind? The bomb fell on the city when he was away from it on a journey to see relatives on the other side of the mountains. He was a young man at the time. He was walking through the mountains when there came the burst of light. He turned his face toward the city to see what had caused it, and the light damaged his vision. He was sixty kilometers from the blast, but its power was great."

"A lot of people died there."

"Yes. Millions in one instant."

"All of your father's family?"

"Most of them. Those who dwelt in Tehran."

"But what did he do then?"

"He wisely hid himself in the rocks until the shock wave had passed, then he walked onward to the place where the other relatives lived. His eyes could see nothing, and he became lost at times, but his mind was a most excellent one, and he remembered the road well enough, for he had traveled it numerous times before. In the end, he found his relatives in their village by the Caspian. They took him in. He was at that time a graduate of the university. Everything he had once lived for was gone, but he kept the knowledge he had learned, and he passed it on to others. For the remainder of his life, he taught languages to village children. In time, he married a woman of the village, and I was born there. When I grew older, it became possible for me to study at the university that had been established in New Tehran, which was then a much smaller place than it is today."

"A hard life", I said.

"It was a beautiful life in many ways. My father has now passed away. I remember his beautiful smile, his calm voice, and his wisdom. He had immense hope in life. He taught this to me."

"Out of such tragedy and horror ..."

"Yes. But man grows as he overcomes suffering, does he not?"

"Does he? And what about the dead? Why is this our fate?"

"The acts of horror need not be our fate", Dariush said. Then, pausing for a moment, he sighed. "Yet our condition changes little, generation after generation. Such is our infinite capacity for self-deception."

He regarded me thoughtfully, as if seeking confirmation that I understood. Or perhaps he sought to impart something more to me. But I could think of nothing to say.

With a sudden change of expression, he smiled and stood up.

"Neil, it is late. And I must learn ten more Kashmiri words before I sleep. I bid you a good night."

"Good night, Dariush", I said as he walked away down the concourse.

Day 1417:

Stron, under the strong influence of a beverage, admitted to me that the whiskey he drinks and sometimes shares with me is not from a diminishing supply.

"Ah, the black market", I said. "I've heard rumors."

"I wouldn't buy any of that rot-gut they concoct in the boiler room. I make it myself. Though I have to admit my supply of corn is obtained through certain channels in the alternative economy."

"Do you sell your product?"

"Do I look like a whiskey baron? Naw, I *consume* the stuff!"

"And sometimes share it with friends."

"If they play their cards right."

Day 1461:

Fourth anniversary. Nothing noteworthy happened today.

Oh, before I forget, I found in my inbox this morning a text message from Dr. Étienne Pagnol, the biologist. No salutation or explanation, just two quotations:

"La génération spontanée est une chimère." (Spontaneous generation is an illusion.)

—Dr. Louis Pasteur

"I have been looking for spontaneous generation for twenty years without discovering it. No, I do not judge it impossible. But what allows you to make it the origin of life? You place matter before life and you decide that matter has existed for all eternity. How do you know that the incessant progress of science will not compel scientists to consider that life has existed during eternity, and not matter? You pass from matter to life because your intelligence of today cannot conceive things otherwise. How do you know that in ten thousand years one will not consider it more likely that matter has emerged from life?"

—Dr. Louis Pasteur

I was impressed by the talk Pagnol gave in the auditorium a few months ago. He and I have never met or exchanged communications, before or since. How on earth did he get my private e-address?

I wrote a courtesy reply and clicked send:

Thank you for note. Thought-provoking. Best regards. Hoyos.

Day 1471:

By coincidence or by his intent, I finally met Pagnol. He approached me in the library on deck B, where I happened to be doing some broad-ranging research on Pasteur. My *max* had not produced the quote's source reference, though it offered millions of articles about Pasteur, one of the greatest scientists of his age, and of all time. Typing the quotation into the library's terminal connected to the ship's mega-computer produced only a handful of articles containing the quote, each of them tainted by snide (and scientifically spurious) attempts to debunk Pasteur's theory of *biogenesis*—life comes only from life, he believed. All these centuries after Pasteur, no one has yet proved scientifically that life can arise spontaneously. Most irritatingly, there is nasty mythological thinking in these supposedly rational critics. Bad science. The stink is unmistakable. I wonder, do they ever have a good look at themselves in the mirror as they mouth off about people like Pasteur?

Anyway, I had a chance to thank Pagnol in person. He told me the quotes came from an early biography. We then discussed *biogenesis* dispassionately, without commitment, though I emphasized that I remain undecided about the question of the origins of life. He thanked me warmly for the inaugural lecture I gave several years ago. I thanked him for his lecture. I told him I hoped to read one of his books. He told me he wanted to read one of mine. We parted.

Day 1492:

In fourteen hundred and ninety-two, Columbus sailed the ocean blue. In twenty hundred and ninety-seven, the *Kosmos* sailed all the way to heaven (or just a tad short thereof).

Did I mention that Dariush urged upon me the novel *Moby Dick*? I've just completed reading it. The story is quite fascinating, and the author especially intrigues me. What kind of consciousness could have produced such a work? Written 250 years ago, at a time we now consider to be primitive in terms of general knowledge and technology, the book reveals that people in those days had an inner life that was richer than we suppose. Maybe they were a whole lot richer than we think *we* are.

Dariush has given me a list of other nautical novels to track down in the libraries (more than three hundred titles). My interest is piqued in the sense that ancient voyages were often very long, and the stories may tell me something about the way mariners coped with their enclosed spaces and their own brand of infinite sea.

(List attached.)

He urged me to begin with five specific titles: *Treasure Island* by R. L. Stevenson; *The Old Man and the Sea* by E. Hemingway; *The Rime of the Ancient Mariner* by S. T. Coleridge; *Billy Budd, Sailor*, by H. Melville; and *Heart of Darkness* by J. Conrad.

"Why these five?" I asked.

"They will launch you", he said, not really answering my question.

Day 1518:

Well, here I am back in my room after two weeks in the recovery unit at the B surgery clinic. I crumbled to Pia-pressure and let the team of neurosurgeons (including her) cut open my leg, my ankle, and my foot. While they pottered around in there, I had a nice peaceful sleep—such lovely drugs they have these days. When I came out of it, I saw a ring of kindly faces looking down on me as if I were a baby in a bassinette. Swaying gently, I then thought I was lying in a little boat. I heard tinkling bells and singing, and for a few seconds I smelled the perfume of lilies. Is this my funeral? I wondered.

It wasn't. Now I am laid out on my own bed with fluffy pillows, a stack of maritime disaster books beside me, and my leg from knee to toes wrapped in a cast of dark blue, inflexible fabric. It has a flickering digital light panel along its side, signaling that inside, hundreds of electronic needles are stimulating neural connections. There's no pain, just a faint tingling sensation, which is not unpleasant. Next week I have to be up and walking about. I'm losing muscle tone in my thigh from lack of use.

Day 1527:

Three times a day I shuffle up and down stretches of my concourse, dressed in T-shirt and short pajama bottoms. It makes passersby nervous (yikes, an old man in his underwear!), though the cast gives me some credibility. There's pain now, but nothing I can't live with. I don't like taking drugs, regardless of how wonderful they make me feel. It's odd to look down and see that my foot is flat, to sense the bare sole and toes touch the floor as they should. It will be interesting to see what the rest looks like when the mummy is unwrapped.

Back to my bed, I go. Early this week, Dwayne dropped in and helped me relearn the protocols for the *max*'s film channels. He also enlarged the screen and showed me how to enhance dimensions for the older films, made before the 3D era.

Despite my earlier determination to avoid the e-drug, I enjoyed it a lot. More and more it seemed. Finished with one film, I immediately wanted another. And another. One day I watched six from the first half of the twentieth century, most of them kind of bloodless, with cowboys and feathered Indians spinning in ballet twirls and plopping into the dust, falling from high rocks in the desert or from roofs in cardboard wild west towns. During the late twentieth century and well into the twenty-first, things got messier—a "realism" so intense

95

that when one of the good guys got shot and blood and entrails were splashed across the screen, I jerked upright on the bed and yelled, "Noooooo!", my heart pounding.

I won't describe the details. Let me say only that in the dozens upon dozens of films I watched, the majority exhibited a slavish devotion to every hideous detail of human death in degrading forms, costumed, of course, with cowboy hats and six-shooters. As always, there were plenty of horses, but these creatures alone were computer generated, due to the anti-cruelty-to-animals laws.

Exhausted, zinging with unrelieved adrenaline, I switched to a documentary film about the making of westerns during the latter half of the twenty-first century. By then, the entertainment industry had grown to the size of 32 percent of our continental economy. Moreover, whole sections of the American Southwest had been "mandated" as culture preserves for the making of films, including grand canyons and painted deserts. Finally, I learned that many of the actors who played victims had chosen to be killed, since the industry gave a generous endowment to those willing to sacrifice themselves in this way for the good of the country. I find this incomprehensible, considering the self-preservation instinct in human nature. Maybe for some it was the only way to leave an inheritance to a child or a loved one; for others, perhaps, it was a productive form of suicide.

I switched off the damned *max* and tried to forget the protocols.

I grew up in one of those few places on Earth where hardly anyone owned a digital wall screen. My parents wouldn't allow one in the trailer. They tried to discourage me from watching it at the homes of my friends the Aztecs. Imagine how hard this was on me. Imagine what it was like walking into a shopping mall beside your four-foot-six-inch-high mother, and you, yourself, age fourteen or fifteen, are not only a foot taller than her, you are also a member of a visibly underprivileged minority, you are not handsome, and you are more or less crippled. The mall is filled with electronics shops that your mother tries to speed you past. But when you halt in your limping tracks, mesmerized by a sex scene on a screen in a shop window, or people being blasted into bloody bits, you want desperately to see more. Your mother reaches up and clamps her hand over your eyes and drags you away.

"*Mamacita*", you protest all the way through the mall, "stop putting your hands on my eyes! I am not a child! It's just pretend!"

"It is *el ojo del diablo!*" she cries loudly, making the kind of public scene that prompts strangers to laugh at you—we're quaint little Hispanics airing our familial conflicts, live drama for bored shoppers. It's so humiliating you want to run away from home.

Fortunately, around that time, I was also getting deeply interested in physics, and when I went away to college, I had already become obsessed with the subject, and was, as well, antisocial and an appreciator of solitary silence.

Day 1535:

This evening, I completed the last of Dariush's five recommendations. Interesting tales, most of them with a dose of death as part of the plot. Not death as entertainment, however, but death entwined with moral complexities. These books are quite different from modern fiction, which I've never been able to read without falling asleep or suffering from nausea. It seems that human beings had different minds way back then.

One of the novels, *The Rime of the Ancient Mariner*, was spoiled by its heavy-handed moralism. A sailor shoots an albatross and the judgment of hell falls upon him. The one by Conrad also left me ill at ease. What on earth was Dariush thinking when he recommended these?

Day 1548, The Unwrapping:

It was pretty ugly, I had to admit, even though it was my very own. Yup, there were the healed surgical incisions and the two white scars from my pocket knife. But the twisted muscles and/or ligaments (whatever the heck it was that got messed up inside years ago) now looked better aligned. What a pleasure to see that my ankle and foot no longer bent at the wrong angle, which was the result of favoring it for so many years. The calluses built up over more than half a century's walking on the edge of the foot are still there, but no longer leathery.

My new leg is half an inch shorter than the other. I will have to walk with a shoe insert now, if I want to avoid throwing my other bones out of alignment.

Day 1550:

Mmmm, it's doing okay. I walk and walk and walk. It really hurts, but it's pure pleasure not to hobble-lurch any more. I still limp—I will always have a limp. The shoe insert fit well in my cowboy boot, since the boots are three sizes too large for me anyway (some years ago I purchased on the black market my last pair of diamondback snakeskin; only one size had been available at the time). When I slipped my feet into them, I found that they were both comfortable. And they looked good—real good. I resisted an impulse to swagger down the hallways with my thumbs hitched in my belt, reverting to juvenile male, cowboy mode. I made do with clipping and clopping rhythmically for the first time since my adolescence.

Day 1552:

Now for an unexpected memory from my childhood:

On the morning of my fifth birthday, our car broke down, and my father didn't have enough money to pay for a tow truck or a mechanic. I observed my mother's worried face, anxious over the demise of her plans to buy party things at a store in Las Cruces, and got worried myself. I looked at my father's stoic face and felt suddenly uplifted by his confidence—which might have been authentic. He smiled down at me; then he picked me up and tossed me onto his shoulders, where I sat with my legs dropping down over his chest and my hands tightly squeezing his forehead. We used to call this "the camel ride" (as distinguished from piggy-back).

"Come on, Benigno, let's go for a walk", he announced. "I've got a big surprise for you."

Thus he packed me into town, easily an hour's walk in the sun. He was sweating hard but whistled lively tunes all the way. At a dime store, he purchased a bag full of party favors, and from there, we walked hand in hand to a nearby hardware store. In this establishment, he purchased a little red tricycle—my first. Heedless of the family finances or the state of the world's economy, I leapt onto it with glee, my joy unsurpassed, and pedaled my jolly way out onto the sidewalk while my father negotiated with the proprietor the compiling of some debt.

That done, we cycled to the last street leading out to the desert, and onto the highway. I must have giggled all the way. He walked behind, alert to traffic. Whenever a car approached, he would lift both me and the tricycle into his arms and step off the pavement. After the car passed, I was back down and off like a shot. Nearing Sunnyview Acres, we turned onto the side road that led to our village, and here the surface became more difficult for me to pedal. The old tarmac was bumpy, rutted, strewn with gravel, and increasingly scarred by heat fractures. It was a rough ride.

"Papa!" I complained loudly. "Papa, the road is broken!"

He laughed and said, "*Sí*, but *we* are not broken."

Day 1660:

Reading my way through the novels on Dariush's list, I've overdosed on nautical themes. I slipped back into e-addiction for a few weeks. *Ojo del Diablo!*

I didn't feel like watching the death-culture films. Instead, I watched a good deal of science fiction from the previous centuries. It was pretty funny stuff, though the fantaseering class got better as it steadily grew. After the inaugural century, however, the filmmakers were unable to resist throwing gobbets of gore at the audience while manipulating us with terror, horror, *deus ex machinas*, *diabolus ex machinas*, and every primitive instinct known to man. Nauseated, numbed, entranced, I finally realized what was happening and switched it all off, wishing I had a wholesome old hatchet to whack on the head of my *max*.

Day 1705:

This past week I fell again. I must say in my favor that I only watched the nine film versions of the ancient tale of *Pinocchio*, based on a book written by an Italian during the nineteenth century. I preferred the earlier film versions, yawned through the animated one made by some guy named Disney, loathed the famous remake from the twenty-first century (Pinocchio discovers his adolescent sexuality on the Island of Bad Boys), and relished a twentieth-century Italian one (charming, sad, beautiful), and ended up wishing I could become *a real boy*.

Day 1708:

Downloaded the e-book edition of *Pinocchio* from the library. Read it and loved it. There was a better mind at work in this story than the minds of those who created the films. Lots of ironic black humor and moral complexities, including some surprising details. For example, when the little conscience-cricket gets on Pinocchio's nerves, the puppet boy smashes the cricket against a stone wall, and the creature's brains go dribbling down the cobbles. Looks like things could be gruesome way back then.

Day 1826:

Five years completed, four more to go.

On a whim, over breakfast I asked Xue if he would like to trade rooms with me. Facing forward to our destination, I'm on the port-side of the ship, he's on starboard. I suggested it might offer a little variety, keep the left and right hemispheres of the brain limber and negotiating with each other. He had no strong objections to an exchange, but then thought it would be too complicated, considering our *max*es. He explained that the *max* is sealed into each desk as a permanent component. It can't be removed and packed along with you when you move house. Nor does the computer have a dock for copying files onto a portable *memor*. The desk itself would demand an engineering degree if you wished to dismantle and transport it to another room. Thus, Xue is wedded to his, and I am in uneasy cohabitation with mine. Ah, well, I'll stay put where I am.

Dwayne dropped off an anniversary gift. I found it on my desk top with a note attached:

This stuff won't hurt you. Black-market. If you talk, I die. Flush this note.

No signature, but I know who wrote it.

The polyplast bottle contained an aromatic fruity liqueur. I took a hesitant sip. Peach flavored. It had a very pleasant effect on me, far stronger than what they serve in the bistros.

I called him on voice-*max*, the private number he had given me, and said, "Thanks for the gift."

"Yup."

"That was real nice of you. Wish I had something to give in return."

"Not necessary."

"I flushed what you asked me to flush."

"Uh-huh."

"Were you serious about the word *die?*"

"Nope. But it could make my life tense if word gets around."

"Barter system flourishing?"

"Yup."

"Want to come by my room? We could discuss astrophysics."

"Uh ... okay. I get off shift at five. Can I drop in around seven?"

"Yup", I said. "Bring an extra glass."

Promptly at seven, a hand rapped at my door. I said, "Open", and there stood Dwayne.

"Well, come on in", I drawled. "Take a load off your feet."

His mouth twitched microscopically into what I took to be his expression of enthusiasm.

"This is really great liqueur", I said, extracting the bottle from the cabinet. "I haven't been a hard drinker for eons, but a fellow could change his mind after a sip or two of this. Did you make it yourself?"

"Nope. Fair trade. Man in hydroponics makes it."

"You shouldn't tell me such details. What if I'm tortured and I squeal on you?"

"Dr. Hoyos, a guy like you would never talk."

"I appreciate the compliment, Dwayne."

He handed me an authentic shot-glass—real glass. I got out my standard-issue polyplast cup and poured us both a drink.

"What on earth did you trade for this elixir of life?"

"Did some jiggery-pokery on a guy's *max.*"

"Taught him protocols, eh?"

"Nope. Turned off the listener, but coded it so no one knows it's turned off. We recorded a random sound presentation, isolated with old firewall 2019.3 that I adapted and back-turned seven times in layered e-loops so anybody listening hears nothing but snores, showers, and films."

"I didn't know you were a programmer."

"My hobby."

I glanced at the *max* on my desk.

"And what, exactly, do you mean by listener?"

"Don't worry", Dwayne said with a mere hint of a grin. "I did the same to your *max*."

"You what!"

"Hope you don't mind. But I figured you hate those guys as much as I do."

"I don't hate anybody, Dwayne. Who and what are you talking about?"

"I know you hate the way they rob us of privacy. I can tell. I see you head-butting them all the time."

Ah, yes, *them*. Doubtless, he meant my occasional disregard for ship's rules.

"They don't rob us of privacy", I said. "It says in the Manual that the *max*es in residential rooms are each protected by a firewall."

"Well, sir, that's what they say. But it ain't so."

Ay caramba! I will bypass the angry comments that subsequently erupted from my mouth.

"A minor question", I said, when I had calmed down and had poured each of us another inch of peach ambrosia. "May I suggest, my friend, that *you* are guilty of invasion of privacy? Hmmm? Hmmm?"

He bowed his head, nodding and nodding. "I know, sir. I know. I shoulda asked your permission. But I figured you'd be better off not knowing they'd been listening in on you."

"Really? And what else of mine did you invade?"

He looked up at me with hurt in his eyes. "Nothing."

"Did you listen to my voice journal, read my paper journal?"

"Nope", he said.

Somehow I knew he wasn't lying. We sat in silence for a while.

"You're some weird cowboy, Dwayne", I muttered at last.

"Yeah, that's true", he mumbled, looking like a whupped puppy.

"You never say much, do you? There's a whole lot goes on inside that head of yours, so why don't you ever talk?"

He shrugged. "That's why I'm here."

He handed me a sheet of paper that looked like the newsprint one sees in museums—yellowed, stained, torn, smelling of age.

On it was penned in old-fashioned calligraphy:

My father's father was a 16-year-old boy when he was incarcerated in a German prisoner of war camp during WWI. He was very tall and had lied about his age to get into the army. For the rest of his life, bits of shrapnel worked themselves out of his body. He was in constant physical pain for nearly 50 years. The pain pushed him in the direction of morphine addiction and alcoholism for the rest of his life. He died at age 65, fully in grace, faithful to the sacraments, living in a basement room in the home of one of his sisters. He was a man with nothing ... only himself and Christ. I never in my life heard him speak a word, because I never met him. He had been banished from our family by my grandmother, who spun the myth that condemned him. She said he was a bad man. It took years for me to piece the true story together. He was a good man.

His absence was a silence, made by the wounds he suffered and the poor choices he made in trying to overcome them.

Certain kinds of silence are holy, the ground of being as presence, a life as a living word.

Other kinds of silence are evil, caused by the external suppression of free speech.

Other kinds are caused by the internal self-suppression of speech due to the terrible blows of injustice that destroy trust, creating suspicion of all other men: "No man can be trusted", laments one of the writers in the Old Testament.

Poor mankind, poor mankind ...

"Who wrote this?" I asked.

"One of my ancestors. Great-grandfather or someone back then."

"This is a very old document. The First World War was almost two hundred years ago."

"I know. I looked it up. Learned a lot."

"Uh-huh. Reading history can be illuminating."

"Depends." He paused, frowned. "Depends on what history y'read."

"Well, it was a long time ago."

"Yup. People were sure different in those days."

"It seems they were."

Seems? No, they *were* different. I remember some of the old people I knew when I was a boy. And my parents. And that's *recent* history.

"We've forgotten things", said Dwayne.

"I agree."

103

"Some of it wasn't so good, but some of it might've been the best we ever had."

"There's not much we can do about it now, is there?"

"Guess not. That's why I'm reading stuff like this. Figured it would be a long trip, so I brought along a bundle of old family papers."

"Discovering your roots, so to speak."

"Yeah. I thought you might be able to explain some of it."

I sighed, said nothing.

"Like what, really, is a sacrament?" he said.

"A what?" I said, covering. I know full well what it is, but I don't go around admitting it to just anyone.

"A *sac-ra-ment.*"

"Didn't you search it on your *max*?"

"I did. It gave me a couple thousand references, and I got the gist of the thing. Or the gist of what those people thought it was. All the articles are cross-referenced under 'Cult' and 'Cultic religion' and 'Dysfunctional mystical sects'—things like that."

"I see."

"That's why I'd hoped you wouldn't mind us talking about the old days, when you were a kid."

"The old days?" I frowned like an ol' cowpoke. "When I was a boy, things were pretty much as they are now—not quite so fast, but only by a hair."

"People like my ancestors would have known a very different kind of world."

"Yes, and, as you say, there were some bad things about that world. World War I was nasty enough, WWII was vastly worse, and WWIII, well, let's not get into that."

"Uh, I never heard about any World War Three."

"Exactly. The slaughter was worse, just archived under a sanitized name. You say you've read the history?"

"I saw the vids", he shrugged. "They taught us even less about it at school. But now that I'm doing some deep reads, I'm patching a lot of it together. I can tell they taught us stuff with twists in it. We didn't get the real thing."

"Yup, you gotta watch out for those twists, Dwayne. So many twists these days, it's hard to find a straight patch."

"They had twists back then too. What I don't get is why everyone in Western civilization was Christian, but they did all that evil."

"The ones who did it weren't really Christian", I said. "Where did you grow up? Somewhere in Nevada wasn't it?"

"Uh-huh. Small town named Antelope."

"Were people mostly good or mostly bad in your hometown?"

"Mostly good, I think."

"Ever see real evil there?"

"Yup."

"Did everyone do the evil?"

"Nope."

"Was the evil committed, perchance, by people who had some position of authority in town?"

"Now that you mention it, yes. They called in state authorities actually, with federal backup. Only they didn't say it was evil. They said it was something we needed. Not everyone went along with them. A few people got themselves arrested for making a protest against it, people I knew. Their kids were taken to a state orphanage. I don't know what ever happened to the parents because they didn't come back—leastways not when I lived there. Antelope was kind of a backwater, you see, most people just trying to live quiet lives, working hard, making no trouble for other folks."

"And did the authorities explain to you that they were doing their evil only in order to help make you, the quiet folks, into better citizens?"

"Yeah. How did you know that?"

"Just a wild guess."

"Well, I wouldn't want to jump to conclusions. Maybe those people who went to jail got home again. Maybe they got their kids back."

"Maybe." Maybe, but I don't think so.

"I never found out", he went on. "We moved to Sacramento the next year, and I entered college there."

He told me more about the following years, his first job, a tech position at an aerospace company, and then the steps leading up to his presence on the *Kosmos*.

At the end of his account, he fell silent, lost in thought, with his eyes on the floor and elbows on knees, arms dangling.

He broke the silence by clearing his throat and looking me in the eyes, his expression troubled, straining toward something elusive to his thoughts.

"You know, when I was reading up on the Christianity cult, I came across a saying by one of their holy men. I can't get it out of my mind. He said, 'We are losing the basic memory of mankind.' "

"Losing the basic memory of mankind? What was his name?"

"Can't remember. Somebody shot him dead."

Dwayne and I talked for another couple of hours. His sentences got longer, mine got shorter. In the end, we made a pact to meet more often and to discuss the "real stuff", as he called it.

Day 1828:

"We are losing the basic memory of mankind."

I can't get it out of my mind either.

This afternoon in the lounge, Maria Kempton said to me, "You're awfully quiet lately, Neil."

"Just thinking about a lot of things."

"Not getting housebound are you? Cabin fever?"

"No, no, nothing like that."

"That's good to hear."

"Maria," I said in a lowered voice, "did you know that our rooms are monitored?"

"Monitored? What, by audio you mean? Good heavens, I don't think so. Why would they do such a thing?"

It's interesting how everyone speaks about some nebulous, invisible over-authority as *they*. Who these people are is never defined. And I don't think anyone is referring to the flight crew way upstairs on the top deck.

"Why would they do such a thing?" she asked again, more amused than disturbed.

"I'm not sure. Perhaps they're keeping an eye on our mental health."

"Whatever for? We're all grownups, and besides, this is a ship full of very intelligent, very responsible people—all of us."

"Maybe some sociologist is doing research—you know, the first interstellar flight, a closed environment, a unique study group."

"A bit far-fetched, Neil. They couldn't do that without government approval."

"This is a government ship."

106

"Yes, true, but ..."

She told me not to worry and returned to her knitting.

Day 1829:

I have made an effort to keep up with this written journal, but there's a subliminal drag on motivation. Regarding my voice journal, I asked Dwayne if there was a way we could prevent any monitoring of my *max* files. He looked solemn and murmured that he had already "fixed" that.

"What do you mean, *fixed*?" I asked. "And when did you do it? I haven't been out of my room for days, except for meals."

"Uh, actually, I did it all in one shot, fooling the audio snoop, blocking *max* access, installing unbreakable file encrypt. I did it around the end of year one."

I just shook my head. "And how did you get access to my door code?"

"That was fairly simple."

"Well," I huffed, "it looks like I'll have to change my code every hour on the hour."

"That'll sure keep your fellow passengers out. But the codes aren't airtight, since there are override commands to unlock a door if someone forgets his code. Every day somebody or other forgets. But don't worry, I keyed in an override of the override. If they ever want to have a look around your room, it would slow them down."

"I don't follow you."

"It's kinda complicated. Anyway, just give me a call if you ever have problems."

"What kind of problems?"

"Let's say you get summoned to the principal's office for being a bad boy in class. Let's say they ask you some casual questions about your *max*, ask you if anyone's been tinkering with it. They might tell you the ship's master computer is blinking a warning that there's a glitch in your *max*, and they'd like to send a tech guy in to see what the trouble is."

"You're saying they'd make it sound innocent as apple pie."

"Yup. And it'd be your proof. It'd tell you that they're real miffed, that they tried to get into your *max* and figured out they've been blocked. They'd have to be cagey about finding out just *how* they were blocked, because that would be a dead giveaway of their secret. That would be telling everyone on board that whoever's in charge of surveillance is reading our secret diaries. Then they'd have to deal with the uproar. They wouldn't want a revolt on their hands. So they'd be real subtle about it."

"Thanks for the heads-up."

"Yup."

"Another question: Whenever I go searching on the *max*, can anyone else see where I'm going, read what I'm reading?"

"As we know, the *max* is theoretically a self-contained unit. That's what the Manual says, and that's what they told us at pre-departure briefing, right?"

"Right."

"And we've discovered that they can jump right through standard firewall for some reason known only to themselves, right?"

"Right again."

"Well, they must want to keep tabs on us in a bad way, because they also implanted a back-up micro trail leading in and out of each *max*. It's a circuit that monitors and cross-checks all the regular air-wave traffic in and out of your *max*. It's also how they would read what you've been surfing."

"In my case, there's no harm done. But what about you? Wouldn't your research into the Christian cult make trouble for you?"

"I fixed it. Sent them on a false trail. Did the same for yours too. I mean there's probably about a thousand *max* units on board, and it would need a lot of manpower to check out where everyone's gone surfing. But if anybody turns his eye on you and wants to track you, what they're going to find out is you're real fixated on astronomy and poisonous snakes."

"Clever, Dwayne, very clever. In fact, I am fixated on the latter topic."

We sat there for a while, nodding and nodding, staring at the floor.

"You've been pretty thorough", I said. "Is there any chance you might have overlooked something?"

"Such as?"

"Anything, really. Take for instance the tapeworms and botflies they use back on Earth."

"The what?"

I described the nano-pests that had infested my home, and how I regularly zapped them.

Dwayne smiled. "Oh, those. I used to call 'em flutterers and burrowers."

"Seen any on the *Kosmos*?"

"Nope. Years ago, I put together something nanoid of my own. It alerts me whenever they're around. Haven't had a bleep since we left home."

"I wonder why they don't use them here. Rare is he who even knows they exist."

"Right. But imagine the curiosity that would be aroused if people started seeing all kinds of flutterers and crawlers on board. I think DSI reverted to the older form of surveillance because they know that a lie and a friendly machine can do the job just as well."

"Or do it even better. No one trusts a creeper; everyone trusts their computer."

"Yup, extension of the self."

"Owner of the self, if you don't keep it in line."

"Keep it in line? I'd say that's a tall order for most folks."

"Not completely. We can simply choose not to use it."

"True, but life is less efficient without the dang thing."

"And more real."

His eyes went all abstract, and he tilted his head a little, musing on a topic that he had probably given plenty of thought to on his own. I expected him to hold forth on the old cliché of tools reshaping those who use them—the slave becoming the master. But instead he returned to our original discussion: "The other day you asked me if I'd read your paper journal."

"Don't worry, I believe you."

"I just want to remind you that there's no way you can encrypt a journal like that. Anybody who gets into your room could read it."

I hadn't thought about this—despite the high IQ of yours truly.

"I just figured I should mention it, Neil. You're probably working on a lot of scientific things, right? And you don't want other people reading it. Maybe you should keep that kind of ultra-private stuff for encryption."

I nodded my thanks.

"Uh, did I just hear you call me by my given name? The name *Neil*?"

"Yup."

"Shake hands, pardner."

We shook hands.

"Dwayne, there are a few people who I think should know about this situation. Would you be willing to do some tinkering for them too?"

He paused and silently tossed it around in his head.

"I'm sure the others would find some way of compensating you", I prompted.

He looked up sharply. "Not necessary", he said, hardly moving his lips.

After he had gone, I dismantled my shaving razor, and using the blade, I cut a discreet slit on the wall side of my mattress. Into this hidey-hole I inserted journal pages that could make problems for others. I reassembled the razor and had a good nap.

Day 1833:

Putting my best foot forward, so to speak, I approached four people and broached the subject with exquisite tact.

Xue took it serenely, but his eyes went cold.

Dariush just look perplexed and began to digest it.

Maria went into total denial.

Pia looked very disturbed, and blushed. What she said is worth noting: "I had no idea, no idea. This is awful. It's so cynical. We're not laboratory rats. I keep a lot of very private things on my *max*."

"Things that have nothing to do with your work?" I asked.

"That's right. You see, I've grown very close to another person on board. We text each other every day, since we're not often able to get together for a meal or a drink."

"Your shifts are different?"

"Yes. And he's in the flight crew. They don't come downstairs all that much, and of course we never go upstairs to KC."

"I know someone who can help", I said.

Day 1865:

Xue, Dariush, and Pia now enjoy ultra privacy. None of them know Dwayne's name or where he works. We prearranged that he would do the job when they were out of their rooms. A hacker *par excellence*, he accessed their door codes without a hitch.

I suggested to Pia that she bring up the topic with her friend, if she feels he can be trusted. She assured me he can be trusted, but he's in a highly sensitive part of command—Navigation—and his personal quarters are also on KC, so there would be problems getting to his *max*. Pia and her beau will have to make do with paper love notes for now.

I fume over the lies we've been told, though I try to maintain my perspective. My guess is that even if everyone on board learned that they are under surveillance, a majority would shrug. Only the very oldest among us remember a time when state surveillance was no more than modestly invasive (monitoring of cell phone and e-mail traffic). We are, to borrow a term, surveillance immigrants while the younger ones are surveillance natives.

How do we inform them? How do we raise the right questions, generate real thought about the right to privacy and the wrongness of invading it? I wonder if they would even care.

Day 1999:

Here are a few more random observations:

Despite the wildly fluctuating clothing styles (women mostly) and the humdrum uniforms or dull civvies (men mostly), everyone wears incongruous grip-slippers. Everyone, that is, except me (barefoot mostly, cowboy boots when I can get away with it) and Stron, who wears real leather brogues (illegal) and emanates an attitude that inhibits anyone from making trouble over it.

More on social relationships: Well, this topic is so complex I won't even attempt an exhaustive description. A sampling of fields will do. The group mood is generally cool to tepid, constantly buoyed up to the level of optimistic, efficient friendliness. Definitely an urban mode of behavior. Nevertheless, there have been breakdowns: For example, three-dimensional Scrabble has become the cause of a certain loss of objectivity in the lounges. The game keeps people's minds agile, but I have noted in players and onlookers a growing amount of emotional investment in winning or losing. There have been angry arguments, sparking intervention by social facilitators.

Then there's the love thing. There is a lot of it, as I mentioned before. Who knows where it all goes. It's conducted in relative privacy (by which I mean outside of *my* optical field, though not, presumably, outside that of the Watchers). Thus any analysis of mine can only be based on insufficient (even faulty) observation.

Are there friendships on board, as in *real* friendships? Yes, there is at least one set of friends, and I'm involved in it. A mysterious thing is friendship. In its own way, it's a kind of love, or quiet affection, without demands or expectations. It's an affinity with certain kinds of other people, those who share an interest, or a common goal, or ideals, or heck, they just like each other.

According to the official e-newsletter, we are all "friends", a "team", a "community", a "family". This weekly missive from the Department of Social Infrastructure contains plenty of happy-face material, augmented by newsy items and announcements, reminders of coming entertainments and activities, public talks, educational programs, etc. Also the "news" from Earth, which is stale due to the distance it now must cross to reach us. Moreover, the details seem rather thin to me, since the murky doings of our home planet are ever tense and complicated. Of course, journalism has always been carefully tailored for positive-attitude-building and group cooperation, but it seems to be even more so since our departure from Earth. Is there no bad news anymore? Has mankind really achieved in so short a time such universal cheer, cooperation, and progress?

Due to my inability to obtain an objective reading of both my home planet and this soaring embassy of the said planet, I must now resort to random samplings, as follows:

Sample 1: In the African restaurant one night, not long past, I am seated alone at a table, spooning corn mash, spiced with red peppers, into my mouth. Seated alone at a nearby table is an extremely short woman about seventy-five to eighty years of age. She is heavily wrinkled, sipping from a martini glass that contains a clear liquid, leaving red lipstick stains on the glass, as she reads from a book. I am close enough to see that the letters on its cover are from the Cyrillic alphabet. With a brooding expression, she mutters to herself from time to time. She is wearing a medical staff uniform, with a gold *caduceus* pinned to the center of her chest, a winged stave entwined with snakes. Perhaps she has just come off duty and is having a drink before heading for home.

I am toying with the idea of leaning over to engage her in a conversation when from the corner of her eye she spots me looking at her. Her chest inflates with outraged dignity. If she had quills, she would have bristled them, maybe thrown a few at me. She glares ferociously as if she is about to open her mouth and tear a strip off my vanity. I look down at my bowl of mash and resume spoon-feeding myself, pretending that none of the aforementioned really happened.

"You rude man! Vye are you looking at my scar?" she says in a low threatening tone.

"I wasn't", I reply. "I didn't see a scar."

"You are lying! You ver looking!"

She slams the book down on the table, and raises her voice: "Alvays, alvays, the fools! You are Amerikanits. You are old man and old baby."

"Really, Madame!" I protest.

Now I notice a slight scar that disfigures one of her eyebrows.

"Stupid, stupid, stupid", she mutters, shaking her head, and then to herself: "They know nothing—nothing! They have not suffered!"

Displaying rather dramatic dignity, she drops from her chair and, with a toss of her head, stalks toward the exit.

Later, checking through the main computer's *Kosmos* personnel file, I find her listed under the medical department, spotting first her photo and then her bio. She's a very famous Russian psychiatrist, and she works on deck A.

Leaving all curiosity aside, I make the decision to avoid Concourse A as much as possible.

Sample 2: Another night, this time in the Euro restaurant on deck A (yes, yes, I know, but resolution weakens, pain fades). At a nearby table, two middle-aged men are eating spaghetti and "meatballs", refilling their wine glasses from a straw-wrapped, rotund bottle of chianti. They are talking loudly and laughing, joking and teasing each other. My three years at the Fermi Institute in Milan had given me enough Italian to understand that they're making puns based on the topic of anti-gravity. The terms they're using are highly technical, so I presume they're engineers.

As it turns out, one of them is from the city of Siena in Italy, the other from Florence. The jokes become jibes. Within minutes, the banter becomes an argument. Soon, both of them are red in the face and gesturing wildly with arms and hands.

"Ha!" says Siena. "Your *little* city, so pretentious, so *young!*"

"The city of Dante and Galileo", retorts Florence.

"The city of the Medici!" shouts Siena. "A city of poisoners and usurers."

"*Basta!*" shouts Florence. "What about your Borghese poisoners! What about your pathetic Palio di Siena! You kill more people with your horses every summer than all the victims of the Medici in history!"

"*Ridicolo!* Firenze kills with poison, Siena with accident!"

"You don't even use real horses any more, just the holograms, but the people get crushed just the same! No longer the horses trample; now you must trample each other. You *love* all that blood on the cobblestones of your very ancient, very *cultured* city!"

The roaring goes back and forth for quite some time. In the end, they embrace and part from each other with kisses on the cheeks, followed by "*Ciao! Ciao! Ciao!*"

Sample 3: Perusing a painting in one of the art alcoves on deck C, I am the unwilling witness to a torrid dialogue between a young man and woman, both of them wearing regulation DSI suits and ties. They careen into the alcove entangled in each other's arms, their emotions flailing in equal measures of desire and anger. The mood tabs behind their ears are flashing lurid colors. Either they don't see me standing there a few feet away from them, or they don't care.

"I told you, I told you", says the male. "She means nothing to me."

"But I saw you together!" says the female. "I saw the way you were with her."

"She started it. I couldn't resist."

"Couldn't resist? If you really loved me, you would've resisted."

"You don't understand. It was just one of those things that happen."

"Just one of those things that happen? You're saying it's all right that one of those things happens because I wasn't there? If I'd walked in ten minutes earlier, it wouldn't have happened?"

"Yeah, it wouldn't have happened."

"It *would've* happened at some other time? Is that what you're saying?"

"Honey, you just don't get it. I told you, she's *nothing* to me. I love *you*, babe!"

"I love you too, babe" (sounds of choking, sniffling, sobs).

"Look, I gotta get back to work. I'll see you later."

114

"Will you call me? Give me a call on *max* when you get off shift, okay?"

"It's better we don't talk on *max*."

"Why?"

"It's just better, that's all."

And so forth. Mind-numbing, nauseating, Pavlovian-Machiavellian drivel.

"Excuse me, babes", I mumble as I brush past them, desperate to get out of that alcove.

Sample 4: Feeling restless one day, I'm in the library containing hard-bound books, searching for something to read. I'm sick of sea stories and would also like a change from astronomy and physics. There's another person present in the room, a man in his late twenties, standing exactly in my path, blocking my view of the literature section. I expect him to notice me and courteously stand aside, but he stays where he's parked, head bent over a leather-bound copy of Shakespeare's poems. I peer surreptitiously and see the page opened to the heading: "Sonnet 30".

I clear my throat and say, "Do you like those old writers?"

He looks up and stares at me. There are tears in his eyes.

"I see you're reading Shakespeare", I say. "I haven't read any myself, but I hear he's pretty good."

"Leave me alone", he murmurs irritably.

"What?"

"Why can't people leave me *alone*?" he seethes with great intensity, as if I have offended him personally

Offended myself, I give the same back to him:

"My apologies!" I growl in a tone that would have withered a cactus. *You arrogant, rude little twit*, I silently add.

He abruptly leaves the room, taking the book with him.

I assess what I've seen during the short encounter: young, handsome, intelligent, literate, contemptuous, and wearing a very fine suit of clothes and real leather shoes. Obviously a successful human being, lacking nothing. His every quality exudes superiority. I doubt he ever had to struggle to get where he is.

Wanting to find a name for the object of my resentment, I go to a computer terminal and check through the *Kosmos'* personnel site. I have only a face to go by, but I find him soon enough. He's the nephew of the President of the World Federation.

Sample 5: I'm in the middle of my aerobics hike, choosing deck B on this particular day. One circuit of the ship equals 2.5 kilometers. I try to do three circuits daily in order to keep the old heart pumping and the muscle tone (such as it is) at survival level.

As I pass one of the wide staircases leading up to Concourse A, I am astonished to see what I take to be a hard-boiled egg bouncing down the steps, all by itself. It hits the hallway floor and rolls across to the opposite wall, bounces, and comes to a stop at my feet. It's a golf ball.

From the direction of the stairwell erupt high-pitched shrieks, or yelps, and down comes a scurrying black cyclone of fur that could be a cat or a dog or a squirrel. It's a dog, barking unstoppably at a decibel level guaranteed to wreak havoc with the human nervous system.

The animal is spinning in circles, trying to get its miniature canine jaws around the golf ball and not having much luck. The ball keeps spewing out of its mouth, covered in slobber, ricocheting back and forth across the hallway.

"Feedo! Feedo!" comes a semi-human screech from above. I look up and see an apparition, a very old man coming down the stairs, holding tight to the railing, taking one step at a time. He is carrying a golf club over his shoulder. He is wearing white tennis shoes, white mini shorts, and a fluorescent orange muscle shirt, on which is stamped an image of the *Kosmos* and the words:

Raydon Aerospace Technologies
The 22nd Century is OURS!

Out of breath, he stares at me with bulging eyes.

"Help me, help me!" he pleads.

"How can I help you?" I ask, genuinely perplexed by this request.

"Feedo needs to catch the ball and bring it to me. You have to get it into his mouth."

"Oh", I nod, and kneel down to grab the golf ball. The dog lunges, and I capture it, then insert the ball into its mouth. The shrill barking ceases, and the tail wags so hard it became a blur.

"Thanks, buddy", says the man with what I now, belatedly, recognize as a California accent. "You're a great guy!"

"Well, I'll be on my way now."

"No, no, you have to bring Feedo upstairs to my place. Would you do that for me? I'll make it worth your while."

"No payment necessary. I'll carry Feedo up for you."

"Hey, you're too good t'be true, boy."

Yeah, right. Well, he's old and fragile, I tell myself. I'll be like that someday.

I could describe in greater detail the monologue that follows, but would rather not. I've been writing these samplings for two hours now; I'm tired, I'm old, and I'm feeling real cranky at the moment.

The elderly gentleman is Mr. Don Gunn. He's the founder and majority shareholder of Raydon Aerospace. He's one of the two trillionaires on board, his wife being the other. They occupy a suite in the forward region of Concourse A. He likes to play golf in the cross street that borders his living space. His dog was named by his wife, whose name is Ray, short for Raydawn. The dog's name is "Fideaux". Don explains to me during our ascent to his floor that this is a very clever pun on the old doggie name, Fido. "It's French", he tells me, then adds that he calls his pet *Fee-dough* because he has made a lot of money in his life. He gleefully asks if I see how it's not just one pun but two? I tell him that I do see. Actually, I spot three but don't bother.

Finally, we arrive at his suite, where we are met at the open door by a Filipino manservant, who takes Feedo from me with a long-suffering expression, and stands back as Don enters his home. As an afterthought, Don invites me in for a drink. I politely decline. A quick glance through the doorway tells me that the entry hall is floored with marble and the palatial living room has wall-to-wall carpet, luxurious couches, easy chairs, and lamps, as well as a huge vidscreen in a corner, before which sits a tiny, mauve-haired lady who appears to be in a trance—watching a soap opera. There is also a soaring stone fireplace, burning what I'm pretty sure are real logs. I smell genuine wood smoke. I also smell what I think is beef-steak frying on a kitchen stove somewhere within. I begin to salivate.

Exercising a bit of moral fiber, I wish him well with his golf game and beat a dignified, though hasty, retreat.

Day 2191:

Sixth anniversary. Ho-hum. More revelry in the hallways. What a happy bunch we are.

Yesterday we passed the "advance probes" that were sent out to Alpha Centauri many years ago. I presume that we will soon launch our own array of telescopes, which will fly in formation with the ship and give us even better triangulation, with superior composite photos of our destination.

I tried to swim in the afternoon, but the pool was too crowded. Had a nap instead, then returned to the inland sea just before midnight. A couple of other crawlers were present—strong, silent types. We didn't get in each other's way.

Day 2222:

I like the mathematical beauty of this day. On a whim, this morning I decided to begin my approach to Stron McKie, to let him know we're inside a laboratory rat maze. I've held back from doing so until now because I suspected that, first, he would fly into a rage and, second, he would storm about the ship creating havoc in his attempt to galvanize an organized protest, probably under his very own leadership. William Wallace with a sword and a rant, losing all credibility and, if he is intemperate enough, giving away clues that could lead to Dwayne. More worrisome, his general slash-and-burn approach to human relations would disable any effective revolt. I am working on my own plans in this regard.

We met over lunch at the end of a long, long vacant table in the cafeteria.

"I think you'd enjoy this novel", I said as I handed him my e-book reader, with some alluring text of *Billy Budd* on the screen.

"I don't read friction", he said, not extending his hand to take my offering.

"*Fiction*, not friction."

"I say *friction*, not fiction. I never read the stuff and I never will. I don't like being force-fed somebody else's subconscious fears and desires."

"This one's pretty good", I countered. "If you read it as a nonfiction account, I think you'll find it interesting. It's about what can happen when things go wrong on a long voyage."

"Well, stop nipping my hide, and hand it over."

As he was tapping page buttons and reading a few lines, I whispered my news to him, hoping that no one could electronically overhear us. How pleasantly surprised I was to discover that Stron did not fly into a rage. He looked up and scowled with pleasure.

"I figured that out during the first six months", he growled.

Taken aback, I exclaimed, "And you didn't tell me?"

"What good would that have accomplished, laddie? Did you bring a set of microsockets in your baggage? Do you know how to reprogram that box of beasties?"

"I'm afraid not. But you might have warned me. I would have guarded my words, watched what I dictated into the *max*."

"Stopped singing in the shower?"

"Yes, that too."

"And by breaking your pattern, getting all secretive, you would have drawn their beady little eyes in your direction."

"Maybe so. But tell me, what have you done about it?"

He picked a piece of "bacon" rind off his plate and began to chew it with relish, his eyes twinkling as he examined my face.

"I have my ways."

"Such as?"

"I know enough about the *max* to insert a sound recording that plays at random. I add to it from time to time. I sing ballads in my inimitable voice, recite the collected works of Bobby Burns in dialect, read long extracts from my books, which would numb the mind of anyone listening in. Business as usual, you see."

"Do you keep private records on the *max*?"

"You mean my fantasies and moonshine recipes? Nay, lad, I'm not that stupid."

"No diary?"

"Just a completely boring one. I mention you in it a few times."

"Yeah, I jotted down a few boring notes about you in my journal."

"I recorded only the worst things", he laughed. "The cowboy boots, the twang, the pathetic limp. I also preen my own cultural camouflage, the kilt and sporran, the longing for haggis and my bagpipe, my filthy moods, my petty jealousies. Just enough to let them think we're idiosyncratic, silly, old scientists who are so naïve we wouldn't ever suspect what they're doing."

"We *are* silly, old, idiosyncratic scientists."

"So we are. However, we're a bit more than that, wouldn't you say?"

"I think so. In any event, there's somebody I know who can do some deep fixing on your *max*."

"Would it cost me anything?"

"Feeling tight-fisted today?"

"No, no, I just like to know the price of things."

"He does it without charge, on principle. He's young, and he's an undiscovered genius."

"Sounds like a good lad. Does he drink?"

"Yup."

"I'll pay him."

Thus, this evening while Stron and I played chess in the lounge on deck C, gathering onlookers and spicing the air with Scottish epithets, Dwayne quietly did his work.

Day 2235:

Today we made a little experiment. Dwayne and I decided to drop by Stron's room without warning. On the way there, Dwayne told me that two weeks ago when he arrived in Stron's room to do the job, he had found a polyplast flask sitting on the *max* with a note under it: *To the Mysterious Stranger, with thanks.*

"It was very good whiskey", he added.

We knocked on Stron's door and heard a muffled grunt from within. The door disappeared, revealing the interior of the highland castle in all its disheveled glory and the master himself sitting at his desk, looking surprised that someone other than service personnel had come calling. Considering his temperament, we may indeed have been his first real visitors. He wasn't very welcoming, but after some whispered appeal to the "revolt" he did agree to admit us.

When we were inside, he barked: "Shut yerself, y'damn door!" Which it did.

While Xue's room is pin-neat, Stron's is situated at the other end of the spectrum of human habitation. It is a squirrel's nest. It is not only messy, it is obsessively messy. Pathologically messy. I won't even attempt a coherent description of what I saw, because the room was not coherent. There was a clay mug full of dry heather stalks that had scattered their seeds or petals over everything, as well as sports trophies topped by silver curling stones. There were photos of humans, dogs, moors, and constellations beaded to the four walls. And I must not fail to mention the ingenious jerry-built alcohol distillery he has running inside a lockable closet, very small but productive apparatus, judging by the number of polyplast bottles he has stored there, each filled with an amber fluid.

"Who are you?" he demanded of Dwayne.

"The Mysterious Stranger", the latter mumbled.

Grumbling to himself, Stron cleared books, papers, and less enlightened debris off the bed and bade us sit down.

The three of us discussed our plan, and then we set it in motion:

First, Dwayne deactivated Stron's new privacy codes. With me sitting beside him, Stron then keyed in my e-address and voice-*max*ed a message to me. He said: "Neil, this is Stron McKie. I've been thinking. Sometimes I wonder if they monitor our rooms and our files. Am I losing my mind, or is there something in it? If they *are* peeking on us, I dinna like it. I have a mind to make a stink."

He signed off and let Dwayne take over. When the privacy was reactivated, we shared a chuckle, and then Dwayne and I went straightway back to my room. There, he deactivated my privacy code, and I checked my inbox. Stron's message blurted through the room.

I clicked *reply* and said: "Stron. I can't imagine why they would do such a thing. It's all in your imagination. Time to cut back on the whiskey, lad."

I signed off, and Dwayne reactivated the privacy.

Day 2236:

Very interesting. This morning, less than twenty-four hours after our experiment began, I received mail in my inbox, a text message. (See attached print-out):

> Dr. de Hoyos,
> We have not yet had the pleasure to meet.
> As a member of the organizing committee for the *Kosmos'* educational, cultural, and scientific enrichment programs, I have been asked to contact you with a request which we hope you will find of interest. As you know, due to the length of the voyage, the factors of psychological atmosphere and morale are a constant challenge in onboard life, in a reduced environmental habitat that is unique as a psychological/social configuration. Of course, these are normal components in a great venture such as

ours. Though I have so far observed an excellent attitude among us all, there is, as can be expected, the potential for unhealthy tendencies to lethargy and withdrawal in individuals.

For this reason, the committee continues to offer a variety of programs that will generate interest and motivation, including our regular public lecture series. You will recall that you honored us by delivering the inaugural lecture six years ago. It was a resounding success, stimulating much thought and discussion for months afterward. The ship's archivist informs me that the recording of your talk continues to be regularly accessed. I wish to thank you again for your generous agreement to give that brilliant and moving presentation.

Since that time, we have completed two-thirds of the outbound stage of the journey. The committee would therefore be most grateful if you would consider giving another public lecture, on any topic of your preference. If this request meets with your approval, I would be pleased to discuss the details of time and venue at your earliest convenience.

Could we meet tomorrow, say at 1000 hours?

With cordial best wishes,

Dr. Elif Larson, PhD, DSoc, DG/GK

Deputy Director, Department of Social Infrastructure

I sent a reply, telling the man I'd be happy to accept his invitation and would appear promptly at 1000 hours at his office door, if he wouldn't mind sending me the physical address.

Within five minutes I received his answer:

Delighted.

Concourse C, DSI annex, Room 712.

See you then.

Best.

I did a quick search on the *max*. Eight thousand-plus articles on the life and times of Elif Larson. He is a Norwegian, just over forty years of age. Adjunct professor at a number of Nordic universities, founder of an Institute in New York City devoted to his theories. Often a speaker at conferences on "the deaggressivization of humankind". Winner of prestigious awards too numerous to mention. A successful facilitator of group well-being in global conflict situations. He specializes in a field that he made "famous" (I never heard of it), called "Gemeinschaft/Gesellschaft Kinesiology".

I looked it up. *Gemeinschaft* is a term for a form of community determined by local geographical proximity (one's village, one's neighborhood, one's family). *Gesellschaft* is a community formed by selectivity: choosing one's relationships from broad geographical and social resources, according to personal preferences. This distinctly urban practice has become the global norm.

He's a social worker.

Day 2237:

Oh boy. Oh my. Oh, what a slick operator—a genius in his own right. Let me describe my meeting with him.

Promptly at ten o'clock this morning, I presented myself before the doors of Gemeinschaft/Gesellschaft Kinesiology in Outer Space. Peering through the transparent barrier, I waved at a young woman typing merrily at her desk. She spotted me, said something inaudible into her *max*, and the double doors divided, permitting me entrance. As she hurried around the desk to greet me, any reticence I might have felt was dissolved by her friendly face and the enthusiastic hand-pumping she gave me.

"Dr. de Hoyos, it's an honor, sir, *an honor*! Please come this way; Dr. Larson is expecting you."

In the inner sanctum, Dr. Larson arose from behind his desk as a benevolent force of nature. He was a huge man, by which I mean unusually burly, though not fat. His face was a boy's, glossy, handsome, and smiling, his countenance aged only by a receding hairline and the token crows-feet at the edges of his bright, warm eyes. He looked like somebody's worldly-wise but kindly uncle standing duty at the barbeque in the back yard. The heartiness of his massive handshake nearly crushed my liver-spotted old claw. All told, this was a fellow well designed to disarm the most antagonistic of clients.

In interests of legal accuracy, I had brought along my lapel button recorder, a lovely item that I had purchased some years ago through the black market in Singapore. To the uninformed eye, it was no more than a tiny gold disk, with an image of a flowering cactus, encircled by the letters ACGA (Association of Cactus Growers of America). The flower sucked up every word spoken in its vicinity.

I will not transcribe the small talk (why waste time, why waste good paper?). Suffice it to say, that his manner throughout our meeting was relaxed and utterly charming. Moreover, he had done his homework. First, he enthused about my Nobels, my presence on the ship, and my willingness to give another lecture. Then he asked about certain details in my "recent" articles in scientific journals, things he had found stimulating but, he confessed, oblique to him. I explained the problematic parts; he asked supplementary questions (actually, quite good ones), and as they tapered off, we got down to the real, if unstated, purpose of the meeting.

We were now facing each other across his desk—actual wood, I think—with steaming coffee served in genuine porcelain cups and saucers. His hands were clasped before him on the desk top, conveying outreach toward me. My hands were folded neutrally on my lap, though every other part of me communicated pleasure and relaxation. I acted as if I were soaking it up with dignified, greedy abandon.

"I'm really tickled, Dr. Larson, that you've made such an effort to understand these concepts. Very few people are able to do so."

"Please call me Elif", he smiled.

"Elif. And mine's Neil."

"Thank you, Neil. I hope I'm not becoming tedious when I say what an honor it is to have you on the ship."

"Not at all", I responded with a maidenlike, verbal blush. Good heavens, what can one reply to flattery like that?

"We were impressed by the response to your inaugural lecture. I must say in confidentiality that no subsequent talk by others has prompted such a positive reaction."

"Thank you."

I mean, *What*? I mean, don't be a ridiculous elf! I had no feedback other than about twenty people asking me for the name of the symphony's composer. Xue's talk in the second year was superior to mine, stunning actually, so good that I almost suggested to him (Xue) that he should forget this ink-drawing business and get himself onto the lecture circuit. Dr. Pagnol's talk on species adaptation was also a corker. As was Dr. Teal's on anti-matter.

"Of course, we've had some fine speakers during the past six years", said Elf. "The committee feels that, on the whole, they have made an invaluable contribution to the psychological well-being of the community."

"I feel the same, Elif", I said, nodding sagely. "Of course, it goes without saying that a healthy community won't always have uniform feelings. In any given community, there's always something of a split between the *Gemeinschaft*ers and the *Gesellschaft*ers."

I had done my homework too. He paused for a few seconds. His expression was no less affable, but the eyes now looked at me with imperceptibly closer attention. He continued: "Yes, it can be a problem. Fortunately, in an intentional community such as ours, a truly global community, *Gesellschaft* is the overarching dynamic of social interaction. There aren't any local neighborhoods."

I nodded in affirmation even as I silently disagreed. You bet there are local neighborhoods on board, Elf. Very close-knit ones.

"The wonderful thing is," he continued, "we'll never exhaust the riches of the great minds we have with us. That's why we're asking our most successful speakers to recommend other scientists whom they feel would offer stimulating presentations. Would you be open to this?"

"To suggesting speakers' names?"

"Yes. Anyone you think would interest a large audience. You see, there is a tendency to individual isolation during a lengthy journey like this. The more people experience each other in public encounters, the more they will feel they're part of a *community*."

Elf, I'm getting just a little tired of that word.

"Smart thinking", I nodded. "We're lucky we have staff who're sensitive to those aspects of life. You know what scientists can be like."

He chuckled understandingly.

Gazing at the ceiling of his office, I frowned as if in deep thought, as if I were going over a mental roster of champion speakers. He waited patiently.

"You know", I said, "I think we need Xue Ao-li to give us a lecture on mathematical anomalies in particle acceleration."

Elf nodded politely. "Yes, Dr. Xue would be good."

"Then there's Dr. Pagnol on species adaptation. And Dr. Teal on anti-matter."

"I think they already spoke on those topics. It would be somewhat repetitious."

"You're right. Now, who else?" I murmured to myself. "Mmmm, who else?"

"There's Dr. McKie. He hasn't spoken yet."

"He'd be great on astronomy", I said.

Elf's face continued to smile, but tightened just enough that I knew we were zeroing in on the radar beam.

"He'd be excellent", Elf said with a slight adjustment of his sitting position.

"Would the committee invite him? Or would you like me to ask him personally? He can be a little rough around the edges. Not really a community buff."

"That would be a help, I'm sure", said Elf. His face slid quietly into an expression of qualified concern. "I admire Dr. McKie's work very much—very much." He paused, as if thinking over my suggestion. "I am a little puzzled by him."

"Oh, in what way?"

"He doesn't seem all that happy to be with us."

I threw my head back and grinned knowingly. "That's just Stron's mannerism. He relishes his reputation as a grumpy old man."

"One wonders if he would be grumpy before a podium."

"I have no doubt he would be. But it's part of his charm. I think the audience would love it."

"Perhaps you're right."

"Have you met him?" I asked. "You'd enjoy him."

"I haven't met him face to face." Elf shook his head with an interested smile, feigning enchantment by Stron's reputation. "I hear he's quite an eccentric."

"He is indeed."

"He has some wild theories, I hear."

"As a scientist, there's none better. Outside the field of astronomy, however, he can be opinionated. Full of quirks and quarks, so to speak. People sometimes think he's a bit paranoid, imagines crazy things. It's his act. It's just his way of having fun. I don't know what you've heard about him, but you shouldn't take it too seriously."

"Oh, I never would. We all have quirks and quarks."

"Too true. It's what makes for an interesting community." I gave it three seconds and asked, "So, would you like me to invite him to be a speaker?"

"Let me run this by the committee first", said Elf, furrowing his brow. "I have to follow protocol, and I expect there'll be a number of names put forward."

"Of course. Just give me a call if you need me. I'm at your disposal."

He rose and offered his hand. I rose and accepted it. We smiled congenially at each other, and he conducted me to the door.

"Oh", I said, as if recalling a half-remembered thought. "We need to confirm the date and venue of my talk?"

"Ah, yes, please forgive me." He went back to his desk, bent over his *max* day-planner, pursed his lips, and said: "How about the first Monday of next month, 1900 hours, the main auditorium on Concourse A?"

"Sounds good to me."

"Then it's definite."

With that, we parted in a cloud of mutual friendliness, congratulating ourselves for having accomplished so much, so brilliantly, in so short a time.

I headed off to Stron's room. He was at home, and once I was inside he demanded a blow–by-blow description of my meeting with Larson. First, I gave him a thumbnail sketch and summarized by saying: "It's not exactly proof, but the timing does seem to indicate that they overheard our fake dialogue."

"It does indeed", Stron growled, as he poured me a finger of his latest brew.

"On the other hand, we shouldn't jump to hasty conclusions", I went on. "It's entirely possible that we're not quite on the mark about this."

"We're so on the mark, Neil-lad, that we split the shaft of the arrow that's lodged dead center in the bull's-eye."

"Maybe it's not as sinister as it appears. What they're doing is unethical, of course, but they probably mean no harm."

"Neil, listen to yourself. Unethical *is* harm."

"But he made no direct accusations, didn't even ask probing questions."

"Worse and worse. I'll bet he's a Freudian-slip-pouncer—the most odious kind. He laid a honey trap for you, and you stepped right into it, which is to be expected."

"I'll admit I caught the faintest whiff of honey. But nothing that would make your feet stick to the floor."

"Did he ever-so-casually bring up my name?"

"Yes, but that was well along in the conversation."

"He's good. He's very good. Which means he's dangerous."

"Maybe so. However, in the interest of keeping perspective, let's ask ourselves if all this amounts to anything. What does it matter if they suspect we're onto their tricks? The fact is, they don't know anything. And even if they did, what could they do about it? Clap us in irons and throw us into the brig?"

"Hardly. But they could make life damn uncomfortable—put the pressure on us, isolate us, demonize us in the eyes of other passengers. And worst of all, they could refuse us permission to land on the planet with the exploration teams. They might even ruin our reputations in the history books."

"Mine's already ruined. I'm a convicted criminal, actually. Didn't you hear about that?"

"No! Tell me all about it."

I did. And he laughed. Then we called it a day.

Day 2251:

Last night I watched an old film called *The Wizard of Oz*—primitive fantasy, but it had a pretty girl with a nice voice, skipping along a yellow brick road.

This morning I awoke before dawn, soaked with sweat, overcome by a feeling of stark terror. This is strange, because I hardly ever remember my dreams, and haven't suffered from a nightmare in decades.

In the dream, I was franticly scurrying about the *Kosmos* trying to convince people that we were all being listened to and watched by "them". The accusation was denied by the authorities as paranoia. None of the passengers and crew believed me.

I was dragged by Elif Larson to an enforced session of psychological counseling. I was strapped to a chair and left alone with the psychiatrist. She was a very short woman wearing dark sunglasses and dressed in a skin-tight, one-piece, synthetic jumpsuit that was not flattering to her figure. She rocked back and forth on her office chair, scowling at me, saying nothing, taking long drags on her cigarette holder, from which protruded a burning filterless cigarette. The room was dense with the cloud of noxious tobacco smoke. Her face was wrinkled with extreme old age and deformed by a scar slashed across one eyebrow and the length of her cheek. Her hair was long, straight, and dyed blond. I felt totally frightened by her—not because of what she might do to me but by what she was.

She smoked cigarette after cigarette, rocking and staring at me, rocking and staring, from time to time spitting bits of tobacco onto the floor. She peered at me as if I were an interesting specimen that she was about to vivisect—as soon as she has finished her cigarette. I could tell that she would enjoy my screams. She would write an interesting paper on the way I died in agony.

But to my vast relief, she gave me a crooked smile and rasped in a deep Eastern-European voice that she believed me. She declared that she could tell when people were repressing, projecting, and transferring, and she was sure that I was not repressing, projecting, or transferring, she said, because we really were being persecuted. Even psychiatrists get persecuted sometimes, she added with a defensive tone. Then followed a long, long lecture, full of crazy things such as her desire to be a circus performer, the lady who stands on the back of a galloping pony, balancing on one foot.

"Oh, yes", I agreed, nodding emphatically. "You'd be very good at it."

She dropped from her chair, and now only the top of her head was visible above the desk. She rounded the corner, and I saw that she was less than four feet tall.

"You patronize me!" she screamed into my face. "You look down on people of my stature! Admit it, admit it!"

"No, no, please believe me, I don't look down on you, except physically."

"Vat do you mean by dat?" she snarled dangerously.

"I mean I didn't choose to be tall," I whined, "and you didn't choose to be short."

She began screaming at me again, spittle and tobacco flying in every direction.

At that point, DSI guards burst into the room. They had been listening through surveillance.

"Are you brainwashing this man properly?" they shouted.

Without answering the question, she glared at them and whipped off her sunglasses in order to stare them down. Their fear of her was too great, and they backed out of the room.

In a rage, she untied me, and stated that we would now go to inform the whole ship that DSI is the secret police. We ran out into the hallways and tried to engage passersby, but everyone shook us off.

Suddenly, out of nowhere Elif Larson appeared with dozens of henchmen. They tied up the psychiatrist and did the same to me. We were hauled off to a torture chamber deep in the bowels of the ship, and there we were strapped to seats facing an enormous vidscreen. Madness ensued—madness, madness, madness! The worst tortures were the programs we were forced to watch. If we closed our eyes, buckets of cold water were thrown in our faces. We were forced to see everything—everything! Daylong interviews with television stars, Disney musicals, Hollywood love-stories.

"You cannot do dis to me!" screamed the little lady. "I am psychiatrist! I am *psychiatrist*, I tell you! I know vat you are doing to my mind!"

We were taken deeper into a special section of the ship, into a large white room without windows. From behind a curtain came the sound of whirring machinery, clanking metal, thuds, beeping, and other cyber noises: A screen lowered from the ceiling, and more programming was shown to us. We were forced to watch hours upon hours of mind-numbing golf games from the twentieth through the twenty-first centuries. The psychiatrist lost consciousness. I screamed; the psychological pain was so great. I begged them to kill me. But they would not let me die. I struggled and yelled until, without warning, the curtain was drawn aside, and I saw inside, controlling everything on the ship, the Wizard of Oz.

My beloved little Scottie dog was dragged in by his collar. He had been captured in the arboretum. Elf took out a pistol and shot him in front of my eyes.

"Noooooo!" I wailed.

"You're not in New Mexico any more, Hoyos", he cackled.

Suddenly, there was a tremendous roar and bang. The *Kosmos* lurched, and we all toppled to the floor, torturers, guards, the wizard, the psychiatrist, and myself. The ship had been rammed by an alien space vehicle. A crowd of little green men, shorter than the psychiatrist, stormed into the room. The aliens' eyes were huge, black, and saurian, their bodies like spider monkeys.

"You must call us your Little Friends", declared their leader. "We come in peace."

At this, all the aliens burst into hysterical laughter. Then they pointed their rayguns at us and started firing. I crawled out of the room, and stumbled to my feet, trying to run away, trying to warn the others onboard, but then I saw that the bodies of my shipmates littered the floor everywhere. I dragged my bleeding body along the concourse, crying out, "The horror! The horror!" I woke up.

(*Ay, caramba!*)

Day 2252:

On the first Monday of the following month, the condemned man enjoyed a last meal in the Indian restaurant (whew, hot, hot, hot curry!) and a modest glass of dry Madeira wine. Afterward, I went down to Stron's room and knocked, since we had agreed to walk together to the auditorium on deck A.

"Aaargh, where's my dirk when I need it?" he grumbled as he knotted his bright red tartan necktie in preparation for departure.

"What's a dirk?" I asked.

"A clever weapon we Scots devised for inflicting pain on invaders."

"Don't tell me you forgot to smuggle one on board?"

"Tried to, but they spotted it at security in Africa. Confiscated it. Didn't want me hijacking the ship."

"They took your ammunition too, I presume."

"A dirk is a knife, laddie, more precisely a dagger."

"Oh."

I flipped open my blazer and exposed the kit strapped to my belt. I unbuttoned it and showed him my old fold-knife.

He grinned. "Boys' own adventures, eh?"

"Yup."

"How'd you smuggle that little item onboard?"

"Being a cripple has its advantages."

He laughed. "I sure wish I was deformed."

I closed it up again and buttoned the kit. Back to nice, harmless astrophysicist.

As we climbed the staircase from B to A, he said, "Now here's a thought for you: Let's suppose there's intelligent life on AC-A-7. Objectively speaking, wouldn't that make *us* the invaders?"

"You have a point. The AC-A-7-lings' view of the matter would be different than ours."

"Precisely. Fortunately, that's probably not going to be a problem. There hasn't been a sheep-bleat from the planet, ever. None that's

131

detectable by any instrument mankind has invented. On the other hand, this doesn't mean they aren't communicating, if they're there. They could be using waves we can't measure."

"Stron, if there is someone waiting for us on AC-A-7, and you think we're the invaders, why did you agree to be part of this expedition?"

"Ach, I wanted to make sure the aliens have some idea of their options, reassure them we're not *all* arrogant exploiters. I come as a *person*, not as an ambassador of the human race."

" 'Greetings, fellow sapient beings, I come in peace!' That approach?"

"Right, that approach."

"Very nice, but can you really side-step your species of origin?"

"Yes, I damn well can. I'm no puppet of official policy. If we meet any little green fellows, I'll introduce them to Stron McKie, not to my species."

"Hopefully they'll get the distinction."

"Why wouldn't they? I can be a charmer, you know."

"Er ... yes."

As we shuffled and bumped our way along Concourse A in the direction of the auditorium, which was in the forward part of the ship, Stron nattered a steady stream of quips. But I could tell he was nervous by the way he kept yanking tufts of white hair out of his ears.

Approaching the wide entrance doors, we realized there would be a good crowd in attendance since a fair volume of conversational buzz came from within, and more people were converging from both directions of the main concourse, as well as its cross-avenues.

"Well, Neil, here we are. Get ready for battle."

"I wish we'd painted ourselves lurid colors, Stron, and brought our claymores."

He grimaced and pulled out a few last strands of hair. "Nay, nay, the wrong approach entirely. Tonight we are going to be dignity incarnate."

He slipped past me and entered the auditorium alone, lest we be identified with each other and a conspiracy suspected too early in the game. I stood outside for a few minutes, shaking hands with people, making chat and observing Stron from the corner of my eye as he took his seat in the front row, beside three of the five Nobel men. Pagnol and Teal were also in the row, along with a few other scientific luminaries.

The auditorium seats six hundred. Large as it is, it's a room without echoes, due to the acoustic-friendly walls and carpet. The rows slope gently down to an orchestra pit (empty now, though it is sometimes used by musicians for pick-up concerts). The seats are maroon fabric over soft padding, as comfortable as an armchair. And tonight, it looked like a majority of them were filled. I estimated that two-thirds of the passengers and crew were present. This surprised me greatly, since my talk as advertised would be on the topic of "Psychological Physics".

During the planning stage, I had taken the precaution of throwing a handful of stardust into the eyes of dear Dr. Larson, explaining to him that I would begin the talk with the astrophysics of our journey, then tie it into my own early work that had made the ship possible, and then bring the presentation to a climax by using a simile—the comparison of the mutual gravitational pull of bodies in a solar system to the mutual influence that members of a community have on each other. The celestial titans, I would assert, maintain each other in a delicate equilibrium, much as we sustain each other onboard the *Kosmos*. The talk would end with a ringing call to a renewed sense of responsibility for each other's well-being. In a word, *Gemeinschaft-Gesellschaft* kinesiology.

He loved it. He ate it up. He unleashed all his powers of promotion and advertisement. And now the splendid night had arrived.

One of the event's organizers, Dr. Skinner, the director of DSI, walked me down the center aisle toward the elevated stage. In passing, I noticed Dwayne in the back row, hunched over a book. Pia waved shyly from mid-audience; Maria smiled maternally at me; a few isolated individuals began to clap. A smattering of applause accompanied me up the three short steps to the stage. My heart pounded.

The podium was a nostalgia item, a historic work of art, a platinum and polyplast sculpture representing a soaring rocket ship penetrating outer space. The rocket's exhaust trail formed the podium's trunk, the rocket itself was the support of the reading platform, which was a tilted transparent disk, representing our home solar system, with an illuminated sun the size of a grapefruit designed to throw light on a speaker's papers. The planets orbited it in slow motion as smaller, colored spheres.

Skinner took the podium and began his introduction. Blah-blah-blah—my awards, prizes, honors, achievements, books—blah-blah-blah. Why does that sort of thing make my flesh crawl? Maybe because it's too much like the hawker's prattle of an auctioneer? Does it threaten my humble persona? Or does it unmask my secret pride? Anyway, throughout the preamble, I stood to the side, smiling inanely like an old crackpot, with my fingers fidgeting nervously behind my back. Thunderous applause followed. I shook hands with Skinner and stepped forward to the podium.

For a few seconds, I paused, and in my mind's eye, I saw a boy dancing in a desert, singing and shaking his bells. I pushed away the thought and began.

Let me say in summation, and with only a modicum of pride, that I shone. I was articulate in a way that flowed naturally, balancing scholar and showman so subtly that none in the audience (save for my co-conspirators) suspected a vaudeville act. I was witty. I was Nobel-ish. I was twangless. I gripped them and moved them. Step by step, I led the audience through the outline I had given to Elf.

When I had reached the point in the talk where I was to compare solar systemic equilibrium to the equilibrium desirable in human communities, I paused for dramatic effect. During this brief hiatus, I looked around the hall significantly. You could have heard a gyroscope topple over. There in front of me sat a scattering of peers, gazing up with fond interest. There in the back row sat Dwayne, who (to my irritation) was still hunched over, reading a book. There in the middle sat Pia, beside a flight officer whom I took to be her "special friend". The breast logo on his uniform sparkled with its three little stars. Beside him were two other sparkling officers, and there were more like them throughout the audience. To my extreme left, in the front row, sat Elf and the director of DSI, side by side, leaning forward slightly, smiling their encouragement at me because they knew that the big juicy plum of the evening would now be presented. The famous scientist would deliver their agenda in an irresistible package.

"As we have seen," I began, "the mutual gravitational pull of bodies in a solar system is a magnificently balanced symphony of physical forces. Our home system is most impressive to us in this regard, because we know it best; it is ours. The Alpha Centauri system presents an even greater complexity. These two systems are involved in a choreography of celestial titans, with their planets revolving on their own axes even as they circle their respective stars, which are in kinetic balance within the larger body of our local star cluster, within the massive spiraling of our galaxy, which is locked in the mutual gravitational pull of members of our own local galaxy cluster, which in turn dances with super-clusters, onward and outward with the expanding universe, and all of it splendid and beautiful. All of it is the courtship and marriage of unimaginable forces maintaining each other in a delicate equilibrium."

I paused and caught my breath.

"It has sometimes been said that these colossal forces are similar to the mutual influence that members of a human community have on each other. Insofar as we do affect each other, this is true. Yet the simile is weak, and threatens to become superficial, for not a single human being onboard the *Kosmos* can be reduced to an unthinking force. We can harness the atom, but we cannot attempt to absolutely control men's wills, nor their capacity for rational thought, nor their hunger for freedom, without grave risk to man himself. To condition him, to determine him according to arbitrary theories of his nature—his perpetually elusive and mysterious nature—is to deform him."

A sweeping glance informed me that Elf and his buddy were beginning to look a little concerned. Both were listening intently, both leaning forward, both with fists under their chins and forefingers laid along their cheeks as if they were deep in thought.

"Has not our entire history until now proved this truth conclusively? We continue to make the same mistake, age after age. We confuse imposed governance for legitimate authority. What, then, is legitimate authority? Is it not a mutual contract between free beings who agree to apportion their fields of responsibility and levels of decision-making, according to their gifts, while maintaining accountability, and placing above all other social considerations the necessity of mutual respect? If this is so, we must conclude that rare indeed has been its exercise in the history of mankind."

Again, I paused. Now Elf and Skinner were no longer smiling. Their brows were furrowed unpleasantly, their heads tilted at an angle of inquisitive worry.

"That is why I am grieved this evening", I continued. "I am grieved most of all that we have learned so little from our past. For this reason, I must now refer to a disequilibrium in the conduct of onboard life. The electronic surveillance of all of us has continued unabated since our departure from Earth. Each of our personal computers in our private rooms is monitored. Nothing typed or spoken into them goes unexamined. Someone, somewhere on this ship, has total access to your most deeply private conversations and thoughts. They are read or listened to by unseen people to whom you gave no permission to do so."

At this point, heads were turning in the audience, people murmuring or whispering to each other. Elf and Skinner were on their feet and striding toward the stage, Elf waving his hand as if to brush aside everything I had just said, or to send me a cease-and-desist order. Regardless, I pressed on.

"No one asked me if they could listen to my voice journals, read my mail, listen to my mail, or track where I surf in the great sea of knowledge."

Now the audience broke out in rumbling conversation. A few people rose to their feet, shaking their heads, while others sat in frozen concentration, not so much perplexed as alarmed and unable to decide how to respond.

Now Elf and Skinner reached the steps and tripped hastily up to the stage.

The head of DSI approached me with courteous body language, but he gripped one of my biceps painfully. Elf, eyes scowling but mouth smiling broadly, put his hand over the sun (apparently doubling as a microphone) and said, "What the hell are you doing? Say good night and get off this stage."

His voice boomed throughout the auditorium, the sound doubly amplified. Startled, Elf glanced at the sun and banged it with his fist. While he was thus distracted, a number of people moved in.

Stron McKie pushed himself between me and Skinner and disengaged the latter's meaty paw. Xue, Pagnol, and Teal, stepped up beside me, facing the audience.

"What Dr. Hoyos has told you is true", Pagnol said, his voice booming. "I am Dr. Étienne Pagnol. For those who do not know me, I am assistant director of the biology department."

One by one, the others identified themselves and confirmed the truth of the message. Five more men and women joined them— doctors all, figures in various sciences, as well as the two other Nobel laureates who had been sitting in the front row.

By now, Skinner and Elf were livid, but trying unsuccessfully to give the impression that they had things well under control, that the accusation was groundless.

Elf tapped something on his lapel and growled *soto voce*: "Turn off the damned sound system." His words echoed loudly.

By then, all the people in the audience were on their feet and about two-thirds of them were making their way toward the stage. Some called out questions.

"How do you know this? Can you prove it? Why would they do such a thing?"

"Consider this", I shouted, though there was no need to shout. "Consider that the public talks we've enjoyed since the beginning of the voyage are always accessible, *live* in real-time, through your *max*. Doesn't that tell us something? If they can broadcast into your *max*, why wouldn't the flow go outward too? They designed the ship's communications systems, and it would be no great effort for them to implant code that walks right through your individual firewalls."

Elf whispered into his lapel, "What do you mean it doesn't work? Use the override. Cut the feed to the rooms. And cut the power to the hall. Do it *now!*"

His whisper boomed, and at that point, he realized he was showing his cards to the audience. He shut up and stood aside, letting me continue, but with every bit of his nonverbal mountain of flesh proclaiming his adamant rejection of what I was saying. I was as perplexed as he was, wondering why the sound system was behaving the way it was, and why something was preventing the power cut to the auditorium.

"Consider also," I went on, "that pre-flight briefings informed us, and the Manual itself states, that our rooms are our personal spaces—so they called it—and that we can do whatever we wish in them. The Manual further states that each of our *max*es is an autonomous sealed unit, intended exclusively for our private use. Read the Manual, page 1013. It's all there."

Now a few dissident voices were shouting objections, while the majority of people were calling out for more evidence.

And that was the rub. I had no hard evidence. None at all. This cold fact momentarily disabled me, and I began to falter.

"Ladies and gentlemen," said Stron, stepping in, "I'm Dr. McKie, head of the on-planet astronomy team. And I tell you that what Dr. Hoyos has told you tonight is the truth. You ask us for evidence. This is not a court of law. This is not a police forensic lab. But I will ask you this: If you were lying on your bed after a shower, undraped shall we say, and you spotted an eyeball at the keyhole of your door, and then you donned your coverlets as fast as you could and raced out into the hallway to catch the culprit, and failed, would you then say to yourself, 'Naw, I was dreaming'? After all, you don't have the Peeping Tom by the scruff of his neck, not even his eyeball in your tight little fist. But you know you saw that eye looking in on you. What any sensible person would do at that point is to try to track the culprit."

"That's just suspicion, that's no evidence!" someone shouted.

"The smell of a skunk is no evidence that a skunk has walked past. You can't see it, can you? Can't pick it up. Can't photo it. Should you then say, 'Naw, there's no skunk here!'?"

"Maybe there is no skunk here. Maybe it's a figment of your imagination."

"Try stepping on the figment in the dark, laddie."

Which made a few people chuckle, and others look thoughtful.

Even so, we were on the verge of losing the audience, when Xue stepped in and raised a hand, calling for silence. He was known by all, and was generally so well respected that people stopped talking and listened. Here was an instance of the strategic superiority of self-mastered dignity over the more unstable manners of the idiosyncratic (by which I mean people like myself and Stron).

Calmly, quietly, Xue said: "I am in total concurrence with the position of Dr. Hoyos and Dr. McKie, as well as the others you see before you. Our agreement on the truth of these troubling assertions is not, as you have correctly said, hard evidence. However, at the very least they should be examined objectively. I therefore propose that an investigative committee be formed, composed of representatives from the science teams, the flight crew, and if they wish to be part of it, the Department of Social Infrastructure. In this way, it may be possible to find a conclusion satisfactory to all."

The audience, for the most part, erupted with applause.

Elf stepped forward and said, "Of course, the Department will be part of any investigation, if it should be decided that one is necessary, which I am fully convinced it is not. I can assure you that there are no grounds—*absolutely* no grounds—to these allegations. They began as a suspicion in the mind of Dr. Strachan McKie, and then it began to spread as speculative gossip. It was then gradually inflated into a so-called fact in the minds of a handful of people associated with him. Now, through this ridiculous piece of theater, we must contend with disruption

and the potential for division, which could negatively affect the outcome of our mission. We are a team, we are a community, and the
role of DSI was precisely formulated by global authority to assist in
that communal sense, as well as to offer remedial efforts whenever it is
threatened by the irrational elements in . . ."

The first half of this declaration went over somewhat limply. He
sounded too much like a team leader trying to revive the spirits of a
crowd of rain-soaked, mosquito-bitten campers. The second half of
the declaration went largely unheard, because the sound system quit
suddenly midway, to the relief of all except, perhaps, Elf himself.

Then the lights in the auditorium went off, leaving only the tiny
glowing dots along the aisles, showing us the way out.

As I made my way past the row closest to the exit, I noticed Dwayne
in the gloom, still hunched over, reading his book by the light of its
pale green glow. More than a hundred people had congregated outside the doors, and they pressed close around me and our small band
of accusatory scientists. Elf was among us too, and it quickly became
a one-on-one exchange, with the others listening. Elf had regained
his composure and his public style.

"Dr. Hoyos," he began, in a quiet, courteous and saddened tone, "I
am really at a loss for anything to say. I feel strongly the need to
convince you—"

"I'm sure you do, Dr. Larson."

"I feel strongly the need to convince you that these allegations are
without any basis in reality."

"Dr. Larson, I'm curious to know how you came to the conclusion
that these allegations originated with Dr. McKie."

"People have mentioned his suspicions", he shrugged innocently.

"No, Dr. Larson, you overheard Dr. McKie and myself speaking
about our suspicions. You overheard it by surveillance of our voice
communications through our *maxes*."

"That's absurd", he protested.

"My sentiments exactly. Eavesdropping is an absurd activity, a symp-
tom of something lacking in a person—or, on the other hand, an
excess of unhealthy curiosity."

"You don't need to get personal in your accusations."

"What is more personal than what you've been doing to us, and to
everyone on board? Everyone, that is, except yourself. You don't eaves-
drop on yourself, do you?"

"This is ridiculous", Elf mumbled. "Doctor, I think you've been overstraining your imagination. Dr. McKie has infected you with his fantasies."

"Dr. Larson, how do you explain the fact that no one outside of Dr. McKie and myself have ever discussed Dr. McKie's thoughts on the matter? Yet this evening you seem to be very certain he is the cause of the trouble."

Stron was clearly enjoying the exchange, grinning, nodding in affirmation of my points, but he held himself back from interfering. Elf looked somewhat flustered, caught red-handed, but he covered it deftly. The hundred or so people around us were listening with close attention, their eyes flicking back and forth between us.

"You're quite mistaken", Elf said. "Dr. McKie's wild opinions are common knowledge. A number of people have mentioned it to me."

"How many?" I asked.

"It doesn't matter how many. My point is, it's common knowledge that he has some harebrained theories and expounds on them to anyone who'll listen."

"That's getting personal", said Stron with a wicked smile.

Elf nodded summarily, as if he had rested his case.

"Gentlemen," I said with an uplifting air, glancing at my co-conspirators and the surprise co-defenders too. "We've had a lot of excitement tonight. I'd like you all to be my guests at supper. Would anyone object to Chinese food?"

"I would", said Xue.

None of the others took him seriously, so it was agreed that we would all go downstairs to the Asian restaurant on deck B.

I turned to Elf and Skinner. The director of DSI had not yet said a word, but he was boring holes in my skull with his eyes.

"Won't you join us for supper?" I asked (with relative sincerity). "It might defuse the situation. I'm sure we can sort this whole thing out tomorrow. For now, maybe we should just shake off the tension and enjoy ourselves."

"No thank you", said Elf. Skinner merely tightened his lips.

With cold looks, they turned on their heels and strode away along the concourse. Me and my band of merry men, ten of us, went off in the other direction.

We gathered around a long table in the restaurant, replaying the night's proceedings and speculating about what would be the outcome.

The mood was elevated, the banter perfect for shaking off tension. I noticed that people seated at nearby tables kept looking at us. Some may have been in the audience; others may have watched the whole thing on their *max*es and experienced the disturbing sensation of sudden revulsion for their closest electronic friend. Did they see us as bearers of unwelcome news, the messengers who should be shot, I wondered, or had the message hit home?

Xue leaned over to me from across the table and said, "Dariush asked me to send you his apologies. He wanted to attend your lecture, but he's in bed with a bad virus."

"Poor man, I'll go see him tomorrow."

"He said he would watch it on the *max*. I'm not sure if he saw the shenanigans at the end. They may have cut transmission at that point."

The waiters were loading platters of steaming food onto the table when a finger tapped my shoulder. I looked up. It was Dwayne.

"Enjoy your book?" I asked.

"It wasn't a book. Sorry about the audio volume."

"You did that?"

"Yup. Thought we should catch reactions. Rigged it into the ship's public speakers too. Did a back-feed on it. There were just over four hundred people in the auditorium. Sixty-seven people watched it in their rooms."

"And there I was feeling hurt by your lack of attention. You really came prepared."

"Yup. Figured something like this would happen. You did great, by the way."

"Well, you were magnificent, the unsung hero of the event."

"Yup."

He looked uneasily over his shoulder.

"Gotta go."

"See you tomorrow?"

"Sure. I'm off shift at five. 'Bye."

He was gone.

My guests looked at me questioningly, wanting to know who the young man was. Due to Dwayne's clandestine ministrations, they had been enjoying privacy in their rooms for some time now, but none of them had seen him at work, didn't even know his name. Only Stron had met him face to face.

"The lad's a mysterious stranger", he informed the others. "Comes out of nowhere, does his job, and disappears back into the night."

This was greeted by several knowing "ahs". Smart people that they were, they pursued it no more. We topped off our meal with *huangjiu* rice wine and sips of authentic whiskey. The gathering went on until nearly midnight, at which time, we stood up rather unsteady on our feet, heartily congratulated each other on our blow for freedom, and wended our weary ways home to the privacy of our rooms.

Day 2253:

This morning I woke early, had a soothing shower, walked my imaginary dog in the arboretum, and listened to Mozart. At seven, the sun and the singing birds were switched on, and I went upstairs to the cafeteria on my floor. There I enjoyed a nice breakfast of poached egg on toast and a cuplet of real berry juice.

Afterward I dropped in to see Dariush, and found him lying listless on his bed, the blanket under his chin, surrounded by water flasks and medications. A book on Sanskrit lay open on his lap. In terms of personal clutter, his room was about halfway between Stron's and Xue's, though the clutter was mainly books—non-digital, cloth-covered books, stacks of them.

"I thought we'd beaten the common cold", I said.

He sneezed. "We have. This is another sort of virus, I am told. My physician has given me something to help with the aches and pains. It surprises me that we are still vulnerable to these invisible enemies."

"Me too. You would think our bio-pool is small enough to track down every last one of the varmints and exterminate them."

"Unfortunately, they have the habit of taking up residence in our very selves. We are ideal hosts."

"We'll get 'em, Dariush; we'll get 'em."

"Your talk was excellent, Neil. I had the pleasure of watching it here. It was a blend of fine content and quality of expression. I honor you for it."

"Thank you. Did you see it all?"

"I saw everything until the lights went off in the auditorium. It was most revealing, especially the attitude of the two gentlemen who attempted to dissuade you from concluding your remarks."

"Yes, that was an amusing part."

He smiled wanly, and his eyelids closed against his will.

"You had better rest, Dariush. I'll look in on you later, if I may."

He nodded absently and I left.

Back in my room, I was just preparing to write down in my paper journal a few more thoughts that had arisen from the foundation of my freedom-responsibility comments the night before, when there came a knock at my door.

I said, "Open", and there stood two serious men, staring at me as if they were apprehending a criminal in his lair. Identibadges clipped to the breasts of their suits informed me that they were representatives of DSI.

"Won't you come in?" I said graciously.

"We're here to accompany you to an interview with Dr. Larson", the older one said.

"I haven't made an arrangement for an interview", I replied. "And I'm rather busy right now. Please ask Dr. Larson to contact me if he would like to arrange a meeting. We can discuss the possibilities."

"I'm sorry, sir, but you're to come now."

"On whose authority?" I asked, more amused than anything.

"The authority of the Department, sir."

"I'm a scientist", I said. "I'm not working for DSI."

"Yes, but you *are* under its authority."

"Am I? This is the first I've heard about it."

"It's in the Manual", said the younger one, helpfully.

"Would you show me?" I said with a smile. "Come on in and let's have a look at it."

They stepped inside while I searched for the thing in my desk drawer. I handed the book to the older one, who keyed an entry and brought on screen the heading:

Department of Social Infrastructure
Subsection 128; Article B-43.
Guidelines for authority protocol in conflict situations:

In the event that conflict situations arise, in which one or more parties to the conflict refuses to enter into counseled negotiations, it is incumbent upon the duly appointed agents of the Department to use reasonable inducement of the said party, or parties, to cooperate with efforts to achieve a just solution.

I looked up at my visitors. "You're the agents?"

They nodded. The elder pointed to a paragraph further down the page:

Article B-44:
In the event that a party refusing to cooperate has, by all reasonable means, been informed of his responsibility to participate in negotiations, and has persisted in non-compliance, the said agents are authorized to assist him bodily in attendance at the said negotiations.

"Assist me bodily, hmmm? Am I being arrested?"

"No, no", they hastened to assure me.

"Sounds like police to me. Sounds like I'm being taken into custody against my will."

They looked embarrassed, but would not budge.

"You have to come now, sir", said the elder.

They didn't clap me in manacles, but they did walk me down the concourse to the elevators, an agent on either side of me, just to make sure I wouldn't get lost on the way to the offices of DSI, and would arrive without mishap. My gendarmes were not hostile, though they were resolute about fulfilling their duties.

As we walked along, I told myself: "If you have nothing to hide, there's nothing to fear. They cannot intimidate you for no reason at all—it's a free planet. You have a right to be yourself. And if they try their cold, official tricks on you, just remember that deep inside they all crave love, maybe collect butterflies for a hobby, and every one of them has a mother somewhere!"

My spirits were not uplifted by my pep talk. I did indeed have something to hide, in fact a good deal to hide. There was, for example, the clandestine privatization of at least twelve *max*es, maybe more than that. Did they know about it? Had they guessed? And if so, would they want to discover who had done it? Would they interrogate me relentlessly? Would the other scientists who had stood with me on the stage be called in for questioning? If so, would they make a reference to the Mysterious Stranger? Would this provide the authorities with a lead that would become a track winding deep into the forest, a trail of bread crumbs ending at Dwayne? And if that happened, would he be penalized in some fashion?

It was possible that none of the aforementioned would happen. It was possible that Xue's call for an investigative committee would be heeded and the surveillance brought to a halt. Maybe. I hoped so. It would depend on the plausibility of our allegations and on how convinced the audience had been. I wondered if they would stand firm in the face of official denials and intangible evidence. The greater majority of people on board were highly intelligent and highly disciplined in their own fields. But how would they handle a problem based on no clear empirical data, on accusations that looked too much like unprovable theory? They were scientists, and this was a strength of sorts. But the fatal flaw of scientists was their tendency to ignore or downplay anything beyond observable and recordable phenomena. They were as liable to emotional influence as anyone else—perhaps more so.

I was duly delivered to the front office and handed over to the winsome secretary. Her earlier enthusiasm seemed to have waned. She did not enthuse at all, she did not smile, she did not take my hands in hers and pump them. Guardedly, politely, she led me into the inner office. The Grand Elf rose from his desk and, surprisingly, stuck forward his hand for a shake. I shook it. The secretary absented herself and closed the door behind her.

Exquisitely nuanced sparring ensued. As is now my custom when encountering officials, I had set my lapel button to voice-activate recording. As camouflage, I had also brought my fountain pen and a sheet of paper, on which I would jot down disposable notes.

"I see you want to make notes", he said.

"My memory isn't what it used to be. I hope you don't mind."

"Not at all."

He folded his hands across his belly and regarded me with a thoughtful expression.

Exhaling a mixture of regret and perplexity, he said, "I can't understand why you did such a thing. It was really irresponsible."

"So is invasion of privacy."

"There has been no invasion of privacy."

I did not bother to reply to this. I felt calm, buoyed by certainty about the justice of my position. I merely watched him, and my silence communicated volumes. There was nothing hostile in his expression, not even a mote of defensiveness. We just looked at each other, and as the seconds ticked away, I began to realize the extent of the abyss between us. It also struck me that he was as convinced of his position as I was of mine. There were no signs of guilt in his face or manner. Unless he was a gifted actor (which in hindsight, I think he was), he appeared to be a man with nothing burdening his conscience.

"I repeat", he said to break the silence. "There has been no invasion of privacy."

"A moot point, if official policy—stated or unstated—is based on the belief that there is no privacy to invade."

"Stated or unstated, you have privacy."

"In the bathroom, you mean?"

"In every cubic centimeter of your quarters."

"Is the *max* considered my personal possession?"

"It's ship property. But, of course, it's entirely yours during the voyage."

"Yet, I suppose an argument could be made that it is both entirely mine *and* entirely yours. We are a team, after all."

"Yes, we're a team."

"A community."

He frowned. "Your behavior last night significantly undermined the sense of community on the *Kosmos*. I'd like to know why you took it upon yourself to do that."

His tone of voice was not threatening, with no hint of the police interrogation. It was a friendly little chat tone, man-to-man. Nevertheless, I felt my defensiveness rising.

"It was my duty to do so", I replied evenly.

"Your duty? A duty based on speculation and gossip?"

"Based on an experiment."

"What experiment?"

"Elf, I'm not quite clear why you've brought me here today. Is this an interrogation? If it is an interrogation, I would like to know on what authority you're conducting it."

"The full authority of my Department, which has been entrusted with the social security of the community during the flight."

"To the point of arresting people?"

"Call it what you will. The stipulations in the Manual clearly define—"

"I've read the pertinent paragraphs in the Manual", I interrupted. "They're vague legalese. They could mean anything you want them to mean."

"Not at all. They are clearly spelled out."

"With nauseating euphemisms."

"There's no need to become emotional, Dr. Hoyos. Why are you so emotional about this?"

"Why are *you* so emotional, Dr. Larson, though you are masking it very well? Very well indeed, I must say."

He emitted a mild snort along with a scowl.

"You referred to an experiment. If it's such a conclusive one, why not tell me about it? If you think something is wrong about the conduct of shipboard life, this is the very place to raise the issue."

"Unless you, yourself, Dr. Larson, are the problematic issue."

"What do you mean?" he said in a quiet voice.

"When Dr. McKie and I discussed the surveillance, we did it through our *maxes*. Hot on the heels of that I received your kind invitation to meet, even though during the previous six years I had neither seen you nor heard about you."

"Purely coincidence."

"And during that first conversation you ever so subtly brought up the topic of Dr. McKie and his harebrained theories."

"I did not say 'harebrained'."

"You have a good memory. And you are correct: at our first meeting you used the word 'wild'. Last night it changed into 'harebrained'. There had been an emotional shift in the wind."

"Of course there had been. Something insignificant had become a threat to the collective health of the community."

"In what way had it become a threat?"

"You know very well that these kinds of suspicions breed unrest and divisions, setting off a chain reaction that can create havoc for efficient social communications, not to mention undermining scientific research on AC-A-7."

"Efficient social communications? I wonder what that is? I wonder, too, if mankind has ever achieved such a thing?"

"Part of my job is to ensure that it happens."

"Whether we want it or not?"

"Do you *like* confusion and suspicion? Do you enjoy those feelings, Dr. Hoyos?"

"Not very much, Dr. Larson. But they are preferable, by far, to imposed serenity."

"Imposed!" he snorted again.

147

"Subtly imposed, insidiously and relentlessly imposed without our knowledge. I think you have fallen into a very old mental trap, Dr. Larson. You mistake uniformity for unity."

"A play on words. They are the same thing."

"They are very much not the same thing. Uniformity is brought about through manipulation. Unity comes about through a conscious effort made by free and responsible people."

"You call yourself responsible, I suppose?"

"Yes, I do. Your Department would lift certain responsibilities off our shoulders, wouldn't it? You would do it for the highest motives, wouldn't you? But have you considered what is lost in the process?"

"For the sake of your hypothetical argument, I would say that strife is lost, as well as division, inefficiency, confusion, the irrational tendencies in human nature. And you wish to preserve these?"

"I wish to maintain our right to make our mistakes and learn from them."

"Well, you've surely made a very big mistake. You call a coincidence a proof. You have no tangible evidence for your accusations because there is no tangible evidence."

I leaned forward and looked him straight in the eyes. "Oh yes, there is evidence. You are doing exactly what in my talk last night I said you are doing. I have very tangible proof."

"Then produce your proof."

"That is what you want, isn't it? That's what this meeting is really about. And if I were to give it to you, and not to a committee of investigation, the proof would disappear."

"Ridiculous."

"You know it and I know it."

His face flushed red. He said nothing.

"Let it go, Dr. Larson. People are more responsible than you think. You've spent too much of your life waist-deep in fixing dysfunction. Cut those little micro-lines leading into our personal *max*es and let us live our own lives."

Still, he said nothing, just examined my face with a whole lot of analyzing going on behind his eyes. There was a new look there, one that worried me. Too late, I realized I had given him an important piece of information. No one but a person very astute about computer technology could have discovered the micro circuit. And I was clearly not that sort of person.

"Has anyone been tampering with your *max*?" he asked in a deceptively quiet voice.

"Why do you ask?"

"It could be that this fabricated crisis is the product of some hacker's game."

"I don't think so."

"Why not?" he asked, and again the specter of the intelligent hunter materialized in those cool and calm eyes.

I had said too much. He knew it and I knew it, and he knew that I knew.

I stood up.

"I think our meeting has come to its conclusion", I said. "I am most willing to convey everything I know to the committee of investigation."

"There isn't going to be a committee of investigation", he said without rising from his chair. "Thank you for your time, Dr. Hoyos. My secretary will see you to the door."

Day 2254:

I've alerted the others by word of mouth, telling them that there will be no committee, no investigation. Most of them were upset by the news, in their non-emotive fashion. A few looked resigned. Xue was particularly disturbed, by which I mean his face went totally immobile, and his eyes became like a deep, cold lake. In the end, we concluded that there's not much we can do about the situation, except to keep discussing it with passengers and crew, one by one.

DSI has sent out an official response, delivered to every mailbox on every *max* in the ship, worded in typical smarmy socio-speak: a statement that the Department had concluded, after a thorough investigation, that there is no basis whatsoever to the allegations. Followed by remedial soothing and stroking of raised hackles. They are masters of putting out spot fires.

Dwayne has not called me. I have refrained from calling him in order to keep suspicion away from him. I'm now wary even of his secret mail-code. If the authorities are onto us, they may put a team to work and crack all unauthorized channels.

Maintenance personnel are changed periodically. Dwayne was my cleaner, dustman, yardman during years one, three, and five. Not since then had he had an official reason for knocking on my door. It goes without saying that even a lowly servant in the egalitarian universe is free to visit the exalted ones, and this he had often done. But I now guessed that he, like me, was wondering if they were watching my door to see who I conspired with.

Do the hallways have surveillance cameras? I don't see any sign of it, but, on the other hand, new technology may have been developed, a seeing eye in the ceiling or walls, too small to be detected by the human eye. I must watch that I don't become paranoid. Reasonable discretion, yes, but I must guard against fear taking hold. Once they make you afraid, they've won half the battle. Frightened people opt for uniformity. Free people opt for unity.

Dwayne is smart—smarter than "they" are. He's lying low.

Day 2255:

Pia rapped on my door this morning. What a lift to my heart when I saw her standing there. She's my appointed physician, so if they do have watchers on duty, there needn't be any suspicion cast on her. Just to make sure, I exclaimed through the open doorway:

"Dr. Sidotra, how nice! Do you have my test results?"

She looked blank for a second or two, then said, "The urology report is causing me some concern. That's why I didn't waste time making an appointment for you. I thought we should discuss this as soon as possible."

"Won't you come in?"

She hesitated, then began to blink rapidly, involuntarily. Was it a disinclination to be alone with a man in his room, or was there another reason?

"Why don't we take a walk?" I suggested.

As we set off on a stroll along Concourse B, she said nothing at first. There was no need to discuss urology, since I hadn't had a test in years.

"Is there something wrong?" I asked.

"Can we find a private place to talk?"

"I know just the spot."

Down the staircase we went to deck C, and ten minutes later arrived at an art alcove containing a Renoir painting of a family in a park.

"Neil," she began, "your presentation was tremendous. I was so proud of you and the others who stood up like that. I felt sure it would blow the lid off the surveillance. Now I'm not so sure."

"Why? What's happened?"

"You must have seen the mail from DSI."

"Yes, I saw it. They stomped pretty fast, I'd say. There's not going to be an investigating committee, since they've completed the investigation and found that all hands are clean."

"How convenient. The fox investigating the crime in the henhouse."

"Precisely. Nice of them to save us all that trouble though."

"Neil, there's more. The morning after your talk, I received a DSI requisition for all your medical records. I refused on the grounds that such records are strictly confidential. Then they sent two of their people to talk to me, and they showed me some article in the Manual that takes precedence over doctor-patient privacy. I told them that nothing—nothing—takes precedence over medical confidentiality, but if they could show me any law to the contrary, made on Earth by a legitimately elected government, I would consider their request."

"And what did they say to that?"

"They basically told me, in the nicest possible language, that *they* are the Law onboard this ship. Even that didn't budge me." She stopped, tears welling. "Neil, they just walked around me and opened up my records terminal. They had some kind of code that jumped over my security password."

"I see. But what were they after?"

"I think they were looking for something that would call into question your sanity."

"My sanity?" I laughed, torn between anger and disgust. "Well, I've never been overly endowed with that stuff."

"You're a very sane man, Neil. You know that. I know it too. But they were looking for anything that would discredit you. They wanted to find out if you're on anti-depressants or sedatives, anything that alters brain chemistry."

"I do well enough altering my brain chemistry without taking pills."

"Please stop joking." She took three deep breaths. "I gave them a piece of my mind they'll never forget. They found nothing, just your wrist and leg surgeries and the general check-up I gave you last year, vital signs, the annual EKG. When they realized there was nothing useful to them, they asked me point-blank if I had sensed any personality change in you lately, and if I had considered prescribing medications for it. They told me it would be *advisable* to do so."

I patted her shoulder. "Every ship has rats, Pia. Don't let it get under your skin."

"It *is* under my skin, and on a number of issues too. I filed a formal complaint."

"Hmmm. Now that the subject has been raised, may I ask who is the final arbiter of complaints?"

"DSI, of course."

"The fox and the hens."

"I also filed a complaint with the ship's captain."

"Really? Do we have access to him? I thought the command crew were not to be bothered by people below KC deck."

"That's what the Manual says. But you remember the friend I mentioned to you, the one I've grown close to?"

"I do. Was he in the audience the other night?"

"Yes, he was. Paul thought your talk was great. And he's as angry about what you've uncovered as I am. Of course, I told him about it some time ago, and we've been more careful about our messages. But when you brought it all out into the open, he thought it was time to get moving."

"In what way?"

"He's talking to his friends up on KC. He has a few of them convinced that the problem is real. Not everyone believes him, but enough of them that it could make a difference."

"You say you've sent a complaint to the Captain."

"Paul wrote a letter outlining everything we know. He and I both signed it. He gave it to the Captain this morning."

We fell silent, pondering.

"There's more. I have a friend in the clinic on C. She told me that DSI got into the records terminal of one of her colleagues, Dr. McKie's physician. He's also Dr. Pagnol's."

"So it looks like the Elf is really waging full-scale damage control here."

"The Elf?"

"The deputy director of DSI. El-if Larson. He's a cagey character, Pia, and I advise you to avoid him. If you should ever have to talk with him, be careful."

"You don't need to tell me that. I'm beginning to understand a few things about what goes on in this ship. It's all so reasonable and democratic, isn't it?"

She suddenly put her hands to her face and began to cry. I put an arm around her trembling shoulders, and patted her distractedly.

"There, there", I murmured. "There, there, now, it's going to be all right."

For some reason, this made her laugh. She dried her eyes and gave me a few shoulder pats in return. Then we went our separate ways.

Day 2269:

The past two weeks have been existentially creepy, by which I mean, I suppose, that my social *Gesellschaft* has gone all strange on me. People shift away, avoid me, or if a meeting is unavoidable (for example, the food line at the cafeteria), they grow vague, say platitudinous things without eye contact. Politeness rules all such exchanges. Beneath the tactful manners is suspicion. They are no longer convinced we have a problem. For them, *I* have become the problem, though they don't voice this. It's as if the curve in space is manifesting through the curve in men's perceptions.

On the other hand, a few have approached me quietly. They are convinced we have a big problem, despite DSI's disclaimers. They're worried. I'm worried too. Not a word from Dwayne. I sent him an inquiry through his secret code address. It wasn't blocked, wasn't bounced back to me, but after I did a cross-check, the auto-mailer informed me it had not been delivered. It gave no explanation.

I called the maintenance main desk down on PHM and complained about too much dust in my room. The man on duty assured me that a cleaner would be sent up as soon as possible. I asked if he could send one of my old maintenance guys, a fellow named Dwayne—he'd left his pen in my room, and I wanted to return it to him. The voice on the other end of the *max* told me there was nobody named Dwayne working for the department.

About an hour later, a cleaner showed up and dusted my room with a vacuum sweep, though there wasn't much dust to speak of. He suggested I might want to be more regular with my suction bath. I asked him if he knew a guy named Dwayne who worked in his department. He shook his head, and said, no, there was no one by that name working in Maintenance—never had been.

"Anyone on your staff who's in his early to mid-thirties, dark-haired, lean, kind of quiet, American origins."

"That describes several of us", the man answered.

"I'd like to meet them."

He shrugged. "Sure, if you want. Come down to M anytime. I'll mention it to the boss. Course, you'll have to get security clearance first. They don't let anyone onto our deck who isn't cleared for it."

"I see. Where do I go to get clearance?"

"Just drop by the DSI office on deck C. They'll give you a pass and temporary code for the elevators."

"Thanks."

Just drop by DSI and ask for a code? Uh, nope, I don't think I'll be doing that.

"Would you mention to your coworkers that Dr. Hoyos in B-124 is looking for someone in your department and has forgotten the exact name?"

"Sure, no problem. Mid-thirties, dark haired, sort of American, you say?"

"That's right."

"Will do."

After he left, I got out the Manual and checked through the index and found personnel, sorted into departments. Nobody named Dwayne was listed—not in any department. I now realized he had been using a pseudonym.

"Good for you, Dwayne. Good thinking", I murmured to myself.

However, this did not solve the problem of how to reach him.

Day 2273:

Remembering that he had once told me his personal room was on Concourse D, I went down there and roved along the corridors on the chance that he would pop his head out of a doorway. No such luck. I spent a day or so wandering thus, and people passing in the corridors began to eye me with uneasiness.

These long, long walks were beneficial to my health, though not to my mood. There were three main corridors or avenues stretching the length of the ship, starboard, port and center, each of them just short of a kilometer long. There were numerous cross streets, each a quarter of a kilometer long (I estimated thirty of these). There were hundreds upon hundreds of doors on this floor alone. All were numbered, but only a small minority had personal name cards magnet-beaded beneath the numbers. A few balloons and other decorative items relieved the monotonous décor. There was nothing in the Manual that would have prohibited affixing one's name beneath a number, but I supposed most people wanted to be *Gesellschaft* about their personal spaces, handing out the room number only to their selected friends.

It was like wandering through Manhattan hoping to run into an acquaintance. From time to time, I stopped pedestrians along the way and explained that I was looking for a friend but couldn't recall his room number. Some of them took this at face value, but a larger number had either seen my talk or heard about it, and recognized me. They had also read the DSI denials, which put me in a pretty bad light. Invariably, people were courteous, but none of them divulged the information I was looking for—*if* they knew it. A few made tactfully expressed comments about the need to preserve unity and to avoid paranoia. The phrasing of their advice was straight out of the DSI sooth-and-desist letter.

Clearly it was a hopeless cause, unless I wanted to become the ghost that haunted deck D, or worse, be categorized as the deranged old man who needed to be institutionalized for his own good.

Day 2275:

I had an inspiration. In one of the library terminals, I word-searched the main computer for *Kosmos*, found a million links, and then narrowed it down to sites referencing staff and passengers for the big expedition. Again, a lot of links, thousands, actually. On the main official site for the voyage, I noted that the last entry had been made a day before departure from Earth. And there I found what I'd been looking for: a complete list of personnel, each name accompanied by an identiphoto and short biography.

It took a few hours to go through, and when I reached the end of it I stood back with my heart thumping unnaturally. According to the companion article, this list included every person who would be on the ship, a total of 676 individuals, none excepted. But nowhere in all those photos had I seen Dwayne's face.

I knew that he was on board. I knew what his face looked like. He was no phantom. But he simply wasn't there. I cross-referenced to maintenance personnel and discovered fourteen young men who visually fit his description, but none of their faces were his. Fearing that I might have sped too quickly through the photos, I entered more cross-references to every other department. Again, nothing.

I went back to my room to think about it.

Dwayne—whoever he was, whatever his name really was—had been deleted from the files. Why?

I examined the possible explanations:

Perhaps he had never been entered in the files. An oversight? Hardly. Not on an expedition as well-planned as this one.

A stowaway? Maybe. But if he was a stowaway, how would he have managed to procure a job in Maintenance, taking his shifts year after year? If he had been a fake cleaning man, surely Maintenance would have sent the real cleaners to my room on schedule, and the duplication of labor would have come to my attention. Not once during the three six-month shifts when he vacuumed the hallways and scrubbed my room had anyone else shown up.

He was a master cyber-hacker. Maybe he had deleted himself from the files. Now this was a possibility. But why would he do it? It struck me that he would do it only if he felt himself endangered in some extreme way. But this did not make any sense. Our controversy with DSI was heated and unpleasant, but surely it wasn't dangerous.

Was Dwayne a "plant", a "mole", quietly working for the authorities? Obeying orders, had he been taking the psychological pulse of a few select passengers? Perhaps a stress-test on potentially problematic individuals such as Stron and myself? Or was a grander study under-way, originating in the fervid imaginations of the director of DSI and his assistant, the deputy director? Was Elf, even now, writing a thesis for a new degree to add to his name? After all, the voyage was abso-lutely *sui generis*, a first of its kind, prime material for a unique experiment.

Of all the possibilities, this last one began to make more and more sense to me. It all added up to a project, approved from above. After all, how could a janitor have come by skills that outwitted a computer system as sophisticated as ours? Maybe he hadn't outwitted the system.

Maybe he had been going through the motions just to pull the wool over my eyes. I never saw him at work. No one had seen him do what we conspirators believed he had done. And wasn't it odd the way he and I shared so neatly our Southwest riders-of-the-open-range culture? A bit too good to be true, that one.

Still, I had spent a lot of time with Dwayne, or whoever he was. I hadn't spotted a single false note in him. The things he had told me about his past rang true, flavored with the hint of sagebrush and sadness, a world lost. A real person carrying real grief and raising real questions. The real stuff, he had called it.

I examined all the possibilities again, and none of them quite matched the situation.

Opening up my *max*, I did a search one more time, arriving at the list of passengers and crew I had just read on the main computer. It gave me the same total of 676.

I'm not sure why I did it, but I then flipped through the earliest entries in my paper journal and came to the page where I had written a summary of people on board, according to categories. The total was 677. I was off by one. I'd been guilty of mathematical mistakes before, but I now recalled how interested (and careful) I had been while doing the number breakdowns and totaling it up. Yes, 677. I was sure of it.

The main computer and the *max* both said 676.

It then struck me that I had printed out the official list of personnel six years ago. I flipped through pages and found it inserted between some initial pages of my journal. I counted the names carefully, and arrived at 677. I did it again just to be sure. And a third time: Yes, the original list contained 677 names—but none of them was a Dwayne.

This could only mean that the main computer had been revised. It also meant that my *max* had been "corrected" as well, which meant that it was no longer protected. This might mean that it had never been changed by Dwayne, or it might mean the opposite—it had been privatized but the block had been detected and removed.

Taking the staircase to another concourse, I entered a different library and found a vacant terminal. There were several people in the room busy at the other terminals. I accessed the main computer and entered a search. All the official and primary links offered the revised number. I keyed forward to an innocuous-looking three-hundredth link and clicked on it. It was the site of an Earth-bound astronomy club devoted to the *Kosmos* and its then-impending voyage.

Enthusiasts and dreamers had created a complex site, and it was well done. Once I was inside it, I searched for a passenger/crew list, and suddenly there it was: Pages upon pages of names appeared, each accompanied by the individual's position and his photograph. The total was 677. The file was dated two days before departure from Earth-base.

I wondered if whoever was overseeing onboard surfing would be able to track me. They wouldn't know who I was, but they would know that someone was looking at potentially damaging information. I scanned down the site's pages to Maintenance and there, among the department's two hundred employees, his face looking back at me, was Dwayne.

His name was David William Ayne, born in Antelope, Nevada. Graduate in process engineering from a college in Sacramento, California. He also had a graduate degree from Stanford University in computer science. Listed also was his employment by the very aerospace corporation he had told me about, as well as his specialization in digitalized testing of alloy stress environments.

I closed the page, deaccessed, and walked as quickly as I could back to my room.

Day 2276:

In a quiet corner of the cafeteria on my concourse, over breakfast this morning, I presented these discrepancies to Stron, Xue, Étienne Pagnol, and Dariush. Each in his way pondered what I told them, saying little. In the end, none of them seemed alarmed, though none took it lightly.

"At worst, I suspect they're isolating him for the extent of the voyage", said Stron.

"That is a lengthy isolation", Dariush commented. "It would be hard on him. I ask myself why they would do it."

"Because he knows the truth", I answered. "He knows the truth conclusively, while we who believe him have only our faith in what he told us. We have no evidence that would stand up in court."

"And thus we are a relatively small threat to the administration", said Xue.

"We're easily dealt with. We're small spot fires they can put out with a toe of their shiny shoes. In fact, they have done so."

"Yet if that is the case, the deletion of his records from the ship's database seems to me an extreme and unnecessary measure", said Pagnol.

"It does", Stron scowled. "It means they feel threatened in a big way by this lad. It's not just the surveillance he knows about, you see. He also knows they've been lying to everyone."

"And if that came to light, it would destroy the equilibrium of . . ."

"Of social infrastructure", said Stron with disgust.

"It is most informative that so many sites on the main computer have been altered", Dariush said in a milder tone. "Does this not seem to you a concerted effort to delete all references to David Ayne? Of course, there are too many sites for them to change at once. It seems they are going through them one by one, and this would demand a great deal of time, since there are thousands."

"Neil, you say you checked a site very far down in the link list?" asked Xue.

"Somewhere around the three-hundredth link."

"It might be useful to find out how far they've got with their deletions."

We decided to access terminals in libraries on each of the four concourses. I told them the name of the little enthusiast site, and we split up in order to check it out.

Gathering again over lunch, huddling in relative isolation at the far end of a long table in the cafeteria on deck D, we compared our findings. The deletion had been done on the site, and random checks beyond that narrowed it down still further. Someone was hard at work eliminating any reference to David Ayne, and was now past the eight-hundred mark.

Xue had taken the trouble to transfer onto his pocket *memor* a photo and biographical data from a randomly chosen site beyond the one-thousand level. His wasn't an ordinary port-*memor*, he explained, but a new test model which worked without circuit contact. He'd brought along the print-out, which he said he had made through a *max*.

"How did you do that!" Stron protested. "*Max*es don't have ports for *memor*s. Besides, we have to assume that none of ours are safe anymore."

"Right", said Xue. "That's why I took it to a friend—who shall remain unnamed—a friend whom the administration doesn't realize is connected to our little revolt. He's fairly high up in one of the science departments and has a *max* in his office to which my *memor* can speak—both downloads and uploads. He kindly permitted me to print out

David's biography on his *max*. It took a few seconds. We deleted any trace afterward."

"Hopefully, his office *max* isn't monitored", I suggested to Xue.

"It may be. It probably is. But the file was multiple-encrypted and numerically named. I doubt that anyone would be able to crack it and see just what it was."

We all bent over the sheet he held in his hand.

"That is the man who spoke to you briefly in the restaurant", said Pagnol.

"The Mysterious Stranger", murmured Stron.

Later that afternoon, we rechecked the site where Xue had obtained it. We found that this, too, had been scrubbed.

"Either someone's working very quickly," said Stron, "or they have a team on it. It smells like a team to me."

"What puzzles me most", I said, "is that this deletion business isn't going to be very effective for them. After six years, David would have made friends with people on board. At the least, he would be known to his coworkers. And they'd probably ask around, wanting to know where he'd got to."

"Neil, you say you checked with the people in Maintenance?"

"Yes, but that was before I had a real name to give them. We've learned that *Dwayne* is a pseudonym. And his general physical description matches quite a few men in that department."

"Even so, a face and a personality are unique. Surely, someone on that level has noticed his absence."

Xue said, "We have a photo and bio now. I think it's time for a focused inquiry."

Day 2277:

Thoughtlessly, I sent a text inquiry via my *max* to the maintenance address, asking for contact info for David W. Ayne. There was no reply from M department. I e-voiced a call, but the M desk did not respond. Within the hour, there came a knock at the door, and there stood my two old friends, the agents from DSI. They were as courteous as before—and as determined. I was *required*, they informed me, to attend another meeting with Dr. Larson.

I now wear my button recorder at all times.

Elf did not greet me with a handshake. He did not use my name. There were no preliminary warm-up comments.

"Why have you had me arrested again, Elf?"

He rolled his eyes. "You are *not* being arrested."

"You mean, I'm free to walk out of this office, having decided on my own that this is not a productive encounter?"

"That remains to be seen. Please sit down."

"I regret I'm very busy right now. If you'd care to make an appointment, just send a request to my *max* address. I'm sure you know it. Good day to you."

I turned to go.

"Who is Dwayne?" he said to my departing back.

I sat down on a chair and faced him squarely. It took a few moments for me to calm my nerves. He watched me coldly from the other side of his desk.

"The real question here", I said through my barely controlled anger, "is *where* is he?"

He shook his head as if he had just heard something incredibly irrational.

"I repeat, who is Dwayne?" he said in a quiet voice.

"You know who Dwayne is", I countered. "You know his real name, and you know he works—or worked—in Maintenance."

"I know that you made an inquiry to that department eight days ago, asking for someone with that name."

"And how would you know this, if you aren't keeping everything under surveillance?"

"A report from the department crossed my desk, as it does every month, listing all inquiries and requests for nonscheduled services. It's a routine *pro forma* document for the archives."

"If my inquiry was so *pro forma*, why have you taken such pains to bring me here for a little chat about it?"

"Because I am concerned about you."

"Oh, really?"

I knew he was lying. He was only interested in ferreting information out of me, anything that would tell him how much we knew. His approach also revealed that he was determined to maintain the veneer, and was not yet ready to use heavy muscle.

"Dr. Hoyos, ever since the night you gave your talk, a talk based on completely unfounded suspicions, I have been concerned about you."

Ah, warm-hearted elf that he is, he *cared* about me. It suddenly struck me as so absurd that I laughed.

He tilted his head a little and looked even more concerned.

"This has been a long flight", he went on. "Close confinement has its psychological effects."

"I find there's plenty of elbow room."

"Does it seem that way to you? Even so, there is always the sub-conscious dynamic, the accumulation of unacknowledged stress. And we know what happens to us when that occurs."

"Do we? Well, I don't know. Tell me what happens."

"The human mind projects its undeclared fears onto quite ordinary situations. Shadows become dangerous presences, whispered conver-sations become conspiracies against you, the normal comings and goings in people's lives begin to look like tragic plays."

"Yes, it's a danger in human psychology", I nodded.

"I'm glad you see it. I was wondering if maybe you'd like to talk with one of our staff psychiatrists. Sometimes a person can sort things out for himself, but with a professional to guide the process, a sense of balance can be restored more easily."

"A sense of equilibrium", I murmured in apparent agreement.

He smiled understandingly. "We all have our down moments. Even the gifted and famous." He smiled again. "Even Nobel prize winners."

"Where is David Ayne?" I said.

His face froze, then on cue, his brow and mouth furrowed into an expression of perplexity.

"Who?"

"You know who I mean. What have you done with him?"

He shook his head in perfect bafflement. "I'm sorry. I don't know what you mean. I haven't done anything to anyone."

"Where is he? Do you have him locked up somewhere on the ship? You've got him isolated somehow, against his will, I'm sure."

"We've locked up no one. And who is David Ayne? There's no one by that name on the *Kosmos*."

"Oh? Have you memorized the personnel list?"

"In preparation for our meeting, I searched through the ship's entire personnel records for anyone named Dwayne, because that is the name you inquired about with the maintenance department."

"I just asked you about David Ayne, and you instantly told me he wasn't real."

"I have a comprehensive knowledge of the list."

"You have him in a holding tank somewhere."

"That is simply untrue", he replied in a reasonable tone. "It's your inflamed imagination getting out of control again."

"Elf, it is simply a fact."

He did something with his lips, a half-smile tainted with the suggestion of a disgusted smirk. It was a subtle expression that lent itself to various interpretations. To the uninformed observer, Elf might have been no more than a professional caregiver momentarily wearied by the pathetic convictions of an irrational patient.

"Elf, that is a sneer on your face. You should see yourself at this moment. A sneer is contempt. It's an indelible sign of loss of objectivity. It is very, very unscientific. And your dissembling really worries me."

"It's you who should be worried", he muttered.

"Really? And what are you going to do to me? Make me walk home?"

His eyes grew colder as he prepared a retort.

"Elf, surely you know the dangers of projection and transference. Get a grip on yourself, or you'll become a victim of your own fixation. You wouldn't want to become dysfunctional, would you?"

He snorted, and still he said nothing. He rocked a little on his creaking chair, lips tight, one hand fisted on the desktop, the other out of sight on his lap.

"And while we're discussing the unreality of David W. Ayne, can you tell me why all references to his name are being systematically removed from the main computer? Of course, he's already been deleted from the private *maxes*."

Now he jerked forward, pointed his index finger at me, and opened his mouth to say something. "Listen to me, you——"

I cut him off. Switching to my quiet but authoritative tone (one rarely used in my life), I said, "That is an aggressive gesture. I believe that both of us are committed to the deaggressivization of mankind, aren't we? So I suggest you put your finger back where it belongs, and while you're at it, wipe the rage off your face."

He flushed beet red and rose from his chair, his impressive chin jutting forward.

"Ah, primitive threat-gestures", I smiled. "Don't shake your horns at me, Elf."

"Get out of my office", he seethed through clenched teeth.

Day 2282:

The day following my interview with Elf, I received a message delivered by hand from the Department of Medicine, signed by the director of DM himself, inviting me to a "consultation". By which he meant, as it turned out, a series of psychological tests, as well as some tests of body chemistry—including brain chemistry. I agreed to do them all, since while it's true that I feel generally low, and sometimes at night I'm agitated and sleepless, this is the result of natural worry over a missing person. I think I am relatively sane. There's sadness but no depression. I decided it would be good for DSI to know this, since doubtless DSI will be receiving copies of the reports from DM.

I still haven't seen any test results. Maybe no news is good news.

Day 2300:

Three weeks have gone by since my nasty interview with Elf. Periodic checking of the main computer now confirms that all references to David have been deleted. Of course, immense as it is, it is not connected to Earth's databases, as far as I know, so the original sites may still be intact somewhere back home. For the time being, however, David does not exist. I made other searches into the sites of institutions where he had studied or worked. Officially, he was never there.

I hope they let him out on AC-A-7. It would be too cruel to bring him all that way and not let him see it. Perhaps he's being held in some security suite and allowed to watch films, maybe even the public visual presentations of the ship's progress through the heavens.

Still no word from DM about my medical test results.

Day 2307:

Transcript of my lapel button recording: The speakers are me and Dr. Arthur (I'm not sure if this is his first or last name), a senior physician in the medical department.

Arthur: Thank you for coming in, Dr. Hoyos. We have the results from all your tests, and I wanted to discuss them with you.

Hoyos: Excellent. I've been wondering about them.

Arthur: We did a comprehensive battery of tests, as you know. Your profile is giving us some readings that concern us.

Hoyos: Biological or psychological?

Arthur: Frankly, both. They're always interconnected, of course.

Hoyos: Of course.

Arthur: The results indicate CDS, clinical depression syndrome, as well as—

Hoyos: I don't feel in any way depressed. Sad now and then, but not depressed.

Arthur: Depression is nothing to be ashamed of. It strikes everyone at one time or another, usually in high-stress situations.

Hoyos: That's true. However, I don't feel depressed.

Arthur: It may be that you've put another name to it. What I would like to suggest is that you try some medication that we'll prescribe. It will ease the symptoms.

Hoyos: That's kind of you. However, I don't seem to have any symptoms.

Arthur: Dr. Hoyos, if I may, I think you do have significant symptoms. There are irregularities in your brain waves as well. The scan shows no abnormal growths, thankfully, so we can rule out tumors as the cause. This indicates that there are other causes.

Hoyos: Such as?

Arthur: Intense emotional conflict, with resulting alteration of brain chemistry and subsequent negative effects in thinking patterns.

Hoyos: What kind of effects?

Arthur: You may be experiencing painful cyclical thinking, perhaps obsessional thoughts.

Hoyos: Paranoid feelings?

Arthur: That would also be fairly typical.

Hoyos: Typical of . . . ?

Arthur: Why don't you think it over for a day or so. Then you can get back to me with your decision.

Hoyos: That seems fair enough.

Day 2309:

Digital button recording:

Arthur: Good to see you, Dr. Hoyos. Thanks for coming in.

Hoyos: Good to see you too, Doctor.

Arthur: So, how have you been feeling?

Hoyos: Wonderful, actually. I've taken up swimming again, resumed my daily laps in the pool. I'm also studying languages with a friend.

Arthur: Excellent.

Hoyos: I just thought I'd drop by to give you my decision about the medication.

Arthur: Uh-huh.

Hoyos: I don't need it.

[Rustling of papers, protracted silence]

Hoyos: Well, thanks for your good efforts, Doctor. I'll be going now.

Arthur: Dr. Hoyos, uh, it's not as simple as that. You see, the medical team has made another thorough study of all your results, and there is consensus that these medications would help you.

Hoyos: But I don't need any help.

Arthur: Yes, I'm sure you feel that way. A sense of, well, denial, is usually part of the problem.

Hoyos: You believe I'm in denial?

Arthur: I regret to say, I do.

Hoyos: Well, what can I reply to that.

Arthur: I'm sorry. I know this is difficult for you.

Hoyos: I think it's more difficult for you. Thank you again, and good-bye.

Arthur: Dr. Hoyos, I had hoped it wouldn't come to this. [More rustling of papers, more protracted silence.] I really regret it, sir, but the medical oversight committee has mandated the medication. It's just one small tablet per day. It wouldn't impede your activities in any way. In fact, it would help you feel more positive about life.

Hoyos: You're saying I have to take it.

Arthur: Um . . . yes.

Hoyos: What would happen if I refuse to take the pills?

Arthur: Unfortunately, you would be compelled to take them.

Hoyos: By force?

[In reply to my question, he nodded and dropped his eyes. There was another strained silence during which Dr. Arthur appeared to be greatly embarrassed. He hated what he was doing. Somehow he was justifying it to himself, possibly for humanitarian reasons or for the sake of community well-being, or maybe he was merely joining that long line of folks in the historical tradition of "just obeying orders". If I stood firm and refused to take the medication, what then? I had a flash preview of myself being immobilized by medical orderlies while a pill was crammed down my throat, or a syringe pumped equilibrium drugs into my veins. I saw myself struggling to stop them. I saw report after report being written up about my irrational behavior, my "episodes" of violent resistance, and duly entered into the archives. I saw myself confined to a ward under sedation, possibly under restraints. I saw the scheming mind who was behind the whole thing, and I saw what I must do.]

Hoyos: Perhaps you're right. I should try some medication. Maybe it will help me.

Arthur: Thank you, Dr. Hoyos, thank you.

Hoyos: I guess I really haven't been quite myself lately. Sometimes I imagine things, get upset about it, and then ...

Arthur: It can be so disturbing, can't it? I know how you feel. But I guarantee you'll begin to feel better within days.

Hoyos: That's a relief, Doctor. Thanks. I guess I have been in denial ... a little.

[The poor man smiled and nodded with relief.]

Arthur: You can drop by here every morning and take your pill. The committee mandate says it shouldn't be patient-dispensed. I've e-*max*ed a prescription to the pharmacy, and it'll be here later today. You can begin treatment tomorrow morning.

Hoyos: I understand. In my frame of mind, I might forget to take it myself.

Arthur: Don't worry, you'll be fine.

Hoyos: Thanks.

[He stood up. I stood up. We shook hands.]

Hoyos: Uh, Doctor, my bad leg has been giving me a lot of problems lately. You wouldn't be able to prescribe something for the pain, would you? Getting down here to deck D from my room cost me quite an effort.

Arthur: I'm sorry to hear that. You should see your regular physician about that one. What concourse do you live on?

Hoyos: B.

Arthur: And who is your physician?

Hoyos: Dr. Sidotra. I haven't seen her for a long time.

Arthur: I'm sure she'll be happy to take a look at that leg and prescribe something for it. I'll send a memo to her.

Hoyos: Thanks so much.

[I hobbled painfully to the door of his office, flinching with every step.]

Hoyos: Um, Dr. Arthur, do you think you could have Dr. Sidotra give me the other pill every morning? Her clinic's on my floor. It would save me a lot of grief with this dang leg of mine.

[He hesitated a moment, then smiled reassuringly.]

Arthur: Of course. She can administer it just as easily as I can. And with much less trouble for you.

Hoyos: Thanks again, Doctor.

Arthur: I'm honored to serve you, Dr. Hoyos.

Day 2310:

Early this morning I hoofed it straight to Pia's clinic. Before I had a chance to tell her what was happening, she whisked me away to the nearest art alcove.

"There's no guarantee the clinic is free of audio surveillance", she explained on the way.

When we were secure, she said, "Neil, what's going on?"

"Uh, d'you mean physically, psychologically, politically, or cosmically?"

"Just the first three categories. This morning I received Dr. Arthur's memo, and the pharmacy sent your medication. Are you aware of what this is?"

"I'm very aware of what it is, politically."

"It's an anti-psychotic drug. And I know that you are definitely not psychotic."

"Don't think too badly of Dr. Arthur, Pia. He's a really nice guy. He's just obeying orders."

"I guessed as much. This is not good, Neil, not good in the least. One of the side effects of this particular item is that if you're *not* psychotic, you will develop secondary psychotic side effects."

"You understand why they're doing this?"

"Yes, I do. Your personal dossier will now be full of memos about you needing an anti-psychotic drug. If anyone should want to check into your allegations, they'll attribute your suspicions to mental illness. Also, your behavior will now alter sufficiently to offer them additional evidence that you're living in unreality. It's so good you'll feel no negative side effects whatsoever, and you'll experience some positive ones—positive in the sense that your mood will elevate, and you won't mind at all being considered mad."

"So, I guess it's time to take my little black pill, huh?"

"Not so fast. I have an idea."

Pia was always full of ideas. In short, she wants to give me a *placebo* every morning, and flush the mind-warper.

This is a fortuitous turn of events. I get to keep my mind *and* enjoy daily meetings with this cagey lass.

I asked her if there had been any follow-up on her and her beau's letter to the Captain. Her face grew angrier and she said: "Regrettably, that gentleman informed Paul that he can't do anything to help. There's a twofold problem, he says. First, there's no conclusive evidence to support the allegations. Second, even if there was evidence, he has no authority to override the Department of Social Infrastructure."

"What! He's the Captain."

"Yes, he's the Captain. But it seems that this means something different than the authority of a captain on an ocean-going vessel. He exercises no overall command. He has absolute say on what happens to the body of the *Kosmos*, where it goes, how it goes, when it goes. But he has no say over the human affairs inside it. DSI is in charge of that."

"I thought they were just a bunch of social workers."

"No, they're the *de facto* government. They've kept a low-profile until now because there was no need for them to be heavy handed about it. They're still playing it subtle in order to maintain the general atmosphere of a free society—the team, you see, the community. But the truth is, their authority is absolute."

"*They* are the government."

Pia nodded.

Day 2313:

Each morning I show up at the deck-B clinic and take my placebo. I feel a tad more irritable than ever, and deep-down angry. Normal reactions. I did some careful reading in the Manual. Though the article on authority structure is made palatable with textual brain sweetener, its meaning is clear: DSI is the government. Skinner is the Emperor, and Elf is his assistant Caesar. Skinner the demi-god and Elf the enforcer who can dirty his hands.

I've spent a few days alerting the other conspirators, asking them to back off for a while, explaining the enforced drugging and also the placebo. I warned them that I'll be sending them fake messages to cover what I'm really going to do, and that they shouldn't believe anything I write to them through ordinary means of communication. We will try to speak covertly whenever we can—chance encounters that we hope will look like natural happenstance.

Today I sent a *max* message to Stron, telling him that I'm having doubts about our "theory". Stron replied that he's having doubts too, and chalked it up to too much confinement, boredom, and whiskey. He concluded by saying that he now wonders if he was being paranoid.

We bumped into each other by "accident" in the food line at the cafeteria, chatted about how embarrassed we now feel about our over-reactions, which turned a few ears before us and behind us. Then we proceeded to a lonely table.

He barked an excremental expletive a trifle too loudly.

"A perfectly apt English expression, Stron, but you might want to adjust your style or lower your volume."

"Scatology-heads of the fifth dimension!" he snarled.

"Nicely put", I said. "And it's good to see you so unusually cheery today."

"This is a *coup d'état*", he said, casting a grim look over his shoulder.

"Not really, Stron. They cut the head off real government before the voyage began. They did it to the whole world a long time ago."

"And left us bread and circuses to keep us preoccupied. So what do we do now, Billy-boy?"

"We slowly, slowly pull the wool over their eyes and let them calm down. They're not going to take their eyes off us, but they are going to believe we've been neutralized."

"Maybe we have been neutralized."

"No, we haven't. But we need to go carefully."

"Can you lend me some of your psycho pills? I could use a bucket of those."

"Not on your life. I need you mean and ugly and paranoid."

He chuckled menacingly.

"I need the real you, Stron. But watch what you say on the surface. Be very, very nice."

"I will. I can be a charmer, as you know."

Day 2337:

Today, Stron asked me for my opinion about the drugging situation. He wonders why they haven't called him into Medical for his own set of sanity tests, and his own prescriptions.

"I'm not sure why", I replied. "Probably because it would look strange in the records if all the accusers were suddenly diagnosed as psychotic, and all were forced to submit to silencing pills. Besides, in their eyes, I'm the ringleader, the one who gave the disruptive talk. I have no doubt they're watching you to see your reaction to my change of viewpoint. They've noted you going along with it, and they've concluded that you're no longer a threat, you don't need my kind of medication."

"I'm crazy enough without it."

"That too."

Day 2400:

It has been two months since my last entry in these written journals. My days are spent ruminating in my cell. I keep throwing stardust into the observers' eyes by surfing on my de-privatized *max*, mainly in the fields of astronomy, physics, and other allied fields. It fills the void. David's absence has shown me that every person who enters our lives is present as a unique phenomenon, radiational, gravitational, altering the symphony.

We are powerless. I try to get my mind off the situation by reading everything there is to know about the Alpha Centauri system, over and over again. It presents a wonderful complexity. Streams of information are arriving, and the telescope visuals are also tightening up our view of the planet. Probably much is known upstairs that the flight astronomers do not share with us. Through the public presentations, we receive general knowledge and enhanced impressions. Stron grumbles continually, frustrated by the lack of technical data from a range of instruments.

Every so often I send out happy messages to my confreres, expressing my newfound belief that the surveillance suspicion had been exaggerated in my mind, and was possibly unfounded altogether. In this way, I hope to convince the surveillance guys, especially my favorite elf, that the little daily pill is doing its job. DSI has disappeared back into the woodwork. They remain as an invisible presence, like Death, which haunts us all.

Death, the old bogeyman who is never visible until the last day of your life, never showing his face or his teeth until you resist him. I recall *El Día de los Muertos*, which made its appearance in the village each year of my childhood, a blend of paganism and Catholicism which my parents and Fray Ramon frowned upon. The good father preached strongly against it during his pickup truck sermons, but most of the villagers absorbed his admonitions with no loss of affection for him, and no compliance. They argued that the annual celebration was just something they had always done and their ancestors had always done, a tradition that did no harm. In retrospect, I think the Day of the Dead was a valid enough laughing at death and a less valid compromise with primitive religious instincts. It was a placation, a temporary truce with death combined with invocation of the spirits of dearly departed loved ones. Year after year, Fray Ramon tried to pull the thing back on track, to keep it purely a day of prayers for the souls of those who had died. He enjoyed little success.

The power of culture is immense, especially when it is sensually rewarding. I remember my lust for the white skulls made of confectionary sugar with red candies in the eye sockets that other children were permitted to eat. I remember, too, my fits of temper when my parents stood firm against it. *Ay, ay*, my mother would sigh over me, *mi pequeño chilito*, my little chili pepper. Sometimes I was *mi triquitraque*, her little firecracker. Nevertheless, they did not give in, and early on, I learned the futility of tantrums. Ah, how I loved the thrill of the mysterious, the dancing puppet skeletons, the eerie songs, the food offerings left at the edge of the village with burning candles to welcome the spirits home. The food was always gone in the morning. I have no doubt that the snakes and coyotes of our region grew fat on superstition and that we were plagued by the varmints because they had been trained to expect a free lunch.

But I digress.

Whenever I connect with my friends face-to-face, in covert mode, we talk real. They reassure me that they know my messages are nothing more than cover story. Even so, most of them are now expressing doubts, calling it whimsically, self-deprecatingly, "our conspiracy theory". While no one, I think, has made peace with the fact that David Ayne has been subtracted from the equation, many of us are learning to live with this as an unresolved question, as an unknowable. A few have entirely opted out of our private—hopefully, private—discussions in art alcoves and at the end of long cafeteria tables. I have asked Pia to stay at arm's length from us, since I don't want it known that she remains convinced of the allegations. DSI may know about her appeal to the Captain, but, if so, I hope the letter has been dismissed as one of many initial reactions on the part of passengers and crew.

During our best period, we were seventeen dissidents. Now we are back down to six, including four committed activists—Stron, Xue, Dariush, and myself.

Yet, we have begun to ask ourselves, "Committed to what?"

Day 2405:

Feelings of resignation and the first tell-tale signs of indifference are appearing. Not strong, but symptomatic. It is very difficult to maintain a constant state of vigilance. I talked this over with Xue, and we agreed that now is the time to shake the bushes.

None of us have access to the e-addresses of more than a handful of people. To try to obtain the addresses of everyone on board would be a giveaway. Instead, using his *memor* and the advanced *max* of his unnamed friend, Xue created a new single-page file and typed in the following heading above David's photo and mini-biography:

David William Ayne is Missing

This crew member of the *Kosmos* expedition disappeared on Day 2253, five months ago. His existence has been denied by the Department of Social Infrastructure. Why? His personnel record (see below) has been deleted from all onboard files. Why? If you have seen this man, report it immediately to everyone you know. Discuss it. Ask questions. Think!

I gave Xue six hundred sheets of my white bond, and he took them away for printing, I know not where.

Day 2406:

We met before dawn, as all good conspirators should. We gathered on deck C, not far from Dariush's room, in an extra-large art alcove, containing four facsimile paintings by a twentieth-century artist named

Rockwell. The images, appropriately enough, were titled *The Four Freedoms*.

We counted out sheets, dividing them more or less equally. Xue would deliver his to private rooms on Concourse A. Stron would take B, Dariush would have C, and I would distribute along D, since that was the concourse on which David had lived and one which I had come to know well.

It was now about two hours before sunrise, when people would begin to stir. Much of our distribution would be guess-work, because each concourse had hundreds of rooms, only a portion of which were residential. However, these private rooms were spaced more closely together than service rooms, were arranged like city blocks, and some-times had personalized decorations affixed to the doors, so we stood a fair chance of reaching a majority of people on board.

Xue had contributed a hundred sheets of his own paper, and these extra prints I would later deliver to Pia at my daily pill session. She would in turn deliver them to her friend Paul during their pre-arranged date for coffee later in the morning. He would distribute them among the flight crew up on KC.

Moreover, unbeknownst to me, Stron had given Xue two hundred sheets from his personal stash of paper, and additional prints had been made with them. We now agreed that these should be handed out at the elevators for the maintenance department. All four of us would meet at the D-level elevators after we had covered decks A to D, and then try to engage maintenance staff coming off shift, or going on shift. Of all the people on the ship, these were the most likely to recognize David's face and name.

We headed off to our assigned tasks.

I was concerned about the absence of gaps under doors; my only apparent option was to place each sheet on the floor outside. On a whim, however, I tried slipping one into the hairline between door and floor, and it slid inside. Eureka! This would help avoid detection long enough for people to read the prints.

The daylight was turned on just as I completed my territory. I now had a few minutes to get back up to deck-B medical clinic. There, I met Pia arriving for a day's work, typing her code into the clinic door. It slid open, and we went inside. I took the bundle of sheets for KC from inside my shirt, while she prepared my placebo. She flushed the brain-warper down a sink drain, gave me my sugar pill, and took the prints from me, locking them into her desk drawer. All of this transpired without a word passing between us. I was off like a shot back down to D.

There I stood by the elevators, and while I waited for the others to arrive, I handed out a few dozen prints to workers entering the elevator to go on shift. Invariably, they glanced at the sheet, curious but saying nothing, in a hurry to get to work. Dariush joined me, and he too began to hand out sheets. Now a few maintenance people were exiting the elevators, going off shift.

We had handed out most of our sheets, when one of the workers paused in the hallway and read it carefully.

"I know Dave", he said, looking up at me with a frown. "He's not missing. He was transferred five months ago to P department."

"Propulsion, you mean?" I asked.

"Yeah. That's on the same floor as M, but it's in the rear of the ship, and sealed off from us for safety reasons. Maybe you should check there."

"Thanks for the suggestion. How do I find it?"

He pointed down the concourse. "You'll find the first set of P elevators about fifteen minutes walk thataway."

Xue and Stron had returned by then, and the traffic of workers was tapering down to nothing. With that, the four of us set off in the direction of the propulsion elevators. When we arrived there, the lobby was deserted. It looked as if the change of P shift had already finished, or else this department's schedules were different from M's.

At last the doors opened, and a single worker emerged, looking tired after a long night.

Xue handed him a print, and asked, "Do you recognize this man?"

The other looked closely at the photo and shook his head.

"With regret," he replied in a French accent. "I do not know this man."

"You're sure he doesn't work in Propulsion? He'd probably be doing some kind of cleaning or minor maintenance."

"I am foreman of cleaning-maintenance team for the P department. I know all of the staff. I have never see this man before. Who is he?"

He read the biography, looked up, and said, "You should ask in M department. I think it is they who would know him."

"We did ask", I said. "We've been asking for months. No one has any answers. And as this says, his name has been scrubbed from the ship's computers."

"It is probably clerical error, the bureaucratic problem, no? If he is not on board, then he did not depart from the Earth."

"He is on board. I've talked with him many times since Day 1. Now he's missing, and we want to know why."

The man shrugged. "There is some explanation, I am sure. May I keep this?"

"Please. And here are a few more copies, if you'd care to pass them around."

"Certainly. I hope you will find your friend."

"Thanks."

The four of us climbed up to deck B and ate breakfast together in the cafeteria. People ambled in, some of them clutching the print in their hands, reading it alone over their coffee and toast, or discussing it quietly with others. No one looked in our direction, so we hoped that blame wouldn't be traced to us—at least not immediately. Doubtless, the denials would soon be flooding the ship.

Day 2407:

Yesterday, about two hours after breakfast, Elf came back out of the woodwork. In fact, he pounced. The gendarmes arrived at my door, solemn as ever, and conducted me to the office of the Deputy Director, Department of Social Infrastructure (DDDSI).

An angry elf is a frightening thing to behold. Elves, I presume, say nothing for at least five minutes after you've been hauled into their sylvan offices. They merely gaze upon you with their preternatural eyes, unblinking, their lungs inhaling and exhaling as delicately as the fins of a Pacific fan-fish minnow. He was spooky. But that was okay, because I already knew he was kind of a sinister guy, and his intimidating silence had the unintended benefit of allowing me to gather my addled wits about me.

I love acronyms. The pregnant pause permitted me to toy with a few. Dire Doyen of Daily Social Intimidation. Doctor of Dogmatic Deaggressivization Syndrome Inversion. Dangerous Downbeat Draconian Spiteful Imposer. Et cetera.

I decided to *carpe diem* and break the silence.

Transcript of recording:

Me: Good morning, Elf.

176

[He does not respond. Is he alive? Yes, he just blinked.]

Me: Can you please give me a hint about the reason for our interface?

[Slight quivering of his fins, heightened color in the neck.]

Me: I know—you want to invite me to deliver another talk to the community.

[Face flushes red, eyes begin blinking rapidly, then are brought under control, followed by a deathly cold stare. If elves had tails, this one would rattle.]

Me: Is something troubling you?

[He extends a stiff fingertip and touches a button on the top of his desk. We are now recording each other's silences. When he speaks at last, it is in the tone of a calm, compassionate professional.]

Elf: Dr. Hoyos, I've asked you to come in to see me because—

Me: Elf, you didn't ask. Your agents arrested me and brought me here against my will.

Elf: There is nothing to be frightened of, Dr. Hoyos. The department—

Me: I'm not frightened, Dr. Larson. I'm merely concerned about the police-state tactics.

[He produces an artificial chuckle, but his eyes are going all slitty.]

Elf: No, no, you misunderstand. I'm concerned about your health. Surely, you're aware that there are no grounds whatsoever to the allegations you printed and distributed this morning. The supposedly missing person has never been on board the *Kosmos*.

Me: I'm aware that the points raised in our leaflet are very well grounded. In my discussions with crew members, I discovered that some of them knew the missing person, David Ayne.

Elf: There is no David Ayne in our records.

Me: Of course, that is now the case. However, he was on board the ship and has not left it. Crew members attribute his disappearance to a transfer to another department. Perhaps if you would kindly search all the departments, you will be able to locate him.

Elf: That won't be necessary. This name, this persona, is a figment of your imagination. If these crew members *knew him*, as you call it, why haven't they come forward?

Me: They didn't know he was missing until now. It's a big ship. Now they know.

Elf: Who are these people? If they believe what you say, then they shouldn't hesitate to raise their concerns with the Department.

Me: Perhaps they have concerns about their own safety.

Elf: If they think that, it's because you planted the idea—an unfounded fear not based in reality.

Me: Where is David Ayne? Why have you erased all records of him from the ship's files?

[Elf leans forward and touches the button on his desk. I think he's turned off the recorder.]

Elf: Listen to me, Hoyos, and listen carefully. I will not permit your delusions to disrupt life on board this ship. Your hallucinations are becoming very destructive.

Me: *Arbeit macht frei?*

Elf: What?

Me: An old saying, made popular by another group of social facilitators.

Elf: You think you're funny, do you? Why don't you grow up? Why do you go about the ship playing games like an adolescent who never matured properly? That ridiculous costume you wear, your cultural idiosyncrasies, your pathetic conspiracy theories—it's all an act. But now the act is getting worse and harming other people. If you don't—

Me: The costume and the idiosyncrasies are just a bit of fun, Elf. You should lighten up a little.

Elf: Stop calling me *Elf*, you moron! If you think your Nobel Prize is going to protect you—

Me: Protect me from what, Elf?

Elf [growling in a very aggressive manner]: Stop calling me *Elf*.

Me: Actually two Nobel Prizes.

[*Ay, ay, ay, caramba!* Elf now proves himself capable of extremely crude language. We shall pass on quickly.]

Me: I'm not banking on my prizes, Dr. Larson. I have a bad taste in my mouth from the last time I visited Stockholm. My acceptance speech—

Elf: Yes, yes, I read your acceptance speech.

Me: Of course you would have. It would be in my Security dossier. Somewhat problematic, that speech, wasn't it?

Elf: One of the greatest errors Security ever made was permitting you to be aboard this ship. Your speech in Stockholm—

Me: Did you read the original Spanish?

Elf: I read the English, the Swedish, and the Norwegian versions of that drivel—that *political* drivel.

Me: I found it so informative, so revealing, that all translations, all transcripts (save my paper original), had altered my words. Did you know that? You probably don't realize that I stated very clearly—

Elf: The stench of paranoia came through clearly enough. Don't repeat it.

Me: I said, "Contemporary civilization is poised on the brink of a quantum leap in science, precisely at the time of history when we have regressed to sophisticated barbarism in the realm of ethics. Our civilization is based upon, and prospers by, legalized murder on a global scale."

Elf: Ridiculous. You never said that. And even if you had said something like that, it would prove my point that you are both irresponsible and irrational.

Me: You may recall that they translated the sentence to read as follows: "Contemporary civilization is poised on the brink of a quantum leap in science, having transcended the unethical behavior of the past. Our civilization has overcome through global efforts the barbarian tendency to genocide." There's a name for that kind of translation, Dr. Larson.

Elf: Oh, really? And what name is that?

Me: It's called lying. It's also character theft.

[He snorts, followed by silence and scowls of professional disgust.]

Me: Push the record button again, Elf; there are a few more things I'd like to say.

[He does not comply.]

Me: A civilization that destroys tens of millions of children annually, confiscates about as many from their parents, enforces sterilization and other punitive measures—well, wouldn't you say that such a civilization suffers from a very deadly fixation? So what's one janitor more or less, right?

[He leans forward and taps the button. When he speaks, his voice is the quintessence of kindness and rationality.]

Elf: Dr. Hoyos, the Department is very concerned about your health. I must ask you to reconsider your recent behavior, which I regret to say, has had a disruptive and depressing effect on some of the expedition members.

Me: I can't stop being who I am, Dr. Larson. And why don't you disclose where David—

[His voice drowns me out:]

Elf: Dr. Hoyos, much as I respect your achievements in science—your very great achievements—you are suffering from delusions, sir. It is with considerable personal pain that I must ask you to cease spreading these ugly insinuations. Your increasing habit of instability is jeopardizing the mission to AC-A-7.

[He taps the button. We're now off. He's fuming through his nostrils, his lips so tight they're turning blue. He says:]

Elf: If I hear one more word from you, either today or in the future, or learn about any act or any utterance which even hints at a recurrence of your insane pranks, I will mandate that you be held under sedation in a medical ward for the remainder of the voyage. I cannot afford madmen to roam loose on this ship. Do you understand me?"

Me: I'm rational enough to understand you completely, Elf. Completely. Why don't you just erase me too?

Elf: Don't push me, Hoyos. I will do exactly what I said I will do, if you don't shut up. Beginning now.

Me: [silence]

Elf: Now, get out.

[I got out.]

Feeling very, very shaken, I made my way slowly back to deck B. Little firecracker that I once was, all my powder had fizzled out. By the time I arrived at Stron's room, I was frightened and, I must admit, struggling against a sucking undertow of hopelessness. I knocked.

"Well, we can count our lucky stars", said Stron with a grin when I was inside his room and the door closed behind me. "You're still at liberty, I see."

"Am I?" I murmured.

We both glanced at his *max*.

"It's off", he said. "We can talk."

I shook my head, put my forefinger to my lips, and said, "Let's go for a walk."

So we went out and rambled along the concourse with our heads together. Stron patted his breast pocket repeatedly and pulled tufts of white hair from his ears. At length, we found a suitable culture alcove and stepped inside. There, safely out of line of sight, he withdrew a flask from his inner breast pocket and offered me a sip of whiskey. I took it gratefully, even as I eyed the "art"—a painting of some naked ladies in Avignon. Nothing to provoke the animal appetites, since they looked like pieces of broken pottery trying desperately to look sensual.

I said, "One of the little details Dwayne warned me about before he disappeared is that even when a *max* is powered down, it's always listening. And we can't presume we have privacy any longer."

"It's recording too, I'd wager," muttered Stron, "with an auto-screening program that goes beep and blinks a red light in some far-off office if we use key words like 'bomb' or 'privacy'."

"Or 'dirk'."

"That one would fetch the human analysts. They'd come running."

"Considering our current status as subversives and mission under-miners, I expect they keep live staff on our case around the clock. But there's worse, Stron. I've just had a nasty meeting with the deputy director of DSI."

"How nasty?"

"Very. Want to listen to it?"

I tapped my lapel button, and he stood with his ear cocked in rapt attention, his face cranky, his white eyebrows tufting upward like a horned owl, but his shoulders slumping more and more, until toward the end he looked totally beaten. He sipped whiskey and stared at the floor for a time. Then he sighed and said, "I told you he was dangerous."

I nodded.

"Good thing you recorded that farce", he went on. "It's so inter-esting, the Jekyll-and-Hyde thing—two personalities, two styles—and this is the man who controls our destiny."

"Controls our destiny? I wouldn't go that far."

"The Mysterious Stranger still hasn't put in an appearance, I take it?"

I shook my head. "Nothing. Not even a hint."

"Everyone on board has seen the missing person posters by now. If he was free, I would expect him to send you something clandestinely, maybe something cryptic, just to let you know he's all right."

"I would expect so too. I think it's a bad sign. It means he really is in custody and being held incommunicado."

"They probably made him crack, and he's told them everything he's done."

"Probably. I just don't understand why they didn't slap him on the wrist and send him back to work."

"And why the erasing of his name from every known archive, eh? I'll bet he's lying on a cold slab in a freezer down in the holds. Or maybe converted into anti-matter."

"There's no need to get paranoid", I muttered.

"Neil, who started this revolt?"

"All right, all right, all right. But I never meant it to go this far. I thought we'd blow the cover off a bureaucratic nastiness and settle the business reasonably."

"Aaargh, how did a bright lad like you ever develop such a phobia against extremism?"

"Extremism is irrational and alarmist. It is not objective. It is not scientific."

"Neither is murder and cover-up."

"Right, but let's keep our wits about us, for heaven's sakes."

Stron took a long sip from his flask and said something guttural that sounded like: "*Ufollisutstanswellneronekinseeettinknonswiznstrongnernefererel-quintasthermzilf.*"

"What?" I demanded, because I feared that my co-conspirator might be going daft.

"I said, 'Of folys that stande so well in their owne conceyt that they thinke none so wyse, stronge, fayre, nor eloquent, as they are themselves'."

"Say that again, in English, please."

"That *was* English", he snapped. His chest began to heave with irritation, and he took another sip. I noted that his hair was all askew, as if he had gone to extra trouble this morning before the mirror, as if he regularly messed up his hair to make himself look more eccentric.

He swallowed his whiskey and said, slowly, emphatically, as if explaining something simple to a mentally deficient child: "I said: 'Of fools that stand so well in their own conceit that they think there are none so wise, so strong, and so fair as they are themselves'."

"I see. And that's what you think of me?"

"Naw!" he barked. "I was referring to the powers that be on this ship of fools. It was a quotation. It was a literary quote from a famous text in our native language."

"*Your* native language."

"It's a line written by a bonny Scotsman named Alexander Barclay, who in 1509 translated into English the all-time classic and best-seller, *The Ship of Fools.*"

"I never heard of it."

"The original was written by a Swiss German living in Basel, a fellow named Sebastian Brandt. It was published in 1494 as *Narren-schiff*, and then translated into Latin under the title *Stultifera Navis.*"

Translations into several European languages followed, and more have appeared ever since."

"*Ship of Fools*—any inference intended?"

"Inference and implication heartily intended. It's an allegorical satire, you see. It tells the tale of a vessel populated by the deranged, the silly, or the simply stupid who, as they sail aimlessly along, get themselves into all kinds of trouble, all of it their own making. No captain, no pilot, just a gabble of goosey egoists and nincompoops absorbed in their own petty theories and desires. The Renaissance produced a ton of fables and paintings using that motif. Brandt's was the best, of course."

"And does the story end well?"

"Only if the reader pays attention."

"It was a warning, then?"

"Right. Or a mirror, methinks. The ship crisscrossed the rivers and canals of Europe with its pathetic cargo of lunatics, searching for a fool's paradise—the origin of our modern expression. Some writers and artists were merely mocking the follies of man, but some were mocking the Church, because it was supposed to be the ark of salvation, you see, and in those days it wasn't doing a good job. Disedifying, one might say."

Without asking, I took the flask from Stron's hand and had a swig for myself.

"Which approach did Brandt take?"

"He was a theologian, and a loyal one", said Stron, grabbing the flask from me. "His was true satire, because he wanted to point out how men deceive themselves, with the objective of making people better."

"And Barclay?"

"A godly Scotsman, he made a faithful translation, very witty in its own right."

"And you, Stron, are you a godly Scotsman?"

My abruptness took him aback for a moment. He scowled at me with one eye as he thought about my question.

"Naw", he replied. "Naw, I am not. But equally, Neil, equally—or more than equally—I do not worship in the new church of our times."

Failing to grasp what he meant, I said, "Well, whatever remains of the church is scattered and pretty much underground in our times."

"The new church I refer to is thriving above-ground and controls nearly everything. And do you know what it worships?"

"No."

"It worships *humanity* and no other. Which means it worships some men at the expense of other men. It's Narcissus adoring his own image. And, as you should know, this new god demands an enormous number of sacrificial victims."

I shook my head dubiously.

His brash tone and exaggerated accent went down to the minimum: "The missing children, Neil, the missing children! Why are they missing in untold numbers, eh?"

"Yes, but that's *anti*-religion."

"And thus it succumbs to the worst religious impulses of all. Back on Earth, didn't you ever cast a casual glance beyond the borders of your computer screen or your antiquarian books? Have you cast a probing glance along the streets and avenues of this ship?"

"Didn't you hear what I said to Larson? And what I said in Stockholm? Don't you think I've been taking a good look around?"

"Yes, in a way. And you've concluded that some things are not right. You've been brave and bold about it too, and canny when you need to be. That's why I'm with you in this. But I don't think you really understand how dark it can get."

"Maybe I don't, Stron." I frowned, sinking into my own thoughts, my own confusions.

"Well", he muttered, staring at the floor, "the next move is theirs."

Day 2408:

I awoke this morning to find that DSI had moved quickly.

First, a flood of new visual presentations of our destination appeared in all the panorama rooms on the four main concourses. These were also available for viewing on personal *maxes*. The three stars are now visible "to the naked eye" (the true-scale digital images) as small orbs: two golden spheres and a smaller red coal.

The *Kosmos* has deployed more robot telescopes, coasting in formation like minnows beside a whale, an array spanning about ten kilometers on each side of the ship, triangulating on the Alpha Centauri system. The close-ups reveal massive solar flares on the two larger suns, shooting hundreds of thousands of kilometers out from their surfaces. The new telescopic images of AC-B's five planets are gripping, but

AC-A's eighteen planets are even more stunning, displaying a wide variety of sizes and colors. It is now confirmed that among them only Planet 7 has an Earth-like environment.

There are many distinct features visible: moving weather patterns, clouds, storms, an atmosphere like that of our home planet. The spectrographs indicate a higher degree of oxygen and lower carbon dioxide. No large volcanoes, only a few small ones ringing tectonic plates, producing relatively low atmospheric pollution. There are oceans, and they are water. There are four main continents and five lesser ones; the latter are island masses larger than Australia. The land/sea ratio is different from Earth's: there is more land on AC-A-7, though the seas may be deeper than ours. Due to our distance, depth readings are unreliable.

The land masses appear to be covered with botanical life, unless all that luscious green is colored dust. A desert belt girds the equator, no more than 25% the size of our own desert belt back home. The polar ice caps are smaller too, which indicates a warm, moderate global climate, with fewer extremes. The planet has three small moons (all smaller than our moon). They are barren and cratered, colors respectively bright white, pale brown, and gray.

The audio commentary to these *son et lumière* presentations informed us that, so far, we have received no signals of any kind from AC-A-7. Its night side displays not a single light of human habitation.

It was difficult not to be distracted and enthralled by the presentations. Even as I watched them, a little scene from my childhood arose spontaneously in my mind's eye, though at first I did not understand why.

My mother was painting a *piñata*. She laid a wide brush stroke of crimson red onto the hardened white paper. Beside it, she painted a wide swath of yellow, without touching the red. Immediately, the crimson changed before my eyes: it now seemed orange.

Then it hit me: optics involves psychological interpretation, perceptual subjectivity. Similarly, in a ship where little seems to be happening, where everything is ordinary and tending to become banal, a single voice cries out that a man is missing. This is a stark assault upon consciousness, a stroke of brilliant color. Then, if there suddenly appears all around it other strokes of color that are much more brilliant, the significance of a missing janitor dwindles. The context has changed everything. Clever, clever DSI.

The second response was a tenderly expressed letter sent via *max* mail to everyone on board. Both Stron and Xue told me that theirs arrived about six o'clock this morning. Even I received one. It read as follows:

To all staff and passengers of the *Kosmos*:

Many of you will have seen the unauthorized hand-out sheet distributed yesterday by Dr. Neil de Hoyos. In it, he expressed his concern that a crew member of the ship was missing. The executive staff of the mission to AC-A-7 wish to reassure you that the person he refers to is not missing. The objective reality is that this is a figment of Dr. Hoyos' imagination. While we believe him to be sincere, the allegations he makes are directly related to ongoing problems he has had with his personal health. For the past few months, he has been receiving medical treatment for his condition, which involves disorders in his brain chemistry that result in severe depression and occasional eruptions of delusional behavior. With regret, we must inform you that the distribution of yesterday's hand-out was one such episode.

Dr. de Hoyos is one of the most respected scientists of our times. His accomplishments in physics have earned him two Nobel Prizes as well as many other honors from the human community. He well deserves these honors. It is unfortunate, therefore, that the subject of his private physical and mental difficulties must become public knowledge. The executive committee, after much discussion, and with hesitation, concluded that it would be beneficial for the good of the mission to share this information with you, in order to reassure you that there is no need for concern regarding the allegations, for they are entirely the product of Dr. Hoyos' imagination.

As he continues to undergo treatment, he will participate as usual in the normal routine of onboard life. We encourage you to exercise every effort at kindness and patience toward him personally, for this great man is ever worthy of our respect.

Sincerely,

[signed]

Dr. Karl Skinner, Director, Department of Social Infrastructure

Dr. Elif Larson, Deputy Director

I had just completed a second reading of this masterful bit of trou- bleshooting, when a knock came upon my door, and my two gen- darmes appeared. They explained that they had a mandate to accompany me to the Concourse B medical clinic. What in tarnation is a "man- date"! I'm getting really sick of this kind of verbal sludge. Couldn't they just say "order"? I went along with them, docile as a lamb. Were they about to have me incarcerated and heavily drugged? Possibly, but I took some comfort in the fact that DSI's smooth letter indicated otherwise.

As it turned out, they had been sent to conduct me to see my per- sonal physician. Pia was waiting for us at the clinic, looking cool and professionally distanced from me. Had they got to her too? She explained to me, without losing eye contact, that a change in my medication had been "mandated" and that the pharmacy had already sent it to her. She turned away to a dispensary shelf, and began to prepare my new pill. The gendarmes stood aside, but did not depart; apparently, they would make sure I took my medicine like a man.

Pia handed me a tiny polyplast pill cup, and another of water.

"Here we are, Dr. Hoyos", she said in the deadpan tone of a detached physician.

I tossed both pill and water down my throat, wondering what would happen next.

The gendarmes cordially said good-bye to Pia, whom they addressed as "Dr. Sidotra", told me I could go about my business as I wished, and then they departed.

"Dr. Hoyos," she said, making my heart sink with the formality of it, "you'll be feeling a lot better within days."

"Uh, thank you, Dr. Sidotra. Can you tell me what this new pill is? What is it going to do to me?"

She turned away from me and penciled something on a scrap of paper.

She said: "It's something that will help you with your mood swings. It will also help you stay on an even keel."

She handed me the paper, on which was written:

Placebo. Meet me deck C 2100 hrs. Munch alcove.

"Thanks", I mumbled, and left.

For the better part of what remained of the morning, I shuffled along Concourse C, feeling somewhat depressed in a natural sort of way, but basically still my good old self. I inspected every art alcove on that deck, wondering what on earth a Munch alcove was. "Munch" as in "chew"? Would we meet beneath a painting or sculpture of a mouth? Or had she misspelled a word? Finally, I found it by looking a bit closer at the label beneath a painting of a distressed man with wide open mouth under a writhing, bloody-looking sky. Its title was *The Scream*. It was by an artist named Edvard Munch, interestingly a Norwegian like Elif Larson. Was this Pia's sly humor at work?

Nothing much happened for the remainder of the day. Whenever I ventured forth from my room for meals, the people I encountered in line were invariably kind, patient, and respectful, though they kept their distance. Most did not engage in eye contact, and others passed me in the hallway as if I didn't exist.

At 9 p.m., I went downstairs to C and along the concourse to the alcove, where I found that Pia had already arrived, pretending nervously to inspect the painting with avid aesthetic interest.

I cleared my throat.

"Neil, Neil", she said as she came forward and took my hands. "I'm so sorry about that awful scene in the clinic. I had to do it."

"You gave me a placebo, your note said."

"Yes. Thankfully, the enforcers didn't see what I was doing at the dispensary table. They're supposed to stand watch while you take your pill every morning. After a few days, I think, when they're convinced you're a docile patient, they'll leave it all to me."

"What were they trying to give me?"

"A double dose of your previous anti-psychotic medicine, plus some added ingredients to spike your irrational behavior."

"Pia, thank you. Thank you for taking this risk."

"Now, we need to discuss the appropriate behavior that results from this medication. When you come to the clinic in the mornings, I want you to walk a little more slowly each time and look a little more distracted."

"You mean I should seem sort of not there?"

"Yes, but not too much at first. Day by day, can you become increasingly more apathetic and inappropriate?"

"I'm always inappropriate."

"You should say odd things out of the blue, not really connected to what's being discussed, as if your mind is elsewhere than involved in what's in front of you. You don't have to behave like you're insane, just disconnected. Can you remember that?"

"I'll try."

"I'll be acting like a competent servant of the system, and I'll be somewhat cold to you. It means nothing."

"I know that, sweetie", I smiled and kissed her on the cheek.

She gently pushed me away.

"Neil, we must never—I mean *never*—presume that in public offices or private rooms there isn't an audio device picking up what we say. I've had a pretty good look at this alcove and there's nothing I can see that indicates surveillance. If there *is* something here, well, then the whole thing's shot anyway." She scowled at the ceiling and walls. "But I think we do have some hopes."

"What hopes—and to what end?" I asked gloomily.

"I can't explain that now. What I can tell you is that the Med exec has sent down a memo telling me to keep an eye on you for any symptoms of suicidal thoughts. That worries me."

"Me too. A nice clean suicide would solve all their problems."

"I want you to do something else for me. Will you please go swimming tonight at 0100 hours? If you see that there are more than one or two people in the pool, just go back to your room and wait. Return to the pool an hour later. If there's only one other person there besides yourself, then you can go in."

"Uh, Pia, have you considered that swimming in the middle of the night is kind of a counterproductive strategy? Drowning is a nice clean way to go, suicidally I mean."

"You're not going to drown. Not while I can do anything about it. Please, just do as I ask."

"All right."

"Do you trust me?"

"With my life, lady."

"Okay, then, here goes conspiracy number two."

Day 2409:

Dutifully, I arose at half past midnight, donned my shorts and T-shirt, slung a towel around my shoulders, and went out for a swim. I avoided the elevator, thinking that this would be a typical surveillance hot spot, ideal for overhearing conversations. Maybe they had installed botfly larva here or a tapeworm head. Perhaps not, but I felt that over-caution was the best approach. Descending the stairs to level D and making the long trek to the recreation complex on that floor took about half an hour, so I arrived somewhat later than I had planned. Gazing through the pool windows, I saw that there was only one other person present. The doors whisked aside at my command, and I entered.

The man in the pool was doing laps. I sat on the edge with my feet dangling in the water and watched him go from one end to the other. He did not seem to notice my presence, which is usual with these strong, silent types. I had no idea why Pia had asked me to come here at this time, and thought that she would soon arrive. Doubtless, we would talk in relative privacy and plan a few more evasionary tactics. If she did not appear at the end of the hour, I would go back to my room and try to get some sleep.

Stripping off my shirt, I eased into the shallow end, where I floated and paddled about for a while, keeping my eye on the other swimmer. It was unlikely he would be a suicide assister, but a lot of improbable things had happened during the voyage, and I didn't want any unpleasant surprises. I was very tired, and feeling some nervous strain as well. After a few lateral paddle-laps, I pulled my flagging body out of the water and sat on the edge, catching my breath and dabbling my feet.

I stared a long time at my defective lower leg and ankle. The surgeons had straightened it out considerably, but it was still as ugly as a Sonoran desert toad, and it continued to pain me whenever I walked too long on it.

"*Ay, caramba!* You didn't pay attention", I murmured for the ten-thousandth time since that bad day in the arroyo. "You weren't watching. One slip, one little slip, and you pay for it the rest of your life."

In that state of mild despondency combined with fatigue, I had failed to notice that the other swimmer had come to the edge of the pool and was standing in the water less than ten feet away. His chest heaving from exertion, he had his arms folded on the tiles with his head on his forearms.

"That's a lot of laps", I said.

"I do hundred tonight. It was good", he replied in a Slavic accent.

"Well done."

Catching my eye, he stared at me intently, then gazed at the ceiling, and deliberately in every other direction. Then back to me.

"Dr. Hoyos," he said loudly, "I am sorry you do not feel very well at this time."

"I'm all right," I shrugged.

"It is unfortunate you have—how do you say it? It is sad you feel delusion. I am sorry if my word is not okay, maybe not polite to you."

"Don't worry. The language barrier hits us all."

"Or we hit it", he said in a lowered voice.

I glanced at him. His eyes were communicating something. It was personal engagement of sort, not an indifferent examination of a poor deranged specimen of humanity.

"We have speak cover", he murmured. "Now we speak under it."

"What?"

"I am Pia's friend."

"Ah, you're Paul."

He nodded. "I have things to tell you, for good hope."

"I certainly need a dose of that."

He smiled and raised his voice: "Medication help you, Dr. Hoyos. Don't worry."

I raised my voice: "I hope it helps. Sometimes I think clearly, but then things go strange in my mind. Did you see the paper I handed out?"

"I hear about it. It is imagine, yes?"

"I . . . I think so. Yes, I suppose it was all in my mind. I feel badly about doing that. The missing guy, well, I wonder if he was real or if . . ."

"Yes, because is long flight. Maybe sometimes people hallucin . . . ate. It is problem. But medicine help."

He lowered his voice: "Pia explain everything to me. Down the toilet, little bad pill."

"Down the toilet, little bad pill. But I'm worried about the missing man. Did he go down the toilet too? Or is that another hallucination?"

"Dr. Hoyos", Paul whispered. "Do not fear. I believe you. Some in flight crew believe you. I give your paper to many on KC. I give to Captain."

I gazed at him with new attention.

He continued: "Captain can do nothing under KC level. He is Captain of *Kosmos* but not Captain of people. You understand?"

"I understand."

"Loud now. Cover."

"Okay, you first."

Paul said loudly: "You should go to computer, Dr. Hoyos. See if man you say is gone was really there. I think it not. No man like him is in files. You will see it."

"Yes, you're probably right. It's the sickness. It's my condition . . ."

Quietly, he said: "The Captain has private communication access with Earth-base. Nobody can touch this, only Captain. He only has code. He send message yesterday. It is years to go there. Then, even if swift, it is more years for answer to come back to us."

"What did he say to Earth-base?"

"I think everything. He does not like DSI. They try to boss him sometime. But he make them back down."

Paul switched to loud mode: "Swimming is good for thinking. It will make you happy, Dr. Hoyos. Take medicine, swim, be happy."

"Thanks for the advice. I don't know if I can come often, but I'll try. I feel pretty tired all the time."

"Swim every day. Then you feel good. Like me."

"Like you", I smiled. "You *are* good."

Loudly again: "Okay, now I do ten more laps. Then I go upstairs to sleep."

"Yup, I should go get some sleep too. Nice to meet you."

"Nice to meet you", he said, then whispered: "*Bog blagoslovit vas.*"

Before I could ask for a translation, he flipped back into the water and launched himself toward the other end of the pool.

Day 2410:

The gendarmes roused me at 9 A.M. to conduct me to the clinic. Along the way, I dragged my feet more than usual and yawned a lot. I said things like, "When does the sun come up?" and "I don't remember this street." They did not respond. Dutifully, they deposited me in front of Pia and stood aside as she handed me my cup with the imitation little bad pill. I knocked it back, and then said, "I sure feel sleepy lately."

"That's to be expected, Dr. Hoyos. The medication will help your body rest more easily, which will enable your mind to recover more quickly."

"Oh. That's good. Is it all right if I keep swimming?"

"Yes, swimming will help you relax and take your mind off things. I encourage you to spend a moderate amount of time in the pool each day. But don't overexert yourself."

"I won't. Uh, Doctor, do you know what time the sun comes up?"

She frowned and said, "On the ship, we have regulated periods of light and darkness. Do you realize you're in a space craft, Dr. Hoyos?"

"Oh, yes, that's right. I forgot."

"I'll see you tomorrow then. These gentlemen will bring you."

"Thanks, Dr. Sidotra. These are good boys."

"I can see they are, Dr. Hoyos."

The good boys departed. I lingered a minute, long enough to accept an ironic smile from Pia. She handed me a small slip of paper, which I pocketed.

"Have a nice day", she called after me as I left.

Back in my room, I read the paper, on which she had written: *Feeling hungry? Munch at 2100 hrs tonight.*

This evening we met again beneath the *Scream.*

"I shouldn't stay long", she said. "There's a risk of it being noted that you and I meet outside the clinic." She glanced out of the alcove. "Anyone could walk along."

"Paul's a fine guy", I said.

Involuntarily, her face lit up. However, the blush and flutter were quickly displaced by the studied demeanor of the accomplished physician.

"He's the best, Neil. He's a real man—a true and honest man with more courage than a brigade of DSI agents. We really love each other. We want to be married. But I can't talk about that now. I just wanted to ask you if you have any private notes in your room that DSI shouldn't see. It might dawn on them to have a look around your room."

"I do have notes—a private journal."

"Any names in it? Anything that would tell them they're being hoodwinked?"

"Actually, quite a lot of that sort of thing."

"I'm glad I asked. Listen, Neil, your room is the worst place to store records like that."

"I have it hidden in my mattress."

"That's terribly naïve. Do you think they wouldn't look under your mattress? I suggest that you bring what you don't want them to see to your swim tonight. Paul will be at the pool. If you wish, you could let him keep it in a place they can't touch."

"Are you sure it would be safe?"

"Absolutely. For one thing, he's personally reliable. His word is his life. For another, DSI has no overarching control of flight staff, and no investigative powers on KC deck. Paul says the Captain will barely allow them upstairs, and then only under strictest circumstances. Sometimes territorialism works to the good, and this is one such case."

"All right, Pia. If you trust him, I trust him too."

Back in my room, I took stock of my mattress. After stripping the sheets and blanket off, I upended the foam and had a look at the discreet cut in its side. It wouldn't be easy to spot. One would have to lie down on the mattress to detect anything inside that didn't belong there. Even so, I removed the papers that I had secreted, the ones that I had separated out from my written journal because they either pointed the finger at my fellow conspirators or referred to my other various deceptions and collaborations. Then I read through the bulk of my written journal, which I keep in my book cabinet. I found a few more pages where I had penned things that shouldn't become known, ruing that I had so carelessly left them exposed to searching eyes. These I added to the other secret pages and wrapped the thin stack in my swim towel.

This afternoon, I tracked down Xue and asked him to join me in an alcove. There, we discussed everything that has happened during the past three days. He told me that he and Stron had been called in for chats with Elf, who explained to them in kindly, patient terms, how very ill I was, that I had been diagnosed with CDS and associated problems that indicated the potential for schizophrenia. Savvy guys, they told him they had gone along with the hand-out project only because they had believed in my delusion. He let them go. No mind-warping for them, for which I am truly grateful.

Nevertheless, Xue is very angry—not at me, but at the manipulation/ suppression.

I told him about the button recording of my last meeting with Elf and played it for him there in the alcove. He listened to it somberly, his eyes cold with a look that Genghis Khan would have envied. When he had heard enough, he pulled a tiny metallic wafer out of his suit pocket, pressed it to my lapel button for five seconds, and then replaced it in his pocket. He smiled humorlessly.

"I have made a copy, Neil. I will have my unnamed friend print a transcript, and get it back to you early this evening. I suggest that you give it to the man on KC deck who will guard your records. I will keep a copy for myself."

"Thank you, Ao-li." I paused. To demonstrate that I wasn't entirely self-obsessed, I asked, "How is the Shui-mo going?"

"My skills are developing. Soon I will present you with a gift."

At 0100 hours I went for another swim. Paul was there doing laps, along with three other aquatic types who were also doing laps. After they left, I paddled about for a while, until Paul had completed his daily hundred. As on the night before, we conversed on two levels. Our towels sat side by side on the tiles throughout. He said goodnight and went off for a well-earned sleep with my towel under his arm.

I went back to my room feeling that now there was some hope.

Day 2411:

This morning a *max* message from Dariush. He inquired about my health, and said encouraging things, urged me to take my medicine regularly, and expressed some regret that he had played a minor role in contributing to the "embarrassing situation". He invited me to be his guest for lunch in the European restaurant on deck A.

I arrived there at noon to find Dariush waiting for me by the entrance.

He took my arm in hand and said, "I think we will eat Asian food, not the European, with which we have become overfamiliar."

"I don't know, Dariush. They probably have bugs everywhere. A touch of a button, and they go to Asia."

"Perhaps, perhaps not. It may be that we will have a little time before we are located."

We walked a roundabout route to the Asian restaurant, and to my surprise, Dariush led me past the entrance and toward a staircase. We went down to Concourse C and walked quietly side by side toward the African restaurant in the forward section of the ship.

As the music of drums, flutes, and high atonal chanting grew louder, he said into my ear: "The *max* message will alert them to our meeting. It is my supposition, one that is not without basis, that they will activate listening devices in the European restaurant in order to assess our conversation, and if my words about the Asian restaurant were overheard, it too will be surveilled."

We found a table in a shadowed corner beneath zebra-hide wall hangings and black masks. The music was stimulating and loud, which suited us fine. Dariush had a lot to tell me as we consumed our plates of *jollof* rice with onions and peppers, spicy *fufu*, and peanut stew with soy-chicken.

"You have endured much agitation," he began, "in the pursuit of justice for the young man, David Ayne."

"It's nothing more than what any reasonable person would do", I answered.

"In past ages, this would have been true", he said. "It is a consolation to know that these noble instincts remain within human nature."

"Thanks for the compliment. Or maybe the insult."

"I refer to the power of the contemporary social matrix—the *psychological* cosmos."

"I know, I know. Anyway, you've been part of the revolt too, Dariush. I hope it hasn't made problems for you."

"Only a little. Somehow I was identified as one of the people who handed out the papers. Perhaps there were cameras along our route. Dr. Larson requested that I come to his office for an explanatory interview."

"Did he send someone to guide you?"

"No, I found the offices by my own volition."

"And what did he say to you?"

"He explained your supposed mental condition. He was very understanding, shall we say, both in manner and content. It did not demand more than a moment's reflection on my part to see how they are dealing with the crisis. I listened attentively to his explanation, and expressed regret over this lamentable situation. I said that I hoped it would not happen again. I believe he misinterpreted my response as repentance."

"He was pleased by your attitude?"

Dariush smiled. "Oh, yes, very pleased."

"Well, I'm sorry for the bother."

"It is no bother, Neil. I know that his mind and his mouth are full of lies. Perhaps this poor soul even believes his own lies. And I have not ceased to worry about David Ayne. Yet it strikes me that under the present circumstances we must look for another method of finding him. At the same time, we must not do anything that would prejudice your own position."

"Dariush, would you be interested in meeting the real Elif Larson?"

He gazed at me quizzically as I undid the button from my lapel and slid it across the table to him. I said, "Play." He got the point and put the button to his right ear and leaned his cheek on his hand as if he were resting his weary head. When he had heard the whole recording, he returned the button to me with a look of consternation.

"This is most revealing", he said.

I nodded.

He sat back and turned inward, thinking intensely. At last he looked up and said quietly, "It is interesting, this problem of man's tools. Each tool reshapes the one who is apparently the master of the tool. I ask myself this: At what point does the tool, the servant, become the real master?"

"I'm not sure I know, Dariush."

He pointed to the button: "We are resisting the technological corruption of our humanity with technology."

"We're also resisting with our thinking, our perseverance, our friendships."

"Yes, this is so. In the end, we will find that even the best of tools can do no more than assist us. Certainly they cannot save us."

He lapsed into silence again, staring at the tabletop. Finally, he heaved a great sigh and said, "Neil, I believe the first step, at least in my relationship with yourself, is to resume our studies of Kashmiri—in public."

"If you wish. It would reassure them that things are back to normal, other than my degenerating mental condition."

"Then we will do it."

"Whenever we meet, I'll have to pretend I can't focus for long, and I'll look very tired, more so as time goes on. I may act out a few moderately wild things, just to create an effect. But it's all a ruse. I'm supposed to be on a strong medication that's designed to make me look real crazy, even as it claims to heal my craziness."

"Yes, Pia explained it."

"Pia? You know Pia?"

"That fine young woman introduced herself to me shortly after your talk five months ago. She saw me on the stage with you that night. Since then, we occasionally meet for discussions about . . . reality."

"In an artistic environment?"

"Exactly so."

"She has been busy."

"Indeed, busy and sagacious. I also have come to admire Paul Yusupov."

"Ah, yes."

"So, Neil, how many Kashmiri words do you now master?"

"I'm ashamed to say I haven't added any new ones in recent weeks, and have lost a few that I did know."

"Then we must return to our studious practices."

"Agreed. What about tonight in the Mexican food bistro? Do you like very hot food?"

"I am extremely enamored of very hot food."

Day 2444:

I have felt little inclination to make further entries in this written journal. Doubtless this is because my life is now generally more absorbing than it has been during certain periods of the voyage when I drifted into boredom. I spend a lot of time acting the part of the addled, medicated scientist, causing a certain amount of amusement among my intimate friends. I take care not to overdo it. They play the part (in public) of compassionate caregivers. Privately, I am the victim of a good deal of humorous tormenting. I think this comic element is primarily a pressure release for the underlying tensions we live with.

DSI has again become invisible. After a month of conducting me to my daily pill, the gendarmes have disappeared. I go to the clinic on my own, and Pia files a report to this effect every day. She is compelled to immediately alert the director of the Department of Medicine if I fail to meet my appointment, and he in turn will then inform DSI. So far, this has not been necessary. No major crises mar the passage of days, nothing much changes except our view of the planet toward which we are ever moving.

The panorama images and the specific scientific presentations are gripping. We now know that Planet 7's seas are very deep, at least three kilometers deeper than the utmost depths of Earth's oceans. The mountain ranges on some of the continents are a kilometer higher than Mount Everest. The green zones are indeed vegetation. The small ice caps are not as thick as Earth's. The deserts are not barren sand but are wide grasslands, similar to the African veldt. Their color changes from tan to pale green during the wet periods—autumn through spring. The seasons appear to be consistently mild. Everywhere there are rivers. Large storm patterns are sometimes visible on the oceans, and they occasionally brush the coastal regions, but no hurricanes have yet been spotted.

The three moons are substantial in size but smaller than Earth's, and even if all were in full moon phase at once, combined they would not reflect as much light as dear old Luna.

No orbiting artificial satellites have been detected. The night-side of the planet continues to offer not a spark that would indicate cities or towns. We are still too far away to be able to see traces of less developed activity, such as simple roads and trails. A few months from now we may be able to pick up such things, if they are there. It is possible that the planet hosts a primitive people that has not yet mastered fire, let alone electricity and atomic energy. There may be dangers for them during the night, predators of some kind, forcing them to spend the dark hours in caves or underground habitations. Or the intelligent life of the planet could be totally different from what we know and would expect. Or there may be no one there at all.

Day 2506:

Xue rapped loudly on my door this morning, and when it opened, I saw that he was out of breath as if he had come at great speed. I could also see that he was anxious in his quiet way.

"Neil, Stron has had a heart attack. He's in the medical clinic on deck C. He's asking for you."

Xue gave me more details as we hastened along the hallway to the elevator that would take us to the lower concourse.

"He felt the warning signals while he was writing at his desk. He just had time to get up and open his door before the attack began. He was found lying in the hall outside his room."

"When did it happen?" I asked.

"Two hours ago. I received a call about twenty minutes ago. He's in the intensive care unit, and there's a good chance he will survive. He's very weak."

"I'm glad they called you. There aren't any next of kin onboard—not for any of us."

We were now descending in the elevator.

"I was just with him a few minutes ago. He told me he'd asked the doctors to contact you first, but when they checked their protocols, it seems this was not permitted. I was a second, and permissible. I came as quickly as I could, Neil."

"Thank you, Ao-li."

A few minutes later, after circumventing the bureaucratic blockage at the clinic's front desk, we entered the ICU and found ourselves standing beside Stron's bed. The doctors apparently had done what they could and departed, and the ward contained only the single patient, with a nurse typing into a stats book at the other end of the room. As we stood there looking down at our friend, she finished and left us alone.

Stron appeared to be sleeping. His face was unusually white, his lips colorless, and both arms were wired and tubed. Monitors beeped faintly on the wall above his bed. The beep was fairly regular with occasional flutters, but it wasn't strong. I had observed the digital graphs during my own heart tests in the past, and I now could see that Stron's readings were dangerously weak.

We didn't want to disturb him, but without warning, his eyelids twitched and opened.

"Boys, how nice of you to come", he murmured.

"You shouldn't try to talk, Stron", I said. "You should rest. That's what you need most."

"No pain t'speak of, laddie . . . not now. It was pretty bad until they gave me the needle. I'm all right. But I *am* tired . . . so tired."

"We'll stay with you. Try to go back to sleep."

"Can't sleep. Won't. Feels good to remember the frozen loch and hear the rumbling stones. Click and crack. A sweet sound. And the brooms sweeping clean."

Xue touched my arm. "Neil, I'm going to find the medical staff and see what they can tell us."

When I was alone with Stron, I realized just how much I cared for the old fellow, and what a terrible loss it would be if he didn't recover. I pulled a chair toward the bed and sat down on it.

"Where are we?" Stron mumbled.

"You're in the sick bay in C clinic."

"Aye, but where is the ship?"

"On the way to Alpha Centauri."

This seemed to irritate him, and he closed one of his eyes in order to scowl at me. "I know that. I mean where are we *exactly*? How long have I been out?"

"Not more than two hours."

He sighed with relief. "Good. I thought maybe ..."

"Promixa Centauri is about 0.7 light-years away. Soon we'll begin the veer to get around it."

"What's that in parsecs?"

"I'm not sure. But we're getting close."

He closed his eyes, and for a time, I sat without saying anything, just watching him. I did not want to prompt any more conversation because I could see it was costing him effort—energy he did not have to spare.

Xue returned and beckoned me out of the room.

"The doctor tells me there are blocked arteries in the heart, and two of them look ready to blow. He's trying to schedule a bypass."

"How soon?"

"He doesn't know at this point. He thinks probably before the end of the day. He'll send me a message once he knows. He said we have five more minutes, and then we have to go."

Xue patted Stron's shoulder and went off to find Dariush and Pia to let them know what was happening.

Stron's eyes were open and alert again, staring at me inquisitively. "So, what are they going to do with this old carcass?"

"You're going to be fine", I said in my most avuncular tone. "Just fine."

"Great bedside manner, but the clichés need some fine-tuning", he croaked.

"I'll work on it."

"Neil," he said with a feeble grin, "are you a left-footer?"

"I'm right-handed, actually. That's enough talking now. You mustn't wear yourself out. They hope to schedule surgery for you later today."

"To blasted hades with the surgery. Don't distract me. As I was trying to tell you, we have a saying back home. It's an old belief that Catholics use their left foot when digging with a spade, and Protestants use their right."

"Well, I use both."

"I think you mean *neither*."

"I guess that's true in the sense you mean it—if I understand you correctly."

"I certainly wasn't referring to your fouled-up leg."

"Why do you ask?"

"No reason. Just asking." He eyed me intensely, though the look was (for Stron) a mild one. "I was writing something out for you when this thing hit me. The paper's probably still lying on my desk. You go in and get it. Keep it and read it. Preferably often."

"All right. What's your door code?"

"Chanty-wrassler."

"Could you repeat that, please?"

"Chanty-wrassler. It means a useless, dishonest person."

"An irony, I suspect."

"It was self-descriptive."

"And untrue."

"I wish 'twere so. You know, the thing I hate most about all this isn't so much their nastiness. There'll always be bad guys in the world. The thing I hate most is the way they've forced us to become liars and sneaks. Don't use the hyphen."

"What?"

"Chanty-wrassler. No hyphen, no word breaks, all lower case. Let me know what you think. Visit me again soon. Bring a wee polly bottle with you. Preferably full. Take one for yourself, with my compliments."

"I'll be right back. Now close your eyes and be good."

The code worked, and amidst a pile of refuse on the laird's desk, I found a sheet of paper, with an antique mechanical pencil underneath, where I suspect it had rolled when Stron was struck by the first pain.

The sheet did not have my name on it as addressee, but the tone was unmistakable:

Three snippets for yee t'ponder, laddie:

> Softe, fooles, softe, a little slacke your pace,
> Till I haue space you to order by degree,
> I haue eyght neyghbours, that first shall haue a place
> Within this my ship, for they most worthy be,
> They may their learning receyue costles and free,
> Their walles abutting and ioyning to the scholes;
> Nothing they can, yet nought will they learne nor see,
> Therfore shall they guide this our ship of fooles.

and:

Of the ende of worldly honour and power and
of Folys that trust therein:

On erth was neuer degre so excellent
Nor man so myghty: in ryches nor science
But at the ende all hath ben gone and spent
Agaynst the same no man can make defence
Deth all thynge drawyth, ferefull is his presence,
It is last ende of euery thynge mundayne
Thus mannys fortune of cours is vncertayne

and:

Of disordred and vngoodly maners.

Drawe nere ye folys of lewde condicion
Of yll behauoure gest and countenaunce
Your proude lokys, disdayne and derysyon
Expresseth your inwarde folysshe ignoraunce
Nowe wyll I touche your mad mysgoueraunce
Whiche hast to foly, And folysshe company
Treylynge your Baybll in sygne of your foly

This was followed by an uncompleted personal message:

Neil,
Since your education was sadly lacking, let me explain that the
Baybll above refers to the Tower of Babel and the confusion of
tongues. The mad misgovernance of our ship is—

Beside it on the desk was a rare, clothbound copy of *The Enigma of
the Quasar* by Dr. Strachan McKie. Written on a slip of paper sticking
out of the flyleaf was the following:

For Neil, if he can be caught in a good mood.

I gathered up the book and the *Ship of Fools* notes and returned
posthaste to the clinic, only to find that visitors were no longer permitted, since Stron was being prepped for surgery. I stood waiting at
the front desk, hoping for news, and there Dariush and Xue joined
me. Pia arrived a few minutes later.

"It's usually not advisable to go straight from a heart attack to bypass surgery", she said with a worried look. "It means his cardiac arteries are so blocked that another, fatal, attack is imminent if he doesn't have the surgery."

"Have you seen the readings on his condition?" I asked.

"No. He's not my patient, so I doubt I'll have access to his records."

Xue said, "Why don't we find a quiet place to wait together?"

Pia begged off, since she had to return to duty. Dariush said he would like to spend the coming hours in his own room. I, by contrast, felt the need for company. Xue and I went to the Asian restaurant, but neither of us could eat anything. We made attempts at conversation and in the end gave up.

Day 2507:

Stron died during surgery. After Xue brought the news to my room this morning, I wanted only to be alone. Later, I went down to Stron's room to see if there was anything there that should be handed over to Paul. But the room had already been cleaned out. By whom? And why so swiftly?

I feel too heart-sick to write.

Day 2508:

Today a grand memorial service to honor Stron, held in the main auditorium on Concourse A. I felt haunted by the events of another night when I had been in that room, remembering Stron's flinty handling of the situation. Now, the hall was again full of people. The speeches were stirring, especially one given by the newly appointed head of the on-planet astronomy team, a man who had been a student of Stron's in Edinburgh. The Captain's remarks were brief and moving. He referred to the death as our "first loss". I think most people indeed felt it as loss. Executives of DSI were present but kept themselves on the sidelines, refraining from any attempt to regurgitate pre-digested pablum. If they had tried, I doubt it would have been greeted with anything other than unease or indifference, since it is well known what Stron thought of the department. Even so, life will go on as usual. Though Stron will be missed, the primary concern of the "community" is the expedition—and this will remain so.

I felt his absence keenly during the service. I felt the absence of something else, but I couldn't put my finger on it. Dariush sat beside me with his eyes closed throughout the entire humanitarian ritual. I wondered if he had drifted off, but then he turned to me at the end of the eulogies, just as the recorded bagpipe music began to skirl, and said, "Each soul is a *logos*."

"What's a *logos*?" I asked.

"It is Greek. It means 'word'."

There was no more time to speak because the crowd of mourners was standing now, the coffin being trolleyed toward the exit by members of the astronomy team. We fell in behind, and accompanied it toward the elevator that would take it down to the holds. Stron's remains would be kept in a freezer compartment until the burial on AC-A-7. In the contracts we all signed back on Earth, there's a discreet little section that gives us a choice of where we want to be buried in the unlikely event of our personal demise: "burial" in space, or burial on the destination planet, or one's remains kept in deep-freeze until return to Earth and internment there. Stron apparently chose AC-A-7.

When the doors closed over the coffin, I stood with head bowed, in silence.

Dariush, standing beside me, said quietly, "Stron is not lost to us, Neil. Each person is a unique word, and this is a true word if it embodies its proper role in the celestial language."

But I was in no mood for one of his philology digressions. I turned away from him and returned to my room where I could grieve in private.

Day 2600:

Can it be so many months since I made my previous entry in this journal?

I have turned over my entire manuscript to Paul. Pia urged me to do so, arguing that I remain vulnerable to searches and discrediting. She says that someday a book—the true history of the voyage—will be written. Paul tells me he will guard my accounts with his life. With his life? I think he means it. It's a wonder that men such as this still exist.

Once a month I am required to submit to blood and urine tests. Pia deals with this by adding the correct amount of trace medication to the samples, enough to convince "them" that I am obedient and ill. From time to time, I act erratically in public. A delicate balance is needed here. If, some day in the future, I am called upon to testify about what went wrong on the voyage, I don't want to leave evidence that I was completely insane. Addled and erratic, yes, but I was ever thus!

Recently, I was in a panorama room that I presumed was in the forward section of the ship because the image on the screen displayed the three stars of Alpha Centauri. I spent a half hour strolling to the other end of the ship, interested in what our view to the rear now looked like. Our own home sun, doubtless, would appear as a bright star. Arriving at the rear panorama room, I went in and stopped abruptly when I saw that here too the image displayed our destination. The sudden realization that I could not tell which end of the ship was fore and which was aft left me disoriented. I felt momentarily dizzy, physically nauseated. I returned to my room by carefully following signs. How was it possible that after nearly eight years of living on this vessel I had failed to know the front and back of it? A careful checking of the Manual diagrams showed me where my room was in relationship to Alpha Centauri. I remembered that my quarters were on the port side, and thus the true destination lay to the left whenever I stepped out of my room, and Earth was to my right.

Day 2614:

I spend a lot of time in my room. I sleep, I read. I go out each day for my constitutional walk around the concourses. I walk my imaginary dog in the park. I listen to Mozart. Occasionally I swim. I can write very little.

Every week or so, I wander into one or another of the panorama rooms for a quick glimpse of our destination, feeling some residual nausea whenever I do so.

No sign of DSI staff for months, though I know their watching eyes and listening ears are upon me. Paul asks from time to time, as does Pia, if I have anything new I want them to store away for safe-keeping. I tell them there is nothing new. And this is true.

Dariush and I continue our studies of Kashmiri. It is a welcome diversion. We have more-or-less fluent dialogues in that language, though I doubt if any of them amount to an exchange of celestial *logos*.

No significant events to record, though some dialogues are worth remembering.

Day 2637:

After my tests in Pia's clinic this morning, she wrote one of her cryptic messages on a scrap of paper, arranging an assignation:

Doctor's orders—Rembrandt, 2100, C U there.

This was Pia-wit, I discovered on a scouting trip. In an alcove on deck C, I found a (probably) facsimile painting of Rembrandt van Rijn's *The Anatomy Lesson of Dr Nicolaes Tulp*, painted nearly five hundred years ago. I returned in the evening, and, sure enough, there she was, gravely analyzing the interior of the poor victim's dissected arm.

"Uh, why here, Pia?" I asked, making her jump at the sound of my voice. "Calm, girl, calm. It's me."

"I'm calm", she said, still jittery. "You just startled me, that's all."

"Sorry about that. What's up?"

"I have a few things to tell you. First, you'll be glad to know that the tests are now no more than routine. During the past month, I've delayed submitting my weekly reports in order to see what happens. No one has sent an inquiry. I submit them three or four days late and don't get any feedback. I think it means they're no longer worried about you making trouble. You'll still have to take the medication, but I think you can relax a little."

"Oh, that's good."

"Are you feeling okay?"

"Feeling real sad, actually."

"Well, so am I. The other thing I have to tell you is that the autopsy report on Dr. McKie has been circulated to all medical teams. That's routine as well. It seems pretty clear he had an old-fashioned heart attack, and died during the bypass. Considering his general condition, there's nothing suspicious in this. Without the surgery, he probably would have died within days."

"I see."

"At least we can drop our alert dials down from maximum to moderate."

"Maybe."

"Are you still swimming every night?"

"Nope."

"I think you should get back to it. Will you do that?"

"Yup."

"Don't do it for me, Neil. Do it for yourself."

"You're a real pretty lady. That's reason enough."

She regarded me with a distinctly cool expression and firmed her lips. "A real pretty lady, am I? Let me tell you something, Neil, something you should stick into your prodigious brain and keep there."

"Fire away", I said.

"The very beautiful people and the very unattractive people experience the same suffering. And do you know what that is?"

"Nope."

"No one sees me."

"Huh?"

"My point is, try to hear what I'm saying *as your physician*."

Chastened, I nodded.

"And while we're at it, maybe you should do some thinking about your acts."

"My acts?"

"Your masks, Neil. You've got all those accents, for example. One day you're erudite, and the next you speak only in slang. Are you a rational scientist or a lonesome cowboy?"

"I'm both", I said with a laugh. "Yeah—both."

"I see. Well then, are you a humanitarian or do you despise mankind?"

"Both."

She gave me a look and turned away, preparing to make her exit. We mumbled good night. I dragged myself back to my room, wondering what she was so intense about. What if I'd called her a real ugly lady? What the heck *should* I call her? Is she reacting against men? Against the way men see first the external appearance and then get to know the inner person? Did she have a tiff with Paul?

In retrospect, I see that my self-pity—the self-pity of the unlovely—was the ugliest thing about me at that moment. I gave myself a mental rebuke and decided to resume regular swimming.

Day 2638:

Paul was in the pool last night. I accomplished a few laps toward the latter end of his hundred, and we exchanged eye contact in passing. Later, at the edge of the pool, he inaugurated our discussion in loud mode: "Dr. Hoyos, is good you swim. Stay strong. Healthy."

"I've been getting lax", I replied. "Time to take hold and build the body up."

"You tired?"

"Yes, very tired. Sometimes I forget about swimming. I forget a lot of things."

He winked, and we lowered our voices to continue.

"You have new papers for me, Neil?"

"Nothing, Paul. I saw Pia earlier today. She gave me a lecture."

"She is good in this. She give me lectures too."

"She's very important to you, isn't she?"

"Very", he nodded. Then, after a pause, "She is life to me."

"I can see you care a lot about each other. She told me you plan to be married some day."

"Yes, is possible. She want, I want. But ..."

"But it's illegal."

He nodded.

"What are you going to do?"

"We will see. I have plan."

"Will the Captain marry you?"

"No. It is against rule. Another plan."

"You're a clever fellow, Paul, but I can't imagine what plan you'll bring off."

"You come to our wedding? Please?"

"I'll be there in my best suit."

"Good. We tell you when."

"What do you talk about, you and Pia? The language barrier can't make it very easy for courtship."

"Court ... ship? Ah, for speak loving, you mean? We talk many things together. Many. With love, you have big language."

"I suppose that's true."

We conversed loudly after that, in order to prop up the cover. Then I did another two laps. He completed six in the same period of time, a human dynamo, a paragon of manhood.

When we resumed our conversation, he said, "She tell me interesting stories of Orissa, her India home. I tell her my family story in St. Petersburg."

"St. Petersburg. Where is that?"

"Is old name for Petersburg in Russia. They say no more *saint*."

"Illegal?"

"Yes, illegal to write and print. But we speak it in heart. I tell her Russian fairy story too. She like it."

"Paul, forgive me for asking, but have you read my written journal, now that you have it all?"

"No, I do not read it. If you give permission, then I read."

"You have my permission. You're a good man."

"Me, I am not so good. But I hope I be more good."

I wasn't sure what he meant by this. A reference to morality, his character, his past? I took a deep look into those candid eyes, and saw many mysteries swimming there—a long and complicated Russian history behind them. He looked back at me in much the same fashion, though what he saw I do not know. He said only, "In fairy story, is always love and courage—and treasure. I am guard your journal as treasure."

"Thank you, Paul. It seems to me you are already the man you hope to become."

This silenced him. He seemed lost in his own thoughts for a while, until finally he looked up and said, "There are two kind of guardian of the treasure of others. There is honest steward. And there is dragon."

I absorbed this, wondering at first if he was telling me he wasn't as reliable as I thought, and as Pia thought. Then I realized that if he were unreliable, it was unlikely he would tell me so. Perhaps he was merely laying bare the natural suspicion I might have, in order to reassure me that he is not a dragon.

"Dragons hate water", I said, which made him laugh.

We did a few more laps (me, two; him, ten). As we toweled off, preparing to make our ways home for the night, he again seemed to be brooding on something. At our parting in the hallway, outside the pool door, we shook hands, and he said in a quiet voice, "My ancestor was Prince Felix Yusupov. You know him, Neil? No? Search his name in library. This man's blood is in my blood."

Day 2641:

The name wasn't in my *max*. However, the master computer informed me that the man was the assassin of Rasputin. The single line of data about the prince was embedded in a turgid, articulate rant against the oppressiveness of Christian theocratic monarchies.

After our weekly Kashmiri session, Dariush and I went to the Mexican food café and ate tacos with beer. In our new common language, I asked him if he thought that love was always rooted in carnal desire.

He looked shocked by the question, and later I realized that he was shocked that I seemed uncertain of the obvious—rather, what was obvious to him.

"Absolutely not", he said.

"You seem very sure."

"I am. It is not theory; it is fact."

"But how can one know the motivations of the heart?"

"By trial, by time, by the measure of sacrifice a person is willing to make for the good of the beloved."

"That's true in romance. Many a lover will sacrifice a lot in order to win his prize."

"Yes, but is the lover willing to continue to sacrifice when the prize is no longer desirable, no longer beautiful to his eyes and other senses?"

"It depends on the lover, I guess."

"Neil, think of the most beautiful woman you can remember, the most beautiful you have ever met in your life. Possibly even such a beautiful woman on board this ship. This beauty moves us deeply, not just in the senses, does it not? Why is this, do you think?"

"I don't know", I shrugged. "I suppose it helps with the preservation of the species."

"That is facile, my friend. Terribly facile. When beauty shocks us—I do not mean merely *attracts* us—what does it reveal?"

"Probably that we like it a lot?" I said in an attempt to lighten him up—to no avail, of course.

"Shocking beauty, animated with goodness, the emanation of personality as it should be, brings us to a state of reverent wonder, because it is a glimpse of the beauty of the eternal."

"The eternal", I murmured dubiously.

"And by the same token, if you subtract the visual beauty from the human form, the eternal beauty yet remains, because the source of this beauty is Being."

"I don't know what you mean, Dariush."

"But you are a *man!*" he exclaimed, throwing up his arms. "You are a *human being!* All human beings should know this!"

"Should, but don't. Let me ask you, does what you say hold true when the external form *and* the personality are shockingly degraded?"

"Yes, but then the eyes must look more deeply—with the eyes of the heart."

"The eyes of the heart", I muttered, thinking to myself that Dariush definitely did not do well on beer.

My mind blurring from the combination of abstractions and alcohol, I stood and made excuses, pleading fatigue. I returned to my room and lay down on my bed for a troubled sleep.

Day 2645:

Today, after downing the placebo, I said to Pia, "Do these things make a person extra hungry?"

"Is your appetite increasing?" she asked in her professional tone, cool and loud.

"I have an insatiable craving to *munch.*"

"That may be due to the increased exercise. You're swimming every day now, you say."

"Yup."

"That's good. Continue the regimen as you have been doing. Your cholesterol level is a bit higher than it should be, and we need to work on that. You don't swim alone, do you?"

This was for surveillance consumption. Through Paul, she knew very well about my every meeting with him.

"Sometimes I swim alone."

"That's not advisable, not at your age, and certainly not with the medications you're taking."

"There's usually a few people doing laps. One or two of the flight crew shows up. Nice guys."

"Well, good, but please don't be reckless, Dr. Hoyos."

"All right, I promise."

"What time of day do you usually swim?"

"I go in the middle of the night, when the pool isn't crowded."

"Try going somewhat earlier, say about 2100 hours." She shook her head in dry amusement, "An insatiable craving to *munch*, you say?"

"Yup."

Promptly at 2100 hours we met in the temple of the *Scream*.

"What's on your mind?" she asked.

"Just feeling nosey. Paul told me he has a plan for you two to be married. It worries me."

"Worries you?"

"I had a careful read-through of the Manual, and also the copies of the contracts we all signed before departure. Both sources say there will be no cohabitation on the voyage, no marriages, and no conceiving children. That eliminates rather a lot of human activities, wouldn't you say?"

"Indeed it does. However, from the perspective offered by light-speed and infinity, I think we can overlook a few fine points in the law."

"The administrators of the law might not take such a blithe approach to someone breaking their little regulations."

"I know they wouldn't." She paused and with a huff she added an Indian word (Hindi, I think) that she refused to translate for me.

"I take it that's a pejorative or expletive?"

"It wasn't a superlative, you can be sure."

"Well, Pia, I've noticed that young people, and even the older ones, tend to fall in love despite the little regulations. I presume they've all been exercising heroic restraint during the past eight years."

"If only that were true. If only you could see what I see in the clinic, you'd be appalled. Every other clinic deals with the same thing, every day. And the volume of contraceptives dispensed through the pharmacy machines is astonishing."

"I knew there were fertile people on the ship, but aren't they a small minority? Didn't the contract stipulate that there would be double pay for anyone who was previously sterilized, or accepted sterilization before the voyage?"

"Yes. And the great majority are indeed receiving double pay."

"That's a very stupid policy in terms of the gene pool. I mean, why cut off the genetic continuation of the most intelligent people on the planet?"

"Not to worry, Neil, not to worry. Part of the contract, don't you remember, was the depositing of sperm and eggs in the gene bank before the surgery."

"Oh, yes, I forgot. Why did you say *appalled*?"

She blushed, and her tone of ironic disapproval turned to one of sadness. "Because it's so blind about what life really means. Because we have a ship full of people engaging in sexual intercourse at a frantic, I would say, addictive, pace."

"I assumed there was some activity. But I've seen no evidence of frantic."

She laughed humorlessly. "I wonder why? In any event, most people on board pursue their pleasures desperately, furtively, and serially."

"Hey, Pia, I thought sex was good for us. As in healthy, as in natural."

"Yes," she nodded, "in the right context."

"Context? What context?"

She gave this a moment's consideration then went on with her own line of thought: "There are no moral sanctions anymore, so why are the majority of the sexually active on anti-depressants, and why are so many of the fertile minority on contraceptives and anti-depressants?"

"I don't know why they're depressed, but the furtiveness is just a need for privacy, don't you think? And to avoid angry scenes with jilted lovers, no doubt."

"But why the desperation and instability of sexual relationships? It has all the symptoms of a pathology."

"That's what the old moralists said."

"Yes, and it may be that those old moralists got a few things right."

Pia had used some antiquated terms, and it sounded like her disapproval was more than scientific.

"There is absolutely no life coming from it", she went on. "And very little love, I would say."

"That's no different from the way things are back on Earth."

"Yes", she nodded. "And what a happy planet we are."

"You sound harsh today. This isn't like you."

"Isn't it? Maybe I'm just getting tired of it all—the way everyone treats the pathological as normal. The way people treat their bodies and their hearts like pleasure machines. I'm tired of what this is doing to human nature in the long run. Tired of having to pick up the pieces."

"What pieces? Do you mean there are still sexual diseases?"

"Oh, no, certainly not. Everyone's clean as a whistle now. You know that. We beat the consequences ages ago. There's only one remaining sexual disease we haven't been able to conquer, and never will."

"Which one is that?"

"A child", she said with a ferocity that was unbecoming of her. "A child in the womb."

"Surely that doesn't happen on the *Kosmos*."

"Oh, yes, it happens. It's rare, but it happens."

"Then what?"

"Mandatory termination of pregnancy and sterilization of the biological parents. It's all in the contracts. Didn't you read the fine print?"

I shook my head. "Pia, what about you and Paul?"

"What *about* me and Paul?"

"I mean . . ."

"I know what you mean. The answer is no. Neither of us are sterilized, and we are not sleeping together. And we won't until we're married. Weird, eh?"

"I'm sorry I asked."

She stared at me hard, as if I too were a brainwashed member of the sterile elite.

"Pia . . . I hope this won't sound, well, patronizing . . . but I just want to say that I'm proud of you. I'm proud of you both."

"Proud?" she said in a quiet voice. "Why would you be proud of us? Are you a moralist too?"

I shrugged. "Nah, I just admire resistance."

She gazed at me without speaking, weighing what I had said.

"I don't think it's a mask, Pia. I just feel . . . proud of you."

She swallowed, and her hard expression melted. Tears sprang into her eyes. "Be as patronizing as you like, Neil. It's so refreshing."

I patted her shoulder. She put her head on my chest. I hugged her, kissed the top of her head. She cried. Then we said good-bye and went off in opposite directions—furtively.

Day 2646:

I had a bizarre dream last night. In it, we had landed on AC-A-7. I was exploring a jungle filled with exotic flowers and wild animals with eight legs. I stopped by a forest stream to take a drink from it, my first sip of real water in nine years. Without warning, Don Gunn dropped out of a tree above my head. He was ten feet tall, his skin was blue, and he was naked except for a feather loincloth. Pointing a buzzing golf club at me, he growled in an impossibly deep voice, "Now, you die!" His little dog Feedo was yapping about my ankles. I backed away from them in terror.

I was preparing to take my last breath when out of the bushes sprang a giant Sonoran toad with a wide open mouth, roaring like a lion. The mouth had rows of fangs. It gobbled down Feedo and then hopped lazily away into the jungle, knocking over trees in its path. Don fell to the ground and threw a screaming fit: "Feedo, Feedo, Feedo!"

Mercifully, I woke up.

While eating my solitary breakfast, I wondered what Don and Ray-dawn and Feedo were having for their morning fare. It wasn't worth thinking about, and I glanced around the room hoping for a distraction. I spotted Maria Kempton sipping coffee at a table nearby and went over to her.

"Good morning, Maria."

"Good morrow, kind sir."

"Maria, I know this is out of the blue, but I wonder if you'd mind showing me the photos of your grandchildren again."

"Delighted", she said, reaching for a voluminous purse.

We looked at the beautiful faces for some time, and she told me stories about their interests and activities, their personal foibles, and a surprising variety of fine qualities.

Over a second cup of coffee, she said, "How strange a world it would be without children."

"That *is* our world", I answered.

"Yes, true. Or almost true. Some do get through the screening, though it's really not enough. It's enough for the survival of a depopulated race, perhaps, but not enough for human hearts."

"Well, we've got a taste of a childless world here on the ship."

"A sterile world. Strange, isn't it, Neil, the way we've got everything turned upside down? Health is dangerous; fruitless is good."

"Yup."

"Tell me, if you had ever married, what would you have given your children?"

"You use the plural, Maria. There's volumes of meaning in your word-choice."

"You're a rebel, sir—that I can see very well. So, what would you have given?"

"Horizons."

"What kind of horizons?"

"The desert, for starters. I would have taken them out into the wild open spaces and showed them sunrises and sunsets. I would have tried to give them what I had when I was a boy."

"Tell me, what was it exactly?"

"Some dangers, some adventures, the sight of distant mountains, a glimpse of the wildlife scurrying in the bushes, the smell of mesquite wood burning in a campfire. I would have liked to tell them wonderful stories. Most of all, I'd have given them a sense of the great solitude of the universe—and its beauty."

"Did you live with your biological parents?"

"Yes, I did. We were poor enough and overlooked enough that I made it through the screen without being taken away."

"I'm glad. I was fortunate too. Sometimes when I look at these pictures of my sweeties, I can hardly believe how good we have it. Thank heavens, we Aussies resisted for so long."

"It amazes me that you delayed it that long."

"We're tough when we have to be. The land teaches us that. But city people get soft and dependent. Century by century, our people, like the rest of the world, became more and more lethargic. We didn't have to struggle any more against hunger, weather, the uncertainties of life in the outback. And then we forgot how to do it. So when resistance was needed, we didn't know where to find it within ourselves. You're an independent sort, aren't you, Neil?"

"I try to be."

"It can give you horizons." She paused and a thoughtful look crossed her face. "It has its hazards too."

"What kind of hazards?"

"A person can be too alone."

"Seems to me, Maria, that solitude is one of the great resources of life, and an endangered one at that."

She nodded. "Yes, there's so little silence. But I think that a person can be in reaction to all that's mad about our world and go too far in the opposite direction."

"Become a crazy hermit, you mean?"

"The rugged individualist can be very sane and still lose his way. He can forget he's part of a community; he might even wash his hands of it. And if that happens, he becomes just another kind of victim."

I smiled understandingly, though I wasn't quite sure what she meant. My cabin in the mountains was the great love of my life. My lack of visitors was bliss. Cacti and squirrels were reliable; human beings were not.

"So what's the desert for you, Maria? I know you're dreaming of retiring in one when we get home."

"The desert for me? It's the same as it is for you, Neil. A place of horizons, where one can think for oneself. I want to make a place where my family could live—where we all could live together on the edge of the infinite. And if we can't do that, I want it to be a place where they can visit from time to time."

"And eat your rabbit stew."

She smiled.

"Do you ever visit the desert in a DEC?" I asked.

She gave the question some thought before answering. "I used to. After a while, I didn't like what it was doing to me."

"I know what you mean. I tried it once, and that was enough." I laughed. "Fantasy—especially *very* convincing fantasy—is unreality. And unreality can really screw you up."

Her eyes pooled with tears, and for a moment she seemed to forget I was there. She stared down at the photos, shuffling and reshuffling them in different order. Finally, with trembling hands, she put them back into her purse.

Day 2647:

I went swimming at my usual hour, the middle of the night. I had completed a dozen of my geriatric laps by the time Paul arrived. He pretended to ignore me, dove from the high diving board, and completed twenty of his own stupendous laps before he stopped for a break and swam to the side of the pool where I sat with my legs dangling in the water.

"Hello, Dr. Hoyos. Is good swim?"

"A good swim, Lieutenant Commander Yusupov."

Pia told me his rank some time ago. In the flight crew hierarchy, he is two ranks below the Captain, one of six lieutenant commanders, the heads of flight divisions. He is head of Navigation.

"You are catch breath?" he asked.

I nodded and patted my towel.

In a low voice, he said, "More?"

"More. In it, you'll read about a conversation I had with Pia a couple of days ago."

"She tell me. We have supper at Euro restaurant on A. No Russia food there. But French is good."

"I want to say personally to you what I told her, and what I recorded in my journal. I want to tell you that I am very proud of you."

He was standing chest-deep in the water with his arms folded on the tiles. He cocked his head and gazed at me, his expression grave and attentive.

"Thank you for it", he said quietly.

The remainder of the swim went as usual. When we were preparing to leave the pool, he murmured, "It is good Pia have you. You are like *papa* for her."

I digested this silently and returned to my room.

Day 2648:

Where on earth did I get that paternal feeling? Absorbed by osmosis from my *Papacito*? Probably. I have to say, though, that it wasn't anything like mimicry of external patterns of behavior. It was just suddenly there.

I found a sheet of paper slipped under my door this morning.

Sorry for my moods. Thank you for your patience. I am angry at the world, and I hope none of it rubbed off on you. Thank you for being a good friend. My parents were killed during a riot in our city of Cuttack, Orissa, many years ago. My brothers and sisters were confiscated by the State. I have never been able to trace them. I escaped to Mumbai and entered university there.

Death rules us. Our world has become death's realm, death's sovereignty, and this has been accomplished in the name of life, progress, humanity. I thought I could escape the dark cloud of my memories by coming on this voyage. But now I see that we take the world with us wherever we go. I know also that we must resist it. Is it possible? I think it is—no, I hope it is. Each soul is a world, a universe, really. Thus, our ship carries all that is worst about our race and—I hope—all that is best.

About the pregnancy terminations, let us call it by its true name. In case you wonder if I am involved—no, I am not. I have never done such things. It is handled by another clinic, on Concourse D. The bodies of children are "recycled". Do you understand? Death infects everything on board. We are prisoners.

A holy man, Fr. Ibrahim, once told me that a slave, if he lives for virtue and if he keeps alive within himself all that is good, is a free man. But a man who serves evil, even if he be lord over all our sad Earth, is a slave. The evil man does not know he is evil. He thinks he is free, while all the while he is the slave of numerous masters, for he is ruled by many lies and vices.

We are prisoners, Neil. This ship is a prison. But we are free. Do not forget this.

(It was unsigned.)

Day 2657:

After our study session this evening, I told Dariush about Pia's letter. He surprised me by saying that she had informed him some time ago about the same things.

"They call taking a child's life 'recycling'", he said with a look of profound sadness. "Nothing is wasted. Except human lives. Except the annihilation of the concept of the soul."

Without voicing it, I asked myself, *Do I believe in the existence of the soul?*

As if he had heard my thoughts, Dariush said, "In our civilization's psychological *ecology*, as one might call it, not a single person has eternal value; everyone and anyone is ultimately disposable. And yet one becomes accustomed to this most severe disorder because it is *normality*. This has a cost."

"What cost?" I asked.

"For those who suffer disposal, the cost is their very lives. For those of us who survive, there is a creeping indifference to anything other than one's own survival, which results in increased selfishness, hardness of heart, denial—which in the long range will bring about the devaluation of self. To counter this devaluation, therefore, one flees into pride of accomplishment. Isn't what we *do* the defining measure of selfhood in our society?"

"Is it? I can't agree. Not everyone thinks that way."

"Not everyone, this is true, Neil. Yet very few see further than their own public honors."

"Pia lost her parents and siblings", I said. "Did you know that?"

"Yes", he nodded. "I know."

"It may have prejudiced her view of humanity."

"It may have opened her eyes. I, too, have lost family. My brother and my two sisters were illegals. I was the eldest, and thus I was a legal child."

With sorrowing, quiet eyes, he observed my reaction.

I stood abruptly.

"Were you an only child, Neil?"

The pain that surged up from within was nearly unbearable. I had not felt anything like it for years. Choking, I said good night and left him.

Day 2664:

There has been too much focus on dark issues. I can solve nothing in our situation. Nor can I change the past.

To counteract the magnetism of negativity, I have spent several days going through my old papers that occasioned the two Nobels. My work was a major contribution to progress. *This* is what I gave to mankind.

Day 2702:

Xue and I celebrated our Nobel anniversary by blowing hundreds of *Uni* credits in the Asian restaurant. Somewhere in the middle of the meal I looked at the protein nuggets in sauce, and without warning, phantom images of the hidden "recycling" flashed through my mind.

Old memories too. I don't need to remember everything. It was so long ago, and I can't change what happened.

I killed the pain by inebriating myself with rice wine, and as a result made a grand fool of myself, loudly declaring to everyone in the restaurant that we needed more kangaroo meat in our diet. Angry for no reason, I smashed a glass to the floor. Then I mouthed off to Xue, telling him that Asiatics should try being less inscrutable some time. I was awful. I deserved a kick in my bad leg. Xue tenderly took charge of me and led me by the arm back to my room.

This is not without beneficial side effects, since it adds to the cumulative appearance of my supposed degeneration.

Day 2703:

The morning after my shameful display, I went to Xue's room and apologized to him for my behavior and especially for my comments the night before.

"Ah, dear Neil, you were merely being scrutable", he replied with a smile. Then he presented me with a Shui-mo drawing on pale green rice paper, with little ferns trapped in the fibers. Ink-brushed on it is an elegant swirl, an incomplete circle (or sphere) in mauve ink bleeding into silver, the latter achieved with a combination of white and gray. Three tiny stars dance around the rim of the circle. There are Chinese characters at the bottom of the page in red ink, his pictograph name, and the title. He calls it "Diagram of the Universe".

As a belated NP anniversary gift, I gave him my leather-bound facsimile edition of Edwin Hubble's notebooks, which includes his stunning black–and–white photographs of spiral galaxies, the images which had first demonstrated that galaxies are composed of stars, are "island universes" rushing away from our galaxy at unthinkable speeds.

I also gave him my paperback copy of *The Enigma of the Quasar*, which I had brought on the voyage before knowing that its author would be along for the ride. I had often reread passages in it, appreciating the amalgamation of pure science and philosophy. Indeed, within that old scientist there was a bard.

I had toyed with the possibility of giving Xue the clothbound copy that Stron had bequeathed to me, but in the end I couldn't bring myself to part with it.

Day 2705:

Today I received an official letter delivered by hand to my door, co-signed by the directors of DM and DSI, informing me that my continuing "instability" has caused the authorities to review the "advisability" of me being part of any on-planet exploration teams. They leave me a small loophole. If there is "significant improvement" in my "behavior", my status will be reviewed, and permission to land on AC-A-7 may be granted to me.

   Uh-huh. Just so I don't forget them, they give me a little warning now and then, a jerk on my chain.

Day 2748:

Life continues: I swim, I read, I haunt the hallways, I chat with Paul and Pia in our customary modes, but there is little to add to what has already been said.

   Dariush and I continue our studies. I wonder if there is any word in the Kashmiri vocabulary that he doesn't know. He is obsessed with mastering accents. As for myself, I have now memorized more than three thousand words, a point he reached some years ago. I am also working on perfecting my grammar.

Day 2922:

Eight years down, the final year begins. Nothing changes in ship routine.

   I have been rereading my old notes on anti-matter enhancement combined with fusion power. Also a few articles about Nihman's early work on anti-gravity.

   Anti-matter has been inactive for years. We sail through the cosmos at constant speed because there is no resistance. No thrust is needed.

Day 3135:

Today, we began deceleration. Five months to go (an imprecise measurement, but mentally serviceable, since relativity will speed our clocks as the ship decelerates.)

The robot telescopes flying in formation with us had all been brought back into the holds. The two reverse engines were lowered from the body of the ship and emitted micro-seconds of burst, very small measures of released energy. So small, in fact, that the body of the ship did not really feel it. It was experienced as a faint tremor, but there was no slamming of bodies and possessions into the bulkheads. Everything inside the *Kosmos* would be instantly liquidated if full power were suddenly turned on. Our internal gravity would not be sufficient to resist the g-force.

The bursts will steadily increase in minute quantities and frequency throughout the remaining months, until we are in proximity to the outermost ring of AC-A's planetary orbits. There, the engines will cease their counterthrust of the forward trajectory, which by then will have slowed to about 0.025% of lightspeed. The rear engines will be activated and continue to push us forward at a moderate speed as we navigate through the solar system.

Day 3164:

This morning, I received another letter from the powers that be. They have now concluded, "after a comprehensive review" of my medical condition, that I cannot be permitted to take part in the exploration teams. I have permission to live my daily routine on board the ship, as long as I continue to submit to "proper medical supervision".

So, there it is. This is bad news. Very bad. Nevertheless, I am surprised by my lack of outrage. Xue, Pia, and Paul are outraged for me. Dariush expresses his empathy in less vocal form. They promise to organize a protest among their fellows. Without doubt, their attempt will come to nothing.

I wonder why I have sacrificed nineteen years of my life (if I should live that long), only to come to this.

Despite all that has happened during the voyage, there are moments when I feel the first flickers of excitement over our impending arrival at our destination—so long anticipated. I will not be able to land on the new planet, but it is some compensation to know that I will be able to behold it near at hand. The on-ground cameras, we are told, will transmit a continuous series of images to the public screens, and there will also be special programs on the findings of the various scientific teams. It is with mixed feelings that I realize I will see what Stron and David cannot see.

We are close. At this range, the onboard telescope images reveal a planet that is apparently pristine.

The Planet

Old men ought to be explorers
Here or there does not matter
We must be still and still moving
Into another intensity
For a further union, a deeper communion
Through the dark cold and the empty desolation,
The wave cry, the wind cry, the vast waters
Of the petrel and the porpoise. In my end is my beginning.

—T. S. Eliot, *East Coker*, in *Four Quartets*

AC-A-7, Day 1:

The ship rests. The *Kosmos* will remain at 4,300 kilometers above the mean sea level, positioned over the equator and orbiting the entire sphere once every three hours. (The following day/time references in this journal are shipboard measure, not AC-A-7 days/hours.)

I am sure that no one has slept much. We are all somewhat breathless, gazing for timeless hours at the huge panorama screens.

I am enraptured by the planet's immensity, most of all by its beauty. It resembles Earth in many ways. The long-distance analyses of atmosphere, land and sea formations, the presence of organic life are now confirmed as more or less correct.

It is so beautiful, so beautiful, like a newborn child.

Day 2:

This morning, the shuttle holds were unsealed, and the four ship-to-earth vessels descended, each bearing dozens of satellites that will be positioned in geo-stationary orbits around the planet so that communications with the ship will have no blind spots. These were released as scheduled and are now doing their work.

Day 3:

After returning to the ship, the shuttles were loaded with smaller robot craft for scanning the planet. Again, they descended. Once the shuttles approached the upper layer of the stratosphere, they released the robots to follow their own planned trajectories. Any lower than that and the fringe of the planet's atmosphere would create drag, slowing the vessels and causing their orbits to decay. During the coming month, each will perform a particular task among a host of operational surveys, which includes atmosphere, sea temperature, land-surface temperature, cloud systems, wind patterns, interim above-ground geological and biological analysis. They will also map the entire planet. It is estimated that three to four weeks will be needed for completion of the robots' surveys. Until then, there will be no giant steps for mankind.

The shuttles have just returned to the *Kosmos*, hovering beneath us like a pod of whales—soon to reenter the womb.

Day 4:

The social events in honor of our arrival are incessant. Today is officially Green Day (GD), which according to the daily DSI update newsletter is for the celebration of "interplanetary bio-consciousness". I had forgotten how much I loathed those enforced global rituals back on our home planet. Here, they are being dragged out of the psychological holds, dusted off, and pushed to the forefront with fervent sociospeak. I will not ensludge this journal by describing the slogans and graphics on the banners which have appeared in every public space. The hoopla also attempts to invade our personal rooms through the *max*, whenever one is foolish enough to power it up. Today, we are encouraged to wear green articles of clothing, if we own any. Green scarves and neckties are being handed out by staff. Hundreds of people wear them with playful smiles and a mood of jolly fellowship, as if we are all suddenly Irish, all members of an esoteric clan. There may be real Irish people on board, but if so, I have not yet met them.

I own nothing green. I do have a red bandana from my sagebrush years. I wear it around my neck, celebrating my own private IBD (Innocent Blood Day). I do not promote it vocally since I am hardly a respectable ambassador of my theme, though I am prepared to explain it, if anyone asks. No one has.

I shouldn't be so negative. I am enthusiastic about the coming explorations. Though I will not be permitted to participate directly, I will be able to observe everything on the big screens, as well as follow the special programs, the daily updates in every scientific field. The latter have already commenced, and I watch them via my *max*. Though I hate the thing with a passion, it can be useful. The robot reports and the first nightly summations are fascinating. This is one magnificent planet!

In the fore and aft panorama rooms on all four concourses, the screens display the planet revolving on its axis in real time. People are now always present in each of these eight enormous halls, often dozens of people, occasionally a hundred or more when AC-A rises over the arc of the planet.

Padded benches with comfortable backs have unfolded from the floors, capable of seating hundreds of people at once. I wander from one panorama chamber to another and always find someone sitting there in a trance, just looking, drinking it all in—*breathing* it in. I do likewise, hour after hour.

It is a strange feeling to look at the "real" and experience it as actual, as sensorial, when in fact it is a 3D image. I am never—never—looking out a window onto a solid object. I cannot explain why, but today I felt caged. After nine years of living within the normality of our environment, I suddenly saw in a flash that it is extremely abnormal. I don't even know what I mean. Maybe I just want to breathe fresh air, dip my head into a brook and suck water, get my bare feet muddy, yell and hear my voice echo against a mountain. My old stabs of panic returned. I squashed them pretty fast. I gave myself a rational reprimand, and the radical fear and the aftershocks of anguish gradually receded.

If at some point in the future, dear self, old Neil, you reread this journal in your cabin in the Santa Fe mountains, try to understand that these emotions were acute. As they occurred, I did not experience them as irrational.

Day 5:

After breakfast, there came through every mode of social communication a grand announcement: A name is to be bestowed upon AC-A-7 at sunrise tomorrow. Like smashing a bottle on the bow of an ocean liner at its first launching, baptizing it with champagne.

I wonder what "they" will call it.

I had supper with my co-conspirators in the Asian restaurant. We enjoyed our chop suey and shrimp, then sat back over our rice wine to speculate.

Xue suggested Chinese names, *Meilì de xingqiú* ("Beautiful Planet") or *Meilì de zhenzhu* ("Beautiful Pearl").

I offered the Spanish version, *Planeta Hermoso*, but even as it left my lips it sounded dull.

Dariush contributed two provisional names, the first in modern Greek: *Éna Panémorfo* ("The Beautiful One"). His second was in unpronounceable Farsi, which he translated as "Paradise Child". Very nice, poetic, but we kept hemming and hawing, not yet satisfied.

Pagnol had listened without saying anything, half a mind away from the table conversation. He sat bolt upright and exclaimed: "*O Astre Splendide!*"

"Isn't *astra* the Latin for 'star'?" I asked.

"*Oui, oui*, it is. In the French, however, it means, simply, an orb."

"Hmmm", Xue frowned, "'Splendid Orb'. Expressive, but I feel it lacks something."

At that point, Paul Yusupov happened to walk by our table. I hesitated to catch his attention, fearing that our company might compromise him, but I was curious enough to detain him for a moment.

"Excuse me, Lieutenant Commander, can we ask your opinion about something?"

"Certainly, Dr. Hoyos. It is pleasant to see you. How is your swimming skill these days? Do you still go to pool now we are here in our destination?"

"I've been quite neglectful, I regret to say. Speaking of our destination, we've been discussing a name for AC-A-7. Do you have any suggestions?"

"Many", he shrugged. "I have decided on one. You will understand that this has no significance for the decision that will be made. I correct myself: I mean to say the decision that *has* been made by authorities, and they will tell us when the sun rises."

"Indeed. But what would you call it, if you had the authority?"

"Me, I would call it *Krasivyi Sad*, which is to say, 'The Beautiful Garden'."

"I like this", declared Xue. "More textured than mine, warmer than a pearl yet retaining the concept of beauty."

"A friend of mine has nice one too", Paul replied. "She is doctor, smart person. She say, we should call it *Sundara graha*. Is Hindi language for 'Beautiful Planet'. Now, excuse me, gentlemens. I must go. Thank you. Good bye to you all."

He put two fingers to the temple of his forehead and left us.

I said, "I guess you guys have noticed a certain word that keeps popping up in the languages we've used so far."

"*Oui*", nodded Pagnol. "Clearly this is the result of a first impression that has struck us all—the planet's extraordinary beauty."

"An innocent world", mused Dariush.

"Let us hope so", I said.

Day 6:

The blighters! They have delayed the announcement of AC–A–7's name until tomorrow at sunrise, Day 7. Is this due to scientific considerations or biblical implications? On the seventh day, the Department of Social Infrastructure, having created the world, rested?

Day 7:

The planet's official name is *Mundus Novus*, "New World". Why didn't they just drop the mask and call it *Novus Ordo Seclorum*, "New Order of the Ages"? Or the variant, "New Secular Order". I mean, that is what we now are as a race. It has a long tradition, since even poor old America exalted the phrase for centuries before it became the Earth's slogan.

Day 8:

Mundus Novus strikes me as too *mundane*, too obvious an appellation. Is there no imagination in DSI, or whoever is above the department in the authority structure of mankind? I have no doubt that the name was decided upon more than nine years ago. They saved it for us as a surprise, and now we are supposed to jump up and down and squeal with birthday glee, popping balloons and blowing party trumpets. That is, when we are not breathless with reverence over having named an entire planet after ourselves.

I retch.

Day 12:

How about "Novacain"? Or maybe "Supernova"? Not a correct term, astronomically speaking, but this planet is truly super. On a whim, I've decided to call it simply, *Nova*. This is merely my counterreaction to officialdom. It's also a compromise of sorts, since if there are any intelligent life forms down there, they are doubtless looking up and scratching their heads, calling *us* new.

Day 16:

The robot surveys are pouring information and imagery into the ship's computers. The science departments apparently employ competent media professionals, because every few hours there is a "special" broadcast on the panorama screens.

Today, a presentation on the seas of Nova. Disposable pods were sent down to the ocean surface and began to transmit data—notably the good news that the liquid is indeed H_2O and is approximately 8% less saline than Earth's. Mean temperature of the oceans at surface is 26°C. Unfortunately, the pods became inactive shortly after sending this initial data, either malfunctioning due to water damage or possibly gulped down as somebody's lunch.

High-altitude scans give early indications that the seas are full of life forms. Two weeks from now, the shuttles will land, carrying aircraft and other vehicles that will begin exploration at ground level. Only later in the year will oceanography teams submerge after extensive closer scanning of underwater bioforms. Before plunging their manned mini-submarines beneath the waves, they want to be sure they won't be eaten as a snack by something very, very big.

The new scans also confirm what our long-distance readings told us. The seas are deeper than Earth's, on average about two kilometers deeper, though some trenches are four to nine kilometers deeper than our deepest. Tectonic plates are apparently more stable than ours back home. Nova's sea/land ratio is significantly different from ours in terms of surface covered (more land than sea), yet the greater depth of water makes the ratio of total volume of water to land about the same as ours.

The circumference of the planet at the equator is approximately 47,300 kilometers, which is 18% greater than Earth's. Its mass is 54.8% greater, with surface gravity at 11.2% greater. Its heat emanation is slightly less than Earth's, which probably means an older or otherwise less volatile core.

Day 17:

Atmosphere programs were broadcast all day long. The air down there is eminently suitable for human respiration. There is 27% more oxygen at the surface than there is on Earth, with fewer aerosol toxins than we're accustomed to. The troposphere is 22 kilometers deep, containing 78% of the planet's oxygen and water vapor. Above the tropopause, the stratosphere is deeper than ours, from an altitude of 22 to 80 kilometers, with a mean of 41% more ozone (O_3) than Earth's. The magnetosphere, to put it simply, is magnificent! Combined, all of this will give the landing parties a sense of enhanced vitality as well as greater protection from solar and cosmic rays. Nova's surface gravity means that people who land on the planet are going to feel some weight gain. This will be hard on pudgy folk, great for skinny guys like me. At 170 Earth-pounds I would weigh 189 Nova-pounds. With Nova's superior aerobics, however, this should work out just fine. I must, must break out of my confinement.

Day 19:

The lands of Nova.

Wait! Before I begin recording information, may I remind you, old Neil of the future, that one can know an encyclopedic amount of things about a place (or a person) and not know it (him, her) at all.

So, remember this first meeting. Gaze at this orb, this three-dimensional sphere. See its immense mass slowly revolving on its axis. See it slowly circling its star. See its moons circling it. Notice its choreography in the dance of the eighteen planets.

A sphere pleases the eye, quiets the emotions, disposes every dimension of attention to contemplation. It exists. It is there, suspended in infinite space. It is majestic and dignified and very, very beautiful. Tears come to my eyes, and I do not know why.

It is a feeling of reverent awe. It is a feeling of love.

Down there on its surface, there may be hostile life forms that would end my existence with one bite. Nevertheless, this planet is splendid.

Day 20:

Low-orbit scanners are still mapping the surface, filling in the meridians. So far, the topographical, photo, and heat scans have failed to discover any evidence of intelligent indigenous life forms. There are no ruins of cities or towns. Nothing. No lights on the night side. No roads, no trails, not even a hint that any such communication systems might once have been used, then fallen into forgetfulness as a civilization declined and became extinct. There is nothing that remotely resembles Mayan or Aztec terrain reclaimed by jungle. Rather, the planet seems to be what one might call Edenic.

I bumped into Maria Kempton in the cafeteria food line, and we ate lunch together. She was as friendly as ever, and we did not touch on the topic of my conspiracy theories or my supposed madness. I presume that she considers me sufficiently sane, because she guilelessly and enthusiastically chatted about the findings the biological scans are funneling upward to the ship. Her own role will come into play when the first exploration teams land.

In summation, she told me pretty much what the special programs are telling everyone. Nova is apparently teeming with animal and vegetable life, since satellite scanners and zoom cameras show us that there are countless heat-emitting creatures down there, though we can see only the backs of herding and solitary animals, some quite large. Drop robots have been sent down to selected ground sites, and transmitted multiple images of slowly moving animals, all distant and indistinct. Only rodent-like creatures (estimated to be the size of mice) have approached the pods out of curiosity. One sniff and they wander off in other directions. It is frustrating, this lack of more detailed views, since everything in me yearns to see more and more and more, to learn all that can be learned about the absolutely *new*.

As I mentioned previously, there are four main continents and five lesser ones. All of them are covered with forests, and only near the equator are there savanna regions. Now we know for certain that there are no real deserts, only drier zones where grasslands turn brown for part of the year. Orbiting around AC-A once every 412 days (its day is 31 hours by Greenwich measure), Nova's axis is tilted. Thus, there are seasons. Equatorial seasons (rainy and dry) are not directly related to axis tilt, and have more to do with variations in precipitation according to weather patterns to the north and south.

Presently, it is the beginning of winter near the southern pole, and almost summer near the northern. Winter is mild by our standards. What there is of it can be seen in the dusting of snowfall in a narrow zone surrounding the small polar cap. This zone extends no more than a few hundred kilometers from the edge of the ice to the beginning of forest lands. It is tundra-like, though not fully arctic, and is covered with tens of thousands of lakes or ponds, crowded by shrub brush. The belt of land between the forests and the snowy regions is red, orange, and yellow, which is the result of leaf change on tundra shrubs—in other words, an autumn transition period. It is presumed that the colored lands will become green after the cold season turns back toward the warm, which it will do at the winter solstice five weeks from now.

We cannot thoroughly examine the character of the planet's forests from their canopies alone. At this point, we do know that vast regions are mainly deciduous trees: jungle, rain forest, and temperate wood-lands. Darker regions farther north and farther south are coniferous evergreens. Teams will soon be on the ground, but when you con-sider that only a few hundred scientists will have less than a year to investigate a massive planet, we will learn only a fraction of what can be learned.

Day 35:

Today, the first of the shuttles descended to the surface of Nova. This was the primary advance party, containing the small contingent of armed military, about forty men and women, as well as high-tech war ordnance, and a number of aircraft and ground vehicles.

The shuttle landed on what has been named "Continent 1", the largest of the nine continents. This land mass is enormous, if you consider that it extends from near the equator to the south pole. The distance between the poles, as the crow flies, is just under twenty-four thousand kilometers, making the continent nearly twelve thousand kilo-meters from its northernmost extremity to its southernmost point. The shuttle touched down on a mile-wide grassy plateau above a river in the forested regions, about fifty-five hundred kilometers south of the equator. Because it is technically winter in the south, this offered cooler weather.

With about six hundred other people crammed into the panorama rooms, I watched the first footstep onto the planet. The shuttle cam-eras gave us 3D images so crystal clear that I felt that I was right down there with the landing party. The man who first put his foot onto the soil of Nova was the Captain of the *Kosmos*. Pre-readings of atmo-sphere at ground level (sampled for both oxygen and bio content) indicated an air that is totally healthy for humans to breathe. Nevertheless, everyone kept their masks and suits on, in order not to bring our infections to this environment. The Captain was immediately followed by Skinner, the head of DSI, and then to my distaste, the Trillionaire, who was carried down the ramp by two soldiers. Fortunately, his little dog Feedo had not been brought along. Behind him, to my added distaste, came an energetic male figure in a mask, whom the media announcer identified as the nephew of the President of the World Federation—the rude spoiled brat whom I had encountered in a library years ago. He was carrying a camera and clicking it nonstop in every direction. Within seconds, a swarm of military guys buzzed down the ramp behind the dignitaries and made a perimeter around them, automatic weapons bristling outward in defense. As sensible as this may have been, it soon looked fairly pathetic—even paranoid.

The terrain underfoot was knee high in grass. In the distance, across the river to the east of the landing site, dense forest swept gradually upward to an escarpment of mountains stretching from north to south, looking pretty much like our Himalayas. Behind the shuttle, about a mile distant, another forest began at the edges of our open space and spread westward into infinity. The sky was cloudless, azure blue with bands of pink and lime green close to the horizon—presumably, a haze of denser air thickened by moisture.

The earthlings walked en masse away from the shuttle toward a low rise, where they intended to plant Earth's flag and a rod containing a homing beacon. There was a gasp from us all when some kind of flying creatures burst out of the deep grass and took wing, flying swiftly away over the river. They were no more than a blur: larger than robins and purple colored. We could see them clearly enough to know they were indeed birds and not airborne malevolent reptiles (as imagination tends to visualize the unknown).

Up on the *Kosmos*, we could hear what sounded like birdsongs. There was a variety of unfamiliar calls, with plentiful musical notes, some discordant, but the whole blending into a wondrous symphony. The soldiers at the head of the group startled another group of birds, which scuttled away through the grass and stopped nearby to regard the newcomers. They resembled pheasant, though their heads were peacock blue and their tail feathers bright orange, trailing three or four feet behind them. They uttered low chip-chip-chip cries, but did not seem unduly alarmed by the invasion.

The flag and beacon were planted in the ground, and then followed brief speeches (predictable wording, I need not record it here). The flag rippled in a light breeze, displaying the image of planet Earth on a sea of cobalt blue, surrounded by the word *Unitas* in major languages.

After the speeches were concluded, and memorable media sound-bite comments had been made by the Captain and Skinner for the historical record, we listened to random radio banter. There was a discussion between the head of the military group and a subordinate, who asked for permission to remove masks. Skinner gave the order, and three of the forty military men did so (brave self-sacrificers). They laid their weapons on the ground and inhaled deeply, grinned, threw their arms into the air, and began dancing around. They, like everyone else, had been cooped up for nine years, and now their jubilation was unrestrained. They strode about the area, laughing for no reason, shouting too. One of them ran to the embankment of the river and looked down on the surface of the water, which was about a hundred feet below. He ran back to the group, calling jokes to his companions about going fishing. Presently, a few more men tore off their masks and began running about like children. The elders and dignitaries chuckled, observing the antics for a time, and when it seemed certain that no negative effects were to be had from Nova's air, everyone removed their masks. The precaution against infecting the planet with Earth's microbes seemed to be tossed to the winds. It is evident, therefore, that this thoughtful consideration of an alien environment was never anything other than a token gesture.

Voices called out, "The air's so sweet!", "Pure air!", "Feel the wind!", and similar ejaculations. The grass was full of wildflowers in all the colors, none of them species that we know on Earth. For example, there is a long-leafed plant with a cluster of beads crowned by pink petals, which gives off a perfume so strong that men just knelt down and inhaled it with intense pleasure (again with no adverse effects). Interestingly, there is a kind of bee that swarms the flowers, as large as a bumble bee, uniformly golden, carrying pods loaded with pollen. When some were captured on Don's fluorescent orange baseball cap, where they had congregated in the hope of a new kind of nectar, they buzzed like our home bees, but were found to be without stingers.

Bio-scans revealed no living thing in the immediate environs, other than the birds and a variety of insects. None of the latter bothered the

239

landing party, though there were several lazy inspections by a four-winged butterfly of some kind, bright red and as large as a human hand. There was also a species of something that resembles a dragon-fly, with a foot-long tubular body, iridescent green with eight whir-ring wings. Despite the warmth of the day (22°C), there were no stinging/blood-sucking parasitical insects.

In the absence of perceivable threats, the landing party wandered at random, entirely caught up in the uniqueness of the moment and the sheer joy of entering nature once again, or should I say, a new and undiscovered nature. Close to the river, there were low thickets droop-ing with white berries that resembled grapes. Tempting as it was, no one tried to eat them, since strictest orders prohibited this.

The Trillionaire and his custodians sat on camp chairs by the shut-tle's ramp, Don smiling and smiling, his eyes shaded by sunglasses, chattering at his caregivers, who nodded incessantly but had little oppor-tunity to reply. The Nephew, scion of privilege, his unmasked face now revealed as somewhat aged since I'd last seen it, wandered off by himself, pointing his camera this way and that. Skinner kept close to the flag, where he was the subject of a few more media interviews. The Captain was busy back and forth with the military, and he also rambled farther into the grasslands, accompanied by KC staff. I was pleased to see Paul Yusupov with him.

We watched the panorama screens for hours, envying the people on the ground, yearning to be with them, wondering when our turn would come.

Later in the day, a great deal of gear and several aircraft and ground vehicles were offloaded from the other shuttles that had now landed. The AECs (air exploration crafts) have jet and hover capabilities, and are large enough for two pilots, two scientists, and a collection cham-ber. The LECs (land exploration crafts) are the same shape and size, and are propelled by treads. From my vantage point, it looked like there were about a dozen of each. When the machines had been parked in rows, the military guys began to pitch their enviro tents, in which they would have their temporary quarters, remaining on ground until the engineering team sets up more permanent accommodations dur-ing the coming days.

As Alpha Centauri-A began to set, and her two sister stars shone more brightly in the northern sky, the departure time arrived. Those who had to return to the *Kosmos* did so with obvious reluctance.

Day 42:

We've been watching numerous presentations on the establishment of the base camp—dubbed "Base-main". All four large shuttles are constantly ferrying supplies down from the *Kosmos*, unloading their holds, building mountains of materials.

The soldiers' enthusiasm for Nova seems unabated, though they have imported many distractions to fill their idle hours. They are not permitted to venture beyond the immediate compound until full-spectrum security has been completed and the exploration missions begin. Today, I watched them make a volleyball court, and enjoyed their subsequent play.

Day 43:

This afternoon, soldiers played baseball with the mountain massif as a backdrop, the game occasionally disrupted by flights of purple birds crossing the screen. Pure bliss, that sound of the ball clonking on the bat, nine innings, with some great home runs. However, it had a musical soundtrack of sorts. Sitting on a packing crate beside the diamond, a solitary man made his electric guitar rant and roll, an old hit from a Roadkill album that I listened to endlessly when I was in college. I must be getting old because today I found it nerve-wracking. Mercifully, the A/V people lowered the volume for the captive audience upstairs in the sky.

Day 53:

Nova is not as innocent as we had supposed. Of course, everyone knew that nature would be cruel wherever organic life exists, though I think there is a secret longing for Eden in every heart. The stingerless bee and the lack of carnivorous mammals in the immediate region had raised hopes. Could it be true? Could there really be a place in the universe where violent death does not reign?

During the past week, AEC scanners and LEC zoologists have come upon dozens of species of quadrupeds that exhibit little or no alarm/escape behavior—which means they are accustomed to nothing

241

threatening them. For example, everywhere there are herds of deer-like creatures, which are a little larger than North American deer, mauve colored at the head, the hue sliding into magenta at the rump. The males have bony antler buds; none have yet been found with full racks. Then there is an animal that resembles the South American tapir, chocolate brown with horizontal black stripes. There are also beaver-like rodents, their hides in shades of yellow and twice as large as our beaver. They build dams in the swamps and creeks feeding the river. Unlike ours, they do not build protective lodges; instead, they make open nests on the banks of waterways. With all such creatures, there is a pattern of calm avoidance, a not-get-in-your-way attitude combined with mild curiosity, but apparently no fear. They are uniformly herbivores.

There is an albino, long-haired mammal, a combination of bear and giant sloth, that lives in the foothills of the mountains. After one was anaesthetized by dart gun, the zoologists discovered that its claws are useless for tearing meat, though sufficiently hard to grip tree trunks when it climbs to the forest canopy to chew on leaves and berries. Its teeth are ideally suited for grinding the tough leaves of an aromatic deciduous tree that resembles the eucalyptus. The leaves are arm-length, smelling of lavender rather than menthol. This tree does not produce hard seed-casings but rather a translucent green pod the size of an apple covered with fibrous gel—something like a gooseberry.

The trees of the nearby forests stretch upward hundreds of feet, with few lower branches. The forest floor is covered with ferns that are green or blue or turquoise during the daylight hours, turning pink in the dusk.

The low bushes covered with white "grapes" that were spotted by the river on the first day have been analyzed as high in fructose. The lab rabbits and monkeys on the *Kosmos* devour them eagerly with no ill effects. It was announced that a biologist ate one as an experiment and pronounced it delicious, tasting like lemon combined with mango. The black-market people, no doubt, will soon be harvesting it to make their moonshine.

Along the river shore, there dwells a "duck-billed platypus" of sorts that defies categorizing, very shy, about the size of a hamster, at home on land and water. Apparently, its diet is minnows and miniature frogs (yup, some small-scale killing does happen). As far as classic amphibians go, there is a shell-less turtle and a myriad of larger frog species.

The latter are all flamboyantly colored, but unlike similar frogs in the rain forests of our planet, none of those so far examined have poison glands. They are cacophonous night-singers, deafening, but musically so. They have webbed feet like our home frogs but retain their tadpole tails into adulthood; their eyes are iridescent orbs which can rotate in all directions, doubtless adapted for night vision. They eat insects. None of the aforementioned creatures display fright or flight behavior, nor any aggression toward humans.

I have wandered a bit far from my point. The sad fact is that there is at least one dangerous species on the planet. During the second week of construction of the base camp, two soldiers stripped down to khaki shorts and went strolling barefoot alongside the river. Without warning, a snake darted out of a shadowed overhang of the riverbank and sank its fangs into one man's ankle. The other beat the creature off with a stick, and it darted away into a hole in the sand. The victim fell to the ground and became delirious within a minute or so. His comrade carried him back to the base, and the medical team worked as fast as they could to inject antidotes brought from Earth, but to no avail. Without regaining consciousness, the man died of intracranial brain hemorrhage a few hours after the incident, despite every effort to revive him.

The surviving soldier described the snake to the authorities as less than a meter long, very fast, and aggressive. Searching through computer photos of Earth's snakes, he identified it as similar to the saw-scaled viper common to the Middle East. Analysis of the victim's blood confirmed that the venom is chemically very close to that of Earth's *Echis coloratus*. The venom of this species is extremely toxic, doubly so in the female of the species.

The public announcement has sobered everyone—I think not so much because of the death of a fellow human being but because our myth has died.

Day 61:

The base camp is completed, a square kilometer of human habitation within a bio-detection perimeter fence, high-wire mesh, low-charge electricity, and surveillance cameras. The "deer" bumble into it from time to time, and then go leaping away into the grass to nurse their sore spots, not seriously harmed. More common is the skiff of dead rodents found each morning, killed by the fence, mouse-like creatures with tawny fur and large black eyes. Alive, they are easy to capture, again displaying no fear, only a mild disquietude if they are picked up in the hand. They feed on the wild grains of the grassland. A burrow discovered in the grass by the main camp gate revealed a female and twelve nursing offspring.

The imaginative among us humans have conjectured that these creatures are the indigenous intelligent beings of the planet, since they have thoughtful inquisitive expressions, like that of a ponderous old man looking up from a weighty book, gazing at the inexplicable behavior of unruly children. In fact, they do not learn from their mistakes, and while they refrain from biting us if we pick them up in the hand, neither do they attempt any form of communication known to man. They make barely audible clicking noises when alive (from the throat, not by gnashing of teeth). They are "cute". They die in droves.

Though the carnage is probably regretted by most of us, I doubt that anyone grieves over the snakes that have been zapped by the wire. No more than ten corpses have been found, two species, including the one that closely resembles the saw-scaled viper and another that looks like the gray *malpolon* of the Middle East. The zoologists inform us that they are both virulently poisonous, and thus anyone who goes beyond the perimeter should exercise caution.

The fence now surrounds a compound of twenty prefabricated fiberglass residences that look like giant tubular pills, connected by utilidors to a central kitchen and dining, washing and recreation facility, the whole resembling a spoked wheel. There are also twenty laboratory buildings connected to the outer rim of the wheel. The major scientific teams are busily at work, gradually expanding their areas of research deeper into the continent. Certain staff will rotate back to the *Kosmos* monthly, allowing others to pursue studies in numerous sub-fields of each discipline. Botany, zoology, biology, and geology have pride of place. Next come the physics and chemistry people. There is a lot of grumbling in the *Kosmos* cafeterias, because all the scientists want to spend the entire year down there, not caged up in our superb orbiting prison, reading incoming data. Nevertheless, the authorities are adamant that all research must be done according to the planning originally worked out more than nine years ago.

Though he is not a grumbler by nature, Dariush laments with a forlorn air that no indigenous civilization has yet been discovered, not even a trace. The philologists and archaeologists are commiserating with each other, trying to keep themselves distracted by focusing on the marvels that the natural sciences are discovering.

Every day, dozens of missions head off into the hinterland and return with copious samples of flora and fauna, which are given preliminary analysis in the base labs, then ferried upward to the ship for further studies and storage. The information is continuous, torrential, often astounding. Everything is new, and yet we are examining only a small fraction of biological life.

For example:

There is a four-legged mammal, similar to the flying squirrel, with wide weblike skin flanges which when extended become "wings", allowing this creature to soar from tree to tree, often hundreds of feet at a time. It eats fruit and builds spherical twig nests suspended from branches, in which it raises its young. Its calls are like that of a song bird, but when captured (a very easy thing to do, since it also forages for nuts fallen on the forest floor), it sits in the palm of the hand, gazing at its captor with interest. It will fall asleep on one's shoulder.

On the other side of the mountain range, southeast of our base, there are large fresh-water lakes, hundreds of miles in circumference and very deep. The fish in them are abundant, their species completely, well, *fishlike*, living on insects and whatever they find to eat beneath the waves. One species resembling the lake trout is the size of a tuna. A salmon-like fish is twelve feet long, and tastes just as good, according to reports by the official tasters. All pre-dinner and post-dinner analysis confirmed that it was quite healthy for human ingestion. There are no exact matches with Earth fish, but so close are they in form and function that the marine biologists and ecologists have named a few, such as the *Salmo novus*.

A zoologist has returned to base with vid images of a mammal dwelling in the warmer regions farther north. About thirty feet long from hoofs to ears, it resembles a giraffe, with four stiltlike legs and an elongated neck, though its head is proportionately larger than a giraffe's. Like the latter, it grazes on the upper branches of deciduous saplings. Its hide is cream-colored fur with gray vertical neck flashes. It travels in "family" groups, male, female, and three or four off-spring of varying heights, and these are in close proximity to other families, forming what one might call tribes, which in turn are part of more populous nomadic groupings of their species that move slowly and peacefully across the landscape. This is the largest land mammal found to date.

Other images display a magnificent horselike creature that ranges across the savanna grasslands. Though its head bears some resemblance to that of the oryx antelope, its body is equestrian, about one and a half times larger than our horse. Its hide is cream-colored fur with a wide red-brown collar and breast. It enjoys breaking into a headlong gallop occasionally, prompted, I would guess, more by playfulness or an excess of energy than by fear, for the zoologists wander freely on foot among herds of the creatures without disturbing their grazing habits.

Apparently, the shallow coastal waters are full of "whales". The low-orbit robots inform us that the seas are heavily populated with these and similar creatures. According to the scanners, they give off heat and thus are warm-blooded. They are uniformly white. Marine biologists conjecture that they are calving at this season, and may usually, throughout most of their lives, live in the deeper waters of the oceans. Manned oceanography teams begin their research next month when the shuttles will offload mini-subs on the north coast.

Day 65:

Due to the loss of one staff member to snake bite, all teams must now wear fang-proof protective apparel and carry venom antidote with them whenever they venture beyond the compound. I wish them good luck, because antidotes are not infallible.

The unfortunate soldier was buried at a specially designated cemetery site on the rise of ground at the edge of the compound, beside the flag. He was given full military honors, recorded music, a stirring speech by the Captain, and suitably mournful words by Skinner. Marking the grave is an aluminum obelisk, surmounted by a blue orb on which is inscribed the soldier's name.

Stron was interred the following day, with the same honors. I was not permitted to attend physically, despite the fact that he was a close friend. The entire astronomy team was shuttled down for it, as well as numerous other star performers. I watched the ceremony on my *max*.

I shut the thing off when Skinner began to recite his artificially grieving and genuinely self-serving eulogy.

To console myself, I opened Stron's book on quasars, the copy he'd
left to me before he died. Since his death, I haven't had the heart to
open it. To my surprise, I found a personalized inscription penned in
the flyleaf:

> To Neil, fellow voyageur,
>
> Whoever looks deeply into the cosmos, and continues to look,
> cannot rest content with what he observes through the tele-
> scope. If he persists with courage and honesty, he will ask him-
> self about the meaning and end to which the whole of creation
> is oriented. Once one veil is removed and our gaze penetrates
> deeper into "space", we are faced with intellectual challenges
> and metaphysical ones.
>
> Time is not omnipotent. Time is not our god. The Grand
> Theorists of *Stultifera Navis* assert that, given enough time, any-
> thing is possible—anything! In a world lousy with epistemolo-
> gists, no one thinks to ask how we *know* that time is endless.
>
> Call me a throwback, if you wish.
> Fraternally,
> Strachan McKie

"Stron, Stron", I murmured to myself, closing the book. "Where
are you now?"

Day 70:

Metaphysical? Time is not our god? What's that supposed to mean?
His message to me reveals an aspect of the man that I hadn't
expected, despite the fact that in his preface to his book on quasars
he refers to "intelligent design" and the "theory of evolution", both
of which are still politically charged expressions. Even so, in the
main text, he never reveals where he stands on the matter. I find it
difficult to believe that Stron was a "Creationist". He was quirky
enough to enjoy playing around the fringes of the Flat Earth Society,
just for fun, just for its shock value. I think he may have been telling
me to look further and deeper than (he presumes) I usually look.

247

Judgmental right to the end, he was. Still, it's hard to dismiss the questions posed by a genius.

There is so much to be learned from the seemingly limitless forms of life we have found that it would be easy to overlook the implications of context, that is, the universal patterns. First of all, there *is* life here. Why life? Why not just a periodic table of elements, as is the case with most of the planets discovered by man? Unmanned probes to the other seventeen planets of AC-A have sent back images that demonstrate there is no teeming life on any of them. However, on the two planets closest to Nova (AC-A-6, one step nearer to the sun, and AC-A-8, one step farther from it), landing modules obtained dust and rock samples that contained primitive "nuclei-bearing eukaryotes", which Maria Kempton tells me are a form of life. Atmospheres on the seventeen are inhospitable to higher forms of life.

Second, it is phenomenal that Nova has produced organic life with ranks identical to Earth's—kingdom, phylum, class, genus, species, etc. As on Earth, there is an astonishing diversity of specific living organisms, yet they are all within distinct categories, either plants, fish, reptiles, birds, mammals, fungi, or bacteria. Without exception, the properties common to them are their carbon- and water-based cellular composition, with complex organization and inheritable genetic codes.

I say *phenomenal*, as in a phenomenon according to the strict meaning of this term. Yet it is undeniable that behind each and every dimension of phenomena there is order, coded or otherwise. Stron seems to consider (at least as a possibility) a universal or meta-universal Designer using a common "language". I prefer to stretch myself further, to comprehend a necessity entirely based in atomic determination. Totally outside my field, of course, but I can speculate.

Day 75:

The soldier guys have set up a basketball court. First, they mowed the entire compound, then they worked for days grading a level spot into a regulation court, sprayed it with fast-set syntho concrete, set up poles with basket hoops, and without further delay threw themselves into the game. Some of the younger science guys have joined in. I've been watching hours of the stuff, wishing I could be down there.

Day 76:

A mini golf course has been made. A mini electric golf cart whirrs around it. A mini Trillionaire putters away on it.

Ay caramba!

Day 85:

More exotic creatures on the big screen:

Hundreds of butterfly species have been captured and categorized, though there must be many more kinds, since several new ones are found each day. Some are very tiny and luminescent at night, like fireflies, though they display a range of colors, not just our home planet's pale green neon. Some flash off and on, others are constant. Generally, the majority of butterfly species are two to three times larger than Earth's common ones, such as the monarch. Others, though few by comparison, are three and more feet from wing tip to wing tip. One bizarre species has a tiny head and beak that looks disturbingly like a hummingbird's—though it is without doubt a kind of insect. Its head is ruby red, its wings magenta with black edges.

Very common is a bird like a turkey in appearance and habits. It has a call that's different from ours (raucous as a crow's), and it can fly short distances on its huge wings. Earthlings are slaughtering them in great numbers, and for the first time ever, we are served real meat in the cafeterias. I am told it is quite tasty, though not quite like turkey or chicken; more the flavor of a free-range ostrich that's been too greedy in a cabbage patch. Easy to kill, they gaze at you calmly as you walk up to them while they're pecking in the grasslands, gorging seeds even as they are hit over the head with a stick; they look momentarily surprised then drop dead without a quarrel.

There is a benign lizard north of here in the warmer zones, as large as a komodo dragon, slow moving, with five-fingered "hands" and opposable thumbs. It climbs trees at snail pace and eats mainly the antlike insects that swarm the branches. It also has chameleon characteristics. Put any color beside it, and suddenly its skin looks as if someone threw a bucket of garish paint over it. Zoologists have tried using artificial color swatches designed by the computers, and to these the chameleon skin swiftly adapts (though a bit slower than its

249

instantaneous response to colors native to its surroundings). It matches the artificial colors exactly within a few seconds, hues that we haven't yet found on this planet. What on earth is happening at the cellular level, or molecular level, is anyone's guess. The labs are busy night and day on this one. Some vivisection experiments are underway, I hear. Not very "green" behavior, if you ask me. However, the pursuit of knowledge tends to sweep aside the objections, since knowledge is ever the deity to which sentiment must pay obeisance.

There have been some outraged cafeteria discussions, which I picked up from nearby tables. I overheard one lab person telling a friend that the "chameleon" screams like a human baby when it is subjected to the scalpel—even under anesthetic.

The "giraffes" continue to fascinate the zoologists, since they have a more complex social organization than other mammals we have so far found. One team isolated a very young one on the edge of a "tribal" group, intending to sedate it and bring it back to the base camp. When the dart brought it down, it emitted a single alarmed squeak. Without warning, the thirty or forty larger animals broke into a gallop and came to the rescue, surrounding the afflicted one. They did not attack the scientists, who had backed off, some at a run. Instead, the animals commenced a rapid high-step pounding of the earth all around the victim, flattening the grass, chopping it into fibers, as if seeking to destroy invisible predators with their hooves. One scientist suggests that this is behavioral adaptation as protection against snakes. Needless to say, the team beat a hasty retreat, leaving the young one asleep. Its two parents stood over it trumpeting from their long necks, a sound we hadn't heard until now, very different from their usual low-pitched bovine noises. Even as the AEC got airborne, the team saw dozens more of the creatures converging from all directions.

Day 86:

A knock at my door late in the evening. There in the hallway stood a man, looking at me with a mixture of worry and uncertainty.

"Can I come in?" he mumbled, showing me the sheet of paper that my fellows and I had distributed a couple years ago.

"Let's go for a walk", I said. We headed toward the nearest staircase, went down to Concourse C, and along it until we found an art alcove.

It was one I hadn't visited before. Or maybe the exhibit had been changed. I don't pay much attention to that sort of thing. A quick glance at the "art" within convinced me that this was an excellent place to talk, since it was a hologram sound-and-light display by someone unavoidably famous named "Artanarchist" who had lived in the early twenty-first century. It was noisy and distracting, but good cover.

"Do you remember me?" my visitor began.

"Sorry, I don't."

"Remember the day you were handing these out at the maintenance elevators? I told you that I recognized the picture as Dave Ayne's. At the time, I believed he'd been transferred to Propulsion."

"Oh, yes, I remember you now."

"At first, I thought it was a case of bureaucratic mix-up."

"Bureaucratic mix-up? But they said your friend didn't exist—never had existed."

"I know, but I felt it must've been a case of misspelled names—you know, some kind of dumb clerical thing. I figured DSI'd solve the problem. I didn't waste any more time on it. Figured I'd bump into Dave at the fish'n'chips place one of these days, so I just put it out of my mind."

"After all, the accuser was out of *his* mind, right?"

"Uh, right. I'm not so sure now. I'm kind of certain you aren't crazy, doctor, and I have this feeling that something not good has happened."

"Any proof?"

"No, but it's how long since Dave was transferred? It's gotta be at least two years now. I sorta forgot about him, and I feel bad about that. The thing is, lately it hit me that we haven't crossed paths once in all that time—not once—and we used to see each other fairly often outside of working hours, usually at the Irish pub or the Brit's fish'n'chips place. And then there's the computer files. My *max* and the main computer say he wasn't with us—ever."

"Doesn't that strike you as rather odd?"

"Yeah, it's weird. So I've been asking myself where the hell he got to. I did some checking on the quiet with the maintenance people who work in Propulsion, the cleaning people, I mean. They all say the same thing. He never showed up. They never heard of Dave, and they say no one was transferred into their department as far as anyone knows. And P and M are sealed off from each other for safety reasons.

Of course, sometimes duty rosters and personnel schedules can get messed up, and a name could slip through the cracks, so maybe he got transferred to another place on the ship. The *Kosmos* is pretty big."

"But this doesn't explain why you haven't bumped into him. Do you know where he lived?"

"His room number you mean? No, we weren't close friends, just working buddies. But then most of us are like that down in M."

"Do you know if anyone else was close to him, a girlfriend maybe?"

He shook his head. "I'm not saying he didn't have a girl, but I didn't see it. He was the kind of guy who kept to himself mostly, liked to read his book on lunch break, went straight home at the end of shift. Nice guy, but never said much. You know, the sort who doesn't get invited to parties—not that we can have much of a party in our rooms. A four-people party ain't no party."

"How did you find my private room number?"

"I followed you home one day. Saw you in the cafeteria and trailed you back here."

"Why didn't you just stop me in the hallway and talk to me?"

"I ... I don't know. Maybe I had a feeling it wouldn't be a smart move."

"Well, you're right about that."

He glanced nervously around the alcove.

"I think places like this are safe", I said. "What's your name?"

He told me (I won't write it here).

"So, what do we do?" he asked.

"I ran out of ideas a long time ago."

"Maybe he had an accident, and the authorities aren't broadcasting it because they don't want to upset people."

"I can assure you that the authorities definitely do not want to upset people."

"But I don't get why they'd erase his records. Are they hiding something?"

"Oh, yes, they're hiding something. And I think it'll stay hidden. DSI knows that most people avoid getting upset unless they feel personally endangered. All the tracks have been covered, and we have no way of finding out what really happened. My advice to you is, stay calm and look for opportunities to discuss this with people you trust. But don't tell anyone you've had a chat with me—not anyone."

He peeked out the alcove entrance and scanned the corridor. "Okay. I gotta go."

Later, I went to the library on Concourse A and browsed a few sites that listed *Kosmos* personnel. I checked some of the departments, a slow roll through hundreds of faces and names without pausing at any, and then went to the list of maintenance people. Here too I casually scrolled down the page, and when I spotted my visitor I didn't change my pace. My eyes took in the fact that his face matched the name and employment position he had told me. I kept going to the end, then switched to Medical and scrolled down it. This way, no monitors would register that I had paused over the man I had just spoken with. If he was legitimate, then no one would take a second look at him. If he was a DSI scout, then I was sunk anyway.

Day 91:

We have been here three months now. I'm weary of idleness. At times, I feel I will go insane from frustrated yearnings to experience what every other person on this barge is now experiencing, or soon will be. I suppose there is some compensation in my respiratory system. The ship's oxygen generators have been recalibrated to increase the onboard O_2 and humidity to match the planet's. This, I presume, helps relieve the adjustment discomfort of people who are back and forth between Base-main and the *Kosmos*. It's also a very welcome change for those who don't leave the ship often—or at all. I seem to have more energy these days, and generally, when I'm not feeling frustrated, my mood is showing some improvement. The shuttles are constantly descending and ascending, day and night. The base has been enlarged to twice its earlier size, double the living space. There are now forty "pods" with ten private rooms in each. At any given time, about four hundred people can be in residence there. The on-ground labs are growing in number as well. According to the media presentations, the *Kosmos* holds are continually being stocked with Nova's animal and plant life, as well as tons of mineral samples. We are told that geologists have found rich deposits of precious metals in the mountains and staggering oil reserves beneath the surface. New and exotic chemical compounds have also been discovered, and samples obtained for bringing back to Earth. Even so, a year will not be enough time to fill the holds to capacity.

At our usual study session and bistro drink this evening, I asked Dariush if he knows when he will be able to land on Nova. He sighed and told me that the archaeologists and language people now have bottom position in the scientific hierarchy, since there still is no indication of native sapient beings on the planet. However, all scientists (in fact everyone on board except me) will be able to land at some point. His week at Base-main is scheduled for next month, unless it is bumped by new discoveries that other science teams may make. When he does finally touch ground, it will be as a tourist.

He seemed patient enough about the matter, but I could tell he was low in spirits.

Day 92:

Placebo at the clinic as usual today. Pia handed me a note, and said aloud, "Here's a list of some good exercises for your leg muscles, Dr. Hoyos. Please consider doing them."

"All right", I murmured.

Back in my room, I read the sheet of paper without interest, then noticed that penciled on the margin was the following:

Wedding soon. Will you come?

Will I come? Whaaaat! I wouldn't miss it for the world—for two worlds actually.

Day 93:

I went swimming last night, hoping to see Paul. He was there with another man about his age, both of them trying to outdo each other in laps. I dabbled my toes at the edge while they thrashed up the water. Later, there was a scant minute to speak together clandestinely.

"You come our wedding?" he whispered.

"I'll be there. Just give me some warning, and I'll dress up nice. Oh, and I'll need an address and street map."

He laughed. "No need map. Somebody take you, Neil." Then, louder, "Keep taking pill, Dr. Hoyos. You will feel better. And swim more. I not see you swim too much these days."

"Yup, too tired these days. Me go sleep now."

He winked and dolphined away into deep water.

Day 105:

Today it was announced that throughout the coming week all four shuttles will be used to transport mini-subs to the shores of the seas and major oceans surrounding Continent 1, as well as materials for the building of the mission bases for marine exploration. There's a flurry of activity everywhere on board and a lot of traffic in space and across the skies of the planet.

Day 108:

Pia beamed at me while she was handing me my pill cup.

Scribbled on a scrap of paper she surreptitiously passed to me: *Press your best suit. Tomorrow. Be ready after lunch.*

I grinned at her, but when I tried to squeeze her hand, she backed off and frowned, morphing into her professional mode.

Back in my room, I flushed the note.

Day 109:

Early this morning, I had breakfast in the cafeteria and returned post-haste to my room. I showered, shaved, brushed my teeth, then dressed in my finest—black suit, white shirt, and my uttermost special bolo tie (hot purple cord, silver tips, and a bluestone toggle clasp). I pulled on my cowboy boots and sat down on the edge of the bed like a boy waiting to be taken to his first rodeo.

At 1:30 P.M., there came a knock at my door. I said, "Open", and there stood a young black man I vaguely recognized but could not place. He was wearing a flight staff uniform with wings above the three stars.

"Dr. Hoyos, can you come with me?" he said in a British accent, warmed by a hint of Africa. Of middling height, he had a dazzling smile and looked cocky enough to take on the world.

"Where do you want to take me?"

"I think you can guess."

Then I recognized him as one of the fellows who swims with Paul now and then.

Once we were both out in the hallway, he offered his hand for a shake. "I am Chukwueloka Ibani. Now we must hurry."

"Right, let's go! We wouldn't want to be late for this one."

I had to scuttle quickly along the concourse in order to keep up.

"You may call me Eloka, if you wish", he said over his shoulder. "Paul calls me Loka, and so do many others."

"You're African", I said disingenuously, since race and citizenship are rather fluid categories these days.

He shot me a benevolent grin. "Nigerian. Biafran. Igbo. Raised in London. Legally a Brit. Citizen of the World-State. A mouthful, aren't I?"

"You're a whole meal, Loka."

"I'm sorry about your leg," he apologized as we plunged down a staircase at top speed, "but we must economize on elevator trips today. We're taking the quiet route."

Arriving on level D (with my leg beginning to ache in earnest), I silently hoped that we were close to wherever the wedding would take place. No such luck. We walked for fifteen minutes to another staircase, and there we went up! On deck C, we turned left and walked along to the next stairwell, and again went down! Finally, finally, we reached what I presumed was the rear of the ship.

"Not much farther", he assured me.

Arriving at a nondescript single elevator in a side street, he punched a code into a console beside the door, and it whisked open. We stepped inside, the door closed, and we dropped to the bottom level.

On PHM, we exited into a cavernous hall that looked like the largest railroad station I'd ever seen, about eighty feet high and hundreds of feet long—so long in fact that the chamber continued on past the point where the ship's curve blocked my view. Numerous chains and motorized pulleys dangled down from above, along with a few AECs looking like model airplanes hung from a bedroom ceiling.

Over the years, I had pieced together a mental layout of this level. Maintenance was in the ship's forward section; the Holds for food and samples storage were in the midsection (by far the largest); and Propulsion was in the rear section. These were sealed off from each other, and also sealed off from this side-concourse for shuttles, which ran along the portside of the ship, beginning closer to the front and ending farther toward the back end. I supposed there would be access from here into the samples-and-specimens hold, but I couldn't see it.

Dozens of people hastened this way and that, displaying no interest in us, focusing on their tasks. There were numerous parked exploration vehicles waiting to be on-loaded, and others being lowered from the ceiling on chains. Along the outer wall were pressure-lock bays so large that a shuttle could have sidled inside through any one of them with plenty of room to spare. There was only one in port at the moment, with its loading ramp down and a crew of men trolleying mini-subs into it. I followed my guide into the shuttle, and he led me through its hold, which was crammed with materials, including half-a-dozen subs.

One of the crew informed Loka that the consignment was now completely loaded, and they saluted him farewell.

"You're a pilot", I said, when we were alone.

"A shuttle pilot", he answered. "But I double duty on the AECs from time to time. I hope you're not prone to air sickness."

"What!"

"Ready for a ride?"

"You're not serious."

"I'm never serious, but we're definitely going for a ride."

"A wedding in outer space?"

He shook his head with a grin. "A wedding on a planet."

Speechless, I let him conduct me to the portal of a sub. Ducking inside, I saw that it was a tubular, low-ceiling chamber, with a cockpit for pilot and copilot, and immediately behind it, two seats for guest scientists and an empty storage chamber for carrying collected specimens, the latter space about ten meters long and walled with inbuilt aquariums. The passenger compartment was equipped with a front windscreen and side windows like an ordinary jet craft. Loka pointed to a guest seat and asked me to strap myself in. Then he handed me an oxygen mask.

"I doubt you'll need this, since the whole shuttle's pressurized", he explained. "It's just a safety precaution in case there's a breach. I'll be flying the shuttle itself, way up front there, so you're going to be alone for the trip. Just sit back and enjoy the ride. I'll see you on the ground."

He went out the sub's portal, pressure-locking it behind him. Through the pilot's window, I watched him making his way forward through crates of gear in the shuttle's hold. He climbed a few steps into the craft's big cockpit, and the door closed behind him.

Then the shuttle's loading door was shut and pressure-locked. The hold was windowless. I couldn't see a thing. A few minutes later, I heard the massive bay doors closing, followed shortly by beeping and an intercom voice announcing depressurization of the bay. I was sealed inside the belly of a sardine, which was inside the belly of a tuna, inside the belly of a whale. Nervously, I checked my vital signs, sniffed the air inside the sub, and concluded that all was well.

Then I felt a rumble, which I presumed was the *Kosmos'* outer port doors opening. The seat beneath me begin to vibrate, and after that, the sensation of gravity gradually declined. It was the first time in my life I had experienced this, and it was both thrilling and disturbing. I began to hyperventilate, as if the loss of gravity meant the loss of oxygen, which of course it didn't. Within a minute or so, I got the hang of the thing.

During the foregoing embarkation sequence, I had been twiddling with my fountain pen as a distraction from nervousness. Now it slipped from my grasp and went spinning in a time-lapse cartwheel, then it slowed to a hover in front of my eyes. I retrieved it, clipping it securely inside my breast pocket.

In what seemed like no time at all, I felt gravity returning. My body was again a weight pressing into the seat. Then came a gradual increase in sound, a dull roaring, which I presumed was the shuttle hull meeting with Nova's upper atmosphere. It continued for some minutes, the noise and force of gravity increasing as the engines pro-pelled us down and forward in an arc of descent.

Where were we going?

As if in response to my unspoken question, I heard a disembodied voice say over the sub's communication system, "How are we doing, Dr. Hoyos?"

"Just fine, just fine", I answered.

"Good. We'll be landing in about five minutes from now. Don't undo those safety belts until I come and get you—face to face, understand?"

"Understood", I murmured.

With that, the roaring increased, and then the forward propulsion eased off, replaced by the sensation of a soft vertical descent. In less than a minute, the seat shuddered, and there was no more motion. The engines ceased, and I was left staring out the windows at nothing but packing crates.

I sat there for some minutes until the sub's portal whisked open and in stepped the pilot. He helped me unbuckle and then handed me a bright orange jumpsuit.

"Please put this on over your civvy clothing, sir. That way, you won't be so noticeable when we go outside. There's a lot of activity out there, mostly engineers and marine biologists. They're all wearing these, so you should blend in okay."

"Is this really necessary?"

"For you, it is. Mobs of people are taking off-duty joyrides these days, but you're a marked man. You're not supposed to be down here, and if you get spotted, I'm in big trouble."

Standing up demanded a little more effort than was usual with me—the weight gain—and I thought to myself that given enough time on this planet my body would adjust by growing more muscle. For the moment, I felt as I sometimes did after packing in too many carbohydrates during a holiday.

When I had finished putting on my camouflage, Loka handed me a polyplast construction hat, also bright orange. I put it on my head, and without further ado, we left the sub and proceeded to the shuttle's offload ramp. As I walked down it onto solid ground, my heart beat faster and my mouth dropped open, sucking in air. I couldn't get enough of that air—so sweet, so pure. I stopped in my tracks at the bottom of the ramp and just took in my surroundings.

The dome of the heavens soared over us, cloudless except for a few feathers of high cirrus, the horizon unbroken by hills or mountains. I heard bird calls and the faint rhythmic rush of waves striking a beach or perhaps rocks, though I could not see the ocean. The day was very warm, and I began to sweat.

The shuttle had landed in a field about a hundred yards from the mission base, which looked from a distance to be well along in construction, since half-a-dozen residence pods and lab buildings had already been erected inside a wire fence. LECs and motorized trolleys were heading toward us along a graveled road, each of them carrying several orange-clad men, the crew who would offload the shuttle. As they approached, Loka raised his hand in greeting, and there were a few jolly exchanges between him and the crew. But we did not slacken our pace as we walked toward a parking lot adjacent to the shuttle's landing pad. This was a compound where air-exploration vehicles had been lined up beside a traditional runway.

"It's going to take them a few hours to offload", said the pilot. "I have permission to do some sightseeing until they're finished."

He headed straight to the closest AEC with its distinctive jets, tail fin, and retractable wings. When we entered its portal, I found that the interior was the same as that of the sub, though its collection chamber was lined with empty cages. The pilot went forward to the cockpit and took his seat before a bank of instruments. He told me to take the copilot's seat beside him, and I gladly complied.

As I belted myself in, Loka talked into his communications system, telling the computer where he wanted to go. It was all given in degree coordinates, so I was none the wiser for this. However, I could tell from the digital map screen between us that the computer was tracing our route in an illuminated blue line even as he dictated it. We would cross the north coast and go out over the sea for some distance, then fly parallel to the shore for a while, then loop around and head due south into the heart of the continent. Flight plan completed, he pressed a button, and the engines began to hum.

Speaking into his communications again, this time to a responding human, he informed the other that he'd be away from base three or four hours and would be back before nightfall, when he would take the shuttle back up to the *Kosmos*.

"You got my flight plan?" he asked.

"Got it", came the reply. "No other traffic for 400 k's. The sky's yours."

"I may deviate a little and do some sightseeing. Haven't seen those mountains yet."

"No problem", said the voice. "But keep your eyes open. There's a lot of traffic around those ranges—geology teams and off-duty sight-seers. Switch to satellite tracking as soon as you're in the mountains. Have fun."

"I shall do."

The view through the front window rotated, and then the AEC began to roll forward to the end of the runway.

"I could have lifted us vertically before powering the jets," said Loka, "but I love the feeling of the old-fashioned take-off, don't you?"

"I've never experienced one", I replied. "But I'm willing to learn."

"Super, let's go!"

The jets hummed more intensely, and suddenly my body was flattened against the seat as the grasslands raced past. Within five seconds, the craft was airborne. Glancing out my side window, I spotted the base camp, with the huge body of the shuttle beyond it shrinking fast, then a line of beach stretching from east to west, and below us the rippled surface of the ocean. Numerous white creatures were breaking the surface and diving. I exhaled, exhilarated.

"It's a thrill", my companion said. "I never get tired of it."

Ahead on the vast expanse of the ocean there were no islands, nor could I see the mainland of another continent, though I knew there was one beyond the arc of the horizon. The ocean floor sloped downward, turning the water from turquoise to amethyst blue.

"How deep is it?" I asked.

He checked an instrument on his dashboard.

"Two hundred meters and dropping fast toward the rim of the coastal shelf. Close to the shore, it's about thirty meters deep. You can see the bottom with the naked eye, the water's that clean. Want to see the wildlife?"

He switched the map to vidscreen. Suddenly, the calm empty ocean was crowded. Sonar, radar, and other scanners were digitally integrated to give near-virtual pictures of what the unaided eye could not see. He zoomed the image, and despite our speed, I could see that beneath the surface the white "whales" were present in great numbers, traveling in groups of ten to twenty, with smaller calves cavorting around them.

"How big are the white creatures?" I asked.

"Very big. They average about forty-two meters long when mature. That's bigger than Earth's blue whale, which is the largest mammal that ever lived on our planet, bigger even than the largest dinosaurs."

"So they *are* mammals."

"Absolutely. Warm-blooded, nurse their young, travel in family groups, as you can see."

"Amazing. Have the marine people got close to any?"

"Not yet. They tried to, but the whales are pretty good at preserving their privacy. They're smart. They're very smart."

"Maybe they're intelligent."

"Oh, they're intelligent all right. But it's simple animal intelligence, same as the giraffes the zoologists found. They don't have a developed language, though they have a variety of calls. The underwater blokes have begun recording it, and they're wracking their brains to decipher the patterns. So far, there's not a broad range. They think it has to do with simple communication about food, mating, travel and social order, just like our whales."

"Do they resemble our whales?"

"Here, have a look—this was our first close-up shot, three days ago."

There appeared on the screen a series of vids taken underwater from a distance (the whole body), and it did look like a whale or perhaps a narwhal minus the tusk. Intermediate distance showed various sections of the body. A single, brief close-up of the head revealed that it had a high frontal cranium like a dolphin's, indicating massive brain size. It turned its blue eyes on the sub approaching it, then heaved away in an astounding parabola into deeper waters, disappearing in seconds.

"Apparently, they aren't hostile to us in any way," Loka said, "not even defensively so. But they are extremely shy."

Now he switched from vid to map screen and banked the AEC to the west. We flew in this direction for ten minutes, with the mainland on our left, a flat expanse with no discernible rises in the topography. Inland, there were forests, threaded by rivers draining into the sea. On the southern horizon, the atmospheric haze thickened, pale pink with a hint of low purple shadow beyond it. We were now flying at an altitude of three thousand meters, and I guessed that the shadow was the beginning of the highlands leading to the mountains, hundreds of kilometers south of us.

After crossing a narrow peninsula that jutted far out into the ocean, the pilot banked again, and we headed back toward the shore and into the continent.

The next forty minutes captured my attention totally. This was the largest of the continents, with its northern coast just below the equator and its southern coast near the pole. We crossed a variety of climate zones, ranging from coastal equatorial to subtropical to the regions of dense forest, territory that steadily rose above sea level into foothills of the mountains. There were three parallel ranges, each of them thousands of kilometers long, the central massif crested by the planet's highest peaks. Near the midway mark of our north/south trajectory, the pilot slowed the craft to less than half speed and banked into the east, dropping between two of the ranges. We flew on for a time, cruising down a wide valley and descending ever lower. Below us, I could see countless waterfalls pouring from the snowfields on the heights, the headwaters of great rivers. In the valley bottom, there were lush marshlands and copses of deciduous trees on "islands" of slightly higher ground.

When we were only a hundred meters above the treetops, the pilot flipped a switch and said, "We're invisible to radar because of the mountains."

"You turned on the satellite locater signal, right?"

"No, I think we can dispense with that."

"Oh, then the satellites will spot you visually."

"No, I just turned on masking."

"Why?"

"This way, nobody traces the flights that are meeting today and asks why we all converged in one obscure spot. It also avoids the satellite scanner pointing a zoom on the wedding. We're about to commit a crime, you realize."

"Yes, isn't it splendid!"

Without warning, he banked to the left at a terrifying angle and flew into a canyon. Now we began to climb at a steep pitch, and shortly after, we passed over a ridge, at which point, he cut the jet power, dropping us precipitously into an alpine glen. Suspended thousands of meters above sea level, it was a bowl of grass, ringed by very high white peaks. In the center, there was a lake that one might be able to throw a stone across, brilliant turquoise in color. Surrounding it was a little grove of pale green trees.

The AEC descended by hover onto a gentle slope near the edge of the woods. When we came to a halt, the pilot killed the power and decompressed. The portal whisked open, and cool, perfumed air poured in.

Leaving the craft, I saw that the ground underfoot was moss, speckled with purple and red flowers. Bees hummed all around us—stingless, I hoped. There were birds too, small warblers of various colors darting here and there.

"You can take off the monkey suit", said Loka, to which I readily complied.

"Have you been here before?" I asked him.

"A few times. Paul's been here with me, and that's why he chose it for the wedding."

"Where's the happy couple?"

"They'll be arriving soon. Let's go look at the lake."

We walked into the woods on a soft carpet of moss. There was little other undergrowth, only a few ground-hugging berry bushes. I was fascinated by the trees most of all. They were white-barked, like birch, though their leaves were spear shaped. From every branch, there hung clusters of what I took to be either an unusual arboreal flower or the tree's seeds. They looked like elongated crystals, and the effect of the whole was that of a chandelier. They were semitransparent, and as they swayed in the breeze, they created a lot of light refraction and a quiet background tinkling. I plucked a handful and shook them, listening to the little chimes within. I smiled and felt a spontaneous desire to sing, to dance. I decided to take them home and stuffed them into the outside pocket of my suit jacket. The whimsy or nostalgia passed quickly, and I walked on through the trees.

Emerging from the woods, we entered a grassy meadow at the edge of the lake. The grass was a shade of blue, and so short it looked as if it had been cropped by sheep. The basin of water was a near-perfect circle of shallow limestone, fed by rivulets that tumbled down over a series of rills in the glen, combining into a creek that cascaded over a low waterfall into the lake. It was an enchanting place, and I was very glad to be there, my first real encounter with Nova in its natural state.

Not long after, we heard a humming in the sky and saw an AEC descending vertically, close to where ours was parked. A few minutes later, Paul Yusupov came striding through the trees with a beaming face. Behind him came another young man in flight crew uniform. Greetings and back-thumpings were still being exchanged when a hum in the sky drew all eyes, and a third AEC descended beyond the treetops.

"She's here", Paul breathed, patting his breast pocket, inspecting the ring he found inside it, combing his hair with his fingers, looking suddenly nervous.

Perhaps because I had anticipated a simple contractual ceremony, possibly with the Captain present, I was surprised when Pia and three other people stepped out of the trees and processed toward us. Pia was dressed in a white sari and golden slippers, her black hair braided in loops about her head, with a long white veil pinned to the back, trailing behind her. Beside her walked Maria Kempton, and behind them came the pilot of their AEC, and finally, of all people, my friend Dariush.

For the moment, there was a great deal of joy in that hidden valley, though it was mainly wordless. The betrothed had eyes only for each other.

Dariush began to busy himself with things he had brought along, a kitbag and a folding table. First he set up the table near the edge of the lake. That done, he covered it with a white cloth, and put candlesticks, a golden cup, a big book, and other items on top. While he was rummaging in the kitbag, Pia approached me with a warm smile and wet eyes.

"Neil, I'm so happy, so happy", she began. "Thank you for coming. I . . . I want to ask a favor of you. Would you give me away?"

The term was unfamiliar to me, since I had not attended a wedding since the days of my childhood.

"I'd be honored to," I said, "but you'll have to tell me what to do."

"It's easy. You and I go back into the woods, and then when the ceremony is about to begin, you bring me to the altar on your arm and give me to Paul."

Altar? I wondered.

"Ready, Neil?"

"Ready."

So we walked back into the trees, turned around, and then she took my arm with her hand. I noticed that her eyes were shining, her hand trembling a little.

Now as we approached the group, I saw that Dariush had pulled a white robe over himself and was standing behind the table with his arms open wide to greet us.

Paul stepped forward and took Pia's arm. He shook my hand, said, "*Spasiba*, Neil", and then the betrothed turned to face the altar.

Yes, an altar. I had seen only two in my life, and one had been in ruins. The only functioning altar I had ever seen was the tailgate of Fray Ramon's truck, way back when I was a boy.

A whole lot of impressions flooded in now. My throat was choked up, and I felt my heart beating fast with an emotion that I really couldn't have defined, if I had been able to, if I had wanted to. I stepped back a few paces beside Maria, who was dabbing her eyes with a handkerchief and radiating some mysterious feminine happiness.

On Paul's side, the three pilots stepped up beside him. Suddenly, they raised their heads and began to sing. It was a full-throated, deep-voiced chant in a language that I guessed was Russian. Paul smiled throughout with surprised delight. When the song was over, he laughed and said something quietly to his best man. (I later learned that the best man was a Russian. The other pilot was a Pole. Historically, Poles have little love for Russians, but he and Loka were good friends of Paul's and had taken the trouble to learn the song in the groom's native tongue.)

"Fr. Ibrahim, we are ready", said Pia. Now Dariush further astonished me by making the sign of the cross. Everyone else but me did the same, though the two Russians did it a little differently. I strained in my memory for the way it should be done, knowing that when I was a child I had made that gesture too. But I was distracted by the sudden confounding of my assumptions about my friends. Dear to me they were—very dear—yet I now felt shaken with the realization that while I loved them I did not really know them as well as I had thought I did—Dariush most of all.

It was a Christian rite. Moreover, it was a Catholic Christian rite, a wedding Mass. Moved, perplexed, and a little stunned, I knelt and stood, and knelt again, following the others' lead, feeling ancient memories returning. The wedding ritual took place in the middle of it. During that part, the best man stood behind Pia and Paul, and held little gold crowns over their heads. They exchanged rings. Dariush blessed the couple. They held hands thereafter. I did not hear their words, for I was completely involved in the seeing and the feeling of the thing. The soft burble of the waterfall filled my ears.

Then followed the rest of the Mass, and as it progressed, I felt something else stirring inside me. It was a combination of longing, pain, regret. Regret over what I had lost, I supposed, though I could not remember exactly what I had lost or how I had lost it. Then I recalled my numerous childhood communions, the happiness I had sometimes felt after receiving that little white host on my tongue, the sensation of gentle, sweet fire slipping into my heart. How many years had it been since I had experienced that—since I had even given it a thought? Nearly sixty years.

Now my mind wandered farther away from this beautiful valley high in the mountains of an alien planet, wandered back across the infinite sea of space to a little place in a desert. I saw myself as a child, singing and dancing while reaching upward. What was that about? What had I been doing? Toward what unknown mystery had I been yearning, blind and happy in my innocence?

I was pulled back to Nova when the others knelt down to receive communion. Only Maria held back, though she too knelt and gazed thoughtfully at the host. I stood apart from them all, for I no longer belonged to that faith. I had always stood alone in human society. And I would remain so.

Finally, the groom and his attendants sang another chant as Dariush solemnly made a sign of the cross over us.

The bride and groom kissed, and we broke into applause, then rushed forward to congratulate them.

As the wedding party made its way back toward the woods, I stayed behind with Dariush and raised my eyebrows at him. He smiled sheepishly. After helping him pack up his gear, I accompanied him through the trees in the direction of the AECs.

"Fr. Ibrahim, is it?" I murmured.

"Fr. Ibrahimi, to be exact, Neil."

"And you felt no need to enlighten me all these years?"

"I did feel the need. Perhaps you recall that I was most interested in your Spanish culture. There were a number of times when I was about to tell you, but—"

"But couldn't bring yourself to drop the other shoe."

"I regret I do not understand what you mean by a shoe."

"A figure of speech. Well, I'm glad to know now."

"You are neither disturbed nor disgruntled by the revelation?"

"I'm surprised, but it doesn't put my shirt in a knot."

"A shirt and a shoe. Neil, I hope you will understand my failure of communication. These times—"

"I understand. I just wish you'd trusted me more. I was raised a Catholic, you know. I ain't one now, but some of the best people in my life were believers. I wouldn't ever blow the whistle on you."

"Whistle?"

We said no more, since we had emerged from the woods and were walking into a full-blown celebration. The bride and groom stood holding hands, smiling beatifically, gazing into each other's eyes. Maria was happily weeping, and the three male attendants were popping open a champagne bottle and distributing glasses (real glass). These disparate pilots—flax-haired Jan, ebony Loka, and swarthy Vladimir—shared a common joviality and fondness for making toasts, which they raised continuously and with increasing frivolity, until Paul called a temporary halt.

He darted back to the AEC he had arrived in and returned within seconds strapping a sword and scabbard about his waist. Clicking his heels together, he faced Pia and withdrew the sword. Standing at attention before her, he lifted it high with the hilt at the level of his heart.

"To you, my Pia," he declared solemnly, "I swear that with this sword and with my whole being I shall guard you all the days of your life. We will love each other into eternity. From our union will come forth many children, who will be our great treasure. I will guard them and lead them in all ways, with you as my companion forever."

With that, he sheathed the sword and dropped down on one knee. He took her ring hand and kissed it. Standing, he said no more, and the rest of us knew that silence was best now. These two were swimming in some fathomless sea unknown to us, and it looked like they had gone beyond all time.

Pia whispered, "*Kinyaz Pavel.*"

"*Knyaginya Pia*", he replied.

Later I was to learn that *knyaz* is the Russian word for "prince", *knyaginya* for "princess".

Maria, practical mother that she was, cleared her throat and went to one of the AECs and retrieved a picnic basket and some blankets. We all returned to the lakeside and spread the blankets on the grass, sat down, and commenced the wedding banquet.

There were more toasts, food, stories, tears, laughter. I cannot describe everything now, but for my future remembrance, let me say that this bright shining moment will remain forever as one of the finest experiences of my life.

Day 110:

Yesterday, after the celebrations, more supplies were offloaded from one of the AECs, including cooking and sleeping gear. Paul and his friends erected an alpine dome tent by the waterfall. He and Pia would spend their honeymoon in the valley, since both of them had arranged for a week's vacation from their departments. Outside of our group, no one would know where they were. As far as the authorities knew, they were two unconnected people, among many off-duty *Kosmos* staff, who were spending their free time as guests of Base-main and taking excursion flights here and there on the continent. It was a common thing to see "couples" go away alone together, as long as they reported in to the base at regular intervals. Romantic weekends were not illegal. What Paul and Pia had done was definitely illegal, and though they weren't in the least worried about it, they wanted to begin their life together in blissful solitude, without official scrutiny.

As the rest of us were preparing to depart from the valley, I raised the topic of dangerous predators. In answer, Paul unsheathed his sword and revolved it slowly over his head with a grim expression, making us all laugh. Then he patted his jacket pocket and withdrew from it a hefty old pistol that "would bring down a mastodon", he assured us. There would also be a perimeter e-fence whenever they slept. Moreover, they would have radio communication with the other Russian, who was stationed at Base-main, twelve hundred kilometers to the northwest. In an emergency, Vladimir could be here within twenty minutes.

With more blessings, final words, embraces all around, we boarded the three AECs. Maria, Dariush, and myself would be taken separately to different mission bases, and there we would catch shuttle rides back to the *Kosmos*. I donned my orange monkey suit and strapped myself into the copilot's seat beside Loka. Two hours later, I was back in my own little room, orbiting the planet.

Day 112:

I have been enjoying myself in the libraries, accessing satellite-streaming vids of every section of Nova. The resolution is very high quality, and I worry that the newlyweds will be spotted from above. I have just spent hours looking down on the mountain tops of the central range, zooming in so close that creeks draining the high snowfields were the width of my finger. Just in case there were any monitors tracking computer use, I examined closely a number of hanging valleys to the north of the one I most wanted to see. Working my way down the range, I finally found it with the help of the degree coordinates that Loka had written out for me.

There it was! Yes, the tiny circular lake, the stream cascading into it, the white foam of the waterfall, the ring of trees, the surrounding alpine meadows. I zoomed in as close as possible and noticed a big rock that I couldn't remember being there. Then I realized I was looking down on the roof of the tent—on screen it was about the size of a fingernail. A swift scan around it revealed no trace of human presence. I zoomed out and went on to the next valley, and continued like that for another hour, looking into nooks and crannies that held little interest for me but laid a false trail. Perhaps it was unnecessary, but I felt it best to be extra cautious.

Day 115:

I had supper with Dariush this evening in the Asian restaurant. We conversed entirely in Kashmiri, replaying our amazing adventure in quiet voices. There is still no word on when his language team and the archaeologists (now considered redundant) will have their courtesy week on Nova.

We did not touch on religious topics. I cannot bring myself to suddenly switch gear and call him "Fr. Ibrahim". I have known two other priests in my life, Fray Ramon when I was a child, and an unnamed man whom I met briefly with my father in sad circumstances. They both seemed to be very decent men, living heroic, if clandestine, lives. There is no antipathy in me toward Christians, though I am troubled anew, as I have not been since my youth, by the suppression of religious freedom. Why, in our very democratic home planet, is there such suppression?

Day 116:

Cloud cover over the mountain ranges—it's raining down there.

Again, supper with Dariush. Today, we ate in the Mexican food place. It wasn't crowded, since so many people are away downstairs on the planet. We both are trying to reconfirm our friendship, despite my radically changed concept of him.

We drank beer and ate "tacos" with real nova-turkey chunks in hot sauce, sprinkled with authentic green onions grown by botanists in the shockingly rich soil of a garden near Base-main. The "turkey" was my first real meat in more than a decade. My previous carnivorous act had taken place in a ravine in the Santa Fe mountains, a squirrel roasted on a spit over a bonfire (both acts illegal). Despite my fondness for eating fellow creatures, I felt guilt then and a degree of indigestion now.

I asked Dariush (in Kashmiri) how he had come to know that the other members of the wedding party were Christian.

"Nine years is a considerable length of time, Neil. One senses another's condition in the soul. Then small things are said, not dangerous words, but enough to hint that there is a kingdom within the closed gates. Do you know what I mean?"

"Uh ..."

"It is a metaphorical and a literal kingdom."

I did not reply to this, and he went on: "In time, doors open, little by little, as trust grows. Then comes speaking with words and mutual recognition of our shared *communio*, our *logos*, because we have for a long time been speaking with a language that does not rely on vocabularies."

"I see. And did you pray together during the voyage?"

"Yes, this was not very difficult for us. However, for the holy Mass it was necessary that we came together in small numbers, four at a time, changing the room each Sunday. We offered the sacrament with silence, speaking the words soundlessly with our lips and our hearts."

"Even Pia?"

"Especially Pia. Her parents were martyred because of the Faith."

I was roundly taken aback by this. She had told me they were killed, but I had presumed it had happened in a race riot of some kind. What else didn't I know?

"Maria Kempton too?"

"She is Evangelical—secretly, you understand."

"And those boys in the flight crew, the Nigerian, the Pole, and the Russian?"

"Yes, very fine young men, risking everything. If it is ever discovered ..."

"And Paul?"

"He remains Russian Orthodox, and he too is a believer in Christ."

"Are there others?"

"Yes, there are others." He paused. "I trust your good intentions, Neil. You are my friend. You would not betray us. Yet in these times, the less that is known ..."

"What I don't know can't hurt you?"

He nodded. "I may tell you this at least, that among those of our close associates who resisted the surveillance, all are approaching the Lord, searching and thinking. All are praying."

"Even Xue Ao-li? I find that hard to believe."

He smiled sympathetically at me. I shook my head in amazement, unable to say any more.

My friendship with Dariush is one of the enigmas of the voyage. In the ordinary course of events back on Earth, I wouldn't have given him a second glance—an overly serious linguistic scholar is hardly the type of person one invites to go hunting rabbits, nor with whom, in inebriated moments, one indulges in the murkier waters of dark humor. So, who is he, really? And more to the point, why am I drawn to him?

Well, I suppose it's because he is honest, sympathetic, short on ego, long on interest in other people. He is in turn an inquisitive mind equipped with an astonishing memory, a lover of the basic human things (stories, boats, Persian delicacies, poems, spicy food), a kindly observer of the diversity in human temperaments, a delighter in the surprises of ethnic cultures, and an amateur, though somewhat naïve, sleuth. There is nothing duplicitous in him. At his worst, he is tediously didactic—intrusively so, in rare moments—but I can live with that.

It's probably a good thing that I came to like the dusty old relic before I found out he's an agent of a disreputable cult. (Yup, even me ain't immune to stereotypes).

Day 117:

Sunny and clear. I resumed touring in mountain valleys via the library computer. When I came to the beautiful valley I zoomed and spotted two small forms in the water near the waterfall. Pia and Paul swimming. I smiled and moved quickly on.

Day 118:

The newlyweds are home!

Did I just write *home*?

We tossed caution to the winds and hosted a supper in the Indian restaurant for the returning lovers. Dariush and I invited Xue and

Étienne to dine with us, and they accepted. Conspicuously moping over our drinks in the restaurant, we looked pretty much like a reunion of defeated conspirators. The walls, I noticed, were decorated with brilliantly colored paintings on silk, portraits of Hindu deities for the most part. Many of the images illustrated the spurious activities of a sensual, blue-skinned god, whom Dariush explained was Krishna—their version of the supreme being.

Pia and Paul arrived ten minutes later and took a table near ours, pretending to ignore us. Maria was eating alone at a table next to them, and leaned over to chat with Pia. Not long after, the three intrepid pilots just happened to pass by and were invited to sit down with them. Innocuous banter between tables developed casually until Xue in a jocular, recordable voice invited everyone to join us. It all looked so coincidental. We pushed the tables together, rearranged seats, and commenced our celebration proper.

They had had the most splendid week of their lives. They looked supremely happy together. Their love overflowed, infecting us all. They told us many details about their time in the valley. The close-cropped grass, for example, was grazed by the "deer" that range widely over the whole continent. The mountain subspecies has a hide that's closer to white than magenta. The creatures were shy but never frightened, and Pia fed grass to some of them from her hand. They liked syntho biscuits too, but spat out protein bars after a few bites. The furry, mice-like creatures were also much in evidence, not shy, very curious. There was a water bird that came only at night and kept them awake longer than they would have wished, though they didn't mind it. Its calls were haunting, like that of our loons. There were no snakes.

One day they had climbed to the height of a lesser peak overlooking the north-south valley dividing the ranges. Below them they saw rivers and wild meadows in the thickly forested bottomland and lower flanks of the mountains. Though they knew there had never been an indigenous civilization on Nova, they enjoyed themselves imagining that there had once been farms and cities in that valley. Pia pointed out a line, or a narrow depression, that ran across the valley from the central massif to the next range. There were trees in the gap all the way, but they were less dense than in the surrounding forest.

"A natural formation", she said. "An old river bed, I think. I pretended it was an ancient road. And Paul saw castles."

"Castle in cloud", Paul laughed. "This road go into a pass through the far range. Above it on both sides I see *kremlins*."

"What do you mean?" Dariush asked, with sober attention. "Did they look like fortresses?"

"Just rocks sticking up", he shrugged.

"Did you hike down to the valley bottom?" I asked.

"No, we just look from high. Is too nice where we are."

"Could you see where the road began?"

"No, nothing. It look like maybe five, maybe eight, kilometer north of us, but I cannot see it hit our mountains."

The subject was changed, and the party continued. Maria, bless her, took a little bottle from her purse and handed it to the newlyweds.

"I saved this for your return, dears", she informed them. "It's a wine that someone—I won't say who—has made from the nova-berries that were found on the day we arrived. Everyone's gathering them and bringing loads of them up to the ship." She smiled. "Against regulations, of course. Take it home with you for your first night back on board."

"Oh, that is so kind. Thank you", said Pia, kissing Maria's cheek. We all grew quiet, and in our thoughts was the question: Home? Where would this new family find a home?

"But where will you live?" Maria asked.

"We've been working on that", Pia replied. "This is absolutely confidential, but I know I can tell you." She lowered her voice to a whisper: "Paul informed the Captain that we're married. He was delighted for us, but worried about the illegality because if DSI ever found out, we'd be in serious trouble. I couldn't just move upstairs and live with Paul in his room on KC deck. And it's ridiculous for him to come sneaking down to my room whenever he's off shift. So the Captain hatched a plot."

We all leaned forward intently.

Pia raised her voice to normal. "I've been transferred to the medical clinic on KC deck, and their resident has been transferred down to my clinic on B. You see, there's been another incident of snake bite. This time, it was a man in Navigation, a friend of Paul's who was on leave at Base-main. He went hiking in the forest near the perimeter fence. He was alone at the time, and without warning, he was struck in the ankle by one of the nova-vipers. It was a male, which can be deadly enough, though its venom is more slow-acting than the female's. He had a pocket communicator with him and called for help. While he waited, he injected himself with antidote. He was up in my clinic within the hour. They brought him to me because I'm a specialist in tropical medicine and spent a few years in Indonesia dealing with this sort of thing."

"And he survived?" asked Xue.

"He's recovering. For a while, I thought we were going to lose him. It was a close call. The DM has mapped out lectures for me to give to all medical staff. I begin the series tomorrow."

"But how does this solve the problem of your living arrangement?" Maria asked, *soto voce*.

Pia returned to a whisper. "The Captain had a meeting with the DDM and the DDSI, and argued quite forcefully that flight staff are of utmost importance, and if any of them die, it could jeopardize the return flight, which would mean we all become victims."

"Victims?" Paul grinned. "I like this planet so much, maybe we stay, yes?"

"In the interim," Pia continued with a flash of eyes at her husband, "I'll be living and working on KC deck as part of their crew."

"And we live in our own house", Paul declared, beaming.

"The situation is somewhat different on KC than on the other levels", Pia explained. "For one thing, the flight staff's personal rooms are larger, maybe 50 percent longer and wider. Also, they can be expanded by connecting two rooms, which isn't the case with the room structures on A to D. So you see, as of tonight, we'll have a very nice little apartment."

We all burst into applause.

I leaned over and kissed the bride on the forehead. "Smart lady", I whispered.

"Thanks, pardner", she shot back. "Smart husband, actually."

Paul and I shook hands.

"Well done, Paul."

"You come swimming soon, Dr. Hoyos. Thank you each for this good supper and pleasant discussions. Pia and me, now we go upstairs. Very tired. Goodbye to you all, most excellent friends."

Followed by an outbreak of grinning, back-thumping, and bear hugs. To hell with surveillance! All in all, this has been a thoroughly satisfying day.

Day 120:

A rap at my door this afternoon, interrupting my nap. There stood Dariush.

"Let us go for a walk, Neil. I am having the most interesting thoughts, based upon minor discoveries, though speculative in nature."

We ended up in an alcove on level C, beneath a painting by someone named Pietr Breugel the Elder. It was a work of hideous genius. I checked the title: *The Fall of the Rebel Angels*.

"Right up your line", I said to Dariush.

"I do not understand, Neil. Please, no idiomatic conversation today. There are new facts I have discovered, which I wish to relate to you."

"Sorry. Go ahead."

"First, I must explain that I was most intrigued by what Pia and Paul told us regarding the road and the castle."

"Dariush, I know you're disappointed there's no civilization on Nova, but I hope you haven't started seeing things that aren't there."

He held up his hand to silence me. Patiently, he continued: "I guard myself against this fault with great diligence. However, to satisfy my curiosity, I visited a library computer and accessed the vids for Nova's surface. Just as described, there is a line in the terrain—a very straight line."

"Nature can create such lines."

"Yes, this is true. Nevertheless, there are other unusual features."

"Such as?"

"The 'kremlins' Paul described are there. From the satellite, one sees what he could not have seen with his eyes. Towers of rock viewed horizontally and at an angle from another range—a line of site approximately twenty-two kilometers in length—appear to be nothing other than natural formations. Seen from above, it is revealed that each tower is hollow, with much rubble all around it and within it. These structures are above the tree line, high enough that no forest and little vegetation has encroached."

"Even so, nature is capable of making all sorts of mysterious formations. The eye interprets—"

"Yes, the eye interprets, which is always a danger in terms of accurate analysis. However, when I switched to topographical maps, I learned that the road bisects exactly the distance between the two castles or towers."

"Are you serious? Exactly?"

"To within a meter. This is mathematical precision, which indicates intelligence."

"Not necessarily, Dariush. As a physicist and mathematician, I can assure you that the universe is based upon mathematical precision, and it does not indicate intelligence."

"On this, we are disagreed."

"Yes, we are."

"There is more. The road, for example, cuts directly across the valley that separates the ranges in a line that is also mathematically precise. That is most unlike the form of any known ancient river bed."

"If so, why haven't analysts spotted it as potential evidence of intelligent life and flagged it for investigation?"

"The planet is immense, and every one of its hundreds of millions of square kilometers is rich in new discoveries. Presently, all human minds are focusing their attention on the natural and geological sciences."

"All right, but surely computer analysis would flag it."

"Possibly it has already done so. It could be years before anyone reads the flag, perhaps only on future expeditions. We would not hear of it, and as I say, human attention is now elsewhere. A computer note about a topographical anomaly is of little consequence compared to the overwhelming amount of astounding new discoveries in the other sciences."

"True, but ..."

"As far as I can tell from above, we have an inexplicable trough in the valley bottom, beginning at the base of the central mountain range, and extending at roughly a ninety-degree angle. The road's angle of trajectory crosses the valley without deviation from its course, entering the pass that cleaves the western range. At the entrance to the pass, above and equidistant to it, are the two towers."

"What's on the far western side of the pass?"

"It is difficult to know at this point. You see, the route descends into the west, and where it leaves the mountains, it is at a lower altitude where forest covers everything. There are hills, mounds, creek beds, but no trough. There may be ruins of towers there, buried by ages upon ages of forest and consequent soil deposits."

"Conjecture. Pure guesswork."

"Yes, but archaeological finds on Earth have often been a combination of analysis and guesswork."

"This line or trough, which you call a road—if it's so old, why hasn't it been filled in by soil deposits?"

"It may have been. Again, it is a hypothesis, but let us say that a people who once dwelled here, very remote from us in ages past, dug a deep defile in the earth as a kind of royal road leading to a significant site in the central range. If it was paved with stones or some other form of biological-resistant material, such as the case of the Via Appia in Italy, it might delay the encroachment and infilling for millennia. The Appian, after all, is more than two thousand years old and is still used."

"Yes, but it's kept exposed by feet and wheels."

"Indeed. Yet if all transportation and commerce were to have ceased on it two millennia ago, would we today know of its existence?"

"You have a point, Dariush, but really we don't know a thing about what's down there. And this unknowing leaves too much room for wild imaginings. Maybe the trough is a fissure in the earth, a fault line that happens to be straight. In a universe as big and complex as ours, it's not beyond statistical probability."

"You may be right, Neil. But there is another detail I should point out. I made certain calculations and discovered additional mathematical data. I accessed a map of the continent on my personal *max* and printed it. On it, I ruled a line from the northernmost tip of the continent to the southernmost. Then I made a lateral line from the most western point to the most eastern. I checked the degree coordinates for the intersection, cross-checking it on topographical and visual print-outs. The lines intersect at the base of the mountain precisely where the road ends."

"That might be coincidence. Maybe you drew your lines impelled by an *a priori* assumption."

"An eager prejudice? Or was I testing a theory? Would you care to come with me and look at the pictures?"

We went to his room to have a look. His desk was covered with topographical maps, satellite photos, and copious notes. I sat down on his chair and looked carefully through the material. In the end, I had to admit that he was right.

Because his *max* was omnipresent in the room, to preserve privacy he keyed a music program that launched a loud and frantic Persian piece. We put our heads close and spoke in Kashmiri, just above a whisper.

"It's a coincidence", I murmured.

"Another unusual coincidence", he replied, with a certain dry tone.

"But look at this, Dariush", I said, pointing to the visual map. "The road, as you call it, ends abruptly against the mountain face. There's nothing there, no ruins, no artificial topography patterns, just a scary amount of vertical rock."

"Yes, which may indicate a cave, a mine, or perhaps a cliff mural. It might have other purposes that we cannot see via satellite."

"But definitely no city."

"No city", he shook his head. "Not even a town, I would think."

"Well, it doesn't make sense why smart creatures would build such a thing—a road to nowhere. And here's another thought: Pia and Paul's wedding valley is less than ten kilometers from the exact center of the continent. They just chose the spot because it looked lovely, and it was in a remote area. A pleasant happenstance, not a mathematical mystery."

"Think further, my friend. Pia and Paul are humans. They were exercising intelligence. If a significant event or monumental construction also appears in that very place, might this not indicate another intelligence at work?"

I frowned. "Maybe. But you'd have to find out if it is, or isn't, a purely natural event."

"And that is what we surely must do", he said, with an inquiring look. "Are you willing to embark upon another adventure?"

"Always."

Day 121:

My new doctor at the clinic is the transfer guy from KC. Pia reassured me that he is totally savvy. I will continue to receive a placebo every morning and will not, it is to be hoped, go crazy at any time in the near future.

During a swim in the pool last night, Paul confirmed that the doctor can be trusted. He's a flight officer in his own right, also a surgeon. The man dislikes DSI's ways, and a good many other things back on Earth, though he keeps quiet about it generally. A real subversive, he has agreed to change places with Pia so she and Paul can be together. That's heroic self-sacrifice, I'd say.

279

This morning, a dialogue of sorts, beginning verbally, then completed on a scrap of paper:

The doctor, I discovered, was fiftyish and oriental.

"Good morning, Dr. Hoyos, I'm Lieutenant Commander Nagakawa."

I made a flash decision to play the idiot for the sake of surveillance. "Good morning. Are you Chinese? I have a good friend who's Chinese."

"I'm glad for you. I'm Japanese. I have a good friend who's American."

"Oh."

"It's hard to tell you people apart. You all look alike."

I laughed. His eyes crinkled, his mouth curled at the edges. Sometimes probes like this are amiable attempts to puncture the racial barrier, albeit rather lame ones. Race fascinates me, though I am no racist. I love Xue like a brother—the brother I never had. I esteem him infinitely more than many a Waspa (White Anglo-Saxon Post-Agnostic) and some Hispanics I've known. The lieutenant commander's swift riposte told me we were on the same wavelength.

"So, Dr. Sidotra informs me that you haven't been feeling well lately."

"Yeah, I keep forgetting things. Sometimes I imagine bad things and think they're real. But not so much any more. Mostly, I just feel freaky and don't know why."

"I understand. That's why it's important to keep taking your medication."

He handed me the pill and a cup of water. I tossed them down my throat. That done, he scribbled on a scrap of paper and showed it to me.

Placebo. Paul says don't forget to swim.

I nodded that I understood. He crumpled the paper and soaked it under the dispensary tap, then fed it down the drain, along with a little bad pill.

Slightly louder than was needed, he said, "The medication can make some patients drowsy and listless. I suggest you keep up a regime of exercise. You could get run down if you don't do aerobics daily. Walking and swimming are the best."

"I love to swim."

"Excellent, but I recommend you never swim alone."

"Okay. Uh, Doctor, when are we gonna go home?"

"Home?"

"Earth."

"Ah, yes. According to the schedule, we'll be heading back in about eight months from now."

"Okay. Well, I gotta go now. 'Bye."

"See you tomorrow."

"Yup."

Day 127:

I had a strange dream last night. A young Indian girl, a teenager with a lovely face, came to me with a golden dish, full of steaming food. She knelt before me and said, "Try to eat more *pitaji*."

I woke up feeling very lonely. This evening I went to the pool at my usual hour and found Pia and Paul doing laps. During a break, I told them about the dream and how the girl had been asking me to eat something called "*pitaji*". Was there really such a food? Pia looked at me curiously and said, "Sounds like you dropped a comma. In Hindi, *pitaji* means 'father' or 'papa'."

I guess it was one of those inexplicable items the subconscious mind throws up now and then. Perhaps it was the flashing of an obscure neuron connection established when I gave Pia away (Indian, female, love, paternal, etc.). Maybe it was an imaginative detail from the life I might have had, or a word spoken by my girlfriend half a century ago.

Day 140:

At last, there came a day when a watershed of distracting social events on the *Kosmos* coincided with resumption of continuous shuttle flights, creating a flurry of activity that would help cover another clandestine landing on Nova.

There was little warning. I had only just returned to my room after breakfast when there came a knock on my door. There stood Dariush and one of Paul's best men, the Polish shuttle pilot.

"Ready?" he asked.

I grinned and pulled on my cowboy boots real fast.

The three of us took the route through the maze that had led to my previous trip. This time, however, the shuttle hold was empty, since needed materials had already been delivered to the planet. The shuttles were now mainly occupied in bringing the findings on Nova up to the *Kosmos'* storage holds.

In the cockpit, Dariush and I strapped ourselves into seats immediately behind the pilot's. I was tense with anticipation because my previous ride had been totally blind, my experience of departure, transit, and arrival completely sealed inside containers. Now, I watched the bay doors rumble closed, and then beeping and announcements warned that the bay was being depressurized. When the outer door opened, the shuttle simply slid into space, assisted by bursts from its side propulsion vents, until it was free of the great ship. Now gravity was gone, and additional short bursts maneuvered our vessel in a slow, rolling tangent that brought her nose toward the planet below us. The intoxicating view of a three-dimensional orb suspended on the deep waters of the abyss rose up in front of me. Then the rear propulsion units were powered on, and we accelerated downward in what looked like a precipitous plunge that could only end in disaster. I kept my wits by focusing on the heavens all around me, the black infinity crammed with the most brilliant stars I had ever seen. It was impossible to look in the direction of AC-A's flaring disk, but I could look out the port window at her two sister stars without flinching, though their magnitude was the most intense I had ever seen with my naked eye.

When the shuttle hit the upper rim of the troposphere, the pilot eased out of the dive and the angle of descent steadily lessened. Now our velocity declined and friction roar increased as we penetrated the lower atmosphere, and finally we were coasting over an ocean in the direction of a huge land mass. The rear propulsion units ceased, and the airspace jets took over, maintaining a moderate speed that would prevent us overshooting our destination. Within minutes, we were flying east of a mountain range, going ever lower, decelerating all the while, until we were now only a few thousand meters above a plain.

"We'll be landing at a geology and mining station", said the pilot. "As soon as we touch down, you must dress yourselves in the orange suits. Fr. Ibrahim, Dr. Hoyos, we will transfer to an AEC very quickly, so please be ready."

"How much time will we have for exploration, Jan?" Dariush asked.

"We'll have plenty of time. The station teams will need six to eight hours for loading the cargo."

He killed the jets and hover took over. We touched down lightly a minute later, and the portal in the shuttle hold hissed open. Dariush and I unbuckled, dressed rapidly in our monkey suits, and followed Jan down the ramp onto the ground.

This station was more developed than the marine base I had seen, with twice the number of pods and additional large hangars or storage sheds. Beyond the compound, the mountains loomed close, though they might have been ten miles away or forty, since their height made distances deceptive.

We walked to a short runway adjacent to the shuttle's landing pad, boarded an AEC, and prepared for takeoff. Jan established radio communication with a voice in the station, confirmed a flight plan, and with a smile, he pressed the "go" button. Contrary to my expectations, we did not rocket forward along the runway. We ascended vertically with only a background hum and with nary a tremble in the craft. When it reached a thousand meters, the jets were turned on, and we accelerated southward along the line of the mountain massif, climbing to a higher altitude as we went.

Unlike the flight we had made on the wedding day, we were now on the eastern side of the most eastern of the three ranges. Our pilot soared upward and banked to the west, taking the craft high over the crests of two ranges and then down into the valley that flowed north-south between the central and western range. He banked to the left and followed the valley southward. Not long after, he descended still further and eased back on the forward thrust. Ahead of us in the green bottom lands, a faint shadow-line cut straight across from the western mountains on our right toward those in the east. As the line approached, Jan brought us down to a hundred meters above the trees and switched to hover power. I looked upward at the heights and peered at the two towers of stone. Though still distant, they were distinct enough that I could see they were singular oddities in the alpine zone above the tree line. Dariush was staring at them too.

Our pilot turned the craft away from them and commenced a slow cruise toward the central range, following the depression in the terrain. Its trajectory was just as the satellite maps had shown us. Now, however, we realized that only high-altitude reconnaissance would have spotted the entire configuration, its undeviating course through the surrounding forest. From ground level, or near the ground as we were, it looked only like forest growing out of a dip in the bottom land. Yet the crowns of the trees within the trench were ten to twenty feet lower than the adjacent trees, and this phenomenon was continuous from the pass all the way to the opposite mountains. A trail of low trees was a common characteristic of dry riverbeds that have been encroached with the passage of time, yet old channels of that sort always took a meandering course. In marked contrast, our trough or trench did not seem to vary its route across the valley, a distance that looked to be around twelve or fifteen miles. I asked Jan what the actual distance between the ranges was, and he checked something on his instrument panel.

"Approximately 19.9 kilometers", he replied.

At this lower altitude, we noted another distinguishing feature of the trench. Along the upper edges on both sides, there was a band of trees standing higher than those of the forest stretching away in all directions. This too was consistent along its entire length.

As we neared its termination point, we slowed to full hover before a flat cliff face that soared vertically a thousand meters or more before breaking up into rougher formations.

"Should we land?" the pilot asked.

"Yes, please, Jan", Dariush replied.

With that, we began to descend, and nestled into a gap in the woods near the cliff, not far from the edge of the trench.

When we disembarked, the three of us immediately set out to learn more. First, we climbed upward through the trees growing from the mound bordering the trench, a sloping wall about twenty feet high. Arriving at the top, we then crossed forty feet of level ground and came to the brink of the trench itself. Gazing down, we saw that it was crowded with woods, though its foliation was thinner and the trees spaced farther apart, as if the soil was poorer in the depression. Even so, it looked entirely natural, for the forest floor was thick with moss and ferns and old fallen trunks.

I picked up a dead branch for use as my walking stick, and after a nod to each other, the three of us made our way slowly downward. When we reached the bottom of the trench, we glanced in every direction, looking for old stone ruins, monoliths, anything that would give evidence about its makers. There was nothing.

"But where does this thing go?" Jan asked.

Now we turned our eyes to the very end of the trench, a few paces away from us. There were no markings on the cliff face that we could see; nor was there a natural cave or an artificial one. Abruptly halted by the lack of anything that would point to an answer, as if our rational minds had collided with the stone itself, our imaginations now began to fly about in every direction.

"If this trench was man-made, it may have been a canal for funneling water to the lowlands beyond the western range", I suggested.

"A plausible explanation, Neil," Dariush replied, "yet the western range is amply endowed with snow packs and rivers that would supply the west. There would be no need to drain this central range."

"Yes, you're right."

"Was it a road to carry materials from mining operations higher in the mountains?" asked Jan. "At one time, there might have been chutes funneling ore down from above. Here in this spot vehicles could have received the ore and transported it to smelters beyond the pass."

"It's possible", I said. "But I don't think anyone has found evidence of industrial activity beyond the mountains."

"None", said Dariush. "I have checked the maps carefully from here to the western rim of the continent, and there is not a single topographical anomaly that would indicate buried cities or industrial sites."

"They may be buried very deep", Jan countered.

"Perhaps. If they are there, they would be of great antiquity, covered with ages upon ages of detritus."

"Surely there'd be a few standing buildings", I said.

"If they were made of stone and once stood very tall."

"You say that this road ends at the far side of the pass."

"Yes, there it ends, or disappears, since beyond that point the natural verdure blankets everything. At this latitude on the planet, the forests are lavish at altitudes lower than these mountain valleys."

"Well, it's a complete mystery", I murmured, shaking my head. "As long as we're exercising our imaginations, why don't we take the AEC higher and see if there are any remnants of mining operations up above?"

"Shall we do it?" asked Jan.

"A moment longer, please", murmured Dariush, walking in the direction of the cliff face. He stopped in front of it, his head moving this way and that, then tilting back as he gazed upward at the soaring mass. The surface looked uniformly bare for a thousand meters or more. As far as we could see, there were no marks on it, other than the random scorings of time and a few shrubs growing out of small cracks.

"No street signs", I said to Dariush. "No door."

He nodded, yet his face told me that he still wasn't satisfied.

"Let us look higher", he said at last.

We climbed back into the AEC, and Jan fired it, and we were airborne. Slowly, he elevated the craft on hover power, at a rate of ascent that covered about a hundred meters per minute, plenty of time for our eyes to inspect the features of the rock face. Half an hour later, we reached a titanic fracture in the mountain's flank, and paused, suspended above the valley, peering closely at every detail. It lacked any trace of roads, shafts, or caves, and there was no access to the heights above. It had been created by the forces of nature. We continued rising for another hour until we reached the peak, none the wiser.

After that, our pilot took us on an extended tour all around the peak and through nearby hanging valleys. Presently, we found ourselves gliding over the site of Pia and Paul's wedding. There we descended in order to take a short break and, I think, to relive a little of that beautiful day.

"Excuse me, gentlemen", said Jan when we had landed and depressurized. "Now I will have a nap." He pulled his cap down over his brow, leaned back in his seat, and closed his eyes.

Dariush and I exited through the portal and walked into the woods in the direction of the lake. There was a good breeze blowing, and the trees were swaying, creating a symphonic effect of light refraction and the sound of tinkling bells.

"The crystal forest", mused Dariush.

"A perfect name for it", I agreed.

When we came to the glade by the lake, we noticed a disc of compressed grass where the newlyweds had pitched their tent. On the shore near the waterfall, I found two letter *P*s made with pebbles, linked with the letter *t*—or maybe it was a plus sign.

Dariush stopped and silently gazed at the lake's riffled surface. With his right hand, he made the sign of the cross over it. From his pocket, he removed a capped jar, which he opened. Then, with thumb and forefinger, he took from it a granular white substance and threw it into the lake in four directions, his lips moving all the while.

"Blessed salt, Neil", he explained when he was done. "A symbol, a sign with authority. I claim this place, and this planet, for the Lord of the universe, our Savior."

"Does it need claiming?" I asked, with a note of skepticism.

"It is his, for all things were made through him, by him, and for him. Even so, there is a war in the heavens."

"A war? There hasn't been a war for nearly a hundred years."

"I mean the war that will last until the end of time. And thus, this little place may need reclaiming. I have also prayed that the entire planet will come under Christ's sovereignty—if it has fallen, as ours once fell."

Out of respect for the man, I voiced no further objections. Though I did say, half-humorously, "Well, we've yet to meet Nova's Adam and Eve."

"We have, however, met its serpents", he countered.

We smiled at each other, and by unspoken agreement left off any further theological discussion.

Deciding to amble around the lake, we first hopped on step-stones across the brook that fed the waterfall. I slipped and soaked my boots. I was about to pull them off but hesitated, debating with myself about the danger of snakebite. Overcoming my fears in the end, I went bare-foot for the remainder of the stroll. It felt so good to walk on the warm blue grass, to inhale its perfume, to feel the cool breeze on my cheek. The crystal symphony simultaneously stimulated and consoled. All in all, it was the most enchanting place I had ever seen; in fact, it was perfection. We circled the lake within minutes, soon finding ourselves again by the waterfall. I sat down on the grass and dabbled my feet, drowsy under the influence of the burbling waters, the crystal forest, and the little songbirds that had appeared, soaring in the air above us.

Dariush knelt down beside me. He remained motionless for a time, and I presumed he felt as I did, well contented and so soothed that he had no need for distracting conversation.

At one point, he raised his right hand again and made the sign of the cross over the mountain on the other side of the lake. That done, he resumed praying, still kneeling, his body upright. He was immo-bile for longer than seemed natural, his face in repose, his eyes closed. I watched him uneasily, feeling somewhat impatient, but kept myself occupied by observing the valley's unequalled beauty.

Suddenly, he groaned and struggled to his feet, agitated, his eyes moist with some pain.

"What is it, Dariush?" I asked.

He looked at me then, and I saw in his expression a sorrow that seemed to have no cause.

"What's the matter?" I pressed.

"A great evil has occurred here", he said.

"Here?"

"Not in this meadow. It occurred nearby."

"How would you know such a thing?"

"From across time, I feel the presence of terror, of despair."

Trying to reason him out of whatever mood had struck him, I said, "How can that be? There's no evidence that a civilization ever existed here. No evidence at all. That road—well, is it really a road? We don't know anything about it."

"There *was* a civilization here. And great was its evil."

"Maybe you're imagining it", I said doubtfully. "Maybe it's something subconscious, like a resonance of your family memory of the bombing of Tehran."

"It is different, Neil."

More doubtful than ever, I recalled how on the voyage Dariush had desired to find a civilization on this planet, and how disappointed he was when the surveys discovered nothing. Had he mixed his disappointments with his myth of good and evil?

He gazed at me with unfathomable grief, or pity. "I hear and see it in my spirit", he said.

Around us the birds swooped. The brook spilling into the pool continued singing as before. The breeze was scented with the perfume of flowers. The sky was cloudless, deep blue in the sunlight of AC-A and her two sister stars that shone by night and by day. All about me was tranquility, the pleasurable sensations of benign nature. I could not have imagined a more innocent place.

"There's nothing here", I said. "We're alone."

He looked at me strangely and said, "We are never alone, no matter how far we travel from our home. The birth and the crucifixion are ever present on the body of the Alpha and the Omega."

It was the kind of symbolism Dariush used whenever reason was inadequate—or inactive. Now I was convinced that he was projecting a primitive fear onto this pristine world. I said none of this. Yet he knew me well enough to guess my thoughts. Or it may be that my face betrayed my general disbelief and my more specific doubt about his irrational intuition.

He sighed and said, "Jan is waiting. Let us go."

We returned to the AEC and prepared for departure. Because Jan was running out of time, we were unable to inspect the towers. He took us directly back to the shuttle, and soon enough, I was in my room on the *Kosmos*.

Day 141:

After our evening language study, I presumed that we would take our customary drink together in the bistro. But Dariush begged off, claiming that he needed to rest.

"I'm sorry if I seemed unresponsive this morning", I said.

"There is no need to apologize, Neil. I understand how it appears to you."

"Well, I know something disturbed you. What puzzles me is that you felt it in the most unlikely place on Nova."

"Yes, a place of great beauty, an island of harmonious tranquility."

"It's certainly that. But then, the whole planet is a marvel."

"I think not the whole planet."

"Your feelings again?"

He nodded. "The little hidden valley may have been a refuge. Perhaps souls fled there from the evil surrounding them."

I did not argue with him, for the incident by the lake had been a clash, or more accurately, an exercise in mutual discomfort, a disequilibrium between us, the natural outcome of his myths in conflict with my reasoning.

Before turning away to go to his room, he sighed and murmured pensively, "We have brought the Earth to this planet. We have brought our knowledge of good and evil, for it is within each of us. Our proud voyage has infected this beautiful world."

"So, you think that whatever you felt down there in the crystal forest was about *us*, not about some evil civilization that once existed here."

"Of this, I am uncertain. It could be that two evils meet in this place."

"Why not two goods meeting in this place?" I countered.

He gazed thoughtfully at me, and once more I felt the eerie discomfort of standing on the edge of unknown mysteries, beautiful and dangerous. Simultaneously, they attracted and repelled, yet they had no visible form.

"We should sleep", he said abruptly.

We bid each other good night, and I returned to my room to make more notes. I went swimming at my usual hour and passed on my latest ruminations to Paul.

Day 157:

Dariush tells me that he has informed the archaeology team about the "road", the two towers, and the mathematical oddities. They are excited by the news and are in dialogue with other science teams and with DSI, negotiating to mount an expedition. Considering that the "evidence" is rather slim, it might take some time for the authorities and their committees to come to a decision, which would demand the rearrangement of the already overextended exploration priorities.

In the meantime, there is nothing to prevent us making sorties on our own.

Day 159:

Today, we made another visit to the mystery site. This time, we were flown down by Paul's best man, the Russian pilot. Paul had decided to accompany us as well. His Slavic temperament was in the forefront of our party, a mixture of high intelligence and capacity for intense focus, combined with an emotional spectrum that seemed much broader than the Anglo-Saxon, Persian, and even the Spanish. He was, in a word, excited.

"Fr. Ibrahim," he declared emphatically as we left the geology base behind and soared up into the mountains on an AEC, "tell me again the detail and omit no part."

So Dariush filled him in on every aspect of what we knew, though this was hardly conclusive.

"It *is* a road!" declared Paul. "I *know* it is a road. And no road lead to nothing. All road come to a place for reason, yes."

"Yes, I believe so", Dariush replied. I kept my own counsel, refraining from blurting out that many times in my life I had stumbled across surprising things, only to find they had a natural explanation, if one was willing to dig deep enough. Then I recalled the cube of turquoise I had found in the desert when I was a teenager. A big surprise, that one. Even so, we were banking an awful lot on outcroppings of rock and a depression in the planet's shield, both of them probably flukes or freaks of nature.

Nevertheless, I felt my own excitement rising. The afternoon would be a pleasant, if imaginative, diversion.

As we flew down the middle of the valley, Paul, who was sitting in the copilot's seat, leaned forward and pointed at the swiftly approaching trench line.

"There it is! It is what I saw. Now I see it more." With an animated face and exaggerated gestures, he turned to us and shouted, "It is a road; it is a road!"

His fellow countryman smiled ironically at him, muttered something in Russian, and began the descent.

"Volodya, can you take us first to the kremlins?" Dariush asked. Without reply, the pilot changed course and turned to the right, ascending by hover toward the nearer of the two towers. We slowly glided over it, and looking down into its core, we saw that the satellite photo had been accurate. It was hollow.

Of course, the tower could have been created by geological forces, for it looked not unlike the natural rock towers of Arizona. Its thick walls were broken, with at least half of the circumference shattered and lying in piles at its base. The standing portion appeared to be about sixty meters in height above the surrounding terrain. It was uniformly covered within and without by what I took to be thick moss or alpine vines, and was in several places cracked by the roots of bushes growing in crevices.

"Can we land?" I asked.

"The surface is bad," said the pilot, "but if you wish, I will hover a few meters above it, if you do not mind the ladder."

He brought the AEC slowly down to a height just above a steeply pitched slope of jagged stones beside the tower, then he depressurized and opened the portal. Paul hastened back into the middle of the craft, found the high-tension cord ladder, and unrolled it over the side. That done, he simply scrambled down it onto the ground.

Vladimir locked the AEC stable in the air, and the rest of us descended, me last of all. For the thousandth time in my life, I cursed my bad leg, cursed all the damnable serpents in the known universe. But this mood quickly passed. Just being there was a thrill and a challenge, more than making up for the difficulties.

As we picked our way carefully toward the nearest tower wall, a portion of which had collapsed, I saw that the pieces looked like shattered slabs of granite, furred with gray lichen. Moreover, avalanches of debris and smaller scree had assaulted the area in times past, making a confusing jumble.

Paul was the first to arrive at the tower's base. There he paused, staring down over the remnants of the wall into the hollow core, waiting for the rest of us to arrive.

The interior was little different from the exterior, in that, here too the bottom was strewn with rubble. However, because there was not much sunlight and no soil within, there was less overgrowth of vines and moss. Now we could see that the interior was definitely circular. In fact, it seemed very near a perfect circle, which had not been observable from the outside. Paul leaped over the wall, and clinging to a vine, he rappelled himself down to the bottom. There he proceeded to pull branches and clumps of moss from the walls. The other Russian joined him, and soon they had cleared a patch, which Dariush and I could not see, since it was immediately below us.

Both men suddenly paused and took a few steps back. They looked up at us, mouths open, speechless.

"What is it?" I called.

Paul cleared his throat and said in a shaken voice, "We are not alone in the universe."

Day 160:

I am writing in my room on the *Kosmos*. Last night, after a day of astounding discoveries, I returned to the ship quite exhausted. I was able to complete the foregoing notes, and then fell asleep without knowing it.

I awoke at 5 A.M. this morning, and went for a thoughtful walk in the arboretum. It now seemed a cramped and tame place. I sat and listened to Mozart for a while, and realized at one point that I had tears in my eyes. A strange sensation, emotionless. I put a stop to it and went off to get myself breakfast in the cafeteria, where I sat staring at nothing as I ate.

The truth that we are not the only intelligent beings in the universe is one that gives an initial shock, yet it needs absorbing. For the moment, we know very little. Were they visitors to this planet? Explorers like us? Colonizers who gave up and went away? Are they out there still on some nearby star? Or was this always their home? If the latter, have they died out entirely, or is there a remnant of these mighty people still alive on Nova, living very differently from the way they did at the height of their power? Indeed, were they people at all—as we conceive intelligent life to be? We do not know what they looked like, what they thought, why they did what they did. We know only that they were here.

I have just returned to my room and now will complete my notes on yesterday's events:

"We are not alone in the universe", Paul had said.

He beckoned us to join him, which both Dariush and I did at much risk, considering our age and my infirmities. We arrived safely at the bottom of the tower and there beheld what our friends had seen: The portions of the wall they had exposed were huge rectangular blocks, unmortared, precision made, with uniform dimensions. Dariush leaned close to inspect the seams. I stepped back and gazed all around me. About halfway up the highest standing portion of the opposite wall (the side overlooking the valley), the broken edge of a shelf or a floor support projected into the room. I could see no windows, for the wall was matted with the foliage of vines, as it was on the outside.

Vladimir was wearing a backpack, and from this, he now removed a hand-held instrument. He activated it, and as he turned around slowly, it shot light beams in every direction. Adjusting his position step by step, he narrowed his coordinates until he had found the chamber's precise center.

"It is a perfect circle," he told us, "31.79 meters in diameter."

"Of course, a system of measurement different from ours", said Dariush to himself.

With another instrument, Vladimir took a sonar reading that, apparently, was able to penetrate stone.

"There is a floor 6.35 meters below the exact center of the room. It is metal. The instrument is having trouble identifying the metal, but it is certainly not iron or steel. It may have lead content or be an alloy that mankind has not yet developed."

He fiddled with something on the instrument and took another reading.

"Measuring from the floor below to the top of the intact portion of the wall, we obtain a height of 95.37 meters."

Dariush did some mental calculation and said, "The height of the tower, then, leaving aside the question of a roof or cap, is precisely three times the diameter of the interior."

"Volodya, are there any openings in the wall?" I asked.

"Let me see", he said and pointed the instrument at the intact section, scanning from left to right, rising a little with each pass. Above the ledge or floor support I had spotted, he stopped.

"A window. Circular. It is 3.179 meters in diameter."

This demanded no complicated math. "One tenth the diameter of the tower's interior", I said. "They may have used a base-ten, decimal number system."

"Did they have ten fingers, I wonder?" Dariush mused.

Vladimir said, "The window is completely closed by organic material. Vine branches, I think."

He retraced his steps to the exact center, and digitally confirmed its position on the planet by longitude and latitude. That done, we climbed back out of the tower and returned to the AEC. It took only a minute to cross the pass and alight next to the other tower. Its condition was as poor as the first, with no significant differences in its structure that we could find. A reading of its dimensions revealed that it was an exact match of the first. The latitude/longitude coordinates were also recorded, and then we were airborne again. Our pilot plunged us down into the pass and swiftly out of it, heading due east along the trench in the direction of the mountain face on the other side of the valley. All the while he was taking readings from instruments on his flight panel.

Farther along, he shook his head and spoke in rapid-fire Russian.

"What is it?" I asked.

"It is very interesting", Paul replied. "He say this road is like arrow, very straight, to within a fraction of single degree. His instrument algorithms averaged numerous laser measurements from left bank to right bank and discovered the position of its center line. Now we learn that this line meets the line between the two towers in exact equal distance. Do you know what I mean?"

"Like a letter *T*?"

"Yes, like that. But it is so precise it is brilliant, brilliant. It is within a few centimeters of perfect symmetry, he is thinking."

Vladimir slowed the aircraft to hover, then descended into the trees, landing not on the embankment but in a gap inside the trench, close to the cliff face. We disembarked into the soft undergrowth of aromatic ferns and walked without undue effort toward it. I noticed that Vladimir frequently consulted the instrument in his hand.

Now we stopped before the impassable blank wall of stone where we had stood three weeks before. Vladimir took a few steps to the left and one step forward. His instrument began beeping.

"What is it? What have you found?" I asked.

"Only an abstraction", said Vladimir, whose English was more polished than Paul's. "The mathematical line, the road's axial line, it ends ... here." He put his finger to the wall.

"It is also the geographical center of the continent", Dariush contributed.

"But there is nothing here", said Paul. "There is no mark, no sign."

"Yes, and if all this precision was so important to them, why did they not leave a marker of some kind?"

"There may be one here," I said, "but if this side of the valley is anything like the other, it's buried. Volodya, does your magic gismo detect any metal below us?"

Our pilot employed not one, but three instruments, before looking up and shaking his head.

"Nothing."

Paul, Dariush, and I stared at the soil beneath our feet. And then, instinctively, we bent over and began to pull loose rocks away from the base of the cliff. It was a Herculean task, more a case of mad optimism than reasonable use of energies.

"Wait", said Vladimir, turning his back to us. He tapped on one of his instruments and paused a few seconds.

"I am triangulating on the center of each tower, the place where the windows are situated. Both windows, significantly, are facing this point exactly. Why?"

None of us had any answers. We watched Vladimir frowning to himself, tapping again, and reading the results.

He looked up suddenly and said, "From the center of those windows, two hypothetical lines can be drawn. If we posit that the lines would meet here at the mountain, exactly where the trench line ends, then we may have a means to learn more."

Paul, who was the head of Navigation for the *Kosmos*, seemed to get the point sooner than I did. He nodded emphatically. "*Da*, yes, of course. The road's axial line is horizontal, and the lines from the towers would *descend* even as they *converge* toward the apex where these three lines must meet."

"Must?" said Dariush with a frown. "But this is speculation."

"I agree, Father", said Vladimir. "However, *if* the apex is exactly here, and if we also consider the precision of all measurements we have discovered so far, would it not indicate, at least as a possibility, a determined relationship of two converging tower lines with the main axial line?"

"I see your point. It *is* a supposition, but one worth considering."

Vladimir nodded emphatically. "So, you understand, gentlemen—*if*, as is supposed, we do have the meeting of all lines exactly here, we are left with one uncertainty."

"Do you mean the depth?" I asked.

"Yes," Paul affirmed. "He is telling us there is something below, may be, but we do not see how far down is it."

Vladimir turned his instrument screen toward us, and we crowded close to look.

"Ah", I said. "We've been thinking two-dimensionally. Your machine has been thinking three-dimensionally, and has proposed a convergence of all lines exactly where they touch the rock face, somewhere beneath the ground we're standing on."

"If my theory is correct, and the coordinates for all lines are correct, the convergence point is approximately 2.78 meters beneath your feet, Dr. Hoyos."

"Really? This kind of guesswork is probably way off the mark."

"Then let us discover if I am a good or bad guesser."

With that, we resumed pulling loose rock away from the cliff. Paul went back to the AEC and returned shortly with a kit box that contained a variety of implements. One was a pneumatic bar with a chisel point. A squeeze of the handle drove it a foot length into hard ground, shunting rocks to the side. There were also a suction hose and two traditional shovels. Even with such tools, I could not sustain the physical labor for long. I tired first, and Dariush had to stop to catch his breath not long after. Eventually, we just sat down on the ground and watched the two young men throw themselves into the task.

Working as a team, they wasted no effort, and within an hour had cleared away a concave basin about nine feet wide by four feet deep.

"If we are right," said Vladimir, "we are very close. Maybe we will find a door, or the top of a door. Maybe a key in a lock. It will shake the whole mountain and crack open a big golden gate."

"Inside is fairy palace full of big gold coins!"

"And a big red dragon, Pavel!"

They were still laughing when both of them suddenly froze. Paul dropped to his knees.

"We have find something", he exclaimed.

Dariush and I hurried to the edge of the pit and there beheld both men down on their knees brushing dirt away from the exposed cliff face.

"What is it?"

"Is markings in stone", murmured Paul. "Not many, but big. Look."

I looked and did not see much at first. There were a few wedge-shaped incisions in the stone. Chiseled below them was an outline of the feathered tips of extended wings, like those of an eagle or an art angel. Another hour of digging brought to light a winged, manlike creature, with a horned head and a three-eyed, humanoid face. From beneath the navel of the naked form protruded something like a spear, its sharp tip pointing to the left, while the face was half-turned to the right. Its legs and feet stretched downward, three times longer than its torso, each of its ten toes extended into claws. Its arms stretched horizontally, ending in claw-like hands. Clenched in its left hand was a feathered arrow. In the open palm of its right hand, there was a shape like a flame.

The four of us stepped back and gazed at the image for some minutes, stunned to silence.

"Is this what they looked like?" Paul asked, speaking as if to himself.

"It is a cultic symbol, I think", said Dariush. "It represents a celestial being or a god."

"I hope so", I murmured, for I did not like the feel of the character depicted here.

"This was made by good artist", said Paul.

"The style is sophisticated", Dariush replied. "The hand of the one who carved it was sure of what he was doing."

"It is like an Egyptian carving," said Vladimir, "in the temple of pharaoh."

"It is similar to Egypt's cartouches, only in the sense that both are pictographs incised in stone. And both are elegant. Here the similarity ends."

"Isn't there a winged god in Egyptian cosmology?" I asked.

"Yes," Dariush answered with a nod, "but in their bas-reliefs and painted murals, pharaohs' artists took pains to create an effect of natural human anatomy. Though stylized and hieratic, depictions of their gods were clothed and retained subtleties and warmth, united to divine principles. Their cosmology was mistaken, and I believe influenced by evil spirits to some degree, yet there was ever a human element in it. This figure before us seems quite inhuman—in fact, evil."

"He looks like a man", objected Vladimir. Then with a shrug he added, "A man with three eyes."

"And claws", I said.

"And horns", said Paul.

"In any event, we are too close to its discovery to be able to interpret it properly", said Dariush. "We must learn its context. Perhaps there is more below, still buried."

The younger men again began to dig, taking care not to scrape the cliff with their tools, lest they damage anything.

A few centimeters below the feet of the "god" an incised line appeared, running straight down into the ground. Carefully, Paul dug away gravel and some larger rocks. Another hour of excavation increased the size of the pit and exposed a further three feet of descending line. Finally, a few more shovelfuls cleared away debris, and the line ended at a disk-shaped incision.

Hastily the men worked on, and soon it was apparent that a broader and more complex scene had been carved on the mountain's face:

There were three disks ranged side by side, each separated by about a foot length. The largest was in the center, approximately half a meter in diameter (the line touched its top). The one on the left was slightly smaller. The disk on the right was no more than an eighth the size of the others.

"Do you think—?" I began.

"Dig deeper", Dariush insisted.

"Yes, yes", said Paul, shoveling frantically. Vladimir stepped back and watched him.

We did not have long to wait. The vertical line continued its descent beneath the central disk. A few more scoops of gravel unearthed its destination—a horizontal row of spheres of varying sizes—eighteen of them. The line touched the seventh from the left, and there it ended.

"You understand what we are looking at?" said Paul.

We all nodded in the affirmative.

Everyone sat down at once, Dariush and I at the rim of the excavation, and the two young men in the dirt and rubble. For a time, we could say nothing.

By now the sun—AC-A—was setting beyond the teeth of the western range. Vladimir stood up and dusted off the trousers of his uniform. He put his instrument to the disk of the hieroglyphic AC-A and checked the readings. He shook his head. Then he placed the instrument to the smaller disk of its seventh planet, and now the instrument began beeping steadily.

"As I thought", he smiled. "I am a good guesser."

"A *maximum* good guesser", declared Paul, leaping to his feet and punching him on the shoulder.

The other laughed and checked his wristwatch. "The hour is late", he said. "The shuttle at the geology base will be loaded. We must return."

"We will come again soon?" Dariush asked.

"As soon as it is possible."

Day 184:

It is out of our hands now. Dariush reported our findings to the archaeology team leader, and he in turn approached DSI. With only a little hesitation, the DDSI mandated a full-fledged exploration team, including the archaeologists, Dariush's linguistics people, and engineers for excavation of the site. In practical terms, this has been swiftly translated into the building of a mission base in the valley between the towers and the cliff mural. It is nearly completed. Media programs on the *Kosmos'* panorama screens have shown the establishment of a compound with a perimeter fence, ten residence pods, and working annexes for examining any artifacts that may be discovered, as well as an AEC landing pad. The base is situated on the higher ground overlooking the trench, midway between the towers and the cliff.

Quite rightly, the discovery has been attributed to Dariush and his detective work. Thankfully, no one has inquired about who went along for the joyride. I have melted away into the invisibility of the dysfunctional. With all the attention now focusing on the site, sneaking downstairs for more on-ground adventures is impossible. The region is being strictly supervised "for security reasons", which probably means for the purpose of preserving a heritage site, protection of artifacts, and preventing amateurs from stomping all over the place with their little pails and shovels. While I regret my exclusion, I know that my friend will be telling me everything, and I can also watch what happens via 3D programs, some of them in real-time.

The news of the discovery has electrified the entire crew and all science teams—the thrill, the mystery, the shock of the incontrovertible fact that we are not alone in the universe. It is interesting to listen to the common themes that arise in overheard cafeteria discussions and the official commentary in media presentations: Were they colonizers, or were they tourists like us? Or were they native to the planet? And where are they now? Did they have wings and three eyes, or were those details only symbolic? What, really, did they look like?

Day 186:

Beautiful news today.

Paul and Pia invited me to be their guest at supper in the restaurant on deck A—the European menu. We ate French, which is to say that there were some exquisite sauces on the nova-turkey. We drank ersatz wine and sipped from a smuggled flask of real nova-berry liqueur. The former tasted superb, the latter sweet and somewhat green, still fermenting but much more satisfying than the standard chemical composition of the "Bordeaux".

After the meal, the newlyweds leaned forward, beaming, Pia blushing.

"We are expecting a baby", she whispered.

I laughed and threw up my arms in jubilation.

"Hearty, hearty congratulations!" I erupted too loudly. "May he, or she, be the first of many!"

"Shhh, shhh, Neil", said Paul putting a finger to his lips. "Please, we do not wish to advertise our criminal activities."

"Oh, sorry. Still, it's wonderful news. The best!"

"Yes, but we'll have to be careful", Pia said, with a wrinkle of her brow. "Fortunately, we're living on KC deck, where we have some protection. But if word reaches DSI, there's going to be a struggle. We would have to defend our child, because he or she is an illegal on more than one count."

"I see. Hopefully the Captain will be sympathetic."

"We tell him last night, and he like this", Paul replied soberly. "And so will be many of flight crew, I think. But not everyone. Soon, my Pia become very big, and then we cannot hide it."

"You could stay upstairs until the baby is born", I said, turning to her.

"I can, and will. I'm pretty sure we'll avoid compulsory abortion. But that doesn't rule out confiscation after the baby's born."

I felt my scalp begin to tingle, and a primitive anger rushing upward from some forgotten chamber of my psyche.

"They not do this", whispered Paul with what can only be called a deadly smile. His eyes became steel as he patted his jacket pocket.

"Your mastodon gun?" I asked.

He nodded.

"I am civilized man", he said in a deceptively calm voice. "But if barbarian try to hurt our child, I will make him ... how do you say ... *extinct*."

Yes, barbarians like Skinner and his Elf, and all the barbarians just like them who control the entire world.

And that prompted a thought: They controlled our home planet. To a great degree, they controlled the floating micro-world of the *Kosmos*. But could they really extend their grasp so far as to control all life on our newfound land? Perhaps this unpopulated planet needed human beings, as many as we could provide.

"How attached are you to Earth?" I asked.

Pia and Paul reached for each other's hands.

"You read our thoughts", said Paul.

Day 197:

Dariush is now living in the archaeology station in Tower Valley, as we have come to call it. However, every few days he returns to the *Kosmos* by shuttle, ostensibly because he is not willing to have his private library ferried down to the somewhat Spartan station, and he needs to study his unique collection of resource materials in search of any similarity between Earth's ancient languages and the hieroglyphics inscribed above the winged creature. Apparently, even the omniscient ship's computer does not possess the text of certain ancient manuscripts. He has a private room of his own down there, but it is noisy at all hours with youngish types talking in the hallways, partying, etc. "Like a cheap hotel", he says. "The walls are thin." I believe he also returns to the ship in order to reconnect with his co-religionists for prayers together, and for his secret Mass. This is probably his main reason.

The AS-VT (archaeology station, Valley of the Towers) is not yet fully operational, and until it is, no further excavations have been undertaken. All other stations continue to send great quantities of material up to the holds, mineral samples and biological specimens predominantly. The quest for utilitarian knowledge remains our global religion. I, too, did my part in making this utilitarian voyage possible, though I remain (privately) an anti-utilitarian humanist—my version of religion, I guess. Or maybe I'm just a survivalist.

Dariush told me this evening what I had already learned via the special media program: Excavation of the mural site begins tomorrow. He will have to be down there in case linguistic findings turn up. The hieroglyphics obsess him.

"Despite the wedge shape of the incisions, which is reminiscent of Mesopotamian cuneiform, they do not truly resemble any script produced by the races of Earth, as far as I can see", he said. "If there were a marked similarity, we might have been able to begin deciphering them."

"So, you've hit a blank wall."

"Not entirely. In the inscription, there is the indelible earmark of language. Because it is short, I have isolated only sixteen distinct 'letters' or, in laymen's terms, a partial 'alphabet'. However, there is no Rosetta Stone, so to speak."

"And you have no idea what it's telling you. But it has to be about the picture, doesn't it?"

"Possibly. The inscription could be the name of the winged deity—I am convinced it can only be a cultic image, not literal. Or it may speak about the nature of the solar systems of Alpha Centauri. Possibly it refers to something very different."

"Do you remember the line in the mural that heads straight down into the soil beneath it?"

"I think about it constantly. Especially I ponder that it probably indicates a subsidiary progression, which we have still to see in its entirety. The god creates the systems of the three sister stars, and then from the middle star, which is clearly AC-A, the line traces downward to the subsystem of her eighteen planets. And then ..."

"And then the line continues downward from the seventh planet—Nova."

"Yes, and this is the most exciting part. Where will that line lead us? Will we find an ancient map inscribed in the stone? Will it show us a continent, then a valley, then the ruins of a city, and finally a buried archive? Tomorrow we will learn more."

Day 199:

I will try to be brief, since I don't want to be away from the panorama screen too long. This is what they have found:

Yesterday morning an excavation machine began its work. First, it penetrated the soil at a spot in the center of the trench, five hundred meters out from the cliff, digging a test shaft straight down. The shaft reached the hard bottom of the trench at 1.29 meters below the surface, confirming preliminary electronic readings. The base was stone. The shaft was expanded and the debris funneled up to an examination field beside the station, where the soil and organic material was put through a giant sifting machine that delicately screens everything falling into its mouth, checking for artifacts (nothing found, so far). More of the stone pavement was then exposed and found to be made of flat, artificial blocks, exactly the same dimensions as the large blocks of the tower walls. Mathematically precise, the surfaces and sides of the blocks had been cut, not chiseled. Several were removed and taken above ground for further examination. Beneath them was found hard-packed gravel, and below that were more layers, the strata approximately 105 meters deep, with intermediate layers of paving blocks separated exactly by a depth of 1.59 meters. At the very bottom of these levels was solid rock, the roots of the mountain chain. The depth of 105 meters down to rockbed is the first departure from the consistent mathematical gymnastics performed by the aliens. Doubtless, they broke their obscure rules only because of the subterranean configuration of the mountain roots. If this is their home planet, dare I call them "aliens"? Well, they are alien to us.

A number of interim conclusions have been reached by soil and geology experts:

Though the figures are not absolute, it is estimated that the road was last used circa fourteen hundred years ago by Nova reckoning, the figures adjusted for the different length of its year and the character of the planet's seasons, based on a theoretical 3.5-cm rise of soil deposits per century. This translates into somewhere between two thousand and twenty-one hundred years ago by Earth time.

When the road was actually built is anyone's guess.

Measured from side to side, the stone pavement is 31.79 meters wide—which is also the towers' diameter. Its borders remain perfectly aligned along the entire length of the exposed section.

There can be no doubt that it was designed to bear heavy loads. This is further indicated by a discovery that came late in the first day, when the excavator machine had exposed nearly twenty meters of road in the direction of the cliff: traced along its bed are three parallel "tracks" of mineral deposits, which the station metallurgist has sampled and examined. It is iron oxide. He believes it is the remnant of completely oxidized rails. These lead straight toward the cliff base, which is still buried under soil and debris fallen from the mountain over the centuries.

No one has attempted to dig deeper at the cliff face beneath the winged creature, since the archaeologists have decided upon another methodology. The excavator will continue to expose the road until it is very close to the cliff, a few meters away, and then the remainder of the work will be done by the archaeologists, using more delicate tools.

Tomorrow excavation resumes.

Day 200:

Unfortunately, another death occurred today. One of the geologists working at AS-VT, a young woman, went for a stroll down the embankment in the direction of a pond three kilometers north of the station. This shallow body of swampy water is the last remnant of the lake that once filled a great part of the valley. There are very similar geographical features south of the road, and it is now believed that the embankments once separated two large bodies of water. In other words, the road was a causeway. That it was sunken, not raised as one would expect a causeway to be, is further indication that it must have been used for bearing unimaginable weights, and thus it needed the mountains' rock bed to support it. An ordinary raised causeway, even one greatly reinforced by alien engineering, might not have provided enough support.

I regret to say that the victim died of snakebite. Her body was found by the shore of the pond. She was wearing a swimsuit at the time of her death. She had neglected to bring antidotes and a communicator with her. Since the distance back to the station was too far to run, she may have panicked, shouted for help, and then quickly become delirious. Brain hemorrhage and asphyxiation followed shortly.

Excavation has been suspended until after the funeral.

Day 201:

A memorial service and burial at Base-main this morning. Many scientists and other personnel had flown in to grieve and give eulogies. The deceased woman had been popular among her colleagues. I watched a half-hour biography program on my *max* last night. Poor girl. If she has family back home on Earth, they will not hear about her death until 4.37 years from now.

Now the cemetery beside the flag is crowned with three aluminum obelisks, each surmounted by a blue orb symbolizing our home planet. Stron's and the soldier's were the first ones. Let us hope there will be no more.

Day 202:

A new detail has come to light. As the excavation resumed and several more meters of soil were removed, it was noticed for the first time that the roadbed sloped downward, a fact that had been overlooked during the previous work, so gradual was the grade. Only when the machine's driver looked back did he see that he was slightly lower than he had been at the beginning. Surveyors scurried down into the trough and took readings with their instruments. The resulting data

305

showed that the slope had been there all along. Further readings taken at sample spots (5-km, 3-km, 2-km, 1-km, and 0.5-km distances from the cliff) revealed that, for a good deal of its length, the road's ratio of decline had been a constant 0.3179 meters of drop for every 31.79 meters of length—need one be surprised? At a distance of 0.6358 kilometers, however, the angle of descent increased, and continued to increase.

By late afternoon, the excavator was only twenty meters from the cliff, and the roof of his vehicle was well below the forest floor. I could see there was growing excitement among the station staff gathered along both sides of the pit, and plenty of us held our breath on the *Kosmos*, where I think a majority of those on board had crowded into the panorama rooms to watch the real-time 3D. I had a good place near the screen on deck B, and noticed Dariush standing at the edge of the excavation, as close as he could get to the mural.

When the machine's scoop and suction arrived at a point only ten feet from the cliff face, the driver began to work more slowly, in order to avoid damaging anything that might be buried there. By then, the archaeologists were peering at his every move and shouting cautions and directions. When the scoop had removed all soil and debris to within a foot, they called the excavation to a halt.

Everyone stood still and gazed downward, and a few seconds later, the media people got their cameras positioned so that we could see too. The pit looked to be about thirty meters deep. The road had proved to be a colossal ramp. But, why a ramp? And where did it go? Would this phenomenal feat of engineering end only at a blank wall?

The excavator was removed, and two mobile hydraulic platforms were driven down the pavement to the base of the excavation. The platforms were raised to the level of the mural, and a horizontal walkway extended between them. Five archaeologists boarded it and knelt down, their faces close to the head of the three-eyed god. Without delay, they began to brush a patina of dried earth from the hieroglyphics, the winged creature, and the line leading to the three solar symbols. The hydraulics lowered them as they scrubbed and dusted their way downward.

At last, they reached the lowest level that Paul and Vladimir had unearthed, the row of eighteen planets. Now their activities proceeded in studied earnest. Carefully, they used trowels to scoop away the mixture of soil and rock, centimeter by centimeter it seemed, with a suction tube taking away the debris. The incised vertical line was more and more exposed as they worked on.

At every stage of descent, two assistants worked on either side of the archaeologists' platform, breaking up the thicker layer of soil covering the cliff, with additional suction tubes removing the material. In this way, the entire cliff face was exposed little by little, lower and lower. It must have taken hours to accomplish this, but I had lost all sense of time.

There came a moment when the team on the walkway stopped as one man, and then they all leaned forward with their heads close to the rock.

"The line has ended at a fracture", called an archaeologist to no one in particular. "It looks horizontal." He measured it with a bubble level. "Yes, it's level. It's an artificial seam."

They dug away more soil, and one of them cried out, "Stone blocks!"

Three hours later, the entire cliff face was exposed, and there we beheld what could not have been detected by instruments alone: cut into the mountain wall was a gateway, as wide as the road, and as high—31.79 meters square.

It was filled with close-fitting rectangular stones, exact duplicates of each other, their joints so tight it would be impossible to pass a razor blade between them. There was no mortar.

The bottom row of blocks sat upon the end-blocks of pavement, indicating that the barrier was added after construction of the road, possibly ages later.

Incised in the central block in the middle of the wall, equidistant from left and right, top and bottom, was a simple arrow shape with pointed head, feathered hilt, and a shaft, which, when measured, proved to be 3.179 meters long. Why, of all things, an arrow? It points to the north, so there may be important findings to be had in that direction—perhaps another entrance or a city?

Silence fell on us all, above and below.

Day 203:

Committee meetings are underway, though their discussions and decisions (if any) have not yet been reported. Dariush has been involved in some of the meetings. He tells me that various possibilities are being assessed: Should the wall be penetrated by removal of a single block, which would open up a portal sufficiently large for a man to go through? Or should a larger "door" be opened by cutting into it with a nuclear micro-blade, permitting machines and technology to enter? How thick is the wall? How dangerous is it? Would it collapse? Had it been rigged to destroy robbers? Is there more than one layer of stone? Instrument readings tell us nothing here, since the beams are deflected for reasons we do not understand. It may be that the backside of the wall is lined with a metal unknown to us. A test bore into the base of one of the towers has revealed that its circular floor, situated beneath tons of rubble, is an unknown metal, exhibiting no oxidation, black in color, and impenetrable by all our instruments. It may be that the gate wall is reinforced with the same element.

We wait. The mountain also waits, resisting us with its implacable face.

Day 205:

At sunrise, the cutting began. Elevated to the top row of blocks, the remote-control nuclear scalpel sliced into the wall at the point where the vertical seam met the horizontal seam at the gateway's upper right corner. Electronic feedback from the machine revealed that the block was 0.3179 meters thick, beyond which was a very thin layer of metal coating the backside of the stone. The beam penetrated both and then encountered no further resistance. There were no adverse effects.

The blade cut slowly downward, following the vertical seam until it reached the seam of the block below it. Then the blade shifted ninety degrees and moved left along the horizontal joint toward the wall's center. At the end of the block, it turned and went upward to the "roof" or "lintel" of the gateway, turned again to the right, and completed the rectangular incision. There the machine was halted and withdrawn.

The hydraulic lift was elevated to that level and suction apparatus affixed to corners of the block. The hydraulic reversed, rolling backward up the ramp, drawing the block outward. There was a low scraping sound of stone grinding on stone, and then the block was free of the wall. The hydraulic's engine wheezed under the tremendous weight, but the machine managed to continue its reversal away from the cliff.

It drove slowly up the ramp in the direction of the station, where the block would be deposited for examination. Watching the whole event on a panorama screen in 3D real-time, I noticed that the reverse side of the block was non-reflective black—perhaps the same mysterious metal of the tower floors, if metal it was.

The panorama hall was filled with silent people completely absorbed by what was happening below. The staff on the ground had held back until the completion of the procedure, no doubt fearing booby-traps set for grave robbers. Now, curiosity swept aside all hesitations, and the scientists and engineers crowded forward to the edges of the pit. The gaping orifice in the face of the mountain was an open door, rather a window. It was lightless, as if darkness itself had become tangible.

Remote-controlled probes were sent into the space through the window. Shortly after, they returned their readings, which were digitally broadcast across the base of the screen and duplicated by a narrator's voice reading aloud the same data.

The interior atmosphere was normal air. It was dry, registering near-zero humidity. Though stale and saturated with mineral dust particles (probably stirred by the inrush of outside air when the window was opened), it was free of any chemical or bio toxins that our instruments were capable of detecting. There were also minute quantities of biological "dust", but this was dead. Samples were taken by the probes, and then they were withdrawn for intensive analysis in the station lab.

Now the remote-controlled vidprobe was inserted and its high-power lights turned on. The image of the hidden world beyond the wall suddenly filled the screen.

At first glance, it was a cave, which had been expected. Then as our eyes adjusted, we saw that it was not a natural cave. It was a hall made by intelligent engineering, with square, featureless walls and ceiling cut from the living rock. As the cameras rotated in all directions, we saw many other things at once:

The hall was enormous, as wide and as high as the gateway itself. Its floor was merely a continuation of the stone roadway that led into it, with the difference that three raised tracks or rails were visible, leading deeper into the mountain. Though the probe's light system was capable of illuminating hundreds of meters ahead, its beams dissolved into nothingness when it focused in that direction. A beam for measuring distance was fired into the gloom, and it reported that the length of the chamber was 3.179 kilometers. No obstacles had been encountered in its trajectory; it had hit a square wall of stone and bounced back. At this early stage, therefore, we could only conclude that the chamber was empty.

Day 206:

The chamber is not empty. It is difficult to write about what has been found, for the lucidity of language collapses before what it must describe. I will therefore attempt a sequential account, and perhaps my powers of description will improve as I go along.

Early this morning, the nuclear scalpel widened the window by two more blocks and then cut downward all the way to the road. By noon, an open door had been made in the wall, and in the early afternoon, the first exploration vehicles entered—three LECs with combined tread and hover capabilities. The entire archaeology team and the linguistics team (including Dariush) rode on the vehicles, as well as a few media people, who would send back images of what (if anything) lay deeper in the chamber.

At first, there was not much to see, only a continuation of the bare walls and ceiling, and of course the rails leading into the dark. The LECs had plenty of room to follow alongside the rails. The road's floor was now level.

It did not take them long to reach the end of the chamber, and here they came to a stop before a second wall of stone blocks. What might have been a radical disappointment was, instead, cause for further excitement. First of all, they noted that the lowest level of wall blocks sat upon the road's paving stones, dividing them in half, indicating that the road might possibly continue onward beyond the wall—if it was indeed a dividing wall and not a dead end. Most importantly, they found incised in the center block, far above their heads, a duplicate of the three-eyed god. Cut into the block immediately below it was another "arrow".

An animated discussion followed, concluding with the advance team requesting that the nuclear scalpel be sent in to them. Not long after, the machine arrived. Within minutes, it had made its initial cut, and jubilation erupted all around when the instrument registered more empty space on the other side. Within an hour, a door was opened and a single LEC entered the inner chamber, several of the scientists following it on foot. A few steps beyond the doorway, they stopped in their tracks and gasped. The cameras entered last, and then we were able to see what greeted their eyes.

The first impression was that of a sun—a sphere of fire, a star—floating just above the floor ahead of them. They did not question how near or far away it was, because the space around them seemed to be as huge as the outer chamber. Instinctively fearing the heat of solar flames, the scientists drew back from it. However, the driver of the LEC moved his vehicle closer, and then objectivity asserted itself. He switched off his headlights, and instantly, the sun was extinguished, leaving the room in darkness. He switched them on again, and the sun returned. Now we realized that it was an object made of highly reflective yellow-orange material. It gave off no heat whatsoever.

Walking cautiously toward it, the team approached to a distance of ten meters.

"Gold", someone said. "I think it's covered with gold."

Instruments were pointed at the thing and registered its composition as stone with a veneer of pure gold.

It was not as large as was first thought, only 3.179 meters in diameter. Its underside was at eye level, and the whole was supported by a thin black rod, piercing it through the vertical axis line.

Dariush stepped closer and walked all around it.

"No hieroglyphics", he said, when he had completed his inspection.

"A symbolic AC-A, I think", said one of the scientists.

By now, the other two vehicles had been driven inside the chamber and taken positions on either side of the sun, pointing their headlights further into the receding shadows. The vid people aimed their cameras in that direction as well.

Again, all voices fell silent, for there in the distance loomed an immense black form, an object of indeterminate shape that might have been a hundred meters distant or a thousand.

"I get a reading of radioactivity", said one of the scientists. "Below hazard level."

"From the sun?" asked another.

"No, it's coming from that thing, whatever it is."

"How far are we from it?"

Another scientist, who was standing beside the sphere, pointed his instrument and said, "My reading says it's approximately 318 meters from us."

"I really hope we're not walking through the innards of an alien power generator."

"It's possible, but a plant as huge as this seems primitive for a race capable of building the road and the chambers."

"Maybe their technological development was lopsided."

"We don't know anything about them, other than they were great road builders."

"The Egyptians and Mayans were great builders too, and they didn't even have electricity."

"Well, let's take a look. If you find any on/off buttons, don't touch them."

In the end, their hunger to *know* shunted aside all reservations. They climbed into the LECs, and their drivers moved onward in the direction of the object. Additional mobile vehicles entered the chamber behind them, and now a convoy was on the move. Neither eyesight nor vid could discern anything more about the amorphous mass, regardless of how close they came to it—only that it was non-reflective and very big. The thought crossed more than one mind that it would prove to be a tomb.

The vehicles in the vanguard braked before a low object that was now visible immediately in front of them, a cube of black stone, waist high, standing between them and the massive structure. Passengers got out of the vehicles and walked around the cube and approached the monolith, which was about ten meters from the cube.

It sat on the three rails, which looked improbably fragile beneath the weight they were bearing. The forefront was rounded with a point like the head of a bullet. It filled two-thirds the width of the chamber and came close to brushing the ceiling, but of its length nothing could yet be seen. Two LECs drove on into the gaps on either side, and the drivers radioed back that the thing was very long. As they continued, they also communicated with each other.

"The sides are curved", said one.

"Black all the way", said the other.

"Grooves on the side."

"Same on my side."

"Equally spaced holes, ten of them."

"Same here. They look like vents. This is some big reactor."

"Or one hell of a spooky machine."

"Vertical lines, a rectangle on the side of the thing, maybe a service entry."

"Radioactivity increasing, but still beneath hazard level. Should I turn around?'

"No, let's keep going to the end. Meet you there."

"We have protrusions along the sides, like tubes swelling gradually, the longer they get."

"Same here."

"I'm at the back end. The tubes stop here."

"There are dorsals."

"Dorsals?"

"Like fins between the tubes. I think there are retractable components too. Did you see the grooves?

"I just thought they were grooves."

"They look like wing bays."

"Are you saying this is a ... ?"

"Yeah, it's a space ship."

Day 207:

With these words, one of the greatest discoveries in millennia was immortalized. "Space ship". The phrase sounded incredibly banal, an old cliché learned from a boy's comic book or a bit of dialogue in a low-budget sci-fi film from the earliest era of motion pictures.

"Yeah, it's a space ship." I want to erase the memory of what that driver or engineer said. It should be stricken from the record. But it won't be, and on second thought, perhaps that is best because this is mankind in action, after all, with sublime and banal forever entwined.

Thousands of photographs and scan diagrams were recorded that first day, and are now being analyzed.

No entry point into the vessel has yet been discovered. The portal, or suspected portal, is being examined minutely, but no incisions have been made in its seams. The surface material is still unidentified, and resists all instrument probes.

But we know the following about the ship:

It is 31.79 times longer than it is wide, thus it is the shape of an arrow—a rather fat-shafted arrow.

There are no windows.

The only external features are the "fins" and the faint seams in the "grooves", which could be bays for retractable wings. If there are wings inside, they are folded tightly and sealed.

The "tubes" appear to be propulsion units, since the radioactivity has its source near the rear end of the craft. The ends of the tubes are holes, plugged and impenetrable.

Nowhere along the entire surface is there evidence of damage. The "nose" or tip of the "arrow" displays no micro impact holes typically found on rocket-style, atmosphere-piercing vessels such as those once used on Earth.

The black surface continues to confound the metallurgists and chemists. They know it is a kind of unidentified metal. It is not the same material as the thin black coating on the backside of the stone gate. The ship's skin is extremely hard, certainly harder than any alloy mankind has developed. The nuclear scalpel succeeded in penetrating the skin only a fraction of a millimeter before shutting itself off due to overloading its power system. Repeated attempts have ended in the same manner. However, minute particles were collected where the incision was made, which one might call the "sawdust" from the cut. This was taken up to the *Kosmos* labs and analyzed under our best mass spectrometers/spectrophotometers, and while they failed to determine the metal's atomic weight, it was found that molecules of sand or glass, possibly the remnants of superheated clay, were present.

The investigation has progressed only this far, as of today. Engineers are attempting to re-rig the nuclear scalpel in order to give it greater cutting power.

Xue came to my door this evening and asked me to go for a walk with him. In an art alcove, he told me that DSI had called a meeting of the directors of all the science teams, held at their head office on deck D. Xue had been invited in as an advisor. In short, they want to know if anti-matter can be used to penetrate the ship's exterior, if the forces that gave us half-lightspeed on our outward journey can be harnessed in such a way. Xue informed them that it was a risk. Theoretically, an anti-matter beam could act in a way similar to that of the scalpel, but because we don't know what material the ship is made of, its matter could react negatively. It could simply explode in our faces, or dissolve into nothingness, or any number of other possibilities. The executives of DSI nodded as if they understood, then mandated the engineers to make a new tool.

"They want to produce a black hole the size of a pinpoint", said Xue, shaking his head. "It is very tempting for me, as you can well imagine. However, as I said, the risks are considerable."

"They could practice on the metal floor in the tower", I offered. "It looks like the same substance."

"Yes, I thought of that. And suggested it."

"Will you be involved?"

"I have offered them my paper on anti-matter reduction—entirely theoretical at this point, but I believe reliable. This would give them the parameters of what to avoid. Of course, they're smart enough to know those things for themselves."

"Let us hope so."

"I will probably function as the quality-control man, making sure they don't come up with anything that would violate the physics. Also, I would need to explain a few things from your own work. Do I have your permission?"

"As long as you promise not to blow the planet to smithereens, Owly."

He smiled. "I'll try not to, *Nil*."

Day 208:

While the new tool is being developed, the exploration of the chamber continues.

Until now, there has been total focus on the ship. Today, attention has turned to the hundreds of stone blocks embedded in the chamber's walls, a long row on each side of the ship, each block separated by a distance of 0.3179 meters.

Archaeologists have asked permission for one to be cut from the wall as a test, to see if it covers a tomb or a storage chamber for artifacts. Dariush tells me that the team cannot go forward with this until DSI gives permission and mandates the use of the nuclear scalpel. This I find supremely irritating. Why do such decisions have to pass through the fetid bowels of social infrastructure? What's to decide? It's plain what's needed! I feel certain that DSI derives so much pleasure from the exercise of power that it savors the exquisite sensation of making people wait. So everyone waits.

And waits.

Day 209:

The archaeologists, feeling somewhat frustrated, filled their idle hours by investigating the black stone cube that sits on the floor close to the ship's nose. As expected, its dimensions are multiples of our favorite number. Interestingly, the top is subtly concave, like a shallow basin. Thirteen pencil-thin grooves radiate outward from a symbol at the center of the basin.

The symbol may not be a symbol as such, and only purely decorative. It is a circular incision with thirteen smaller circles surrounding it, their rims all touching the central one. Each of the small circles, though they are of varying sizes, is the starting point of a groove. The grooves radiate toward the four edges of the "tabletop", cut the edges, and run down the sides, where they disappear into small holes in the floor. The cube sits upon a larger rectangle of the black metal. A second metal rectangle is embedded in the stone floor halfway between the cube and the nose of the ship, flanked by the two outer rails. Here, it would appear that the central rail was removed ages ago by the ones who originally made the chamber and/or interred the ship. Metallurgists have determined that the rails are a kind of steel, mainly iron, with carbon and another component that gives it extraordinary tensile strength.

Day 215:

In the late afternoon, I received a voice message from Dariush in my *max* inbox:

Hello, Neil.
I will be returning to the *Kosmos*, arriving by shuttle at 5 P.M., in order to consult my books. Perchance, will you join me for supper at a cafeteria or restaurant of your choice? I hope you are well and taking your medications faithfully.

I quickly sent a text reply:

> Feel okay, some days not so good. Bad dreams all the time. Taking my meds, but I wonder if they're helping. How about Mexican, 5:30?

Hopefully, this would be adequate cover.

At half past five, I stood by the door of the Mexican bistro and beheld Dariush coming toward me along the concourse, head down, looking very weary.

We greeted each other and then went inside. The place was bereft of customers, and so we were quickly served at the bar.

I lustily consumed my tacos and "cheese" while Dariush sipped at his cup of water and stared at the table top. He picked at his basket of tacos from time to time but dropped the uneaten chips back into it without a nibble. When I was full, he turned his bloodshot eyes upon me. I could tell he hadn't been getting enough sleep during the past few days.

"May we go for a walk?" he asked in a subdued voice.

We ambled here and there on the concourse for awhile, and then almost by default we took an elevator down to the arboretum. It too was deserted. The "birds" were off; the sky above was a deep blue with a few "stars" appearing.

We sat down side by side on a park bench.

"You've had quite a wait, my friend", I began. "But I expect DSI is as curious as we are and will give permission for opening the wall blocks soon. Do you think they contain the aliens' archives?"

Dariush nodded and said, "It is probable."

For a moment, I was sure he would launch one of his philological lectures. Instead, he put the palms of his hands to his face and bent over, his head almost touching his knees. He began to sob. I was more shocked by this barely audible weeping than I would have been if he had erupted into loud shouting. To see this most scholarly and quiet man so overcome with emotion left me at a loss for what to say or do.

Without thinking, I pitter-patted him on the back with my hand and made silly consolation noises which I had, I suspect, learned from my mother.

"Oh, oh, *pobrecito*, Dariush, *estás tan triste*", I murmured. "*¿Qué te pasa, ahora, qué te pasa? No te pongas triste, no estés triste. Todo va a estar bien.*" (Rough translation: Poor Dariush, you're so sad. What's the matter, now, what's the matter? Don't be sad, don't be sad. Everything's going to be all right.)

When he had composed himself, he told me about new discoveries, which had come to light after closer inspection of the rectangular metal floorplate, situated halfway between the cube and the ship's nose.

Three days ago, an archaeology team penetrated the rectangle's end seam and elevated it a few feet, discovering that it was balanced on an unseen axle or bar in its middle. Though the archaeologists did not rotate it fully, they raised it enough to observe that a stone staircase leads down to another level beneath the chamber containing the ship. Their lights did not penetrate far enough to see anything other than the steps disappearing into the darkness below.

Next, the archaeologists, with the aid of engineers, entirely removed the floorplate. Now armed with powerful searchlights, they descended the staircase. Dariush was with them. Arriving at the bottom, they found that the lower chamber was very large. It was filled with skeletal remains. Those who went down there could not proceed far, since stacks of bones blocked their passage. However, they noted that in all directions every space was filled as far as their eyes could see and the lights could penetrate. If, on further exploration, it is confirmed that the heaps of the dead continue uninterrupted to the farthest reaches of the chamber, it would mean that hundreds of thousands of bodies have been interred there, possibly millions.

Examining several dozen skeletons near at hand, the archaeologists learned much about the race that had built this extraordinary monument to their lost civilization.

The aliens were humanoid, with bodies and craniums shaped like ours. However, their skulls were disproportionately larger in relation to their skeletal frames, compared to our human ratio of cranium to frame. They had two eye sockets, not three, and there was nothing in the spinal region to indicate wings. They were much shorter than we are. The tallest of those examined were less than four feet in height. The majority of skeletons were markedly shorter than this, giving rise to speculation that there was more than one sub-race or "breed" (I use this term for lack of a better one) within this alien race. This is indicated by the fact that the taller ones, the minority, had a ratio of cranium size to body size that is closer to ours.

Messages were sent upward to the station and to the *Kosmos*, requesting additional staff to help bring some of the remains out of the crypt.

Within the hour, two physicians and a forensic specialist arrived, along with other station staff, carrying body bags. Every effort was made to load the skeletons intact, but their great age proved their undoing. They tended to fall apart into individual bones when they were moved. They are presently being reassembled in the lab at AS-VT, in preparation for further examination.

Now I must write about one of the more disturbing details of what was found. Dariush explained that the archaeologists thought at first that the chamber was a mausoleum, and he had concurred with this, thinking that it may have been a tradition of this race to bury its dead "in community", not in individual graves. One of the party suggested that it resembled an ossuary such as those found beneath certain ancient monasteries on Earth where burial space had been limited. It was then argued that Nova offered more than ample space for burial. The discussion continued as the archaeologists stepped this way and that through mounds of bones and skulls. Then came a sudden silence.

Now they were facing the area directly below the cube on the floor above. They could see thin shafts of light from the holes in the ceiling— the holes in the upper floor—to which the cube's grooves had led. Beneath this corona of light beams, they noticed a dark shape and pointed their lamps at it.

It was a sculpture carved from a massive block of gray stone. More than ten meters high, it was a three-dimensional embodiment of the celestial being or "god" inscribed on the cliff face above the gateway. All the details were there. It had uplifted wings. Its head was horned and had three eyes. Its legs stretched three times longer than the torso, ending in the elongated feet, with the difference that the base of the sculpture was a stone sphere that it gripped in its toe-claws. The arms were extended horizontally, and the claws of one hand held an arrow. The other hand was open with palm upward, though it lacked a carved depiction of flames. Dariush concluded that real fire once burned there.

In another important detail, the sculpture was different from the incised images on the cliff face and the inner wall. The neck and head were tilted back at a 90-degree angle from the body; its mouth was wide open, and into that gaping hole, thirteen light beams fell.

When Dariush had completed describing all this to me, I didn't know what to make of it. The whole scene was just too weird. We both got up and walked through the park toward the arboretum exit, saying nothing.

As we stood in the concourse, preparing to go to our separate rooms, Dariush said, "I am sick in my heart, Neil."

"I can understand that", I said. "All those skeletons and then a nasty shock from a sinister-looking statue."

"If this idol, and the altar above it, were used for what I suspect, then we have found a memorial of the unthinkable."

"The unthinkable? You could be misinterpreting the scene."

"Possibly. But I do not think so." He shuddered and murmured, "I feel very alone—alone in an ocean of evil."

I put a hand on his shoulder. "You're not alone."

Without warning, he said, "Will you pray with me?"

"Pray?" I asked, alarmed by his request. "I . . . I'd like to help. Really I would. But I'm no good at praying."

"It is the intentions of the heart that matter. If you would but trust—"

"Listen, Dariush, I know that what you saw in the cellar seems pretty grotesque, but it may not be what you suspect it is. And even if it is, it happened ages ago. You should get some sleep, and tomorrow you'll feel better about all this."

He gazed at me silently for a few moments.

"I must find Dr. Nagakawa", he whispered.

Day 217:

This morning, I knocked on his door, because I wanted to tell him that I had reconsidered his request and would try to pray, though a prayer of mine wouldn't be worth much. Did I believe in the soul, did I believe in a benevolent, overseeing God? I wasn't sure. Even so, I believed that Dariush was my friend, and this was good enough for me.

But he had gone. He was already back down on Nova.

Day 218:

The public presentations are short on details, short on imagery too, just plenty of learned commentary by the archaeologists and quick photos of the monster in the cellar and the limitless fields of body remains—info bites, image bites. Attention is being deflected back to the aliens' ship, and to the mysterious blocks that run along the walls on both sides of it.

Yesterday, one block was surgically removed, and behind that single slab were found ranks of rectangular metal plates standing on end and leaning against each other—hundreds in this chamber alone. The vault was found to be not very big, just over three meters deep, the same in height, and three times wider than the aforementioned dimensions (our now familiar measurements, I will not repeat them again).

Several plates were removed for examination. They are covered in hieroglyphics, finely inscribed. Dariush's team is making photoscan records of them, and preliminary analysis will begin soon. Though faintly oxidized, the script is not obscured. The metal is like bronze, an alloy constituted of copper, tin, and a third unknown element. One test plate was easily cleaned with a noncorrosive solution.

Today, more blocks were removed from the walls, and they all contained the metal plates inscribed with the indecipherable script. Thousands upon thousands of them. A linguist's paradise!

A program on the panorama screens reported the progress in making a new kind of tool that may be able to open the ship. There was a short interview with Xue and other interviews with the designers and engineers, plus a few diagrams and computer simulations of how it will work. The team is a month away from an initial test, which will be performed on the rotating floorplate leading to the crypt, since it appears to be the same substance as the ship's outer coating.

This was followed by a program about the towers, which have been stripped of all the organic growth. The rubble covering the metal floors has also been removed. An archaeologist gave his analysis of the towers' construction and his speculations about its purpose—an astronomy center, he thinks. If so, why have no artifacts come to light?

Then came a half-hour program about the skeletons being examined in the AS-VT labs, and the more intensive tests being done on them in the labs on the *Kosmos*. There were interviews with experts, who conjectured at length about the aliens' habits, appearance, and attitudes on death and the afterlife. An artist had created an imaginative rendition of what they may have looked like. He made them hairless and green-skinned (shades of our myth of the little green men), more or less humanoid, with bulging black eyes that gazed expressionless into the infinite and terrifying cosmos. The whole lot of it was guesswork, dressed up in highly articulate language that told us nothing.

321

Sadly, there has been another snakebite victim, a technical worker on a research mission to Continent 5—this is one of the lesser continents, situated in the northern hemisphere on the other side of the planet. There will be a media biography of the man later tonight, and burial at our cemetery at Base-main tomorrow. Our fourth death.

I have already watched about eight hours of presentations today, and my eyes are sore. I'll go for a swim, then maybe tune in to the biography of the deceased.

Day 219:

I went straight to bed after my swim last night. This morning I woke late and turned on my *max* to watch the funeral, which was already in progress. There weren't many mourners, I noticed, just a few stiff-looking guys and Elif Larson. The eulogy delivered by the Elf was brief and platitudinous. The obelisk was erected over the plot of soil that covered the deceased's body. The mournful music began, and the voice-over narrator began his account of the young man's short life. Disgusted by the expression on Elf's officially grieving face, and the subtler pomposity lurking behind it, I was about to shut down the *max* when suddenly onto the screen flashed a photo of David Ayne.

The narrator's summation continued:

William D. Aynes, known as Dave to his friends, came from Sacramento, California. A graduate of Stanford University in computer science, he worked as a technician for a subsidiary company of Raydon Aerospace during the years leading up to the *Kosmos* voyage. He signed on for the expedition to *Mundus Novus* because he had been interested in astronomy from childhood.

For some years he was a member of the ship's maintenance department, before his transfer to a special project attached to the Department of Social Infrastructure dealing with metallurgy statistics. It was in this capacity that he had undertaken a one-man flight to Continent 5 three days ago. A pilot and a part-time prospector back on Earth, he told colleagues that he wanted to make a preliminary investigation of C-5 to see if it would prove to be as rich in mineral deposits as C-1. Two days ago, the automatic distress signal was activated, and a rescue team was sent out. It followed the homing beacon and located the AEC flown by Aynes parked near the mouth of a river that flows into the equatorial sea. His body was found on the shore nearby. He was not wearing protective boots and leg gear at the time, nor had he carried antidote with him.

William Aynes will be missed by his friends. His passing is a loss to the *Kosmos* community. He will long be remembered.

Music, fanfare, mournful trumpet notes, sunlight flashing off the obelisk, end of program.

I groaned, my heart hammering hard.

Then came a one-minute image of the Earth flag rippling in a breeze, accompanied by stirring patriotic music (global version), concluding with a sober voice-over reminding the audience to wear their mandatory protective gear when venturing beyond security perimeters, and to carry snakebite antidote with them at all times.

I stared at the screen, seeing nothing for a few moments as the full impact hit me.

A special presentation began, featuring the scientists who were examining the skeletal remains found in the crypt. There was a sweeping vid of a sea of bones, a few still shots of a reconstructed skeleton, followed by several computer-generated images of what the aliens might have looked like, extrapolated from the anatomical findings. There was a variety of little men—all eerie.

I shut down the *max*.

Day 220:

A good deal of information had been compacted into that biography of my fellow conspirator, and a good deal of unanswered questions as well. It was a neat package. Too neat.

First of all, where were the friends who would miss "Dave"? Had they attended the funeral? Who were the men standing by the grave, and why did they all have a common ambience—the hardened mercenary-in-civvies look? Was the "metallurgy" special project listed as an activity in the roster of the ship's science departments and subdepartments? I would check this later, not through my home *max*.

Had David been an agent of DSI all along? Had the accidental death uncovered this? Had he avoided his old fellow conspirators because we were no longer a case that needed studying? Because we had been neutralized?

My suspicions produced question after question, all of them directed at David, whoever he really was; all of them tainted with resentment, the feeling that we had been royally (or should I say, democratically) used.

Then the counterarguments began.

He had sweated as a cleaning man for a number of years, which, it seemed to me, was rather overdoing a cover story, if indeed DSI had been merely checking out a handful of eccentrics. Though I am not particularly astute at reading human character, not once had I sensed a false note in my conversations with David. His had been a real personality.

And why, above all other considerations, had such a concerted effort been made to erase his records from the ship's computers?

Why, moreover, had the executives of DSI gone into meltdown over our tiny little revolt, and an even worse reaction when we inquired into David's absence?

I thought about it all for many hours, tossing the contradictory scenarios around in my head until I realized I was going in circles. And the more I thought about it, the more it seemed to me that the funeral and public biography might be the cover story. And if this was the case, what was the reason behind such elaborate disinformation? David's death may or may not have been accidental, but the cloak of lies pointed to something. Was he killed, not by a viper but by a two-legged snake? Or an elf? Or a skinner?

I was still brooding over this dark possibility when a slip of paper was pushed under my door.

On it was written: *Pitaji. Pool. P+P.*

I went swimming at my usual hour, about 3 A.M. and found the pool comparatively crowded. There were five people present besides myself, and I knew only two of them—Paul doing laps like a turbine and Pia demurely sitting on the edge, dabbling her feet. Beneath her modest bathing suit, her tummy was beginning to swell a little.

I did a few geriatric laps from one side of the pool to the other. Our eyes met, and she nodded slightly. She looked troubled.

I stopped to catch my breath a few feet away, and said, "Good evening, Dr. Sidotra."

"Good evening, Dr. Hoyos", she replied in a cordial tone that implied no close relationship with me.

"David?" I whispered.

"Juxtaposition", she whispered back, then pushed herself off the edge and swam away.

It was my turn to sit and dabble. What on earth had she meant by *juxtaposition*? Later, Paul thrashed past me, churning up a wake, and after a couple of more lengths, he stopped for a rest, his chest heaving, head on his arms, his face toward me. We performed our usual loud cover talk, and then he whispered, "Pia say we meet Rem-brant."

"When?"

"Tomorrow night, twenty hundred hours, she and me are off-shift. Now she is wait for autopsy your friend."

"Was she involved in the autopsy?"

"No. She know somebody."

Day 221:

I knocked on a few doors this morning, trying to locate Xue, Dariush, and Pagnol. No one was home. I then walked by a circuitous route to the library on Concourse B, where I accessed a computer terminal. A search through the ship's main website, as well as through several primary websites dealing with the voyage, showed me that the list of personnel now numbered 677. Our missing number had been returned without explanation. I searched through all the science departments' staff lists and couldn't find David in any of them.

"Where are you, where are you?" I seethed through clenched teeth, knowing they had reinserted him somewhere.

I checked a number of sites that concerned themselves with the *Kosmos*, including the ones far down the line beyond the eight-hundredth site level. All along the way, I learned that the records had been recorrected to read a total of 677.

Cross-checking a few randomly selected sites, I found David at last. He was listed as a statistician working for DSI. I keyed my way back to the ship's main site, picked my way through its maze, and sure enough, I found him in a little office with the title "metallurgy research statistics", a section of a subdepartment of DSI. It had only one employee.

There was his face; there was his revised name; there was his revised bio, concluding with a footnote: "Deceased. Accidental death. *Mundus Novus*", followed by the date of death.

Now I remembered the list of staff names I had printed out for myself during the first days of the voyage, more than nine years ago. It had been the source of my notes on types of personnel. Among them was a nonspecific category I had called "odd and sundry experts in extremely obscure fields". (See my print-out, pre-departure, Earth base—Africa.) At the time, I had not paid any attention to the names nor to the schematics of their departments.

I returned to my room and rummaged through the shelves in search of that personnel print-out. Fortunately, I had not passed it on to Paul with the rest of my written journal, since I had presumed it would be a public-access document, and thus there was no need to hide it. I found the papers tucked away between some science journals, and confirmed what I suspected. There was no office of metallurgy statistics. Moreover, this document contained the original biographical information, and it was quite different from the new official version. Here was the solid evidence that his name had been changed, along with certain details of his life. I hid the papers inside my shirt, then checked my mail.

There were three messages:

Xue had sent me a text message saying that he was away for several days at a base on Nova, involved in a crucial stage of developing "research technology". He mentioned his regret over the recent death of a member of an exploration team. He reminded me to take my medications. Of course, he knew that I knew about his project, so this, along with the reference to the meds, was nothing more than a smoke screen. Between the lines, he was telling me that he was thinking about the meaning of David's death.

Pagnol sent a friendly voice message, also with a passing reference to the recent death. He noted that people were now being more careful about protection from snakes. He too reminded me to take my meds.

Dariush sent a voice message, telling me that he would be returning to the *Kosmos* this afternoon and giving me his time of arrival. He wished to consult a book on Assyrian cuneiform, since rational intelligence, he said, might follow universal principles in the formation of language. It was only a theory, but he wanted to assess it by comparing Assyrian patterns with emerging patterns he thought he detected in the aliens' script. He made a simple reference to the "regrettable recent death of a crew member" and hoped there would be no more such accidents. He reminded me to take my meds.

At 4 P.M., I met Dariush coming out of the elevator on his deck, fresh off his shuttle flight. He looked unspeakably weary, but insisted that we go for a walk. We went down to deck D on the nearest staircase and proceeded along the concourse in the direction of the arboretum.

My heart skipped a beat when I saw Elif Larson walking toward us from that direction, swinging an attaché case in one hand and smiling to himself. My fists clenched and my teeth gritted. As we neared each other, he looked up and frowned.

"Dr. Larson", I exclaimed in an eager voice. "Did you see the aliens? Do you think they were green or blue?"

He scowled without slackening his pace and did not answer me, sweeping by as if I were a bug or a chimera.

He had gone a few steps past us when Dariush stopped and called after him, "Dr. Larson!"

The Elf paused, turned around, glanced at his wristwatch, and muttered, "Yes?"

Dariush looked at the man without expression and in a freighted tone that was quite uncharacteristic of him, he said: "*Qui legitis flores et humi nascentia fraga, frigidus—o pueri, fugite hinc—latet anguis in herba.*"

"What?" barked Elf irritably.

"A line of Latin poetry, sir. A reference to a beautiful world, though one fraught with perils."

"Yes, yes, very nice. I expect you're working hard at deciphering the archives in the cave. Well, I'm busy too. I'm late for a meeting." Turning on his heel, he strode away.

"What did you say to him, Dariush?" I asked when the Elf was out of earshot.

"I said, 'Gatherers of flowers and ground-strawberries, fly hence! O children, a cold snake lurks in the grass!' It was a moment of weakness on my part. I hope I have not violated charity."

"Well, you won't get a slap on the wrist from me."

"It is from Virgil's *Eclogues*. You must read this magnificent opus one day, Neil. I will lend you my copy, if you wish."

"Okay, if you agree to read Conrad's *Heart of Darkness*. I'll lend you my copy."

"Recall that it was I who first introduced you to that estimable book."

He smiled wanly, and we entered the Mexican bistro. Over a suitably hot repast, I described to him in a low voice what I had learned about David's files.

"Why has there been this change of names?" he said. "Why the subtle shifting of initials, nicknames, a letter added or subtracted?"

"Smoke and mirrors, Dariush. Now you see him, now you don't. Then you see him again in a new costume. Only, now he ain't talking."

"It seems to me that there can be only one reason for it. If the death were ever to be investigated, or if David's absence for the past many months were suspected as unlawful incarceration, the authorities would be able to deny it. They would attribute it to poor record-keeping, a clerical error."

"Sounds like a snake in the grass."

"Yes, there is a snake in the grass", he nodded.

After that, he went off to consult his books, and I returned to my own room.

At ten o'clock this evening, I went downstairs to the Rembrandt alcove—the anatomy lesson—Pia's wit again, or perhaps a late-blooming symbolic tendency.

She and Paul arrived shortly after the hour.

"What did you mean by *juxtaposition*?" I asked her.

"Neil, did you notice how the accidental death occurred precisely in the middle of the most dramatic discoveries? The attention paid to the death and funeral were short-lived, preceded and followed by the most fascinating programs."

"Yes, I noticed."

"That's distraction by juxtaposition, swamping the perceptions with stronger stimuli. It's also an ominous sign."

"In what way?"

"Because it means the time of his death was chosen", said Paul.

"We don't really know that", I said. "It may be one of those coincidences. I've had times in my life when everything went wrong at once. We used to call them 'a week of calamities'. Everyone gets a week like that at some point."

Pia shook her head. "I might have reserved judgment too, Neil, but there's more to tell you. I have a physician friend in the deck-D clinic, where autopsies are performed."

"Have you read the autopsy report?"

"Yes, all clinics received a copy. It tells us that the victim died of snake venom. However, microscopic analysis has revealed that the body had been frozen and thawed before its supposed death."

"What!"

"David's body had been frozen for approximately thirty-nine months before it was thawed and then deposited on the shores of Continent 5. Someone killed him, someone stored him away for all that time. Then he was thawed out at the right moment, the corpse flown to C-5, the distress signal and homing beacon activated, and then whoever did it flew back here to watch the tragic tale unfold."

"So this is how they're covering their tracks", I said.

"Yes, death by accident, and a nice clean autopsy report for the archives."

"But won't there be an uproar when all the physicians on board read it?"

"There is no mention of the freezing in the report."

"Why not?"

"At first, the doctor didn't know what had really happened. He had his doubts about the cause of death—or I should say, he maintained an open mind about it. That's the proper approach for any forensic pathologist. He was also concerned about the way the directors of DM and DSI wanted a quick autopsy and report. They had talked up the fact that the cause of death was obvious. And so it seemed. But the doctor is a perfectionist, and he didn't like the way the directors stood by, breathing down his neck, eager for him to complete his findings so they could file it. Usually, after an autopsy report is filed, all lab samples taken from a body—blood, urine, stomach contents, bone marrow, etc.—are destroyed. That's standard procedure. But the lab people hadn't yet been notified that the report was completed, so they were still holding onto samples until told they could do so. After the report was officially filed, the doctor went personally to the lab people to inform them. He obtained the samples and made his own analyses in private. He found that the lab had done its work correctly. However, he submitted the samples to other tests, including a look at everything through an atomic microscope."

"What did he find?"

"Of course, he found fresh venom traces in every sample."

"But that means David did die on the planet."

"Not necessarily. The most disturbing evidence he discovered was in the molecular condition of cells. The crystallography tracks in the hemoglobin revealed conclusively that the body had been frozen for around thirty-eight to thirty-nine months."

"But it doesn't add up. You say the autopsy showed he died of venom . . ."

"We know there have been no snakes on the *Kosmos*. Moreover, the venom found in David's body is the same as that found in the other victims, and matches exactly the *proteases* samples taken from AC-A-7 snakes—specifically the viper-like species that resembles our sub-species Crotalinae on Earth."

"I don't understand. What are you saying?"

"He died of asphyxiation and heart failure caused by radically lowered blood pressure, which is typical of *proteasis*-induced death. But cardiovascular damage can have other causes. The presence of venom in his system could also be obtained by other means."

"Such as?"

"Immediately after thawing—if the body had been quick-frozen after death—all body fluids would again become mobile and fresh, manipulable. His blood could have been recycled through his system, and the venom added during the process."

"You're saying he was murdered."

Pia nodded. "My friend thinks so. It seems that everything points in that direction. Why else would such discrepancies be present, especially the freezing, followed by a cover-up?"

"Obviously, whoever did this felt confident that no one would discover it."

"They didn't consider that scientists also have intuitions."

"Has the doctor reported his findings?"

"Not yet. He's feeling somewhat anxious."

"He does not want to die of snake bite", said Paul.

Pia continued: "After your talk three years ago, Neil, he began to ponder things with more circumspection. He's a good observer. He didn't know if your accusations about surveillance were based in reality. He had nothing to go on, nothing that would convince him, but he kept the file open in his mind, though he didn't discuss it with anyone. Then he saw your poster about David being missing. He saved it, and now he knows that the dead man is the very one the administration said never existed."

"Never existed but has now been found", I said. "Hopefully, there are a lot of people on board like this doctor."

"Hopefully. Until now, he had spotted nothing really out of the ordinary in medical protocols. Of course, when he told me about his autopsy findings, I told him about DSI's and DM's efforts to turn you into a psychotic. He argued that you were mentally ill and needed the medication. But even as he said it, I could tell he didn't really believe it. I also confessed my failure to administer the pills."

"That's a risk, Pia", I said. "Can you trust him? What if DSI spooks him and makes him retreat into complicity to save his own skin?"

"That might have been a problem until now, but no longer. Bad prescriptions can be the result of poor diagnosis, which can be explained away as human error. But murder can't be explained away. And there the good doctor draws the line. He told me he's convinced we're dealing with a tyranny. The worst sort of tyranny, he said, because it disguises itself as benevolent, reasonable administration."

"What will we do about this tyranny?" asked Paul in a low, Slavicly dangerous voice.

No one had any suggestions.

"Maybe we should meet this doctor", I said. "Pia, would he be willing to talk with us?"

"I've already asked him, but he declined. However, he did write a complete report on his findings—albeit a private report. He's going to give me a copy, which Paul will store for safekeeping as soon as I have it. The doctor insisted that he remain anonymous in word-of-mouth conversations and e-communications. Accusers are a tainted bunch, you realize, with little credibility and absolutely no means to overthrow the regime. He thinks that justice will be done only when the ship returns to Earth. As long as we're under DSI authority, anything we say can be denied or drowned out by their countermeasures and distractions, and all to no good effect. In the meantime, he's going to try to discuss this with others on the quiet."

"And I will discuss with Captain", Paul added.

I stared at the floor, pondering, adding and subtracting.

"He died sometime between thirty-eight and thirty-nine months ago, you say?"

Pia nodded. "You gave your talk on Day 2252, Neil. Just under 39 months ago."

"I see."

I suddenly found myself incapable of speech. I murmured good night and went back to my room.

(Note to myself: Get this most recent entry into Paul's hands as soon as possible. If it's found in my room, I will have a week of calamities.)

Day 222:

Paul has the unofficial autopsy report, which the Captain has radioed back to Earth base. My notes are also safe and sound. I want to murder two people on board, need I say who? Murder or justice? I could not, would not, do it. Still, the feeling remains.

Day 223:

Dariush just arrived back on board and will remain here for a few days. We shared a meal in the Mexican bistro this evening, and afterward we went for a walk to an art alcove on deck C, one we had never used before. There I told him about the private autopsy findings.

He fell silent and closed his eyes.

"It's murder", I said, interrupting his prayers. "I *know* it's murder. But would we be able to prove it in court?"

Mute and glum, he shook his head uncertainly. We remained without speaking for a time, staring at the floor, both of us feeling quite helpless.

Hoping to break the looming paralysis, I asked Dariush if he was making progress in his work. He answered in a subdued voice that, yes, there was progress. Upward of four thousand tablets had been removed from the archives, with more being removed and scanned every day. Projecting from the number of wall blocks still to be opened, the tablets so far examined represent a fraction of what may be archived there.

"Are the hieroglyphics telling you anything?" I asked.

"Unfortunately, we do not yet have a key. As I mentioned to you before, there are patterns emerging, and a greater variety of 'letters', so we know it is a language. Of course, we have known this from the beginning. Our problem now is to find the decryption that unlocks it. I am going carefully through some of my own books to see if I can find anything helpful. I have a sense that it is there, lost in a forest of my old materials from Earth."

"You think their language may be like some of our ancient ones."

"I do not know. It is a sense, a feeling. Not necessarily even a productive scientific feeling. Intelligence, however, has a nature of its own, transcending all our world's races and stages of civilization. It is possible that this alien race, much like us in several ways, developed similar language patterns."

"So you're not talking about a decryption key as such. You mean some kind of vague template."

"Yes. And if the aliens were intelligent, as we know they surely were, and their brains were like ours biologically, it points in the direction of common development of logic and communication. The symbols would be different, arbitrary, that is, yet the processes would be similar if not the same."

"I see. You're searching for a needle in a haystack, but at least you have a haystack to look at."

"Precisely."

For a moment, he seemed to lose focus, his eyes clouded with distractions, or worry. I did not press him for more discussion and let him run to the end of whatever line of thought he was silently pursuing. Then to my surprise, I saw that the dark look was there again—the one which had so haunted him the day he asked me to pray with him, when he told me he was facing an "ocean of evil".

"You're thinking about David", I said.

"Yes, Neil, I am. And also about the Temple of the Ship—"

"Is that what you call it now?"

"The archaeologists have given it this name, since clearly it was a site built for religious purposes."

"Also scientific and archival."

"For them—the aliens—there was no distinction between the three. Their scholarship, their science, their cult was a single unity."

"Well, it's true they had hideous art, but they were also very advanced. Not as far as we are now, but still ..."

"Advanced? Yes, in terms of technology. But why have we found no cities? And this art you speak of was not merely art. The celestial being in the crypt of the Temple was an idol. Moreover, this idol drank copious amounts of blood—the blood of the aliens. There is so much about their society that remains inexplicable."

"And that's all we know."

Now he looked directly into my eyes. "Neil, we have learned that all the skeletons examined in the crypt, without a single exception, were children."

"Children? They were very small compared to us, that's all."

He shook his head. "The forensic people have completed their studies of the remains. Samples were taken from every skeleton type, ranging from the shortest to the tallest. All samples indicate that the bone cells were in growth stage when they died."

I stared at him, not wanting to believe it.

"Maybe the adults were buried elsewhere in the huge vault", I suggested.

"It is true that it is immense, and there are millions of skeletons. However, the hall was explored to its limits and numerous samples selected in every quadrant. Some of the remains were found to be very ancient, others more recent. But they are all children."

"So, it was a communal tomb for their children."

"No, Neil, it was not a mausoleum where they merely interred their dead. It was a temple where they performed human sacrifice."

My throat closed and the hair stood up on the back of my neck. I said nothing, just stared at him unable to speak.

"Neil, please excuse me. I must return to my studies now."

I could see he was overcome with emotion and did not want to talk any more. I watched him turn away and head off down the concourse. Like a sleepwalker, I returned to my room and lay down on my bed.

Day 224:

I awoke in a sweat, yelling, "No! I left it behind!"

For a few seconds, I saw a spiral staircase shining before me in the darkness. It had been part of the dream, I knew, but now I saw it with my eyes. Trying to clear my vision, I blinked rapidly, and the image faded, though it remained in my mind.

Then I remembered I was on a great ship in the heavens—floating above a heaven in the heavens. I was a scientist, a man of reason, devoted to objective reality.

I switched on the bedside light, threw off the covers, and sat up. Looking down at my hands, I saw they were clenched on my lap. They were old brown hands, wrinkled and roped with blue veins. My bare legs and feet were old too. The scar was there, as it always had been there.

The dream had terrified me, leaving me with a feeling of unbearable pain. It screamed at me, though I was now fully awake. *You must look at this, niño*, it said. *It has been buried in the dark for too long.*

Slowly, my heart ceased banging in my ears, and the rapid inflations of my chest returned to normal. I did not think of the monstrous idol in the Temple of the Ship. I did not think of the uncountable victims hidden away in that dark cellar of evil. Instead, I looked at the thing I did not want to remember: the journey I had made with my father when I was nineteen, the day he took me to Santa Fe to register me for my first year of college.

We were about halfway between Las Cruces and Santa Fe, traveling on an old gravel road that was rarely used after the twelve-lane expressway from El Paso to Albuquerque had been built thirty years before. This superbahn was straight as an arrow and permitted speeds of 180 km per hour. Our route, by contrast, was a rough one, and it sometimes dwindled to a single lane. It passed through a valley east of the Rio Grande that was appropriately named Jornada del Muerto, very dry and with few human habitations along the way, then it climbed laboriously through the San Andreas mountains. Occasionally, we passed old people leading donkeys, and sometimes a traveler making his way from nowhere to nowhere on foot. My father would stop and ask such solitaries if they wanted a ride, but they always took one look at our decrepit Hydra with its stinking compost tank on top, thanked us politely, and declined.

Our intention was to cross over into the northern end of the Tularos Valley on various little-used side roads, and in this way, we would bypass the old ruins of White Sands missile site and Alamogordo, and finally swing around Albuquerque and arrive unnoticed in Santa Fe. As was often the case, that year my father could not afford the vehicle insurance, nor the plate registration fee, and he hoped to avoid being spotted by the police.

For this and other reasons, I felt anger against him that day. I did not let it show, but I brooded and brooded, and sweated and sweated in the late August heat, nursing my many grievances against life. Why was I so angry? Sixty years later, I do not recall the reasons exactly. I have a memory of resentment against the bubbling in the tank above my head, the stench of rotting organics that escaped through a leak, and the inefficiency of the old methane compressor, the squeaking and rattling, the whine of the motor. I had a headache from the heat that was stewing my brain inside our tin pot of a car. I hated the broken air conditioner that we could not afford to fix, the stings of insects that hit my arm hanging outside the open window, the smell of my father's body, which so often went unwashed because our water well was not deep enough. I hated my leg and ankle, my stupid ears, my secondhand clothing, my battered suitcase in the trunk, and of course my social status, which was as low as one could legally go and remain alive.

I had received a scholarship to the college only because I was (so they told me) a genius at physics, or at least a potential genius. This was my single resource. I was about to be thrown into a community of strangers—beautiful, privileged, young people who would take one look at me and decline to know me. Already I did not like them.

Thus I was tense with determination. Determined that over the long haul I would outshine them all intellectually, and in the short haul that I would arrive on time for registration, demolishing the common prejudice that my people were unreliable, unambitious, and unconcerned about the pressing matters of life, such as watching the clock. *Mañana* would no longer be my motto. Henceforth, *Per ardua ad astra* would be my motto (I had recently read this phrase in an astronomy book, and was insufferably proud that I had memorized it).

Sure enough, the car chose the worst possible moment in my life to break down. There was an ominous little "pop", followed by chuff-chuff-chuff, a wheeze, and then we rolled to a stop. Instantly, the sun began to broil us.

"*Ay, caramba*", my father mumbled, which made me angrier. I think I rolled my eyes and exhaled through my nostrils.

"Well, let's see what the matter is", he said in his patient tone, the tone that irritated me most.

So we got out of the car and walked all around it.

"What now?" I asked abruptly.

"I don't know. Maybe I should look at the tubes."

"Maybe you should", I shot back in a tone that lacked our usual solidarity in trials. My disdain was just below the surface, and rising.

This drew a swift glance from him, and I felt sudden shame for my rudeness. Without comment, he opened the fuel-access hatches on the roof, and the front lid covering the engine that he had jerry-built from the far superior (though unrepairable) original motor.

"Ay, ay, ay", he muttered as he checked all the components, one by one.

"What is it?" I demanded. "Do you see anything?"

"It looks okay to me. I don't understand it."

To make a long and horrible story shorter, let me say that after two hours of tinkering we gave up trying to find the source of the trouble. My father sighed and unrolled an old tarp he kept stored in the trunk, and tied it between two *piñon* trees to make us some shade. We sat down on the ground under it and drank from our water bottles. Neither of us said anything. My life was in ruins.

"Why do we sit here?" I said after some time had passed.

"Maybe a car will come along", he replied. "It will take us to a service station. There we can hire a tow truck."

"But we have no money."

"I have *Uni* credits", he mumbled, not very convincingly. I had two hundred *Uni*s coded into my personal card, but I wasn't sure if he knew. After a short struggle with myself, I withdrew it from my hip pocket and handed it to my father with a facial expression that would have chilled the heart of the hungriest beggar.

He stared at the card and then delicately took it. He did not thank me; he did not say anything at all. He merely held the card in his hand and lowered his head, covering his eyes with the palm of his other hand.

I was very embarrassed. I had never heard my father weep before, not in all my long life of nineteen years. Generally, he was a most confident man, never daunted by setbacks and blows. But now, strangely, he looked defeated.

"Why do you cry!" I exclaimed, more a protest than a question.

He did not answer me, did not look at me.

Is this my father? I thought to myself. *Is this what I have been given!?*

The injustice of it, added to the constant burdens of our life, our endless striving that never got us anywhere, now hit me full force.

"Why are we so poor?" I shouted. But the question needed no answer. We both knew that our family was on the bottom of things because he could not make enough money to raise us up.

"Why are you and *Mamá* always so sad?" I threw at him. "Why do you cry? Why does she cry all the time?"

This was unfair of me. The truth is, while he could not be called a jolly man, he hardly ever seemed despondent. And my mother rarely cried. Both of them were calm, generous people, full of good thoughts and kind words, and were ever involved in valiant attempts to make "our village" a welcoming place for the world's unwelcome people.

Still, he said nothing. I was staring at him when we heard the clippitty-cloppity of donkey hoofs and the tinkling of little harness bells. Looking up, I saw an old man coming along the road toward us, leading a burro. He was smiling, his eyes twinkling beneath the shade of his straw sombrero; his silver handlebar moustache was quaintly long, the skin of his face and hands dark brown. I resented him mightily. He was the embodiment of *mañana*. He had no worries, no responsibilities. He had a four-legged vehicle of his own, and such vehicles perpetuate themselves. Cars did not give birth to little cars. Even the poorest of the poor were better off than me!

The old fellow came to a halt beside the car and shook his head over it.

"*Ay, ay, pobrecito, estás tan triste*", he said in a sing-song. "*No te pongas triste, no estés triste. Todo va a estar bien.*" (Oh, oh, poor little one, you're so sad. Don't be sad. Everything will be okay.) Whether he was addressing us or the car, I do not know.

My father slowly rose to his feet and went over to him. The stranger gave him an encouraging smile, and then without another word, he peered under the hatches on the roof. He reached inside like a blind surgeon and felt all around with his very ancient fingers.

"It is the blood vessel of the *automóvil, no?*" he said in the high voice sometimes used by very aged Mexicans. "*Señor*, the hose is crack and pull from the heart. You make the wire around it, *el coche pobres* is fix, *sí*."

My father tinkered as directed. The old man watched, humming to himself. My father got into the car and turned the ignition, the motor rumbled, and our chariot sat there in front of us, vibrating nicely and ready to go.

"The pressure hose", my father said. "That's all it was."

He got out of the car, rummaging in his pockets for some money to give the old man, but this was only a courtesy gesture, because there was nothing in the pockets.

338

"*Nada, nada*", the old man waved it away. Then he turned and led the burro off the road and into the desert. He passed beyond a thicket of mesquite, and we saw him no more.

My father got in behind the steering wheel, I jumped into the passenger seat, and we continued our journey.

I don't think we said a word for about forty miles or so.

Somewhere east of Albuquerque, he handed me back my card, keeping his eyes on the road.

"I am sorry, *Papacito*", I murmured shamefacedly.

"Benigno", he replied and said no more.

More time passed.

There came a moment when he cleared his throat. "You ask me why we are sad all the time. Does it seem to you we are always sad?"

"No, *Papa*, you are not."

"Your mother cries one time a year, I know."

"Yes. It worries me. She will not tell me why. Never has she explained it to me. I can see no cause for it. Why does she cry at the end of July every year? For three days she cries. Every year. It is very strange."

"There are reasons."

"Can you tell me the reasons?"

I watched his face closely. A wave of sorrow washed across it.

"You are a man now", he said. "Perhaps the time has come for me to tell you. For a long time, you have known that the world is a hard place. You can see with your eyes that we have guarded you from the evil all around us, and I think you have discovered that we guarded your thoughts as well."

Still, Benigno, the world is a dangerous place, my mother had called after me when I strode confidently out into the desert, the day a rattler struck me down.

I said nothing. I did not want him to speak negatively about the world. I knew that the world had problems, even serious ones. But my life was beginning. There was promise in it. Maybe I would become a genius. I had a scholarship. I did not want him to tell me, as he had done so often before, that there was much wrong in the way people thought and the way they lived.

"Why does my mother cry?" I asked, hoping to steer him away from general criticisms of the world.

"Your mother cries because there is a great suffering in her heart. Long ago it happened. We have wanted to tell you, but ..."

"What did you not tell me?"

"Neil", he said. He always called me Neil when he was about to speak of the gravest matters. "You once had a brother and a sister."

"What?" Stunned, unable to absorb what he had just said, let alone understand it, I stared at him with my mouth open.

"When you were a year old, we conceived a child, *Mamá* and me. There were two children in her womb, twins, though we did not know this at first. Later, when she became bigger, Fray Ramon brought a doctor to us. He was a good man who did work for free. He brought an instrument and put it on her belly, and we watched the *niños* swimming around inside. We could see it was a boy and a girl. Very pretty, very strong they were."

As I listened to him tell the story, my throat choked up, and I stared straight ahead through the windshield. I did not know what to feel. I felt only that I did not want to hear this.

"We hid her pregnancy. She never left the village after her belly could no longer be hidden. Your grandmother lived with us then. Do you remember her?"

"No", I said. Looking back, my memory produced only vague impressions of several old women with gray hair, the ladies of the village who were like grandmothers to any and all children.

"The people were accustomed to guarding such secrets", my father continued. "They did not report us to the police. There were other illegals among us. Do you remember the red blossom children?"

"Yes. They always ran into the desert when the police came."

In our village, mothers or grandmothers often painted little flowers on the hands of certain *niños* among us—not all of the children, just some, the illegals. They made a game of it, because they did not want to frighten the little illegal ones. Whenever the bell rang, the red blossom children knew that they must hide. In the chaparral and sage bushes, they could not be found. If they remained hidden until they were called home by their mothers, they received sweets.

"The police always come fast. They give no warning", I said.

"Yes, and that is why we made the trailers into a maze."

"We are a town of crazy streets. I thought it was because people are stupid."

"It is because people are smart and because they love their children. Later, the police and the social workers used the heli-floaters and heat scanners, so it was not so easy to hide. The fathers of the village dug holes in the earth beyond the edge of the village and covered them with plywood and sand. Little caves. They were dangerous because of snakes and scorpions."

"I used to play in them."

My father took his eyes from the road and gave me a severe look. "That was foolish, Neil."

"We thought it was part of the game. The older ones helped the little ones. *Mamá* used to ring the bell."

"Yes, the mothers took turns watching. If a strange car came along the road or a hovercraft appeared in the sky, they rang the old brass bells—the same as the one your *Mamá* uses for the *piñata* feasts. There are many bells like it in the village. The children stopped playing and hid themselves."

He grew silent again.

"Where are my brother and sister?" I asked.

"I do not know who betrayed us", he said in a shaken voice. "Maybe no one betrayed us. It is possible the police just came that day in the hope of finding something. They checked every trailer. I was away at work. Your mother was napping in our home at the time. Your grandmother had taken you for a walk, wrapped up in her *tilma*. When *Mamá* heard the bell ringing, she got out of bed and tried to go quickly into the desert. But she was eight months along, very big with two babies inside, and she could not walk well. She did not get far before they spotted her."

Now I was frozen inside. It was the strangest sensation in the world, to feel nothing emotionally, with the hair lifting on the back of my neck, my fists tightly clenching, my heart pounding, my throat closing, my lungs struggling to breathe.

"They took her away to a hospital. They cut the children from her womb. They killed them, Neil. They killed them. And then a doctor did something so that she could never again have children."

"What did you do?" I asked in a choked voice.

"I could do nothing—nothing! I searched for her. I went to Las Cruces and banged on many doors. The police would not tell me where they had taken her. The department in charge of these things would not tell me. I hit one of their men. I spent six months in jail because I hit him."

"And my mother?" I gasped.

"Three days after they took her, they returned her to the village, to our home."

As he drove onward, I observed my father's face. Never had I seen him look like this. Never. Until the day I die, I do not want to see another look like that on anyone's face. I saw a grief so deep it was fathomless, beyond my comprehension, then and now. There was an old anger in it too, an utterly helpless kind of anger. All these years later, I wonder if there was also despair. I don't doubt that he had feelings of despair. Yet I think there was no absolute and final despair, because of what happened later that night.

I can't write any more today. I feel sick. I feel helpless. Why has all this come back to me now? I want to kill the people who killed my brother and sister. Sixty years have passed, and I still want to kill them. I am watching myself kill them in my mind. Why does this pain not stop?

Day 225:

Look at it, Neil. Look at everything and see it. Why have you tried to bury this? Why have you turned away from it throughout all these many years? Was the pain too great for you? Is a man a man if he does not face the worst with courage?

But where would courage have taken me? What would I have done? What *could* I have done? Learning the truth of my family's history left me in a state of rage and dread, and for neither of these was there any outlet.

As our car approached the outskirts of Santa Fe, the sunset was a violent red over the city.

"Take me back to Las Cruces", I said to my father.

"You must not miss the registration", he replied, shaking his head. "There are only a few hours until it closes."

"Take me back to my mother!" I demanded.

"Neil, you cannot go back."

"Take me back *now*!" I yelled and burst into tears.

He pulled over to the side of the road and idled the engine. He sat with both hands on the steering wheel as I sobbed.

"You must go forward", he said quietly.

"To what! To what!"

"You must go forward into your life."

"No, I will go back. I will go back, and I will find the killers. I will destroy them!"

"If you kill the killers, you too will become a killer."

"No! I will bring justice."

"Justice? What do you think is justice?"

"I don't know. I don't care. But I will make them pay for what they did."

"Only you will pay—it would destroy *you*, not them."

"I hate them. Truly, *Papa*, I hate them. I will hate them all my life."

"Do not hate them. They do not know they are evil. They are blind. If you hate them, if you kill them in your heart, they will not die. They will rise up again and again within you, and they will kill your heart."

"I will make them suffer!"

"*You* will suffer. And your mother and me will suffer too."

"There is no other way!"

"There is another way, Benigno. I will show it to you."

What did he show me? He showed me a ruin. A ruin within ruins within ruins.

We drove on into the brightly lit city, which was filled with speeding cars and happy laughing people on the sidewalks, the noise of bars and dancing halls, and billboards with 3D advertisements for beautiful people living beautiful lives. I hated it all. I hated every passing face. As we navigated slowly along a street called Alameda, young men and women in expensive cars sneered at us as they roared past at high speeds, and some of them made rude gestures. All around us towered new office buildings and hotels. We turned off this main thoroughfare onto a side street and went north. The whole block looked like a junkyard of rubble and machinery for demolishing buildings, with a few standing structures that looked very old.

My father turned left into an alleyway and parked the car. We got out, and he led me across the street into the maze of ruins.

"What is this place?" I asked.

"The cathedral once stood here, San Francisco de Asís, where for centuries men worshipped God. They have torn it down to make a grand hotel."

I had never entered a church before. I knew what they were because from childhood onward I had read about them, heard stories about

343

them, and seen their ghostly forms from a distance. I had been baptized by Fray Ramon in the plaza of our village, and had worshipped all my life at the tail gate of his pickup truck. When I was a little boy, my father had sometimes taken me to remote adobe missions in the hills, but these ancient buildings did not have priests in residence and were boarded up, locked with police seals, or enclosed behind barriers erected by historical preservation agencies. Whenever we visited one, we would kneel in the dust and pray, then quickly leave before we were seen.

"We are trespassing in our own home", my father now said to me, in a voice just above a whisper.

His solar flashlight lit the way ahead of us a few steps at a time. We climbed over piles of concrete, crawled under barriers, squeezed through fence slats, and came to a shadowed building of large yellow blocks. The beam of light played over the doorway, the padlocks, the police notice, the other signs warning us away. Undeterred, my father led me around the building and into what looked like a yard full of wheelbarrows and stacked stones. Beyond these, we came to a wooden shack leaning against a high chain-link fence.

"We will speak to the watchman", he said.

He knocked on the lintel of the low doorway, for only a blanket covered the opening.

"*Mi amigo*", he called in a low voice.

An unseen hand pushed aside the blanket, and the light of an oil lamp flowed out to greet us. Then a man stepped out into the dark. I could not see his face, but I could tell by the way he embraced my father that they knew each other well. As they whispered together, I could not hear their words.

The man took us through a canyon of construction materials, and led us deeper into the shadows behind the building we had first examined. There my father pointed his flashlight at a spot on the wall close to the ground, and I saw a wooden trap door, white with cement dust. The watchman lifted it, crouched down, and went inside, with my father and me following on his heels. I could see next to nothing as I climbed a few rickety wooden steps behind the men. At the top, the watchman opened a door with the sound of squealing hinges and scraping wood, and I found myself standing inside a low-ceilinged room that contained only a countertop along one wall and cupboards with open shelves. The smell of mice was strong. I heard the hooting of an owl somewhere above my head. Broken glass crunched beneath my shoes, and I dragged my bad leg through it carefully, fearing that I would fall and cut myself.

Next we passed through an open doorway into a larger space.

"I will make a light", said the watchman. He took two candles from his pocket and set them on a table at the near end of the room. When they were lit, their glow illuminated the immediate area, and I saw that the table was a slab of flat stone upon two stone uprights. It was cracked in several places, with pieces broken off, and covered with spray-painted graffiti. The surrounding walls had been defaced in the same way.

"The light might be seen", my father said.

"No, we are safe. After vandals broke the glass, the windows were covered with plywood until a decision is made."

"So there is still hope?"

"*Un poco*, a little. The government wants it razed to the foundation. The historical agency wants it restored. A museum, they say. Perhaps they will save only the work of San José."

"If they try to save it by taking it elsewhere, will it not be destroyed?"

"*Sí*, this is a danger. It is very old, and no one can explain why it stands. No one has ever been able to explain it. Yet it is not indestructible."

Turning to me, my father said, "This is my son. His name is Neil Benigno Ruiz de Hoyos. Neil, this is my friend. I cannot tell you his name."

The nameless man extended his hand to me with a smile. I shook the hand and dropped it. Now I could see that he was in his fifties, with a toil-worn face haunted by a lifetime of troubles. In the flickering shadows of candlelight, he seemed furtive to me, repugnant. Yet there was kindness and intelligence in his eyes, and I wondered why I was not permitted to know his name.

"So you have brought him here to see the gift?" said the man.

"He has need of it now", said my father. "Will you show him?"

"Of course."

The man took the candles from the table and carried them into the darkness. We stepped off the low platform onto a brick floor and followed him. I halted abruptly and gave a yelp of fright when out of the shadows came a huge red shape like a monster opening its jaws to devour me. My father took my arm, drawing me closer.

He played his flashlight over the great beast.

"It is a fire engine", he said. "Once this was a station where men defended the city from fires. In the old days, houses were made of wood, and sometimes they burned down and people died. No one has driven this machine for many years."

Now we stood before the front of the vehicle. It was like a truck with a huge head and long body. It sat upon concrete blocks, its tires missing. It was something like a modern car with two glass eyes, but its front was not flat like our cars. It bulged forward with an open mouth and broken metal teeth. Above the teeth was an iron motor with wires sticking out of it, and a completely shattered windshield. There were seats inside with torn fabric and coiled springs.

"A little farther", said our host.

As we walked toward the end of the room, I saw that the ceiling was far above us, and that, directly ahead, the space behind the truck contained a high balcony. On the left side was a structure of some kind, rising from the floor to the balcony.

I peered at it curiously, for never before had I seen anything like it. It was a staircase spiraling upon itself, with many wooden steps and a railing. It seemed to hang there in space, for there were no beams holding it up.

"What is this?" I asked, amazed.

"Would you like to hear its story?" the watchman asked.

"Yes", I said curtly.

"About two hundred years ago, some nuns came to Santa Fe mission to build a school for poor children. They themselves had nothing, only their faith. In time, the school was built and generations of children were taught here. Of course, the school and convent were destroyed during the persecutions—before you were born, when your papa was a boy. This building was the school's chapel. It was called the Loretto Chapel. It was not destroyed because the staircase was considered a marvel by local people. The government closed it eventually because they said it encouraged superstition. Later, they turned the chapel into a fire station. Even so, no one had the heart to destroy the staircase."

"What is a nun?" I asked.

My father and the watchman looked at me and furrowed their brows, struck by the sudden realization of my ignorance. My father was

346

especially embarrassed, since it was he who had neglected to teach me all that I should have known about life.

"They were holy women, dedicated to God and full of love", he said.

The watchman continued: "The sisters asked an architect to design the chapel, to make it look like a famous chapel in France, which was a very beautiful one. But the architect made the design with a serious flaw. He forgot to make a staircase to the choir loft."

"What is a choir?" I asked.

"A group of people who sang songs to God during the holy Mass. For hundreds of years, perhaps thousands, there were such lofts in many churches. Construction of this chapel was begun in the year 1873 and was completed in 1878."

"I have always wondered why the sisters did not think about the part that was missing", my father said.

"Yes, it is a puzzle why they did not notice it immediately", the other replied. "Were they and the architect blinded to the omission for a purpose? We do not know. But I think it is a happy fault."

"What happened then?" I pressed, for I wanted the story and not their conjectures.

"The sisters were having many troubles financially. They begged for money and materials. They prayed, and God always answered their prayers, though sometimes slowly. Beautiful glass windows were sent to them by sailing ship from France to the port of New Orleans, and then by paddle boat to St. Louis, Missouri. There the windows were loaded onto wagons, pulled by oxen and horses, and taken along the old Santa Fe Trail to this place. A long journey. A long, long journey." The watchman's face clouded momentarily, and he shook his head in sadness. "So far, so far they came, only to be demolished all these years later by rocks and machine gun bullets."

"Even so, Pedro," said my father, forgetting that I shouldn't know his friend's name, "even so, thousands of children prayed in the light from those windows. They looked at all that beauty, and perhaps they felt God's warmth in it."

"Yes, this is true", said the man. Then he continued, "When the sisters realized their mistake, they asked builders in the region to install a staircase to the loft. But all of them said they could not do it, because a staircase would take up too much space in the chapel, and it would make all liturgies uncomfortable.

"The sisters began a novena to San José the father of the Holy Family and the patron saint of carpenters, asking him to intercede for them, to find a way through their impossible problem."

I opened my mouth to ask another question, but the man anticipated it.

"A novena is a series of nine days of prayer, Neil. And their prayers were really an act of faith, because they had no more money, and they did not know where they would find a carpenter who could build a staircase that would not fill their chapel with steps, leaving less room for people. So they prayed and prayed and trusted in our Lord's generosity and the care of the saint.

"On the final day of the novena, a man came to the door of the convent. He was very poor, with only a donkey and a toolbox and the goodness in his heart. They could see he was a good man. The nuns in the old days, they knew these things. He asked them if they had any work for him. He told them he was a carpenter and could build wooden things and repair even badly broken things. They asked him if he could build a staircase that would be safe for the *niños* to climb, and small enough so it would not crowd the chapel, and would last a long time. Those sisters, they really knew how to ask for the impossible.

"So the carpenter went to work with only a hammer and saw and T-square. It took him six months to complete it. He designed the staircase himself, and made every part of it, great and small; he carved even the wooden pegs. There are no nails in it, only pegs. On the morning after the day he finished, the sisters went to pay him, for they had found some money by begging. But he had already gone. He never returned. They knew nothing about him.

"Over the years, many engineers have come to look at this staircase, and they cannot understand why it does not collapse. There is no central support beam and according to their rules this staircase should collapse. But it stands. Sometimes I go up and down on it when I am alone here. I am never afraid. It is strong, and no one can explain its strength. Then and now, the best minds do not understand it. It is two perfect spirals of 360 degrees—a helix, they say. It has thirty-three steps. We cannot tell what kind of tree this wood came from; it is not like any wood in our region. There are no records of how such wood came to be here."

He looked at me and smiled. "Would you like to climb it, Neil?"

"No", I said quickly, for it did not look strong at all. It looked like a dream hanging in the air.

"I have climbed it", my father said. "And I weigh twice as much as you do."

"No", I shook my head adamantly and took a step back.

The men let me be. They wandered over to the staircase, and both of them, perhaps unconsciously, stroked its banister, looking upward through the spiral to the roof. As they talked with each other in quiet voices, I went back to the fire truck and inspected the metal ladders clamped to its side, a coil of rotting hose, and the driver's cab. I took one of the candles and crawled beneath the machine to inspect its underbelly. Its complicated parts seemed to me a greater wonder of engineering than the staircase.

While I was crawling there on the floor, I was hit with renewed force by the reality of my missing brother and sister, and the anguish my mother had endured. I backed out and struggled to my feet.

I saw that the men had returned to the raised platform and its table, which I now knew was an altar. My father's friend was seated on the top step in front of it, and my father was kneeling before him. What they said I do not know. When the watchman made the sign of the cross over my father, I understood. He was hearing his confession and absolving him.

I glared in outrage, wanting to cry, to shout, to scream that their beliefs could not stop evil. More than ever, I wanted to find the men who had hurt my family and kill their evil by killing them. A black devouring fire full of stench was boiling within me, and at the same time, it terrified me.

Now my father stood up and called to me in a gentle voice.

"Neil, it has been a long time since you made confession."

I stared at him coldly, and retreated another step, shaking my head. "No", I said.

There was a world of meaning in that single utterance: I had left all that behind. I had forever departed from our hiding and fearing, our status at the very bottom of the world, our criminality. My father was a good man—too good. I did not want his religion with its enormous demands and its few rewards and endless failures. *My* religion was about justice in *this* world, and I would continue to express my single dogma by killing as many snakes as I could trap or stalk, and, if possible, the human snakes who had made my parents suffer.

349

I told myself that this would have to wait. I would not return to Las Cruces immediately nor in the near future. I would register at the college in an hour from now. I would conquer that institution and climb. I would become a scientist, maybe a mathematician, maybe a master of physics, but in either case, I would become a man to be respected. I would be the genius they told me I could become, and for me there would be no more creeping into ruins and sandpits to escape the hunters. Red blossoms had never been painted on my hand, but they had been imprinted in my heart. From now on, I would never again permit such a brand to wound me. My heart would be cold. It would be as hard as steel, harder than an old wooden stairway. I would rise by my own strength.

"No", I said again as both men waited.

Then the priest stood up and came to me. "I understand", he said with sympathy, putting a hand on my shoulder. I shook it off.

"Neil", my father exclaimed, offended by my rudeness.

The priest glanced at the staircase. "You will have a long road to travel, Neil. Life will take you to places that you cannot now know. But always, always, you must look up."

I looked down at my feet, because I did not want, at that moment, to meet his eyes.

"You must look up", he said again. "When it seems most impossible to you, a way will open before you."

Without answering, I walked past him and limped to my father's side. "*Papa*, I want to go. We must hurry if I am to register on time."

And so we did.

Day 226:

I studied in Santa Fe for four years and never returned to the chapel. It was demolished at some point, but whether or not the staircase was saved, I do not know. There is now a forty-story luxury hotel on the site of the cathedral, and on the site of the chapel, there stands a ten-story steel cube, which houses the state offices of DSI.

Scholarships took me to other universities. Every summer, I returned to Sunnyview Acres for a week's vacation, unable to spare any more time than that, due to research projects at institutes in Europe and Asia. Long before my first Nobel, I won prizes, and with the award money, I was able to help my father buy his own dump truck and relieve my mother of the necessity of working at the café in Las Cruces where she had slaved for years. Later, when I was teaching at Princeton, I offered to buy them a house. Though they were touched and grateful, they declined the offer. They loved the village too much, and the remainder of their lives was spent there, hiding illegals and feeding those who could not find work. My father died of heat stroke in the cab of his truck while working on an irrigation canal during the terrible summer of 2074, when temperatures soared to 120° Fahrenheit in the shade, 49° Celsius. My mother lived a few years longer, preserved by the air conditioning unit I had installed in the trailer. Her life was expanded a little by the addition I built onto it, and the deeper water well I paid for. She loved to garden and gave away most of the food she grew.

We never spoke of her missing children, I don't know why. As my early successes mounted one upon the other, I buried the subject in my memory and left aside my homicidal impulses. I think I continued to hate, but the hatred gradually subsided into a bedrock of resentment against the way things were in the world—a system that I vowed to myself I would always beat. No one would know my thoughts on these matters; no one would ever know my heart. I had moments of weakness, however, notably my speech in Stockholm, but I was getting older then, more confident that the government would not dare to erase me from the social spectrum. I was right about that, but wrong about hoping my words would make a difference.

Until her death, my mother still made *piñatas* for *los niños*, three times a year. Every July, she cried for three days.

Day 239:

I have been unable to write during the past two weeks. I try to distract myself from the old memories, wounds freshly opened. Nor do I want to think about what lies below my feet on this planet. I've watched hours of baseball and basketball games, even a few films. I stare at my *max* screen and realize that I am no longer seeing anything on it. I have completed rereading Stron's book, which has helped me to reorient a little. I pace the hallways. I swim at odd hours, alone. Why do I want to be alone with this pain? What is happening to my mind? I haven't seen Pia and Paul since our discussion about David's death. I miss them. Pia's pregnancy must be showing. They are staying upstairs, as far away from DSI as they can get.

Poor sleep, more nightmares.

I have asked around, and no one I talk to recalls seeing any presentations on the findings of the forensic people who worked on the skeletons—the shocking fact that these are the remains of children. If what Dariush told me is true (and I have no reason whatsoever to disbelieve him), why hasn't this become news?

Day 245:

A tremendous breakthrough today, jarring me out of my stupor. At last, a city has been discovered. It happened this way:

For some time now, surveyors have continued to make probes into the road that crosses the Valley of the Towers, at regular intervals along its length. In the rubble-strewn pass through the western range, avalanches had buried the road too deeply to tell us anything. However, on the far side of the pass, probes picked up the route again, where there were no more rockfalls and only the natural deposits of organic material built up over millennia. The lower the road went into the western plain (which extends without interruption to the sea), the deeper the overlayer of soil they found. The forests are denser there, tropical in fact. About three kilometers from the last outcropping of the foothills, they lost the road. Random probes executed in a 180-degree arc soon found it again. The road had veered toward the north, gradually straightening out as it headed west-northwest.

The route continued onward for a distance of twenty-two hundred kilometers, ending near the mouth of one of the major rivers draining the continent. And here the probes began to hit a complex grid of buried cross streets or avenues. Detectable by the on-ground instruments only, all of the above findings had been invisible to the satellite scanners.

By human standards, the city is not a large one. It is 3.197 kilometers on three sides, presumably square. Its irregular westernmost side is eroded by the action of the sea. There are no ruins visible even at that end, though probes indicate traces of a grid of streets and cross streets beneath the seabed.

There is renewed excitement on board, as well as numerous presentations on the panorama screens. Interviews with experts and survey teams are feeding us plenty of data, combined with stirring scenes of the jungle meeting the ocean, the river's estuary, colorful wildlife, as well as conjecture heaped upon conjecture.

Full-scale archaeological investigation of the site begins next week.

Day 258:

Dariush is below on the planet. There were more new discoveries today. This morning, archaeologists working in the Temple of the Ship moved the black altar off of its metal base, and when the plate was removed, three sets of inscribed tablets were found beneath it, embedded in the stone floor in separate compartments. The topmost tablet of each was flush with the floor, face up. A program I watched informs us that the tablets are made of pure gold. An archaeologist expressed the opinion that these three hard codices could very well be "documents" relating to the foundation of their civilization, or, alternatively, relating to the purposes of the temple. If they can be deciphered, they may tell us a good deal about this race.

Day 267:

A media presentation on the first tentative efforts to unearth the city. Sonar mapping has given the information that the walls of the city buildings are intact, though roofless. There were no exceptionally tall structures. Oddest of all is their uniformity. The overwhelming majority of them (98 percent) share their side and back walls with identical units. If each unit represents a family dwelling, or the dwelling of an individual, there could have been no more than a few hundred thousand residents of the city. All streets are geometrically precise, both north-south and east-west, at 90-degree angles to each other. The whole gives the impression of a beehive; though by contrast, bees would appear to be more creative.

There are a myriad of objects buried below, presumably "man-made" vessels of varying shapes and sizes that may have been used for

353

food storage. A test shaft descended 29 meters before reaching the top of one dwelling or cubicle, and the floor was reached at a depth of 3.179 meters below it. Careful excavation brought to light the information that it was a two-room unit with a single window and door opening onto the earth-packed street. The walls and floors were brick, smoothly plastered with a limestone veneer. Clay pots, ocher and gray, were found in one of the rooms and brought intact to the surface; they are elegantly shaped and heavily glazed but lack decorations. When opened, one tightly sealed pot contained grains similar to spelt-wheat. Nearby were traces of oxidized metal cooking implements. If fabrics, rugs, or tapestries were once extant in the room, they had long ago dissolved. There was a brick bed frame with two skeletal remains lying upon it, the bones largely disintegrated. Gold fillings were found in the teeth of the remnant skulls. There were no personal adornments such as rings or beads of any kind. Time has erased much of what this house once contained, leaving only stone or gold and traces that give little explanation of the life that was lived there.

In a wall niche, there was a small stone sculpture of the winged three-eyed god.

Day 285:

The city site is swarming with archaeologists and engineers, as well as their skilled helpers.

Two dozen shafts have been dug at evenly spaced distances. They reveal uniform stratification of soil, lacking any volcanic deposits such as that which entombed Pompeii and Herculaneum. Indeed, the closest volcano is a small, dormant one, fifteen hundred kilometers to the northeast. Upper layers reveal three periods when the river flooded its banks and covered the city, but this was long after the city died and was buried by the slower accumulation of detritus.

At this stage, it is difficult to know how and when all life ceased within it, but the early findings indicate a time roughly the same as the age when the road in Tower Valley ceased to be used. The greater depth of the city is attributed to the heavier soil deposits laid down by the more intense biological life in a tropical forest at sea level. To this must be added the minor river floods and also the likelihood of sea storms of unusual strength sweeping inland at one or more times during the fourteen hundred Nova-years since the city's demise.

Day 287:

More alien remains have been found in the dwellings, all in the same state of disintegration. Most of the units have one or two such skeletons. Radiation dating and atomic microscopy place the age of death circa fourteen hundred (+ or −) N-years ago (between two thousand and twenty-one hundred Earth-years ago). A distinctive feature, however, is that their height is considerably greater than that of the remains found in the temple. Theorists are now saying there were two races here: one tall, one very short; one master, one servant or possibly slave to the other. The gold teeth fillings in the taller race indicate that *it* was master. Yet the careful entombment of the smaller race indicates that the latter enjoyed the more exalted status. Such is the theory, such is the conflicting evidence.

I find it very odd that the public presentations never mention the forensic discovery: that the remains in the temple are those of children. Why is this not being openly discussed? Compared to the two-races theory, it is equally possible that the remains found in the city were adults and the sacrificed were their children.

But if only a few hundred thousand "adults" could have lived in the city, why are there many times more this number interred in the temple? Are there other buried cities? Exploration has been limited, and even this has focused on one continent only.

Day 292:

More and more dwellings are being excavated. They reveal a perplexing uniformity, an urban planning extremely efficient but devoid of art (with the exception of the nasty little god sculptures), and lacking open spaces where numbers of people could gather. Were there no parks, no temples, no libraries, no gardens? It resembles a sterile warren. Was this a slave city? If not, was it the home of a self-regimented master race whose distinguishing feature was their stupefying unoriginality?

We simply do not know.

Day 310:

I was wrong about something I wrote a few weeks ago. Apparently, for the past month, low-orbit scanners with newly augmented capacities have been focusing all their instruments on the surface of every continent, re-examining them kilometer by kilometer. Now the findings are being presented to the public: only Continent 1 displayed any feedback indicating the possibility of buried cities. After concentrated effort, three more cities were discovered. There is one near the northern edge of the continent, also situated at a river mouth. There is another on the eastern side of the mountain ranges, farther south in the cooler latitudes. The fourth is in the wide valley between the central and eastern ranges, about four hundred kilometers south of the Temple of the Ship. Traces of roads have been found near all of them, and though surveys are not extensive, the roads appear to lead in the general direction of the Temple. There are hardly enough archaeologists and engineers to go around, but small parties have dug shafts in each of the newly discovered cities and found (at least, at first glance) that they differ in no way from City 1.

In the suburbs, so to speak, there are industrial ruins on a small scale, forges, brickworks, cement plants. Splaying outward from the urban cores are networks of irrigation canals. It would seem that agriculture was a major occupation of these people.

Day 316:

Another presentation about the aliens' ship, mainly interviews with scientists in various fields—metallurgy, propulsion, aero- and thermodynamics, etc. Though the craft has not yet been opened, scientists have determined that it was propelled by atomic energy. Its fuel supply was not great in mass, and the low level of radiation indicates that most of the unstable isotopes have already decayed.

Long ago, its initial thrust would have been impressive, one atomic engineer speculated. He went on to say that the ship was probably designed for a single journey from solar system to solar system, or a few such journeys at the most. If so, where did it come from? Once launched, it could have traveled great distances from any one of thousands of nearby solar systems, but how could it have sustained life during the extremely long duration of such journeys? Did they have anti-matter? Or did they have something else that brought them even closer to lightspeed?

Day 321:

Just before dawn, Dariush found me sitting on my bench in the arboretum, listening to Mozart. Without explanation, he asked me to come with him to his room. I could see that something was troubling him because his eyes blinked rapidly and his face was flushed, his customary paternal expression vanished. Walking hastily a few steps ahead of me along the concourse, he seemed barely conscious of my presence. When we arrived at his room, he sat on the bed and gestured toward the desk chair, saying nothing. I sat down and looked at him expectantly.

"What's happened?" I asked.

With trembling hands he picked up a thin stack of paper from the desk. "It is difficult", he murmured. "It changes everything."

"Everything? What do you mean?"

He glanced at the papers and closed his eyes.

"Tell me, Dariush."

"The tablets. We have made progress in translation."

"Really! That's tremendous news!"

"Yes, insofar as the meaning of codices have become translucent—though not all the words—we can read the archival records."

"This is an astounding breakthrough", I exclaimed.

"Astounding", he whispered.

"What do they say? What do they tell you?"

"There are thousands of tablets, as I mentioned to you last month. The linguistics team is presently scanning the final hundred thousand. Until now, we were unable to decipher any of them, neither by cyber-analysis nor by human labors. We exerted every effort at cryptanalysis, but lacking a key, we made no progress. For my part, I have focused my attention on the three gold codices that were found beneath the altar—each composed of several plates.

"Three days ago, a thought came to me. Because the codex characters are not dissimilar to our Mesopotamian cuneiform, I decided to run a new scan through the main computer, testing again for character identification."

"And that broke the code!"

357

"In the beginning, it did not. Yet after repeated attempts and adjustments of coordinates, a word appeared—a single identifiable word—then another. At first, I believed it was the product of random chance."

"Like the monkeys at typewriters composing a Shakespeare play, if given millions of years to do it?"

"Like that, I thought. But it was not so. The two words unlocked five more. Then we were faced with new obstacles. Though we cannot say this codex is cuneiform in the strict sense, its characters are similar in this regard: they are not alphabetic; they are syllabic, interspersed with a low percentage of logosyllabic, that is, ideograms and pictograms. In the codex I examined, there are 146 characters with assigned values, and many of these I presumed would have multiple phonetic values. This was an additional clue because the Babylonian Bisitun inscription, for example, has 150 characters with multiple phonetics. The characters are different, yet the pattern is nearly identical." Dariush paused. "Babylonian has approximately 600 characters, the Hittite about 350, and so forth. A codex with only 146, therefore, while still very difficult, is yet within the capacity of cryptanalysis. You realize this is more complex than our Roman alphabet with 26 letters or the Greek with 24."

"Yes, I can see it would be."

"Even so, the computer was able to isolate a number of signs that appeared to be distinctly proto-Semitic in form. Many were close to the Akkadian, others remotely similar to Old Elamite. Still others seemed to be Vannic, and among the latter were entire phrases that resembled what the Assyrians called Urartu's script."

"Then it's a hybrid of several languages, a Rosetta Stone for this civilization."

"No. It is a coherent language of its own. The print-outs yesterday revealed this."

I pointed to the papers in his hand. "Is that a sample?"

"A sample of utmost importance. This is the text of codex-1, the oldest of the three 'enshrined', one might say, beneath the altar in front of the ship. It appears to have been highest in significance to the people who once lived here. The three are dated at periods separated by many hundreds of years."

"How old is this one?"

"Approximately nine thousand years, by Earth-reckoning. Testing on the plates' isotope decay, though providing only raw dating, confirms its age, give or take a hundred years."

"In any event, very old."

"Yes. And it is an account of events even older than the time of writing. I have just now completed a careful check of the wording."

"May I see it?"

He handed me the sheets. Before I could begin reading, however, he said a second time, "Neil, it changes everything."

"Everything? In what sense?"

"Our understanding of history. Of civilization."

"Their civilization you mean?"

"We suspected early on that they had not arisen spontaneously from this planet. The dearth of ruins indicated this. Now we know that only one continent had cities, despite their ability to make long journeys. This indicates a small population. There is no archeological evidence of primitive stages preceding their last era. Their achievements, as far as they went, were not typical of gradual progressions over long historical periods."

"You're saying they came here from somewhere else?"

"Yes. I thought at first that it might have been in the region of Barnard's Star, or CN Leonis, or even as far as Sirius."

"Maybe farther still."

He shook his head negatively. "Their technology would not have permitted it."

"They could have been dropped off here by a race with superior technology, like ours is now."

Dariush did not respond to this. He continued, "As you will see, I have inserted punctuation for the sake of clarification. My annotations are in brackets wherever a word was either indecipherable or was meaningful but inexact by our standards. In the original codex tablet, proper names are logo-graphics enclosed in a square or rectangular incision in the plate."

"Like an Egyptian cartouche."

"Neil, please read the text."

I read: [Document inserted]

Of the Coming

The chant of Dumu-er-se-tim [literally, "Child of the Underworld" — D. I. Mirza] of the up-leaving. This is the road [way of] departure. [To] the Lord of Night-gods, [be] praise. [To] Nisaba and Haia, god-protectors of scribes, [be] praise.

Thus did the Night-gods come to Akri-mun-zi
And bid him hearken:
Obedient, he slashed his body with the knife.
He burnt his hair and ate the ashes.
Three times he walked in the pit of the venom-snake.
Three times he lived and made chant of it.

Three times he called forth the Lord of the Night-gods, [name].[1]
The Ap-kalu [sage-priest] performed the summon[ing] rite
With sacred [literally, "spirit force of the Night-gods"] sacrifice.[2]
[When] all rites were fulfilled
Then did the Night-gods speak unto Akri-mun-zi
From the mouth of the Ap-kalu.
[He said:]
"You will make a ship to break [penetrate] the blanket [literally,
    "cloak-water"] over the earth [land, world],
For the sky-god [your] enemy is about to do an ill [evil, catastrophe]
    unto mankind.
In this ship you will journey on the sea above,
Unto a heaven in the heavens, which I will show you.[3]
I will point the road [way] to the triple-fires;
    [they are] lights in the heavens.
Of the three, one is lesser, a flame of copper [literally, "red-metal"];
Two are flames of gold and the greater of these is your destination.
Of the greater are born the eighteen[4] and the seven[th] is yours."
"Our ships go only upon rivers and lakes," said Akri-mun-zi
    to the Lord of the Night-gods.
"We see no flames in the heavens, for the blanket covers all.
It does not make a gate [literally, "opening in a wall"]."

---

[1] Here, along with his title, the over-god's proper name is used for the first time in the codex. The hieroglyphics are unique to his name, presently undecipherable. — D. I. Mirza

[2] Literally, "spilling human blood"; this may or may not signify the death of the sacrificial offering. — D. I. Mirza

[3] My phrase, "a heaven in the heavens" for the literal, "a god-realm [singular] in the god-realms [plural] above-waters". — D. I. Mirza

[4] Numerical values are represented pictographically with a symbol of the human hand. One hand with fingers and thumb extended represents five. The latter capped with a slash represents ten. Thus, eighteen is represented by a single hand with slash, beside which is a single hand without a slash, beside which is a hand with three fingers. The hands are linked by a single underline. — D. I. Mirza

The Lord of the Night-gods answered:
"Yet will I show you the making of marvels and strong devices
to carry you up unto the sea."

Then did the vision-men under Akri-mun-zi
Receive dreams of wonder-iron and the hand-craft [skill] to make it.
Unto others did the serpent-head come forth from
The mouth of She-Who-Sees-Far[5] and say unto them:
"Go up to the mountains of Ara-arath and dig into the earth for
the burn-stone [possibly "stone that burns"]."
When Akri-mun-zi was 380 years old[6]
His son, the noble [exalted] Akri-mun-té, brought forth from the
earth
The stone that makes sick with tumors and burns flesh
[of] man and animal.
He stood afar and did not touch the stone; thus he did not sicken.
Many[7] servants died; their deaths [were] slow; [there was] weeping
in the city.
The Lord of the Night-gods received their sacrifice.

In the dreams of Akri-mun-té, the Lord of the Night-gods showed
him the making of forges and devices
To hold [uncertain meaning, possibly "harness, use, employ"] the
power of the burn-stone in the tubes [uncertain meaning, literally, "hollow reeds"] made of the new iron that does not bleed
[possibly "rust"].
Forth from it came the flame of the Lord of the Night-gods.
Many [circle-hand] died and the tubes rose unto the blanket; [they]
did not return.
Then unto the noble [exalted] Akri-mri, the son of Akri-mun-té,
came the voice of the Lord of the Night-gods in a vision and
said:
"Now you will make unto my praise a greater [tube].

---

[5] Presumably a female idol in the royal temple.

[6] The number 380 is represented by three hands surmounted by a single horizontal line,
which is surmounted by ten vertical checks, then follows eight hands surmounted by a
slash, the whole underscored by a single line. The sum is estimated, yet is consistent with
other verifiable numerical values such as eighteen and seven. — D. I. Mirza

[7] "Many" is represented by a single hand within a circle, number uncertain. — D. I.
Mirza

A house for one man shall you build within [it].
You shall ride upon the sky-arrow and see far."
Akri-mun-zi was 420 years old and Akri-mun-té [was] 390 and Akri-mri [was] 310, when Akri-mri rode upon the sky-arrow and went up into the blanket.
He did not return. The Night-gods received his sacrifice.

Akri-mun-zi was 431 years old [when] Krani-mhrod, one in [the] thirteen[th] generation of the body [literally, "seed"] of Akri-mun-zi, began to make a tower unto the heavens of marvel[ous] invention.
[Thus] no more should the sky-arrows point to the heavens on the slopes of mountains.
Krani-mhrod said unto the governor [literally, "King's-steward"] of the lands:
"The Lord of the Night-gods commands me."
Taken [was] he unto the King [unnamed, possibly Akri-mun-zi himself. — D. I. Mirza].
The King said, "Krani-mhrod, what is this you say unto my steward?"
Krani-mhrod answered him: "The Lord of the Night-gods commands me. I must build a ship to mate [literally, "have sexual intercourse"] with the tower unto the heavens. The sky-arrow will fly up in this way, and the hands of the sky-god [our] enemy cannot pull it down.
In this way will your servants go unto the heaven in the heavens.
The sky-arrow must have a house within [it] for one hundred people and journey-animals for food and drink and their fodder. We must carry the sacred [literally, "force of the Night-gods"] serpents for ritual in the heavens."

"Do then what the Lord of the Night-gods commands", [said] the King unto Krani-mhrod.
It was done.
Akri-mun-zi was 500 years old, and Krani-mhrod was 147, [he was] yet young when the sky-arrow was completed.
Within it was the house for men and beasts, much food and water, and devices for replenishing [literally, "making-again"] water and air.
There was a sacred place for the serpents.
Three moons passed and day unto day the servants filled the sky-arrow with goods for the journey.

Yet all men were in fear of the journey, for none before had returned
   in the small sky-arrows that did fly.
Krani-mhrod said unto them:
"It is the will of the Lord of the Night-gods that you depart,
For this is to shame the sky-god [our] enemy.
You will not return, but you and your women and your offspring
   will live
In the heaven in the heavens. And I shall go with you."
Still, the people were in fear.
Then did the serpent head appear after long absence
   from the mouth of She-Who-Sees-Far
In the temple of the Lord of the Night-gods.
The serpent said:
"You shall not die. You shall live.
Marvels I will show you. Above the blanket is a wondrous sea,
   and you will go upon it as wind fills the sails of the river-boats.
The earth is round as fruit of the vine, the blanket is thin.
It is not [a] wall made by the sky-god [your] enemy. It is but water.
In the heaven in the heavens you shall be as the Night-gods
   and walk to and fro among us."

Then did the people take heart [literally, "strength came into them"].
They filled the ship until full.
Then did the Ap-kalu of those times speak unto the King:
"Now you must command the people to enter the sky-arrow.
No longer is it to be called a sky-arrow, for it must have a
   name.
Its name shall be after the beast in the swamp-forest
   that is sacred to the Lord of the Night-gods."
"I will name it as he commands", said the King unto the Ap-kalu.
A great [indecipherable]⁸ was captured by men in the swamp-
   forest, and brought unto the city. Many died in [its] capture[ing].
Great roaring it made, and its breath was fire without flame, for the
   drops of it burn holes in flesh. [Its] claws cut into pieces a bull
   given unto it, [though] the beast was caged [literally, "bound in
   iron-house"].

---

⁸ The pictograph combines the serpent sign, the name of the Lord of the Night-gods,
and that of a four-legged beast with a long tail. —D. I. *Mirza*

It was mighty. It was [obscure pictograph][9] unto the Lord of the Night-gods.

In the seventeen[th] day after the full moon, in the month of departure [literally, "ship up-going"], word was brought unto the King:
"O King, we bear tidings of amusement [literally, "bring laughter to the mouth"] [said] the message-bearers. "A man builds another sky-arrow."
"What sky-arrow is this?" [said] the King. "I have granted no permission for it.
There is but one and it is the heavens-ship named [pictograph of the beast]."
"This is so, O great King, [yet] he builds it", [said] the message-bearers.
"Where does he build?" [said] the King.
"He builds it in a place of no-waters, in the forest beyond the mountains", they answered the King and trembled.

Then did the King consult She-Who-Sees-Far and the Ap-kalu.
These two said as one voice:
"The sky-god is shamed. He is angry.
The sky-god has spoken unto a fool in the forest,
Commanding him to build a ship in mockery of the great heavens-ship."
And the King said unto the seers:
"This makes insult to the Lord of the Night-gods. Break up [its] metal as salvage [literally, "find-save"] for my forges."
"It is great in size, O King, and made of wood", said the Ap-kalu [in] his own tongue. It was not the god speaking through him.
"Then I send a host of my men", said the King. "They will burn it."
Once again the Night-god spoke in the mouth of the Ap-kalu:
"Many [hand within circle] times many [hand within circle] men must you send forth to burn it. Slay the fool in the forest, you must. Slay also[10] his woman and his sons and their women. When

---

[9] The pictograph is complexified by the signs for "offspring" and "servant". — D. I. Mirza

[10] My punctuation. Alternative is: "Slay the fool in the forest. You must slay also …", etc. D. I. Mirza

364

you have burnt the ship, O King, you must bury the ashes in a pit and cover it with stones [so that] nothing remains in memory [of it.]"

Then did the King send a great company of men unto the forest.
There they found the ship and its makers at work with wood,
With mallet and axe and teeth-saw in the old way.
They dropped their tools and stood silent when they saw
The host that ringed them all about.
The eldest, white of hair, knelt on the earth, and all his offspring and their wives did as he.
"You plead for my mercy", said the Captain of Hosts. "Yet no mercy shall be granted, for I come at the bidding of the King, and he bids you [to] die."
The old man lifted his head and he said:
"Not to you, do I kneel, O Captain of the King, but to the one who bade me make this ship."
"This is a ship upon dry land", said the Captain. "It is a fool's ship, for it is too wide for the river or the lake, and too heavy for bearing to [those] waters."
"Soon, O Captain, the waters will come to the ship", said the old man.
And all the host laughed.
"Before you die, tell me who bade you make this thing", said the Host-Captain.
The old man said:
"The one who is above the blanket of waters. The one who made the flames in the heavens and this earth and all living things that move upon it."

The Host-Captain answered:
"The Lord of the Night-gods made them. He did not bid you make this wood-ship.
The Lord of the Night-gods commands that you will die."
The old man said:
"I do not speak of that one. He who you name makes only death and confusion [literally, "mix-thoughts"] in the minds of men. Your god is not seen with the eyes, yet his serpent shows him well enough."

Then did all the host fall into rage at this insult.

The Host-Captain gave command, and the men moved to enclose the ship and its makers with fire-torch and sword and other diverse weapons.

Yet they stopped and could make no near step;
     they could move no closer than a spear-throw.

Some hurled their spears, but they fell short.

And the Host-Captain and the host departed,

For consultation with the King and the seers.

When they had come unto the King, the King said:

"Is the fool in the forest no more?"

"O Great King," said the Host-Captain, "a hand unseen stops us and the fool yet lives."

"What hand unseen is this?" said the King.

"I do not know", said the Host-Captain. And the King slew him in the court of the palace.

Then did the King consult She-Who-Sees-Far and the Ap-kalu.

These two said with one voice:

"The sky-god is shamed. The sky-god is angry. Yet he is small.

He bids a mouse to build a box of wood to mock the great ship.

The mouse will die and all his offspring with him.

Go now and make great sacrifice in the face of the fool and his ship."

This the King did.

The King and all his host, and many others of the city went down unto the forest.

There they found the fool and his offspring at work with wood

And mallet and axe and teeth-saw.

When they saw the great numbers of the King-Host, they fell to their knees and bowed their heads.

"You plead for my mercy", said the King unto them. "Yet no mercy shall be given to you,

For you mock the Lord of the Night-gods and you mock the great ship and you mock me who am the King of all the lands. Now you must die."

The old man stood and looked from afar at the King, yet his voice was strong.

He said:

"O King, I work with my hands.
At the bidding of the one you call sky-god,
The one who is the Sky-father over all."
When [they] heard [it], the seers fell into a frenzy, and the King fell
     into a rage.
The old man in his folly spoke onward:
"There is but one God and he is Sky-father.
There is but one God, and he is maker of all things.
There is but one God, and he shall crush the serpent."

At this, the King gave command, and the host rushed forward to
     slay the fool and all who dwelled with him, and [to] burn the
     ship.
But they fell back, and none could account [for it].
Then did the Ap-kalu speak:
"The sky-god makes a wall not seen by the eyes.
The sky-god is shamed. He is angry. Yet he is small.
We must make the sacrifice."
And all men withdrew a ways and the sacrifice was prepared.

[Now follows a description that is heavily loaded with hiero-
glyphs, indicating ritual significance. The ratio of pictograph and
ideograph to straight text increases fourfold in this final portion
of the codex. It is dominated by the signs for blood-letting, the
serpent, the name of the Lord of the Night-gods, and sexual
intercourse. The following is an approximation. — D. I. Mirza]

In the place of no-waters, the Lord of the Night-gods made victory
Over the small god, the sky-god.
With us he made victory, for we gave unto him
First three children [literally, "the small who speak"]
And ten more cut from the womb [literally, "mother-belly"],
     [undecipherable pictograph] in pieces.
     [Undecipherable text] their scream[ing] is the chant of praise.
The King gave the fruit of his body,
     one son and one daughter from his house, man and woman grown,
     unto the fire.
     [Undecipherable text] their scream[ing] is a chant of praise.
Then the host did [pictographs for sexual intercourse and blood-
     letting] upon one hundred children.

367

[Undecipherable text] their scream[ing] is the chant of praise.
And their bodies [undecipherable pictograph] unto the fire.
Unrobed, [literally, "flesh-without-cloth"] in the light of flame-
    torches and the sacrifice fires, we circled the wood-ship.
We made the serpent-dance. All the host made the coil
    from the time of light-fade until the blanket awoke.[11]

At this point, Dariush broke my concentration when he reached
over and took the next two sheets of paper from my hands, leaving
me with several still to be read.

"Pardon me, Neil", he said with a note of severity. "What follows
is extremely graphic in describing the ritual activities. I think there is
no need for you to focus on it. The foregoing indicates well enough
what occurred."

"May I proceed?"

"Yes, please continue."

When the sky-blanket awoke, all the host lay down upon the ground.
They slept unrobed, their bodies with blood and ash anointed,
And full of the fruit of the vine.
The King slept in his tent [literally, "journey-sky-cover"].
Krani-mhrod and Nih-kri-zi slept with him in the tent.
The Ap-kalu alone, and one other, stood with eyes open,
With eyes upon the wood-ship.
I who write this was the other. I am Ti-shmi, the scribe [literally,
    "he who keeps the King's memories"].
Ap-kalu and Ti-shmi saw the fool come forth with his sons.
They came near to us, and the unseen wall did not stop them.
We cried the alarm, but none of the host awoke.

Then did the fool and his sons dig a pit in the midst of the camp,
    [while] all about them slept.
From the coming of the light until it began to fade, they dug [it].
Ap-kalu and Ti-shmi, [we] two sought to rouse the King,
    [but] he slept and would not awake.
As the light grew less, the fool and his sons gathered the bodies
    from the sacrifice stone [possibly "altar"] and placed them in the pit.

---

[11] Presumably, this means the dawn, when the diffused light of the cloud cover returned.
— D. I. Mirza

368

This was insult to the Lord of the Night-gods,
For many bodies were yet unburned, and the Lord of the Night-gods
   commands burned flesh, for it is sweet to him.
All the pieces they placed in the pit.
With buckets, they gathered the pools of blood and poured them
Into the pit. The day was [very][12] hot.
We sought to stop them, [but] the arms of the Ap-kalu are old
And the arms of Ti-shmi are not-strong; one is withered.
And still none awoke.

The fool and his sons covered the body-pit with soft-soil.
They knelt upon the ground and made many tears and loud cries.
The Ap-kalu and Ti-shmi cursed them by the power of the Night-gods
   [but] no closer did we approach; there was the wall of the sky-god.
When they were done, they turned their backs to us.
The fool looked not our way. He shielded his eyes
And went back unto the wood-ship.
The Ap-kalu and Ti-shmi this we saw; [we] two alone.
The blanket night was upon us,
And still the King and his hosts slept and nothing would awake them.

When the blanket light returned,
Then did all men arise and were hungry
And they ate.
To the King went the Ap-kalu and Ti-shmi and spoke
[of what] the fool had done.
Then did the Ap-kalu in the King's presence and the presence of
   the lesser seers of the temple, go into a trance [literally, "the Night-
   god fills him-speaks"]
The Lord of the Night-gods spoke through his mouth,
And some saw the head of the serpent coming forth from the hole,
   as it is with She-Who-Sees-Far.
The Lord of the Night-gods said:
"See now, you are victorious in the test
   [which] I have given unto you.
You have harkened to my command.
Yet now I do a more great thing [and it is] this:

---

[12] "Very" is represented by a hand in circle with stroke through middle. — *D. I. Mirza*

I leave the fool to his work.
I leave the wood-ship not burned.
I leave it as a sign for you and all the peoples,
Of sky-god folly, for the wood-ship is far from water.
Yet my heavens-ship [name of the Lord of the Night-gods and the beast]
Shall go up.
The sky-god ship is a nothing, for it goes unto no-place.
The Lord of the Night-gods-ship is great, for it shall rise unto the heaven in the heavens."

Yet Krani-mhrod was not destined [literally, "hand of the Night-god directs"] to depart unto the heavens.
When he awoke in the tent of the King,
He stood for a time and listened to the account of [what] the fool had done.
Then he fell to the ground and rolled upon it,
    raving [literally, "babble-speech of the insane"] came from his mouth.
It has not changed unto this day. He is in the house of the ill,
    [he is] bound by cords [lest] he destroy himself;
    he is preserved [kept alive] because he is King-blood.
In his father's place, Nih-kri-zi, the son of Krani-mhrod, was chosen to rule the ship in the fourteen[th] generation of the body of Akri-mun-zi.
He shall prove the sky-god small.
He shall prove the Lord of the Night-gods great.
[Name of the Lord of the Night-gods] is greatest in the heavens for he has overthrown the sky-god.

Then [said] the Ap-kalu unto the King:
"The sky-god is shamed. Yet the sky-god is angry.
We must make sacrifice unto the Lord of the Night-gods
    [to] rebuke the sky-god."
It was done.[13]
The great beast that is sacred to the Lord of the Night-gods
Was brought unto the ship in [its] cage and it was fed

---

[13] This short line is followed by the symbols for blood, sexual intercourse, and a hand within a circle—signifying "many". — *D. I. Mirza*

With one hundred children [alive] who entered its mouth.
Their scream[ing] is praise unto the Lord of the Night-gods.
Five cities gathered in the plain for the departure [literally, "up-going"]
And all the people were in the plain with the King and the Ap-kalu.
Then the burn-stone was struck within the sky-ship
And the fire of the Night-gods came from its tail.
High-reaching, it climbed up the sky and went into the blanket.
It pierced the blanket. As the gods had told, the blanket is thick
    water.
Above it we came unto the great sea that is constant night,
Yet [it is] full of the flames of the Night-gods.

To honor the Lord of the Night-gods, who is mighty.
To honor Nih-kri-zi, who rules this ship.
To honor Nisaba and Haia, god-protectors of scribes.
Through my hand, I, Dumu-er-se-tim, called Ti-shmi, [made] this
    chant.

[Codex-tablets, gold-hieratic-1, Temple of the Ship, AC-A-7; 27.51
degrees S, 18.35 degrees E. Translation: onboard KC main computer: Scan/cryptology: KC-y09-59858a; Adjusted scans/
cryptology: KC-y09-59858a-b-c-d (the source decryption is d).
Additional translation analysis and annotation: Dr. Dariush Ibrahimi Mirza, Cambridge University, staff Philologist, *Kosmos* expedition, AC-A-7. Ship's chronometer: Day 320 since arrival AC-A-7,
Mundus Novus.]

I looked up from the page, unable to say anything. I shook my head
in disgust. When at last I found my voice, I said, "Thank God these
murderous wretches are extinct."

Dariush took a deep breath. "Neil, these people came from Earth."

Day 322:

My first reaction was disbelief.

"They couldn't have come from Earth", I said. "That's impossible."

"Why do you think it is not possible?" he asked.

"Because . . . because we know our own history. There was no developed technology before the modern era."

"Do we, in fact, know with absolute certainty our own history—the history of mankind?"

"Yes, we do. Just because this chant or religious fantasy seems similar in a few details to our own biblical myths doesn't mean it was connected to us. So we have a man building a wooden ship. How unusual is that? If, as you once told me, intelligence creates universal patterns, then the aliens could easily have had experiences similar to ours. Wherever there are trees and water, men make boats."

"Are you saying it would be a product of universal intelligence for two men on two different planets to spend their lives building two massive ships in a place far from water, for no apparent reason?"

"You're presuming that Noah existed, Dariush. You're also presuming that the biblical flood happened as the scriptures tell it."

"Yes, I am believing this."

"It's a myth. It's *our* myth, and maybe another race light-years distant from us had a similar myth. Or maybe it was a scribe's dream."

"Neil, the dream was real enough that it was carried through the vastness of space and recorded in gold."

"Cult documents of our own primitive civilizations were sometimes made of gold. But their dreams had no basis in reality."

"Have you read the Epic of Gilgamesh or the Epic of Atrahasis?"

I shook my head.

"These are ancient poetic flood accounts. The Sumerian, Akkadian, Babylonian epics are part of a larger body of flood literature from the ancient world, including folklore and myth among many peoples. A great deluge occurred, and the stories of it share crucial details with the story of Noah."

"All right, I see your point. But how do you *know* they weren't fiction?"

"Have you read about the findings of Leonard Woolley at Ur and Nineveh, and those of Dr. Field at Kish, or those of Kathleen Kenyon at Jericho?"

Again I shook my head.

"In the early years of archaeology, the very deep flood deposits in those and numerous other sites in the Mesopotamian basin were thought to be a localized flood—immense in size and destructive effects, but still limited. Later, geologists discovered overwhelming evidence that the flood was far greater in size, covering most of Europe, India, Africa, and Asia as far as the Himalayas, and even parts of North America.

Why, for example, are there the same flood deposits and a great salt lake on the Iranian plateau, the Dasht-e Kavir, thousands of meters above the level of Mesopotamia?"

I shrugged. Where did he get his information?

"I have walked on this very desert, Neil. It is in my homeland, bordered by mountains. Geologists confirm that in ages past this vast, sterile plateau was a fertile region surrounding a fresh-water lake."

"All right, but look at the Dead Sea. We know how it came about— the ocean spilled in ages ago, the evaporation—"

"The Dead Sea is nine times saltier than the ocean. And it is twelve hundred feet *below* sea level. My beloved Caspian, the largest land-locked lake in the world, is also saline, though only one third the salinity of the ocean. Yet it is *above* sea level. The Kavir, as I have said, is far higher still, and there are similar high-altitude salt lakes elsewhere on our planet."

"Okay. Let's say, for the sake of argument, that there was a world-wide flood—or nearly worldwide—in the Earth's distant past. You're still not addressing other details in this scribe's chant. For example, his planet was covered by a thick cloud layer. The aliens knew darkness and light, night and day, but from what he says, they never saw the stars or the sun until the day their arrow went up."

"There is a theory that the Earth was once surrounded by a dense layer of cloud, heavy with water. If this is so, it would explain many things, and could further dispel our presumption that the flood account is myth."

"How?"

"If you read Genesis carefully, you will see that during the generations following Noah the ages of individual men are recorded. With each passing generation after the flood, the lifetimes of men steadily decline until they reach our present 'threescore years and ten'."

"But that could prove the earliest accounts were just ancient lore, exaggerated and wildly imaginative."

"Or it could point to a cosmic catastrophe. If the dense cloud layer was broken—let us say by a comet or asteroid, if not by the direct hand of God—then solar rays and other cosmic rays detrimental to man's health would then for the first time penetrate the atmosphere and begin our genetic degeneration."

"A theory", I murmured. "A theory with many *ifs*."

"In the flood account, it is written: *All the fountains of the great abyss burst forth, and the floodgates of the sky were opened.*"

373

"Which could mean anything—such as a severe localized flood in Mesopotamia."

"Yet it is written that the crest of the waters rose fifteen cubits higher than the highest mountains. Then there is the *bow in the heavens* established as a sign that God would never again destroy mankind by flood. It is recorded as an unprecedented phenomenon. Yet rainbows appear only in skies where sunlight pours through broken clouds."

"But where is there any evidence of an advanced civilization before recorded history? There's nothing, Dariush, nothing of any kind."

"Geologists inform us that worldwide catastrophes have occurred during the history of our planet. The Earth has several immense impact craters, any one of which could have set off a chain of events, such as unthinkable tsunamis and shifting of tectonic plates and the axis of the planet. We have theories that attempt to explain diverse prehistoric phenomena separately and sometimes together, but we have no absolutely reliable map of the past. Within various scientific fields, there is much controversy over the chronologies and causality."

"Granted, Dariush, but you're jumping to some enormous conclusions here."

"I am merely speculating. *If*—yes, I will dare to use this word—if a cataclysm with global effects occurred during Noah's lifetime, is it not likely that everything preceding him would be swept away, and what remained would be buried beneath very deep deposits of sedimentation?"

"All right, I'll grant you that too—*if* it happened."

"There is also the question of the greenhouse effect created by the pre-flood cloud layer, which would have made a warm, humid environment permitting luxuriant botanical growth and large creatures. *There were giants in those days*, the scriptures tell us. These factors, combined with the longevity of man during that period, would enable a civilization to develop rapidly. It would not need to expend so much of its energies on survival. This would have changed with the collapse of the cloud layer."

"Everything you're saying is interesting, Dariush, very interesting. But it doesn't in the least prove that the aliens came from Earth."

In answer, he merely handed me another sheaf of papers.

"What's this?" I asked.

"This is the translation of the second set of codices found beneath the black altar. It was written many hundreds of years after the arrival on AC-A-7. The author is unstated, yet the style is close to that of Dumu-er-se-tim, called Ti-shmi, the Child of the Underworld. A different hand, a different mind, but the author was of this culture.

"The document recounts the past, which at the time of writing is already very distant. He speaks of the 'sacred arrow' landing in a wide, fertile plain between mountains and sea. Then follows the establishing of a city, of agriculture, mines, forges, social hierarchies. There was a slave class, a priestly class, and an overarching cultic life that determined everything. The Night-gods spoke into their ears yet remained invisible. The Lord of the Night-gods was their supreme deity, and he too was invisible. Yet through the mouth of a later Ap-kalu, he commanded the people to carve an image of him and instructed them in the rites associated with it.

"The document describes a sickness caused by the 'burn-stone'. It is the cause of deaths, since the ship's fuel was removed from its safe compartments after arrival on the planet and enshrined in the city temple. The burn-stone is sacred, and those who touch it will die by the hand of the Night-gods. Now, the fuel must be put back into the ship's safe compartments, and the people are commanded to coat the entire vessel with a material the Night-gods tell them how to make. The people must then carry the ship into the mountains and enshrine it in a new temple they will construct by cutting deep into a mountain. A road must be built on which to carry it.

"The new world is rich in resources, yet the people are unhappy. They are longing for the world they left behind, a world that had no harsh sunlight, where the air was thicker and all things grew more bountifully."

Dariush paused.

"Even so," I said, "this doesn't necessarily mean they came from Earth."

He thumbed through the document and handed me the final page.

"This is a scan of an image on the bottom tablet of codex-2."

It was a print-out of a photo: a gold tablet inscribed with circles. In the center of the page was the largest circle, the only one with symbolic flames radiating from it. Revolving around it were thirteen circles and ellipses of varying sizes, with increasing radii. Eight planets and five small planetoids. The third out from the sun was the only colored one—intense blue.

375

"That is an inset stone", said Dariush, touching it with his finger. "It is lapis lazuli."

Inscribed beside it were typical alien hieroglyphics.

"What do these letters mean?" I asked.

"It says, *The Beautiful Planet*." He pointed to additional symbols beneath the third sphere. "These signify 'domicile' and 'origins'—in other words, *home*."

We talked throughout the morning and into the afternoon, by which point, my friend was finally overcome with fatigue, and I sensed it was time to leave him so that he could take some rest. We agreed to meet again in the evening. I returned to my own room, sat down on the bed, and tried to digest it all.

"We are not alone in the universe", Paul had said that day at the tower when we first discovered evidence of intelligent life on the planet. Yes, we are not alone, and now it seems that our close encounter with an alien race is not what it appeared to be. We are like a man wandering from room to room in an empty house, turning a corner in a hallway, and suddenly seeing another man standing there, gazing back at him. And then he realizes it is a mirror and he is looking at himself.

Day 323:

That evening, Dariush and I met at the bistro. Both of us picked at our meal, saying nothing, staring at the food, at the table top, at our own non-thoughts. By wordless agreement, we went for a walk along the concourse, back and forth, from one end of the ship to the other.

To break the silence, I asked him about the contents of the third gold codex.

"Instructions for rituals," he solemnly replied, "dictated by their god."

"A sacred document", I said.

"A sacred document from hell", he murmured.

Before we parted, he told me that he and the chief of Archaeology have reported the decryptions to DSI and also to the expedition's archivist, who will file it in the ship's main computer. According to the executive's instructions, those who know about the successful

376

breaking of the "aliens'" code are to keep their findings to themselves. The matter is "under further investigation".

Day 324:

I have felt little interest in reading the Bible since my middle teens. The only copy I ever saw in the open was the one Fray Ramon used at Mass, and it disappeared along with him sometime during the years I was away at college. My mother owned a Spanish-language edition, disguised as a cookbook, and after her death, I gave it away to a neighbor in our village. Searching through the *Kosmos'* main computer, I discovered that there is no complete text available, only fragments quoted in the countless articles demythologizing or debunking the book.

But, as I was to learn, our ship does indeed carry copies of the Bible, all of which were smuggled on board:

I asked Dariush if he owned one. He admitted he had an edition in Persian Farsi, and another in Armenian. He showed them to me in his room. They are disguised as philological texts with fake titles on the covers.

Xue owns a Mandarin edition, disguised as a treatise on quantum mechanics.

Pagnol owns one in the French language, disguised as a compendium of "recent" (now ten years old) discoveries in microbiology.

Paul Yusupov does not have a copy, but he informed me during our late-night swimming session that he has memorized the Gospel of St. John—in Russian. I asked if he had perchance memorized the book of Genesis. Regrettably, he had not. He offered to write out a translation of John into English, warning me that it would probably be a clumsy one. I declined, explaining that I wanted to begin at the beginning.

Finally, it was Maria Kempton who came to the rescue. She owned an English-language edition, published in the year 2040 by the "bishops' conference" (whatever that is) of Sri Lanka. Holding it reverently, she hesitated a moment, then put it into my hands.

"It's not disguised", I exclaimed. "How did you get it on board?"

She smiled. "Neil, you do not understand women's purses. No man has ever got to the bottom of them."

"I know they exist", I shrugged. "I've seen them. My mother owned one. But *why* they exist is another question entirely."

"It's our little secret—*our*, meaning the other half of the human race. I'm afraid I'm duty-bound not to explain it to you."

She agreed to lend me the book after extracting a solemn promise that I would guard it with my life. I'm reading it.

Day 327:

Paul tells me that the *Kosmos* will remain in orbit around Nova for another 108 days, our stay extended to make up for the first month when we were unable to land, plus an additional month due to our projected schedule for investigating the ship.

"How is Pia?" I asked.

"Very beautiful. Very big."

"Are people on KC deck sympathetic? Any problems?"

"Some are happy. Some are silent. They look at her belly when they see her, but I do not know what they think."

"This is the dangerous time", I said. "There are a lot of people in the flight crew. Not everyone is like you."

He patted his pocket. "I know this. I am ready."

Day 328:

I learned from Dariush that the archives in the Temple of the Ship have all been opened, scanned, and auto-translated. His small team of linguistic experts, ten philologists and ten assistants, will be fully occupied between departure from Nova and arrival on Earth—nine very interesting years of study—and doubtless the archives will be examined by scholars for centuries to come.

Dariush said: "You realize, Neil, that several hundred thousand bronze tablets have been scanned. It is impossible to read more than a fraction of them. Thus, we selected codices primarily for the purpose of obtaining an overall chronology. We searched for phrases such as "one hundred years since the Coming", "one thousand years", "two thousand years", and in this way we were able to isolate sections of text that gave us the general outline of their history. We now know that the records were written over a period of 6,900 to 7,000 years, and were archived chronologically from the front right wall beside the ship's nose, backward to its tail, then across the rear wall of the chamber, then proceeding along the left-hand wall toward the front of the ship."

He explained that the texts taken from this counter-clockwise route through the past reveal that the aliens' dating system was based on the longer Nova year. For example, many documents are headed with passages such as, "Three hundred years after the Coming, in the month of three moons" or "Eleven hundred years after arrival in the heaven in the heavens", etc. The figures below have been adjusted to represent Earth-years. Dariush emphasized that the dates closer to our own time (within four thousand years) are the most accurate, but dates become increasingly more inexact the farther back they go. As far as we know at this point, the history of the "aliens" on this planet is roughly as follows. [Insert]:

Chronology compiled by Dr. Dariush I. Mirza

ca. 9200 years B.P.[a]	Departure from Earth (+/− 100 years).
Uncertain	Transit time to Nova.
9160 to 9150 B.P. (+/−)	Landing on Nova (also uncertain, estimated).
ca. 9150 B.P. (+/−)	Naming of planet for their deity and their continent for the "beast that is sacred to the Lord of the Night-gods".
9050 to 9000 B.P. (+/−)	Building of first city (City 1).
	Inscription of gold codex-1.
8900 to 8000 B.P.	Era of expansion and rapid population growth; establishment of City 2 (north) and City 3 (east).
8700 B.P.	First mention of declining longevity of individual lives

---

[a] B.P. = Before Present. — *Zheng.*

8000 to 7980 B.P.	Population demographics peak and begin slow decline. Social unrest. Punitive measures.
7980 to 7960* B.P.	Building of road and causeway. *Estimated completion date.
	Establishment of City 4 (south), excavation of mountain for Temple of the Ship.
	Inscription of gold codex-2.
7960 to 7955 B.P.	Transportation and internment of Ship.
ca. 7955 B.P.	Institution of Temple Rites, inscription of gold codex-3.
7940 to ca. 6800 B.P.	Era of slow population recovery, renewed demographic growth, regulated sacrifices, wealth.
6800 to 6500 B.P.	Second era of gradual population decline, but still above replacement rate.
6500 B.P.	Deity demands increased number of sacrifices.
6500 to 6100 B.P.	Era of recovery, relative stability.
6100 to 5580 B.P.	Breaking of civilization into city-states, regional alliances, betrayals, minor wars.
ca. 5580 B.P.	Reimposition of continental control, one state, one religion, strictest regulation of language, culture, social behavior.
ca. 5580 to ca. 4200 B.P.	Era of stabilized demographics, civil order maintained by force, ongoing purges of all innovative corruptions of original language and culture; sustained totalitarian theocracy (with minor outbreaks of rebellion).

4200 to 4185 B.P.	A major war, followed by genocide of populace of rebellious city and its administrative region.
4185 to 3400 B.P.	Era of imposed relative stability, accompanied by slow population recovery.
3400 to 2700 B.P.	Declining demographics.
2700 to 2600 B.P.	The "gods" declare temporary reduction of human sacrifice, stimulating a century of recovery.
2600 to 2250 B.P.	Resumption of sacrifices, followed by longer, gradual decline of demographics.
2250 to 2140 B.P.	Demographics falling below replacement rate.
2140 B.P.	"Plague" first reported.
2125 B.P.	Universal plague, population decimated.
ca. 2100 B.P.	Second universal plague, massive reduction of population due to combined plague deaths and increased sacrifices demanded by the "gods".
ca. 2064 to 2061 B.P. (+/− 10 E-y)	Records end, the final Sealing of the Temple to protect the ship from "fires in the heavens". Road ceases to be used (depth of soil cover and dating of human remains in temple). Deaths of last living persons of the final generation (dating of human remains, Cities 1 through 4).

In summation, they lived on this planet for approximately seven thousand Earth-years. Their civilization ended twenty-one hundred E-years ago, give or take a decade.

Day 329:

I slept poorly and awoke in an irritable mood.

After I had knocked back my placebo in the B clinic this morning, Dr. Nagakawa asked me, "Do you like art, Dr. Hoyos?"

"Not really", I mumbled, wondering if he were going to mess with my cover.

"You really must see Hokusai", he went on as if he hadn't heard me. "There is an excellent print on our very own deck B, precisely three alcoves forward of the Asian restaurant."

"I can never figure out the front end from the back end."

"I do recommend you take a look at it. Very soothing for the nervous system. If you wish, I could show it to you when I am off duty at 1700 hours. Would you like to see it?"

"Okay", I murmured, not enthusiastic. Doubtless he would introduce me to something zennish like a drop of water falling into a placid pool of water, or the sound of one hand clapping. Just what I didn't need.

Promptly at 5:05, I stationed myself at the entrance of the Asian restaurant, and a few minutes later, Nagakawa came serenely walking down the concourse. Without saying a word, he bestowed an obscure look upon me and led me to an alcove farther along the route.

Inside, I saw an exquisitely oriental image of a gigantic ocean wave about to crash down on slender, open-topped boats filled with Japanese fishermen.

"This isn't soothing my nervous system", I said.

"Its title is *Tsunami.*"

I nodded to affirm that I got it. The image had caught my attention, and I didn't want to clutter the experience with chatter.

As I stood there absorbing it, he mumbled something in Japanese that sounded like *genshy back oo dam.*

"Pardon me?" I asked.

In reply, he handed me a little slip of paper. "Good-bye, Dr. Hoyos." And he was gone.

After another deep look at the print, I sighed and read the slip of paper.

He had written:

> *Waga yado to*
> *iu bakari de mo*
> *suzushisa yo*

"Our home"
in these words
already freshness

—Kobayashi Issa (1763–1828)

What on earth is this about? What's Nagakawa trying to tell me? Let's go home, but let's pass through a gorgeous tsunami to get there? Life is dangerous but beautiful? Or is it, Life is beautiful but dangerous?

On the way home, I decided to make a flying visit to a library computer terminal. There I accessed an omni-translation program, keyed Japanese to English, and typed *genshy back oo dam*. No results. Then I tried variations on the phonetics, and suddenly there appeared on the screen:

Genshi bakudan: "Original Child Bomb".

No explanation. Just words dangling in space. At first, I thought it was a meaningless fluke. Of course, as a physicist and a neighbor of Alamogordo and Los Alamos, I knew the phrase very well. And then I wondered if it wasn't a fluke after all. If not, why had the good doctor mumbled it in that place at that moment? I deaccessed and returned to my room.

Is the whole world going cryptic on me? It's hard enough figuring out the true history of the universe, and now I must deal with the true history of late civilization, not to mention the society I've been living in for the past ten years. I thought the ship was mainly populated by scientists. Now I find it's populated by apostles of art and religion. And they all—all of them—keep handing me documents. Why do they do it?

I don't understand anything!

Day 331:

Today another extraordinary discovery: the anti-matter tool now completed, a test was performed on one of the metal floor plates removed from the temple. An anti-matter device releases ten times the amount of energy as a nuclear blade but does it more finely and slowly. Xue's invention (or reinvention) used a minute quantity of anti-matter injected into a subcritical mass of plutonium—a rather antiquated working fuel, but one that proved to be effective.

383

Both plate and machine were flown to a site within the central range, hundreds of kilometers north of AS-VT, a deep gorge embraced by sheer mountain walls, a natural fortress that would help contain possible negative effects. The tool was operated by remote control at a safe distance. It slowly, relentlessly made an incision of molecular thinness, cutting the plate in half. There were neither explosions nor implosions, nor the disappearance of anything more than a thread of matter along the cut line. Xue had done his work well.

The tool was flown back to the temple, and there it began its painstaking labor of slicing away the veneer covering the ship. The first incision was made at midpoint along its length, four lines around the rectangle of fine grooves, which many people believed was a portal. The work was slow-going, with frequent changes to the speed of cut, as the machine continually adjusted itself to the varying relationship between protons and anti-protons in the black veneer. Unlike the nuclear scalpel, the tool did not overload and shut itself down. The veneer was found to be (on average, with minor irregularities in the surface) 0.03179 meters deep.

By the end of the day, the incision was completed and then the great moment arrived: the outer plate was affixed with suctions, removed easily, and then lowered to the floor. Behind it was what looked very much like a portal. The metal surface was featureless, and the seams were so tight that nothing could be inserted into them. Now the nuclear scalpel went to work, slicing into the seams with relative ease. The portal was cut and removed, revealing that the hull was over two meters thick, with layers of walls enclosing the dark cavity within. Now probes with mobile eyes were sent inside for a preliminary look. As we watched on the panorama screens, the vidlights lit up a cavernous interior that was, at first glance, an enormous empty tube.

Closer inspection revealed that the walls were covered with a maze of tracks that looked like computer circuits, and numerous pipes that ran the length of the chamber. The whole appeared to be colored uniformly dull gray. When the cameras pointed to the left, or nose, of the ship, we saw that the cavity ended some distance from the portal at a floor-to-ceiling bulkhead. This was broken by several doors at three equally spaced heights, with cross-walks at each level and a central staircase uniting them all. It much resembled the atrium of an ocean-going liner. Little by little, more details came into view:

Instruments reported that the atmosphere inside was normal air. There were no toxins present, only a minute quantity of dust, which was composed of degenerated mineral elements with no biological content, living or dead. The dust was faintly radioactive, below the level dangerous to human health. The entire atmosphere was suctioned out and replaced with clean air suctioned in from the valley.

Along both sides of the base of the central chamber were numerous connected metal cubicles with open doorways, like two rows of cheap apartments divided by a street. The probe went into one of them and found it empty, with the exception of a metal shelf on one wall, low and wide enough to be a sleeping platform. It also sent out readings of the interior dimensions, which proved to be precisely the same as those of the dwellings in the cities. If these were passengers' rooms, they had been cramped quarters. The probe entered several other cubicles (there are a total of ninety in the chamber) and found them to be identical. There were no windows in any of them.

At three levels above the cubicles, flanges ran the length of the chamber, each with evenly spaced sockets, which may have once supported floors for bearing cargo. The chamber's length was one third of the ship's, with another third in the unexplored forward section, and the final third in the aft. Another bulkhead closed off this latter section, and like the forward bulkhead, it was punctuated with matching doors. Here, by contrast, the surface was covered with the veneer of black metallic substance, including the doors, which were identifiable because they are slightly recessed.

By the end of the day, specialists in aeronautics, nuclear engineering, and archaeology entered the ship and inspected the central chamber. No artifacts were found.

Day 332:

I ate breakfast with Xue in the cafeteria this morning. He is "upstairs" with us for a couple of days in order to take a break from weeks of hard mind-work and the constant tension of the watchdog. He needs to relax in his serene living space in the company of his little poet on the deer.

"No black holes, Owly?" I asked.

He wiped symbolic sweat off his brow and cracked a Xueic smile. "None so far, Nil, though there's always hope."

He tells me that duplicates of the tool have been made. Two are now busily peeling away strips of veneer from the ship. A third is cutting into the floor of Tower 1 (the one we discovered).

He says that penetration of forward and aft sections through the bulkheads is being delayed until more of the ship's outer covering is off. The experts want to see a good deal of the exterior exposed before doing any internal surgery. Though there is no guarantee, this may help avoid making mistakes with the anti-matter tool blindly cutting into sensitive material—there will surely be some kind of crucial technology inside. The rear third will be examined last, since the black alloy's resistance to radioactivity may be shielding us from lethal doses.

Day 335:

A mountain of veneer sections is growing in the entry hall of the temple. The ship is nearly two-thirds exposed now, with only another ten or fifteen meters, over the nose, to go. The ship is beginning to shine, silver in color and reflectivity. Its surface is being cleaned by swarms of engineers, metallurgists, and maintenance people on hover platforms. Some oxidization, very light. As is the case with the outer veneer, this alloy is unknown to us, extremely hard, and probably of equal or greater heat/friction resistance than the metalloid alloys of the *Kosmos'* outer hull. Again, there is a lot of head-scratching over the strange mixture of the "aliens'" highly developed technology and their less-developed social order and culture. In the media presentations, there is not a word about their planet of origin. No public discussions on the nature of their religion. No mention of human sacrifice. No analyses of the appalling depersonalized cities. Where are the anthropologists when we need them!

Dariush and I met for supper in the Mexican bistro this evening. I asked him the above questions. He did not reply directly, but after some silent musing, he said, "Neil, behind every anthropology there is the lure of ideology. By the same token, behind every ideology you will find a determining anthropology—and this latter is the more dangerous."

I wasn't sure what he meant. Fearing an abstract lecture, I changed the subject.

Day 336:

The nose of the ship is now completely exposed. Its tip is an embed-ded crystal cone that resembles white quartz. It is not natural quartz as we know it, but something like it in the mineral realm. A kind of synthetic diamond perhaps, polished to a shine, displaying no facets or cracks or other flaws. The metal surrounding the gem is pitted with innumerable microscopic impact holes, as is the ship's skin a long way down the body, the pattern tapering off gradually.

Day 337:

The floor of Tower 1 is not a floor. It is a ceiling. Beneath it, there is another circular chamber with the same dimensions as the upper sec-tion of the tower. It was discovered when a piece of the floor/ceiling was cut and removed, large enough for probes to enter. Ongoing exca-vation of the surrounding terrain reveals that the tower extends well below the mountain's rubble surface.

Probe cameras reveal a complexity of machinery below, as well as all manner of unidentified objects. At this early stage, it is conjectured that the floor/ceiling was lowered and raised by hydraulic mechanisms that elevated it to the level of the shelf I spotted on that first day, immediately below the circular window. On the walls, equidistant from each other, three tubular metal columns support the floor/ceiling. They appear to be telescopic in the sense of cylinders within cylinders.

Day 339:

Excavations on Tower 2's exterior, as well as cutting of its floor/ceiling, reveal that it is an identical twin of the other.

Today, a team went below, through the hole in T-1's floor, armed with plenty of lights and audio/visual remotes. Within this lower cham-ber, they found innumerable small mechanisms neatly arranged on shelves inset into the walls. The instruments were composed of ground glass lenses integrated with calibrated rods, and were in all likelihood used for astronomical purposes. Taking up the remaining wall space, open archival shelves contained a large number of bronze tablets similar to the ones found in the Temple of the Ship. These, however, were mainly what appear to be stellar diagrams, each with its symbols and a line or two of script—yet to be translated. The room also had a set of hydraulic columns (let us call them that for the time being). There was another singular oddity: in the center of the chamber, resting on a vertical support rod of black metal, was a perfect crystal sphere, transparent except for a faceted red gem in its core.

More cutting into the floor of this level revealed yet another chamber below. It too contained a set of hydraulic columns, with the addition of metal housing for a machine that apparently powered the columns. There was nothing more in the room. Its floor is the bedrock of the mountain.

In short, there are three chambers: the lowest contains the fundamental hydraulics of the whole system, lifting the ceiling/floor above it, and the uppermost ceiling/floor above that. In the middle chamber is the second set of columns, the crystal sphere, instruments, bronze tablets. Above that is the roofless open section we first discovered months ago.

Day 340:

The machinery in the basement is a single unit the size of a small car. It once had access or service doors, but these long ago seized shut. One was cut open, and inside was found a complex mechanism of cylindrical pistons and valves designed by a long-dead engineering genius. There were crystals that may have been light nodes, hieroglyphics inscribed in the metal in which they were embedded, levers that could not be moved, and embedded circuits similar to our computer circuits on Earth, though the conduction tracks are much larger than ours. There was a single hollow compartment the size of a thumb, where a fuel pellet would have been deposited. The compartment is believed to have held atomic fuel, since a trace of radioactive dust remains there.

Engineers are fascinated by the mechanism and say it all makes sense (at least to them). They believe that with a little rewiring, plus reoiling of the hydraulic pistons and application of a power source, the columns might be made to function. We have no atomic fuel pellets that would fit, and the danger and time cost in producing one is prohibitive. Instead, the engineers want to bring in a mobile generator and hook it up to see if the system still works. The columns themselves are a fairly simple matter, since they each have valves for injection of lubrication fluid.

Day 342:

The forward section of the ship was entered today, after technicians cut into the central door on the lowest tier of the bulkhead. Here is a first survey report on what was found:

Three floors still intact.

The lowest floor:

It contains ten chambers or "apartments" that were probably residences for priority passengers or crew. Each unit has two or three connecting rooms. They are bare except for the sleeping platform. No artifacts of any kind. Inscribed in the metal walls in a few of the rooms is a solar system, clearly our own, with the sun and eight main planets in proper proportion, plus the five main planetoids, including Pluto and Charon. Inscribed on the wall of every room is an animal form—reptilian with wings. Wide hallways separate the rooms.

There is a large dining area, with a stainless steel table and benches still intact. Next to it is a kitchen with a variety of cooking machines. The latter had their energy source in a circuit umbilical rooted in the wall, a square wire covered with a thick glassine substance that crumbles at the touch. (Was electricity the primary energy grid for the ship? If so, is the harnessing of electricity another universal product of intelligence?) In this room, there are also round sinks made of a metal similar to stainless steel, as well as pipes, taps, and drains—all displaying minute quantities of oxidation, which is minimal due to the near-zero moisture content of the air. There were countless empty shelves on every wall, and a pantry with more empty shelves.

A room across the central hallway contained toilets, ten side-by-side holes in a single, seat-high metal shelf, the holes funneling into conduits beneath the bottom floor. There were no windows anywhere throughout this level. There were no elevators for transport from floor to floor, only staircases.

Middle floor:

The entire space is coated with a thin black substance (a paint, not hard metal). The room is devoid of artifacts or furnishings. The floor is flagged with black stone tiles (our usual dimensions).

389

At the end of the room closest to the ship's nose sits a black stone cube the same size as the one outside, though lacking symbols and runnels. Inscribed on the wall above the ship's internal "altar" is a reptile with wings.

Immediately above the head of the reptile are three holes, each measuring 3.179 centimeters in diameter. When a light probe was inserted into the central hole, it was discovered that the opening is the mouth of a tubular channel leading to the tip of the "quartz" cone in the nose. There are faceted transparent crystals along the path, which measures 3.179 meters in length. Shouts came from outside the ship; observers standing on the temple floor noticed that a brilliant beam of light shot from the cone and continued in a concentrated line toward the distant wall of the outer temple gate, kilometers away from the ship. The probe light was turned off, and the beam died. The probe light was low strength, and thus we have learned that this device (for lack of a better word) amplifies light dramatically.

Later, the light was turned on again; the beam shot out as it had before. Its line was traced to a point on the chamber wall immediately above the temple gate. Now it was discovered that three circular holes (each 3.179 centimeters in diameter) were present there, a fact which had gone unnoticed until now. The light from the ship entered the center hole. The acrid smell of burning dust and a few wisps of smoke came from within. The light source in the ship was turned off and the beam died. A low-wattage probe light was inserted into the center hole in the temple wall, which was the mouth of a tubular channel leading toward the exterior cliff face. Along its path were more faceted transparent crystals. The other two holes were the same, though the crystals in one were amethyst color and the crystals in the other were ruby red.

The outer ends of the channels were blocked by stone. The light was turned off and withdrawn. Measurements were taken, and it was found that the channels led to the three eyes of the winged deity inscribed on the cliff face.

Day 343:

This morning, archaeologists on hover platforms reinvestigated the large external mural of the winged deity. With a little tapping, it was discovered that the incised lines of the eyeballs are seams. These were cut out and stone plugs removed. The holes are the pupils of the eyes.

Again, a low-power lamp in the ship was turned on, and a beam of light shot through the temple, entered the central eye channel, exited the cliff face and continued on across the valley, entering the pass.

Unaware of these experiments, workers in the tower radioed a query, asking about an intense beam of nearly blinding light that had appeared below them in the pass and continued onward into the west.

I learned much of this while having supper with Xue in the deck-B cafeteria. He said: "Neil, I don't have a lot of time this evening. I've been asked to participate in a new investigative team, which includes three astronomers and two optics specialists, Dr. Hoang of Seoul University and Dr. Cowan of Rinmen Beijing University. I just came from a meeting with them. We're working on collating the preliminary data regarding the light beams and the temple ship. At this point, we know that the light of a man-made, 40-watt lamp, when directed into the hole within the ship, exits the ship at a magnitude perhaps a thousand times stronger than the source. It passes through only one of the three orifices in the mountain wall, and exits the cliff face at an even greater magnitude, not measurable at this point. We experimented by placing a metal plate over the cliff exit hole, and within a few seconds, the beam burned through the plate. Its trajectory over the valley brought it straight down the middle of the pass."

"Was it a weapon of some kind?"

"I do not know. Actually, I think not. Remember, we have directed a beam outward from the ship as an arbitrary experiment. It is equally likely that these prisms were intended to direct light *into* the ship."

"A power source, then."

"Perhaps. Or it might have been associated with astronomical observations."

"I've been wondering about the astronomy towers. Wouldn't one tower have been enough for reading the heavens?"

"*We* would think so. But the makers of this system could have had purposes connected to their symbology. For example, the winged being had three eyes, hence the three holes. My belief is that there were three towers originally."

"If so, there's one tower yet to be found."

"Our committee reached an agreement with the archaeological oversight committee that a search would be undertaken. We began by excavating at likely spots in the pass."

"That's a large area to search, isn't it?"

"Yes, very large. However, it is relatively straight. If there is a third tower, one dependent on an optimum vantage point, it would most likely be at the highest point on the floor of the pass. This point, as it happens, is exactly below the two towers, and forms a line with them. Add to this the aliens' obsession with mathematical relationships, and I think we will find our missing component in fairly short time."

"You still call them 'aliens'?"

"Dariush has described the findings to me—the remains in the temple crypt, the forensic evidence, and his translations of the early codices. I am convinced he is right about the origins of this race." He paused. "It is merely easier to say *aliens* than to say 'the others' or 'our forefathers'."

I shuddered. "Our forefathers. There's a chilling thought."

"Indeed. Besides, on this planet they *were* aliens. We all are."

"Regarding the missing tower, Ao-li, I can see the logic of your theory, but if there's one situated in the pass, and if its dimensions are the same as the other two, wouldn't it have blocked the road?"

"Not necessarily. The tower could have been constructed after the internment of the ship. In addition, the mouth of the pass opens wide at that point, and if there is a tower there, I think we will find that the road either swerves around one side of the tower or divides and goes around it in two branches, then reunites into a single track after it enters the valley."

"So that's where you'll start digging?"

"Excavation has already begun in the valley, in the shallower soil deposits five hundred meters from the height of ground at the entrance to the pass. However, preliminary instrument readings in the deeper deposits at the approach to the pass indicate that the road has begun to divide."

"Eureka!" I exclaimed.

"I must catch the next shuttle, Neil", he said with a smile, picking up his tray and rising to his feet. "I will keep you informed."

"I really appreciate it, Ao-li. Life on the *Kosmos* is pretty dull these days. You're very kind."

He put the tray down on the table. "Neil, we've been friends for how many years?"

I shrugged. "Lots and lots."

"Do you remember our times at Princeton? And the Loner's Club?"

"Yup, how can I forget? I did it as a joke, figured I'd establish a fraternity with only one member—until you popped up, that is."

"Our numbers instantly doubled. A fraternity with two members. A pity we never grew beyond that."

"It was a relief. Did I ever confess to you that when I put up the poster, I intended it as an antisocial terrorist act, a *kultur kamikaze* free-fall without a parachute?"

Xue shook his head. "I didn't know."

"It was just the kind of fatalistic black humor I used to excel in. Really immature exhibitionism. The psychiatrists would have had a field day on my psyche, if I'd ever let one near me. Don't you remember the crazed drunk who had no friends?"

"Do you remember the lonely Chinese boy who had no friends?"

"I remember meeting an inscrutable super-brain who looked like he needed nobody's help. When you came along, so exquisitely polite and so eager to join, how could I say no?"

"Do you also recall when we began to work together on the anti-matter equations?"

"Un-huh, those were good times. I liked the beer too."

"I remember everything, Neil. I remember especially how you never hesitated to supply the missing elements for my theories."

"As you supplied missing elements in mine."

"For my part, motivation was purely *quid pro quo* in the beginning. And that's one of the reasons I esteem you, despite your cowboy boots and your inability to pay your Mensa dues. You were never a *quid pro quo* guy, never a bargainer, never a trader. You cashed in no chips, and you called in no favors. Never. You were always a giver. And that's a rare kind of person. I would not have won the Nobel without you, and you have not once reminded me of this throughout all the years since then."

"Nonsense. I never would have won the Nobel without *you*."

We left it at that.

Day 344:

I talked with Paul at the pool last night. He looked worried. The director of Medicine has sent a clipped inquiry up to the KC clinic,

393

addressed to Pia, asking why she had failed to attend a mandatory meeting of onboard medical staff.

She replied by voice mail, apologizing, explaining that she had been ill.

There is another meeting scheduled for next week, to be held at the DM offices on deck D. She is "required" to be there. No explanation was given.

If she attends, no one will fail to take note of the fact that she is very pregnant.

"Can't she resign or retire?" I asked Paul.

"If she do this, DSI rule say she not part of KC and must move down to her own room on Concourse B. Then she is under their authority again."

"We sure as hell have a lot of rules in this ship. You should just ignore them. And do keep Pia upstairs. No more strolling down to other levels."

"Yes", he nodded. "Maybe we be safe. Eight, nine weeks and baby is born."

"What is the Captain's position on this?"

"Long time ago, on voyage, he send message to Earth-base about DSI going bad. Now first answer from Earth come back to him. It say, all law for voyage still is law. Follow Manual."

"Wait, wait, wait!" I shook my head. "That can't be. He sent the complaint letter to Earth just before we arrived at AC-A-7. Light-speed there and back, we're looking at close to eight years for a message turn-around time."

"Yes. But he send earlier message about DSI problem in year four, and others later. This is first reply. There will be a hearing—government court—when we return home, when all Captain's message have arrive at Earth-base. Until then, DSI is boss."

"Not on KC deck I hope."

"Not on KC. Is law they have only lower decks."

Day 350:

As excavators opened up more and more of the road, they confirmed the instrument readings, which had told them two roads were merging after a division higher up. Nearing the height of ground at the head of the pass, they unearthed the division, after which the two road branches bent in a wide symmetrical tangent. The pass had suffered a great deal of rubble-fall over the millennia, including avalanches of heavy stuff. The road was now covered to an average depth of forty meters, in some places fifty and sixty meters. Excavation proceeded with slower progress.

Day 353:

Xue was right. The third tower is located exactly where he thought it would be. The whole site has been cleared, leaving the tower exposed down to its base in the floor of the pass.

As with T-1 and T-2, T-3 has a ceiling/floor cap made of the seemingly indestructible black metal. It is undamaged. The anti-matter tool was flown in and an incision made. Men went down the hole.

The bottom two layers of the tower are intact and are identical to those of the other towers. The third, uppermost layer is largely nonexistent, though its collapsed building blocks, before they were cleared away, composed much of the debris covering the lower levels.

The tower is positioned exactly equidistant from the two flanking towers. There is a sphere inside. It too is equidistant from the other two spheres, to within a centimeter.

Beyond the tower, the pass begins its descent into the west. If our mechanics staff were able to elevate the sphere to the height it was designed for, it would have a clear line of sight to the arc of the planet.

On-ground astronomers are busily pointing mobile telescopes westward along the pass, counting the hours until nightfall. Beyond the horizon, the star field will doubtless confirm what the *Kosmos* astronomy people have already discovered: in that direction lies our home solar system. They have made computer-generated star maps, dating back progressively through thousands of Nova-years B.P, calibrated for this longitude/latitude/day-time. Needless to say, the universe is in motion, yet their calculations demonstrate that alignment occurs— probably on dates pertinent to the history and religion of the ones who made the towers.

Day 354:

Further exploration of the interior of the ship was delayed while the foregoing investigations were underway. I should say, rather, that the final third or tail end of the ship remained unexamined. I must now return to describing the forward section and its three levels. To recap:

The bottom floor was exclusively residential—sleeping, cooking, eating, and hygiene for those at the top of the flight hierarchy.

The middle floor was a barren black temple section, containing only an "altar" cube, the incised mural of the Lord of the Night-gods' pet beast, and the three holes leading to the nose cone.

On the morning when the top deck was investigated, I hastened to the panorama hall with keen interest, since this would be our first glimpse of the temple ship's control center, and it would be in real time. The hall on my floor was nearly deserted, since a majority of people are downstairs on the planet. I had a good seat, front row center.

Close on the heels of three scientists, the camera ascended a stairway from its base in the ship's cultic chamber on the middle deck. Arriving at the top, the vid shot went immobile as scientists and media men paused to take in the scene. Before us was a single, long chamber—a hall as wide as the ship and a third its length, tapering toward the nose. The walls were a half-dome tunnel matching the outer hull. The ceiling in the forward section sloped down steeply to the floor, as this upper deck was at the tip of the "arrow". The ceiling, walls, and floor were composed of dull metal plates with barely discernible, welded seams.

As the camera moved forward, I saw that there were five "windows" in the extreme forward end of the chamber. Three of these were slits in the wall immediately above the nose cone, uncannily similar to the pilot windows of our Earth-based mega cargo planes or rocket craft of the early space era. Measurements were taken—each window slit was 0.3179 meters high by 3.179 meters wide. A few meters aft of the nose were two more identical slits, one on each side. The windows were thick transparent panels of a diamond-like material. They were blocked by the external wall of the hull. It is logical to presume that during the ship's voyage the forward windows were not covered by metal. If this is true, the metal was installed over the windows after the ship landed on Nova, or perhaps during the internment of the ship, for reasons that we cannot presently understand.

Now the camera shifted to a tilted "dashboard" beneath the five windows. It was metal alloy with an array of control components embedded in it—fairly simple design, with crystals, levers, and what appeared to be circuit tracks. Centrally positioned were three bronze pads in the shape of human hands.

I leaned forward in my seat, extending my right hand impulsively. Each of the hands had two thumb depressions. For a moment, I wondered if the "aliens" had six-digit hands, but then I recalled that among the thousands of skeletons examined in the cities and temple crypt all hands had five digits. Surely, the hand-pads were designed for control of some kind. Had they once responded to pressure or body-heat? Or did they swivel on unseen axles, forward and backward and sideways? If so, the two thumb depressions might have been designed for control by either the right or left hand.

The dashboard sloped down at an angle that declined toward flat horizontal, though still tilted a few degrees, with its upper side fused to the wall. It ran continuously on both sides of the chamber, forming an elongated letter U. There were no seats in the hall. Floor sockets in front of this countertop followed it all the way, and one of the scientists commented that probably many seats had once been installed here, and were removed after the flight.

I stayed rooted to my seat throughout these hours of preliminary familiarization. Later in the day, another program presented additional findings, with plenteous commentary from analysts.

While the craft is relatively simple compared to the *Kosmos*, it appears to have been designed to meet every basic human need throughout its voyage. The number of individual control panels embedded in the countertop along both sides of the U argues in favor of the theory that all functions on board were controlled from this room, everything from propulsion, navigation, communications, atmosphere, lighting, heat, water, etc. The control panels were each distinct in design, with hieroglyphics inscribed in the metal beside each crystal—the latter were a variety of colors and hues.

The great age of the bronze hands prohibited mobility at first, but engineers succeeded in lubricating one of them and manipulating it on unseen axles. It is surmised that these were the pilot's (or pilots') controls for pitch, roll, altitude, etc., during take-off and landing. A panel was cut out of the frame beneath the countertop, and inside was found a complex mechanism resembling gyroscopes within gyroscopes, with circuit connections from the hands and circuited into the floor. Gyroscopes only work where there is gravity. Were these instruments used exclusively for airflight above planetary surfaces? Did the ship have internal gravity generators as well?

Since the ship appears to have been designed for both air and space flight, it is presumed that when the aft section is opened we will find retracted wings and also propulsion vents for maneuvering in zero gravity.

Cryptanalysis tells us that the hieroglyphics beside crystal nodes on the various control panels are a mixture of mythic references and the purely pragmatic. For example, one inscription reads: *Flame of the Night-gods small* (meaning, "reduce nuclear propulsion"?). Another reads *Beast Sacred to the Lord of the Night-gods wings* (possibly, "extend [or] fold the ship's retractable wings"?).

Sample cuts have been made into the base of the countertop at selected points, revealing only complex circuitry inside.

Though investigators say they feel they are poking about in the innards of a giant computer, it is a cyber-control system with no visual screens. There is perhaps one exception. Embedded in the dashboard immediately above the three bronze hands is a rectangle of diamond-like, transparent material. On the underside of this "glass" is a grid of thousands of hair-thin tubes, which may be akin to our primitive fiber optics. When I saw this, my heart skipped a beat, and I wondered if the "screen" once displayed star maps. Or it may have been the visual terminal for the ship's master computer, which has yet to be located. Strangely, only one such screen has been found on board.

I remind myself that the original crew or authority of this craft did not have an exact picture of their destination, nor for that matter a scientific schema of our home solar system. According to codex-1, written by the Child of the Underworld (thankfully, long-dead), they had a poetic description that was accurate as far as it went. If his account is the sum of what they knew in the beginning, it would mean that the voyage pilots or authorities were given instruction as they went along, with the Night-gods whispering in their ears or through the mouth of the Ap-kalu.

Above it we came unto the great sea that is constant night,
Yet it is full of the flames of the Night-gods.

More suppositions on my part:

The panorama screen presentations have infrequently shown images of our home solar system inscribed on the walls of residential rooms on the lower deck. There is no commentary about this, apparently because our authorities, and especially our very own elfish Ap-kalu, have decided we don't need to get into that. Undoubtedly, Elf and Skinner are still weighing the implications. Knowledge is power, and the power is theirs for the time being. People must wait until *they* decide what we should know. Nevertheless, enough has been seen and enough has been circulated through private conversations that we can guess the motives for the inscriptions. These "aliens" were homesick for their *Beautiful Planet*. Soaring far above the water-blanket, they had analyzed their own place of origins and depicted it accurately. But they had not yet seen their destination, which was only a pinprick of light in a heavens crowded with the flames of the Night-gods.

Man is a naming creature, Dariush once told me. During our out-ward voyage, he often lamented the impoverishment of modern languages, at least as they are spoken and written outside the realm of technical knowledge. He has chided me for my lapses into slang. He has also underlined to me the anomalies in language itself. He asserts that the breathtaking insights of Socrates and Aristotle, for example, or the natural wisdom of an earlier age, such as that of Solon the Law-giver of Athens, are clear indications that man, even on the brink of the prehistoric, was capable of highly advanced thought. Much of it was superior to our own thinking, which we in this era consider to be progressively more advanced than what went before. Early man's conceptual and abstract powers were impressive.

Dariush believes, moreover, that the nature of language itself, its semantics, its semiotics, was more developed during that primitive stage of civilization. For example, Babylon with 600+ letters in its "alphabet" and the Hittite with 350. I am not convinced that larger alphabets relate to any larger configuration of *mind*. It points to something unusual about them, but what? Tyrannical, cruel, power-hungry, and morally depraved, those ancient civilizations had something that eludes me. One would not want to live for a single day in their company, yet . . . yet their mental capacity was different from ours. And perhaps that is what I am straining to understand: As a species, is *homo sapiens modernicus* evolving, or are we degenerating?

Then there is the question of the pre-flood civilization, evidence of which is now staring us in the face. The descendants of Noah had no such technology. Yet the Babylonians and Hittites and all the other races known to us had come from that survivor in his wooden ship. As his family multiplied and spread out over the reborn earth, living to great age and generating great numbers of offspring, did they move farther and farther away in time and geography from the original story of their miraculous rescue? Did the evil in man's nature gradually increase as the memory of the flood dimmed? Did they retain only scraps and mutated versions that they interpreted according to their weaknesses, their desires, and even their growing attachment to evil? Did they lose the basic memory of mankind? Even in those early post-flood generations, had it become for them something of a myth? Was the Nimrod who built the tower of Babel harkening back to stories he had heard about the legendary peoples who lived before the flood? In his pride, in his disregard for the object lessons of his own history, did he desire to emulate the greatness of Krani-mhrod who had built the tower for the "sky-arrow"? We cannot know. We can only speculate.

Of course, in my own way, I am avoiding the implications—I admit this much. If what I have written above is true, then the biblical account is more or less accurate. It displays mythlike qualities, but it is a myth that occurred. The question follows, therefore, that if the biblical account is accurate, what should be my relationship to it? I will think about this later. For now, the presentations about the ship are totally engrossing.

As I said, man is a naming creature. And it looks like pre-flood man was no different from us in this regard. The ship has a name. Which brings me to a significant finding on its flight control deck. On the arched ceiling above the three bronze hands is a mural incised in the metal. It is a winged animal, clearly a reptile. Its wings extend from one side of the "cockpit" to the other. Its spiked head and neck is tilted back, fanged mouth wide open. In its left claw, it grasps the numerical symbol for 100. In its right claw, it grasps a star. Around the star are eighteen heliocentric planets. The star-sun is an embedded gold disk. The planets are merely incised, with the exception of the seventh, which is a blue nodule of lapis lazuli.

Engraved in the metal immediately below the mural and immediately above the front windows are hieroglyphics which say:

Heavens-ship Beast Sacred to the Lord of the Night-gods

These are also the words inscribed in stone above the mural on the cliff face.

Day 355:

A rare privilege. By the Captain's initiative, Xue, Dariush, and I were invited to join him and selected flight staff for dinner on KC deck.

About five o'clock this evening, Dariush and Xue knocked at my door. As we walked along the concourse toward the nearest elevator with access to KC deck, I mentioned to them my uneasiness about my status, wondering how closely I am being watched. Since the invitation had come by word of mouth, not through ordinary communication channels, we hoped that our sojourn would go unnoticed.

Alas, approaching the elevator, we came upon two people who looked very much DSI, one male, one female, both of them grim and determined.

The male stepped forward and said, "Where are you going?"

Xue replied, "We are going up to KC at the invitation of the Captain. A purely social affair."

"It's not allowed", he said.

"It's allowed if the Captain permits it", said Xue, with his calmest Genghis Khan look.

"Well, it's not allowed", said the man with the standard repetitiousness of the imprisoned mind.

Then followed a dialogue that I need not record here. Let me say that it was an uneven match between an intelligent man and a bureaucratic male. Xue was polite and relentless. Whenever the agent was bested, he simply retreated into his zombie instructions. Neither of the two DSI agents carried weapons, and from this we may deduce that the department is so assured of its authority that they presume a word of command is enough to meet any situation, which in this case it was not.

There were a few concluding exchanges:

Xue: I repeat, the Department of Social Infrastructure has no authority over KC deck.

Agent: Yes, but you're standing on deck B.

Xue: Then we will now depart from deck B.

Agent: No, you can't. It's not allowed.

Still, we did not have the access code for the elevator, and it looked like we were in a stalemate. Fortunately, at that point the elevator doors opened, and there stood two uninformed flight staff people, come to bring us on high.

I walked past the agent, but he grabbed the sleeve of my jacket.

"Not you", he said. The female agent stepped close with a purposeful look.

I gave them my ol' cowpoke smile and said, "Sonny, are you a facilitator or an animator?"

"I'm a facilitator, DSI-3 grade."

"And your fellow employee?"

"She's an animator, DSI-4."

"Uh-huh. Well, I can tell you're a couple of good kids in your heart of hearts. You just don't know what you're doing."

"I know we've got orders to follow."

"Well, buddy, I suggest you just go on over to the nearest library computer and type in the following search words, making sure you put quotation marks around the phrase: 'I was just obeying orders.' Then, after you've done that, and after you've read a few articles about that phrase, I'd like you two to go have a drink in the Mexican bistro. You'll be my guest. Here's my *Uni*-card."

He shot a glance at the card and ignored it.

I went on: "Then, tomorrow, I'd like to take you out to supper as my guests. Do you like Asian or Indian? Maybe Afro? We'll talk about what you've learned. Will you do that for me?"

I gave him a paternal pat on the shoulder and turned away while he was digesting this, though he didn't let go of my sleeve. He was still wondering what he should do when the two flight staff waded into the thick of things and herded us three scientists into the elevator. They keyed the code, the doors closed upon the perplexed faces of the agents, and up we went into another country.

Seconds later, the doors opened, and we stepped out into a lobby. There, we were welcomed by a commander, *the* Commander, in fact: the second in command on the *Kosmos*. As I may have mentioned before, the ship is one kilometer in length and a quarter kilometer wide. I can't describe the layout of everything on KC, because I saw only a fraction of it. To say the least, it was big and complex. The residential section is aft. We did not go in that direction but instead went forward along a wide central hallway toward the command centers. We passed several of these divisional wings along the way, identified by signs in various languages denoting what went on inside (propulsion liaison, navigation, officers' mess, medical center, communications, etc.). I noticed a large cafeteria similar to those on the lower decks. There were no bistros or specialty restaurants.

"This really is a city", I said to Dariush.

"One might become lost", he answered.

Xue walked a few steps ahead of us, chatting with the Commander and the other two, who were wearing the insignia of lieutenant commanders, heads of KC sections.

I overheard chuckles and snatches of conversation, dismissive references to the nature of DSI "attitudes". Of course, I already knew that KC people were somewhat independent personalities. Paul's friends, the shuttle pilots, for example, were bona fide mavericks, but I had attributed this to the psychology of the few men in our world who were able to transcend the force of gravity, alone and in charge of their magnificent craft, facing the dangers of the lonely skies and the infinity above.

"They're so arrogant; they think they rule the world", muttered one of the officers.

"Well, they do", replied the other with disgust.

"It's a big world and a bigger universe", said the Commander. "They'll need to print more of their little manuals."

These fellows seemed to have retained the semi-independence of the man of the sea, the man with his eyes on horizons. That their independence was limited by the state of our world and its government would surely be plain enough to them. Nevertheless, the conversation implied that they had made their own judgments about it, had broken out of the mind-box. Perhaps this was possible because the government was as dependent upon them and their expertise as they were upon it. Thus, the uneasy coexistence between the true man in a community of common purpose and the bureaucratic male in a collective of common uniformity.

Such thoughts preoccupied me until we approached a dividing wall near the foremost section of KC—the ship's actual command center. We did not enter it, but instead turned right into a cross street and through a double door into the Captain's personal quarters. This, as it turned out, was an annex with a conference room, three small private rooms (presumably bedroom, bathroom, and study), and a fairly spacious dining room. The Commander brought us into the latter, where we were greeted by a tall, silver-haired man, rising from the head of a long, oval dining table. He was about my age, dressed in casuals, relaxed and warm, but exuding an unstated authority. He shook hands with Xue, Dariush, and me, introductions were made, and then he stepped back to allow Paul and Pia to greet us. Welcoming banter followed. Pia did not get up from her chair but flashed me a big smile.

"How ya doin', *Mamacita*?" I asked, sizing up her belly in a glance.

"Purdy darn good."

"Countdown begun?"

"Yup, six weeks to go."

"Everything healthy?"

"Mother and child doin' well."

"Wonderful, wonderful", I murmured and gave her our customary little pats on the back. I suddenly wished I had a gun to defend her with. But then I saw the valiant Paul, beaming with pride and love, and remembered his mastodon killer and his sword.

The Captain took charge and asked us all to find seats around the table. A dinner was wheeled in on carts, and servants placed steaming platters and tureens before our place settings, which were genuine ceramic plates, silverware, and glasses. I chatted with one of the servants, a Hispanic lad who came from, of all places, Santa Fe. I invited him to visit me in my cabin if we ever make it back to Earth. He enthusiastically accepted the invitation, and added that he would like to buy property and build a cabin in my neighborhood, after he has purchased a home for his mother and father and several cousins. I knew the scene. I knew the scene very well actually, and wrote out my address for him on a paper napkin, which he pocketed with satisfaction.

The meal was a mixture of Earth-origin vegetables grown in the Base-main gardens, plus some small fruit items in salad greens from the ship's hydroponics garden, followed by the main dishes of nova-turkey and nova-salmon, in sauces.

I would like to add as a note of special interest that the vegetables were running with authentic butter brought from Earth by the Captain. This incredible item had been frozen in cold storage and thawed for this moment.

"It must have cost a fortune!" I declared when I put a real buttered carrot into my mouth and closed my eyes in ecstasy.

"It did", said our host with a whimsical smile. "And may I mention, dear gentlemen, lady, and baby, so did the wine. It is black-market, made somewhere aboard this ship, of which I am ostensibly the master. I asked no questions, and no lies were told to me. Please, sample it."

We did. It was nova-berry, aged well. A delightful evening ensued.

Did I mention that the Captain's correct English is accented? He was born in the city of Siauliai, in the "republic" of Lietuva (old Lithuania). He began his career many decades ago with aeronautical studies in Vilnius, Berlin, and Brussels, steadily rising in the world-fleet. He piloted the first expedition to Mercury and was involved in establishment of the Mars base-colony. Later, he was the first man to land on Pluto.

He told us fascinating stories about that "cold, cold" event and about "warm, warm" Mercury. Paul's three pilot friends (Vladimir, Jan, and Loka) were present at the supper and contributed anecdotes as well. As the conversation unfolded, it was clear that they shared a trans-ethnic fondness for dark humor. They kept everyone laughing, even our rather somber Dariush and the gravely responsible Commander. In retrospect, I'm not sure what we found so funny, but perhaps that was not the point.

The conversation turned to the behavior of the two DSI agents at the elevator. The Captain and his second-in-command listened to this latest development, frowning and exchanging looks with each other. The Captain sipped from his wine glass, then leaned back and stared at the ceiling. Everyone else fell silent, wondering what he would make of it.

"How did they know about my invitation to you?" he said at last, as if to himself.

No one replied. Doubtless, the possibility of an informant on KC crossed more than one mind.

"Maybe they are now watching all elevators leading to KC", suggested a lieutenant commander.

"They exceed their limits", said the Captain. "It is, how do you say, *ultra vires*, beyond the law."

"That is unclear", commented the Commander. "We seem to have a gray zone here. They can't countermand your authority on KC, nor invade this concourse. But they are testing the perimeters of their authority, it would seem."

"It is good you resisted them", the Captain said, turning to the two lieutenant commanders who had rescued us. "Nevertheless, it presents new problems. It raises the question of whether or not it would be wise for Dr. Hoyos to return to deck B and other regions below."

"Oh, I fully intend to return to my own room this evening", I answered.

"If you wish. I hope you understand that it will present a counter-test. And I am not certain about defending you down there."

"I may not need defense. There's always a coward hiding inside a bully. I've got nothing to lose, and it would be interesting to call their bluff."

"Neil, it's hardly a bluff", Pia interjected.

"I will lend you my sword", said Paul with a half-smile.

"Do DSI people have weapons?" I asked.

"I have seen no instance of them carrying one", said the Captain. "But I would think they have weapons in reserve, in case of emergencies."

"A talking mouth and the Manual are always enough of a threat", said Jan in a tone of driest contempt. "Or freezing of *Uni*-credits for the really stubborn."

Loka laughed and added, "We have a proverb in my country. We say, the lizard knows the condition of his underbelly, and that is why he keeps it pressed against the ground."

"Let us hope he does", smiled the Captain.

"We also say, the lizard would like to stand erect, but his tail will not permit him."

"Yes, but has anyone ever resisted the lizard with force?" I asked.

Heads around the table shook in the negative. No one had ever witnessed any real revolt.

"My own form of resistance is within the lines of protocol", said the Captain. "Dr. Skinner in a most courteous and menacing letter has informed me that my attitude is uncooperative. He is correct in this. We can be grateful that the designers of *Kosmos* installed private communications for me. I can send messages to Earth-base without our friends in DSI monitoring or blocking. Yet for the time being we are at something of an impasse. We must wait nine years for a proper hearing. DSI knows this. They also know that the authorities at home will want an accounting of their behavior. They will go more carefully now."

Xue said, "They are extremely careful but not invincible, certainly not omniscient. There's the question of David Ayne's death, for example. We have proof that a murder has taken place. We have the private autopsy report."

"Unofficial, written by a nervous doctor", I said. "And we have a bucket-full of coincidences. Even now, we're uncertain about what happened and why it happened."

As our thoughts returned to the deceased man, a pall descended on the company. But there was really nothing more that could be said about the unresolved questions, other than chewing our guesses to death.

Turning to Xue, the Captain asked him about the discoveries in the three towers. Xue gave him a detailed account. One of the lieutenant commanders, the chief of flight-crew astronomy, asked Xue if his committee had now concluded that the towers had been used primarily for astronomical purposes. Xue replied that while no definitive conclusion had been reached, he and his colleagues were fairly certain that the towers were indeed for such purposes. If that was the case, the three spheres were probably elevated and exposed only at night, for reading what was happening in our home solar system, and other systems. The middle sections of each tower were full of star maps on bronze plates. Those examined to date were found to be mapped from a "topocentric" perspective, he said—meaning ground-based, specifically as observed from the towers.

He paused, thinking quietly, then added that he wouldn't rule out the possibility that the towers had been a source of solar power for the ship, supplementary to the nuclear.

"We are uncertain about the full range of energy design. The presence of radioactivity and propulsion tubes at the base of the vessel point to nuclear fusion, but again, how it worked is not yet clear. Next week, when the theorists and committees have all had their say, the rear third of the ship will be opened. Then we will have more facts to weigh."

Dariush now spoke up for the first time. "I concur with Dr. Xue regarding the towers' purpose. All the star maps have been scanned and analyzed by the computer. Decryption of the hieroglyphic text on each map reveals that it is technical in nature. Their vocabulary in this field was quite well developed, and some of it remains obscure to us."

"What perplexes me", I said, "is that the temple tablets, the three gold codices, were written in a primitive style. It just doesn't seem to match with their technological language—and their accomplishments."

"This is true. Of course, they are much older documents. We should also keep in mind that religious codices, even certain nonreligious codices, might have been written in an elitist or gnostic style, that is to say, a form of temple language."

"Poetic?"

"Yes, like an epic poem written in traditional style, one that moves the reader or listener by appealing to subjective feelings. As is the case with our own present civilization, a treatise on biology or astrophysics is rational thought expressed in a different form and style than, say, a poem or a song. The brain's logic faculty is not needed for the latter; the creative intuition faculty is dominant, both in the composing and the listener's inference."

Xue said, "That is so, my friend, yet the poem or song is dependent on a thought or a concept, and is not necessarily irrational. It may be *meta*-rational."

"Mmmm", said Dariush, pondering this, swept into a vortex of his own rumination on the point.

Because few in the room were much interested in this sidetrack, the general conversation returned to the mechanics and optics of the towers and their relationship to the "eyes" of the "god" on the cliff face above the temple of the ship.

Everyone had seen photos or vids of it, but, oddly enough, only a minority of those present had seen images of the god in the temple crypt. I assumed this was because a plethora of scientific and historical material had been discovered at the same time, and thus the sculpture had not captured more than a passing interest. While it is human nature to be fascinated with morbidity, the attraction is a transient one. People can't look at horror for long.

Dariush, returning from his voyage to inner space, now spoke up. He described for us the sculpture's purposes, and added other significant findings, such as the fact that the hundreds of thousands of skeletons in the temple were those of children. He finished with a verbal sketch of the sacrificial rites as they were recorded in the gold codex-3.

People fell silent, frowning, quietly shaking their heads in disgust, or simply staring at the table top. No one knew what to say.

Xue leaned back in his chair and closed his eyes. In his quiet voice, toneless, he recited:

> The great snake lies ever half awake, at the bottom of the pit
> of the world, curled
> In folds of himself until he awakens in hunger and moving his
> head to right and to left prepares for his hour to devour.
> But the Mystery of Iniquity is a pit too deep for
> Mortal eyes to plumb. Come
> Yet out from among those who prize the serpent's golden eyes,
> The worshippers, self-given sacrifice of the snake.
> Take your way and be ye separate.
> Be not too curious of Good and Evil;
> Seek not to count the future waves of Time;
> But be ye satisfied that you have light
> Enough to take your step and find your foothold.
> O Light Invisible, we praise Thee!

None among the assembled guests responded. Dariush gazed at Xue thoughtfully. Pia's eyes glistened with tears. Paul nodded in unspoken agreement. The Captain stared at his empty glass, then reached for the bottle.

"More, anyone?" he asked, pouring wine into a few glasses held out to him.

"Did you compose those lines?" Dariush asked Xue.

"No, it's by a poet named Eliot. He wrote it one hundred and seventy-five years ago."

"Got any of his poems with you?" I said.

"Several in my head, Neil. I will write out a few passages for you, if you wish."

"Okay", I shrugged.

"Good and evil", said Loka with a sigh. "The old story. It just keeps cropping up again and again, doesn't it, no matter how hard they try to banish the idea."

"Oh, they never banish it, Loka", said Jan. "They redefine *what* is good and what is evil."

"True. But it seems the concept does not go away."

"Because it is reality", said Dariush. "The war in the heavens."

"*Be ye satisfied that you have light*", mused Jan. "This race we've found had plenty of light. They were masters of light."

"The poet refers to an invisible light", Dariush replied. "The ones who built the ship used the forces of physical nature to combat the true eternal Light."

And there it was again, Dariush's theme: eternity, soul, the divine presence, the one true Light versus the appearance of light.

"Perhaps we judge them too harshly", said the Captain. "Without doubt, they had intelligence, yet there was ignorance too. Their evil—may I use this word?—their evil seemed right to them. It was like a light to them. They were wrong, but can we hold them to account for it?"

"A little late for that", I said, feeling sudden anger—strangely, anger against the forgiving people around me. "How much better it would have been if their ship had exploded in space before touching down on this beautiful world. An atomic blast would have wiped them all out."

"You presume to know the meaning of justice, Neil", said Dariush, affixing me with a penetrating look.

I retorted, "It's plain enough to me what kind of justice was needed. Think of the millions murdered by this wretched tyranny. Think of their horrible acts committed against children. Think of the serpents they infested this planet with—a peaceful world, with only natural death until they arrived. They brought it all here."

"And now they are gone. You know the dates, Neil. You know their end approached when the true Light was born in our home world. And later, when he died and rose again, their end came. Then did the true Light spread throughout the cosmos unto infinity."

Dariush was my friend. I did not want to push the discussion to the level of argument where hurtful things might be said. I shrugged and looked away. Doubtless, others in the room were uncomfortable, since this was a mixed gathering of theists and unbelievers, I presumed.

"Stron called us a ship of fools", I laughed half-heartedly. "And maybe we are. How can we know anything for certain? We do our best, and that's all we can do."

Suddenly Paul sat up straighter, made a Russian gesture with his arms, scowled, and declared: "This is not ship of fools. This is ship of clever killers. We have snake on this ship. Not everyone—but many."

Pia put a hand on his arm, trying unobtrusively to calm him.

Xue stepped in with his serene voice: "Our ship is a microcosm of the world back on planet Earth. Our companions on the voyage are people whom mankind considers its best, not its foolish. But without God, even the best are fools—bad fools. We take our humanity with us into the infinite sea."

No one offered a reply.

Without warning, Pia began to cry. The rest of us, all men, felt helpless in the face of this force, the mysterious feminine heart. Or soul. Or whatever it was, absent within ourselves.

Paul put an arm around her and murmured Russian words into her ears. He put his right hand gently onto her belly and held it there.

"I'm sorry", she sobbed. "But whenever I think about that monster in the crypt, I feel so afraid. I saw the photo of it only once. That was more than enough. Sometimes I dream about it. It's alive and it's thirsty. It wants more blood. It wants our baby's blood."

"Shhhh, shhhh", Paul whispered, holding her close.

We made distracting small talk for a time, but it petered out, leaving an uncomfortable silence. By unspoken agreement, we three guests from the lower decks stood up and thanked the Captain, preparing to make our departure. I leaned down and put an arm around Pia's shoulders, kissed her cheek, thumped Paul's back, and bid them good night. They got up and kissed me in return, then left for their apartment. The Captain and the pilots walked the rest of us to the security elevator.

"Thank you for coming", he said as we stood in the KC lobby, waiting for the elevator to beep its unlock code.

"Thank you for protecting this good couple", I said to the Captain. "If there is anything we can do ..."

"Continue giving your encouragement, I think. She has protection here, though it isn't airtight. Paul is upset because earlier today the director of DSI sent a formal letter, couriered by the hand of an agent, demanding that Pia return to deck B and surrender herself for termination of pregnancy."

"They know!" I groaned.

"Yes. Someone in the flight crew has informed them. It is impossible to know who has done this, but it was unrealistic to expect it to be otherwise. Paul said that this is a ship of clever killers. He was expressing strong emotion, of course. Yes, there are killers on the *Kosmos*. But I believe the greater problem is in the majority, those who would never participate directly in it. They are silent accomplices, either informants or passive look-the-other-way types."

"But you are not", said Xue, with a note of admiration.

411

The Captain dropped his eyes and sighed. "I am a grandfather. I have one grandchild. If the world were different, I would have many."

His eyes clouded, and we asked no more questions.

The elevator doors opened.

"Good night, gentlemen", he said with a salute. We three civilians saluted him back.

Day 356:

Postscript: Last night, arriving on deck B, we exited the elevator to find four DSI agents waiting for us. They stepped forward.

Two of the pilots had accompanied us, Vladimir and Jan. Now the Pole advanced and handed an envelope to the agent in charge.

"Letter from Captain to Dr. Skinner. Copy to Dr. Larson", he said coldly. "Captain has sent message to Earth-base about this situation. DSI will not touch Dr. Sidotra. If she or her child is harmed, DSI will be broken, and you will go to prison. Understand?"

The agents said nothing, but they took a step back.

"Captain says Dr. Sidotra stays on KC and DSI will stay off KC, totally. Do not ask. Do not argue. You just obey. Understand?"

"You can't hide a baby on this ship", one of them dared to say.

Jan gave him a look that Vlad the Impaler would have admired. In a low Slavic rumble, he said, "If *you* can hide a murdered man, *we* can hide a baby. Now, go."

They went.

Xue, Dariush, and I shook hands with the pilots, thanked them, and said our good nights. They stepped into the elevator and were gone.

"Well, here we are in DSI country", I said. "Any idea what we should do?"

"I think we will not be bothered for the time being", said Dariush. "Forgive me, but I must return to working on a text that was found in the walls of the central tower. The scan reached me this afternoon, and I would like to run it through cryptanalysis and then examine the results. Will you excuse me?"

This left Xue and me alone in the echoing hallways of Concourse B.

"Asian?" I asked.

"I'm Amerasian actually", he smiled.

"I mean ..."

"How about a nice quiet bistro, Neil?"

"An excellent proposal. Are you fond of exceedingly hot snacks?"

"I abhor them. Why not Irish beer?"

So we went down to deck D, and no one bothered us along the way, nor in the pub, nor at any time during the rest of the evening, nor today (so far so good).

In the pub, we sipped at our beers and replayed the evening.

"Looks like they're backing off", I said.

"For a while, perhaps", said Xue. "They will doubtless need to have numerous meetings in order to assess the situation."

"Let's hope they have nine years of meetings."

"Let us hope so."

But his expression told me he didn't think we would be that lucky.

"That was an interesting comment you made about rational and meta-rational. Sometimes you perplex me, Owly."

"In what way, *Nil*?"

"The stereotype. The emotionless oriental prodigy. Do you still have that slide rule?"

When he and I first met at the inaugural meeting of the Loner's Club, he had stepped out of the amorphous mass of humanity as a midget wearing thick, rimless eyeglasses; he was dressed even more nerdishly than my good self (his highly polished black shoes had two-inch soles, topped by a cuff of thin vermillion socks, blue trousers, white short-sleeved shirt, buzz-cut hair, the face of a twelve-year-old Buddha, and what looked like an antique manual slide rule poking out of his shirt pocket (along with five multicolored clip pens).

"So, you remember the slide-rule."

"How can I forget it, Owly? It shattered many of my assumptions about life, society, the history of the universe, and the destiny of the entire cosmos."

"If only I'd known, I would have brought two and given you one."

"How could you? Your grandfather was deceased by that time, wasn't he?"

"You remember him", he said, and for a moment, his face betrayed an inner emotion. "About the extra slide rule, I was speaking metaphorically."

Xue's slide rule was a manually operated analog computer—the kind that was used during the pre-computer era. Handmade of ivory, it was mind-stunningly complex, demanding actual brain work with the assistance of its numerous sliding bars, on which my fraternity fellow worked out logarithms, roots, trigonometry, multiplication, division, and a host of other functions. Later, as we got to know each other better, he tried to train me how to use it. I mastered a few functions, but it always seemed to me an enormous waste of time. I owned no less than three pocket computers that performed the same functions with much less brain and mechanical involvement. Yes, sometimes the batteries died, and sometimes I had no money to buy replacements, but it sure freed up my time for other things. Such as moping over unreachable girls. Brilliant me, I also had a problem with vodka as pain-killer in those days.

I never met Xue's grandfather, the man who made the amazing slide rule. He died in Beijing a year or so after seeing his little grandson, age nineteen, off to Princeton for his first year of post-doctoral research at the Einstein Institute for Theoretical Physics. I was still working on my doctorate at the time. At first, Xue had seemed to me an alien life form. An admirable alien life form, but still ... There were no points of connection other than physics, loneliness, and nerddom.

Xue had undoubtedly found me and my culture to be nearly incomprehensible. Later that year, after he had come to trust me, he told me a lot about the old man he loved so much. I even saw tears in his eyes for the first time. He sorely missed his family back in China. He also tried to interest me in Chinese poetry, which he explained would be a healthy antidote to excessive specialization in our field. I was not interested.

Sitting in the Irish pub, nigh on sixty years later, we are old men. We have accomplished much. We are soon to die. We are soon to be noted in histories of science. I love him as a brother, very dearly actually, but I can't say I really know him, not soul to soul.

Did I just write *soul*?

Well, it's a serviceable word.

"Ao-li", I said, somewhere after my second cup of ale. "Did your grandfather make the little sculpture of the poet on the deer?"

"No." He smiled. "My great-grandfather made it. He gave it to my grandfather. My grandfather gave it to my father. My father gave it to me when I left China."

"You have two treasures, then."

"Do you have treasures, Neil?"

I couldn't think of an answer. What were my treasures? My boots? My pocket knife. Maybe the turquoise cube I'd given away to Pia? My cabin way up in the Santa Fe mountains? The carapace I'd surrounded myself with for these past many years, in privileged isolation?

"Memories, maybe", I said. "Those are probably my treasures. The goodness of my parents. Their love for me. The little bits and pieces of life they gave me out of their poverty. A few words, fragments of meaningful conversation."

"Of the conversations, what do you recall most often?"

I had to think about that. And when I saw it I was surprised.

"Mostly, I remember the things they said that told me who I was."

He nodded. "It is the same for me. We receive life so unthinkingly, often ungratefully. And this may be, in part, one of the causes of our worldwide devaluation of life in these times."

"What they've done to mankind is evil."

My use of the word made Xue pause and gaze at me silently for a few moments.

"One wonders constantly how it happened", he said. "How did man cease to know himself?"

"We got distracted. We didn't pay attention. We stopped listening. Those gifts you were given, Ao-li, were messages from the past, weren't they?"

"Yes, my forefathers were speaking to me, handing down to me their love, their countless sacrifices, their belief in me, embodied in a concrete form. And they are speaking still."

"Do you ever feel lonely?"

He smiled again. "Lonely? I suppose I feel it sometimes. It is the human condition. But I think, Neil, that this passing sense is a sign written in our innermost being, a longing for what is beyond our limited vision and cognitive powers."

After a third beer, I said. "Did I ever tell you what a fine word you are to me?"

"You have told me in many ways, many times. You have not resorted to the primitive medium of spoken language."

"I should have said it. I should have told you how grateful I am, how honored I am to know a man like you."

He did not reply. For both of us, this was a veer toward the unstable realm of emotions.

"Neil, you were a word to me", he said at last. "And you still are."

I shook my head, wondering what kind of "word" I could possibly be for the man.

I said, "If I had ever married, if I'd ever had a child, maybe many illegal children, I would have liked you to be an uncle for them. I would have been so happy to see you teach them to use a slide rule, or read a poem, or get to know a wee little fellow sitting on the back of an antlered stag."

Now he grinned. "When can I come for a visit?"

"It's a bit late for all that. But we can dream."

"We can dream."

"Care for another beer? It's on me."

"Thank you, but we must now put a pleasant cap upon the evening's festivities. I must be up and about at five in the morning. Tomorrow we will try to elevate the tower floors."

"Keep me informed?"

"I'll keep you informed."

We shook hands and he left.

I went to my room, looking over my shoulder in case DSI agents suddenly jumped out of the shadows to drag me away. But none appeared. I slept poorly that night and was in and out of consciousness, dragging bits of dreams with me. In one, I saw brown-skinned young people diving from a boat into deep cool water. They were my children. The children I didn't have. Maybe the children I might have had. I can't remember details now, but the spiral staircase was there too. Another of those synapse blips, I suppose.

Day 357:

Not much to report by way of developments. No harassment from DSI. Both Xue and Dariush are below on the planet for a few days, engaged in their respective work at AS-VT.

True to his word, before he left, Xue gave me half-a-dozen sheets on which he had penned some poetry, including the snake poem that had made Pia cry. He says this writer's work is *persona non grata* back on Earth, and thus he had committed a few to memory. I like this guy Eliot. He's so refreshingly dire; no happy-think for him. I passed the poems on to Paul for insertion in my journal.

Day 359:

This morning a brief e-voice message from Xue to say that engineers installed a generator in the base of Tower 1 and connected it to the ancient wiring of the original power source. The circuits were conductive and "live". The hydraulic pistons were refilled, and the three columns on each level (total of six per tower) were lubricated. This, combined with experimenting with the levers (which turned out to be switches), succeeded in elevating the bottom floor/ceiling, which simultaneously elevated the top floor/ceiling. There was a din of squealing and groaning as the telescopic tubes were used for the first time in two millennia. Yet they were wonderfully designed, and the whole operation proved to be ridiculously simple.

The uppermost floor came to a stop beneath the broken shelf in the top chamber, which when intact would have made a rim to inhibit further rise. The sphere stationed on its rod at the radial core of the floor was now level with the center of the circular window. Sunlight pouring into the chamber from above passed through the prism inside the sphere, emerging as a thin beam, shooting outward through the window and hitting the cliff face on the other side of the valley. There, a panel of metal had been affixed to the mural, large enough to cover the eyes, since Drs. Hoang and Cowan had predicted the beam, concerned that it might do some heat damage inside the temple. The beam struck the metal at the position of the monster's right eye and began to burn through. This was reported immediately by radio to the people in the tower. They covered the sphere with a canvas hood, and the beam instantly died.

Tonight we watched a panorama presentation about these experiments. An astronomer explained that the spheres were used by their makers to amplify starlight, and were not intended to direct the full power of solar rays into the temple. Night experiments began after sunset today. We'll hear more about this tomorrow.

Day 369:

Green Day again. A year has passed since the previous exercise in elevating our cosmic sensitivities, or "interplanetary bio-consciousness" as it is called officially.

There are few people onboard the *Kosmos* at present, so the green banners, scarves, and neckties were scarce here. Down on the planet, however, festivities were in full swing. On the panorama screen, I watched a few celebrations at various stations, dominated by an incompatible mixture of ecological cant and jargon and an any-excuse-for-a-party attitude, seasoned with mystical music.

One particularly nauseating performance occurred in the temple itself. There, accompanied by the piped-in music of flutes and drums, a bevy of maidens danced around the black altar cube. They were dressed in diaphanous green gowns that left nothing to the imagination. Somewhat frenzied, nearly erotic, and definitely euphoric, the ten young women twirled and pranced and sang in praise of a cosmic "lord" who held fire in one hand and arrows in the other. Their choreography resembled a coil, winding and unwinding hypnotically as they chanted. At the head of the dance, leading it all, was the old Russian psychiatrist lady who had been so offended by me looking at her scar years ago. She was now without doubt far into her eighties, which was unfortunate, since her gown was the flimsiest of all, nearly transparent.

With flailing arms, she repeatedly let fly full-throated cries rising from her arching abdomen, a crone-nymph on hallucinogens. As the event progressed, a soft, male voice-over informed the viewers of our need to reconnect to primitive "spirituality", which entailed, apparently, a "rediscovery of the phallic" (thankfully not acted upon, at least not on screen, as far as I know, which isn't saying much) and a "reintegration of light side and shadow side" for the sake of universal harmony.

(*Ay, caramba!* I turned it off and went for a long walk.)

Day *370:*

Today has been occupied with repeated practicing on the columns in all three towers. They are fully functional. Continual lubrication has lessened the squealing and groaning, and they now slide one inside the other with greater ease and speed.

The spheres are kept covered between dawn and dusk, avoiding all exposure to direct sunlight.

During their night experiments, astronomers at Tower 1 reported a powerful influx of star light, with the creation of a very thin beam that crossed the valley, striking the protective metal covering on the cliff face, burning a pin-hole in it, a few millimeters deep.

No one has yet come up with an explanation of how the whole optical arrangement worked to produce star maps. One hypothesis is that the alien astronomers manipulated light through the numerous hand-held bronze and brass instruments found on the shelves of the middle chambers in all three towers. Since each device contains lenses and prismatic crystals, light beams may have been redirected onto screens within the towers, and then copied exactly onto the inscribed stellar map-plates. Alternatively, the plates themselves may have been the screens, and the map was burned into the metal by the very light that came from their source stars.

Needless to say, for the time being, it is all conjecture.

Day 378:

Astronomical experiments have been continuous throughout the past three weeks. Working only during the darkest hours of the night, the astronomers have tried applying various hand-held instruments to the sphere. They believe some apparatus is missing, perhaps only the framework that would have held the instruments in proper place for the production of maps. In any event, our attempts to replicate the old bronze plate maps have been stabs in the dark, producing only unidentifiable patterns on our own screens erected within Tower 1. It is the same with experiments in Towers 2 and 3. The results are random conglomerations of burn holes, and the computer can find no match with true stellar maps. If maps were once made with this configuration of instruments, we simply don't know how to use them.

Day 380:

I have been wondering over the lack of panorama presentations on the opening of the tail section of the temple ship. It may or may not have been done. This morning I knocked on Xue's door in the hopes that he could tell me something about it.

I heard his muffled "Open" in Chinese, and the door disappeared into the wall. He was sitting on his bed with a book open on his lap. He closed it. I recognized it as the Bible disguised as quantum mechanics.

"Neil, I was just thinking about you. Come in."

"Do you read this often?" I asked, pointing to the book.

He glanced at the *max*. I nodded that I understood.

"The wave particle duality still bothers me after all these years", he said. "There is an applicability of Planck's Constant that we need to investigate, mathematically, I should say."

This was intentional gobbledygook, and we both smiled, knowing that if any monitor folks were listening, they wouldn't know the difference and would begin shutting down their higher brain functions in order not to be bored to death.

"I was surprised when I discovered you owned a book like this", I said.

"I find it most helpful. It opens vistas of cosmic theory that cannot be blocked by our normal scientific presumptions about the duality of energy and matter."

He then spun me a complex equation designed for public consumption. It was gibberish. I chuckled and said, "Brilliant, Dr. Xue, brilliant!"

He continued: "I regret that this volume is in my own language, and thus is not accessible to you. Everyone should read it and ponder it. Were you able to locate one in Spanish or English?"

"In English. However, the author belonged to neither of those races, and thus we have potential difficulties with the translation. I struggle with the wave-particle duality especially."

"Ah, yes, the uncertainty principle. Perhaps you should discuss it with Dr. Mirza. As a philologist, he may be able to help you."

"His worldview is within certain restrictive parameters, I feel."

"I believe he is not a restricted man. He is something of a polymath."

"Or a peculiar savant."

Xue shook his head. "No, he is not. Which becomes increasingly apparent the more one gets to know him."

"I know him very well."

"Do you?"

Again, impasse.

"Where did you get the book?"

"My father gave it to me. It was his grandfather's. A rare volume, you understand. Priceless, actually."

420

"Another gift."

"I think the greatest one."

We had proceeded as far as we could go in this line.

"Ao-li, I came by to ask you if there has been any progress on the temple ship. Has the rear section been opened yet?"

"The initial cut into the bulkhead will take place the day after tomorrow."

"Why have they waited so long?"

"There were concerns about the radioactivity. Interestingly, the black alloy that originally covered the ship is a material which blocks radioactive particles to a considerable degree. The atomics people are concerned that inside the propulsion section we will come upon a reactor that is not in decay, as we first supposed, but is nearly as potent as it once was. The presence of mild radioactivity within the rest of the ship, despite the black shield, seems to indicate this. To open it up could mean exposing staff to lethal doses of radiation."

"So they've been thinking of ways to get around this?"

"Yes. Level-A hazardous material suits with air supply will provide some protection. But how much protection is not known at this point. When the incision is made with the anti-matter blade, the results will be carefully monitored. Once the cut is completed around a very small segment of the shield layer, the instruments will record the intensity of radiation coming through the original metal of the exposed bulkhead. If the *roentgen* units are too high, the shield fragment will be reinserted and the propulsion section left alone. That would be a disappointment to many people, due to their desire to learn more about the technology that powered the ship. However, if the rads are within acceptable limits, they will cut open a single door and enter that section."

"Who decides what are acceptable limits?" I asked. "And another question: Won't there be a risk of nuclear material spreading out into the temple itself, and beyond into the valley? A lot of people would be affected."

"Yes, that is the worry. It's why there have been so many delays. They have now weighed the risks against the potential rewards."

"And endangering human life is not a major factor."

"As always", he whispered.

He opened the book and pointed to a passage. The Chinese characters were unintelligible to me, and I glanced at him curiously. He took a clip pen from his breast pocket and wrote on a slip of paper. He handed it to me and I read:

For lo, the day is coming, blazing like a furnace,
When all the proud and all who do evil will be stubble,
And the day that is coming will set them on fire,
Leaving neither root nor branch,
Says the Lord of hosts.

(Malachi 3:19)

"Who is he?" I asked aloud.

Xue penned his reply: *The last prophet of the Old Testament.*

He stood and said he had to go catch a shuttle flight. I walked him to the elevator. There was no conversation between us. I was disturbed, but unable to explain to myself why I felt this way.

To my surprise, he withdrew from the inside pocket of his blazer the ivory slide-rule I had last seen when we were young men at Princeton. He slid the middle section from it and turned it at right angles, inserting it into a perpendicular groove. It was now a white cross.

He said nothing. I met his eyes. He then reassembled the slide rule into its usual position, and handed it to me.

"Will you keep this for me until I return?" he asked.

"If you wish", I said. "May I ask why?"

Without replying, he gave me a long look and then entered the elevator. When the doors closed, I went back to my room. I did not know what to make of it, but I knew he had entrusted to me one of his most precious possessions.

Day 384:

Dariush and I met at the bistro this evening. I brought up the subject of the temple dance, asked him what he thought about it.

In answer, he just closed his eyes and sighed deeply.

"Poor people, poor people", he eventually murmured.

I did not press him on the matter. To change the subject, I asked him if he had come across anything especially interesting in his recent translations. He said, yes, it was all interesting; every day brought more to light. For a moment, he looked irritated, which was quite unlike him.

"Neil, the translations have been expropriated by DSI. They have decided that it is not in the best interests of the expedition to release the truth about the origins of the ship. For the time being, most of our people believe that aliens created it."

"Do you mean to say that you can't look at your own translations?"

"The archaeology and philology teams can *look* at them. We may continue to translate and refine them, but we are not permitted to publicize our findings. This is why there have been no media presentations about the archives. You realize that most people are more interested in the technology than in the minds who made it."

"Yes, that's true. I must admit, Dariush, that I'm not much different than other people in this regard."

"It is the dimension of *logos* again."

Oh no, I thought to myself, here comes a lecture.

"Neil, if you are a true *logos* and I am a true *logos*, then there is the possibility of the *dia-logos*—a true dialogue."

"True dialogue? What is true dialogue in a world like ours?"

"Our world is drowning in communication, but starving for genuine *communio*—the union of true communion."

"True communion. I wonder what that is."

Not to be dissuaded by my lack of enthusiasm, Dariush pressed onward with his theme: "Profound communion, the flow of celestial language, becomes possible when we are speaking on the firm foundation of the *Logos*, the Word who became flesh, the One who redeemed the universe."

"Redeemed the universe?" I murmured. "Does the universe seem redeemed to you?"

He gazed peacefully, compassionately, into my eyes. I did not like it. I did not want to hear any more of his theological dissertations.

"Now is not the time", I whispered.

"When is the proper time?" he gently replied.

"Why do you waste your efforts on me, Dariush?" I erupted. "Why do you even like me? I'm a hard case."

He smiled at me with affection. "You do not know yourself, Neil."

I shook my head, wished him a good night, and returned to my room.

Day 386:

At 6 A.M., a knock at my door woke me from a dream. In it, I had been wading into ocean waves, breaking on a beach of white sand. Seven young people were with me—children and adolescents—the two youngest holding my hands. All of us were laughing and leaping together into the breakers. They were my own children. Looking back to shore, I saw a woman, their mother, waving at me. I felt intense joy.

Regretting the loss, I shook off the last of the dream and groped my way out of bed.

"Who is it? What do you want?" I said through the closed door.

"It is I", said a muffled voice.

"Open", I grumbled.

There stood Dariush and the Russian shuttle pilot, Vladimir.

"Neil, let us go for a *walk*", said my friend in a low voice.

"This is early for a constitutional stroll."

"I invite you to take with me a very long walk upon a beautiful mountain", he whispered. "Are you interested?"

"Ravenously."

"Good. Our excellent friend Volodya came to me just now with a message from Pia and Paul. They cannot leave KC deck, but they have asked that you and I return to their wedding place and leave a memento of that great event."

"*Kosmos* departs for Earth on Day 435", murmured Vladimir. "Our opportunities to clandestinely visit the planet will be very few from now on."

"Then this may be my last chance."

We followed the pilot on a circuitous trail through the ship that brought us to a single elevator on a side street of Concourse C. We went down to the lower deck and boarded a shuttle without being observed. As before, it took the usual route out into space and precipitously down to the surface of Nova, leveling off over the ocean east of Continent 1. We landed at a geology base, donned our orange suits and hats, and boarded an AEC for the short flight into the mountains.

Our approach was from a direction we had not taken during the previous flights. Avoiding the great north-south valley, where there was a good deal of ground activity and air traffic, we came up over the range from the east and dropped softly into the bowl of the beloved alpine glen.

When we stripped off our suits and walked down the ramp onto the moss, the pure air invigorated me, and the chiming bells of the woods delighted my ears and my heart. Birds swooped low over the little lake; the waterfall burbled pleasantly.

"I'll really miss this place", I said to Dariush.

"I too am loath to leave it", he replied. "It is like a portion of the world restored to Eden."

"We'll remember it when we're back on Earth."

"Yes. Now we must absorb every aspect, that it might live in our memories as a sign."

A sign? I wondered. Well, I suppose the place was a kind of sign—of love, of the eternally renewed hopes of wedding days. Of kindness and good fellowship. Of beauty.

The three of us stood by the lakeshore for a time, just listening, looking, soaking it all up.

Vladimir turned to me and gave me a piece of paper. I read:

Neil,

Will you permit me to make a memorial of the gift you gave to me years ago? I know that you gave it to me as something that is very precious to you, the little cube of turquoise. Paul and I treasure it greatly and do not lightly part from it. I hope you understand. Some day when we are back home, we will look up into the heavens, and we will see a bright star and know that on its best planet there is our cube. It is so much smaller than the evil cubes in the temple. But it is infinitely greater and more beautiful. It is, in a sense, a word that we leave behind us. Thank you for giving us such a word, for enabling us to "speak" it.

Pia

Vladimir gave me the turquoise, which sat in the palm of my hand, radiating its astonishing blueness under the warm sunlight.

"They ask that it be planted beside the waterfall", he said. "Will you do it, Dr. Hoyos?"

"Of course."

We climbed up the low banks of the lake and stood beside the rim of the falls. I put the cube down on a bare rock, wondering if it would remain there undisturbed for eons. Perhaps Pia and Paul's child or grandchild, or a person further down the line of their generations, would return on a future expedition and find it, recalling the ones who had left it here for him.

Dariush closed his eyes and prayed for God's blessing upon the young couple and their baby, and for all the lives that might come from them. He also prayed for the countless souls who had once lived on this planet.

Prayers completed, Vladimir and Dariush made the sign of the cross.

Immediately after that, the Russian peeled off his uniform and jumped into the water below the falls.

Dariush and I stood above, laughing as he hooted and thrashed about.

"I am, I regret", Dariush commented in his most ponderous manner, "a little too old for that."

"Me too", I said. "I'd hate to cross an infinite sea only to drown in a pond."

"Nevertheless, Neil, I think elderly gentlemen are still permitted to walk. Shall we?"

"Let's do."

We walked for an hour, circling the valley twice before returning to the shuttle for a lunch that Vladimir had packed for us. He was now sleeping, stretched out on a blanket by the falls. We two older men ate sandwiches and drank from water bottles. As we finished off the meal with succulent nova-fruit that tasted like a cross between kiwi and sweet lemon, Dariush gazed up at the snow-capped peaks around us, lost in his own thoughts. The afternoon had begun.

"I would like to climb higher", he said at last. "How is your leg? Would you care to come too?"

"My leg's no worse than it's always been. Let's go."

Because the sun was high and the air hot, we took a route up the lower slopes leading to the purple shadows cast by a mountain on the north side of the valley. The footing was easy going on soft turf, and the first traces of scree that had slid down from above with the passage of time. It was a gray shale, very small fragments.

We soon passed out of the sun's glare and saw a herd of deer higher on the glen, where the mountain proper began. They did not startle as we approached, and merely gazed at us for a few minutes before wandering off, nibbling grass as they went.

Dariush and I sat down on a rock to catch our breath. The rise, though gradual, had demanded energy we were not used to exerting.

426

I was seventy-eight years old, and he wasn't much younger. For a time, we gazed over the valley, with its blue alpine lake, the pale green woods surrounding it, and on the far side of the trees, the AEC. By the falls, our pilot was still stretched out, asleep or drowsing.

"Higher?" asked Dariush. I nodded, and we resumed our climb.

We had not gone far when he paused and stood for a moment looking at a darker shadow at the base of a cliff directly ahead of us, about thirty meters away. He said nothing, but walked toward it with a purpose.

When we arrived there, we saw what had not been evident from below: a low crawl space about three feet high. I'm sure we would not have entered it to investigate, if Dariush had not spotted something on the rock above the opening. Though overgrown with lichen, it looked like a crude image cut into the stone. He scraped away the growth, and we saw what was clearly the shape of a deer, no larger than a hand. Facing it was an image of a bird, the same size.

"This is interesting", he murmured. "Who could have made these?"

"They look old", I said.

"Yes, very old. It may be there is a cave inside. Perhaps it was used long ago as a shelter for hunters during inclement weather."

He removed a flashlight from his pocket and pointed it into the dark recess below the images.

"Not a cave. It is a natural tunnel, an irregularity in the mountain. I confess I earnestly desire to look within."

"Well, if you must", I said dubiously. "Let's hope there are no saber-tooth tigers in there."

He dropped to his knees and crawled inside. I followed with some reluctance, though my interest was piqued.

We had gone a few feet through this tunnel when it took a turn, rising and to the left. A minute's crawling brought us to the end, a stack of flat stones that blocked any further progress.

"Too bad", I said. "Time to go back."

"Wait, Neil", said Dariush with excitement. "These stones were laid by human hands, and it was done from farther within."

He began to push on the topmost stone. It gave a little, and then toppled away into the darkness beyond. I crawled up beside him, and together we pushed away more stones. When the passage was clear, we crept onward, Dariush first and me at his heels. As he flashed his light around, we saw that we were now inside a small cave. We stood up, the tops of our heads brushing the roof. The air was dry and smelled of dust. The floor was fine gravel and sand. The entire space looked to be no more than ten feet wide by fifteen or eighteen feet long.

"There's nothing here", I said.

"There is something here", he replied with an odd tone of certainty.

Foot by foot, we investigated the cave, until by accident we stumbled upon what looked like human remains. Though coated with dust and sunken into the gravel floor, it was clearly a skeleton, curled in the fetal position.

Dariush knelt and inspected it carefully. "A child", he said. "Or a young adolescent, judging by the length of the femur and fibula." He flashed the light about the skull. "There is no damage to the cranium, and I can see no broken bones. It seems to me that this person died in sleep, not by violence."

"Sickness or starvation perhaps?"

"Perhaps."

He pointed the light along the bones of one arm, which extended out from the rib cage, with the hand and fingers resting on a pile of flat stones. This pile was neatly arranged, a rough rectangle rising two feet above the floor. Dariush sat back and thought for a few minutes. Then, with deliberation, he removed the top stones and looked down into a cavity within.

"There is another skeleton", he said. "Also a child."

"I wonder what brought them here?" I asked. "What was their story? We'll never know."

"The deer and the bird seem to indicate that they were here for a time. Time enough to leave a mark of their presence."

"Someone else could have made the images. I don't see any tools here."

"These children may have used a stone to chip the image into the cliff. As you saw, it is crude, not incised mechanically."

Thinking that there might be tools or artifacts within the "tomb", we removed more stones, fully exposing the remains. And that's all there was—simple bones, a life interred in an unmarked grave, without history, without explanation. Yet the position of the other skeleton showed us that at least one had grieved.

When we had finished removing all the cap stones, we noticed that the wall by the feet was twice as thick as the one at the head. Dariush directed his flashlight at that end, and now we saw that a double layer of slate fragments had been stacked inside the outer wall. He removed the top one and inspected it closely. There was a sharp inhalation of breath, silence, and then he said, "Hieroglyphics."

We removed every slab that had hieroglyphics, twenty in all, the thin slate covered in the ancient script we had come to know from the temple archives. The inscriptions looked to have been scratched with a sharp stone, the letters crudely executed, as if by an immature hand.

"Can you read them?" I asked Dariush. "Do they make sense to you?"

"A moment, Neil", he replied, slowly poring over lines on the tablets.

Without explanation, he arranged them side by side on the floor, sometimes re-reading one or another and changing their positions.

"This is it", he said at last, exhaling loudly. I could see that his hands were trembling.

"What does it say?"

"It is a chant. Or a song. Yes, a song, I think. It tells the story of these two. Shall I translate it for you?"

"Can you do that?"

"I may not have every word exact, but the meaning is more or less clear to me. It is the mind of a young person, not complicated."

And so we sat with our backs against the cave wall, and Dariush picked up the first fragment of slate. Like the others, it was an irregular piece with broken edges, about a foot wide by a foot and a half long.

In his quiet voice, he slowly recited the following:

I Kitha-ré write this.
My mother took me and said,
"Kitha-ré, now you are about to become a woman,
For your body shows the first signs.
You have been chosen to be among
The chosen of the Lord of the Night-gods."

I cried and said to her:
"I do not desire this."
She put her hand over my mouth, and she was afraid
Because of my words, but none heard what I said.
And my father hid his face.
In the dark when sleep was upon the city,
I heard them weeping.

With the sacred hundred I went.
We departed at the rising of the sun,
borne in vehicles upon the Great Road until the setting of the sun,
And we came up unto the mountains of the Temple
Of the Lord of the Night-gods,
That we might see the sacred heavens-ship
And thence be taken into the Lord of the Night-gods' mouth.
Yet I was afraid.
Pho-rion was with me, the one who is dear to me.
Yet I was afraid.

Unto the Temple we came, and the guards led us within.
The ninety-eight who were with me took the drink that gives sleep,
And ate the mash that hastens the blood flow.
I made as if to eat and drink but I did not,
And none saw me.
In the forecourt of the Temple, the hundred lay down on the floor
for sleep.
Pho-rion did as me: he ate and drank not, and was awake.
And none saw him.
We two did not sleep. Tomorrow we would die.
He touched my hand.

The lights were extinguished, and the guards stood near;
At the Gate with their lamps, they stood and watched.
Then did a man of light walk in through the open gate,
The light was in him and around him; he was like a god.
The guards did not see him, though their eyes were open,
And the three eyes of the Lord of the Night-gods,
The all-seeing eyes in the stone above the gate,
They did not look upon him.
Who is this? I thought.
And I was afraid.

He came to me and touched my head.
"Kitha-ré, do not be afraid", he said to me.
"How do you know my name, O Night-god?" I asked him.
"I am not a Night-god", he answered me.
"Who are you, and why do you come to me?"
Pho-rion lay as one struck by a spear;

His mouth was open as he watched and listened.
"I am a servant", said the man of light. "I am sent by the Sky-
father unto you."
I said, "The Sky-father of old was broken. He was angry and he
was shamed.
He is no more."

The man of light said, "The One you call Sky-father is Creator of
all things
And he lives. In him, there is no evil."
"What is evil?" I asked.
"It is that which hurts you and would take away your life."
I said, "I do not desire that my life be taken from me,
Yet it is the will of the Lord of the Night-gods."
He said, "The Lord of the Night-gods is evil.
The Lord of the Night-gods is like unto a serpent.
And this day he is broken."
"How is he broken?" I asked, for I did not believe him.
And I was very afraid,
For the man of light had spoken words-that-bring-death-to-him-
who-speaks-them.

The man of light touched Pho-rion's head
And Pho-rion quaked at the touch.
He was very afraid.
"The Sky-father has heard your cries unto him", said the man of
light.
"I did not cry unto him", I said.
"You cried unto him when you were at work in the fields.
On the day when Pho-rion who is dear to you was with you;
You were among the tall plants for cutting the harvest,
And no others were nearby to see you or hear you."
"How do you know this?" I asked.
"The Sky-father saw you and listened," he said, "when you two
raised your arms
Unto the sky and desired to go up into the heavens."

I did not answer him, for he had seen what no man could see.
For on the day when Pho-rion and I had raised our arms,
Music was in our mouths (it is forbidden),

431

And we made as if to fly with our feet (it is forbidden),
And we shook the seed pods that make sounds sweet to the ear (it is forbidden),
And we desired to go up into the heavens.
That day we desired not to be among the chosen of the Lord of the Night-gods.
We cried together in the fields of harvest, for there was no escape.
We held each other
And we said, "We cannot go up into the heavens, for there is no path,
And we will die."

Then did the man of light take our hands,
We two, Pho-rion and me,
And raise us up.
Though the guards were awake, they did not see us;
They did not see the man of light lead us to the gate.
We went out unto the road under the stars.
And he took us from there down through the forest unto the great lake.
There we came upon a little boat at water's-edge,
And the man of light bade us enter it with him.
He poled the boat down the lake.
He made music come from his mouth.
It was sweet to our ears,
Though we did not know his words.

Far from the lights of the Gate he brought the boat to shore.
We got out, and he took our hands and led us by a little path.
The path went high into the mountains.
We were sore tired in our flesh with climbing, Pho-rion and me.
We were afraid in our hearts, for we had fled
From the will of the Lord of the Night-gods.
But when fear came again upon us in this way
The man of light said, "Do not be afraid."
For he knew our inner thoughts.
The sky beyond the great mountains grew pale
And still we climbed.
We came to a high place between two mountains,
The sun sailed up into the sky.
And we saw a wondrous place below us,

A small valley, with a lake and fall of water, and trees with music in
    them.

Here we stayed.
We lay down on the grass of this place, Pho-rion and I,
And we drank of the water that falls into the lake.
And the man of light said unto us:
"Now you must take your rest.
This place is hidden from the eyes of the Lord of the Night-gods.
I will keep watch over you."
As we fell asleep in the shade of the music trees,
He kept watch, standing tall above us.
And when we awoke there was a fire burning,
In a circle of stones, with baked bread and fish.
We ate it and it was good.

We walked with him in the valley, and he told us many things.
"Soon you will go unto the Sky-father," he said.
"You will not fall into the mouth of the Lord of the Night-gods
    who is evil.
For the Father sees you and loves you."
"What is this word, *love*?" I asked.
He answered, "This word is the spirit of the Father,
The Father who desires only to give you life.
The Father who would feed you and take away your hunger.
The Father who desires not to take your life.
The Father who put into you the little heart-fire that makes Pho-
    rion dear to you,
And into Pho-rion the little fire that makes you dear to him."
I said unto the man of light, "Fire burns the flesh. It is pain."
"There is another fire", answered the man of light.
"This fire gives happiness. It is warm and gives light. It does no
    harm unto you.
This fire is within you when you cry out unto the listener
Whom you cannot see with your eyes,
When music comes forth from your mouth,
And when you make your body move as the birds of the sky."

"These are things which I desire", I said. "I do not like screams
    and blood."

433

The man of light said, "Such are not praise unto the Sky-father."
"Then the Sky-father is not evil", I said.
"The Sky-father is love. He is not shamed. He is not broken.
On this day, in a far world, he passed through shame and pain and
  death,
And this he took upon himself for your sake."
"Where is he that we may see him?" Pho-rion asked.
This was the first-speaking of Pho-rion.
"You will see him", said the man of light unto Pho-rion.
And Pho-rion was no longer afraid.
I Kitha-ré was no longer afraid.
"When will we see him?" I asked.
"In forty days, he will go up into the heaven beyond all heavens.
"In forty days, you will grow ill, Kitha-ré, for there is even now a
  sickness in your flesh.
In your flesh, Pho-rion, this sickness has only begun,
And thus you will live a time longer than
She who is dear to you."

Pho-rion took my hand.
"We will die?" he said to the man of light, and the fear returned to
  his eyes.
"Your bodies will pass away into the earth for a time", said the man
  of light,
"Yet no evil will touch you,
For I will stand guard over you, though no longer will you see me
  with the eyes.
Then you two will go up unto the heaven above all heavens.
You will see the One who has died in your stead. You will see him,
And music will come from your mouths on that day,
And your arms will rise unto him, and he will embrace you,
For he is love.
Then will you understand what I tell you now,
And there will be no more fear."
Yet I wept because I did not desire to die.
I did not desire Pho-rion to die.

"You will have sorrow but a little while", said the man of light.
"And after it, you will have joy without end."
"What is this word, *joy*?" I asked.

434

Now for the first time did a smile appear upon the face of the man
    of light.
"Joy is soon to be yours. Until then, you must wait to learn of it."
"Forty risings and settings of the sun?" I asked.
"Yes, for you. For Pho-rion, fifty risings and settings."
"That is long", said Pho-rion.
"When it is completed, you will know it is short.
Even so, I set a task for you."
"What task is this?" I asked.
"You must make music come from your mouths.
You must make the words of this music,
Which shall tell the story of our meeting.
You shall write the words upon a stone, and another stone.
There will be many stones."

"What stones are these?" I asked.
"They are in the place I will show you", he answered.
Then did he bid us rise and walk with him.
He led us unto a cave in the rocks upon the breast of the mountain.
We went inside it and sat down. It was warm and dry.
"Here you will live for forty days", he said unto me.
And unto Pho-rion he said:
"Here you will live for fifty days. And ten days you will sorrow,
Until you too sleep in the earth."
"I will be alone", said Pho-rion.
"You will feel alone, but you will not be alone,
For I am with you.
And after this time you will see Kitha-ré once more;
Never more shall you be parted."

The man of light poured water over our heads from a bowl,
And he spoke names.
"These are the three names of Love", he said,
"And they claim you for themselves.
The three eyes of the Lord of the Night-gods are in mockery of
    these names,
For the serpent desires to be as them, but he never can be.
So too the heavens-ship in the temple is in mockery of the Sky-
    father,
To escape his will.

Yet it will be broken.
The mouth of the one that drinks blood will be broken
And rendered unto dust and be no more."
"When will this be?" I asked.
"It will be after an age of years", he answered. "After a time, and yet
    another time."
This we did not understand, Pho-rion and me.
He said, "I bid you write it as a sign for those who will be in this place
In an age that is yet to come."
"We will write it," we said, "though we know not many words."
"You know enough", said the man of light.
He placed his hand upon our heads.
We closed our eyes, and when we opened them,
He was no longer there.

We have written our story in music that comes from the mouth.
The man of light has gone from our eyes.
Yet we feel him close.
We are not afraid.
I am ill, and I lie down on the soft soil of the cave. I do not rise up.
Pho-rion holds my hand.
Who are you who reads this?
Do you hold it in your hands after a time and another time?
Do you see my face?
Can you hear my voice?
Do you listen to the music that comes from my mouth?

I Kitha-ré write this.

Dariush pointed to a few lines in a cruder script at the end, reading:

I Pho-rion help Kitha-ré write this.
I lie down.
I sleep.

Day 387:

I couldn't write any more last night. I am not a sentimentalist. I do
not enjoy tragedies. They make me fall into a rage that has no outlet.
No outlet at all.

Even so, the story of Kitha-ré and Pho-rion seizes me with awe. Sorrow too, and love for them (these strangers I do not know, these poor children who died two millennia ago).

Let me finish the account of that day. Dariush spent a long time praying over the bodies. He blessed them with the sign of the cross. He knelt and for a few moments put the palm of his hand on the foreheads of their skulls. To other eyes, it might have seemed grotesque, macabre, but I didn't feel that way, not at that moment. Dariush quietly wept, but he smiled as he wept. I hung my head, grieved and confused.

We covered Kitha-ré's remains with stones. We built a cairn around Pho-rion's.

After that, we began the labor of removing the slates from the cave. Back and forth, we crawled until we had made a stack outside the tunnel entrance. There we heard Vladimir calling our names from below, and spotted him standing by the lake, looking all around at the mountains. We shouted and waved, and he climbed up to the cave and helped us with the removal of the slates. We loaded them onto the AEC and flew back to the geology base. An hour later, the shuttle entered the *Kosmos*. I have no memory of us saying anything during the return journey.

How strange my room seemed to me when I entered it—sterile, a void filled with a man with a void inside him. I understood nothing about my feelings. I only felt them. Long past midnight, Dariush knocked on my door and entered with papers in his hand. He had scanned the slates, which he called "Kitha-ré's Song", and he gave me the auto-translation, annotated with his minor corrections. I've copied his polished version into yesterday's journal entry. It was very close to his recital in the cave.

I thanked him, still so choked that I couldn't say much.

"Do you know what their names meant?" I asked.

"*Kitha* is the word for the water bird that warbles like a loon, and *ré* means 'the heart of'. *Rion* means deer, and *pho* means 'force of' or 'strength of'."

Then he left me to ponder the meaning of it all.

Day 388:

Last night, another strange dream: I am standing on the shore of a lake filled with floating water lilies. There are snow-covered mountain peaks in the distance. It is twilight, the sky striped with hues of red and violet. I am watching a brown-skinned, teenage boy who is seated on a chair by the lapping water, concentrating on sheets of paper on a music stand. A large cello leans on his shoulder, and in his right hand, he holds a bow. Lifting the bow, the boy is about to begin playing.

"What is your name?" I ask him.

He looks up at me, smiles, and says, "You know my name, *pitaji*."

A light flashes from horizon to horizon.

"We have to get out of here!" I yell.

"Why?" the boy asks, gazing at me curiously.

The lake bursts into flames.

I wake up gasping for breath, my heart pounding.

Is he my son, the one who I might have fathered if I had chosen another path? Is he the past that could have been? Is he the future? Is he a translation of Kitha-ré and Pho-rion into a single symbol? Or is he just more flotsam from my disordered mind?

Day 390:

A momentous day in terms of the expedition. The rear third of the temple ship has been entered. Radioactivity was within acceptable limits. Inside were found all manner of machines for water and oxygen regeneration, very unlike ours but identifiable by their ventilation and water pipes, which once fed the rest of the ship. A good deal of the upper space in the chamber is filled by spars that support the retractable wings. These are two immense isosceles triangles sitting on their cradles, once manipulated by gears and hydraulics that long ago seized shut. Between them hangs a giant gyroscope, connected by circuitry to the wall and to the wing gears. This construction is in fact three gyroscopes one inside the other.

Dominating the whole chamber is a nuclear reactor, caked in the black alloy that greatly reduces radioactive bleed. The fuel inside, though thousands of years old, undoubtedly has lost only a portion of its strength. It provided the thrust through the four main propulsion tubes at the base of the ship, and also fed a wheel of smaller cylinders connected to vents encircling the body of the ship, clearly designed for maneuvering in zero gravity.

There was a three-hour presentation on the panorama screens this evening. Xue was one of several scientists interviewed, but he was not given pride of place, since primary interest is focused on the ship's aerodynamics and nuclear physics. He had only a sixty-second sound bite, in which he pointed out that there were a number of odd features in the tail section that suggested major changes had been made to the ship after its landing on the planet. He drew attention to three small holes halfway up the bulkhead wall (with a three-second still photo of them). They were first noticed when the black alloy veneer was removed from the bulkhead on the mid-ship side. Xue said that it was initially believed these were for nonmechanical circulation of air within the ship. Alternatively, there may once have been pipes passing through the holes, funneling heat from the reactor into the forward sections during space flight. In his opinion, he thought these explanations were superficial, since the ship has other more efficient circulation apparatus.

He concluded by pointing out that there is a pattern of triune holes in the temple complex and emphasized that the presence of these newly discovered holes should not be overlooked or hastily dismissed as insignificant. The next visual/sound bite displayed manipulation of the giant gyroscopes, which, despite their age, still spin nicely. This was followed by other fascinating presentations.

Day 391:

Two minor developments, just for the record:

The Captain sent down to me the elevator codes for KC deck, couriered by hand. In the accompanying note, he renewed his invitation to move my personal quarters upstairs. Of course, I will not do so. Despite his concern, for which I am grateful, I feel this would only add to the siege mentality.

The Captain also said that if I wish to remain on deck B for the time being, I may have some degree of immunity, since he has warned DSI to keep their hands off me, and off anyone else in the ship, for that matter. He cautioned me against using normal e-communications, since *max* messages in and out of my room are probably monitored around the clock, and thus I should not rely on making a call for help that would only be blocked by DSI before it reached KC. He suggested that if I am ever in need of emergency sanctuary, I should get myself to the nearest KC elevator as quickly as possible.

After reading the note, I went for a stroll and located the one closest to me, a fifteen-minute walk forward on deck B, on cross street 22, between the portside and central avenues.

Second development: A note from Dariush, slipped under my door while I was napping, tells me that he will be at his office in Tower Valley for the next three days, assisting with decryption of hieroglyphics on mechanisms in the rear section of the temple ship.

He concludes by assuring me that the slates bearing "Kitha-ré's Song" are safely archived with Paul. He is concerned about the way every translated document is expropriated by DSI. He worries, I think, that the song might disappear due to its religious implications.

Day 392:

One never knows what will happen in this universe. As a precaution, I made a trial run, escape mode. It took me 12.5 minutes to reach the KC elevator, and another fifteen seconds to access it with the code. In total, the time between leaving my room and stepping out into the lobby of KC was 13 minutes. Not bad, but if something should happen unexpectedly, would I have that much time?

Arriving at the lobby, I asked a staff member if I could speak with Paul Yusupov. When he joined me a few minutes later, we had a pleasant chat. Mother and babe in the womb are doing well, he says. Pia is "*bolshoi*—very, *very* big.". She sleeps a lot, or reads, putters around the apartment, makes flower arrangements from a variety of Nova blossoms brought by their friends the pilots.

I gave him my most recent entries in the journal. We also discussed the ancient song Dariush and I had discovered. He said he had read the translation and had been moved by it. He was glad that in some way the boy and girl had been present at the wedding. I told him how pleased I was to leave the turquoise cube by the falls, as a memorial of their marriage. He thanked me, and then apologized that he had to get back to his crew. They were beginning the remote warm-up practice of navigational protocols—test runs for departure, six weeks from now. The ship's computer will do the real work, he explained, but it was important to have human back-up and oversight. The procedure was all very familiar to his men, but it was best to keep it fresh in the mind. I said something about how easily we forget important things. He replied that we are always making trivia into crises and crises into trivia. Once again, I saw depths in the man that would not be immediately obvious to acquaintances. A boy with a sword, yes, but he also has a reflective mind.

Day 401:

The baby is born! A girl!

She's a week early, and it was a long, hard labor, but mother and child are doing just fine. I haven't seen them yet. The news came via my favorite Igbo-Brit, who tapped on my door, grinning from ear to ear and blurting the news in a loud voice. Doubtless DSI also learned about the birth at that instant, via my *max*. Well, so what! Let them try something. They'd regret it.

"Paul says Pia needs a few days' rest and then people can visit", said Loka. "You can pop up anytime on Day 404 or after. Just use the code."

"Give them my love."

I am eager, I can't wait. But yikes! Loka gave away a whole lot of information in two short breaths. The Elf and his sylvan band now know I have a code, and thus if they wish to take me into custody, they will do it by surprise. Following on that, the gamut of disinformation ploys will be ever at their disposal. They could make me into a serial killer for the records, a madman who had to be incarcerated in their prison. Or shot while resisting arrest.

Maybe I should move upstairs. No, that would be capitulation.

Day 403:

Dariush was aboard for a few hours today, ostensibly to do research in the main computer, and more importantly to visit the newborn baby. He stopped by my room for a few moments. We went for a walk.

"I bear some messages for you, Neil. Pia and Paul are looking forward to you meeting their child tomorrow, if you can come."

"Whaaaat! *If* I can come! I'll be at their door before sunrise."

441

"I have just come from her baptism. Her name is Katherine Teresa. She is very healthy. She is brown-skinned and has her mother's eyes. There is plenty of Paul in her as well. She is very beautiful."

Dariush handed me a slip of paper. On it was written a mixture of numbers and letters. I smiled, recognizing a quirky algorithm Xue and I had worked on in our youth.

"This is from Ao-li?"

"Yes, it is his door code. He asks that you retrieve his most favored book—the one you have discussed with him. He asks also that you bring this book and a sculpture of a deer to your room."

"My room is hardly a safe place to keep them. Why does he want me to do it?"

"He did not say. He mentioned, however, that he is currently embroiled in a controversy with fellow committee members and with other committees involved in the examinations of the towers and the temple ship."

"Did he explain what the trouble was?"

"He believes they are pressing for discoveries in a hasty manner. Our time is running out, you see. Departure is thirty-two days from now. Under the laws that govern the expedition, all personnel must return to Earth, since debriefings will be extensive when we arrive there. It is hoped that the findings and papers written by the scientific teams, with no member excepted, will generate the global funding for a second expedition. Xue argues that what we have already discovered will ensure a second expedition."

"I don't understand. What are you saying?"

"Several teams are desperate to have a major discovery to bring back to Earth."

"We have tons of major discoveries!"

"Yes, but they want a gem to cap their crowns. They want to power the ship. Our own mobile generators have been unable to do so—only the very simple hydraulics in the towers respond."

"Power the ship? You mean they want to make it fly?"

"No, that is still in the realm of the fantastic. For now, they hope to reenergize the circuit systems, including functions as simple as the original lighting and as complex as the glass tablet in the command center, which they believe is a computer screen. If it is such, it could give them potential access to digital archives they think are embedded somewhere on board. This may enable them to extend the wings, analyze the bronze hands' relationship to the wings, test the gyroscopes' relationship to the command center, and activate many other functions."

"Have they figured out how to access the original power source?"

"Not yet. And this may be a blessing, since the forces within the reactor, though dormant, could prove to be more idiosyncratic than we suppose. Dr. Xue is arguing for extreme caution."

"And so he should! It's bad science—very bad science—to tinker with powers like that, not knowing how they really work."

"Xue believes that the ship's propulsion and internal energy both came from the reactor, but how it was done he doesn't know. Neither do the nuclear physicists know. The latter are convinced that there was a bi-level system, one for propulsion and a secondary mini-reactor for powering the ship's internal systems."

"On what do they base their conviction?"

"There does appear to be a second component on top of the main reactor, less than a tenth its size. It has three small orifices on the side facing the front of the ship. The holes are presently sealed with the anti-radioactive veneer. They are aligned with three holes in the bulkhead. In the opinion of the nuclear physicists and technicians, they were apertures through which power cables once ran."

"That's jumping to a big conclusion when we're dealing with nuclear power."

"They are desperate to make a tremendous achievement."

He checked his wristwatch. "Neil, I must go. I am behind in my translations, and the shuttle departs half an hour from now."

We bid each other farewell. I went directly to Xue's room, retrieved his Bible and his iron deer, patted the little poet on the head, and returned to my own room.

If Xue really had been thinking straight, he would have asked Paul to retrieve them for safekeeping.

Day 404:

A DSI agent was standing in the hallway when I left my room this morning. He didn't say a word, but he followed me to the cafeteria, and after I had my breakfast, he followed me back. Then I led him on a merry chase, zigging and zagging in a random pattern throughout the maze of deck B, all the while getting ever closer to street 22. By the time, I arrived there, I had turned so many corners that his guard was lowered, and he was lagging half a block behind. I turned onto 22 and hobble-hoofed at my top speed to the KC elevator, typed in the code as fast as I could, and stepped inside. I didn't look back. The doors closed and I went up. I don't know if he spotted me.

Paul ushered me into the bedroom of their apartment. Pia was lying on the bed, eyes closed, looking serene, if a little drawn. The baby rested under her right arm, swaddled and flawless, her large black eyes regarding me with total consciousness.

I knelt down beside the bed and kissed the baby's forehead. She began to cry, waking up Pia.

Pia and Paul let me hold her. I had never experienced this in my life, not even long ago in our village. The grandmothers had always monopolized that sort of thing, and my paternal instinct was entirely latent then.

Now it blossomed—flooded, actually. I was in love. I was totally in love.

"Do you like her, Neil?" Pia asked.

I nodded up and down in the affirmative.

When I was able to speak, I whispered, "Katherine Teresa."

For the longest time, I gazed enraptured at her little face as she gazed back at me. Finally, Paul the knight-prince tapped my shoulder and said that the baby needed to nurse now; it was time for me to go. I gave the princess back to her mother and babbled inept congratulations to her parents. We concluded with handshakes, hugs, and final kisses.

On my way back downstairs, I kept thinking, O mankind, why, why are you so blind, when you can have this!

RETURN

"Say quick", quoth he, "I bid thee say—
What manner of man art thou?"

—Samuel Taylor Coleridge
The Rime of the Ancient Mariner

Days no longer have meaning.

I write to preserve my sanity.

Why do I preserve my sanity? After all that has happened, am I still sane?

Is there hope beyond the end of all possible hope? Is this the animal spark within us that keeps us going when the worst occurs—and beyond the worst—darker than the mouth of the blood-devourer?

I did not mean to do it. It did not begin that way.

It began with an accident.

No, it began with a lie.

*

I will try to remember how it was.

The day after I visited baby Katherine, Dariush unexpectedly returned to the *Kosmos*. He found me in my room and insisted that we go for a walk, in order to talk privately.

He said, "Neil, I am disturbed. I have completed translation of a scanned codex in the central tower. It is a bronze plaque embedded in the wall above the sphere."

"What does it say?" I asked.

Without answering, he slowed his pace, and we turned aside into the next art alcove we came to. There he read to me from a sheet of paper:

To you who come to us from the stars,
We open wide the path between the plentiful lakes.
Pass over the low bridge between waters and know it as the high
    road.
Our god welcomes you unto the household of his light
In this heaven in the heavens.
Three towers are his eyes, the light of his glory shines forth from
    them.
Our heavens-ship sleeps until you come,
And though we are gone, we give it unto you
In honor of your light, be it soon or in ages hence.

We are lords of the thirteen of the star in the west,
Which the towers will show you.
We are lords of the eighteen of the star that is nigh,

Which is three flames of the Lord of the Night-gods.
Open the gate in the wall and behold.
Open the eyes in the towers to the flame of the Lord of the Night-
    gods.
His day-star in full strength will give power to the ship,
So you may know its greatness and rise up on it,
As we once rode the arrow of the gods.

Dariush frowned and met my eyes.

"Interesting", I said.

"They are inviting visitors from other worlds to share in their glory and power. Their power *is* their glory, you see."

"And you find this disturbing? I wouldn't read too much into the poem, if I were you. It's just more of their myths."

"It is telling us to do exactly what Xue is warning the other scientists not to do. I am worried."

"The only thing that disturbs me is bad science, Dariush. Blind methodology—that's what we should be worried about."

"Neil, there is a profound unease in my soul. It is like the day we visited the beautiful valley. I blessed the water of the little lake, and then there rose up within me the ancient voices of terror and despair. Do you remember?"

"I remember."

"The feeling is the same. Something is wrong, but I do not know what it is. I believe we should not so quickly obey these instructions from the past. They were evil men."

"But proud of their accomplishments and eager to display them."

"Yes, proud. I ask myself, in the darkness of their pride, were other spirits moving?"

This was theology. I did not trust it.

"What does Xue think?" I asked.

"From his perspective, he is adamant that we must learn more about the optics and the operations of the ship before exposing it to the full power of the . . ."

"Of the eyes of the god."

"They are more than eyes. As you know, they are a brilliant invention entwined with a most odious mythology. The myths have no power over us spiritually, but the inventions may yet have power. Moreover, Neil, man has not ceased to be vulnerable to falsehoods."

"Falsehoods? Why would they lie to us? They wanted us to admire them extravagantly, maybe even to bow down in awe before their memory."

"Perhaps", he frowned, dropping his eyes in private thought for a moment. "Perhaps. I hope that is the nature of their evil, and no more."

"Well, it's not your responsibility. I suppose once the committees read this, they'll make their own decision."

"I will refrain from submitting the document. I fear it would only be an added incentive for them to proceed thoughtlessly."

*

But Dariush had not considered other factors. He had auto-translated the hieroglyphics through the main computer, and this meant that someone, at some point, might read the document. And it was read. Then it went out of his hands and into the hands of the blind.

Human motivation is subtle. The blind cannot "see" their own blindness. And I am no different in this than any other man. I cannot now piece together exactly how it came to pass that the authorities obeyed the instructions from the old lords of the night. Perhaps there were whisperings in their own ears. Perhaps it was only the whisper of ambition. I wonder in retrospect if they lusted for that gemstone, the ultimate discovery, because they felt certain it would eclipse the harm they had done during the voyage—murder and injustice in other forms. Did they think that a court of inquiry back on Earth would overlook their crimes and call them misdemeanors in the face of such a tremendous accomplishment? I do not know what went on inside their minds. I know only that DSI gave the final permission.

It was, I think, a week or so before our scheduled departure from Nova that the announcement was made. The media proclaimed that we were on the verge of a great breakthrough, a triumph to bring back to Earth.

I tried to contact Xue, but he had not returned to his room since the last time I saw him. He sent me no messages—or none that got through. My *max*-mail to him went unanswered. Dariush was also absent from the ship.

In the panorama presentations, interviews with the heads of committees were broadcast simultaneously with images of the towers, the cliff face, and the ship itself, silently waiting. Of all the committee members who spoke, only Xue was absent. The document Dariush had translated was narrated and extolled. The incentive was in place, adding fuel to the other reasons, spoken and unspoken.

The procedure was described in advance. The spheres in the three towers would be elevated before dawn of the next day. They would remain covered until noon. The plugs would be removed from the "eyes" of the mural on the cliff face. When the sun's azimuth and altitude were optimum, the spheres would be uncovered and their prisms would configure optical beams to enter the temple and strike the cone at the ship's nose, passing through more triune holes and prisms until they struck the three small orifices of the mini-reactor in the rear of the vessel, melting the black veneer and contacting the devices within. The concentrated solar power would activate the mini-reactor, and the ship would awaken.

The next morning, after a sleepless night, I got up early and made my way to the panorama hall on my deck. A few people were present, watching the live programming that had already begun. For the most part, these were maintenance staff, since a majority of the scientists were down in the valley and temple, as close to the ship as they could get.

I watched the raising of the hydraulic columns in split-screen, the left shot taken from within one of the towers and the right from an observation point about a hundred meters distance from it. Then the camera cut to a wide pan of all three towers, clearly visible in the pale light of dawn. The central one lacked its upper walls, and so its sphere was poised erect on its supporting rod, exposed but hooded. Since the two other towers higher on the mountains had retained much of their upper walls, the light beams would be directed from the spheres through their circular windows.

A short experiment was made with the last of the faint starlight in the west. Three miniscule beams shot through valley and hit the mural's eyes, which were protected by a steel plate; the beams burned pinholes in it. The spheres were re-hooded. A hover platform was elevated to the face of the deity, and technicians removed the plate and then extracted the stone plugs from the eyes. A close-up view showed an optics man placing the plugs on the floor of the platform. It descended to the ground before the open gate, and the technicians went inside the temple. The sun broke over the mountain tops, and then we waited.

Interviews with technicians in the towers and the ship's aft section continued throughout the morning. Shortly before noon, the main screen switched to the area immediately around the ship. There seemed to be about a hundred specialists milling this way and that or entering and leaving the portal at midship. Then came an interview with a nuclear physicist standing in front of the reactors. Pointing to the great black mammoth and its little appendage perched on top, he explained that the ship's designers had prudently separated the energy functions of propulsion and inboard power; they had done so in order to ensure that life support systems and other internal functions would not cease in the event of a shut-down or accident in the major reactor. In a few minutes from now, he enthused, we would observe the ingenious process by which the "aliens" had either regenerated or augmented their core fuel. They had probably used a similar method during their flight across the stars, and had adapted their optics for on-ground solar generation after they had made their base on this planet.

Now the panorama screen divided into four panels side by side. On the left was the wide scan of the three towers. Next, the cliff face, with a close-up of the winged god staring out over the valley. Then, the temple's innermost chamber, with a view of the ship's nose and people still milling about, talking animatedly and checking instruments. The excitement was high. Finally, the screen on the right, the interior of the rear section, where the nuclear physicists had gathered, staring at the reactor or smiling at the camera.

Suddenly, there appeared a commotion by the portal entry on the third screen. I looked closely. It was Xue struggling his way up the ramp, and then head to head with a scientist who stood at the portal with his arm held out to prohibit entry. Xue was shouting at him. I heard a few words such as "fission" and "isotopes" before military men ran up the ramp and hustled him down to the chamber floor and out of sight. I wondered what Xue had been trying to do, and where he had been taken.

The countdown began: Five minutes. Three minutes. Two minutes.

The narrator was at the one minute mark when I saw on the screen a figure run out of the temple gate and leap onto the hover platform. He jerked its control lever and rose at high speed, just as the narrator began, "ten ... nine ... eight ..."

The camera zoomed for a close-up. It was Xue. He bent and picked up something in his hand. He was holding a stone plug and frantically trying to pack it into the central eye.

"Three ... two ... one ..."

Simultaneously, the spheres in the towers were uncovered, and three beams shot across the valley, the central one horizontal and aiming for the middle eye, the other two converging. It all happened at light-speed, but I saw it as if in slow motion. I leaped to my feet just as a beam hit Xue's right hand.

"No!" I yelled. "Ao-li, no!"

There was a flash, and his hand burst into flames. He flinched but did not waver. He was using both hands now, and with whatever muscle or bone power was left to him, he still tried to block the beam's entrance. But it was too late. The other two beams were inside.

Xue jerked backward as his arms exploded; then he spun as the beam struck the side of his head. He toppled off the platform and hit the stone pavement far below.

Now all four screens displayed the progress of the beams: across the valley, through the eyes, through the temple, converging on the nose cone, through the midsection of the ship, through the three little bulk-head holes. They were now burning their way through the black veneer on the mini-reactor.

All four screens went white for a micro-second, and then they went black.

I stood there staring at the blank wall. Panting, my mouth wide open in a silent yell of protest, I was desperate to know what had happened, desperate to save Xue, even though he was beyond all help.

The people around me in the panorama room were on their feet too, anxiously discussing what they had just witnessed, shocked by the accident that had befallen the scientist at the cliff face, perplexed by the sudden loss of visual contact.

"O God, O God", I groaned, as I hurried as fast as I could down the concourse in the direction of my room. Inside, I powered up the *max* and keyed in the program for the temple experiments. Blank. Only the words: *Transmission Interrupted*.

I keyed in the satellite view of the planet. And there was Continent I with a bright star blazing in its center, in the middle of the mountains. I zoomed and zoomed, and then I saw what I had dreaded, what I had somehow known I would find, though I had not admitted it to myself.

The entire valley between the western and central ranges and for a distance of sixty kilometers or more north and south of the temple was engulfed in flames, a massive fireball still spreading outward from its brilliant core of light. Thick clouds were rising around a firestorm that would form into a mushroom cloud greater in size than any that man had ever made.

Hardly breathing, I tapped the negative zoom key, and the continent shrank until the eastern and western oceans were visible. I zoomed on the western coast and saw heavy waves speeding away from the shore.

I checked Base-main, northwest of the temple region, and saw that it had not been directly hit by the blast, though the buildings were shaking and AECs were tipping onto their sides, with fissures spreading in the earth. People were running in all directions.

The same thing was happening everywhere, as if the continent itself had been shattered, like a rock thrown at a mirror, the splinters radiating outward. The extinct volcano in the northeast was streaming a trail of vapor. Herds of mammals were galloping panic-stricken on the plains; whales were diving toward deep water beyond the continental shelf. A shuttle parked at a marine base fell into the sea as the ground beneath it collapsed.

I zoomed out and saw that the brilliant star at the center of the catastrophe had begun to fade, replaced by an engorging cloud so dense and so high that its cap must be reaching an altitude of twenty or thirty kilometers.

I sat down and stared at the unfolding horror.

A hundred, two hundred kilometers from the epicenter, forests were flattened. The distant savanna regions were hazy with grass fires.

Xue was gone. Hundreds of people had been vaporized.

Where was Dariush? He had been absent from the ship for days. I went out and hurried to his room. Hard knocking on his door elicited no response. I found the nearest elevator and went down to the lowest level. But the elevator would not unlock for me, and I remembered that a special code was needed for accessing PHM.

After pounding the door with my fist, I went back up to B and hastened along the concourse until I found street 22 and the KC elevator. Using the code, I entered it and punched the PHM button. The elevator took me down, and at the bottom it opened.

I was now in the section of shuttle bays. Only one was in port, and its loading platform was open. A few people scurried about with anxious faces. I spotted Jan heading straight for the shuttle and intercepted him.

"Do you know what's happened?" I asked.

"Yes, I know", he said with a look. "I'm going down there. I have to save what I can."

"Don't go near the epicenter. Don't go anywhere near the middle of the continent; it's all radioactive. It's spreading too, so get out as fast as you can."

"Loka's shuttle was in the valley. We have lost him. Many people died. There is a second shuttle at the marine station in the north. A third was in transit up to the *Kosmos*. That one is safe. It turned around and is heading for Base-main to see if there are survivors."

"Then there are only two shuttles left. The one in the north fell into the sea."

Jan's face darkened, and he looked away.

"Was it Vladimir's?" I asked.

"Yes, it was his. He may still be alive. I will go there too and try to find him."

"I'm coming with you."

"No, Dr. Hoyos, you cannot. You must stay with the people here. I think we have lost half our population, maybe more. Down there— down there on this planet, it is very dangerous. Radiation is only one thing. There are seismic problems and bad weather because of the blast." He paused. "Do you know how it happened?"

"I do."

"The three-eyed god did this, yes?"

"He did, and his makers did, and so did those among us who were like them. Dr. Xue died trying to stop them."

"Then he too is gone. I am sorry. He was a good man."

Yes, a good man. We never guessed how good until the end.

"I have to go now", said Jan.

He entered the shuttle and sealed the hatch. A minute later, the bay doors closed, and the alarm started beeping for depressurization.

I took the elevator up to KC.

Paul and Pia were in their apartment, sitting side by side on a sofa, holding the baby. Pia was weeping silently. Paul had his arms around her.

He leaped to his feet when I entered the room.

"You hear what happen?" he cried.

I sat down and told them what I had seen on the panorama screen and my *max*. I related what Jan had said, that Loka was gone, and

454

possibly Vladimir. I described Xue's last minutes. Pia, who had been napping at the time, had missed it all. Paul had been watching on a screen in the navigation section. I had interrupted him in the process of telling her.

"Has anyone heard from Dariush?" I asked.

Stricken, they shook their heads.

"Is he not aboard?" Pia asked.

"The last I heard from him he was heading down to AS-VT for several days."

"Oh, no! Oh, no!" she sobbed.

"We do not know many detail now", said Paul. "Maybe he is okay."

Our eyes met, and we looked away from each other.

I stood up and told them I was going to search for Dariush. I would contact them if I learned anything. They nodded mutely.

But where would I look?

I tried the offices of translation and archaeology. I tried his room again. I checked our favorite library in the hope that he might have dozed through everything, slumped over a book. But he was nowhere to be found.

The next few hours were confusion. The order of our world had been shaken to the foundations. Who were dead, who were living, who had barely survived? We would not be able to assess our situation until the two shuttles were back on board with the remnants of the expedition.

The people I passed in the halls either bustled along, manic with useless purpose, or they were wandering disoriented. Perhaps others were in their private rooms staring at their *max* screens. The cafeterias were empty, as were the bistros and recreation centers. I don't think I saw a single scientist, and it struck me that a good many of them, perhaps the majority, had been down on the planet, busy at their duties in the mission stations or congregating in the temple valley for the great moment.

I went back up to KC and spoke with some junior staff, offering to help in any way I could. But I really had nothing to offer, and they knew it. They suggested that I return to my room and wait there. The Captain would soon address the crew and passengers via the ship's communications system.

*

I sat in my room and waited. And at some point during those hours I knew the truth of the matter. I knew that it had not been an accident. It had not been the result of hasty miscalculation. We had been lied to by the aliens—the aliens who were ourselves. They had deceived us. They planned it for us. It was waiting for us, even though we would not fall into their trap until two thousand years had elapsed. They could wait. They had the patience of serpents. And their malice.

Xue's slide rule was inside my jacket pocket. I took it out and slid its bars back and forth distractedly. I made a cross with it. I unmade the cross.

I wanted to pray for his soul. As a boy, I had done that for people who had died. I had prayed for my parents' souls when they died—there was that much faith left in me then. Since then, nothing.

What was this nothing, this no-thing inside of me? It was an ache, a void, a yearning so deep I could not fill it. I could only look down into the dark well of myself and wonder if there had ever been anything there. Like all the wells of my childhood, all the arroyos, all the inner reservoirs of tears, I had dried up in a desert. I *was* the desert.

I had been instrumental in the deaths of all these people. I had provided the key to the creation of the *Kosmos*. I had brought them here. And later, I had ignored Xue's and Dariush's warnings, their profound intuitions. Again and again, those intuitions had proved to be right, and my objections wrong—my eminently rational objections—my skeptical distancing from their supposed irrationality. But they too had played their parts. Dariush's persistence had opened the path for discovery of the temple. Xue had helped me find the logic that made this ship, though in the end it had been my inscrutable friend who gave his life trying to stop the unthinkable.

The unthinkable had now happened. It was real. It was history, the past and the future fused in a fireball of the inescapable present.

I wanted to die. I wanted permanent escape. But I still feared death—that at least was left to me.

*

I had not slept the night before, and the stress of the day now overcame me. I lay down to rest my body for a few minutes and slipped into a light doze.

I dreamed of the spiral staircase in Santa Fe.

456

I awoke not knowing how long I had been asleep, minutes or hours I could not say. Rubbing my eyes, groaning with fatigue and grief, I was afflicted by an old memory. I had not thought about it for decades and now it returned in great force. I was seventy-eight years old, and I was a boy again.

It was the day my father drove me to Santa Fe for my first year at university. Scene after scene flashed past: the car breaking down, the old man with his burro and tinkling bells. The story of my murdered brother and sister. My resentment, my rage, my hatred. Then came the fire engine and the watchman named Pedro and the spiral staircase. Finally, my father's confession. And my refusal to do as he had done, to kneel before God's servant and admit my sins, asking for forgiveness. It all swam before my eyes, and I sat up in order to dispel a wave of dizziness.

My father and I had left the chapel and returned to the car. He checked the street map, and then we drove off to find the university's registration office.

He said nothing for a time. I was silent too, wrestling with my emotions. There were so many of them—all bad.

"Benigno," he said at last, in his quiet gentle voice, "in every man, there is a desire to rise."

I did not reply. I knew that whatever he was about to say would be pious and wise. But I had finished with all that. I wanted none of it.

"There is for each of us a struggle", he continued. "It is like climbing a mountain. Like climbing that staircase in the chapel. But the destination can sometimes be different from what we wanted."

Heaven or hell? I silently answered, supplying the predictable and inevitable conclusion.

"A man may strive for a heaven of his own making, and find himself in hell."

Just as I had predicted!

My father went on: "He may find himself in hell and not know how he got there."

"What world is this, then?" I fired my rebuttal at him. "What kind of universe, that we who are blind can step into hell and be found guilty of it?"

"We choose", he said. "We choose many things along the way. And the choosing sets our course. And that is why a man must not choose blindly. If he makes a wrong course, he can change it, right up until the end of his life, but then it is harder. That is why we need God to guide us. He would guide you, if you'd let him. But he will not force you to obey."

"He just drops us into hell if we don't."

"You are wrong, Benigno", he said, his voice breaking. "That is not how he is. *We* choose hell. We choose to reject his mercy. He shows us a spiral staircase that leads up to Him. He climbs beside us, and within us too, if we let him. He wants to help us. But we so often insist on going alone."

Yes, he was right about that. I preferred alone.

I loved my father. I loved his goodness. But I was not like him. I would climb my own staircases. I would *make* my own staircases.

"Do not forget him, Neil."

"I won't, *Papacito*", I said, relenting a little. "You shouldn't worry so much about me."

*

Had Xue suspected that a catastrophe was looming? Or had he only exercised scientific caution? Did he foresee that something more than a nuclear accident was about to happen, that it would be a bomb, prepared deliberately far in advance for those who would one day trigger it? He had shouted "isotopes" and "fission". But I think his frantic last-minute attempt to stop the explosion was an act that could only be impelled by certainty. He knew what would happen, and he knew he would probably die trying to prevent it.

The little reactor on top was the fission trigger for the larger cache of fuel, which became the fusion bomb. Like a hydrogen bomb, only a thousand times greater in power. What fuel did they use? Neither liquid deuterium nor solid lithium deuteride seem likely. It was probably an element unknown to us, derived from the minerals of Nova.

*

I slept again, and dreamed about a planet covered in fire with a black puncture hole in its center. I awoke in a state of terror, afraid that a chain reaction had spread throughout Nova and that it was burning below my feet.

I powered the *max* and keyed the satellite view. The planet was still there, revolving serenely on its axis, with its seas and all but one of its continents as they had been before. Over C-1, there was a thick haze,

458

streaming westward across the ocean with the prevailing wind currents. I zoomed on the central mountain ranges, but the cloud cover was too thick to see anything—dirty brown, purple, and gray, with numerous patches of flame where the remaining forests still burned.

When I keyed to the ship's main communications site, a media announcer appeared, speaking in midsentence: " . . . indicate that radioactivity is highest in the center of the continent but is spreading on the hurricane-force winds generated by the explosion. Three extinct volcanoes have also erupted, and earthquakes of magnitude 10 and higher on the Richter-Mercalli scale have devastated Base-main and all the mission bases. Two shuttles and their pilots have survived the disaster and are returning shortly to the *Kosmos* with the last of the survivors. One is due to enter port within the next twenty minutes; the other is preparing to lift off from the geology base on the eastern side of the mountains. The number of survivors is not yet known. We will update this report with the latest news as it happens. Stay tuned to *Kosmos Media*."

This was followed by the Earth flag rippling in the wind and emotional background music. Then a recital of the Earth Charter by a man's voice in tones of infinite wisdom. Then a recording of a children's choir singing on the shore of an ocean, 4.37 light-years away. I gazed at their shining faces, wondering who they were, wondering if they had all lost brothers or sisters. If so, they were survivors too. I switched off the *max* and went out.

Within minutes, the KC elevator brought me to the lowest deck. There I waited in the shuttle concourse, among a group of people from all the departments, including cooks and cleaning people, flight officers, and a number of medical staff with a line of gurneys ready to roll. I saw no DSI uniforms, and something dark in me hoped that the department staff had all been in the valley at the time of the disaster.

The Captain and his second-in-command stepped out of an elevator and joined us.

Two of the bays were open and empty; the third was closed and silent. The fourth was beeping its pressurization signal. A shuttle had arrived.

*

Thirty-nine survivors were brought out on stretchers and gurneys, or stumbled down the ramp on their own. Few were those without the marks of the disaster upon their bodies and faces. Many were showing preliminary symptoms of radiation burn, though they surely would have been hundreds of kilometers away from the epicenter.

I felt certain I would momentarily see Jan coming out. Instead it was Vladimir, carrying one end of a stretcher, with Dariush on the other end, whispering to the form lying on it. It was Jan, groaning, his face red and blistering, his hands lifted beseechingly.

The medical staff took over and began to ferry people by elevator to the clinics on the decks above. The Captain and Vladimir accompanied them. I went up in a large elevator with Dariush. The cubicle was crowded, with two semi-conscious people on gurneys, a doctor and three nurses, and other wounded, who were stunned and weeping.

I caught Dariush's eye.

"Are you all right?" I asked.

"Yes. I was on the shuttle coming back to the *Kosmos* when the blast occurred. We turned around in mid-journey and headed to Base-main."

The elevator came to a halt, and the doors opened. It was deck A. The medical people rolled the gurneys into the hallway and raced toward the clinic. I caught Dariush by the arm and asked, "What did you find at Base-main?"

"Among the many dead, I found the body of our friend Étienne."

"Oh no, not Pagnol too!"

"We carried into the shuttle all the bodies we could find, and the few survivors. After that, we went around the coastal regions trying to locate people at the marine bases. The turbulence was severe. When we landed at the northern marine base, Jan's shuttle had already landed there, a safe distance from the sea. We ran to the base and found him pulling those still alive from the buildings—there were not many. Then he saw Vladimir's shuttle capsized in the sea not far from the shore— the new shore, for the land had collapsed. Even as we watched, the base slid into the water. Jan ran to the edge and dove in. He swam to the shuttle and pulled himself up on it. He banged on the sides, but there were no answers from within. He used his remote to open the portal. When it opened, the vessel began to fill with water, sinking very quickly. He dove in through the portal, and a minute later he brought Vladimir out."

"But who flew this shuttle back to the *Kosmos*?"

"Vladimir. You see, he was unharmed. When his shuttle fell into the sea, the hatch had been open, though he was able to close it with his controls in the pilot's cabin, leaving the craft partly submerged. But he was trapped in an air pocket in the cabin, and the command controls became inoperative. He could not open the cabin door. Jan used his remote to open the hatch, and then he swam inside the ship and opened the pilot's door. A moment longer, and they would both have been pulled to the bottom and drowned."

"Jan's badly burned. It looks like radiation burn."

"It must be. He never came close to the blast, not even to the secondary fires far out from it. He went around the rim of the whole continent, stopping at every base that still existed. He saved many people, though it now looks as if he and they were exposed to radiation."

"You say you went to N-1 on another shuttle."

"Yes, I transferred to this one in order to accompany the survivors. The other shuttle went back south to the geology base, the only station Jan hadn't checked. I hope they have got away."

"I hear they'll soon be lifting off, or maybe already have."

"On the return flight, Jan collapsed, and the symptoms of burn appeared. His sufferings are only beginning, Neil. I must go to be with him."

"Yes, of course."

I followed Dariush as far as the medical clinic, where we met the Captain leaving.

"How bad is it?" I asked.

"Very bad", he said quietly. "Fr. Ibrahim, I suggest you see the people in the clinic. Some are calling for you. Dr. Hoyos, you are welcome to join us on KC deck. I think Pia would appreciate your presence."

We boarded the flight staff elevator, and in the KC lobby, we parted. Several executive officers were waiting for him there, crowding him with requests for instructions. He hurried forward to the command center, and I went in the other direction, toward Pia and Paul's apartment.

I found Pia sitting alone on the sofa with the baby sleeping beside her, the tiny face serene, the little hands raised as if in surrender. The sleep of total trust. Only moments before, I had seen Jan in the same position, his hands reaching upward, not in surrender but beseeching relief from intolerable suffering.

Pia looked up as I entered the room.

"Dariush is alive", I said. "He's on board."

461

I sat down in a chair opposite and told her what I knew.

"Thank God", she breathed. "Thank God."

"Where's Paul?"

"He's gone forward to the command center."

For an hour, we remained in the silence of waiting, as if we floated in a zone without orientation, neither up nor down, forward nor backward. When the insistent cry of the baby grounded us at last, Pia nursed her. I tried to make small talk, straining to find hopeful things to say. But in the end, it was she who comforted me:

"We'll get through this, Neil. We're going home soon, and then this nightmare will be over. We'll have many good things to remember."

I couldn't keep my eyes off Katherine Theresa. Her face and miniature hands were so beautiful, so completely dependent—a world reborn in that tiny form.

Paul returned and told us the latest developments.

"The Captain just addressed the ship", he began. "The other shuttle crashed during take-off from geology base. No one survived. Now only Vladimir is pilot, and we have one shuttle safe with us. Everything we bring to this planet is gone."

For a moment, I felt a pang of loss for my turquoise cube. Then I thought of Kitha-ré and Pho-rion, and lamented them too. I did not think of the missing *Kosmos* staff. Perhaps their deaths were still an abstraction, as if the shock wave of the detonation had not yet passed through me.

But Pia felt it. Paul and I maintained compartmentalization, our male brains enabling us to function in the midst of catastrophe. Were we to collapse in a state of horror or grief, it would help no one, least of all the dead. We needed to remain strong, to preserve order, to ensure the survival of the expedition.

"More than four hundred are missing", Paul continued. "Maybe more will die from the radiation, those who have returned to us. We have lost most scientists, all but two pilots, and Jan is now very ill. All military are gone, some DSI, many maintenance people on mission bases, some cook, some doctor."

"And *Kosmos* flight staff?" I asked.

"Most are safe. Few were on ground. All navigation people are here. We will go home. Soon, when robot surveys finish record of radioactivity and damage to C-1."

"Is there any hope for more survivors?"

"There is a little. We have receive only two distress signals. Two subs in the northern sea were underwater when the blast wave pass. When they realize what is happening, they turn and go away from C-1. They have some damage from seismic turbulence in ocean, but nothing bad. They are together near shore of C-2, five people, marine biologists. They stay inside subs because of fall-out."

I suddenly thought about Maria Kempton. I asked if they knew where she had been when the bomb went off. Had they heard from her?

"She's in her room", Pia said. "She's fine, though shaken like the rest of us."

"Volodya goes down to C-2 now", said Paul. "Is dangerous but he will bring biologist back."

I could see that they needed to be alone for a while. I said good-bye and returned to my own room.

Though I wasn't hungry, I knew I should eat. Around the usual suppertime, I wandered into the deck-B cafeteria and came upon kitchen staff sitting at the tables, talking quietly among themselves. Some sipped from cups of coffee, a few openly smoked cigarettes. Where had the tobacco come from? Had it been smuggled from Earth, or had it been grown on Nova? They glanced at me then looked away. Some were red-eyed, some looked angry; most were still stunned. One responsible cook pointed to the row of steaming containers at the food counter. I served myself, sat down alone, and forced myself to consume whatever it was.

Throughout the evening, I watched the satellite view of the planet on the panorama screen. People wandered in and out of the hall, shook their heads, covered their mouths with a hand, stifled their sobs, left for elsewhere.

The high winds generated by the blast were still raging, but I could see that a good deal of airborne debris was falling into the ocean in the west. The atmosphere above C-1 was still too dense to make out ground details. When sunset in that hemisphere darkened the continent, it was clear that countless fires still burned beneath the clouds of smoke. I wondered if all the forests would be gone by morning.

Restless, I went down to PHM to see if Vladimir's shuttle had returned to port. It was there. A flight technician told me the pilot had brought the biologists back safely. I returned to my room and fell into an uneasy sleep.

*

The next day, I tracked down Maria Kempton and returned her Bible to her without comment. She was stressed and distracted, and I was glad she didn't ask me if I'd read it. If she had, I might not have been able to restrain my bleak thoughts about life, providence, and the fate of the universe.

I returned to my room and flipped through Xue's Chinese edition, examining annotations he had penned neatly in the margins, his underlined passages, and some inserted notes, all in Chinese script, as alien to me as the temple codices. It struck me how closely the letters resembled cuneiform. Had his people come from one of the sons of Noah? I closed the book and put it onto my shelf beside the deer and the slide rule, realizing they were no longer on loan. They were mine, and I didn't know what to do with them.

*

Three days later, a message from the Captain was hand-delivered to me at my room. Maybe the courier had been chosen because he was Hispanic like me. It was the young waiter who had served our table in the Captain's dining room, weeks ago. I had written my address on a table napkin for him, not seriously expecting that he would ever turn up at my mountain cabin.

He seemed happy to see me, like a long-lost cousin. Who knows, maybe he was a long-lost cousin, if you traced us both back to the Aztecs and the Conquistadores.

I asked him how he was coping with it all.

"I have lost friends", he said, his face falling, tears in his eyes.

"I'm sorry."

"You lost friends too, *Señor* Hoyos. I am sorry for this."

What could one say? We were sorry. Everyone was sorry. To change the subject, I asked him if he was regular KC staff or just borrowed from the kitchens on lower decks.

"I was an ensign in the navy", he replied. "Then I was seconded to space fleet and chosen for the voyage."

He left and I read the message, an invitation to dine that evening with the Captain.

It was a downcast group of people who met in his private quarters. The Captain, the Commander, Vladimir, a few other flight staff, Pia and Paul and the baby, Dariush, a nuclear physicist named Barton, and myself.

Barton, it turned out, had planned to be in the temple on the day of the explosion, but at the last moment, he had decided to remain on the *Kosmos*. I could see well enough that he was a taciturn, cautious kind of man, which was probably why he had held back that day. British, fortyish, and afflicted with classic academic myopia, he told us that he had considered it unwise to clump all the nuclear physicists in a single room in proximity to a highly unpredictable experiment. He had been influenced to some extent, I now learned, by conversations with Xue.

As we ate a meal of simple vegetables and nova-salmon (the last we would probably eat), he gave an account of the current condition on the planet's surface.

"Low-orbit scans have been tracing the spread of radiation. Significantly, it is declining sharply as it moves westward over the sea, and has fallen to less than 3% strength as it touches C-2. The fall-out is heavier material than we first thought; it and dust are descending by gravity or being precipitated out in the tremendous storms caused by the blast. This is extraordinary good news, to say the least."

No one around the table responded. It was hard to think of anything post-blast as extraordinary good news.

"What's the condition of the epicenter?" I asked.

"It's certainly the worst event in recorded history. The crater is more than thirty kilometers in diameter, and unmanned probes sent into it tell us that it's basically a shallow bowl of fused glass—green and purple glass. The temple mountain is gone, and all the nearby mountains have changed shape as a result of combined blast, earthquakes, and avalanches. The pass through the western mountains is twice as wide now and nothing remains of anything on the temple side of the range. The land everywhere is absolutely barren. It's like a moonscape. Only on the outer rim of the continent are there any remnant forests—however, these are no more than blackened stumps. A few fires are still burning."

"What was radioactivity at the epicenter?" asked the Captain.

Barton gave a figure. "Surprisingly low after four days", he said. "I simply cannot imagine what fuel they were using, or how, precisely, it was brought to the state of chain reaction. This is unknown physics, but in my estimation it would have been a smaller *fission* bomb driven into the mass of nuclear fuel which became the *fusion* bomb."

"I agree", I said. "That's the only way it could have happened. You saw the two so-called reactors in the tail of the ship, I'm sure."

"Yes. And I'm guessing the innocent blighter on top was the fission bomb. Even so, consider this, Hoyos: They may have found some elements not on our periodic table—which, according to our current state of knowledge, is absurd—or perhaps not—I don't know. Now the larger 'reactor' was certainly immense, and if it contained only fissionable material, then it could have created an explosion larger than any mankind has made. And so it did. But this would not account for the colossal size and effects of the explosion. My guess is that the designers of the bomb had interred a much, much larger cache of fuel in a chamber beneath the ship, connected by a hidden channel or channels. Add to this the fact that there are significant seismic faults running into those mountains, and . . ."

"What's happening with the seismic aftershocks?" I asked.

"Declining in number and magnitude. Lava flow from the three erupting volcanoes is decreasing. Two other unstable volcanoes on the closest continents are venting steam but exhibiting no immediate threat of massive eruption."

He went on to say the tsunamis in the southern hemisphere had done some damage to coastal regions, but the seas had absorbed the waves and were nearly back to normal patterns. The planet was big and resilient—magnificent, actually. The other continents appeared to have suffered no great harm, and in ten years time, even C-1 would have regenerated its flora, possibly tree saplings. Perhaps some fauna had survived as well. In a hundred years, all that would remain as evidence of the blast would be the immense glass bowl, though it too would be slowly covered by wind-blown dust, soil runoff, and subsequent organic growth.

Barton had just concluded the above when a flight officer came into the room and addressed the Captain in a quiet voice. "Sir, Sobieski is dead."

Vladimir half-rose from his chair and exclaimed in a stricken voice, "Jan!"

Dariush stood and excused himself, saying he would go to the clinic now.

Paul covered his eyes, and Pia put a hand on his arm.

The Captain stood, speechless for the moment. Then, in a quiet voice, he too excused himself and left the room.

Soon after, we all went our separate ways.

Barton suggested we find a place to talk. We took the elevator down to deck D, the concourse on which he lived. He wanted another drink, he said, and I had no reason to object. We entered the Indian restaurant, the doors wide open and no sign of customers or serving staff inside. I took a seat at a table, and he went behind the counter to see what could be found in the way of alcohol—anything to numb our feelings. He brought back two cold beers.

"What a bloody disaster", he snarled. "We're in a hell of a mess. We have one shuttle left and only one pilot for it."

"That's more than enough for when we get back to Earth. Besides, the base in Africa will have other shuttles to come up and fetch us."

"True", he nodded. "Sorry. I didn't mean to sound bitter."

Bitter? I wondered. What was his bitterness compared to mine? Mine was a vat of acid. He didn't know yet. He hadn't added it all up. He was sharing a drink with the man who had made it happen.

I knew this was false guilt, or half-false. I hadn't *made* it happen. But there were a whole lot of people dead or dying because I had made it possible for them to come along on this great adventure.

"Have you seen any DSI staff?" I asked.

He scowled. "None so far. Hopefully they all got fried."

It was a harsh thing to say, wishing people dead. It matched my own emotions of the moment. How satisfying to see the bad guys shot, just the way it should be, just like a cheap western.

"You know," Barton continued, oblivious to my thoughts, "Oppenheimer said it when he observed the first nuclear explosion, the bomb he helped make. As the fireball and mushroom cloud rose up into the sky over New Mexico, he quoted the Hindu scriptures."

"*I am become Death, the destroyer of worlds*", I said.

"That's right. That's the one."

"It was from the *Bhagavad Gita*, the *Song of God*."

"What god was that, I wonder?" Barton snorted.

"It was Krishna", I said, pointing to a blue-skinned deity in one of the wall paintings. "The supreme being in disguise, you see. He was quite a slaughterer, this supreme being."

"Aren't they all? One wonders which of them is the front-runner in the body-count department."

"Oh, Krishna was right up there with the best of them. For example, he explained to a warrior named Arjuna, riding into battle on a chariot, why it was permissible for him to slaughter his grandfather, his teacher, and his other relatives. You see, when Arjuna spotted his family among the enemy host, he got cold feet, dropped his bow, and refused to fight."

"Decent of him."

"Then Krishna the great lord of the universe gave him a stern lecture. 'Arjuna,' he said, 'this isn't worthy of a hero like you. Your duty is to fight. Those who have joined forces against us must perish. Attachment to friends and relatives should not stand in the way of your duty.'

"'How can a man know his duty?' asked Arjuna. And Krishna replied: 'Don't think of the results. Don't say, 'These people are yours, and others aren't yours.' You have to understand, my boy, that everyone who is born has to die. Justice is more important than people.' And then the zeal to fight returned to Arjuna—he picked up his bow, and went forth to the battle."

"Lovely", said Barton sourly. "And where's the justice down there on *Mundus Novus*?"

It was a good question. It was rhetorical, of course, but it needed to be asked, and indeed I asked it, though I kept my thoughts to myself. It struck me that people are always real and that Justice, by contrast, is a debatable topic. Justice, justice, so often reshaped by those who would wield it, depending on their cultures and myths, depending on whether they think they are supreme beings or isolated bio-mechanisms floating alone in the universe. Which one were you, J. Robert Oppenheimer? And why did the occult mythologies of the East have such appeal for you? Was Krishna better than the God of your ancestors? Or was he just a lot more like you? You considered yourself beyond guilt, didn't you? You looked original sin in the face, as you once confessed in a candid moment, and you didn't recognize it.

"Original sin", I murmured, realizing that Barton was staring at me, waiting for a response.

"What?" he said as if he'd never heard the term before. Maybe he hadn't.

I shrugged. He finished his beer in a gulp and pushed back his chair.

"Good night, Hoyos. I need some sleep."

After he left, I found another bottle of beer in the cooler and drank it on the spot. I also searched for vodka and found a flask of the synthetic kind. I took it with me to my room and sat down on my bed, staring at my feet. I sipped from the neck of the flask, and I thought a little. Then I took some swigs that burned all the way down, and I thought some more.

Why did we of the enlightened West call our first nuclear weapon, the "Trinity" explosion? This god, our defensive god, gave birth to an "Original Child", who burned and obliterated our family, so that they would not kill us, we were sure; we were very sure it was right and just. And so we did it again and again.

Oppenheimer once said that when a man of science sees something that is technically sweet, he goes ahead and does it. Only later, after he has enjoyed his technical success, does he think about what he has done. That is the way it was with the first atomic bomb. That is the way it was with us on Nova.

Oppenheimer, Einstein, Bohr, Fermi, Teller, all you who preceded me in our great calling, you were riding on the wrong chariot! Didn't you know what you would unleash? Didn't you realize you had launched an age in which millions upon millions would be obliterated by your rational brilliance, your light of the lord of the night-gods?

After I drank the vodka to the last drop, I felt good—real good.

"Here's to the heroes of science!" I raised my arm in a toast. "Here's to heroes of the deaggressivization of mankind!" I lurched to my feet and stumbled into the bathroom. "And here's to a hero like you!" I declared to the man staring at me in the mirror.

*

Departure was delayed and delayed. There was still a thread of hope that we would receive more distress signals from individuals or from isolated beacon posts where a remnant might have gathered. None came.

Finally, the Captain gave us the statistics of our demise. Broadcasting live through the all-ship communications system, he told us that of the 677 people who had departed from Earth ten years before, two had died on the outward bound journey, two more had died of snakebite on Nova, 459 had died in the blast and subsequent firestorm and earthquakes. Of the forty survivors brought back to the ship, thirty-three had since died.

This was a total of 496 dead. We were now a group of 181 people living on a ship designed to comfortably accommodate a thousand. We were less than a third of the original voyageurs.

After the Captain had concluded speaking, I powered up my *max*. None of our on-ground cameras had come through the devastation, but our satellite cameras were still in operation. I accessed the real-time vid images of C-1. The skies were clear over the continent, which now was a gray landscape speckled with patches of charcoal gray. Even the glass bowl at the epicenter reflected no light, since falling ash had covered it. I zoomed to the central mountain range and crept southward past the crater toward the place where the beloved valley had been, only five or so miles from the blast. It was gone. The mountains that once had held it in a close embrace were broken, though portions of them were still standing. The lake and the crystal forest had vanished. The cave of Kitha-ré and Pho-rion was buried under a thousand meters of shattered rock. All the plentiful snowcaps had melted, and numerous canyons were filled with dirty cascades of run-off.

Base-main was a junkyard covered with dust. I zoomed to the hill where the flag had been unfurled more than a year ago. The site was barren, the flag gone. However, there were four sparkling beads nearby, vaguely blue, which must have been the toppled globes of the grave-markers. Beneath the ashes lay the bodies of Stron and David and the other two victims.

*

Departure seemed an anticlimax. The flight staff, nearly a third of our total number, were busy in the command center. The remainder of us watched on panorama screens as the *Kosmos* did a slow roll away from the planet, though visually, it seemed to the eye that the planet was suddenly leaving its orbit and spiraling upward out of sight. When the ship reached its proper plane and bearings for the return voyage, the cameras adjusted and Nova came into view again. We were now on the side of the planet in daylight, facing three continents that had never been explored, except by high-altitude scan surveys or token visits by subs and AECs. We had left our view of dusk over C-1, and now as the main propulsion engines ignited, morning was spreading across C-4 in the northern hemisphere and C-5 in the south, with the smaller C-6 floating on the ocean east of them, midway between the two. Nova seemed as serene as ever. Though a bomb had destroyed C-1, the other eight continents still radiated their lavish green—life irrepressible. But it was not really irrepressible, I knew. A few more bombs like that and the planet would have become a sterilized orb.

*

The Captain invited everyone to move up to deck A, since this would bring us into closer physical proximity, offering more opportunities for daily encounters and reducing the tendency to isolation. Some of the private rooms, on closer inspection, were found to be suites for the privileged. Now everyone learned that there had been an appalling discrepancy between the single rooms of most people and the residences of very important figures such as the trillionaires, the nephew of the World President, Skinner, and others who had rated a higher place in the classless society. We looked and ogled and admired their former lifestyles (they were, after all, dead). I found it interesting that no one moved into those luxury suites. They were converted into social lounges and game rooms.

Don and Raydawn's fireplace, with its real logs and real flames, became a huge draw. There must have been a dozen reasons why fire was an outrageous risk, but the former tenants had got away with it, and we did too. The boost to morale was more than worth it. Love of the true hearth appeared in all hearts. Though the ship's systems functioned perfectly as always, maintaining a constant comfortable warmth, people would often kneel before the fire and extend their open hands toward it—an instinctive gesture. I did it myself, inhaling the incense of burning apple wood, cedar splints, and aged pine knots as I ached with longing for my cabin. I became territorial over the issue of splitting kindling and starting the fire in the morning. I was the first to locate the wood shed, a room just down the hall from Don's place, eighteen by forty-eight meters by three meters high, with three quarters of its wood supply still there. From then on, I reigned over it like a benevolent tyrant.

There was a lot of mixed emotion when it was discovered that a freezer compartment in the ballroom-size pantry attached to the trillionaires' suite contained hundreds of beefsteaks and limitless shelves of prepackaged Cajun food. There was also a wine cellar that staggered the imagination. When these rooms were first opened, lowly staff just stared, feeling delight at their newfound abundance and, I think, some resentment against the idle rich. In any event, the steak was gone within a month, consumed by us all at communal feasts. These feasts helped cement the fellowship among us, which would be crucial, considering the nine years still to be spent in each other's company.

The deck-A cafeteria was the main place where the ship's company ate. A majority of the food service staff had died at the bases on Nova, and the surviving cooks became highly valued people. Like self-respecting cooks everywhere, they did not stint on their creative abilities and foraged daily for specialty items in the vast holds of PHM. They continued to serve us with dedication and good humor, and we the idle less-than-rich were deeply grateful for it. In fact, we revered them.

Our social order was now considerably changed. There were too many missing executives in all the departments, except for KC. Certain flight staff people had natural leadership skills that were not dependent on rank, and these good men and women helped in the initial stages of organizing division of labor. Among us all there was a general mood of generosity that helped pull us together. We became that which the combined powers of our home planet's government had failed to make—a team, a community.

Inexplicably, considering the crisis we had endured, certain undefined atmospheric tensions seemed to have disappeared. Social gatherings tended to be less planned and less class conscious: for example, maintenance people would joke around with, or engage in serious discussions with, the high-tech people; lieutenant commanders would go courting among the nursing or laundry staff—respectfully, with new manners. Smoking cigarettes and drinking various forms of contraband—both illegal activities—were now open practices. I think there may have been DSI people at public gatherings, but none who appeared in uniform. If there were animators or facilitators present, they did not bother to reinforce the old rules. A lot of "mandates" had been abandoned without a vote being cast or a shot being fired. It was our first, though transient, experience of freedom. Perhaps most people realized that if we wanted to return to Earth without killing each other or otherwise going mad, we would have to take responsibility for our little society. There were no enforcers, no responsibility police.

I might mention at this point that my area of expertise was cleaning public washrooms—a task for which I volunteered.

*

During the second week after departure, the *Kosmos* was still cruising at relatively low speed under nuclear propulsion, passing through the orbits of AC-A's outer planets. Within a few days, we would be in open space and altering course for home. Anti-matter would be initiated, and we would begin acceleration toward our maximum velocity.

Late one afternoon, I was lying on my bed reading Stron's book on quasars. I was missing my old friend, wishing we could talk over all that had happened. Ao-li kept coming to mind too. On a whim, I flipped through a little hand-bound booklet I had found a few days earlier among the scanty belongings in his room—*Beijing Poems*. I now saw that it was a collection of verse he had written when he was a young man. I wondered why he had given me poetry written by Li Po but had not given me his own. Had this been due to his natural diffidence, or to the intimacy of his reflections—had he been writing only for himself?

Dated more than fifty years ago, the poems were penned, not printed; the text was Chinese characters on one page, with the English translation on the facing page.

The first was titled "Departure".

By the gate of your small orchard, three trees in blossom,
I take my leave of you, knowing that I shall never again
    eat its fruit
(for the sea is wide).
With a bow that veils your hidden tears and silences mine,
    you bid me go.
Yet I cannot go.
This once, breaking the customs of time,
I kneel and kiss the old hands that carved the sign of covenant,
the ivory word you made for me.
I carry it, I carry you
Into the heartless land.

I wanted to read more, but I choked up and couldn't go on.

My door was open. Like many others on board, I was no longer as intent on preserving my privacy. Perhaps I hoped for a visitor to drop by and save me from myself.

Paul appeared in the doorway.

"Neil, hello. Would you like a big swim with me in pool?"

I sat up and wiped my eyes. "Thank you for asking, Paul, but there's no longer any need for us to make clandestine cover stories."

I put Xue's booklet carefully away on a shelf.

"Would you like to read my dark ruminations?" I said, rummaging for the most recent pages of my journal entries.

"Is a good book?" he asked.

"A bad book. My journal, I meant."

"Ah. Yes, I would like to read your new thought. So, no swimming for you?"

"No swimming for me."

"Okay. Pia tell me you will say no. Now, plan number two. She want you to visit for supper in our house. Will you?"

"Yes, I'll come."

"Okay. Eighteen hundred hours, our place."

I knocked on the frame of their open doorway at 6 P.M., welcomed by the sound of the baby making cooing noises and the aroma of Cajun cooking. Pia had done some plundering in the trillionaires' pantry, I realized, and was completing last-minute preparations in her small kitchen.

We sat around the table in the dining alcove, with our knees touching throughout the meal, and tried to make happy talk. But it didn't fly too well. I could see that something heavy was on their minds.

"What is it?" I asked. "What's wrong?"

Pia answered: "Nothing's wrong, Neil. It's something Paul and I have been discussing over the past week. We should have been thinking about it and praying about it long before this."

"About what, may I ask?"

"We're going back to Nova."

"But it's too late. The ship's coordinates are set for Earth, aren't they?"

"Yes, it cannot be change now", said Paul. "We must intersect with her orbit at a specific time and place; you know how it is."

I said I didn't really know how it was exactly, though I could guess. As he expanded on the astronomical data and technical side of things, I realized what they were planning.

"The shuttle?" I interrupted.

They nodded.

"But you aren't a pilot, Paul."

"Volodya is pilot. He is coming. Others are coming too."

"Does the Captain know?"

"We ask permission. He tell us yes, go."

Once again it struck me that this was one unusual captain. By giving his permission, he would doubtless be breaking all manner of global and fleet rules.

"When?"

"Tomorrow morning, Neil", Pia answered. "And that's why we wanted to talk with you. Not to say good-bye but to ask you to come with us."

"Back to that planet? What about the radioactivity? What about Katherine's future, her health, the risks?"

"Does she have a future on Earth, our illegal child? Where would we hide her? How could we raise her in that sterile place, ruled by madmen and tyrants?"

"A dose of rads can be tyrannical too."

Paul said, "Dr. Barton tell us whole planet is now about same as rads on Earth from atomic weapons, long ago. C-1 is worse, but it is falling fast."

"That's unlikely."

"It's true", Pia answered. "He showed us the instrument readings, and the Captain verified them. Whatever it was that exploded had a short life unlike any of our nuclear material. No one knows what it was, but we have a reasonable assurance that we'll survive."

"Surely, you won't go anywhere near C-1."

"Not for a long, long time. We've talked with everyone who wants to return, and we've agreed on C-4, the second largest continent, on the other side of the planet and every bit as good as C-1 was."

"I see. Will you be taking an axe and a box of matches with you?"

"The shuttle can hold over a hundred people for a three-week flight, as well as enough food and survival equipment for a year. It will give us a head start, building a village and farms."

"Watch out for snakes", I said with a note of bitterness.

"You come too", said Paul.

I shook my head. "Sorry. You don't need a decrepit old cowpoke to carry around on your backs while you get started. I think I'll just stay on this ship and go home to my own mountains. Besides," I said, averting my eyes, "I destroyed what we had on Nova. I killed all those people."

"Don't be absurd!" Pia erupted fiercely, leaning toward me.

"Daedalus, that's who I am", I snorted bitterly. "I made their wings, and they flew too close to the sun."

"But how could you have known! We were tricked by those monsters. We were seduced, and we believed them."

"Yeah, well Xue didn't believe them."

"Don't start taking on guilt that isn't yours, Neil, not now. That would be a lie on top of a lie."

I disagreed, but I refrained from saying so.

"I'm touched by your concern, Pia. But I need to return to Earth and tell my part of the story. Maybe the authorities will learn something from this. I can do that much to make up for—"

"Stop. Stop it now. Stop apologizing for inventing the wheel. You need to hop on the cart with us."

"How many of you are going?"

"About sixty definites. Maybe tomorrow morning some undecideds will show up."

"You've been busy."

"You missed a few meetings. Don't you read your mail?"

"Nope."

"Well, now you can think about it. Think about it seriously and carefully. We need you."

"You don't need me."

"We need physicist", said Paul. "Dr. Barton is not going back to Nova."

"The last thing in the world you need is a theoretical physicist."

"Okay, is true, physicist is not so important. We need *old* people."

"What?"

"We need *dedushka*, the grandpa. We have three or four grandpa and grandma only. Not good. Not enough."

I almost laughed it was so quaint, so ridiculous.

"Well, if you can find me a rocking chair", I mumbled.

Pia put a hand on mine. "You'll consider it, won't you?"

"All right, I'll consider it. Let me sleep on it."

Paul told me that the departure next day would be at 0800 hours. Presuming upon my capitulation, Pia instructed me to bring all my possessions, including the latest installments of my journal, if I had any.

As I made my way back to my room, I knew full well that I would not sleep and that I would not consider their invitation. I would not be returning to Nova.

But I resolved to do one thing for them. I would get into the ship's records of orbit scans. I would erase the good news about radioactivity. I would give testimony at the debriefings back home. I would write papers and articles. I would tell the authorities that

476

Nova would be uninhabitable for another thousand years. That way, Earth's glorious expeditions would go elsewhere and leave my beloved people alone. Undisturbed, they would have a chance to build what mankind might have been, and might yet become. I would smother the lies of our ancestors and our contemporaries with my own little corrective lies.

I wrote *beloved*, didn't I? Yes, I loved them. They were the family I never had. But I knew that in the long run they would be better off without me.

*

After a terrible night of tossing and turning, I went down to the shuttle bays at 7:45 A.M. and stepped out of the elevator bearing nothing in my arms. The Captain was standing with a group of people by the shuttle's loading ramp, shaking hands and giving his final best wishes. Paul was among them, and I noticed that he had his sword and scabbard strapped to his belt. Pia stood beside her husband, looking resolved. When she spotted me without baggage, her face fell. She turned away and lowered her head.

As I approached the edge of the crowd, I met Maria Kempton, who was carrying a knitting handbag, a backpack, and her purse.

"No roo pie for you, Maria?" I asked.

"Something much better, Neil. Aren't you coming with us?"

"Nope."

"That's a shame", she said sadly. "A real shame. I think you'd thrive on Nova. You're a pioneer kind of fellow aren't you?"

"No longer. My adventuring days are over. All the best, Maria. You were good company on the voyage."

"You too. Burn my thesis for me, would you?"

"Glad to. Don't look back."

I'm not sure what made me say it, but thoughtlessly I blurted, "Maria, what about your grandchildren?"

Her face froze, and then it just seemed to collapse into a haggard mess, her eyes as bleak as anything I had ever seen. She covered her face with her hands and hunched over, as if defending herself from a coming blow. She made a sound like a moan or a subdued wail.

I put an arm around her shoulders.

"I know, I know, it's the hardest part", I murmured sympathetically. "It won't be easy to leave them behind."

Her whole body shuddered in a paroxysm of grief that bordered on despair. Finally, she looked up with haunted eyes and sobbed, "I don't have any grandchildren. I don't have any children either."

For a moment, I thought I hadn't heard her correctly.

"But the photos . . ."

"I took them at a school, a long time ago. Strangers. Beloved little strangers. I never had a family of my own. Edwin was . . . they made him do it, you see . . . never to have children. If he wanted to do research, if he wanted to get ahead, he had to have the surgery. We fought about it. I told him I didn't need a comfortable life. I needed a child. *We* needed a child. But they wore him down."

"So you pretended you had a family."

"We loved each other. We really did. But he was so afraid."

"Your knight?"

"He *was* a knight in the beginning. And later, he felt he'd made the worst mistake of his life. We planned to build that cabin in the Simpson desert when we retired. We were going to make a place where we all could live, you see. We'd take in any illegals who escaped into the outback, any runaways who made it through the screen. Hide them, help them grow, love them."

"You'll have a real family to look after on Nova. They need you."

She nodded as she dried her eyes. "The story gave me moments of happiness, Neil, as if the dream was more real than reality. And I couldn't let go of it. I'm so sorry. I didn't want to lie to you."

"They turned all of us into liars, Maria. But now there'll be no more lies. You'll have a chance to be what you always should have been."

She gave me a hug and went up the ramp. Others were going inside too.

I spotted Dr. Arthur hustling toward the ramp, clutching a variety of items and pulling a wheeled crate, which I suppose was medical equipment. His face flushed red when he noticed me eying him coldly. He stopped in his tracks and headed in my direction with a cringe in his body and facial expression.

"Dr. H-Hoyos", he stammered, dropping his eyes.

"The great escape artist", I murmured through clenched teeth.

"Try not to hate me", he said in a pleading tone, his eyes filling with tears.

"I don't hate you", I snarled—my tone implying, *I just despise you, Doctor.*

478

"I had to give you that prescription. They made me do it."

"*Made* you do it?"

He nodded up and down and still would not meet my eyes.

"Your fear made you do it", I said in a cold voice. "You didn't have the courage to resist them."

"That's true. And I didn't know *how* to resist them. I am very ashamed of it. I betrayed everything I believed in as a physician. It was the worst mistake of my life—and I will regret it the rest of my life."

"Uh-huh", I said with a nasty curl of the upper lip. "And I see that you're off to the next stage of your life."

"Forgive me", he pleaded in a small voice. "Please forgive me."

"Sure", I snorted, "I forgive you."

I turned my back on him.

He grabbed the sleeve of my jacket. "I . . . I tried to redeem myself, Dr. Hoyos. I was the physician who performed the autopsy on David Ayne. I'd lied about one person's life—yours—but I thought I could make up for it a little by getting to the truth of another person's life. They killed him, and when I realized what they'd done and how they'd done it, it opened my eyes. I understand a lot of things now that I didn't when they used me."

"Okay", I murmured halfheartedly. "Thanks for telling me."

We stood face to face for a few moments, looking at each other, thinking who knows what. I had no more words to speak, and neither did he. He turned away and went back to the ramp. I made my way toward Pia and Paul through clusters of people locked in tearful embraces.

I stuck out my hand to Paul. He shook it and grimaced. "Is too bad. We won't forget you."

I turned to Pia. She was crying. I put my arms around her and the baby.

"Bye, girl."

"Bye."

I wouldn't let her go. Or maybe she wouldn't let me go. Paul and the Captain were silently regarding us.

And then it happened:

The elevator doors opened, and Elif Larson stepped out, followed by three men and two women, all carrying weapons—little hand-held pistol affairs that I had never seen before. Maybe they were designed to shoot bullets, maybe they fired e-volts that merely stunned.

The Captain stepped forward to meet them.

Enough to say that it went the way of all showdowns. Elf verbally laid down the law, backed up by his gang—or was it a posse? That was the question wasn't it? On what side of the law did people stand? What exactly was the law, and did it any longer apply to our situation? Was Elf *ultra vires* or was the Captain? The Captain argued. The Elf restated the law. He insisted that everyone must go back to their rooms. The Captain insisted that all those preparing to depart should now board the shuttle.

The Elf raised his gun and pointed it at the Captain. Calmly, the latter slowly lifted his arm and pushed it aside. The gang or posse bristled their weapons menacingly. Paul and three other young men bristled in return, fists clenched, gathering around the Captain.

"Back off", said Paul to the gang. They didn't back off.

Paul pulled his mastodon gun from his pocket and aimed it at Elf's head. It was a high-caliber Russian army pistol, very old, but dangerous looking. He cocked the trigger.

"Go away to your office", said Paul. "Go back to Earth and scare children and mothers. We are going to another place."

He had just finished saying this when one of the gang fired at him, a line of blue light that buzzed as it hit Paul's shoulder. Another flash struck the side of his head, and he fell to the floor unconscious. Pia screamed and ran to him.

Suddenly, it was a free-for-all, full of punching and wrestling and blue flashes striking off in all directions. Paul had dropped his gun. I bent and picked it up, aimed and blew a hole in the floor at Elf's feet. He flinched and aimed his weapon at me. I sidestepped and tripped (there is something to be said for bad legs). The blue flash missed me by a centimeter. The young men were now wrestling weapons from the DSI crew, and I kept firing at the floor and at the ceiling until the gun's chamber emptied. I didn't hit any flesh, but I shook a lot of people up and added to the general confusion. I suspect that most of our assailants had never before heard the report of a gun. Throughout their short, conditioned lives they had preferred to hypnotize, to immobilize, and then walk in and dominate. Several of them suffered hard punches on their chins and were disarmed. Then our guys hustled them back to the elevator and kicked them inside. The Captain had by then seized Elf's nasty little weapon and proceeded to walk him at gunpoint to the elevator. Elf was livid. Elf ranted. He threatened and raged. When our facilitators of social infrastructure were all safely inside the elevator, the Captain punched a code into the console, the doors closed, and our adversaries were whisked away to some other part of the ship.

"Quickly, now", he said to the rest of us. "Go on board and tell Vladimir to prepare for depressurization."

Paul was lifted and carried into the shuttle, Pia hurrying along beside him.

There was no time for last good-byes. The portal ramp was just beginning to rise when two men came jogging down the concourse as fast as they could.

"Wait, wait", cried one of them.

It was Dariush. The other was my doctor, Lieutenant Commander Nagakawa.

The Captain ran into the bay and waved to Vladimir up in the pilot's cabin, signaling through the window that he should delay a minute longer. The ramp lowered.

Then the oddest thing occurred. Dariush knelt down on the floor before Nagakawa and bowed his head. The doctor lifted his right arm and made the sign of the cross over him. Dariush stood, they clasped hands, and then the doctor ran up the ramp and went inside.

The portal closed, the bay doors closed, the depressurization bell rang, and I stood there helpless, realizing I would never again see my friends. Then they were gone.

*

Why had I not read the list of survivors? In retrospect, I see that I had abstracted those whom I didn't know, or who were of no immediate concern for my life. All those I had grown close to were either dead or accounted for.

But why had I stopped reading my mail? Was it because I preferred my habit of splendid isolation? The autonomous self adrift in a giant city-ship, fed by others, loved by others, selfishly nursing my wound? If I had extended more than cursory interest in the general condition of our remnant community, I might have looked beyond the enclosure of my pain, my guilt (or false guilt—who knows?). I might have seen that Elf was alive. Instead, because I had heard by word of mouth that Skinner had been vaporized, I presumed that his deputy had been with him on the day of disaster. Not so. Oh, lamentably not so.

There were more confrontations, but none involving weapons other than the human mind, the human tongue. The ugliness of power struggles need not concern me here. Let me say that Elf backed off with his gang, and we did not see them again for a time. They did not frequent deck A. D was entirely their terrain. There were now only 114 people on board, and DSI was intimidated, I believe, by the sizeable body of energetic, determined men on the flight deck.

*

As I look back at those first weeks after our departure from Nova, I recall my feelings when the *Kosmos* received a message from the shuttle that it had safely landed on C-4. I went to my room to be alone, and there I wept from relief and gratitude.

Vladimir had first flown around the planet at an altitude of thirty thousand meters, at a latitude that brought the vessel over the tower valley. Instrument readings were taken continuously and demonstrated that radioactivity was definitely in decline over the entire globe, though somewhat higher above the epicenter. Even so, here too it was falling and was now just above the hazard level. I was puzzled by this, since the magnitude of the blast indicated a massive fission-fusion bomb, which implied that it was very "dirty" and would contaminate the world for years to come. But it did not. Was it a neutron bomb? I found it hard to believe that's what it was, because a neutron bomb would have created a blast very much smaller than a classic nuclear weapon, though destroying all life within its radius. In our catastrophe, the characteristics of both had been evident. I think we will never know what was used. I would have liked to discuss this in depth with Barton, but he took his own life six weeks into the voyage. His body was buried in space.

*

The messages from the shuttle were a relief, but I think a few of us regretted our decision to remain on board the *Kosmos*, myself among them. Later, all of us would regret it.

The shuttle landed in a wide upland valley on C-4, a lush wilderness of mixed deciduous forest and natural grass pastures. Winding through the valley, coming down from a mountain range on the northern horizon, a river ran cold and clear, teeming with fish.

482

The people renamed the generic shuttle *Pioneer*. Its fuel was irreplaceable, but there was enough left for foray flights that would help them get acquainted with their new homeland. They had plenty of maps.

The men were busy in the forests bringing down trees for cabins they would build, using older laser saws and sometimes two-man bow saws (unbelievably, half-a-dozen had been found in the holds before the pioneers left the ship). In the interim, people were lodged in tents. Their mood was high; they felt they were at the birth of something beautiful, a humble renaissance, a new chance for the human race. As a contingent of the race, they were few in number, but they had more than enough people to begin the regeneration. A majority of them were young. There had been marriages soon after arrival. There were already three pregnancies, which was a heartening portent for the future—four children at the very beginning.

Paul was recovering from the wounds in his head and shoulder. He was fully conscious and itching to get back onto his feet, so that he could build a cabin for his family. The winter in that region, though mild, would be cold enough. They needed to stock up firewood, to dry the fish they were catching in abundance, to prepare for the tilling of soil and a spring planting.

My inbox contained several messages from people on Nova. There was one from Paul and one from Pia (worded with her old Pia-wit). There was even one from Vladimir, exhorting me to watch over Dariush. In addition, Dr. Nagakawa informed me (I think tongue in cheek) that I could cease taking my anti-psychotic medications. He urged me to "contemplate Hokusai".

The influx of unblocked mail told me that DSI no longer controlled the airways. Later, I learned that messages from Nova were being sent directly to the Captain's private communication channel. They were forwarded from there to recipients throughout the ship, without interruption by the monitors. It looked like Elf and his band of un-merry men had backed off definitively. Yet I wondered if they were merely biding their time, lulling us into a false sense of security.

*

Dariush and I no longer met regularly, though we made a point of getting together often enough that I knew there had been no waning of our friendship. There was a quality of sadness in him, however, that I had not seen before and which I attributed to the loss of people dear

483

to him. Little had I realized how close he had been to Xue. We talked about him one evening as we sat in the deserted Mexican bistro, where we had gone for old times' sake.

"He was the same age as me", Dariush said. "Yet he became as a son."

"Did he ever show you his slide rule?" I asked.

"Yes, and he explained its origins too. There is a history behind that man, one full of unknown sufferings, dreams, and hopes. His was a sacrificial life."

"He was always self-effacing, but he knew what to do when it was needed."

"This is true." He paused and regarded me thoughtfully. "How little we understand the people we care about. How little we know them, really."

This was more an indictment of me than it was of him, though I don't think he intended it as such.

I changed the subject: "Barton is dead."

"Yes, I heard."

"He did away with himself."

"He blamed God, Neil. He blamed God for everything that has happened. I tried to reach him, tried to explain to him that we should look to ourselves for the cause of these evils."

"Maybe so, but why didn't God prevent it?"

"God did try to prevent it. He was moving in my heart and in Xue's also, sounding an alarm bell. For my part, I did not listen as well as I might have. I could have done more, spoken more loudly. But in the end, I did not know enough, and I doubted. I worried that if I cried an alarm it would be dismissed as the irrational fear of an elderly scholar who had no connection to the problems of physics. Even so, I should have tried."

"That's hindsight. You can't beat yourself over the head with it. You didn't design that bomb. You didn't make it detonate. And after it went off, you tried to save what could be saved. Don't you think that counts for something . . . in God's eyes?"

"Yes", he nodded. "Yet I know that we do not live perfectly in the will of God, always attentive to his promptings."

"If he is God, why doesn't he speak louder, so we can hear him?"

"He does speak. In a multitude of forms, he speaks. Yet our human nature does not want to hear what he says. We choose our own paths;

we prefer to rise on our own terms. For us to accept that someone higher is speaking with authority—an ultimate authority over our lives—would cost too much, we think. Thus, we make ourselves more deaf. We turn our eyes and ears in other directions."

"He could still give us a good shake and catch our attention, couldn't he?"

"Neil, he has just given us a good shake. But will we learn from this? Will we see what is so plainly before our eyes? Man without God becomes a slave of the old gods, those demons, or else he becomes his own god and falls into another kind of darkness."

This was his theology again, his myth. I preferred a universe without gods of any kind, good or evil. And I knew he was probing this element of my interior life. He was really asking me if I had made a god of myself.

"How can a man rely on anything?" I replied to his unspoken question. "How can a man know his duty and what true justice is?"

"Are your questions rhetorical, Neil? Or are you asking me for my thoughts?"

"Whatever, Dariush", I shrugged.

"It seems you wish to be good on your own terms. You are a man of fine qualities, in many ways, a noble person, a man of courage. Yet you are also proud, for you think yourself alone in the universe."

"I don't think I'm alone. Here we are talking together, aren't we?"

"Yes, but you feel very alone."

Well, he was right; ultimately I did feel that way. But I wasn't going to admit it, and I certainly wasn't going to fuel his argument.

"Your qualities were given to you through your parents' sacrifices", he went on. "And other gifts were given to you as you grew and went out from your family into the world. Did you create these out of nothing?"

"I've done my best with what I have."

"What you have? Do you think of these as your possessions? Can you not see that everything was given to you? God gave them to you."

"Where was God when Xue was burned to death and shattered on the pavement?"

"He was with him . . . and in him."

I frowned, thinking to myself that his theology or philosophy was a version of the endless variety of consolations humans clutch onto when the unthinkable occurs. I had mine, he had his.

"I believe in people", I declared. "I believe we can make of our lives whatever we choose."

"I believe this too, Neil. Within the limitations of our nature, this is so. Yet is there not a crucial element missing from your equation? If we choose blindly, we so often choose according to the impulses of what is unredeemed within our nature, or unpurified, I should say."

"I thought your Christ redeemed everything."

"Fundamentally, it is accomplished, yet the final part remains."

"Accomplished but not accomplished?" I said, frowning.

"Science and our countless electronic servants tell us that all things are accomplished by the flick of a switch. We live surrounded and sustained by linear circuits. Thus, existence is perceived as a mechanism."

"That's a rather sweeping generality."

"Perhaps."

"And I fail to see your point."

"My point is, time cannot be reduced to a mathematical equation and no more than that. From the perspective of eternity, we will, I believe, see the unfolding of human history as a drama that transpires in the blink of an eye. But we who are still within time cannot yet see it."

"Answer me this, Dariush: In this blink of an eye, why are so many of Christ's followers suffering? Why haven't they changed the world for him?"

"We change the world in the most important way. First, we labor to conquer ourselves, and then to resist the spirit of the world. I know you grieve over the way the world is. It is your solution that is wrong."

"Really? What do you think is my solution?"

"You strive always to prove yourself superior to the world and at the same time to make yourself apart from it."

I don't know why his words inflicted such sudden pain. I suppose I felt he was judging me. In answer, I merely shrugged. I reached for my cup of ale and drank in one gulp until it was empty. Then I stood up, preparing to make my departure in a cordial manner.

"The point is, Dariush, I have no way of knowing if your God exists or not. And frankly, I don't care."

"You care", he said.

I smiled patiently, conveying my affection and pity for him.

"Neil, if the redeeming light of Christ were to go out of the world, mankind would swiftly fall into greater darkness—and then the world would be ruled not only by errors. It would be ruled by the diabolic."

An image of the beast in the temple crypt passed through my mind, and then, strangely, an image of little children with red dots on their hands scattering into chaparral bushes, to hide.

I shook my head. "I'm very tired. Let's call it a night."

*

There was another significant conversation, though it ran along different lines. One day as I sat alone in the library on deck A, staring at the floor, he came into the room carrying a sheaf of paper.

"I wondered if I would find you here", he began. "I have learned something important. These are translations of archival records from the period immediately preceding the internment of the ship."

I sat straighter. "What do they say?"

"They say a great deal. During the past few days, I have tried to learn more about their thinking, their planning."

"You mean why and how they made the bomb?"

"Exactly. A philologist-archaeologist must be something of a detective, you realize. Of course, hundreds of thousands of scans were auto-translated, and the bulk of them were awaiting intensive analysis when we return to Earth. Only a small minority had been subjected to further refinement by human analysis."

"Such as the three codices under the temple altar."

"Also Kitha-ré and Pho-rion's song. A few other documents as well. However, in an effort to understand the minds behind the catastrophe, I tried word searches of the entire body of archive translations."

"Words like *bomb* and *explosion*?"

"Yes. There were no results, of course. The bomb's designers were clever enough to know that we might stumble across such references, alerting us to the danger. Moreover, they presumed that the bronze tablet in the tower exhorting us to focus the three lights of the sun into the eyes of the god would be sufficient incentive. They felt sure we would fall into their trap, beguiled by curiosity. And so we did."

"And so we did. But what have you found?"

"You recall that we posited the construction of the road and causeway between the years 7980 to 7960 before the present. The excavation of the mountain for the making of the temple was completed during the same time period."

"And the transportation and internment of the ship took five years."

"That is correct. This probably occurred in the time immediately leading up to 7955 B.P, because that is the year when temple rites began. However, the final sealing of the temple occurred at some point between 2064 to 2061 B.P."

"Nova-years or Earth-years?"

"Earth-years. I adjusted the codex dates to our chronology."

"Then the ship has been sitting in the temple for around eight thousand years, and waited in the dark for two thousand of those years. But when did they make the bomb?"

"I am uncertain about this. However, I thought it unlikely that they would have created such a malevolent device, one so vulnerable to the sun, before the last moment. If that were the case, it would surely mean it was made shortly before the sealing of the temple. And on this supposition, I searched more diligently through the archives dealing with the final hundred years."

"And ..."

"There was too much material to read. Let me say that it was a horrifying portrait of a society going mad. There were plagues and revolts, countered by increasing suppression and regulation of their society, a proliferation of laws and police and military. The temple sacrifices grew in numbers even as their population declined. They understood that in practical terms this was a mistake, but the gods demanded it, and their belief in their gods assured them that it was the only path to survival."

"From the plague, you mean?"

"From that. But more significantly, their astronomers were recording 'lights in the heavens' which had appeared in the direction of 'the beautiful planet', their planet of origins. They were told by the Night-gods that the 'servants of the sky-god' were gathering for a great battle and were coming to wreak vengeance on those who had escaped. Thus, more and more sacrifices to the Lord of the Night-gods were demanded in order to augment his power." Dariush paused, frowning, doubtless worrying about my theological limitations.

"You realize that there can be no such augmentation in purely spiritual terms", he continued. "It is the evil one's nature to compound murder upon falsehood. It was the unleashing of his hatred. As his sphere of influence shrank, he sought to destroy everything he could in the realm of living creatures."

"Uh ... but why the bomb?"

Dariush looked down at the papers in his hands.

"It took them ten years to make, and they began the project not long after the first sightings of a new 'star over the star of the beautiful planet', which is how they expressed it. Later, there were more celestial phenomena, 'fires in the heavens', which they called the 'warriors of the sky-god'. What these were exactly, and how they were manifested is not clear in the records. But one thing we know is that Nova's rulers felt threatened in a way they had not for thousands of years."

"And they thought a bomb would protect them?"

"No. They conceived it and built it as an act of vengeance against those who would come from the stars as servants of the 'sky-god'."

"Which, as it turns out, we are not."

"Some of us are." He paused for a moment and went on. "After selecting the archival material dealing with the hundred years leading up to the moment when the ship was locked behind the mountain gate, I searched for words such as *fire* and *flames* and *light*. I found that during the final ten years before the closing of the archives, these words appeared with increasing frequency, always in mythic terms and euphemisms."

Dariush held up a sheet of paper.

"This translation is from an archive tablet inscribed shortly before the final sealing of the temple. It tells of a prophecy that came through the mouth of the last Ap-kalu. He speaks of a people who will come from *the beautiful planet* in another heavens-ship. They will be servants of the sky-god, and they must be destroyed as the final insult and shaming of the sky-god. When the codex was composed, the rulers of Nova knew that their days were numbered. Their population had by then declined to a fraction of what it once was. Their cities were mostly empty, save for the one we call City 4, the last to be built and the last to fall into silence, unremembered for millennia. There, the rulers and religious hierarchy lived among a remnant population, with more and more dying every day. Even then, they demanded that the sacrifice of children must continue."

"You call it a prophecy. But how would their gods know the future?"

"The evil spirits could not know the future. Yet they could anticipate it. I think that the realm of the evil beings is one of fear as well as hatred. Thus they feared that the 'sky-god', who had been born on Earth and had overcome their dark lord on that planet, might one day go farther and bring the war to Nova through his servants.

489

And thus they whispered in the minds and hearts of their human vassals."

"Is there anywhere a mention of how they built the bomb?"

"Nothing that we would call science. Like other major documents, it is poetic in nature, expressed in terms that were meaningful for them but remain mysterious to us. Here is an example: *'Two flames of the Lord of the Night-gods lie sleeping in the belly of the beast that is sacred to the Lord of the Night-Gods'*—their name for dragon."

"And their name for the ship."

"Yes. Like a dragon, it is an entity that flies, it is consecrated to their evil deity, and it is deadly."

"What else does it say?"

"The text continues: *'One flame is lesser and one is great. The lesser will awaken the greater, that the light of the Lord of the Night-gods may shine forth, be it soon or in ages hence. Then shall the sky-god be shamed as in days of old, and all shall bow down and remember the one who ever rules the heavens.'* "

Again Dariush paused in his recitation.

"Go on,", I said.

" *'Prosperity and reward, the Lord of the Night-gods brings to the realms of man. Thus they will know that he bestows both good and ill, and those who follow him shall soar and know that they are gods.'* " Dariush cast a glance at me. "Here is the final entry, Neil: *'The gate is closed, and the chant of finding is placed in the middle tower on the high road that leads to bliss. The chant will show them the way.'* "

"The gate is closed?" I objected. "Wouldn't this mean the scribe was interred inside the temple? He would have archived the tablet and then lain down to die."

"Not necessarily. The gate may have been closed, leaving a single block open for the scribe to make his exit. No adult skeletal remains have been found in the temple crypt, despite our searches in all its sections. Though the millions of skeletons have not all been examined, the thousands that have been are, without exception, those of children. I think it likely that if the scribe had died there, his remains would be fairly close to the staircase or near the sculpture of his god."

"Well, it's a moot point. The deed was done. The chant indeed showed us the way."

Dariush sighed. " *'Those who follow him shall soar and know that they are gods.'* The ancient temptation, you see."

"Yes, I see", I replied. "And I see more than that."

"What do you see?" he asked expectantly.

"I see what religion does to human minds."

*

Throughout the following weeks, I performed my cleaning tasks, lit the kindling in the fireplace, and fed the fire with larger pieces of wood, ate meals regularly, and tried to walk a little every day. I sat in the arboretum sometimes, and after locating its audio control panel, I resumed my early morning habit of listening to Mozart. Music as wave of spirit? Was there really such a thing as spirit? Was spirit sub-subatomic energy? What then was personality? What was beauty, and why did it affect the human bio-mechanism as positively as it did the plants? When I noticed that some of the smaller bushes were wilting for lack of water, I located the irrigation controls and took over that task as well. Mostly I kept to myself, restless and brooding.

I recall sitting among the soothing trees early one morning. I had by then found a way to silence the artificial birdcalls. That day, I felt indifferent to the usual music and left it off. There was a control for the sounds of wind, however, so I set the volume to low, sat back on the park bench, and closed my eyes.

I was again in the desert of New Mexico, perched on a fallen mesquite tree. My father was beside me, and at our feet a campfire crackled as it consumed twigs and the dead husks of bean pod. Sweet smoke was in the air.

Benigno, he said, *I'd cut off both my legs if I thought it would help you walk straight.*

"How does a man walk straight in this life?" I whispered aloud. "How can a man know his duty?"

There is right, and there is wrong in this world, my son.

"This I know, *Papacito*, this I know. But where are the borders?"

The borders are not east and west, Benigno; they are not north and south.

"But how do I find them?"

Look up and you will find them.

"Look up to the sky?"

Look up to the heavens above the heavens.

"But that is what the aliens told us, the aliens who were ourselves."

491

I speak of another heavens, the true heavens which you will find.
"But it is too late for that now."
Only when a man's last breath has ceased is it too late. Turn now and climb.

The campfire crackled as I threw another handful of bean pods onto the flames. They burst and flared, their sparks rising into the blue sky above the desert of New Mexico.

I opened my eyes, and my father was gone.

*

Turn now and climb, he had said. But where would I turn? How would I climb? Gazing upward at the ceiling four stories above me, I watched electronic clouds passing across the illusion of infinite blue.

I returned to my room and sat down on the bed. I opened Xue's Bible at random and stared at the inscrutable text, straining toward what I had lost. I could only sense it and did not know what it was. An impressionist memory-bank of origins perhaps, *piñatas* and feast days, a thousand times kneeling in the dust of the plaza to receive the host on my ignorant tongue, my mother's tears, my father's inexhaustible courage in the face of defeat. Perhaps, too, I needed to know that Xue had been real. Though he was gone, the volume in my hands was a touchstone of his presence.

*

I remember Dariush as the signal presence during my last portion of life. There is anguish in the memories, because of what happened.

We shared several good exchanges before the end. I recall especially the evening he appeared in my doorway with a whimsical Persian smile on his face.

"Neil, I have come to invite you to a celebration."

"I'm not a crowd person, Dariush, but thanks anyway", I said.

"It will be a crowd of two, my friend. Won't you come? It is to honor a lady well known to us both."

"Pia?"

"Today is December 12th on Earth, and if the space/time continuum has not played us a mischief, we may still celebrate the feast of the Mother of Guadalupe."

"You know about her?"

"Who has not heard about her!"

His remark was highly debatable, but driven by simple curiosity, I got up and followed him.

He led me to the Mexican bistro, and therein I saw that he had been busy. Strings of multicolored Christmas lights had been hung from the ceiling, luminous in the darkened space. Chairs and tables had been pushed back, leaving only a solitary table and two chairs in the center of the room.

I half-smiled, wondering what he was up to. Like a gracious *maitre d'hotel*, he conducted me to the table and bade me take my seat. A white candle burned on the turquoise tablecloth.

From the bistro kitchen, he brought a steaming plate of tacos dribbled with salsa sauce. Back to the kitchen, he went and returned with another serving bowl. Setting it on the table with a flourish, he declared: "*Cucarachas*, Neil. I made it myself."

I burst out laughing. "I think you mean *enchiladas*, Dariush. *Cucarachas* are cockroaches."

He sat down and peered into the serving bowl, filled with tortillas smothered in hot chili peppers and sliced olives. Then he too erupted—a chortling old scholar's laugh, his face turning red, tears of hilarity slipping from his eyes.

Why did we laugh like that? How was it possible we were still capable of laughter? Did we no longer care that so many people had died? No, I think it was because we cared so much, and the silly joke gave us a temporary reprieve from the crushing grief. When we had recollected ourselves, we began to eat. There was a flagon of nova-berry wine too, and a bottle of cold Mexican beer that we split between us.

Later, we sat back and looked at each other. I laughed again. He chortled noiselessly.

"You know, Dariush", I said. "I think a lot about Kitha-ré and Pho-rion. Do you ever feel the way I do, that somehow you knew them personally? That they were part of your life?"

"Every day I feel this. I often reread their song. I try to imagine how it might have sounded when they sang it. Surely, they must have sung it together."

"They probably did."

"I ask myself what they would think if they visited the *Kosmos*."

"They would think they'd arrived at the bliss in the heavens", I said dryly.

"I suppose that is so."

"Or they would have thought they were dreaming. I'm still puzzled by their innocence—if that's what it was. How was it preserved in the midst of their civilization?"

"There is always a spark of goodness in the human heart, no matter how deeply buried in surrounding evils."

"There's always a spark of evil too, no matter how deeply buried in surrounding good."

"Yes, this also is true. However, I would call it a lightless place within us, rather than a spark."

"There's always a killer hiding inside of us. Do you remember the shoot-out the day the pioneers left for Nova?"

"I heard a great deal about that most amazing event, though I arrived too late to observe it."

"At one point, I aimed Paul's pistol at Larson's head. I was just about to pull the trigger. I wanted to pull it, but at the last moment, I pointed the barrel at the floor."

"You couldn't bring yourself to do it?" he asked with a solemn expression.

"I discovered I was quite capable of doing it. But I didn't."

"There is the inheritance of Cain inside each of us. And Abel."

"Yes, well, I suppose that's the case. The problem is, which will we turn out to be? One never knows until the moment arrives."

"One never knows", Dariush nodded.

For a time, we let the subject ride. I hoped it would fade out. It was veering too close to his belief system, and I did not want a repeat of our previous conversation.

But he was irrepressible, as I should have realized.

"Murder in the human heart", he said quietly. "The violence as old as the story of Cain and Abel. Lately, Neil, I've been pondering those two brothers, and it seems to me that in a sense we are like a third brother."

"A third brother?"

"We are witnesses to the scene through the hindsight of history, and yet we are also participants. When radical evil strikes, our instinctive response is to defend—especially to protect the innocent and vulnerable, is it not so?"

"Yes. That's a good thing, wouldn't you agree?"

"It is a necessary and just thing to do. Our response to evil, however, becomes problematic according to the ways we defend the good. In one form or another, this is the test we all must pass through."

"But when you see the evil that goes on back home, all the deaths, all the confiscations of children, the persecution of your religion, don't you ever feel an instinctive flash of horror, rage, and desire to kill the killers?"

"When I was younger, I overcame this instinct."

When I was young, I had nurtured the instinct, then shelved it, biding my time. Throughout the following sixty years, there had been no opportunities to make retributive or preemptive strikes against the atrocities. Always I had searched for a way to stop the killing, yearned to eradicate the killer class in some big decisive way. But I never found one.

"When I was younger", I said, "I did not overcome this instinct."

"I understand, Neil. Yet do you see how the temptation, if it is not recognized for what it is, will grow and grow? Then comes the desire to *definitively* solve the murderous tendency in human nature by applying radical therapy. Is there not a voice inside us suggesting that if we kill enough of the killers, then the world will become safe for good people like ourselves? Do you see how we presume that *we* are good? Is this why most of mankind applauds a world-system of absolute control over all aspects of life, public and private—because we have been convinced this is the only way to abolish violence?"

"That's what DSI is all about", I said. "It's what the world state has given us, and there aren't any other options."

"There are other options. They do not come easily to us, especially for those who must defend the weak. If there had been a third brother back then, on the terrible day when Cain's rage and jealousy drove him to murder, would he not have been put to this test? Driven by powerful feelings, would he have picked up a rock and killed Cain in turn? Would he have called it justice? Would he have seen it as a necessary act for the preservation of peace and security in the lands east of Eden?"

I did not answer him. In a sense, he was speaking rhetorically. In another sense, he was cutting straight to the core of my struggle with life itself. Too often, he had done this to me, engaging me in conversations that gradually drew me into one of his sermons. He just wouldn't leave well enough alone. He was my conscience-cricket, and it was getting on my nerves.

495

"Look, Dariush", I said irritably. "Your beliefs help you to avoid despair. They make you peaceful in the middle of a firefight. They promise you justice in a future heaven, and so you never have to fight for it here and now."

"Do you believe that?"

"Yeah", I said. "Yeah, I do believe that. I like you and respect you as a man, but you make the mistake of always presuming you're standing on the high road, and people like me are unenlightened. Maybe it's the other way around."

"If I have offended you . . ."

"Irresolvable questions", I murmured dismissively. "Have some more *cucarachas*."

He ate a token bite.

I ate one too, and not long after we parted.

*

Little did I know that the third brother would soon become the hand of justice—justice as he saw it. Arjuna rose up in our midst with Krishna standing behind him, pushing him on. Then Pinocchio stood up on his little wooden legs and lurched forward to resist him.

It was during our eighth month outward bound from Nova that the event occurred. We were then cruising at more than half-lightspeed, our navigation set for destination Earth.

One evening, I received another invitation to dine with the Captain. Dariush was also invited. Both of us were in an equitable mood as we walked along Concourse A toward the KC elevator, chatting about this and that. I told him I was concerned about the firewood consumption, that it might not hold out until we got home. He described new translations he was working on, temple codices. He was intrigued by what he called the "the psychology of ritual" and waxed didactic about the differences between cultic mind/brain processes and those of "authentic worship". He said that the abolition of formal religion in our times had created a new phenomenon, the "ritualization of spontaneity", which he believed was not in the least spontaneous or free but was, rather, an unhealthy frame of mind, producing in people a mental shell without a core. This in turn fostered a craving for "neo-transcendent experiences".

"Like that green dance in the temple?" I said.

"Like that serpent dance in the temple", he replied.

496

We boarded the elevator and ascended. The doors opened, and the conversation ended.

As we entered the Captain's dining room, he rose from the head of the table and warmly greeted us. There were new messages from Nova, he said, handing us print-outs. The news was good. A second baby had been born, healthy and full term, obviously the fruit of another illegal conception before departure from Nova. There were now twelve pregnancies. Cabins were being built, fields being turned over for planting grain, tubers, and beans. The pioneers had discovered a mammal that was akin to the bovine. It had been captured without great effort, and the small herd was adapting well to domestication. It produced abundant milk. The colonists were experimenting with making cheese. The wild "turkey" was a prolific egg layer. Hives of the wild stingerless bee had been found, full of honey, as well as wax for making candles. The laser saws had broken down, and there were no materials to repair them, but the manual bow-saws worked well enough. The men had constructed a forge and were making tools such as ploughshares, sawbands, scythes, axe-heads—there was iron in the hills.

The shuttle had exhausted its fuel and had become a temporary barn. Vladimir and two of the other men were building a wooden boat, on which they hoped to go down the river to the sea some day, an estimated three-day journey. Others were building a cart on which they would pile harvested hay from the natural meadows. They hadn't yet come to an agreement on a name for their community, but for now they were calling it "our village". Everyone was in good health.

The Captain declared that the evening's celebration would be in honor of our brave friends, whom he wished were here with us. "Or we with them", said one of the half-dozen flight crew seated around the table. Dariush and I sat down to join them, and friendly banter ensued. A trolley was rolled into the room, bearing steaming platters and bowls. The meal commenced. I was getting a little tired of Cajun food, but the evening as it began was congenial.

After supper, the Captain turned to me and Dariush and said, "Gentlemen, would you be interested in seeing a room with a view?" We both said yes, wondering what he meant.

Everyone went out into the hallway, and the Captain led us through a double door into the forward command center. I had not visited it before, and my first sight of it was overwhelming. Uncannily, it was not unlike the command center of the temple ship, though ours was brightly illuminated, with polished floors and off-white ceilings. Along both walls were numerous modules for particular functions, all lit up with a perplexing array of technology, blinking lights, and computer screens. There didn't seem to be anyone on duty. At the forefront of this long room, or hall, the uttermost command post stood like the wheel of an ocean liner. There was no wheel as such, but rather a sloped curving countertop embedded with large computer screens and more technology. Front and center were three comfortable swivel chairs facing the nose. Above the counter was a twenty-foot-wide horizontal window.

The Captain led us close to it and patted the central chair.

"The hot seat", he smiled. "I don't sit in it much. The ship is basically flying itself, and all we have to do is check instruments once or twice a day and make a record in the log."

I couldn't stop staring at the window.

"It's a digital image", explained the Captain. "Sometimes it seems more real than real. I'm not sure I like that, but it is very pretty."

The view ahead was one I knew from reading star maps. We were heading home. In eight years from now, that tiny star we called the sun would be a massive sphere of fire so bright we would not be able to look at it.

"Can you see the planets?" Dariush asked.

The Captain bent over his console and tapped buttons. The view through the window expanded rapidly, and now we could see our solar system in detail. The sun was the size of a marble and four of the planets were visible as pin heads. He expanded it further, and then we could see Earth, our small blue pearl, a conglomerate of pixels that was halfway between a square and a sphere.

"Not much to see at this point", he said. "It looks like it's still there. Or should I say the light is still reaching us, though it left the planet four years ago."

"Can we look at Nova?" I asked.

Again he tapped buttons, and there it was on the screen with a different configuration of constellations surrounding it. It was large enough that the continents were distinct. Only C-1 looked dead, partly visible as its western coast was swallowed by nightfall. C-4 was in the dawn of a new morning, shining and beautiful. Another zoom took the screen to a valley between the mountains and the ocean. From our present distance, the village was too small for recognition, but we knew its coordinates, knew where it was by the luminous computer dot shining at the bend of a river, twenty kilometers south of the mountains, sixty kilometers north of the sea.

The Captain pointed to the locater dot and said, "We'll be erasing that from the computer memory soon, along with any other reference to the location."

And that is when Arjuna appeared.

Behind us a voice said, "You will not be erasing anything from the memory."

Startled, the Captain and the rest of the crew turned around to see who had spoken. And there stood Elif Larson and six DSI agents in uniform. We had been so intent on the view screen that we hadn't heard them enter behind us. For a moment, no one said a word. We saw that the agents had pistols in their hands, little e-weapons that were either for stunning or killing, we weren't sure which.

The Captain calmly pressed a button on his console and glanced up at the screen. The locator dot disappeared. He pressed another button, and the screen showed our distant home system.

"Get away from that console", the Elf commanded. The Captain did not do as he was told. Instead he drew himself up to his full height and said: "You will immediately leave this deck and return to Concourse D, where you will confine yourselves for the remainder of the voyage, unless you are otherwise instructed."

In reply, Larson removed a folded piece of paper from his inside breast pocket and opened it. He addressed the Captain by name and informed him that he had committed crimes against the government and grave violations of the expedition's mandate. Moreover, he had just been heard planning another crime, the erasure of ship's records, which were the property of the government. There were witnesses.

The Captain's nerves were good. He looked Larson straight in the eyes and said with a voice that betrayed no emotion whatsoever: "It is a matter of supposition whether or not I have committed any crimes. It is a matter of fact that *your* crimes, Dr. Larson, are real. It is that which should concern you. There will be a hearing on Earth, and if you are found to be innocent, you will be released. If you are found to be guilty of murder and other infractions of civil liberty, you will face a prison sentence. I suggest that you would be wise to avoid compounding your crimes with more."

"Obviously, you do not know the law", said Larson.

"I have read the Manual thoroughly, as well as my own fleet directives. You are standing outside the law at the present moment, and I command you to leave this deck, where I am the sole authority."

"The Manual is bigger than you think", Larson countered. "Only my department has full access to the entire body of the laws governing this expedition."

"Oh? Tell me what sort of a law is readable only by its enforcers?"

"An effective law."

"A mockery of true law. Leave this deck now."

"No, you're coming with me. You are being taken into custody."

"The ship needs her flight officers."

"The ship, as you very well know, is programmed for the entire voyage and for docking in orbit upon arrival."

This was true, a point that could hardly be refuted.

"You forget the need for oversight, human monitoring."

"The ship monitors itself and corrects itself in the event of systems error, which has never occurred and never will."

"This crew is also the guardian of fail-safe."

"No more arguments, Captain. You will come along with us now."

"Dr. Larson, I have already sent a detailed account of your activities to Earth-base, along with the sworn and signed testimony of witnesses. Your guns will prove to be very ineffective against a court of law. I should inform you that this conversation is being recorded and simultaneously transmitted to Earth-base even as we speak."

"I don't believe you."

"You would be imprudent to disbelieve me. Of course, it will take four years to arrive there, but within eight years from now, you also will arrive there. Consider this carefully."

Larson grabbed the sleeve of the Captain's uniform and yanked him away from the console.

Now for the first time, I saw the Captain's anger. "Murderer of Siauliai," he growled in a low voice, "destroyer of the hill of crosses."

Larson took a step back and pointed his gun at the Captain.

The six men in the flight crew, who had followed the foregoing exchange as if they were paralyzed, now pressed close to their captain and stared menacingly at the company of DSI.

They in turn raised their pistols and aimed at the crew.

Does it sound like farce? Is it a scene out of a wild west film full of showdowns and shoot-outs, a cliché that has been lived or dramatized a thousand times over throughout our history? Well, that's the way it was.

And to this last, best western I must now add an account of my own part in it. If I were truly honest with myself, I would tear up these pieces of paper or burn them in the arboretum, or simply wait for everything to burn. But I will not.

Tell it, Neil.

During the whole confrontation, Dariush and I had stood nearby, Dariush a step to the right of the Captain and me farther back, both of us within the guns' firing line.

I felt the weight of Paul's Russian pistol in my jacket's right pocket. It was a revolver, loaded, with the safety on. I had carried it about with me ever since the aborted showdown at the shuttle bay. Like everyone else, I had been fairly certain that DSI was deflated and that we would probably have no more trouble from them. Nevertheless, carrying the gun gave me confidence. In part, it was a hankering after my youthful identity as the rider of the open range, the killer of snakes, armed and dangerous. And though I had not seriously believed that Larson was still a threat, it had given me some satisfaction to think that I could protect people from him in the unlikely event that he stepped out of line.

I slipped my hand into my pocket and flipped the safety off.

"Move!" Larson roared at the Captain. His humiliating defeat at the shuttle bay was visible in his gritted teeth, his flaring eyes.

"No", said the Captain quietly, firmly, and turned his back to him.

It happened very fast, no more than a few seconds. Paralyzed by confusion more than by fear, we watched as Larson stepped forward and put the muzzle of his weapon to the base of the Captain's neck. There was a click, a buzz, and the Captain fell to the floor, with a wisp of smoke curling up from his neck. Then Larson stepped over him and pointed the muzzle at the temple of the Captain's head. Click, buzz, the body jumped and lay still.

The flight crew leaped upon the agents, and lines of blue light shot in every direction. At the same instant, I lurched forward and withdrew my gun. Pointing at Larson, I felt the frustrations of a lifetime concentrated in this one burning moment. Larson now saw me and raised his gun to shoot me down, but in his panic, he misfired and then the weapon clicked and clicked and did not buzz.

I heard a voice cry out, "No, Neil!"

I had closed my eyes for a second. Larson would now die, but reflexively, I could not watch myself kill a human being for the first time in my life. I pulled the trigger. There was a tremendous bang, and my eyes flew open.

There, standing between me and Larson, was Dariush with his hands raised toward me. For a moment, he looked me in the eyes, and seemed to nod as if he understood, and then he collapsed. Now Larson was fully exposed.

I blew a hole in his chest. A surprised look crossed his face. Blood spurted from the wound, and he fell to the floor. I was astonished. I had never quite thought of him as a real person—he was made of polyplast; he was made of paper. Now I knew that he was flesh and blood like me.

Then it hit me like a hammer blow that I had just shot Dariush. I dropped to my knees and crawled to him, desperately hoping that the wound was not grave. But he was dead.

*

What did I do then? The DSI agents had been disarmed. There was no more danger. The Captain was dead. Larson was dead. Dariush was dead. Two pools of blood were spreading across the floor.

Did I weep? Did I cry out to God for help? Did I beg him to rewind the tape and record a different scene?

I did none of this. Instead I rose to my feet, and in a fit of insane rage I aimed at the ship's control consoles and fired bullets into them, one after another until the chambers were empty.

Why did I do that?

I do not know.

With shaking hands, I found a few more bullets in my pocket, and inserted one into the chamber. I put the muzzle to my temple. I pulled the trigger, but someone had grabbed my arm, and the bullet whizzed past the side of my skull and shattered a computer screen. Then my arms were pinned behind my back, and the gun yanked from my grasp. Silence fell upon the room. Those of us who were still alive stood there panting.

*

The remaining DSI agents on board were locked away in their own departmental prison, six people in all. The prison was found after a lengthy search, since the prisoners had not felt inclined to give directions to it. It was a maze of rooms and chambers occupying a wing of Concourse D, an entire annex unto itself. There was no reference to it in the ship's indices of services, nor was it outlined in the floor plans as illustrated in the Manual. The diagram of rooms in that area was a deception, a blanked-out zone with a few representative inner wall lines and the whole of it designated as "departmental administration". The room layout proved to be, in the concrete, quite different. It had a dozen detention cells and a medical section as well. I wondered if David had died in it.

Both Larson and the Captain were buried in space. Though I was hardly fit for human company, I attended Dariush's funeral, if funeral it was—a memorial service of some kind. I could barely stand to be there— me, his killer—but I owed him at least this. All those who were not in prison attended. Dariush had chosen that in the event of his death his body be kept in deep freeze until its internment on Earth. Before it was committed to the ship's morgue, several cleaning and cooking personnel and some flight staff knelt before the casket and prayed, among them our young Hispanic ensign. The majority stood back with bowed heads. They were still doing it when I left abruptly, unseen by any eyes. I returned to my room and code-locked the door behind me.

I spent the next week absolutely alone. I did not respond to knocks. I did not look at my e-mail. I had no means to do away with myself, other than by starving myself to death, and this I tried without success. I ate nothing and drank only a little water. Sisyphus redux. Inheritor of J. Robert's mantle. Einstein's Pinocchio. I want to be a real boy. Real boys create and destroy worlds. Real boys create and destroy themselves.

*

It was the Commander who pulled me out of my deadly plunge.

He came to my door one day and knocked. Lying prone on my bed, I did not respond. He knocked again and again. Finally, he shouted loud enough for me to hear him through the walls: "Dr. Hoyos, it's the Commander. I understand why you want to be alone. However, I need your help."

Still, I would not open the door.

"Sir," he continued, "I have the override code for your door, and I could open it from outside. But I wish to respect your privacy. Won't you give me a moment of your time?"

I whispered "Open" in Spanish, and the door disappeared.

The Commander entered my room.

"I know how you feel", he began. "We've all suffered a severe trauma. The Captain was my closest friend. Now I am in command of the *Kosmos*, and I have to ask you to help me. We're in serious trouble."

I got up and went into the bathroom, avoiding looking at my face in the mirror. I bent over and put my lips to the tap, taking a long drink.

"What kind of trouble?" I croaked.

He brought me up to the command center on KC. When we entered the flight deck, staff members were standing or seated before consoles, but any who looked up and recognized me merely gave a solemn nod or looked away, or tried not to see me at all.

The Commander and I halted before the Captain's consoles. There were three main ones within arm's reach of his chair and half-a-dozen others within a roll of the chair. What they were exactly I could not guess.

"We have considerable physical damage, as you can see", he said by way of opening. "There is likely some systems damage as well. This poses no immediate threat, since as far as we can tell the ship is flying true to course, which it will do all the way to Earth."

"What's broken?" I asked, looking around at the several consoles with blast holes in them and shattered circuit modules visible within.

"These three main ones are sub-controls of the ship's master control system—a component of the main computer, in other words. To put it in laymen's terms, this central one is for the nuclear/anti-matter propulsion engines, basically for stop and go. The one beside it is for maneuvering in zero gravity, connected to the auxiliary propulsion engines for changing course. This one over here is for the acceleration and deceleration controls that lower the forward and aft tubes for braking or speeding up."

"Can it be fixed?" I asked.

"We're hoping, and we have seven years to try to do it. The end of that period is when deceleration must begin. Deceleration is a long process. Are you following me?"

"I understand the process. You're saying that if we can't begin deceleration at the appointed time we're going to overshoot Earth's orbit."

"Yes, that's the main problem."

"Are the reactors destabilized?"

504

"No, they're fine. And thankfully, the propulsion engines had already shut down before the ... the incident. We're now coasting through space, you see, maintaining a constant speed. But when we approach the deceleration point, we'll need propulsion functional in order to initiate reverse thrust, a series of micro-bursts that gradually increase over a five-month period."

"And you're getting no response from test commands?"

"That's right. All kinds of circuits are down, and, to be honest, most of us here on deck have only a general concept of how they operate. We understand the buttons and buzzers, so to speak, but not how the neurons are connected."

"Do we have any electronics engineers on board?"

He shook his head. "They were all down at the temple that day, wanting to see the aliens' ship come alive."

"How many nuclear engineers?"

"One."

"Anti-matter people?"

"None, but they wouldn't have been much help anyway."

"Computer technicians."

"Two are aboard, but they weren't the people in charge of checking and troubleshooting the main system. They both are very good at what they do, programming and code analysis and the like, and in a pinch they can do some hard-wiring. But there are limits to their knowledge. Compartmentalization of skills and responsibilities was standard practice during the voyage. The people who could have fixed this are dead."

"In the explosion on Nova, you mean?"

"Yes. Add to the situation the fact that plenty of original design went into the making of the *Kosmos*, much of it protected by security clearance. There were secret protocols as well, none of which we've yet been able to locate, let alone hack into."

"So the technicians don't know what to do."

He nodded and exhaled. "We thought you would be able to tell us a few things. Anything might turn out to be a help. After all, you designed the ship."

"I came up with the mathematics and the integration of the branches of physics involved, not the actual hands-on mechanics of it."

His face fell.

"But I'll take a look and see what I can do."

I stared at the blast holes I had made in the consoles. I could hardly believe I had done that. But I *had* done it, and now I would have to pick up the pieces.

"There were a lot of people firing guns that day", said the Commander.

I glanced at him.

"It was a confused situation", he went on. "You may have saved some of the crew's lives. Those DSI agents looked fit to kill. Indeed, they killed the Captain."

He was being very kind. Yes, I had killed Larson, and yes, maybe this had given the crew enough time to overcome the agents. But I had also killed Dariush. I had shot the albatross, and then gone on a rampage that could well turn out to be the end of us all.

He seemed to know my thoughts, and doubtless this was because the truth of the matter was in everyone's thoughts.

"DSI weapons damaged some of the consoles", he said.

"Give me a few days to think about it", I said at last. "I need to do some brain work. We'll have to search the main computer and familiarize ourselves with how it works. There may be a trail to the master design of the ship's commands. There are other options, which we can discuss after we try a few things."

"Excellent!" he said, brightening.

"Does KC have a master fail-safe control?"

"Yes, but it's damaged too."

"You say there's been no alteration of course."

"None."

"That means there's no damage to navigation control."

"We're hoping that's the case. The N console was hurt but not as badly as others. It was done by an e-charge, not by a bullet. It doesn't mean we're guaranteed control of navigation at the other end of the voyage, but for now we're on the straight and narrow." He paused. "Look, Dr. Hoyos, can I suggest that you move up here to one of the KC apartments? It would be good if you were close at hand. Then we wouldn't have to break down your door every time we need a light bulb changed."

It was an attempt at humor, and a generous one it was. But there was no humor left in me.

"Thank you", I murmured. "I'll stay where I am for the time being. The silence helps me think more clearly."

He looked dubious. "Well, then, can I suggest you start taking your meals with us again. The cafeteria on deck A at the usual hours. It's where everyone is eating these days. Would you consider it?"

"You should throw me in prison."

He looked embarrassed. "No one's going to throw you in prison. You shot the man who shot our Captain. Let's leave it at that."

So we left it at that.

I returned to my room with much to ponder. I no longer wanted to kill myself. That would come later, after we were back on Earth. In the interim, I would help get us all home, and I would testify against DSI during the hearings, and I would do my best to convince the government that another expedition to Nova was the worst idea in the known universe. That was enough to live for.

*

We worked endlessly on the main computer during those first years. One of the technicians was an analyst, and he was also, by his own admission, a hacker. He wasn't the genius that David had been, but he worked his way deep into the system's quantum memory, and during the second year, he found our trail. There came a day when it led to where we had hoped it would lead. I won't try to explain this "thing", this zone or component or coded digital mystery. It would take a very long book to describe how it worked, and even then computer specialists would have a grueling task reading it and understanding it. In short, it was a layout plan for the circuitry of the entire ship. That sounds simple enough. But one would have to know the nature of this circuitry to realize how brilliant and how nearly impenetrable it was. For example, there were three tiers of fail-safe codes for every main system, including propulsion/anti-matter, internal functions, gravity, navigation, etc. It had been designed in such a way that if one fail-safe failed, the second cut in and took over. If the second failed, then the third took over. If the third failed, well then, we were cooked. No one had anticipated a man firing a bullet into a fail-safe over-sight console, the *Über*-fail-safe of the multi-faceted fail-safe system. That is just one of the things I had accomplished on that fatal day. I had blasted a little hole through the ship's immune system, and now we were very, very ill, perhaps terminally.

Discovery of this "zone", however, was only one step in piecing together how the ship operated and how the malfunctions could be corrected. We checked through every computer terminal in the public libraries, hoping to find a wayward back alley that would lead us deeper into the main memory and show us the connections to connections to connections. We word-searched endlessly and came up with nothing. Hacking deeper into the system produced no results.

Throughout several months, every room in the *Kosmos* was ransacked in the hopes that we would find a back-up system that bypassed the main computer with its defunct fail-safes. There were thousands of rooms, each with its *max* that had to be checked, the private ones as well as those of the myriad bureaucratic desks, plus the larger *maxes* in the administration offices of various departments. It was a hacker's free-for-all. We even picked our way through the medical clinics, and I spent one whole day deleting my personal medical records from the files of Drs. Sidotra, Arthur, and the director of Medicine (DDM had died at AS-VT).

I also took pains to go through the computers in the head office of DSI. My personal dossier in the latter was most interesting—and the most sordid. This alone I preserved as evidence, since it showed clearly that my psychotic demise had been carefully planned. There was a file on David Ayne as well, but it had been scrubbed clean, leaving a simple biography and the final notation, "Death by accident, *Mundus Novus*." I checked to see if Pia had a personal dossier, and indeed she did (I was to learn that 675 people had security dossiers, with Skinner and Larson exempted). Fastidiously collected were Pia and Paul's love e-mails to each other, which I left unread. There was a record of her faithful dispensing of the anti-psychosis drug. Somehow they had also come across her protest letter to the Captain early in the voyage. Penned at the bottom of the copy was a note: *Typical superficial alarm response. Otherwise reliable. No further action required.*

I checked into Paul's file. There, I found a long history of security investigations (unbeknownst to the observed man), and, again, copies of the love notes. There was also a psychological assessment (aggressive Alpha-male) and a letter from Larson to Skinner in socio-speak, referring to the head of Navigation as *Potentially troublesome—further surveillance recommended.* Then I checked Xue's and Dariush's dossiers, and in both there were documents tracing their involvement with our early anti-surveillance revolts. The investigation had been closed on both men with the summary notations: *Dupes of Hoyos or McKie, involvement ceased. No further action required.* Other than this, there were brief biographies and academic accomplishments.

Behind the department's bureaucracy section, we found the section where surveillance had been gathered. It was a room with digital recording modules and seats for a dozen staff members. It wasn't difficult to get through the security gates, a matter of hacking a simple access code, and opening up the files for what looked like every *max* on the ship. Residences were listed by individual sub-code numbers. For example, mine was R-B-124. I listened to an hour of my solitary mutterings, snores, and sneezes, etc. Fast-forwarding through days and months and years, I came across nothing but eccentric innocence. My e-surfing had been meticulously recorded, mainly research in the fields of astronomy and poisonous snakes. David had done what he said he had done.

I typed in Xue's room code and heard human breathing and occasionally some whispered Chinese words that may or may not have been prayers. His surfing had always been in the realm of physics and oriental poetry.

Stron's file was vastly more colorful, but, like those of the other conspirators, it revealed nothing particularly damning.

Then I selected random room numbers of people I didn't know. Nosey, unethical, but I was curious to know how far DSI had gone. It produced everything from the intimate to the banal:

A tap of a key, a woman's voice: "... so I said to her, if you bat your eyelashes at him one more time, I'll tell him what you're really like."

Tap of a key, a man's voice: "... yeah, but transistors were always vulnerable to current overload, burning out just when y'needed them."

Tap of a key, a woman's voice: "... Hi, Mom, thanks for the voice mail. I had a great birthday party with some friends. I don't really know if our time is the same as yours any more, but I thought about you all day."

Tap of a key, a man's voice: "... of course the Hydra was a hell of a car. My old man had three over the years, but he always said the magnetos were slowly killing us, like we're strapped inside a magnet, he said, and it was messing up our brain cells."

It was impossible to listen to and read the records of hundreds of people surveilled over the course of so many years. Our crew was forced to concentrate on key individuals in the computer department, and while this offered our best hope, in the end it produced nothing that we could use. We also went through the ultra-secret DSI internal staff records, hoping that we would stumble across a lead. The executives' files were minimalist in quantity and sparkling clean in content. Here too, the files of Skinner and Larson were empty.

We located the wing on deck A where DSI executives had lived. Searching the spacious apartments, we learned that Skinner was a lover of vampire novels. In his desk drawer, under lock and key, was an e-manuscript in progress, titled *Psychopathia Socialis*. It wasn't about vampires; it was about *us*, the space voyageurs. Larson's private hologram screen revealed that he was a lover of razor-board racing and pornography. In neither of these rooms was there a *max*. They may have had portable *max*es in the briefcases they had always carried with them, but these were missing. Their personal offices likewise failed to produce anything helpful.

I felt a certain pathos when I investigated the suite where the Nephew had lived. Though it was next door to Don and Raydawn's place, it was not quite as large and luxurious as theirs. His bedroom was just as he had left it. It resembled the lair of a spoiled adolescent, strewn with clothing and electronic gadgets, including his collection of cameras. There were, however, numerous folios of the very fine photographs he had taken on Nova, mainly landscapes and wildlife. On the bedside table, I found a journal of sorts. Like me, he had used pen and paper. Guiltily, I read a few pages, lying to myself that I might find clues to solve our computer problems. It was pure curiosity, of course. I wondered what it had been like for him, considering his position in the world, this unfriendly offspring of the uppermost echelon of privilege and power. I found that, for the most part, during the past ten years he had struggled with an excruciating sense of depersonalization, a loneliness so deep that he had come close to suicide on a number of occasions. There were several references to his uncle, expressed in tones of contempt, even hatred for what the man represented.

"I am invisible", he wrote early on in the journey. "I am an image. I am defined by a biological accident that places me close to the pinnacle of absolutism."

There was much in these pages that revealed he was a shy introvert, albeit one who was capable of acting the confident extrovert. In his inner life, he felt imprisoned by solitude, ever searching for "the Real", as he called it, ever searching for meaning within the closed circle of himself. Throughout the voyage, he had chosen to live as a recluse because he could not trust that others would value him as a person independent of his status. Now I understood why he had spoken to me so rudely that day, years ago, when I interrupted him in the library reading Shakespeare sonnets.

The final line of the journal, probably written hours before his death in the Temple, reads: "It is yet possible that I will find love. It is not impossible that I will learn to love."

It was all very sad, and I felt some regret that I had not pushed harder to break through the walls of his isolation.

*

In summation, our investigations brought a solution no nearer. Despite our every effort, we had turned up not a hint of an ultra back-up system. This left us no choice but to launch a painstaking search through the holds down on PHM, in the hope that we would stumble across replacement consoles. It seemed to me that it would be a strange oversight to neglect storing replacements for such crucial items, and thus I and my fellow searchers launched a new kind of expedition.

The men in charge of holds were eager to help, and they lent a hand all the way. They opened their records of the manifest, and we pored over these lists, looking for anything that might even remotely be understood as mechanical or electronic. It took us years to go through the stores, as we opened every single box in the onboard warehouses. There were times when I was so fascinated by some of the items we found, I completely forgot for a few minutes that we were racing against time. For example, there were trunks full of glass beads and shiny trinkets (for trading with natives, I suppose). There were boxes of salt and pepper shakers in discordant designs (clowns, male and female donkeys, black and white poodles, film stars). There were barge-loads of women's cosmetics, eighteen thousand tooth brushes, and a far greater number of toothpaste tubes, a mountain of boxes containing condoms ("Nature's Best"), alongside digital clocks and antique wind-up alarm clocks, three cuckoo clocks, an enormous African drum with a synthetic zebra-skin top, a crate full of axes (regrettably unseen by the pioneers when they scrambled through the area looking for things to take back to Nova), a ton of laundry detergent, and so forth. It was like a general store gone mad, and eventually we searchers were numbed by the sheer volume and variety of items, the bulk of it thoughtfully chosen by the quartermasters who had outfitted the ship, but some of it simply bizarre.

We also checked the other major hold, which contained all the samples brought from Nova. A good deal of this was minerals, but nearly half of the space contained endless shelves of flora, small reptiles and amphibians, and microbiological samples suspended in vials of liquid preservative. There were thousands of insect species in display cases, including the flamboyant butterflies. Enormous freezer lockers contained the bodies of hundreds of animal species captured and killed, dissected or vivisected, and preserved for further studies back on Earth. This section was investigated more quickly than the others, though I lingered there a while to placate my curiosity. Many of the specimens were creatures I had not seen on the panorama screen and *max* presentations. I put an end to my diversion, however, when I came across three huge bodies of the giraffe-like creatures hanging from hooks in a freezer locker, a male, a female, and a yearling. The mother's abdomen was splinted open with a transparent pane inserted, showing a dead baby *in utero*.

We also searched through the food holds on the remote chance that a console might have been mistakenly stored in the wrong place. Suffice it to say that the things we stumbled upon pleased the cooks, who were ever ready to try new recipes. The liquor holds beckoned me, but I resisted. Staying sober was now a life-and-death matter.

This search took us well into the fifth year after the gunfight, and it produced no results that would solve our problem.

*

Others had been busy throughout this time, teaching themselves circuitry from manuals downloaded off the main computer. This master brain continued to confound us, since it faithfully performed its maintenance of the internal life-support and life-comfort services. It was like a man who had had a stroke. Some of his limbs worked and some didn't; portions of memory were intact and others weren't. We were endlessly baffled by it, though in a general sense we knew that the damaged sections were restricted to the part of the cortex which determined where the ship was going and how it would get there.

At first, we had believed that only the consoles had been damaged, a circuit connection problem, like the broken spinal cord of a quadriplegic. All his organs still functioned, but he could not control them, could not feel them from the neck down. Above all, his mind was clear. Later we learned, through deep probes into the main computer, that the e-bolts fired accidentally into the consoles on that terrible day had sent charges back down the line and into the computer, jumping circuit breakers and other kinds of safety blocks. It had all happened in less than a second. The damage was not just physical; it was, so to speak, mental.

The *Kosmos* was still on course, relentlessly approaching the year when deceleration should begin. And this was our single most daunting challenge—how to initiate the reverse thrust engines at the precise moment in the precise quantity that would slow us at the right time and in the right sequence, avoiding the alternative disasters of, on one hand, the instant liquefaction of us all by hitting the brakes too hard, and on the other, a continuing plummet through the cosmos at one hundred and seventy thousand kilometers per second, taking us beyond our solar system into infinite space. The latter option seemed preferable by far, for we might live comfortably for a very long time with our resources, like a person in a splendid city who has everything he needs, and never leaves it. Manifests indicated that there was food for a thousand people for ten more years, and we were roughly a tenth that number. The number of pioneers who had returned to Nova was 67, which left 110 now on board. At the very least, we could thrive for another century, unless we slammed into a star in our path, which was statistically nearly impossible, given the vast spaces between stars. However, without exception, we all desired to return to our troubled planet. Despite its faults, it was our home.

The single surviving nuclear engineer was an elderly Czech with a keen mind and limitless knowledge of reactors as sources of energy. He had been hard at work ever since the gun-battle, familiarizing himself with the operation of the ship's unique propulsion functions, about which he had less knowledge. His area of responsibility during the voyage had been the monitoring of the auxiliary reactor that gave us heat and light and hot water. There was a separate primary reactor for propulsion, but its keepers were gone, and so he tried to acquaint himself with this as well. He told us with profound apologies that the mechanics of lowering and raising the reverse-thrust engines, and operating them with proper timing and burst quantity (a function that only a computer program could accomplish), were simply beyond his capabilities. Even so, he spent seven long, mentally arduous years studying the mechanics and program manuals to see what he could learn.

He was often frustrated by gaps in the manuals, zones of information blanked out because of patent or security reasons. He had a fit of temper or two, demanding to know why there was no override code for such blocks, why there was no command center in the propulsion department that bypassed the master computer and bypassed the KC control, why the people who made this ship were so stupid, and so forth. None of us had an answer for him. He became morose toward the end and took to drink. To his credit, he continued to strain himself to the outermost limits of his capabilities, writing new programs that he hoped would reconnect the mechanics to the main computer, though the tests he made with these proved to be useless.

The community was canvassed to see if there might be individuals among them with electronics or computer skills—or any other kind of technical or mechanical knowledge. It was a long shot, but one never knew where a genius or savant might pop up. A few cleaning people stepped forward, and, after hesitating a little, they said that maybe they could figure out what was wrong with the ship's computer. They confessed that they knew how to cannibalize personal computers and had built their own in times past. One man had been a welder back home, and he also knew how to use a soldering gun for finer work. Another told us that before the flight his hobby had been in the field of shortwave radio. When he was younger, he had built several sets from scratch, despite it being illegal. He also knew a lot about radar and analog pulse-density modulation, though his first love was ancient crystal radio sets. So we took these people on and explained our problem to them—rather, the little we knew about our problem. Nevertheless, after years of tinkering and experimenting, nothing effective came from it.

*

The communications system continued to work just fine. Early on, our pioneers knew about our plight, though the time lapse between appropriate responses back and forth grew steadily longer as our distance from Nova increased. None of their company was able to offer solutions. In the same proportion, our communications with Earth-base became ever more synchronized as the distance between us decreased.

During the final two years, they radioed a massive amount of data to us, with the blocked-out information zones supplied. The new material made sense to the computer people, and they accomplished much in terms of transferring operations portions of the damaged "brain" to unused data banks. Again and again, they tried to restore broken or zapped consoles, rebuild and rewire and fire up the circuits, but their trial runs failed to solve our major problem. Despite all efforts, the reverse-thrust engines refused to lower beneath the body of the ship. There was an improvement of neural connections, a rebooting of some secondary functions, but not enough to make deceleration happen.

*

During the month before the approaching deceleration event, I fought a growing despondency. Many others struggled with the same thing. On the whole, this was a time when optimists were sifted from pessimists, but no one could know which of the two were realists.

I, employing my favorite conflict-resolution method, turned to drink. I should say *returned*—vodka, the pain-killer of my youth, my old best friend. I spent a lot of time in the panorama room with a jug in my hand, watching our approaching solar system grow larger. If I had not gone off on a shooting spree seven years ago, if I had not indulged in my little tantrum, we would soon have begun our long, gentle approach to Earth's orbit, right on schedule. Now I would spend the rest of my life in outer space, eating and drinking merrily, if I did not shoot myself.

The Commander had returned the gun to me. Presuming it was my mine, he had handed it over, without bullets, somewhere around year five of the homeward journey. Later, with the aid of some house-breaker skills, I located a box of bullets in Paul's apartment, hidden under a copy of Dostoevsky's *The Idiot* in his bedside table drawer.

Thus armed, I was prepared to meet any eventuality.

*

Now I come to the events that determined the end of it all.

Those of us who had tried to save the ship throughout these past years gathered together in the command center on KC deck to observe the moment when deceleration should rightly have begun. It would be a non-event, we were certain, yet we felt it necessary to be present. We would see that the ship continued to hurl itself placidly into infinity, without resistance, confirming what we already knew.

The moment came and went. Nothing changed on the screen above the command module. There were no shudders from ignition of counter-thrust, which was as it should be, since the reverse engines remained doggedly inside the ship. Now we knew that what we had anticipated would be enacted as fact. Our future lay out there among the stars.

And then the inconceivable happened. A man came running forward from the navigation department and cried out that the maneuver vents had begun firing. The ship was turning a fraction of a degree.

And it continued to turn, degree after degree.

People scrambled in all directions, consulting the intact instrument consoles and those that had been rebuilt, checking readings and shouting out what they were seeing on their screens.

The Commander strode back with the navigation man to his section. I followed them and stood behind them, listening.

"I don't know why," said a lieutenant commander, "but we're turning on a tangential course."

"But what's making it happen?" asked the Commander.

"I have no idea why the maneuver vents are suddenly functional. But they *are* working. They're turning the ship as if we have begun deceleration."

"Will we penetrate the orbital plane according to return flight plan?"

"I'm not entirely certain yet, but if the course correction continues, we may be retracing the outbound flight plan made nineteen years ago."

"What?"

The man looked down at his console. "It's really too early to tell, but the readings are changing steadily, the ship adjusting our trajectory moment by moment."

The man watched his screens for a time. We stood by him silently, unable to assess the meaning of the complex time/space data he was looking at.

Finally, he looked up with a frown. "Factoring our track of adjustment, the computer is extrapolating that we'll be coming in *on* the orbital plane.

"But we're not decelerating."

"I know, sir. And that means we have a situation here. We're bearing on course for intersection with Earth-orbit at too high a speed."

"Could it be a stellar compass error?"

"All the instruments give the same readings."

"When do we intersect with Earth-orbit?"

"It would have been five months from now, if we were decelerating steadily. If we maintain this velocity, and if the auto-navigation continues to correct for the differences between low-speed and high-speed trajectories, we have approximately seventy-two days, *Kosmos* time, before impact."

"Impact?"

"I'm afraid so."

"You mean there's a navigational lock on the planet?"

"It looks that way. We'll know more as we observe the ship's progress."

"Change the course, Lieutenant Commander; put us out into space."

The man bent over his console and tapped command keys, checked his screen, read instruments, and looked up.

"It's not responding."

"That can't be", said the Commander in a calm voice. "If the maneuvering system is working and if it can send data to you, we can send data to it."

"It doesn't seem to be receiving it, or maybe it's ignoring it. It's not responding to commands."

"Then shield the navigation intake, or shut down the N system entirely."

The lieutenant commander tried both and fixed his eyes on his screen.

"It's not responding either, sir. It's got to be an auto-function that's blocking our commands."

The Commander turned on his heel and went forward to his post. I followed close behind him. He clicked the ship's communications network and spoke into it, calling all computer people to KC immediately.

The Commander then sent a message to Earth-base, informing them what was happening.

*

Continuous searches were made in Navigation's innermost control center, deep in the ship's energy section on PHM. But a manual control for the off/on function, if there was such a thing, was never found. In our present situation, the absence of such a mechanism seemed to be an insane omission on the part of the ship's designers. Placing limitless confidence in the KC terminals, they had not foreseen this kind of crisis. Thus, our frustration steadily gave way to feelings of suppressed panic. Weeks passed, technicians came and went, slaved over terminals with shaking hands, but in the end, they threw up their arms in dismay, as perplexed as anyone else.

When the reply from Earth arrived, it was coded top secret. The communications people had decrypted the message and printed it out in plain English for the Commander's eyes only. I was standing beside him when he read it quietly to himself. His face paled, and then he turned to me as if he did not see me. The paper had fallen from his hands. I picked it up and read it. He was instructed by Earth-base, on the authority of the World Federation, to destroy the ship. For a moment, the Commander stared at me, and then he seemed to recognize me. A wave of bitterness washed across his features, but he said nothing and abruptly turned away, heading toward the exit door. I caught up with him as he was entering the KC elevator. He ignored my presence, his face still white, his brow sweating.

We got out on PHM, and made our way swiftly to the propulsion department.

The Czech engineer was sitting in an easy chair beside the main reactor, chuckling to himself as he watched a comedy on his mobile *max*. The Commander tried to catch his attention courteously, but the engineer scowled and ignored him.

The auxiliary reactor was humming, and I could hear the faint whisper of the maneuver vents firing outside the hull, turning us slowly, slowly, toward our final destination.

The Commander picked up the *max* and shut it off. Then he described the situation to the man and instructed him to shut down all electric power in the ship.

"Do you mean flip the switch, boss?" the other asked with an ironic look.

"Shut *everything* off", the Commander snapped. "We have to kill the navigation."

"Turn it off upstairs, why don't you?"

"The navigation commands aren't working."

"With my deepest apologies, boss, but there is no switch down here. I can turn off nothing."

"What! This is the energy source for the ship!"

"Yes, but the designers cleverly protected it from us fallible human beings. No one is allowed to shut off *all* the power with one click. You see, we always need air, we need water, we need—"

"Then how do we do it?"

"You would have to spend two days unlocking the fail-safes for the ship's energy system. This requires three engineers, each with his permission and unique code-key. I can show you the service portal, if you wish. But it won't help you. There are back-up batteries too—somewhere else, not here—navigation will continue to run even if the reactor is shut down."

The Commander fumed, his lips working angrily.

"Put the reactors into meltdown", he barked. "The ship must be destroyed."

The engineer looked at the Commander as if the latter were insane.

"What are you talking about?" he huffed.

"Blow this ship up!"

"A reactor meltdown does not cause a nuclear explosion", said the engineer as if he was trying to explain the obvious to a tedious child. "It will produce steam, yes; lethal radioactive emission, yes; fire, yes; some damage, yes; but there will be no large explosion. Besides, this ship is stronger than the containment building of a power plant."

"Then how do we demolish it?"

"You cannot ... unless ... unless ..."

"Tell me, man, and make it quick!"

"We power up the deceleration tubes from the propulsion reactor—anti-matter-catalysed fusion. Reverse thrust, you see. The tubes fire *inside* the ship, and then we break into pieces. Simple, no?"

"Simple", the Commander murmured. "Then do it—and do it now!"

The engineer put a little flask to his lips and took a long drink from it. He sighed and said, "I have no controls for it here. You must do it from KC."

Back upstairs, we went at a run down the corridors into KC command and arrived at the deceleration console. I closed my eyes, preparing myself to be disintegrated. Command after command was entered, but nothing happened.

None of the anti-matter gurus had survived the blast on Nova. If Xue had been here and given enough time, he might have been able to rig the anti-matter propulsion units to backfire into the ship or, with luck, collapse our entire mass into a microscopic black hole. But he was not here.

Navigation people came forward and informed the Commander that the instrument readings continued to show that the ship was adjusting itself perfectly for intersection with Earth's orbit, and if the present course continued we would impact with the planet within thirty-eight hours.

*

They tried everything possible to change us from a massive missile into a fine rain of debris. On the last morning of my life, when I realized that we could not stop what was about to happen, I returned to my room on deck B. There, I changed my clothing, dressing myself in my fine black suit, which I had last worn for Pia's wedding. White shirt and bolo tie. My old snake knife snapped into its case at my waist. I shined my cowboy boots. As an afterthought, I shaved my face and combed the few remaining strands of my hair.

"It's my party", I snorted at the contorted face in the bathroom mirror.

As I was preparing to leave my quarters, I happened to glance at the poet-deer on the shelf. This in turn led to a bitter last look at Xue's Bible and his slide rule. After filling the revolver chambers with bullets, I tucked the weapon into my belt. Then I went out and found the closest bistro. I took a jug of vodka from its stores and went forward to the panorama hall.

The room was empty. I was relieved because I wanted to be alone for this. I sat down on the padded bench, front row center, the best seat in the house. Now I would watch the greatest epic in the history of film.

The screen was 3D real time. We had just passed Pluto, with about seven hours to go until impact.

Speed gives you relativity. So does alcohol. During those inebriating hours, I laughed and laughed and sipped and sipped. What kind of laughter was this? I do not know. It was black and bitter in a way that I had never before experienced. Not merely the absence of internal light, a dying bird struggling blindly in a tar pit. No, it was something closer to the inversion of light into a deeper inversion of darkness—a psychological mobius loop that twisted upon itself in an infinite descent.

Spiraling ever downward, I looked inward to the fast-flashing film of my life, its unceasing honors, its secret failures. Its losses and helpless rage, its murderous ambitions in the name of justice, the spiral staircase, which I saw myself shattering with an axe. And mixed with these were the dreams I had had during the voyage—the images thrown up by my subconscious—the aged woman in a turquoise sari looking at me with love, the girl bringing me a golden bowl of food, offering it to me if I would accept, urging me to eat, calling me *pitaji*. Then more fractured images: Alvaro with a bullet shattering his skull, my mother with her belly cut open and my brother and sister pulled from her body like rats. My own beautiful children leaping into a lake of floating water lilies, then me leaping and laughing in the ocean waves with them at my side, and the boy playing the cello—my son, or myself as I might have been. I saw the love running through everything, oft-beleaguered love, and love now dying in the suction of absolute despair, the approaching conflagration of all love, the final extinction of love.

By now, Earth had realized we were its incoming nemesis. We flashed through a barrage of nuclear missiles, too fast for them to lock onto us. Then we penetrated mine fields, a needle at lightspeed, passing through a haystack without touching a straw. There were explosions in space behind us as we touched the mines' sensors and in split seconds were beyond their range as they detonated.

Now there were only a few contracting hours left.

The auto-navigation had set the course years ago, locked, fused, fated by my hand. I am become Death, the destroyer of worlds. I had climbed my own stairs. I had *made* my own stairs, and now I would see where they led to. Behind me were several hundred deaths that would not have occurred without my genius intervening in their lives. Ahead of me were billions upon billions of deaths.

I looked at the gun in my hand and pondered it. Should I put the muzzle to my temple and execute the executioner with Paul Yusupov's weapon, Prince Felix' weapon? Shoot Rasputin's demon or *el ojo del Diablo*? Blow a hole in the hole?

Then I wondered if it wouldn't be better, after all, to cut my throat. I patted the kit at my waist, and felt the old knife that I had owned since boyhood, the very blade with which I had incised my leg, stabbing at the poison that would have killed me young. And here it was again, the blade open, hilt gripped in my left hand, ready to slice through the pulsing jugular, my final, futile attempt to defeat the serpent's venom, because *El Día de los Muertos* had arrived at last. This day would kill me, but I would kill myself first and prove my mastery over life and death.

Yes, I can do that, I thought. *I would like to do it. It would be a token repayment for what I have done. But it is the easy way.*

I lowered the gun and the knife.

"No, Neil", I declared. "You are going to watch this to the moment of impact. You will see the ultimate bonfire of your vanity."

The ship passed more mine fields. Earth had analyzed our speed and trajectory. Now, they were detonating all the fields on the chance that the *Kosmos* would be in the middle of one at the exact microsecond when the atomic blast occurred. It was their last best hope, and it was useless. We sped onward through thousands of detonations, and none of them touched us.

"Scatology heads of the fifth dimension!" I sneered. "Always counting on your technology—worshipping it, drugged by it, and killed by it."

Yeah, me too—the biggest scatology head of all time—the killer of killers and the killer of the innocent. The tyrants were all there on the target. And so were the red blossom children.

I could pray, I thought. *I could ask for mercy from the God I don't believe in, the maker of galaxies and wooden staircases. I could ask him to stop this ship. I could beg him to save the billions upon billions I am about to kill.*

For an instant, I wanted to pray for this. But I could not, because hope beyond all hope was not objective reality, because it was not rational, and most of all, because it was absurd to believe the impossible. For I knew that at the end of everything, there are no little old men with burros and jingling bells arriving from nowhere to save you.

"Watch it all", I said aloud. "Watch it all until your eyes are vaporized, the ship is vaporized, the impact crater in the land or the sea is vaporized, and a hole is drilled so wide and deep into the molten core of Earth that its bowels spew out and the atmosphere ignites and death spreads its final word across the face of the earth in a firestorm that leaves nothing behind. You won't feel a thing. You won't hear anything at all. You will fall into the mouth of the Lord of the Nightgods, and you won't even care."

How many hours were left? It did not matter, O obsessive measurer, O calibrator of mankind's end! Matter—anti-matter. Christ—anti-Christ. Time—anti-time. Minutes, hours, days, millennia, eons—all were meaningless.

There was a man standing near me. He had walked into the room without me seeing him at first. Then he stepped in front of the screen and blocked my view. His thoughtlessness enraged me.

"Do you mind?" I growled.

He turned, and I saw he was carrying a little black dog in his arms.

"*Hola!*" he greeted me in Spanish.

"Yeah—*hola*", I said back at him.

"It looks bad", he said.

"You think so, do you?"

"Maybe we'll be okay."

I stared at him and felt a wave of disgust at his naïveté.

"Go away", I snapped.

"I do not want to go away, *Señor* Hoyos", he replied in a quiet voice.

And then I knew who he was. This was the young ensign I had met at the Captain's table. I had written my address on a napkin for him. He was almost a parody—short, chubby, a bit of a moustache, kindly eyes, a thatch of black hair that should have been cut long ago. A white uniform none too clean.

The dog whined and buried its nose in the crook of his elbow.

"This is Feedo", he said. "Poor Feedo, his master and the lady die in the bomb on the planet. I look after him now, but he is very old. He is blind, and he is, you know, not always listening to me."

"You should go to your room", I said. "Lie down and go to sleep. You won't feel a thing."

"But I want to feel, *Señor*. I am awake. I am alive."

"Not for long."

"Is your cabin in the mountains of Santa Fe very nice? I would like to visit you, as you asked me."

"It's nice, but you won't be visiting me there."

"I would like to build a house where my parents could live."

"Well, that's unfortunate. I guarantee you won't be my neighbor."

"They say we will burn."

"That's right. Everything will burn."

"Are you afraid?"

"No", I said.

"I am a little bit afraid. But I think *Nuestro Señor* will come for us."

"*Nuestro Señor?* I hate to tell you, but it's too late for all that."

"It is not too late."

I said nothing. The rings of Saturn rolled past.

"*Nuestra Señora* will help us. She will pray for us."

"You think so? Take a look at the screen. In a couple of hours from now, we're going to smash the biggest *piñata* of all time. And it won't be candy that spills out."

For a time we stared at the big show. He stroked the whimpering dog. I drank.

"*La Madré*, she crushed the serpent's head, *Señor*."

"What is your name?" I asked, though it didn't matter what his name was.

"My name is Manuel."

"The serpent has won, Manuel. He devours everything."

"No, he will not devour everything."

He put the dog on the floor, where it curled up and went to sleep. Then he sat down in the seat beside me, too close. I looked away. What did he want from me? Comfort? A word of hope? Soon he would be dead because of me.

"Go away, Manuel", I told him. "Don't watch this."

He did not look at the screen, the final hypnotic film of man's demise. Instead, he gazed into my eyes and said: "*Pobrecito, Neil, estás tan triste. No te pongas triste, no estés triste. Todo va a estar bien.*"

Stunned, I stared at him. I knew those words!

"What!"

He said it again. Then he knelt down on the floor beside me and began to sing. It was some kind of prayer-song. He closed his eyes and lifted his arms, and the singing went on.

I glanced at the screen and saw Jupiter approaching.

"You must pray too, Benigno", he said.

"Why did you call me *Benigno*?" I shouted, hating his stupid face.

He did not answer, merely increased the volume of his prayer, pleading with *Nuestro Señor*.

I reached into my jacket pocket—I don't know why. To feel the power of a gun or a knife, I suppose.

One of my hands closed over something strange that felt like brittle paper and small sticks. I pulled it out to toss it away and saw in the palm of my right hand a bundle of the seed pods I had collected in the crystal forest on Nova. I shook them absentmindedly. They chimed.

And with that sound, something within me cracked. Tears sprang to my eyes, and I fell backward through time, back through the maze of many years and the complicated paths I had taken, back into the still pure moment when, as a child, I had danced and sang and rang my little bells in a desert. Without thinking, hardly knowing it, I slid from the chair and onto my knees.

I closed my eyes. I could not pray. But I was no longer a vortex of anti-light, no longer a void. In my soul, I saw only what I had once been—my small, young heart as I danced and sang and rang my bells, looking upward into the deep field of the infinite. I saw this and nothing more.

Manuel resumed praying as I wept.

We had just passed Jupiter's moon Ganymede when Manuel suddenly dropped his arms and looked at me with wonder.

"*Señor*, I have seen something. In my heart, I see a room within a room. I see a bridge. And I am the bridge."

"A bridge?"

He stood abruptly and took my hand, making me rise to my feet.

"Come", he said. "There is little time."

Pulling me by the arm, he led me swiftly from the hall and to the closest elevator. Inside, he pressed buttons on the console, we descended, and got out on PHM. From there, we hurried along the concourse to a cross street and turned left on it. Now we were in a section of service bays for the energy grid, a wide avenue bordered by metal doors. I had seen them before, time and again, whenever I accompanied technicians blindly groping inside the ship's complex systems, searching for a solution that had ever eluded us.

Manuel halted before a door on which was printed a large letter *N*. He threw it open and stepped inside. We were now in the entrance foyer to navigation's energy section. A workbench on the wall opposite was littered with tools and small electronic components. Without hesitation, Manuel grabbed a spool of bare copper wire and then sprinted toward yet another door, leading deeper into the interior.

"What are you doing?" I asked, following close behind.

"I see it", he said, striding forward into a maze of structures that resembled a great city at night, with thousands of windows blazing. He merely kept moving, now this way, now that; to the right down a corridor between waist-high boxes with blinking green lights, then left, up an alleyway between walls of circuitry tracks sealed beneath transparent covers. We were ants crawling through a giant computer.

"This way", Manuel muttered to himself, without slackening his pace as he swerved into a cross street of consoles, all their lights blinking orange and red.

"How do you know where to go?" I called after him.

"I am listening", he called back and then turned right into a street of higher consoles and disappeared.

I caught up with him a minute later, where he stood poised on the brink of a canyon about eight feet wide. We both peered into its lightless depths but could see no bottom to it.

"The place we must go is ahead. It is there", he said, pointing to a raised track on the far side of the gap.

He dropped to his knees and unrolled a few feet of wire from the spool.

"Give me your knife", he demanded. How did he know about my knife?

I handed it to him, and with it, he cut through the polyplast coating of a circuit track on our side of the canyon. That done, he slid one end of the copper wire beneath a metal filament and wrapped it around several times, and knotted it so that it would not slip off.

"It is not hot", he explained, turning to me with large, black eyes. "But across this arroyo is another that is hot—you know, electric current is running. These two must connect."

"But how?"

On the opposite side of the gap, the wall was sheer, leaving only a four-inch shelf along which ran the other circuit track. It would be impossible to jump to that side and not fall into the depths.

"A bridge is needed", said Manuel. "You see, there are two roads, one on each side. This one has secret wound far along its track, deep in the body, but the scientists they have not found it. Here is the way to fix."

"B-but how?" I stammered.

He got to his feet, slowly unrolling the spool of wire. Looking me steadily in the eyes, he said: "I will connect. Then navigation commands will work again. No propulsion is fix, only navigation. You must hurry, and tell Commander to change course."

"This is insane! How can you be sure?"

For a few moments, he gazed into my eyes. Then he smiled. "Now, Benigno—*now*, we will climb the stairs together."

Open-mouthed, I stood as one paralyzed, until he said with incontrovertible authority: "Go!"

*

We passed by the Earth with less than a thousand kilometers to spare. And then we continued to plummet into the infinite cosmos.

Hours later, I led the Commander and crew down into the bowels of the ship and found Manuel. In the place where I had left him was a strand of wire connecting the two circuits across the gap. We found his body at the base of the canyon, fifteen feet below. His neck had been broken, the fingers of his right hand burned.

I have tried to imagine how he did it. And I believe it was this way:

He had thought swiftly and planned every action, because there was no margin for error. It must have taken extraordinary determination, because he would know that even as he was about to save the ship—and our world—it would almost certainly cost him his life. First, he had unraveled several more feet of copper wire and cut it from the spool. Probably he clenched the wire in his teeth. After checking to make sure that the end connected to the dead track was secure, he lunged across the canyon with his arms outstretched, hoping against hope that he would be able to grab the housing of the live track on the other side, that it would not break, that he would not lose his grip on it. He caught it and did not fall.

With his body dangling over the abyss, his toes touching nothing but air, his left hand gripped the housing and supported his weight. With his right hand, he used my knife to slice through the polyplast coating at a shallow angle. There would have been a spark when the blade touched the metal track beneath, but the handle was nonconductive material. That done, he dropped the knife, and the clank when it hit bottom told him that it had had a long fall. It may be that he thought his only option after connecting the two tracks would be to drop away into the darkness in order to avoid pulling the wire loose. Or he might have considered a leap back to the other side, though this is unlikely, because the canyon was eight feet wide, and there was nothing from which to launch himself. Or he might have imagined himself gradually moving along the line of housing, hand over hand, toward some better purchase or the end of the canyon. But I do not think so. I believe he understood the power of the forces he was about to connect and what they would do to him. He would be the bridge—and the conductor.

It may be that he paused for a second or two before he took the final step. Then, with his free right hand, he took the end of the copper wire from his mouth and slid it carefully beneath the circuit wire, without touching it, pushing it against the wall, making it loop back upon itself above the live track.

Now he had no choice but to seize the end of the copper wire and jerk it down so that it connected with the track in such a way that it held. Only a second of time was needed to twist it tight—a precious and deadly second. He would have felt a severe jolt and heard a snap even as he let go and dropped away into the fathomless dark below.

*

Manuel's sacrifice needs no eulogy from me, not even here at the end of my private journal, which no one will ever read. What he did was sufficient to avoid the destruction of mankind's home. Indeed, he saved billions of lives.

During the months that followed, as we headed farther out into open space, technical staff replaced the temporary fix provided by the strand of copper with a permanent safe connection. They also followed this previously unsuspected trail, trying to locate the greater internal damage, which Manuel had called "the secret wound, deep in the body". They found some of the source problems, but not all. The repairs were insufficient to restore total navigation control. However, during the second year after our near-collision with Earth, the problem of deceleration/propulsion was finally solved. The units lowered from the body of the ship without fail, and the test firings were perfect. Repeated tests confirmed that we could now change course for home.

But the navigation system did not respond when the Commander and crew attempted to change our coordinates for Earth. Deep within its alchemical mysteries, it had reverted to auto-function. Without permission, without human commands, it had reset our course, and no man now could change it.

The voyage is a wide ellipse through the galaxy. If no further complications develop, and if the stellar compass extrapolations are correct, the ship will arrive in the vicinity of Alpha Centauri approximately forty years from now, at which time, there will be few if any of us left alive.

The others—those who are like Manuel—have not condemned me. They know all that I have done, yet they welcome me. I go to their gatherings. I listen. I wait. Sometimes I hear the bells ringing in my childhood memory. Will I one day sing and dance with them? And even lift my arms, seeking what is . . .

I can write no more.

528

DISCOVERY

35 August, A.D. 258   St. Benedict's Abbey,
                                             26 Mirza Lane, R. R. 2,
                                             Foundation City, Queensland

Most Reverend Nicholas Hoang
Office of the Archbishop
Holy Family Cathedral
439 Ao-Li Avenue
Stella Maris, Queensland

My dear Archbishop Nicholas,

It is my hope that this letter will arrive in the city in time to greet you upon your return home from your sea voyage to the communities in Josephsland. I have heard that the children being confirmed this year are exceptionally well prepared by the sisters, and that their numbers are unprecedented. I know that all three bishops of that continent were most grateful for your offering to assist them with the sacraments. My cousin Mark, the bishop of Tower Valley, wrote to me before my own "journey" to say as much, and mentioned how moved he was that you would remain with them long enough to participate in the blessing of the new museum at the site of the original catastrophe. I pray that this and other events have been very fruitful, and that you return to us in excellent health. May God grant that you will shepherd the flock of the Lord on this our home continent for many more years to come!

If your schedule permits, I would like to come down-river before month's end to give you a personal debriefing. There is a world of news to tell you. First and foremost, the ship is indeed, as we long supposed, the *Kosmos* itself. In the documents which accompany this letter, you will find a summary of our flight with my reflections regarding our findings, and an older handwritten manuscript (in English) which I believe will be of great interest to you. This, as well as my own interim report, I have translated into the Standard Tongue, with attached Appendices I, II, III, IV for Mandarin, Hindi, Spanish, and Pan-Slavic translations (the brothers worked long hours on these). In addition, I am sending you a selection of significant short documents and other items of interest. When you open the package, I think you will forgive me this understatement when you see two of the treasures in particular.

531

As you will find when you read my interim report, it is somewhat informal, and even rambling. It is a collation of my first response to a momentous encounter with the past. For the present, I am still overwhelmed with impressions and quite distracted. I plan to write a more comprehensive history of the events (insofar as our newfound understanding will allow) and, with your permission, submit it to the archdiocesan library when it is completed, with copies to the regional libraries of the four continental governments and five territories. I would, as well, like to donate the original manuscripts to the central archives of the Commonwealth.

Please remember me in your prayers to our Savior, as I pray for you.

Holy peace be with you, in Him,
Abbot Anselm Yusupov, O.S.B.

Interim Report by Anselm Yusupov, O.S.B., on the first boarding of the spaceship *Kosmos*, 15 July to 2 August, A.D. 258 (A.D. 2485, Earth-year, est.).

Prologos The combined efforts of the continental and territorial agencies involved in making possible the flight to the ship were of a character that bodes well for future projects. It was understood by all the governments that our objective in retrieving information was not merely for the enhancement of our scientific knowledge. It was unanimously agreed that the use of any such forthcoming information would involve ethical and moral considerations, which would be discerned at future global conferences.

The flight was, I believe, primarily motivated by mankind's desire to learn more about the history of the expedition that had led to the founding of a new civilization on our beloved planet. Moreover, we hoped that whatever we discovered would significantly enlarge our understanding of our ancestors.

As we know from our own history books, the pioneers landed by shuttle in the southern highlands of Queensland, which was then called Continent 4 (C-4). This occurred in the year that we now call Year One, or foundation year. The pioneers were loath to date their arrival as anything less than the real beginning of man's presence here. The previous year, during which the *Kosmos* expedition had explored the planet and gathered samples to take back to Earth, was certainly acknowledged, but for understandable reasons, it was discounted as a period of transient and often shameful intervention by men in a world of uncorrupted beauty. Perhaps, too, the founders wished to put behind them the moral confusions they had experienced on the ship, and, moreover, to leave behind the horror of the bomb that had destroyed the majority of expedition members.

In any event, for our purposes here, the history of those years needs only a cursory outline:

In the year A.D. 2097 (E-year chronology), the ship departed from Earth, arriving in orbit above Regnum Pacis (then called AC-A-7) by late 2106 E-y. Approximately a year was spent in exploration and gathering data and samples. Then the catastrophe occurred, and in early 2108 E-y, the ship departed on its return voyage to Earth.

As the communications transcripts of that nine-E-year period confirm, the journey was greatly troubled by violence and by technical breakdowns. Little more is known about it because the pioneers' own technology was declining as the shuttle's power source failed. Their focus at the time was primarily on establishing means of survival—food, shelter, heat, health matters, and so forth. Perhaps the psychology involved was also at fault: the desire to escape a past that was riddled with confusion, tyranny, falsehoods, and unnatural death. Lacking the means to reactivate (or repair) even the simplest of wave communication, their last received messages from the *Kosmos* told them only that the ship had narrowly escaped impact with Earth during the year 2117 E-y and had continued its voyage into the exo-solar regions beyond.

At that point, the pioneers' communications system had all but ceased to function, due to the exhaustion of the shuttle's internal power. Propulsion had become impossible during the first year, for lack of fuel, but the solar batteries continued for a time. Eventually, however, all such batteries and sundry other energy sources also failed and could not be restored, despite the best efforts of the pioneers. The harnessing of wind power for electricity would not occur for another two generations, when the first simple electric generators were made. Redevelopment of solar power followed shortly after. Until then, the pioneers' attention was mainly focused on the tasks at hand, though I imagine they cast a glance at the night sky from time to time—and wondered. For them, agriculture was the foundation, and industry, as it grew, remained supplemental and small. One thinks of the myriad aspects of life that challenged our forefathers. With dedication and ingenuity, they applied themselves to the making of brickworks, glass, the water wheel, and grist mill, then the first small paper mill and reinvention of the printing press.

The pioneers had brought a quantity of paper with them, and did not develop their own paper manufacturing until more than a decade had passed. By then, they were entirely without electric energy of any kind, and were reduced to manual copying of documents initially printed from the few miniature hand-computers they had brought with them. These phenomenal machines are now at rest, enshrined in our museums, and it has not yet become possible to make them functional again. While the instruments still worked during the first few years, technical knowledge was looked for in what was called their "memory files", and later in the small number of printed documents obtained before they failed. But these sources had provided little information about the simpler forms of technology needed at the time. Nor could the complex mechanisms developed by Earth's later civilization be replicated. Many aspects of the powers that had brought man to the planet were by then beyond our grasp. Indeed, we have never recovered them—anti-gravity and anti-matter remain entirely mysterious to us in this present age.

In the early years, there was much discussion as to what the planet should be named. *Caelum Caeli*, heaven in the heavens, was considered for a time but discarded because of its historical connotations. Numerous variants, familiar to us all from our high-school texts, were also applied (one thinks of *Nova* and *Sundara Graha*). We know about these mainly through the writings of Dr. Maria Kempton and Dr. Pia Yusupov, who co-founded with Dr. Henry Arthur the first hospital. Cross-references were also derived from the account written by Dr. Neil de Hoyos, the physicist who returned to Earth with the *Kosmos*, and whose journal *The Voyage* (brought here by one of the pioneers) is still required reading for all students in second-year university courses. None of the suggested names for the planet satisfied the pioneers, and only at the first continental congress in A.D. 68 was agreement reached. Thereafter, *Regnum Pacis*, Realm of Peace, was universally acknowledged as the name of our planet.

By the beginning of the third generation, a basic civilization was growing. It was a humane society governed by the pursuit of wisdom, by the constant effort to maintain a freely given unity of mind and spirit, governed most of all by the desire to love and to avoid the destructive errors of mankind's past. There were churches and schools in every village. By the beginning of the fifth generation, there were numerous towns, and a city by the mouth of the Great River had been established—Stella Maris. There, a cathedral was built from the honey-colored limestone brought down from the White Mountains. That same decade saw the establishment of the first university.

From the perspective of more than two hundred and fifty years after the foundation, it is difficult for those who now live in the tenth generation to imagine what it was like for our ancestors. Without doubt, their strength of character, their faith, their overarching concern for the children born to them, enabled them to work with constant sacrifice so that there would be a future for the children—and for us. We who live a quarter of a millennium after them are sustained, often unthinkingly, as the recipients of immeasurable and oft-forgotten generosity.

From among the sixty-seven original pioneers, thirty-six people married, and in the first generation (arbitrarily, I count a generation as twenty-five years), these eighteen marriages brought forth seventy-four children. Most of these first marriages were unions of people in their mid-thirties to late forties. Thus, their child-bearing years were limited. In the second generation, however, there were a greater number of marriages and a larger number of children born. By the third, few people were counting. It was all fruitfulness, it was all a blessing. Love begat love, and the more bountiful the love, the more were the resources of the human community in dealing positively with our practical difficulties and our tendency to sin. Children were the great treasure of mankind. They grew to adulthood knowing they were loved, and they became capable of loving in turn, coming early to maturity and responsibility, for all around them at every moment of their lives they saw the giving of the self for the good of others.

Our people have never been census takers, but in general we know that there are now about 1.8 million people living on the four most populated continents and a quarter of a million more in communities throughout the five smaller Commonwealth territories. Everywhere, families are large and energetic, and, with few exceptions, happy. This is our world. We have all been born into it. It is our home.

It was not so for the original pioneers, who surely would have felt they were strangers in a strange land. It must have seemed to the first few generations that their civilization grew with painful slowness, though by hindsight, it appears to us as rapid development. We need only remember the turning of the fields by men and their ploughs, drawn forward through the rich soil by those blessed creatures the Regnum ox and the massive oryx horse. I think also of their heavy labors felling and dressing the trees with which they built their homes, the gathering of stone for chimneys, the clearing and harvesting of fields for their livestock. Then came gravel roads, the gradual spread of small communities, farms, orchards, and vineyards throughout the valley of the Great River, and into neighboring valleys and beyond. With the passage of time, a second large community grew up on the coast, with its fleet of primitive wooden fishing vessels. And from that came the first sailing ship, which took colonists to Josephsland in the east and Zion in the west and Gilead in the South.

Then, the great leap forward into the age of steam, the building of the first paddle-wheel ship, followed a half century later by the invention of the propeller-driven steam ship, which has made travel across this broad world so much more efficient. And in our own times, the extraordinary appearance of the steam locomotive and the spread of the railroad.

My musing takes me back to a time before these latter events, especially to the fourth generation and the uneasy return to the mountains of catastrophe. Led by Bishop John Adamson, the third successor of Bishop Paul Miki Nagakawa, the expedition discovered the legendary great glass bowl upon which a forest of saplings (now the Old Forest) grew up from the ashes. We have all read the accounts of that day, written by those who were present. There, the bishop offered the memorial Mass for the souls of those who had died on the day of disaster, and for the untold millions who had died at the hands of the evil race that dwelled there in ages past. I try to sense some of what he felt as he stood at this epicenter of darkness. I know well his later reflections on the matter, and those of his companions, the geographers, priests, and historians. We have read that the bishop and his fellow explorers gave little thought to the possibility of lingering radiation. And in their reflections, they ponder the lingering radiation of man's tendency to evil. Though I wonder if the horror had become something of an abstraction, I know that in more than one account there is reference to an undefined sense of presence—an apprehension of millions of ancient voices crying out to God across the millennia of evil's reign. The writings of expedition members lament those victims, but I believe they grieved as much, or more, for the abiding condition of man's nature, which will be our burden until the end of time.

In this prologue, I have rather wandered back and forth across the years. Let me now return to the foundation era, when memory of the original pioneers had not yet begun to fade, for the settlements were populated mainly by their immediate descendants. These children and grandchildren of hope knew the Tale of Origins well, had listened again and again to the account over meals and by firesides and in bedtime stories, and had read about it too, for the pioneers had taken pains to record everything they knew about what had happened during the *Kosmos* expedition, and also about mankind's history on Earth.

It would be well into the second generation before the people could apply themselves to the reestablishment of electric power. In due course, the mineral smelters and forges had produced some basic metals, primarily iron, tin, and copper—though not a great amount of any of these. With the advent of copper wires at the beginning of the third generation, primitive electromagnetic coils were engineered; and in time, the water wheels that had ground our grain so faithfully were adapted to the rotation of motors and the generating of electric current. Following upon that, wave manipulation (the transmission and receiving of radio frequencies) was re-mastered, but not in time for us to learn the entire story of what had happened to the *Kosmos*.

By then, it had been known for several years that a satellite had appeared high in orbit above the equator. Using the single telescope in their possession, the second generation of pioneers had noted its presence early on and had deduced from its orbital behavior that it was a man-made object. Though the image in the lens was too small for identification (no more than a luminous dot), some believed that it might be a ship sent out from Earth. Historians recount that fear gripped the population for several weeks, though it declined throughout the following months until, by the end of the first year of the satellite's arrival, the general feeling had been replaced by one of puzzlement. Why, it was asked, had no landing craft descended? The question would remain unanswered for decades to come. Not until Year 57 (2191 E-y), when radio was reactivated, did they learn that the ship was silent. It has remained so ever since. So, too, the Earth.

In summation, the chronology is as follows, in both Earth years and Regnum Pacis years. Note that the planet Earth had a year of 365 days and a 24-hour day, considerably shorter than our year of 412 days and 31-hour day. One E-year is approximately 0.686 of the RP-year (one RP-year is 1.46 E-years). With apologies to the mathematicians, I am a linguist and historian, for whom the space-time continuum and general relativity remain forever beyond comprehension. I offer this dating schema, therefore, as subject to future correction, in the hope that it contributes to a provisional understanding of the sequence of events:

EARTH-YEAR	REGNUM PACIS-YEAR	EVENT
2097		The *Kosmos* departs from Earth.
late 2106		The ship arrives in orbit above AC-A-7 (Regnum Pacis).
early 2108		The Catastrophe.
		The *Kosmos* departs for Earth.

538

2108	Year 1	Pioneers return to Regnum Pacis on shuttle.
2117	Year 7	The *Kosmos* narrowly misses Earth, and continues on into the exo-solar region (according to last received transmission).
ca. 2160	Year 36	A satellite arrives in orbit above Regnum Pacis.
2191	Year 57	Radio technology remastered; pioneers learn that the object is radio-silent. Neither are any transmissions from Earth detected, then or since.
2485	Year 258	The satellite is boarded, its identity confirmed as the *Kosmos*.

Project development   For two hundred and twenty years, the *Kosmos* has orbited Regnum Pacis. Fifteen years ago, the Commonwealth made the decision to apply a portion of its resources to the development of a small vessel that might one day be able to escape planetary gravity and unite with the satellite, whatever it might prove to be—a great ship from Earth or elsewhere, or a celestial entity of unknown origins. Given the current state of technical development, this was a laudable though improbable dream—at least for any time in the foreseeable future. It was rightly believed that new sciences and discoveries would be needed in order to bring the dream to reality, and that, given enough time, they would appear. It was thought that the project could not be fulfilled before the passage of another three or four generations—or more—but that the effort should begin.

A hundred years earlier, the original *Kosmos* shuttle had been restored (physically, not operationally) and preserved in its museum near the landing site at Foundation City. Though it had been meticulously examined for generations, fifteen years ago engineers and other specialists applied their skills and our then-current state of knowledge in a renewed effort to understand how it worked. We knew from the records that the shuttle had been driven by a combination of fuel propellant and "anti-gravity". The latter device, while entirely incomprehensible to us, was located beneath the interior floor of the hull, and easily identified: engraved on its side were the words "Anti-gravity generator.

Authorized technicians only." It was a self-contained tubular unit that ran the length of the shuttle. Its sealed casing was made of a material (presumably a sophisticated alloy) that had not succumbed to the ravages of time, neither to rust nor wear nor any sign of incisions made by previous investigators. Indeed, the surface continued to resist all attempts at penetration.

The unit was removed from the shuttle and installed in a free-standing framework of light steel (an iron-carbon alloy, one of the benefits of railroad development). The structure was a web of thin girders about the size of a small family home. With much trepidation, the scientists applied electricity to the anti-gravity unit's external circuit portal, hoping to control it by a rheostatic mechanism. Nothing happened. It took some few years for the specialists to realize that there was not a thing wrong with the device. They had to learn by trial and error that what *we* had called electricity ever since the creation of our first primitive electromagnetic generators two centuries previously, was not precisely the same thing as the "electricity" and "electronics" referred to in older documents from Earth. The state of their technology had far surpassed ours many centuries ago. What that was, we could only guess.

Providentially, a genius or two is born into every generation. And one such person was a member of the development team, Dr. Felix Arthur by name. I could not begin to explain what he conceptualized into material reality. Nor can anyone else, for reasons I will explain in due course. We do not understand his invention; we know only that it worked. When standard electricity was connected to it, his device "translated" it and directed energy into the anti-gravity device, and then the latter activated.

Dr. Arthur felt strongly that the pace and the character of modern progress was showing signs of becoming harmful to the human community—especially the question of power combined with speed. He found it convenient to ride as a passenger on the railway system from time to time, since he continued to teach courses at the university, and it would have been a two-day journey from the science base at Foundation City to Stella Maris, if he had traveled by horse-drawn carriage or by boat. Nevertheless, he remained cautious about the train's long-range effects on the body, and especially on the mind. He felt it could very well prove to be unhealthy for men to travel at speeds faster than forty miles per hour (the maximum gallop speed of a thoroughbred oryx horse). I knew him personally, and can verify that he was a reflective, brilliant man to whom a precipitous action or thoughtless utterance was entirely alien, and so I believe his conclusions on the matter were no superficial opinion. We should, I think, ponder his cautionary insights with some attention.

Why then, one may well ask, did he agree to participate in a project that would, if successful, propel men at velocities faster than the speed of sound? In his personal memoirs, completed shortly before his death, he writes that while he at times regretted his involvement, he understood that the benefits to be derived from a reconnection with a "starship" (which he suspected was the *Kosmos* returned) would outweigh the potential dangers of too-rapid technological advancement. Nevertheless, he urged the governmental and scientific authorities to delay for generations to come the application of any discoveries that might be made in the fields of fuel propulsion, the new electronics, and anti-gravity. It remains to be seen whether or not he will be heeded.

To return to the crucial moment when the use of anti-gravity first became possible:

Dr. Arthur plugged a "live" standard electrical wire into his invention and flicked a switch on its side. Soundlessly, it projected a thin pulsing beam of "something" into the power portal of the old anti-gravity device. The thing hummed, remained motionless for a few seconds, and then slowly floated a few inches off the ground, drawing the modern framework with it, though the whole must have weighed close to a ton. Using the rheostat on his invention, Arthur increased the current, and the entire structure rose more swiftly, trailing the umbilical power cord, hundreds of feet long. Careful decreasing of current (combined with a different pulse sequence) made it descend smoothly.

Then came the next stage, the permanent coupling of invention and device and their integration with a third component, which was a large electrical battery that would rise along with the other two, ensuring that no energy failure occurred. One mistake in this regard and years of work would plummet to the ground, shattering any hope of connecting to the orbiting object. Repeated experiments revealed that amplification of current made it possible to lift even greater weights to greater heights. Fearing to do damage to a unique and still mysterious triad, the science team discontinued elevation experiments after it reached an altitude of several thousand feet, bearing a trial weight of three tons. That it worked—and worked unfailingly—was beyond all doubt. Yet it was capable only of vertical lifting. It may have had maneuvering functions in times past, but, if so, we did not know how to access them—and still do not.

During this same period, research scientists had constructed a small petroleum refinery in the subarctic region of Queensland, experimenting with the crude oil pumped from reservoirs beneath the surface. In time, they produced a liquid fuel of heretofore unknown explosive force, which, if properly controlled, might provide additional thrust for escape velocity. It was not then understood that the anti-gravity device was sufficient for this task, that it had no upper ceiling, so to speak. At this stage of theorizing, the planning committees also realized the obvious: that a simple reversal of anti-gravity would not be sufficient to bring a shuttle back down to its launching point. Because the planet revolved on its axis, delicate calibrations would be needed in order to avoid dropping it into a sea or a mountain upon return. Hence the need for a propulsion fuel that would, using calculated bursts of energy released through a system of valves, maneuver the ship at will.

A new shuttle was built, reproducing the design of the original and the more complex internal design. Much of this replication was based on increased knowledge of how the vessel had once operated, though some of the copying was blind. The problem of stabilizing air pressure was minor compared to the challenge of supplying and purifying atmosphere for the projected twelve-man investigative team and two pilots. A considerable quantity of compressed oxygen would be needed. Based on low-altitude experiments, it was initially thought that the interim from launch to arrival at the mysterious orbiting body would be about three hours. This, however, in no way ensured immediate entrance into the vessel, if it was indeed a ship of some kind. From readings of early manuscripts and other documents relating to the *Kosmos*, the satellite gave indications of being a duplicate, at least in terms of its external form. The very-high-resolution observations made with the new telescope at McKie Observatory on Mount Zion in the equatorial region, with its 2-meter lens aperture, enabled astronomers to confirm that the object was at least a kilometer in length, and oval shaped.

If it *was* the *Kosmos*, or a duplicate, then shuttle bays would be waiting for us. They might or might not be closed. If all bays were closed, we still might be able to open one, since we had the command codes for this and other docking functions, left in the record logs of the original shuttle. Moreover, these were described as universal emergency portal codes in the archived, unpublished writings of Vladimir Kirilov, the pioneer who piloted the shuttle's return to the planet at the foundation. Nevertheless, our radio transmission of the code still might not communicate with the code responder in the bay. We had no way of knowing whether or not our radio frequencies were dedicated—could "speak" with each other.

If the shuttle were able to enter the ship, would the bay doors be closable? And would pressurization still operate in those bays? The ship's designers surely would have seen the need for human oversight, providing a manual back-up in case of remote command failure. Yes, but in all likelihood, we would find no one left alive on board after two centuries of orbit; there would be no one there to open and shut the doors and change the pressure.

The questions multiplied: Was there breathable air in the ship? Was its internal gravity still maintained? Was there light and heat? We knew that the energy source had been "nuclear". We understood very little about this form of power generation, and, of course, it was associated with the catastrophe—in other words, it was a dangerous entity. Clearly, mankind had once harnessed it for positive purposes, but how long did its fuel, or its apparatus, last? Had the ship's silence been caused by the death of its energy source?

A year was set aside for test flights that brought pilots up through the stratosphere and well into the mesosphere. The sensation of weightlessness, though expected, was initially a cause of both disorientation and entertainment for the men, but they quickly grew accustomed to it. Oxygen regeneration worked adequately. Reentry was accomplished with only minimal damage (overheating due to too rapid a descent). The designers learned a good deal from these trial flights, and developed a clay-ceramic coating that went a long way toward protecting the hull from extremely high-friction temperatures. Even so, thereafter the shuttle's test flights took much longer to complete, since ascent and descent times were deliberately increased in order to avoid unnecessary stress on the vessel's outer skin.

Test flight   In June of this year, the shuttle made its first full test flight to the ship, with two pilots at the helm. During the greater part of the six-hour ascent, their radio communications with Regnum-base were comprised of operational information. During the final hour, however, the pilots' comments became more exclamatory, the tone increasingly excited by what they were seeing through the cabin window. "It *is* a ship!" they cried repeatedly. "It's immense ... beautiful ... flawless!" As they made a pass from bow to stern, they discovered on one side, close to its underbelly, a single open bay.

"It looks like someone left the door open for us", said one of the pilots.

"Waiting for us", said the other.

With small bursts from its jets, the shuttle maneuvered close, so close in fact that there was a shudder as the two vessels touched, like the hulls of wooden boats bumping into each other without doing damage. The pilot in charge swiftly withdrew, and brought the shuttle level with the open bay. Carefully, he slid it toward the entrance. As he did so, the bay's interior was suddenly illuminated by a bright light. When the craft was entirely inside, one more small burst brought it to the floor. The moment it touched the surface, the bay door began to lower from a recess in the wall above, and a red light began flashing.

Alarmed at first, the pilots did not know what to do. They simply sat there and watched it all, waiting to see what would happen. When the outer door was completely closed, the pilots realized that they now felt their bodies' weight. The ship had internal gravity. Then they listened to a minute or so of roaring-hissing that steadily grew in volume until it abruptly ceased. The red light stopped flashing, and a loud voice that seemed to come from nowhere, or everywhere, announced in several languages: "Pressurization complete".

The pilots remained where they were and waited. And waited. At this point, they should have obeyed their orders and taken the necessary steps to depart from the ship and return to Regnum-base. But they were unsure of how to reopen the door and were also overwhelmed by curiosity. They affixed their helmets to their pressure suits and locked them in place. Taking a few deep breaths, wondering if these would be their last, they agreed to make an experiment. The pilot in charge opened the shuttle's portal, half-expecting to feel its atmosphere rush outward into a vacuum. Instead, the external atmosphere flowed into the shuttle. Now they had confirmation that the bay was indeed pressurized—though with what they did not know. The oxygen monitor for the shuttle's internal air supply showed that some change in the atmosphere had occurred, and that it now contained slightly less oxygen, but the instrument could not indicate what other elements might be present, such as lethal gases or unknown factors detrimental to human health.

Rashly, the copilot opened his helmet, preparing to shut it at the first sensation of distress. He inhaled. Then he smiled.

"A bit stuffy", he laughed. "But good enough for guys like us."

Both men then exited their craft and walked about the bay. On the wall opposite the ship's external wall, they located a large, closed doorway leading deeper into the interior. They had brought Vladimir Kirilov's codes with them, and now they tried punching the numbers into a console beside the doorway. Finally, one of the numbers prompted the loud voice to say: "Access verified." An overhead green light began flashing as the door slid slowly upward. When the entrance was fully open, the light stayed solid green.

The men now found themselves staring into a cavernous hallway or concourse, far longer than it was wide. They could not see either end of it, though here too the chamber was illuminated by overhead lights. The ceiling appeared to be sixty to eighty feet high.

"We shouldn't be doing this", murmured the pilot.

"Yes, you're right", said the copilot.

"If we die, the shuttle stays here—years of work gone in one stroke."

"And no second chance."

"Let's go."

Retracing their steps, they closed the doors to the interior. The copilot pointed out that there was a numerical console beside the huge door that accessed outer space, and he offered to try opening it using one of the codes. The pilot replied that this was a risk: if the door began opening too soon, whoever entered the code might be sucked out with the atmosphere, followed by a painful death, suit or no suit. Alternatively, the code command might have a delay response, giving him enough time to get back into the shuttle and pressurize it. But there was no way of knowing what the timing, if any, was.

Both men reentered the shuttle and sealed it. Then they sat there for a time, thinking.

"It may be automated", said the pilot at last. He lightly touched the anti-gravity button and the vessel lifted from the floor. Immediately, the red light commenced its flashing, and the loud voice announced: "Prepare for depressurization."

A minute later, the atmosphere hissed as it was pumped from the bay, and a bell rang continuously until there was no more air for sound-waves. The red light flashed on and on as the bay door began to rise, then turned green when it was completely open.

"Thank God", both men exhaled simultaneously.

The pilot brought the shuttle out through the wide-open portal and headed for home.

The boarding   And now, my personal account begins:

On the morning of 15 July 258, the new shuttle lifted off from the field base at the science center near Foundation City. We rose straight up into a clear blue sky, ascending very slowly. The first four hours of ascent would be through the troposphere and stratosphere, the next hour and a half through the mesosphere and ionosphere, and finally, when we had escaped the planet's protective layers, came the short half-hour propulsion flight to the ship.

The party was comprised of fourteen people: seven scientists, including an electrical engineer, a chemist, a mathematician, an astronomer, a biologist, a physician, and a person who specializes in the new theoretical field of computer analysis. The non-scientists were our two pilots and a navigator, a representative of the Commonwealth Congress, who is also chief archivist of the continental library, and three historians, one of whom was myself in my combined capacity as historian, priest, and representative of the synod of bishops.

During the first hours of the journey, I felt an increasing sense of awe and love for this work of art that God had made and given to us: an entire world, a world so beautiful, so inexhaustibly rich in wonders. I had until then only imagined what it must look like as a whole. Though the newly rediscovered science of photography has given us marvels of image-making, it cannot convey the colors of reality and has never obtained images of the planet seen from above—seen as a whole. My first sight of it reduced me to tears, and I think my companions felt very much as I did, for we all grew motionless and silent as we gazed out the windows, and there was no speaking among us until later, when we boarded the great ship.

As we left the ionosphere behind, propulsion was ignited, and its thrust caused me to feel the return of a portion of my body's weight. So many marvels all at once! Through the windows, we saw the massive form of the great ship swiftly approaching. Reducing thrust and maneuvering carefully, the pilots brought us in close and then, with small bursts from navigation vents, we entered the bay. The shuttle settled gently onto the floor, a red light began flashing, and the outer bay door descended, enclosing us within.

It is impossible to adequately convey our first impressions. These were various and conflicting, at times psychologically disorienting due to the sheer number of astonishing experiences and discoveries we would come upon within a very short period of time. In a word, we were overwhelmed, sometimes with awe, sometimes by fear, and occasionally by profound respect for those who had remained as passengers on the ship two hundred and fifty years before our time.

As the pilots led the team through the bay into the ship proper, we felt as if we were entering a city. During the following two weeks, the truth that it was a city floating in the heavens was never far from our thoughts. Our life's experience had imprinted in us the subconscious conviction that heavy things up in the air must always fall down, and this was a very heavy thing indeed. At certain other moments, we felt as if we were wandering within the complexities of a colossal machine.

We had brought with us diagrams of the ship left to us by the pioneers. We had all read their memoirs, short and long, which had been published and republished over the centuries. We knew that we were now on the bottom level called PHM, which was divided into three main sections, titled Propulsion (at the rear of the vessel), Holds (the largest section, in the middle) and Maintenance (the smallest, in the forward area). The shuttle bays were on the port side of the ship, in a separate region that ran the length of Maintenance and Holds, with access mainly into the latter. The Holds was divided equally into two separate subsections: food storage and samples storage, where zoological, botanical, and mineral samples brought to the ship by shuttles had been stored for return to Earth.

The committee at Regnum-base had decided beforehand on a program of exploration that would bypass this bottom level and take the team straight up through the four intermediate residential concourses to the ship's command center on KC. It would be the most likely place to find a hub of information.

The possibility that people were still alive on board was remote in the extreme. For two hundred years, the vessel had displayed not a flicker of life, at least none that we could detect. Regardless of the possibility that the first generation of voyageurs might have had children, grandchildren, and so forth, there was simply the problem of food. Pioneers had estimated that there would have been no more than a century's supply at best, even as the number of the ship's company declined. We did not yet know with certainty that this was the *Kosmos*, but it was generally believed to be the original ship. There were, after all, no other shuttles: there were three empty bays beside our own, which fit with what we knew about the condition of the ship at the time of the catastrophe.

Following the plan, we now moved as a body along the shuttle concourse until we reached a set of three doors in the left-hand, or inner, concourse wall. One stood open. Engraved in the wall above the doors was the word "elevator" in several languages. Apparently, the original inhabitants had used these very small room-like mechanisms to raise and lower themselves from level to level. This had played an important role in their lives. Regrettably, the numerical key consoles beside each door did not respond to touch. Within the single open elevator, we found another console with five command buttons, on which was inscribed their destination floors, reading from bottom to top: PHM, D, C, B, A, KC. None of them responded to touch, and throughout our remaining time on the ship we were unable to locate any elevator that still functioned. Why this should be so, we could not guess and did not try to discover, since we had far more important questions before us. A long walk from one end of the shuttle concourse to the other showed us that there were a dozen "emergency staircases" ranged along the route. Only the one closest to our arrival bay had an open door; the others were locked.

Inside its entrance foyer, or stairwell, we found painted on the wall facing us the following words, in the French language, with an English translation:

Ascendez, s'il vous plait. Les habitants de la Kosmos sont ici. Nous vivons à l'étage supérieur. (Please go up. The people of the Kosmos are here. We live on the top floor.)

This was our first confirmation that the ship was the original exploration vessel that had brought mankind to Regnum Pacis. As we climbed upward through successive staircases, floor after floor, we learned that the ship's primary energy source still functioned on every level. We kept our oxygen apparatus by our sides, but the atmosphere continued to be consistently breathable air. We also had gravity, light, and warmth. We did not try the closed doors at any of the landings and proceeded directly toward KC.

Pausing on a landing, which we estimated to be at the halfway mark, none of us were as short of breath as we had expected to be. One of the scientists pointed out that Earth's gravity had been less than ours, and the ship had maintained what was normal on its home planet. We were now, he said, experiencing the benefits of a good diet or fast, with no loss of muscle strength. The comment occasioned smiles all around. I also felt grateful for the years during my youth when I had been an avid mountain climber, before I entered the monastery. Despite my advancing age, I now felt more invigorated than strained. I was also wearing my lightest habit, which I use for summer labors in the garden, and I was carrying little baggage, just my backpack, containing my portable Mass kit, notebooks, and a few changes of underclothing.

With nods to each other, we resumed the ascent. Finally, arriving at the topmost platform where the staircase ended, we found an open doorway awaiting us. Passing through it, we were now in a wide concourse. Pausing for a moment to orient ourselves, we looked left and right down an avenue that resembled a street of unbroken smoothness, as if made of polished limestone, shining with reflected light from overhead sources. Immediately in front of us stood a small wooden table upon which sat a vase of flowers.

I went down on my knees to inspect it and saw that the flowers were not organic but had been made with art and great diligence from tiny pieces of fabric. Handwritten on a piece of cardboard beside the vase was the following, again in French, but lacking any translation (the added translation is mine):

Bienvenue, chers frères.
Nous sommes très heureux que vous ayez enfin venu. Trois d'entre nous restent. Nous vivons dans l'infirmerie, au bout du couloir à votre droite. N'ayez pas peur. Il n'ya pas de maladie. Nous sommes simplement vieux. Je suis bien et je m'occupe des deux autres.
Avec l'amour,
Marie
[Welcome, dear brothers.
We are very happy that you have come at last. Three of us remain. We live in the infirmary, down the hall to your right. Have no

fear. There is no sickness. We are merely old. I am well, and I look after the other two.
With love,
Marie]

I translated for the team members, and without discussion, we turned right and walked toward the end of the hall. Passing through a set of double doors, we entered a section that looked less official, as the "avenue" now suddenly changed to a pavement of soft carpet. Many of the open doorways we passed revealed inner rooms with furniture of unusual design. We peeked inside two or three such chambers along the way and saw beds, chairs, tables, and the most extraordinary life-like images on the walls—photographic, I think, though they were rich in colors. Mainly, these were scenes of forests and seas, and one an unknown city of immense size. Another was a landscape with red mountains rising above a golden plain where nothing appeared to grow.

Finally, we came to a second set of double doorways, on which was printed the word *Infirmary* in several languages. Obscuring half of them was a clumsily painted red cross that was clearly a later addition. We pushed the doors open and stepped inside.

The room was a spacious one, with two rows of beds, still covered by neatly arranged white cloths. One bed, the first on the right side, closest to the door, contained a body. Only a head capped by long white hair was visible, turned away from us. The form beneath the mauve blanket lay in the semi-fetal position, as if the person had just fallen asleep.

The team's physician stepped forward and drew back the blanket and sheet, which began to fragment as they were moved. Beneath these covers was a skeleton. The bones were clean, the flesh long decayed; there was no smell of decomposition in the room. The covering fabrics and those beneath the body were stained, though dry and odorless.

"It is Marie, perhaps", I ventured, and none of my companions replied.

The others stood for a while in silence, gazing down at the sad little form on the bed. Then one by one, they turned away and walked about the room, looking curiously at a variety of instruments on countertops, and into cupboards and closets. I blessed and anointed the body's remains.

There were several items on the bedside table, all coated with a layer of dust: an empty carafe and drinking cup, a few books, a pen, a basket, full of pieces of colored fabric, and a half-completed cloth flower. There was also a small crucifix, carved from wood with not very great skill. It lay upon a few sheets of paper, which I now took up and read quietly to myself.

Her name was Marie Louise Durocher, and she had worked aboard the *Kosmos* as a kitchen assistant and, after the catastrophe, as a cook. She was twenty-one years old at the time of departure from Earth. Ten years later, when the pioneers chose to take the shuttle back to Regnum Pacis, she had been torn between going with them and staying on the ship, but in the end decided to return to Earth because she missed her mother and father very much, and she was their only child. After the near-collision with her home planet, when the ship had begun its long return to "AC-A-7", she had suffered an emotional breakdown for a while, but people had been very kind to her and helped her through it. She had grown strong, she wrote, by serving others. She had known the ensign Manuel, before his death, before he saved the world and its people. They were friends. Later, when she was ill in her mind, she saw him in a dream, and he told her to pray and to trust. It was he who taught her from heaven how to serve, to find healing in this, and joy.

Who was Manuel? I wondered.

Marie had written a good deal more on these few sheets of paper, but the document was short on details and long on reflections about suffering, hope, love, and her faith in Christ. I strained for descriptions, but there were few, only the portrait of a soul and, even this, a sketch.

She had been eighty-four E-years old when the *Kosmos* returned to orbit around Regnum Pacis in Year 36 (RP-y). By then, there were only seven people left alive, all of them very old. Two years later, there were only three people left, all women. During the following year, wrote Marie, "My beloved sisters have passed away into the arms of infinite Love." She had interred the bodies of her last two friends in the "*la mortuaire*", and then waited.

The document clearly had been written during her final days of life, when she knew she had not much longer to live. She wrote that she now understood the pioneers would not come to the ship and rescue her. They might find her body some day, and if they did, she wished to bless them "from beyond the gates of death". She prayed the visitors were in good health and good spirits. She hoped that some among them had come to know *"le bon Dieu"*. If by a miracle everyone had come to know Him down there on the beautiful planet beneath her feet, the world she would never see again, then this was very good, and she was content to offer her *"petite sacrifice"* toward that end.

Her final words in this little memoir were:

I am alone. But I am not alone.

That night, the team gathered with me in a large dining room off the KC main foyer, and I celebrated a Mass for the souls of the deceased. Each morning thereafter, we met for Mass, and often in the evenings for night prayer.

We ate our meals in the dining room also, after warming our food in the adjoining kitchen, since its cooking apparatus was not unlike ours at home, though it lacked our cookers' electric coils, which glow red. These machines had glossy square tiles that looked incapable of doing anything at all, until with one touch of a button they became instantly hot. We slept in the private bedrooms ranged up and down the hall of the KC flight staff residence. The mattresses and coverlets were all in a state of deterioration, dry and fragile, crumbling at the touch, but we had our own bedrolls and blankets.

Throughout the ship, lights were dimmed or raised at regular intervals, leaving only small trains of miniature lights along hallways and in other public rooms, to guide our steps if need be. It left us with an uncanny feeling at first, and imagination could easily have inflated the phenomenon into a grand overseer watching our every move. When we realized that it was the ship's system regulating the illusion of night and day, we adjusted to it quickly.

During the "days", our attention was pulled in a thousand directions. My fellow team members will be writing their own accounts of our exploration. Therefore I will pass briefly over the practically inexhaustible details of our various researches, with a few exceptions. After the first day or so, when they had satisfied their initial fascination for the history and anthropology of the *Kosmos* people, they turned their attention to scientific matters, the gathering of technical information and artifacts.

The physician was perpetually busy in the medical wing, collecting smaller instruments and making notes and drawings of larger machines.

As did all of us, he rued the absence of the newly invented photographic apparatus, which would have made a better record. But there were only six such prototype instruments in the laboratories of Regnum Pacis, and even if permission had been granted for one to be brought along, it would have been extremely difficult to transport about the ship (too large and too heavy for even four men to carry).

The chemist disappeared into the pharmacies, cataloguing and collecting samples from an inexhaustible store of medications.

The electrical engineer applied himself to finding his way into the labyrinth of the energy system, its nerves and entrails, so to speak. Since the ship was still "live", this would be a perilous venture. He found the access portals on PHM on the fourth day, and thereafter we seldom saw him, though he returned to our headquarters late each evening with filled drawing pads and copious notes. Whenever we asked him what he had learned, he usually shook his head in some bewilderment: "Everything and nothing", he said.

The astronomer searched for information pertinent to his field, limiting his activities to the Command center of KC, where there was a division with a large room of its own, labeled *Astronomy*, next door to a room labeled *Navigation*. He and the computer theorist, often assisted by the mathematician, knew that what they sought was asleep within the memory storage in the ship's complex "brain". Daily consultations between the three, and occasionally with the electrical engineer, brought them no closer to accessing whatever that mysterious power had been. Computer screens would light up at the tap of a lettered keyboard, but displayed nothing and responded to no amount of experimental typing on function command keys.

Knowing that their time was limited, these four men grew increasingly frustrated. They had hoped to obtain advanced optical instruments, presuming that these were connected to the astronomy computer terminals. For example, an inscribed label above a screen might say: Telescope 4, Navigation-14. Another might read Telescope 2, Stellar Obs-3. The actual telescopes were surely buried somewhere in the zone of the ship's observation functions, but the locus of these was never found. From accounts of the original journey from Earth, we knew that there were also mobile lenses or "cameras" that had flown alongside the *Kosmos*. Our investigators eventually found their storage chamber in a subsection of the shuttle concourse. It contained several dozen identical "machines", with parts that none of us could understand, other than their glass-like, optical lenses. Though cumbersome, the machines were lightweight, and six were stored in our shuttle's hold.

The pilots and navigator were mainly occupied in the forward section of KC. They reported that several instrument panels appeared to have been damaged at some point in the past, and repaired. Here too they were met by nonresponse from the myriads of components. As a result, they restricted their activities to making exact diagrams and notes on the layout of the numerous piloting and control stations, meticulously drawing any and all labels they found, copying every number, symbol, and alphabetic letter, and their exact positions in the Command center.

Leaving me to my own random searches, the two other historians went off on forays through the several libraries, though their investigations proved to be fruitful only in the single library containing real books—pleasantly heavy in the hand, dusty, and smelling faintly of their bindings. None of these volumes were about technical subjects, being mainly works of the humanities. The electronic "books" and library terminals doggedly refused to activate.

Day after day, as we moved through the ship, we learned that not a single such electronic apparatus would respond to our touch. All computer terminals that we happened upon, both public and private, were found to be nonfunctioning. They lit up at the tap of a lettered keyboard, displaying a glowing blank screen, but would go no further. Whether this inaccessibility was by design or by accident, we did not know, and perhaps will never know.

It made no sense to us. Why did the ship continue to maintain all life-sustaining functions so faithfully, while at the same time it refused us access to even the simplest knowledge reservoirs? Had we misunderstood the meaning of *computer* in the old documents written by the pioneers? Had we misinterpreted certain details in their memoirs? It did not seem so, but then how were we to know for certain? In any event, after the pattern was found to be consistent, we reached the conclusion that either something very far beyond our understanding had broken down, deep in the system, or else the last authorities had simply locked it up and thrown away the key.

We had brought rations sufficient for our two-week stay on board. As it turned out, we need not have done so, since we soon found the food storage holds on PHM. Much of the dried materials (grains, for example) had disintegrated into dust. However, the refrigeration facilities had not failed, and large quantities of frozen foods were discovered, certainly enough for many people's needs for years to come. We thawed a few samples and cooked them in the kitchen on KC deck. Despite the risk, I volunteered to take a test bite of something or other, the name of which (all food packages were labeled) I had never heard before. It was delicious, though the flavors were strange to my tongue. We did not much trust these provisions in the beginning, but by the second week, we were eating them exclusively.

Water was a concern at first. Washrooms, both private and public, still had hot and cold running water. Most spigots had begun to rust, and some produced nothing but screeches of metal grinding upon metal. The ones that did work issued streams of liquid that ran red for a few minutes and gradually cleared. Our biologist examined the liquid closely under a microscope and pronounced it free of biological contaminants. "Of course, they may have nuclear radiated it", he conjectured. "And we have no instruments for detecting how dangerous that is. Judging by what we know from the records, whatever that power was, it wasn't good for living organisms." He shook his head and put a cup under a faucet. "But if *they* drank it, I think we can drink it without harm." And so we did, without any ill effects then or since. The water was odorless and strangely tasteless, as if it were utterly devoid of minerals, reduced to the basic hydrogen and oxygen components. It satisfied the body's needs, and we did not fear it, but we all felt some uneasiness about the substance. Perhaps our feeling was based in mankind's love for living water, or an instinctive sadness over sterility in any form. I do not know.

Regarding the whole problematic nuclear question, there is not much to tell. We knew that it had its base on the PHM level, and eventually we found the rear propulsion section, and an attached section that was the ship's internal energy source. Entrances to both were well-marked with their names and with hazard symbols. We did not go inside, and I expect that we have suffered no loss by leaving well enough alone.

When I began to write this interim report, I had intended to present a linear chronological account of my arrival and exploration of the ship, but I have failed in this, which I expect is due to the mind's sensory overload. It is difficult to configure intellectually—at least at this early stage—our encounter with an older civilization that was far in advance of ours. I fully intend to write a more coherent, detailed account during the year (or years) to come, but this interim report, I fear, must suffice for now.

I will now continue with random moments, images, and, one might go so far as to say, illuminations:

One of the more impressive memories I retain from the time we spent on board is the great central park that had its base on Concourse D and soared all the way up to the ceiling of Concourse A. We located it in short order by simply following a trail of sallow vine tendrils that had spread a ways down the two long avenues bordering the park. All the side entrances were choked with impassible thickets and rope-like vines. With the aid of handsaws and hatchets, the younger men cut a path through into the interior of the forest, where we found the mossy remains of old stone pathways. We who were older followed close behind.

It was a living habitat, chaotic and tangled with a wide variety of plants struggling for life. The air was rank with the smell of rotting vegetation, though it was also mediated by the perfumes of new growth. From some of the trees hung seeds and fruits, from others, flowers. In every direction, great disorder reigned among shoots and saplings and fallen trunks, all of them species I had never seen before. It was a wondrous thing to behold this living memorial of the planet Earth. However, unlike natural forests, there were no insects or birds, no sounds other than the occasional water droplet from the system's hydration apparatus, the snap of a falling twig, or the flutter of a few small leaves wafting down from above.

Looking up through a gap in the forest crown we spied the ceiling, which pioneer accounts had described as looking very much like a real sky. It was now revealed as a sheet of unknown substance, similar to glass, I would think, since it was transparent and reflective. Wherever they struck this layer, the topmost branches of trees had bent back down toward the ground. A few vines had cracked the "glass" here and there, penetrating to the region above, which looked as if it had been painted uniformly black and dotted with numerous instruments for projecting light or imagery.

To penetrate any farther into the forest would have demanded time better expended elsewhere, and so we left with many a backward glance. I asked the biologist how the pollination of flowering shrubs and trees had occurred in the absence of insects. He had no certain explanation to offer, but suggested that gardeners might have done it by hand. I replied that there had been no gardeners on board during the past two centuries. He thought about this for a time, and then said it could have been done by regular cycles of artificial high wind. As an afterthought, he conjectured that members of the original expedition might have unknowingly brought insects back to the ship as stowaways inside clothing.

One night, out of curiosity, he and I unrolled our sleeping pads by the doorway where we had first entered the park. We discussed the possibility that there could still be unsuspected creatures living there, too shy to make a daylight appearance. We had our manual mobilights ready by our sides, in case of need, and drifted toward sleep telling each other about the different findings we had made.

I mentioned the empty swimming pool I had discovered, its water evaporated. He told me about a section in the holds where a large number of creatures from our planet had been stored, including a glass terrarium in which he had found the skeletons of several snakes.

"Are you certain they were snakes?" I asked.

"A label testified to what they were. I also remember the skeleton diagrams from my university textbooks, and these were classic."

"Was the cage locked?"

He laughed. "Oh, yes, the security system was very tight for this specimen. They were poisonous snakes, you recall."

"I remember the stories", I said. "It just strikes me that one or two of them may have escaped from their prison."

"It's possible—a male and female maybe." He smiled slyly, glancing toward the doorway to the forest. "That's the perfect place for them to set up housekeeping."

I knew he was having a bit of fun at my expense, and I enjoyed playing along.

"In all my years, I have never seen a snake", I protested.

"Neither have I," he replied, "but that doesn't mean they aren't here."

"Mmm, yes, we had better stay alert."

He grew suddenly pensive. "There are plenty of references to them in the old accounts of the *Kosmos'* bases on Josephsland. I read that a few people died because of snakes."

"True, but none of our people have ever been harmed during all the years since then. Not even a single sighting of snakes. I think the bomb or its radiation destroyed them all."

"But why were there no snakes on other continents?"

"They were not indigenous to this planet. You know the story of the ancient people who came here thousands of years ago. They brought the snakes from Earth. Because they deliberately limited their human population, they lacked the means for expansion. Perhaps they never wanted it and remained on the main continent in order to ensure strict control over their people."

"Oh, yes, the Lord of the Night-gods", he shuddered. "Dark stuff. Really bad stuff. And they were *very* fond of their snakes."

"Yes, an essential part of their diabolic rituals."

The biologist yawned and rolled onto his side, pulled a blanket over his shoulders, and closed his eyes. "Well, it was a long time ago", he murmured sleepily. "And so far so good. But keep your eye on the doorway, would you please, Father."

"I'll take the first watch."

There came a chuckle, and no more was said. I flicked on my mobilight and finished reading night prayers by its glow. After I shut it off, I did not sleep immediately, but this was due to the overstimulation of the preceding days, not to fear of serpents. Or more precisely, not to fear of the material kind.

I reminded myself that there had once been a garden where no snakes had entered—a place like Paradise, a realm of peace. When the serpent came, our first parents did not recognize it for what it was.

A few hours later, we were awakened by an artificial dawn, as the ship's automated system slowly turned on the lights in the hallways and forest. Without warning, the sounds of various birdcalls issued from the doorway. Startled, we scrambled to our feet, staring at the park's interior.

I burst out laughing when I remembered something from the memoirs of the physicist Neil de Hoyos. He had mentioned listening to artificial "electronic" bird sounds in this very place. It was an illusion.

That day I went in search of what Marie had called *la mortuaire*, presumably a colloquial use of a legitimate French word, by which she probably meant a morgue. In her notes, there had been no indication of where this might be located. She had been very old at the time of her friends' deaths, and I could not imagine her having the strength to transport the bodies far from the infirmary. I searched everywhere throughout KC, paying special attention to each door and alcove in the medical center on that concourse. I found no human remains anywhere.

I had overlooked the fact that two hundred years ago the elevators might still have been operational, and she would also have had medical trolleys at hand. I found the trail the next day when I wandered down to deck A. Distracted by the continual surprises of seeing in the material realm what I had read about in the pioneers' memoirs, I decided on a whim to find the sumptuous apartments of the elderly couple whom Neil de Hoyos, in his account, had called "the trillionaires".

I was gratified when I did find it, for it was no longer as he had described it. It was identifiable only by its marble entrance, the high ceiling of the spacious main room, and a soaring stone fireplace. There was no furniture other than a few rows of simple chairs facing what looked very much like an altar made of wood, covered by a linen cloth. Standing on it, there was an artless wooden crucifix and two candle holders with stubs of melted wax.

Now I recalled that there had been clandestine Christians among the *Kosmos* passengers. I knew also from the memoir of my ancestor Pia Yusupov that a priest had remained on board when the pioneers returned to Regnum Pacis by shuttle. Fr. Ibrahimi Mirza was his name, sometimes called Dariush. He had been warmly remembered by all those pioneers who had mentioned him in their accounts, and greatly revered by Pia. The priest had also been a close friend of Hoyos. It was good to know that after the fall of the tyranny, the surviving voyageurs had been free to practice their faith openly. They had been blessed to have a priest with them, the inestimable treasure of holy Mass and sacraments. The evidence before me pointed to a regular liturgical life.

Though two hundred years had passed since the last Mass, or the last prayers of Marie, had been offered in this room, I bowed my head and gave thanks to God for his providence.

Walking about the altar, moved and grateful for what I was seeing, I smiled when I noticed little cloth flowers gathered about the base of the crucifix. There was a piece of paper folded among the blossoms, and I picked it up to read. It was in French:

O my good Lord, I am the last, though I feel you very close. Yet I do not have strength these days. Assist me, O my good Father, to bring the body of my friend down to join the others. The cold of the burial room is severe, and my hands ache with the arthritis. Donkey that I am, my poor old back cannot push the trolley far. Please give me enough strength to take her to PHM and into her resting place; that is all I ask.

I love you very much.

Your small Marie

I walked to the nearest staircase and went down floor after floor, arriving at the stairwell bottom on the concourse below D. But here the access door was firmly closed and locked. Then I realized that Marie would have used an elevator to transport the trolley and its burden to another floor. I remembered, too, that at our arrival we had found only one open door leading upward from PHM. I retraced my steps to KC, a considerable climb, and proceeded along the hallway to the emergency stairwell that we had used. When I was down at the bottom floor again, I passed through the open doorway into the high chamber of the shuttle concourse.

But where in all the vast maze of this level would I find what she had called the "burial room"? She had described it as a severely cold room, and this could only mean that it was located in a section that had refrigeration or freezing compartments. There were such rooms in more than one section, but I thought it likely that voyageurs would have chosen to inter their dead somewhere in the food holds. They would have frequently visited these stores for provisions, and this, therefore, would be a preferable place for burials, since it was near their daily path and closer to their living quarters. Our team had investigated only a small portion of the section, excited by the alien cuisine we had found, and looked no farther.

Now I made my way along the shuttle concourse, and passed through unlocked doors into the midsection of the ship—the holds. A major subsection of this zone was for samples that were to be brought back to Earth, but that was farther toward the rear of the vessel, beyond food storage, where I now stood. It had freezer storage as well, but I thought that the voyageurs would not have spent much time there.

Where to look?

I guessed that there would be three main avenues and a dozen or more cross streets. They would not have as many rooms as on the residential concourses but enough to consume my time until departure, if I had to look into every one. Though the storage rooms were much larger than rooms on the floors above, most of those I looked into had four to eight levels for the sake of maximum efficiency in the use of space.

I now made a trek through the food holds area in order to orient myself regarding its layout. A rectangle, its dimensions were roughly two hundred meters (the width of the ship, less the width of the shuttle concourse) by three hundred meters (beginning at the maintenance bulkhead and ending at the bulkhead of the samples hold). As it turned out, there were ten cross streets and three main avenues. Each of the latter had five sets of elevators evenly spaced along the entire food holds section. It struck me that the voyageurs would probably have selected a room close to an elevator.

I found what I was looking for on a cross street ending at a set of elevators on the middle avenue. I cannot attribute my success to clever deduction, but rather to the fact that there was a wheeled trolley rolled haphazardly against a wall beside a closed doorway. There were no nearby doors, which indicated that the chamber within was a very large one. Its outer wall was shining steel, as was its door. The handle turned with only a little resistance; the door opened outward with a whisper and a breath of frosted air.

Inside, I beheld a scene I did not at first understand. Here, there were four levels surrounding a central atrium, the levels connected by ramps, staircases, and the room's internal elevator. The three upper levels were empty. The bottom level had the distinguishing feature of a knee-high shelf, about eight feet deep, running continuously around the room's four walls, interrupted only by the doorway. On it were stored semi-transparent containers, as long and wide as coffins, and it took no guesswork to realize that these were the burial containers of the dead. I turned to my right and inspected the first one. There were markings on its surface indicating that it had once contained food of some kind. It was covered with a hinged lid. The container's material, I suspected, was the substance referred to in *Kosmos* accounts as "polyplast", which had served a variety of purposes. It was sometimes described as white or off-white or transparent, and it was adaptable to transformation into many forms.

Upon closer inspection, I noted that there was a slot at the head of each container, with a paper card inserted into it. I now read the one closest at hand. It gave a name I did not recognize from my readings, a date of birth, and a date of death (these were in E-y). I lifted the lid and found within it a human body sealed in a transparent bag. The face was that of a very old woman, wrinkled and serene. On her breast, folded between her fingers, was a wooden crucifix and a small cloth flower. I closed the lid.

The next body was also that of an old woman, her cheeks sunken, perhaps wasted by disease. Here too there was a little crucifix and a flower.

The body after that was an old man, again peaceful, again a crucifix and flower.

Stopping to survey the room, I realized that more than ninety bodies were interred here. I bowed my head and prayed for their souls. Then I slowly walked around the length of the shelves, reading names and dates. It seemed that each of these bodies had been placed according to the date of death. When I noticed the pattern, I continued reading the death dates only.

Arriving at the end of this chronology—in fact, a fastidious track of the community's long decline into silence—I noted the date on the final coffin in the row. It was a day in September of the year 2108 (E-y). I knew that the *Kosmos* had departed on its return voyage to Earth in early 2108. This, then, was the first person to die among those who had remained on board.

Reading the card more closely, I saw that here were the remains of Fr. Ibrahimi Mirza. I dropped to my knees, blessed the body, and prayed for his soul, even as a flood of confused thoughts raced through my mind. His early death meant that the voyageurs had been without the sacraments for their entire remaining lifetimes, unless there had been another priest on board. The memoirs of Bishop Paul Miki Nagakawa stated that only one priest had stayed with the ship. If this was correct, then what I had found in the chapel revealed an extraordinary history of faith in Christ, a community of lay believers who had not ceased to love God and grow in sanctity.

My heart beating hard, I stood and lifted the coffin's lid, desiring to see the face of the priest whom my ancestor had so revered, the friend of many who became pioneers, the close friend of Dr. Hoyos. His face looked as if he were asleep. He was elderly, but by his appearance I saw that he must still have been a vital man at the time of his death. His hands were crossed on his chest, the fingers enfolding yet another carved wooden crucifix and surrounded by an abundance of Marie's little flowers. A piece of paper inserted beneath the frozen hand was covered in her now-familiar script.

I unzipped the bag covering the body and picked up the note. It read in French:

Pray for me, Father, you who were so kind to me when I was young. Pray for your brother who suffers much. He is in agony and despair.

As I shook my head, wondering about her meaning, I noticed that the priest's shirtfront was stained dark red. At first, it had seemed to be no more than shadows, but now as I brushed aside the flowers I saw a great hole in the chest, above the heart.

Gasping, I took a step back. What had happened here! Had Fr. Ibrahimi died by accident? Or had he been a victim of violence? What, or who, had killed him? I stood for a few moments pondering what I remembered about the return voyage. The pioneers had received communications from the *Kosmos*, and in their memoirs, they referred to news about incidents of violence and death. They had recorded no details. Perhaps they had not known any details. On the other hand, they may have learned what happened, but, for reasons known only to themselves, they decided to refrain from passing the truth down to the coming generations.

I kissed the cross in the priest's hands, closed the bag over his body, then lowered the lid, thinking there were many unexplained mysteries here. I glanced at the coffin on my right, and again I was startled. Its label informed me that it contained the remains of Dr. Neil de Hoyos. He had died in the year 2122 (E-y). Unlike all the others, his body had been stored out of chronological sequence. To confirm this, I looked closely at the next coffin in the line. It contained the remains of a man named Manuel de los Santos, who had died in the year 2117. This too seemed oddly out of place. Inspecting the next coffin and all those that followed, I learned that only these two broke the pattern.

I opened Hoyos' coffin. For the first time in my life, I looked upon the face of the man I had so admired when I was young—a legendary person, a figure of gigantic proportions for me, before I began to mature and better understand his inner struggles and his compromises. Even so, I had never lost my respect for him. And now I saw, with a rush of emotion, that clasped in his hands was a simple cross, two rods of white ivory with fine markings on them.

The features were those of extreme old age. He had been ninety-three E-years old when he died. I gazed long at his face, wondering over the brilliance that had once resided in his mind, his long journey through life, his honors and his failures. Here was the man without whom the *Kosmos* would not have been built. Nor, without him, would any of our civilization on Regnum Pacis have become reality. Nor would our people, these millions of God's children, ever have come into existence.

On his chest, there were many flowers. Tucked beneath his frozen hands were two pieces of paper. I opened the bag and picked them up, expecting a little memorial from Marie. Instead I found two writings by Hoyos himself.

One was a passage from scripture, the Book of Job, written with a pen in a handsome script, and initialed *NRdeH*.

The other was in the same script. It read:

> My brothers and sisters,
> Please permit me to rest beside the bodies of my two friends, the sacrificers. That they might pray for Divine Mercy to be glorified through this poor sinner, and that we three might rise together on the Last Day.
> Neil

I closed the lid and left the room, shutting the door firmly behind me.

Later that evening, when the team gathered after supper to report the day's findings, I told them I had located the bodies. When I described the condition of Fr. Mirza's remains, there was some discussion over the possibility he might have been killed. We knew from our older books that the agency called DSI had exercised control in extreme situations by using weapons that could stun or maim. Indeed, they had badly wounded one of my ancestors, Paul Yusupov. But would they have killed people? The memoir written by Neil de Hoyos accused them of doing just that. This was confirmed in the writings of Paul and Pia Yusupov and Dr. Arthur, who believed that DSI agents were quite willing to commit murder—or strategic execution, as the killers would have viewed it. Yet the evidence had been inconclusive.

I encouraged the other team members to assist me in a more concentrated search through the residential rooms on KC, where it seemed the voyageurs had lived in close proximity during their long return to Regnum Pacis. The ship had missed impact with Earth in the year 2117 E-y and appeared again in orbit above our planet in 2160 E-y, after more than forty years in transit. About that voyage we knew absolutely nothing. We thought it likely, however, that people had left behind personal reflections, messages, and memories in the hope that these would some day be read by others.

The team members were reluctant to spend their dwindling time in pursuits that were not likely to produce technological information or artifacts. But the two other historians were willing to assist me, and the biologist joined us from time to time. We opened and searched every residential room on KC. All manner of fascinating things were found, but I must not let myself be distracted by describing these. The most significant items, in my opinion, were personal memoirs, simple auto-biographies, letters to people on Earth, and letters to pioneers—none of which were ever delivered, though they must have given some con-solation to their authors. We did not have time to read much of this material, but a few samplings showed us that religious faith had begun to spread among the voyageurs very early on. One moving testimony, written by a man who had been an agent of DSI, was a classic account of spiritual conversion and repentance. Another author described what could be called his intellectual conversion to Christ. Another spoke of dreams and visions in prayer. In these and other manuscripts, there were often references to "Manuel". In one document, for example, there would be a line about "Manuel's sacrifice". In another, "Without Manuel, where would we be?" In yet another: "Manuel, who was small in our eyes, was the greatest." The mystery grew.

We now had less than a week before departure back to our home base. We forced ourselves to stop reading during the daylight hours, and focused on carrying the manuscript material down to PHM and the shuttle's hold. The historians begged off after a while and threw themselves into transporting library books. They were physically fit, middle-aged men, but the labor of climbing and descending stairs all day long, bearing the weight of those volumes, took its toll. They ate rather more than was their custom and fell into deep sleep early each night.

For my part, I continued to transport the many and various per-sonal writings and the few books that I came across in private rooms. Even as I persevered with this task, I sensed that there was something of vital importance still to be found—something essential to our under-standing of the past, and hence our understanding of the present—that is, ourselves. Every now and then, I would take a break and wander the residential concourses, drifting without purpose into side streets, poking into rooms haphazardly, fascinated by the evidence of complex living habits and social customs. There were intriguing objects of invention to be picked up nearly everywhere, left behind on the day of disaster, unused by the survivors. Nevertheless, my backpack remained nearly empty as I disciplined myself to resist a sort of disguised avarice that had begun to afflict me.

The sense that something crucial to our understanding was still eluding us grew in urgency but had no apparent means of resolution. Praying as I meandered through the streets and avenues, I did not expect a revelation on the matter and certainly invested little confidence in my deductive faculties. I merely roamed at large, soaking up the ethos of the great ship, which we were soon to leave and would never again visit.

One day while strolling along Concourse B without any object in mind, I vaguely recalled that Dr. de Hoyos had lived somewhere on this level. He had referred to his room number a few times in his book, but I had paid no attention to this minor detail. Now as I continued to walk, I glanced at the passing doorways, many of them open, a few closed. It is a marvel of the human brain that once something is imprinted in it, it never thereafter disappears. It may fade, it may even recede from the conscious mind beyond the reach of willed retrieval, but in odd moments, a prompt or some other providential stroke from the rich mysteries of life may suddenly evoke the specific memory without warning. As I passed a room with an open door, I happened to glance inside and noticed absentmindedly that the ancient mattress on its bed had a gaping cut in its side. For no reason that I could offer to myself, I stopped and went in.

A swift examination of the place disclosed nothing to indicate that Hoyos had once lived here. It was stripped entirely bare. When I put my head into the little bathroom, however, I noticed a small piece of paper lying on the floor behind the toilet. Picking it up, I read: "Neil, don't forget to bring your shaving gear. Sacristan needs to be tidy!—Neil."

Clearly, the note was a reminder addressed to himself. I knew that the word *sacristan* was the term for a person who cleaned and minded a sacred place, specifically an altar and its sanctuary. Had Neil wanted to lend his shaving equipment to a person who performed this task? Or had *he* become the sacristan?

Following an intuition, I climbed the main stairway to Concourse A, and went along the hallway to the chapel. Entering it, I felt a wave of peace flow through me. Yes, this had been a holy place, and still was. Though the sacramental presence of Christ was not here, members of his Body had spent long years praying in this room, and listening to the still, small voice of the Holy Spirit. I glanced at my chalice sitting on the altar. Ever since the day I had found the chapel, I had been offering Mass here, accompanied by the team.

Now I did what I had not thought to do during my previous visits: I looked into every room of the old apartment. There was a kitchen, three bathrooms, and adjoining rooms, which I guessed had once been bedrooms, all of them devoid of furniture and decoration. At the end of a short hallway, just behind the wall of the altar area, I found a door that I took at first to be a closet. I opened it and looked within. When I did so, the dark interior become visible as the ceiling began to glow with a faint light. I did not know how to increase its luminosity, but there was enough to see by.

The room was about the size of one of our cells at St. Benedict's, though more austere than the brothers usually keep their rooms. There was a simple platform bed without a mattress. Two blankets were folded at its foot. A hand-carved crucifix hung on the wall. On a bedside table lay a rosary made of knotted string. When I picked it up, its fibers fell apart in my hand.

Turning back toward the door, I noticed a single, recessed wall-shelf in the shadows. I withdrew the mobilight from my backpack and pointed its narrow beam at the shelf. The first thing it struck was a thick, clothbound book. I picked it up and found it to be in a good state of preservation. Opening its cover, I saw that the printed text was in Chinese script. Archbishop Hoang had been teaching me a few words, not many, just the names of apostles and books of the sacred Scriptures. I opened to a section deep between the covers and saw in the header the word *Isaiah*. I opened a section near the end of the volume—*John*. It was a Bible! My excitement expanded into joy as I realized I would be able to bring this great treasure back to the archbishop as a gift.

Again I pointed the beam at the shelf, and my eye was caught by a solid shape on top of a stack of papers. Peering closer, I saw that it was a metal sculpture of a deer with a rack of antlers. Sitting on its back, side-saddle, was a tiny man reading a scroll.

My heart beat faster as I understood what I was looking at. I had read about it and imagined it many times in my life, and here it was in the flesh. Picking it up with both hands, holding it tenderly, I scarcely believed that the moment was real. I was overcome with emotion as realms of memory, imagination, past, and present connected through this small symbol, so layered in meaning. After I had dried my eyes and put the sculpture carefully into my backpack, I resolved to give this second treasure to the archbishop as soon as I returned home.

Now my attention turned to the stack of papers upon which the sculpture had stood. I removed the yellowed, brittle sheets from the shelf and took them out into the hallway leading to the chapel, for my mobilight was fading. Reading the first page, I saw that it was a hand-written document bearing the signature of its author, Neil de Hoyos. Its title was *Return*.

Seated before the altar, I began to read through the manuscript. With growing fascination, I realized that it was a continuation of Hoyos' journal *The Voyage*, and that it contained a wealth of information about the catastrophe and its aftermath. It also described events that had occurred during the ship's return voyage to Earth. One after another, the mysteries were illuminated. The most shocking thing I learned was that Hoyos had been responsible for the death of Fr. Ibrahimi, and had also been the indirect cause of Manuel's death. He had destroyed apparatus in the Command center, causing the ship to plummet out of control toward the home planet. Later still, the ship was driven by the damaged logic of its electronic master onto a wide course through the heavens, bringing it back to orbit above Regnum Pacis.

Even so, the man had become a sacristan. This indicated that he had found a degree of faith at some point after the final words of his second journal—"I can write no more"—were written. Among the last entries in the journal was a mention that the problem of deceleration/propulsion was solved during the second year following the near-collision with Earth. That event took place in 2117 E-y. His death was five years later in 2122 E-y. This was strong evidence that a community of faith had been formed very early on in the forty-year journey back to Regnum Pacis. Hoyos had lived in the room behind the altar as custodian of what by then was already a functioning chapel. Additional confirmation of his conversion, however, was not to be found in the journal but rather in the notes I had discovered in his coffin.

I completed reading the manuscript late in the afternoon. I felt very moved—and shaken. All my conjectures about what had happened during the long journey had been wrong. Other assumptions I had made about people and events were now proved facile at best. I decided to forego eating supper with my teammates and went down to PHM. Entering the *mortuaire*, I went first to Manuel's coffin and opened it. The body within was that of a brown-skinned man in his early forties. Viewed from a few paces away, he could have been mistaken for a youth, but close up I could see the wrinkles about the eyes, the creases in the cheeks, the brush of silver at the temples. The hands were folded over a wooden crucifix that lay on his chest. The right hand was black, the skin burned away, revealing the bones of the fingertips.

I knelt and bowed my head. The surrounding silence was a voluble presence, peaceful, very still, poised in a weightless equilibrium of timelessness. I cannot now recall if I prayed for his soul, but I know that I asked him to pray for me and for the children yet unborn to the people of Regnum Pacis.

Our departure was scheduled for two days later. The team members were unanimous in their conviction that we needed another two weeks on board, a month, if possible. Since our radio reception was nil inside the bay, the pilots took the shuttle out into space for a few hours, floating alongside the ship and radioing the expedition authorities at the science base. When the contact was made, they pleaded for extra time. But those down on the planet could not see what we were seeing, could not understand what we were telling them. In their distanced objectivity, their primary concern was for our safety and that of the shuttle. They insisted that if we had learned the basic history of the ship's presence and what had happened to its voyageurs, and if the hold was full or nearly full of material to bring back, then we should return home on schedule. Relenting a little, they granted us three additional days.

That night after supper in the dining room, we put our minds together and tried to work out an agreement. We had five days left in which to decide what more could be retrieved. Already the shuttle was three-quarters full of cases containing samples in various fields, and numerous small machines pried out of their countertops and walls (including twenty of the computers known as the *max*), and thousands of books.

The historians pointed out that most of the books they had loaded were of broad literary and historical interest, and that fully half of the volumes were not indispensable. They had not read far into any of the texts, but thought that many contained material of dubious quality. The histories, for example, had been present in the library by permission of Earth's global authority, which had been a tyrannical one. Would any tyrant overlook the subversive potential in true histories? Almost certainly, the books were politically approved distortions of the past, and therefore could be removed from the shuttle's hold with no significant loss. There was also some cultural and sociological writing that seemed to be tainted with ideology, and it too could be weeded out.

These two men, with assistance from myself, argued for certain replacements to be made: for example, selections from among the several hundred works of art in the concourse hallways and some heretofore unknown musical instruments found in an auditorium. After much discussion, a consensus was reached that a third of the space in the shuttle hold would be freed for the addition of these cultural artifacts. We spent an entire day loading paintings and musical instruments. Of course, on Regnum Pacis, we have fine paintings and musical instruments (especially winds and strings). But one large item was wholly unfamiliar to us—that is, until I read a label on its underside: *Casals Cello Co. Baltimore 2065*. Yes, a real cello! We will now be able to recreate its sounds, which were once so well known by the people of Earth.

Among the team, there was no disagreement about music, but there was vigorous debate over the paintings. The ship's art, though it was all historically significant, was nevertheless an amalgam of the disorders of Earth's later civilization. There were works of exalted imagination (truth expressed in beautiful forms), and there were works of degradation (falsehood expressed in both beautiful and ugly forms). There was some confusion over a painting I personally selected and carried downstairs to the bay with the help of one of the pilots. It was titled "Fall of the Rebel Angels", a stunning visual panorama of a battle between good and evil angels. It was beautiful and horrible— and true. I argued for taking it with us by employing all my theological wits, and by reminding the team about the evil race who had engineered the catastrophe. In the end, everyone agreed that the painting could be included, albeit with a few bemused looks from some.

Of major concern were the bodies of the voyageurs. Each of us felt deeply about the matter. These were the people who had accompanied our ancestors across the heavens. A minority of the team suggested that we leave all the bodies on board so that the *Kosmos* would remain as a memorial, a kind of floating mausoleum orbiting Regnum Pacis in perpetuity. There was merit to the idea, but the majority of us, myself included, believed that we should bring back some, perhaps all, of the bodies for burial in the living soil of the new world.

However, there was not enough room left in the hold to bring every coffin. The available storage space would be barely sufficient for a total of twenty. With this in mind, on the morning of our last full day on board, we selected from among the deceased those representing the races of the founding pioneers, including African, Asian-oriental, East-Indian, Hispanic, Western European (Anglo, French, Germanic), and Slavo-Caucasian. Three bodies for each of these major groups. All coffins were opened, all names read and recorded, all facial features and skin color examined, and decisions made accordingly. On my insistence, the bodies of Manuel de los Santos, Marie Durocher, and Neil de Hoyos were included in the above categories. By that point, Marie's remains had been put into an empty coffin and carried downstairs to be stored with the other bodies.

In addition, Fr. Ibrahimi Mirza represented Indo-European races, and two others represented Semitic peoples. A single Filipino represented the Pacific Islands peoples, and finally, one whose racial identity was not certain represented the indigenous peoples who had lived in diverse places throughout the old world. This made a total of twenty-three coffins, and there was not enough room for them all. In the end, space was made by offloading ten of the twenty *max* machines that had been stored in the shuttle hold.

On the morning of our departure day, we used the trolley to transport the coffins one by one to the shuttle. This took only a few hours because the freezer compartment was on the same floor and not far from the bay. When all was done, we stood back and glanced around the PHM concourse. Among us, there was none of the usual chatting or banter. The mood was solemn. I knelt down and prayed, and the others joined me silently. Standing, I made the sign of the cross over the ship, and then it was time to go. The pilots entered their cockpit; the rest of us entered the portal behind them and took our seats. The shuttle doors closed.

The bell began ringing, the red light flashed, and depressurization was underway. When the bay's outer doorway slid upward and the infinite depths of space appeared, I felt anew the mystery and grandeur of what the *Kosmos* expedition had attempted, its strengths and weaknesses, its heroism and its errors, the hopes and failures of all those who had journeyed in the great ship in the heavens. Our time aboard had been as fleeting as a bird on the wing, now here, now gone. Soon it would be a memory, like a glimpse of a white whale surfacing and diving, leaving only the impression that it had been there, a sign, a presence, alien and beautiful and free. Man on this ship had not been free, but he had brought the longing for freedom with him, carefully guarded within himself, secret and silent until it was finally released. He had also brought his evil.

As we descended slowly toward Regnum Pacis, the team members did not converse with each other, and I think that all of us were feeling the pathos of the moment, knowing that we were at the conclusion of the last flight to the *Kosmos*. It might be many lifetimes, perhaps centuries, before man would, through gradual stages of development, rediscover the secrets of the old anti-gravity device or those of Felix Arthur's invention.

O God, I prayed silently, *please give us long years to grow in wisdom and grace. We have seen what we need to see. We are a people who honor you and turn to you. You are our life and our hope. Do we need any more than this? O Lord of heavens and earth, do not let us return to this ship too quickly. And if in your providence you deem it better, do not let us return ever again.*

I glanced out the window. The shuttle was tilting to horizontal, preparing for its vertical descent. It was good to see reality again. Inside the ship, we had been blind. There were no windows. Man had relied too much on his artificial sight. He had been enclosed inside a magnificent invention that gave him titanic powers at too great a cost. In the cases upon cases of archival material I was bringing home to my people, there were extraordinary documents that would testify to this. These and other items of historical importance would simultaneously reveal our potential for authentic greatness and our capacity for making a horror of existence: the glory of man fully alive in the grace of his Creator; and the depravity of man when he turned away from that grace and declared himself lord.

I thought back to Neil de Hoyos' book, *The Voyage*, which generations of our people had read, brought to the planet by one of my ancestors. Who among us did not know the final words of that book: *O mankind, why, why are you so blind, when you can have this!*

Little had we guessed that the book was incomplete, that a more terrible (and in a profound sense, more beautiful) addition to that famous work had been written by its author. He had penned it by hand and titled it *Return*, not realizing the irony in the word, believing at first he was on his way back toward the Earth.

I thought of what I had learned about the sacrifice of Xue Ao-li, who was known to us, but not fully known until now. Hoyos' later journal gave us the inner man—the poet and believer willing to sacrifice his life for others. Then I thought of another man of sacrifice: Manuel, who had saved the ship and the planet Earth. A small person, an insignificant person—a soul so beautiful that his humility hid his glory until the very end. For the most part, I thought about Fr. Ibrahimi, whose life and death were entirely sacrificial, embodying both truth and love as a single unified whole.

I also pondered what I had learned about Hoyos himself—Neil, I had thought of him, had always thought of him since I first read his book during my youth. He had seemed to me then a courageous person, greatly at odds with the tyranny of Earth's government and ruling social system, and this he surely was. He had been bold in resistance, highly intelligent, ruthlessly honest, and ferociously independent. I had admired these qualities. I had, in my own small way, tried to emulate them as best I could during my adolescent years, while seeking to avoid the man's bitterness and lack of faith.

In this new journal, I saw something else in him, something which, if I had been more mature, wiser perhaps, I might have better understood when I was young. He wished to be good without Christ. As his friend Fr. Ibrahimi once told him, he wished to be good on his own terms. Neil had rejected the insight. He would face some truths about himself, but not all. He admitted to many faults, but it would be the final and fatal eruption of his rage that would reveal his gravest fault to him, his pride. He would kill an evil man, and in the process, he would kill another, the best man in his life. Then, in a frenzy of despair over what he had done, he sought to take his own life, though he was prevented from doing it. During the years that followed, he resisted the urge to self-destruction a number of times as the ship continued onward toward Earth. But that is not how it ended, because yet another man sacrificed his life.

Manuel had died because of Neil's moment of rage when he had fired bullets into the ship's vital command functions, and this was a truth that Neil could never forget. Thus, with Manuel's death, there came one more test. At that point, Neil might well have taken the precipitous final step toward his personal annihilation—the end of all pain, as he thought it would be. But he did not. He chose to live with his guilt and not to carry it alone. He chose to serve others for the remainder of his life.

Strangely, as I had read through *Return*, its author had more and more reminded me of Dr. Felix Arthur. The two men were of different eras and cultures, and yet their personalities struck me as similar. It may be due to the fact that they were both scientists involved in crucial discoveries that would have momentous consequences for mankind. But I think it was more than this. Could it be that Neil was what Felix might have become if he had not been a man of faith? Could it be that Felix was what Neil might have become if he had had faith throughout his life, if in a moment of wholesome abandonment he had knelt before an authority higher than his own will—before a priest representing Christ himself—and if he then had climbed a spiral staircase, no longer alone?

As I mentioned earlier in this report, Felix Arthur was known to me personally. I first met him five years ago at a meeting in the city, when I was appointed to the team that would one day, hypothetically, board the mysterious object in the heavens. I did not know at the time that he had only a short while left to live, and that because of the man I would board the *Kosmos* far sooner than I expected.

Arthur was highly respected in academic and scientific circles. An astronomer, electrical engineer, inventor, and professor at the university, he was, despite all his accomplishments, a humble person. He was gentle-mannered, polite to a fault, and at times, the composer of dry, though not uncharitable, epigrams. In his free time, he was forever writing and revising a book on the laws of thermodynamics, but I know that his chief love was his family. His wife Eleanor, whom I knew less well than I did Felix, was a woman of warm heart, wit, and wisdom, and she was clearly the sustaining human source of his life. There were eight children, their spouses, and more than forty grandchildren. Doubtless his science was his pleasure, but his grandchildren were his joy, for he presided over the clan with a mixture of childlike affection and paternal dedication. Not one of his grandchildren, for example, failed to receive an annual birthday letter containing a poem, a joke, a reflective quote, along with an unusual seashell or bird feather, and, above all, the certainty of being known and loved as unique. Felix and Eleanor's Christmas parties were a local institution; the decorating of the giant bristle-cone tree in the yard of their modest farmhouse was a ritual that few people of the surrounding shire cared to miss (he used multicolored fireflies and firebutterflies, then released them on Epiphany). An uncommonly loving man, he was loved in return. Only in the final year of his life did he come to have enemies—or more precisely, vehement critics. He responded to the newspaper attacks with great forbearance, without retaliation.

During the year following our first meeting, he had visited the abbey with increasing frequency, in order to ask my advice. I never inquired into the specifics of his research, and he, by the same standard, did not broach the topic. His questions were sometimes about important matters in his personal life, and at other times purely speculative. He was a devout man with a sensitive conscience, and he had a philosophical mind. He was strong and manly in character, yet blessed with a sweet temperament—a not uncommon mix. Never drawing attention to himself, he was very generous to people needing help of one kind or another, especially to families with many children. It seemed to me that if Felix had not been called to marriage he might have become an excellent monk. In the midst of a very full life, he worked hard to maintain a balance of activity and silence: he and his wife prayed the Office together daily and were often to be found in the Science Center chapel, side by side, interiorly recollected.

Though Arthur was twenty years older than I, our relationship had grown into that of a father and son, with myself in the default position of spiritual father. Yet it had the disturbing quality of reversing itself unexpectedly. On occasion, after giving him spiritual direction, I would find myself talking of personal matters that I shared with no one else—unresolved abstractions, my worries about this or that—nothing very intimate or very pressing, but serious enough that I felt greatly benefited by his perspective on matters. We had become close.

I recall especially one of the last conversations we shared. We met by accident at the annual Thanksgiving Festival in the Fields of Praise outside Stella Maris. There must have been more than eighty thousand people there that day, a majority of whom lived in the city and others who had come in from nearby towns and villages. After the celebration Mass had been offered on the high dais by the sea, we hundreds of priests and five bishops went down into the crowds to join in the general merriment and to meet with friends and neighbors.

As a monastic, I did not expect to bump into anyone I knew well, since mine is mainly a cloistered life at St. Benedict's, and Foundation City is far from Stella Maris and a good deal smaller. Most of my spiritual directees are in the north.

Wandering through the crowds of people, I simply enjoyed the atmosphere, buoyed by the contagious happiness all around me. The sky was cloudless, the temperature mild for late autumn. The waiting banquet tables ringing the field would soon be groaning under the weight of the coming feast. I received many kind greetings offered by strangers, and occasional requests to bless crucifixes and scapulars—and newborn babies (always a particular pleasure).

At one point, I lingered on the edge of a lovely spontaneous incident: About a dozen children had joined hands and were dancing in a circle, singing and laughing all the while. Some of them held small handbells, which they rang with contrapuntal abandon (they had brought them for the *Gloria*, but clearly they knew how to put them to other uses). People gathered around to watch, and for all of us, I sensed, it was an unexpected delight in a day full of delights.

More and more children ran out from the crowd and joined the dancers, singing too, though it seemed to me that there was among them no agreement on a particular melody or set of lyrics. Yet it worked somehow, the unplanned creation of radiant wholeness, balance, harmony. It was beautiful, and it touched me deeply.

I had just begun clapping my hands in time with the rhythm when someone, literally, bumped into me, and I staggered, going down on one knee to break my fall. I looked up and saw that it was Felix Arthur.

With a chuckle, he helped me to regain my feet.

"Father Abbot," he declared as he dusted off my habit, "you are out of your orbit!"

"Felix," I answered in the same tone, "you are out of yours!"

"A wandering planet am I", he laughed. "My apologies."

"None needed. How are you, Felix?"

"I'm very well, Anselm", he said with a bit of a smile and a mildly furrowed brow. "Yes, I believe I am quite well, after all."

"After all?"

He smiled again but offered no further elucidation.

"Would you care to sit with me?" I asked.

"Gladly!"

As we walked toward the park near the river's mouth, he explained that he had a free hour before the banquet began, when he would join his wife, who had gone to fetch some of their clan who lived in Stella Maris. We sat down on a less crowded stretch of grass beneath a giant *ficus* tree from which most of the syrupy yellow fruit had already been harvested. We plucked a few remaining orbs from the lower branches and sucked at them without conversing, in a restful mood, listening to the surf on the nearby beach, watching the antics all about us. At one point, a group of young people came by, bearing trays full of glasses, and they offered us white-berry wine. Felix and I sipped and contented ourselves gazing out over the southern sea, at the brightly colored sailboats in the bay, across the river at the capital buildings.

"Spiritually, I mean, or hope", he said cryptically.

"Pardon me, Felix?" I asked.

"I mean I'm *ultimately* quite well."

"Ah, your 'after all' qualifier, which I last heard more than twenty minutes ago."

He chuckled. "Of course, you are no mind-reader, Anselm. Forgive me. Bemused and befuddled am I."

"No more than usual, it seems to me. Or is something specific on your mind?"

"Something specific is definitely on my mind. May I speak of it confidentially?"

"Of course."

"I wish to posit a moral question."

I nodded for him to continue.

"What would you theologians say about someone who made a great thing, quite a marvelous thing, that could benefit mankind, though to what degree, and how, would be uncertain?"

"I would say that the maker of the thing was exercising his God-given gifts."

"Granted. Now add to the equation a few additional factors."

"Such as?"

"What if mankind was not ready for this thing? What if its sudden appearance had the potential for disrupting his understanding of himself and his natural powers?"

"It would depend on whether or not the disruption itself had moral or immoral content, I would say. Would the invention, for example, communicate a falsehood?"

"Not a lie as such. Nor be inherently a lie. Yet it would have the potential—remaining potential only at a certain early stage—to deform man's sense of his place in the hierarchy of creatures."

"You're touching upon the realm of theological cosmology, Felix. A rather significant *factor*, one might call it."

"I'm referring to a kind of power, you see", he went on. "Power combined with speed. Possibly speeds approaching the velocities achieved by our ancestors who came from Earth."

"And look what happened to them? Is that what you're saying?"

"I suppose that's part of it."

"We would have to consider that a tool is morally neutral, wouldn't we?"

"Is it?" he asked, peering at me intently.

"It would depend on the nature of the tool. An explosive chemical compound like the one used to open fissures in our mines is intended entirely for good purposes. It is not inherently evil. Yet it might also be exploded by a malicious person here in our park, taking many human lives to death by unjust violence."

"Speedily and with great force."

"Therefore, to avoid this potential, should we return to picks and shovels when we dig for iron? A pick, after all, can end another's life swiftly in a moment of madness."

"I know these arguments", Arthur said, with a hint of impatience. "I know where they lead, for I have wrestled with them over and again until my brain spins. Remove all tools, all potential for evil through such tools, and a man is still capable of picking up a rock and hitting his brother over the head with it. Perhaps the problem is better examined by asking where, precisely, are the limits—where the benefit of a tool, or an invention of any sort, overwhelms its user and makes of the man an instrument for *its* purpose."

"The analogy is somewhat flawed. The tool has no will, no intelligence of its own. It is man who is ever the problem."

"Yes", he said quietly. "But what can we do with man?"

"*Do* with man? I cannot see that we are able to *do* anything with the human race that would prevent evil from rising within us—either individually or as a people."

"I agree, Anselm. Truly, I understand what you're implying. To attempt to control our nature by limiting freedom in order to prevent evil would be to exchange one form of evil for another."

"Precisely." I paused, wondering what was really bothering him, and where the discussion was leading to. "We have a functioning democracy, Felix, which has not failed us in two and a half centuries."

"Say rather that we have not failed *it*. For democracy is only as good as its people are good."

"Which is true of any form of government, don't you think?"

He fell silent, looking doubtful.

"Leaving aside tyranny", I added.

I pondered the fact that since the foundation there had been no war on this planet, nor had there been much place for sly, voracious politics. The member states of the Commonwealth were at peace with each other, united in common purpose. Nor had there been in their internal affairs any tribal skirmishes, so to speak, no petty battles between villages or regions.

"Consider that we have no armies on any of the continents," I continued, "nor are there developed mechanisms in the social order that would reward the greedy or those who might lust for power."

"We do have police", he said with a frown.

"Of course, every hamlet and city has a few just men who help pull carts out of ditches and remind the young not to carouse late at night to the detriment of their neighbors' sleep."

"Or try to catch thieves."

"Yes, there are thieves among us—and on occasion crimes of passion, such as that most rare and horrible thing, murder. And there is a jail-farm on every continent, though I'm sure you would agree that their residents are few in number."

"I think you are too optimistic about human nature."

I smiled. "I am a confessor, Felix. I know human souls."

"Then you should admit that evil persists in us."

"I do admit it. Moreover, I believe we must never forget it."

"But you see my point, Anselm. Given the wrong circumstances, these impulses within us might grow and grow, might be acted upon by greater numbers of people. Then comes governmental reaction, control, suppression—fostering even worse evils."

"That is always possible, without grace."

He nodded absently at my obvious thought, and said, "I know as well as you do that the crucial thing is faith."

"Yes, the revelation given from above and paid for by unspeakable suffering. The Crucifixion.... And do not forget the Resurrection."

"I don't", he replied with a quick look.

Arthur turned his gaze to the sea and said nothing for a time. I knew that his great mind was churning over a dilemma that he was hesitant to tell me about, and that his great heart was involved too.

Finally he broke his line of private thought and faced me directly. "I have invented something that could propel the people of Regnum Pacis too far, too quickly for our minds, and maybe even our souls, to cope with. Power is enormously attractive when presented as an instrument for bringing about some good. But it is dangerous. And what I'm referring to is near-angelic power. Near-instantaneous knowledge and velocities that are presently unthinkable for us. Illusions of immortality, you see."

"Something that would undermine our experience of natural limitations, you mean? And hence deform our sense of place in the holy cosmology?"

"Yes. Very much the kinds of things that our forefathers thought they had mastered—before the catastrophe."

"Surely, Felix, you are not arguing for ignorance."

"No, I'm asking myself where are the frontiers: Where does pursuit of knowledge become folly; and where should prudence prevail?"

"An excellent question. Indeed, an ennobling search. Yet the answer to this cannot be reached by equations and formulae."

"I know. I'm just asking for your thoughts on the matter."

"You called it a moral question. It strikes me rather as a prudential matter, a question of discerning the will of God."

"And you're a man of God. Give me some guidance on this, I beg you."

It was now my turn to look out over the sea. Infinite it seemed, always beautiful, sometimes dangerous in its powers, sometimes serene; sometimes harming mankind, sometimes aiding us.

"I will pray for you, Felix. I will ask that you be given light on this question and that you will receive it and proceed in good conscience and good peace. Do not be anxious."

He clapped me on the shoulder with his large old hand.

"Thank you," he said. Then came another sigh, and I could see that he was still not at peace.

We both returned to gazing at the sea.

"Somewhere up there, above the equator, is a little anomaly in the sky", he said quietly. "I think it is a ship. My heart tells me it is a ship. If I am right, it is a seed with so much encoded within it that if the seed be replanted on our world the errors of the past might well repeat themselves. Can we risk it?"

"Is not all choice a risk ... an act of hope, a step made in trust? And is there not inherent in all right choice the belief that everything works to the good for those who love God?"

"How many love God, I wonder? In our world, most do, or very many, I should say. But what was the condition of the people who lived on Earth, the ones who sent the *Kosmos* on its voyage?"

"You know as well as I do what they were like. Would it have been better if they had stayed at home? Where would we be now if they had chosen not to cross the sea of the heavens to explore this planet?"

"I understand what you're saying. I can see that the hand of the Creator was upon the venture. But why so much destruction, why all the carnage?"

"Man's freedom, man's choice. Both good and evil issue forth from within the human heart. It is the same in this world as it was in the world of our origin."

"Earth", said Felix with a scowl. "What a hellish place they made of it. And nearly made hell here too."

Troubled, he lifted his eyes to the sky above us.

"Last week I was at McKie Observatory, and I looked at it through the new telescope. Just a pinprick of light orbiting around its sun. It's still there, or was there 4.3 light-years ago. Why the silence? I ask myself. Where are they now? What happened? Maybe we'll never know. But I can't help wondering if the prophecies of Revelation have come to pass."

"I often ponder this very question", I said. "But here we are in the heaven in the heavens, after all. We came from those people, and, for good or for ill, we are a continuation of them. It seems to me that God has not yet finished with salvation history."

"Silence, darkness, absence", Felix went on in his most somber tone. "Did they destroy everything? Or was a remnant left?"

"There is so much we do not know. Is there still a Church somewhere on that sad, old planet, with brave and holy souls continuing to tell the true story against all odds?"

"Are there priests, bishops, even a pope?"

"There must be a successor to Peter still alive on Earth", I said, surprised by my own intensity—and longing. "Perhaps we will one day reconnect with him or one of his successors. Until then, we can be thankful that Rome gave Bishop Nagakawa an indult to ordain priests and consecrate other bishops in the event that the expedition could not return."

"And so we were given a second chance."

"A new beginning."

"Yes," he sighed, "but how will it end?"

"Look at the horizon, Felix", I said, pointing southward over the water. "Can you see it?"

"No, the day is very fair, but the haze obscures the arc of the planet."

"Exactly. Yet it is there. Why do you think we are looking for it, now, at this very moment?"

"The sight is a beauty to behold. It consoles and beckons."

"Yes, but there is more: Does not man look up into the infinite because he knows in the heart of his soul that this is not our permanent home? That he is more than he thinks he is?"

"I suppose you're right. Yes, we know this instinctively—if *know* is the correct word. We are not bio-mechanisms. We are not clever, talking animals."

"The Kingdom of Heaven is within us, though it is not yet realized in its fullness. The Kingdom is beyond us too, and it is for the eternal union that we long."

"The horizon shows us the way, you mean."

"The infinite horizon and the horizon within you are one horizon."

Arthur glanced at me with some uncertainty.

"You will know", I said at last. "Whatever your invention may be, the light will be given and you will know what to do."

Three months after this conversation, he came by the abbey to see me. We had lunch together in the refectory with the brothers, and then we went off to my office for a quiet chat.

By then, it was no secret to anyone in the scientific community that he had invented a spectacular new kind of machine. But what it did exactly—rather, *how* it did it—was a secret known to none save its inventor.

"I received light, Father Abbot", he began without any preamble, when the door was closed behind us. "I have prayed as I have never prayed before, and have arrived at a discernment, subjective though I may be."

"The Lord knows very well our subjectivity", I said. "He communicates with this in mind."

"That is my hope."

"Can you tell me about it?"

"I owe at least that much to you, my friend. It's regarding the machine—the anti-gravity machine. No doubt you've heard about it."

"The whole world has heard about it, Felix, but that is nothing new."

"You remember when we last spoke together, the day by the sea when the children were dancing? I mentioned I had invented something, you recall."

"I remember."

"It is a device that adapts our simple form of electricity to the sophisticated circuitry and energy protocols of the anti-gravity machine we removed from the old shuttle."

"And ..."

"And my invention communicates with it. It works. It works very well in fact. We have been experimenting with elevating considerable weights to high altitudes within the stratosphere. Anti-gravity is now fully functional."

"And will you use it to reach the ... ship?"

"We will use it. However, the grace I received concerns the extent of the use." He stared at the floor for a moment, then looked up and continued. "I am the only one with access to my notes and diagrams. I am seriously considering destroying them. My invention will work only for a limited series of projects."

"How do you know this?"

"I made the thing to be so."

"I'm afraid I don't quite understand."

"Crucial internal components of my invention have a brief operational span. They are calibrated to a certain number of usage events. I have also included an altitude factor. We are guaranteed numerous test flights below the ionosphere, but only two flights to the ship in the heavens."

"You planned it that way."

"Yes, I did."

"What is to prevent other scientists from simply replacing the outmoded parts with fresh ones?"

"The invention is sealed. It has a self-protective function. Any attempt to enter it now would initiate an internal reaction, using white phosophorous, carbon allotropes, disulfide, and various other components that would interact in such a way as to immolate everything inside, rendering it unintelligible to analysts."

"Have you told anyone about this?"

"Only you. Of course, I will inform the other committee members before any more flights are made."

"Good. That is absolutely necessary. You cannot risk human life."

"There is no real risk, as long as the use does not exceed the parameters I've set. The invention is solid and reliable."

"Until it destroys itself. Why did you do it?"

"To set a limitation on what we can retrieve from the ship. It's my hope that the mission team will focus on seeking understanding of the past, and not on new keys to dangerous kinds of knowledge."

"An old debate, Felix—the rights of Science and the rights of Prudence."

"Though I am a scientist, Anselm, I would rather err in the direction of prudence, considering the calamitous mistakes made by the scientists who brought the *Kosmos* to Regnum Pacis, and who probably are responsible for the Earth's present silence."

We regarded each other mutely for some moments. As I pondered what he had told me, I saw that he had a point. Yet his decision had been made, in human terms, entirely on his own; he had consulted no one but God. How well had he heard what God was saying? How subjective had he been, really? Did he have a right to do what he had done? On the other hand, the invention was his own. The materials he had used were his own. He had been asked by the Commonwealth to apply his gifts to the project, but he had never been their salaried employee; he was not paid by anyone. He had rendered a gratuitous service that was already an enormous achievement, one that would in all likelihood be of great benefit to mankind regardless of how few the flights to the ship. Little did I know that he would not live to see this happen. A few months later, he would succumb to a massive heart attack while working in his lab at the science center near Foundation City.

"Will you tell the committee soon?" I asked.

"Yes, at tomorrow's meeting. But I thought you should hear first. You played an important part in the decision."

"Did I?" I said uneasily.

"Horizons, Anselm", he said with a thoughtful smile. "*True* horizons."

He had nothing more to say. Nor had I. We both rose to our feet, shook hands, and bid each other good night. He went off to pray in the abbey nave, and I to the choir, where I knelt down close to altar. The vigil lamp by the tabernacle gently flickered in the darkness, and it held my eyes for a time as peace slowly returned.

It seemed to me that this small light was not like the wavering lamp of human knowledge but was instead a beacon in the great sea of being, pointing to the Presence who is always with us until the end of time, and pointing to the true horizon where he dwells in eternal communion.

"Look up", sang the little flame as it danced. "Look up to the heavens beyond the heavens."

[Handwritten note found on the body of Dr. Neil Ruiz de Hoyos, physicist, contributing designer of spaceship *Kosmos*; born planet Earth, circa 2029 E-y; deceased during voyage, 2122 E-y (10 RP-y).]

Where were you when I established the earth?
Speak, if you are capable of judging!
Who has determined its measure, if you know it,
Or who has stretched the measuring line over it?
Upon what are the bases of its pillars founded,
Or who has laid its corner-stone,
When the morning stars sang together
And all the sons of God shouted for joy?

—Job 38:4–7

NRdH

AUTHOR'S NOTE:

If, in our wild imaginings mingled with speculative thought on what might be, we do not forget that our baleful "folys" are entwined with purest longing for the things that are above, we may better comprehend our horizon. Even so, by long labor, the unknown craftsman, with his hammer and saw and wood, leaves a greater sign: the spiral staircase of St. Joseph stands, as it has for the past century and a half, in the Loretto Chapel in Santa Fe, New Mexico.